I0772716

The Human Inside: Obstinatio

Book 3

By

Y.T. CHENG

For my grandparents.
For getting me to where I am now. Thank you.

Table of Contents

Authorization confirmed: Amborg Files accessed. Welcome back to the A.I. Industries public database. Resuming previous session. Please stand by.

Caution! There may be editing in progress of the following files. Please be patient as the information is being updated for your viewing needs. Files for the Epsilon-Alpha conflict in the year 2137 are now available. Please enjoy.

Hi there!

I'm... uh, where is everyone?? There's no one in here. I thought there was going to be someone here. Oh wait, there's some instructions written down for me. One second.

Ok, uh, I think I read them correctly. Now... alright, the camera is recording and... I guess I just say whatever is on my mind. 6? Are you watching this in a live broadcast? Hello?

Oh, I'm sorry. This is the first time that I'm filling out one of these forms. So, what's with the video recording? Why do I have to submit that? Isn't there an interview process for this sort of thing?

Ok, I'm back. Dr. Vanessa 6 gave me some information to clarify what I'm supposed to do. Sorry about that. Let me just clear my throat, sip some water and... let's get this show on the road!

Hey everyone! I...!

Crap... I messed up. I need to start over. Why is this so difficult?

Alright, I got this.

Hi Vanessa! This is a recorded message to be submitted with my final medical check.

I am Amara Three-Four-Five and I am a Third Group amborg. My supervising amborgs are Angel 999 and Jack 917. I'm their apprentice. Fun fact, most people mispronounce my amborg number sometimes and they often ask me why I say it that way. It's a preference. Like how 297 of the Second Group says Two Ninety-Seven like he's buying a snack from the gas station or how 57 isn't Five-Seven. She says Fifty-Seven.

Anyway, this video is about me getting cleared for active duty. I was on medical leave for about six months due to an injury from our Third Emergency Recall to Brazil. Not... the third trip to Brazil. No, the third recall that was ever triggered in A.I. Industries history was where I... you know, I had a severe spinal injury.

I was in a wheelchair and then on crutches for a while. I'll admit it was agonizing... watching the others go out on mission after mission. You know how it is. I was feeling really isolated at home. I really worried a lot of people when I was brought back home after my injury.

My spine was badly damaged when I participated in that Emergency Recall. Every amborg was summoned to help with the evacuation efforts of everyone off the coast of Brazil. A massive storm was about to hit the mainland and there was no stopping it. It was huge. It just kept building up and... it was such a serious situation. Fortunately, casualties were few but the amborgs all made it in and out of there alive.

I was hit by flying debris and it caused serious damage. A normal human would have died. If they had survived what I went through, they probably would have been fully paralyzed, and the pain would have been excruciating. Dr. Kendrick and... you, 6 have stated how lucky I was. My cybernetics saved me from dying.

Many years ago, The Chief of Security at A.I. Industries was almost paralyzed from a storehouse accident onsite. She was given an experimental spine surgery which gave her the ability to walk on her own two feet again. The same surgery was used by the medical staff to replace my spine. Thanks to that, they got to do a familiar operation on me. After months of therapy and learning how to stand on my own again, I am absolutely confident in my ability to return to the field.

I know that some people have expressed concerns and shared doubts about whether I am ready. I would like to put all that to rest and state that I am prepared to go on my next assignment. I feel that my progress has been amazing. Everything has gone smoothly and I just want to get out of this current state of boredom.

I mean, it's not all bad. A lot of people have been taking time to message me and hangout and it's been great! Most of the missions I've handled on my own make me feel lonely at times. Especially the undercover ones. So many days, weeks and months of work where I had to assume so many identities. Being home here at A.I. Industries is a safe spot for me to be myself and not have to worry about what goes on out there.

Now that I'm better, I think it's time to get back out there. I can't be the only amborg stuck at home, right?

If this whole self-video recording thing is my final self-reflection, then I just wanted to say thank you to Dr. Kendrick, Vanessa 6, and the entire medical staff for all of the hard work that had to go into fixing everything for me. They literally had my back. It's as good as new.

If I am cleared for duty, I'd very much like to volunteer for an assignment.

I'll see you out there! This is me telling you, whoever sees this video, to take care!

Apogee Station
Secure A.I. Data Vault
Emergency Recall plus 4 days
One day before the arrival of the S.C.E. Firestar

"End file."

Serina folded her arms as she watched the screen in front of her minimize and disappear from view. She turned left and lifted her left hand, like she was using telekinesis to lift something invisible.

She was standing inside of a circular room. Scratch that; it wasn't actually a room within our physical space. Deep within the confines of cyberspace, she was looking at old files and footage in her free time. When she was in this form of solitude, time was slowed down and enhanced in comparison to what others would normally experience. There was a unique reason as to why this was possible. Serina was an artificial intelligence.

She was arguably the best A.I. in the entire world, according to what many have said. Her creation was an extraordinary tale at A.I. Industries as well. Serina was the first A.I. that had a human soul. Not the mind of a human or a borrowed personality. She was a former human being, the first to move her entire existence out of her body and transform it into something new.

To the public, she resembles and lives among the other A.I. programs under Dr. Kendrick's care and supervision. The amborgs, a majority of the staff, and a small community in private are the only ones that know her true origins. If it was known to the rest of the world that she was formerly the amborg Serina 43, then she would have a huge target on her back.

Imagine the shock that everyone felt when another 43 from another universe showed up on their planet. Everything changed less than a week ago and now they were here, preparing for a terrifying encroaching invasion from outer space. Planning a defense for something of that scale required a lot of thinking. Fortunately, an A.I.'s fulltime job was to think. Almost every second of the day. Retreating into a personal data vault multiplied her thinking abilities exponentially and she could spend several months there, whereas outside of that space, only seconds would have gone by. If anyone called for her, she could be there in an instant, all those on the outside completely oblivious to the passage of that amount of time.

"I'm so sorry," Serina let out a remorseful sigh. The screen that appeared in front of her showed Amara 345's files. "I'm sorry 917. I'm sorry 999. There was nothing we could do."

There was a loud ping. Then, an echoing voice called out to her. Serina looked upward to the sound of a calm and commanding tone. It was Dr. Kendrick's voice.

"Serina?"

"To be continued," Serina lifted both hands and clasped them together.

Everything began to shut off as she snapped her fingers. A white light appeared above her head as she looked straight up. With a flash of light, she "beamed" herself upwards. In an instant, she appeared in another dark room. The data vault she was in came into view as she looked around.

Quickly, she pulled up a map of Apogee station and located Dr. Kendrick's beacon. Without hesitating, she transmitted herself into the data circuitry of the wall. From there, it was like entering a freeway and she suddenly rocketed along the power lines. In less than a second, thanks to her high speed, she approached an "exit" and transmitted herself into a projection device. With another flash of light, she appeared and gazed upwards at a man in a white lab coat with spectacles. Her small holographic size made everyone else look like giants. Boldly, she looked at Dr. Kendrick with enthusiasm.

"What's up doc?" she smirked cheekily.

"Funny," Dr. Kendrick chuckled as he gazed down at her. "I need you with me while we go have another chat with your other self."

"What about?"

"I do admit that I'm still pretty angry about the fact that she and Angel almost killed each other," he grumbled softly. Then he gave her a shrug and sighed. "But that deadlock did make me curious about a few things."

"Like what?" Serina asked curiously.

"You'll see," Dr. Kendrick replied. He began to walk down the hall. "I just want you there for moral support."

"Right," Serina nodded.

As he continued to stroll down the hall, she floated alongside him. It looked like he was using an invisible wire to pull a balloon with him. She kept a rigid stance as they continued chatting.

"What you really mean is that you want me to record everything she tells you."

"Of course."

"Well, I certainly love information," Serina let out a sarcastic laugh.

"Speaking of which," Dr. Kendrick paused. When he stopped, he turned and gazed down at her again. "What were you doing in the data vault for the last 15 minutes?"

"Spending a few hours reviewing some old footage," Serina answered honestly.

Dr. Kendrick nodded.

"Private?"

He casually glanced at her as they continued on.

"Not really," Serina shrugged. "I was just looking at old files relating to Amara 345."

"Why? You know that looking into the past doesn't contribute to anything we need right now."

"I respectfully disagree."

Serina's response was gentle but firm which semed to irk Dr. Kendrick a little. He crossed his arms as he stared intently at her. She was trying to analyze whether she had touched a nerve and crossed a line. It wasn't easy to get a read on him despite having a strong scanner that could read micro-expressions.

"Ok then," Dr. Kendrick spoke more sternly. "Why do you disagree?"

"There are a lot of numbers that I've calculated and thought about," Serina answered cordially. She crossed her arms and looked up at him. "Let me remind you that it's not good. I think that there are a few amborgs up here in space that need to address a few problems.”

“And by a few of them,” Dr. Kendrick mused, “you mean one of them?”

“Jack 917 has a lot more going on than I realized,” Serina snapped. “Why would you keep me in the dark about him being in prison?”

“He had important matters to attend to,” Dr. Kendrick replied and resumed walking.

“Great!”

Frustrated, Serina threw her arms up as she continued floating after him. She turned a bright shade of crimson red which he saw in the reflection of his glasses.

““Just keep walking away!” she yelled. “917 is one of the best amborgs in the Second Group! He lost Amara 345...!”

“We all did,” Dr. Kendrick corrected her, not glancing back.

“Fine! *We* lost 345 after she went on a botched operation! Then you send 917 and 999, her former mentors, away for some weird therapeutic vacation. Then the town of Silhed literally goes up in flames... he goes on a rampage...!”

Serina blinked and looked away. Dr. Kendrick stopped and turned his head to look at her.

“Surprisingly,” she said, a look of realization in her holographic eyes, “without Angel... Huh, how uncharacteristic. But even after he demolished a gang of ruthless criminals, you sent him away!”

Serina paused to allow her words to hit him. Dr. Kendrick merely nodded, his expression becoming confused.

“Serina, as much as I do enjoy you repeating things the way they happened... Is there a point?”

“Fine!”

A sudden burst of light flickered behind him, which indicated that she had disappeared. He turned his head and began to look around. Then, another flash drew his gaze forward. This one was larger and brighter, and the next thing he knew, someone appeared in front of him, causing him to lean back.

“Ok! I... absolutely didn’t see that coming,” he stated.

He had seen this before back when they were on Earth. Serina was standing before him. Instead of her usual small holographic appearance, she was now a fully sized human, standing directly in front of his path. She wasn't see-through anymore; she actually had a solid, physical body and was now wearing her old amborg jacket from when she was alive.

It was actually a little refreshing to see the original uniform that belonged to his universe's Serina 43.

"Seeing you use this 'body' to interrogate your alpha version in the recording was impressive," Dr. Kendrick nodded approvingly. "Now that I'm looking at it in person, I can see you put a lot of work into it. Well done."

"Thanks," Serina's eyes narrowed as she glared at him. "Moving on. Now tell me what happened!"

"What happened with what?" he replied innocently.

Serina didn't appreciate that he was still dodging the subject. His response sounded so scripted and rehearsed that it sounded like he was covering something up.

"Stop it!" she snarled.

"Or what?" Dr. Kendrick replied defiantly. He crossed his arms and planted his feet firmly. "You'll hit me? With your fake holographic hand? Overload a nearby terminal and try to electrocute me? It's a new low for you if you start threatening me."

"I won't physically hurt you…"

Serina's expression darkened slightly.

"…but I know what will get your attention."

The image of young Serina 43 morphed and dissolved as the image shifted into a different form. Electrical pulses and blocks of pixels flashed across her entire body and Serina took on a new form. Dr. Kendrick's eyes widened.

She was slightly shorter, wearing a white lab coat similar to his own. Her whole body and hairstyle changed, and she was now staring at him behind round framed glasses perched low on her nose. Furious, Dr. Kendrick clenched his fists tightly. Serina had transformed her entire holographic image to that of his late wife, Melissa.

"What are you doing?!" he growled.

The two locked eyes in an intense stare down. In the background, the footsteps of other workers and employees echoed throughout the space station, but as far as they could tell, no one was paying them any mind.

"Tell me the truth about 917," Serina said in Melissa's form. "Did you banish him?"

"No, I did not!" Dr. Kendrick replied immediately.

He looked around and made sure the coast was clear before rounding back on her again.

"Now you listen to me, my young A.I. child. You do not talk to me in that image and you do not, I repeat! Do not ever accuse me like that again! You want answers?! Get rid of that body, *NOW!*"

Instantly, "Melissa" blinked and then nodded. The image dissipated but then morphed into someone else. This time, Dr. Kendrick saw a rather fuzzy and incomplete image of Jack 917 standing before him. It continued to fizzle in and out as Serina continued her light show masquerade.

"For the love of...!" Dr. Kendrick nearly flipped out. "Stop taking on the image of people you know!"

"So, you didn't banish him?" Serina asked as she lifted her hand and pointed at 917's face.

Hearing her voice coming out of a tall and stoic man's body was disconcerting, but Dr. Kendrick impatiently nodded.

"Again, I didn't!" he answered insistently. "What he did after the town of Silhed was destroyed defied our policies! Anyone who takes matters into their own hands, especially an amborg, must face punishment!"

"Why imprison him? You didn't have to do that!"

917's body disappeared as Serina seemed to be struggling to maintain the image. Dr. Kendrick watched, expecting her to revert back to her tiny holographic form, but she appeared to be morphing into one more person. Once the image and pixels stabilized again, Serina made her decision. Dr. Kendrick's expression softened when he suddenly found himself staring in the eyes of Alice Angel 999, 917's best friend.

She was often known to the public as the lone wolf of A.I. Industries. She was efficient and lethal. The only thing that she never liked to show was any emotion. When she was alive as an amborg, Serina was the more outgoing of the two. Technically, each one of them were strong and powerful, but Dr. Kendrick knew them all individually and had unique ways of connecting with all of them. Out of

119 active amborgs, Serina knew that Dr. Kendrick had a soft spot for Angel. His reaction to when Serina used her image said it all.

"You could have sent him away," Serina's voice and 999's voice spoke out at the same time. "Like Thomas 227 when he messed up. He spent months away from A.I. Industries on your orders! Why was it different for 917? Why did you allow him to go to prison and let him stay there?! Are you sure you didn't keep him away from us? The only family he has left?"

Dr. Kendrick held his tongue as he bit his lip. His gaze softened even more as he glanced out the window, where the Earth was visible. When he turned to look at Serina in 999's body again, he conceded.

"First, enough with the impersonations," he said sternly. He made sure that his tone wasn't as fierce as it was before. "I won't talk to you if you continue to take on the forms of other people."

Serina nodded and slowly, pixels reappeared, covering her from head to toe. There was another flash of light as 999 disappeared. Then, Serina's small glowing holographic form popped up before him.

"Second," he continued as he looked at her small glowing form, "I'll tell you what you want to know. On one condition."

Serina nodded quietly to show that she was complicit and accepting his response.

"Finish this session of questioning with alpha 43 and I'll tell you what you need to know," he instructed softly. Before Serina could respond, he lowered his gaze and stared menacingly at her. "Never, under any circumstances, do that again. If you use the image of my late wife to coerce me again, I will find your off switch, purge you and have you restricted back to A.I. Industries in a state of limbo faster than you can say wifi. Not even Robert will be able to sneak you out."

Serina gulped as she nodded quickly.

"Yes sir."

Even though she had no physical body, that response from Dr. Kendrick managed to instill a massive level of fear in her. Artificial intelligence or not, Serina still had her basic emotions thanks to her previous life. She silently admitted to herself that she had crossed a rather personal line.

As he headed down the corridor with Serina floating after him, the mood grew awkward as the sound of his footsteps was the only noise they could hear. Finally, when he spoke again, his tone stern, she braced for the incoming lecture.

"Serina, I am actually disappointed in you."

"Yes doctor..." Serina turned a pale ghostly white color as she looked down at the floor.

"When you were alive, you were the best of the best that humanity had to offer."

His voice trembled with anger as Serina noticed that his footsteps became heavier. She focused on his stomping.

"Vanessa and I saved your life!" he barked. "When you had that knife in your chest, we were all afraid we were going to lose you right then and there! So, we tried our hardest to prevent that! 6 was on the operating table for days! And then Gene told me you were going to die, no matter how hard we fought to save you! I failed your parents!"

If Serina still had tear ducts, she imagined this would be the moment she would begin crying. This type of scolding was incredibly new to her. In her mind, she was committing his emotional outburst to memory so she could examine the data, but she obediently paid attention.

"I made a promise to your parents that I would keep you alive and I broke it," Dr. Kendrick continued his lecture, clenching his fists as he walked. "The best amborg of A.I. Industries was killed in action."

"The promise wasn't broken," Serina spoke softly. She tried to smile reassuringly. "Technically, I came back."

"Quiet!" Dr. Kendrick snapped.

"Ok," Serina squeaked and shut her mouth.

"Now you're one of the most advanced and quite possibly humanity's most powerful achievement in our universe," he declared.

"Are you... complimenting me?" Serina tilted her head curiously.

Dr. Kendrick glared at her which made her go pale again.

"Shutting up," she quickly muttered. "Sorry. Just a little confused where you were going with that thought."

"When you were alive," Dr. Kendrick breathed and spoke intensely, "you were the best. The strongest and the most capable amborg in our ranks. Now that you're a program that travels between our physical dimension and cyberspace, you are levels beyond what you used to be. All those skills and all of the knowledge of the known universe in your mind... and you thought it'd be ok to use that against me?!"

"Oh..."

"Use your abilities against our enemies," Dr. Kendrick instructed while marching away, causing her to frantically float after him. "It's disappointing that you used them against me. You'd better not use it against anyone else that trusts you."

The two of them fell silent as they went to the meeting place that had been agreed upon with alpha 43. When they arrived, they saw that she was there. She gazed at Dr. Kendrick and Serina inquisitively.

"Bad time?"

Dr. Kendrick and Serina exchanged a quick glance.

"We're fine," they both stated.

43 blinked and raised an eyebrow.

"Ok..."

"Although, my following questions might put you on the spot," Dr. Kendrick said bluntly.

"What do you want to know?"

Dr. Kendrick led 43 to their meeting room. As the door slid open, they walked in and Serina floated in after them. When the doors shut, Dr. Kendrick locked them for privacy.

"Things got very emotional since your deadlock," Dr. Kendrick stated. "Naturally, this generates more questions."

"Again," 43 smiled politely, "I am so sorry I lost control of my emotions."

"It was because you almost lost control..."

Dr. Kendrick's gaze lowered and he stared at 43 harshly. She got the message and her light and carefree demeanor faded.

"...that's what raises more questions."

Serina looked at her alpha universe counterpart. 43 nodded and walked over to a chair and sat down. Dr. Kendrick refused to sit, instead he stood in front of her.

"Tell me," he said, "what happened to the amborgs of alpha universe."

"They're all dead," 43 replied.

"All of them?" he asked. "You're the only survivor?"

"There weren't that many of us to begin with and it's a big galaxy out there," 43 nodded grimly. "Every single time I got notified that they were gone, it was like losing a piece of me. Every time."

Dr. Kendrick glanced over at Serina.

"I can relate," he said. "I also want to know about A.I. Industries. I want to know about my wife. I want to know what's happened over there."

43 opened her mouth to speak but Dr. Kendrick held up his hand, which effectively silenced her.

"I want to know..." he breathed. "I need to know... if you're here to protect us."

"O-of course!" 43 stammered as she looked at him and Serina. "I am here to..."

"Then tell me!" Dr. Kendrick scowled at 43 angrily. "If you were so mad about all of that loss you've suffered, can you confidently reassure me... that my family, my friends... are also not going to meet the same fate?"

43 didn't respond, rendered completely speechless while Serina nervously hung in the air.

"At first," Dr. Kendrick spoke again, "I thought it was a miracle that you were here. Like some sort of savior. But Alice managed to expose a side of you that I've never seen before. Not even in her."

Dr. Kendrick pointed at Serina, then jabbed his index finger at 43.

"Can you honestly sit here in front of me... and tell me..." he spoke softly. "Are we doomed? Are we going to walk into a massacre?"

The silence between everyone in the room was just as nerve-wracking as the dead silence of outer space.

CHAPTER 1

Phoenix Down

Washington D.C.
Georgetown University Hospital
2138 August
One Week after S.C.E. Arrival

President Holland kept his head low, his hat concealing his face. Following protocol, he continued to walk discreetly. He successfully passed through security without any issues, made his way to the stairs, and received clearance to proceed to the second floor.

He emerged from the staircase into a nearly deserted area. Only a trio of doctors and a chosen few nurses were present, accompanied by a full contingent of Secret Service agents and armed soldiers. Their sole responsibility was to care for and safeguard one VIP on this floor. While she was important to the public, to the President, she was everything.

"Excuse me, you're not on the scheduled... Oh!"

President Holland quickly reached up and removed his hat. The nurse behind the desk immediately froze when she recognized him. The guards and soldiers had already begun to move in, but also halted in place when they recognized their commander-in-chief.

"Now now," Bill cleared his throat. "Let's not make this a big deal. As you were."

Everyone returned to their stations. Behind him, he heard his lead agent whisper urgently. If there was one thing that always comforted the President, it was listening to his friend Mike express annoyance.

"Sir," Mike sighed. "I told you that these sudden visits wouldn't be cleared by the staff here on time."

"Seeing that I'm your boss, Mike," President Holland chuckled, "you'd think that all of our memos would be delivered instantly."

"With how tense everyone is," Mike stated professionally. "It's not easy getting clearance to sneak you out of the White House anymore."

"Even with everything that's going on," Bill turned to look at Mike and smiled, "I'm trying to remind myself of what I'm fighting for."

"Yes sir."

As they continued walking, his escort peeled away to cover certain checkpoints on the hospital floor. The President asked Mike a quick question.

"How's your family?"

"I had my husband take the kids to his parents," Mike replied firmly.

"You had them go to Texas?"

President Holland looked at Mike, dumb-founded. Mike held a serious and stoic demeanor as he gave his boss a single firm nod.

"If the aliens invade, I want them to be safe," he replied. "Sir."

"Well, Texans are pretty well-armed," Bill stated. Then he shook his head and scowled at Mike. "Also, don't call them aliens. They're visitors. That's an order."

Mike maintained his professional and neutral expression and nodded again.

"Yes sir."

As they arrived at the room President Holland was heading towards, he reached for the door handle while Mike joined his hands together, clasping them in front of him as he stood watch. He had no intention of entering with the President. While gripping the door handle, he glanced once more at the armored Secret Serviceman.

"Mike," he said.

Mike turned to look at Bill attentively.

"Sir?"

"If the planet comes under attack...," he said.

President Holland shook his head and sighed while Mike listened quietly.

"Maybe you should give them a call or text them," he suggested.

"Once I clock off, I always let them know I'm ok, sir," Mike answered politely. "I'll call them later."

"No," President Holland smiled reassuringly. "Call them now. That's another order."

"Sir... I'm still on duty."

"What's going to happen to me in here?" Bill smiled cheekily. "I won't be long."

Bill heard Mike acknowledge him with another "yes sir" as he opened the door. As Bill stepped inside, he could see Mike pulling his phone out of his pocket with a small smile on his face.

Good man, he thought.

His thoughts were interrupted by a sweet and familiar voice.

"What are you doing here?? Honey?"

The occupant of the only hospital bed on the second floor was taken aback, but she appeared very happy to see him. President Holland beamed at his wife, Caroline, the First Lady, and approached her. An older woman seated in the chair beside the bed looked stunned but soon began to laugh.

"Would you look at that?" the older lady chuckled. "Mister bigshot actually came here for a visit! Or am I dreaming?"

"Mister bigshot just wanted to see his wife and his mother-in-law," Bill replied in a smart-alecky tone. "Hi mom."

Bill walked over and hugged Caroline's mother, Barbara. As they pleasantly greeted each other, there was a cry from the bed.

"Oh my god..."

Bill and Barbara turned to Caroline, whose eyes were wide. She looked at her husband with a panicked expression. All traces of her happiness were gone.

"Negotiations failed!"

"W-what?" Bill sputtered. "What are you talking about?"

"They blew up the White House and you managed to escape!"

Bill and Barbara exchanged a quick glance.

"Honey," he chuckled as he casually approached his wife. "If the White House was blown up, I wouldn't be here talking to you. My security detail would have had all of us gathered and sent to a safe and secure location. Besides, I meant what I said."

President Holland gently gave his wife a kiss on the hand.

"I wanted to come and see you."

"But an unscheduled visit?" Caroline took a deep breath, calming herself. "Are you sure this is ok? You have a lot on your plate!"

"Well, that's what a Vice President and the entire cabinet is for," Bill replied. "The country will be just fine without me for ten minutes."

"I suppose that's all the time you get?" Caroline sighed.

"Duty calls," Bill nodded.

"I'm more impressed with how you're staying so calm," Barbara chimed in. "The whole world is witnessing the biggest event in history and he's trying to keep the entire country from falling apart with his merry band of misfits."

"You are so incredibly brave," Caroline smiled reassuringly at Bill. "These last few days must have been so..."

"Memorable?" Bill replied.

"Stressful," Caroline snickered. "But sure, memorable works too!"

"Well, it's not just me doing all this by myself," Bill smiled. "I have many colleagues and friends who are engaged in extensive negotiations and discussions. The visitors from the S.C.E. have provided us with an abundance of extraordinary knowledge and information."

"So, what else did they talk to you about?" Caroline asked excitedly.

"Have I already told you about their spaceships?" Bill asked cheekily, giving Barbara a wink.

"Yes," Caroline sighed, shaking her head. "Tell me something new!"

"Ok, so one of the advisors on that diplomatic team had told me about... drumroll please?"

Barbara began to tap her hands on the railing of Caroline's bed, simulating a rapid tempo. Caroline giggled like a young and excited child, quickly joining in by tapping her hands on her lap.

Bill waved his hands and pretended he was revealing something special.

"Food," he said.

"Yes!" Caroline seemed to light up. "What does their food even taste like?"

Bill put his hand on his chest proudly and pretended to act heroically. He wasn't usually this dramatic, but he always knew that it would cheer his wife up. Hearing her laugh and seeing the way she lit up was more than enough to keep him going. He loved seeing her like this.

"Alright," he began a short and improvised skit when he had their attention. "One of the S.C.E. diplomats had brought their own food. It might be because the food in our universe might not be entirely compatible with their physiology or something like that. It's precautionary."

"Oh ok," Caroline nodded. "Did they bring a cure for lactose intolerance?"

"I don't know," Bill laughed. "Anyway, they offered to let us share a meal. We had a potluck at the White House. After security scanned their food and ours, we had lunch."

"Thanks," Caroline sighed, "for making me hungry now."

"So, we sit down and then..."

The door suddenly burst open, cutting the story short. Alarmed, everyone turned to see who had entered as Mike rushed inside. He was followed by another agent that had come with the President, along with two security drones that marched in behind them.

"Sir! Please come with me!" Mike commanded.

"Mike?" Caroline gasped.

"What is it?" Bill demanded once he saw their serious expressions.

"Mr. President," Mike stated. "We need to go!"

Bill turned and looked at his wife and her mother. Both were stunned, at a complete loss for words. Bill defiantly faced his Secret Service detail.

"What's happened?"

"Your wife and mother do not have code-word clearance!" Mike urgently reminded them.

"My wife is in this hospital bed and unable to leave!" Bill replied sternly. "I'm ordering you to tell me what's happening! We are all under your protection! I will personally vouch for my family!"

Mike glanced at Caroline and Barbara. They both maintained a focused gaze on the Secret Service agents. After a moment of contemplation, Mike let out a sigh.

"Olympus is under attack," he said.

Bill's eyes widened.

"What?!" he exclaimed.

"Bill? What's happening?"

He turned to look at his wife.

"The White House is under attack," he answered.

"Oh my god," Barbara's hand flung to her chest.

Bill glanced at Mike.

"Casualties?"

"We don't know how many," Mike shook his head. "There're no updates coming through. All communications have been lost. We need to get you to safety!"

Bill nodded. He pivoted and rushed over to his wife. She desperately reached out for him and he took her hand.

"I've got to go," he said.

"I know," Caroline whimpered. "Please be careful."

"It's going to be ok," Bill smiled reassuringly. "The hospital is going into lockdown protocol after I'm gone. I'll call you."

"You'd better," Caroline sniffed.

"Mr. President!" Mike called out to Bill again. "Your family will be safe! We have to go!"

Bill let go of his wife's hand, nodded to Barbara, and turned to leave. Once he passed Mike, he felt hands from all of the agents on his back as he was ushered out of the room and urged down the hall.

"Tell me what happened!" he demanded as he tried to keep up with their pace.

"Amborg 125 signaled a distress call to us before we lost contact."

Bill remembered what Marco had been up to prior to surprising his wife. When he had decided to take a break and sneak out of the White House, the few people that he notified were extremely hesitant. 125 had been one of those that had been against his sudden desire to visit Caroline. Despite the initial protests, even an amborg of A.I. Industries couldn't disobey one of the most powerful leaders in the world.

"Is there any way to reach him?" Bill asked.

"Negative."

Getting an idea, Bill pulled his cellphone out of his pocket. The President of the United States didn't actually have a personal mobile device, but this was a special one that was given to him by Dr. John Kendrick. It was a direct hotline to the amborg that was currently in charge of protecting him.

After a few rings, he was able to get through.

"Mr. President?"

Bill sighed in relief. It was good to hear a friendly voice.

"Marco," he said. "What's going on?"

"Communications on all emergency channels and normal frequencies have been jammed," 125 reported immediately. "Just before things went down, an emergency alarm from Olympus was activated! I am moving to your position!"

"No!"

"What??" 125 replied over the phone.

President Holland noticed his Secret Service detail halt in place once the command was given.

"Sir?!" Mike exclaimed. "We need to get you to the nearest shelter!"

"No!" Bill whirled around, his phone still held up next to his ear. "I mean, yes. Get me to safety! But... Marco! Go to the White House!"

He had almost forgotten in the overwhelming rush of adrenaline that surged through him when he was forced out of his wife's hospital room. He glanced anxiously at Mike.

"My kids!"

"Sir, they have agents too! We will protect them!" Mike replied.

"No, he's right!" 125 said. "I'm returning to the White House!"

There were a few reasons why someone would dare to attack one of the most secure locations on the planet. The aim was to either capture the President or manipulate him into committing a grave act. Another possibility was to target other things that were precious to him.

"Mr. President, I am going to call for another amborg to come and protect you!" 125 explained. "I will call you again on this line once I have your kids safely in my care!"

"Thank you Marco!" Bill stated. "Please find out what's going on!"

"125, redirecting to Olympus."

125 hung up the call. Bill couldn't help but continue to worry as he approached the staircase. This time, the Secret Service was not urging him to hurry. They allowed him to descend the stairs at a comfortable pace without any pressure.

"How the hell did the White House come under attack?" he asked no one in particular as they made it to the ground floor.

"Mr. President, we will find out," Mike replied. "But if I may, sir?"

They reached the ground floor and were met by a military escort ready to surround the President.

"Yes?"

Bill breathed as someone handed him a bullet-proof vest. He slipped it on as the soldiers surrounding him and his Secret Service detail gave him a protected space to put on his armor.

"I'm actually really glad that you snuck out of the White House," Mike admitted. "It's good you weren't there."

"I will share that sentiment..." Bill gulped as they began walking again. "Once my kids are secure."

A.I. Industries
Emergency Command Operations

"We're getting emergency alerts faster than we can process them!"

4 and 18 glanced over at Carter who was standing next to a computer terminal.

"Do I need to deploy?" 18 asked.

"Not yet," 4 shook her head as she frowned at the screen. "Carter? Please help me identify who activated a distress beacon first."

"Marco 125," Carter reported.

4 and 18 looked up at the giant screen that held a world map.

"Every single alert on the screen is a city in the capital of each and every country that's part of the U.N." 4 stated.

"And every single one of them was visited... by the S.C.E. diplomatic corps."

18 finished 4's statement and the two of them nodded in agreement.

"At least, we have enough amborgs down here to respond," 4 stated.

"But you're not sure who to prioritize?" 18 asked. "Are you sure you don't want me to..."

"When it's time," 4 replied firmly. "I need you to help be my second pair of eyes."

"Well, we're screwed."

4 gazed at 18 and frowned. She shrugged her shoulders.

"You never ask for someone to double-check," 18 answered bluntly. "This is bad."

"It is," 4 nodded.

She turned to look at Carter.

"Carter," she said. "Please give me the list of all active amborgs out in the field and in reserve."

"Yes ma'am," Carter nodded.

4 looked at 18.

"You're the best training instructor we have and you know everyone's techniques and moves," she said. "Can you go and help 125?"

"Sure," 18 nodded.

She turned and left the operations room.

"What about our friends overseas?" Carter asked.

"Let's have echo and delta group move in," 4 stated.

"Understood," Carter replied as he glowed green. "Movement orders sent out to the First and Second Group teams."

4 noticed something to the left and glanced over at one of the terminals. There was a blinking red light. Each computer had one which indicated that someone was trying to call their direct line. Fortunately, the operator sitting there noticed and answered.

"A.I. Industries E.C.O.," they said once 4 saw the blinking light stop and begin to glow. "Please identify."

4 waited as the person on the other end sent in their proper identification codes. According to their protocol, it had to be a former or a current employee of A.I. Industries that was off site.

"Oh? Mandy? It's good to hear from you. The supervising amborg? Yeah. Let me get her."

The operator turned their head and waved at 4 who immediately walked over. 4 connected to the computer terminal and joined the call.

"This is amborg 4, go ahead."

The caller ID appeared on her display screen and she heard a friendly voice speak.

"4, what's going on? I'm here with Thalia and all the phone lines seem to have gone down."

4 was glad to hear her voice checking in on the emergency channel. The last time she had seen her, Mandy had left A.I. Industries temporarily to search for Thalia Ramirez. She had volunteered since there were no amborgs available for the task.

Mandy had gone with a special group of colleagues to Vegas in an attempt to track down Thalia. The shuttle crew of Echo 209 had gone with her at 4's suggestion so that no one would have to worry about their safety.

"I'm afraid that the situation seems to have escalated," 4 answered quickly. "We've lost contact worldwide with all of our allies. The only ones reporting in are the amborgs. The emergency channels are going to be flooded soon."

"Are we going to die? End of the world?" Mandy gulped.

"As far as I know, we aren't dead yet," 4 replied.

"Oh come on!" Mandy replied frantically in a hushed tone. "You know that when you tell people not to panic, that's when you run!"

"I didn't say that we were panicking," 4 replied calmly. "I suggest that you and the crew of Echo 209 return to A.I. Industries. We need to regroup all of our assets."

"We haven't found Thalia yet," Mandy sighed. "Her friend Wendy said that she stopped by to visit but left early to go somewhere else. She can't have gone far."

"I strongly advise against it," 4 replied. "I am recalling you."

"You're going to recall me while we're acting under an Emergency Recall?" Mandy let out a laugh.

"Your sense of humor remains intact and I appreciate that about you," 4 stated. "However, I am in charge. Please return."

"Alright, I trust your instincts," Mandy sighed. "I'll get Hicks and we'll..."

4 heard a gasp over the line and paused. She glanced at the operator, who shook their head in response. The light on the terminal was still glowing which meant that the line wasn't dead.

"Hello?" 4 asked.

"Kat..." Mandy breathed. "I found her."

"What?"

"Thalia! She's across the street! We need to get her! Someone wave at her!"

4 felt a wave of relief.

"Mr. Ramirez will be quite pleased to hear this," she stated.

"Oh... my... god..."

4's expression was taken over by one of confusion. That response from Mandy didn't sound pleasant.

"Pardon?" 4 asked.

"Thalia's with someone. It's... is that who I think it is?"

"Can the exposition please move slightly faster?" 4 asked impatiently.

"Kat," Mandy breathed. "It's Ariana."

4 paused. The only sounds in the background were the other operators responding to various calls. That name was a blast from the past.

"Are you sure? Our records show that she's..."

"Missing?" Mandy finished.

"Divorced," 4 clarified. "She left... right after the Dominoe Incident. No one knew where she went."

"Looks like Thalia found her."

"I believe you have a mission update then," 4 stated.

"Uh, right," Mandy chuckled over the phone. "For the record, we have discovered Thalia Ramirez and... some other things... does that grant me permission to stay out here?"

"Yes," 4 nodded. "I redact my order to have you recalled. Please take as much time as you need for this investigation."

"Thank you! Call you back later!"

The line disconnected and 4 went back to her position near where Carter was working.

"Was that awkward?" he asked.

"No," 4 shook her head. "It's just... no one has seen George's wife... in a long time."

"If I had to guess," Carter stated, "she was before my time. Is that correct?"

"Yes, you wouldn't have known her," 4 replied. "You were still in your previous form before you got upgraded."

"Don't remind me," Carter groaned.

Like Serina, Carter had also gone through a type of upgrade to his main construct. Around the time of the Dominoe Incident, he didn't have a holographic form like all of the current A.I. models. He was from an older generation of programs that had been long discontinued and recycled.

With the money and the proper facilities, an A.I. could be upgraded. It was essentially an update or patch to keep them up to speed. After Audrey, Carter's owner and David 117's wife, graduated from school, she was desperately trying to find a stable career while dealing with a multitude of problems. Fortunately, Dr. Kendrick was able to help Carter.

Artificial intelligence programs had to be given regular checkups and maintenance every few years. Unfortunately, there weren't a lot of companies that could take him in due to heavy A.I. growth and modernization. Most research institutions and businesses would have seen how old and outdated Carter was. They would have had him replaced by a new and improved A.I. Once he was taken to A.I. Industries, they worked very hard to give him a new form and properly extend his life. Their efforts were successful as he was now living a good life at A.I. Industries.

"Incoming transmission!"

4 and Carter looked at the screen. It showed a first-person perspective of someone sprinting down a street.

"18?" 4 asked. "Report."

"I've made it to the White House," 18 replied calmly. "It's bad."

Everyone in the operations room watched 18's camera as she ran up the north lawn of the White House. She turned her head, and a sleek and shiny space shuttle came into view, sitting quietly on the grass several feet away from the entrance. What got their attention were the bodies scattered around the area.

Soldiers, secret service agents, armored police and even... K-9 dogs were all dead or knocked out. Many of them were feebly trying to get up, calling for help, or trying to stay awake. The rest were all still and lifeless, all from what appeared to be a brutal attack.

"You need an army to storm the White House," 18 stated as she scanned for survivors. "But I'm only seeing the bodies of our own people..."

"We're going to have to comb through the footage of all of the security or body-cam recordings," 4 stated. "Can you connect to any of them and upload them back here?"

"No," 18 replied. "That's what's creeping me out. It's like someone shut off the wifi and I can't... connect to anything electronic once I get closer."

"Proceed with caution," 4 instructed. "You're still broadcasting a live feed and we can see you clearly."

"Yeah, who knows how long that will last," 18 replied as they saw her draw her weapon and begin to slowly walk up the steps to the doors. "4, had emergency responders establish a triage area nearby. We need to upgrade the emergency to a mass-casualty protocol. I'm going to look for 125."

Suddenly, gunshots rang out from behind the door.

"There's still a fight going on inside," 18 declared. "I'm going to go dark. Standby."

"Really?" 4 sighed. "Do you have to?"

"I can't focus on the task at hand if I have people talking in my head," 18 replied hastily. "I'll call you back!"

As 18 disconnected the call and the broadcast from her camera disappeared from the screen, 4 looked at Carter.

"This seems to be a reoccurring pattern," 4 said.

"Well, to be completely transparent," Carter shrugged, "I don't really get anything done whenever someone needs to talk to me or supervise my whole methodology."

4 stared at Carter's holographic form. She didn't appreciate that he had inserted a small pun.

"You are transparent," she grumbled.

"I like utilizing my sense of humor," Carter replied with a polite grin.

"You need to read the room better," 4 retorted.

Suddenly, they received another call. Everyone checked the caller ID and was relieved to see 18's name appear on the screen again.

"4..." her voice spoke to them again, sounding hesitant.

"18, are you alright?"

There was a moment of silence. 4 looked at Carter and he pointed at the glowing indicator light which meant that the call was still connected, but 18 had stopped speaking.

"18? Can you hear me?" 4 repeated her question.

"Yeah," 18 replied. "I'm sending you video footage."

The same screen from before appeared in front of them as 18's camera revealed the whole scene from her perspective. Everyone gasped.

"Oh no," Carter's eyes widened.

"I have President Holland's kids. Both are safe," 18 reported. "But..."

18 approached someone that was hunched over with their back against the wall. Based on the damage, it looked like he had been thrown and slammed into it. Despite the blood, fire damage, and the explosive residue on his body, there was no mistaking the glowing neon stripes of an amborg jacket from A.I. Industries. 4 watched in horror as 18 knelt down to give them a closer look. One glance at the flickering blue stripes on the uniform combined with a patch belonging to the Second Group made their hearts sink into the pit of their stomachs.

"Amborg down," 18 reported. "I repeat. Marco 125 is down."

"I-is he...?" Carter stammered. "Can you check...? Is he...?"

"No life signs," 18 replied softly. "125 is dead."

CHAPTER 2

Firestar Lockdown

**S.C.E. Firestar
Deck 3
Engineering**

*Emergency Transmission
Protocol: 308 - Alpha
Code: 1
General Order: 12
S.C.E. Order: 141
Regulation: 19, Section C*

"Attention! Attention all hands! Ship-wide lockdown initiated! All non-emergency and civilian crew must shelter in place or seek refuge in the nearest designated bunkers! All security personnel and marine detachments engage hostile forces! This is not a drill! Repeat, this is not a drill! Defend the ship at all costs!"

The announcement blared loudly overhead at the first sign of trouble. It kicked everything into overdrive and before anyone could realize the ramifications of what had been broadcasted throughout the entire ship, a massive firefight had broken out within the interior of the S.C.E.'s flagship. Hundreds of lives were now caught in a terrible struggle to maintain control of the enormous vessel.

Amborgs 1 and 2 of the First Group sprinted down a hall as fast as they could. The klaxon alarms and their glowing red lights flooded the passageway. There was no sign of anyone, which was good, but they knew that their path wouldn't be clear for long.

1 received a text message from 2.

Stop. Do you hear that?

1 immediately nodded and texted his reply.

Yes.

They halted in place and raised their weapons. Their plasma rifles began to charge as they assumed cautionary stances. 1 stepped forward and took point while 2 stood behind him. Once they were ready to move, 2 quickly double-tapped 1's right shoulder from behind.

Both amborgs began to move forward slowly, their weapons at the ready in case they had to respond. Suddenly, someone appeared before them.

A uniformed S.C.E. officer who was bleeding from the head was leaning against the wall, slowly heading their way. He was young, likely in his early twenties, and appeared to be fading fast.

"Help…" he groaned weakly.

1 glanced at the three silver stripes on the young man's sleeves, indicating he was a junior officer and had been actively aboard the Firestar for at least a year.

"What happened?" he asked in a hushed tone. "Lieutenant?"

The officer swayed, catching himself against the steel wall to support himself.

"My friends…" he coughed. "We were… going to engineering. We were going to help. I stopped to give directions to another person…"

He lifted his head and turned around. He lifted a trembling hand and pointed behind him, fear in his eyes.

"My friends walked ahead of me…" he gasped. "Then the next thing… I knew, they were all attacked… I saw… I think… Luco… transformed…"

1 glanced sharply at 2. They both gave each other a knowing look.

"Silent Eclipse bot," 2 whispered.

"What?" the young officer murmured.

"Were you followed?" 1 asked.

"My friends…" the officer mumbled.

"He's losing it," 2 replied. "And I hear something…"

1 and 2 turned in the direction the injured man had come from. In the distance, the sound of energy blasts rang out, but as they filtered through the noise, the unmistakable sound of metallic footsteps marching closer became apparent. The sound grew increasingly louder, signifying that something was approaching.

"My friends… they were back there… thrown around… I ran… I was… afraid."

Both amborgs took aim down the hall. The mechanical footsteps continued growing louder.

"I hate creepy hallways," 1 stated.

"Agreed."

The footsteps were now drowning out the sounds of fighting taking place in a far off section of the ship. The noise had become so intense that it seemed like it was coming from all directions. 2 texted 1 again.

Leonard, he wrote, *we were informed that these... Silent Eclipse assassin drones are... infiltrators, right? Like... mass-produced Terminator commando droids?*

Those are two different franchises, 1 replied.

Not the point. They can disguise themselves as anyone. Right?

1 and 2 glanced at each other. Perhaps... they had looked in the wrong direction too hastily? They both whirled around.

The wounded officer was still there, trying to stay on his feet. He wheezed and stumbled a little, catching himself on the wall and leaned heavily against it.

Ok, so... what do you think? Is he a robot? 2 asked.

The blood sure is convincing, 1 replied.

Could be CGI or a hologram. Should we shoot him?

1 stared at 2 in shock, but they both maintained a fighting stance.

You want to shoot an unarmed wounded man?

I don't want to! 2 texted back immediately. *I was asking if we should!*

Wait! 1 replied as he looked at 2. Why did we both turn around??

2's eyes widened when he realized their mistake.

I thought... I was going to check the officer while... you kept watching the hall.

They both turned back around, but it was too late.

A dark, hulking humanoid robot slapped 1 and 2's rifle's out of their hands before they could even pull the trigger. Without missing a beat, they moved to engage the assassin droid in close quarters combat. They coordinated their strikes in an effort to take it down.

On the left, 2 attempted to pivot and execute a high roundhouse kick with his right leg, but the drone ducked to evade it. On the right, 1 tried to throw a punch, but it was blocked, and his fist collided with metal. Fortunately, it wasn't too painful, but he could feel a stinging sensation after hearing a metallic clang.

The drone stood, lifted its leg, and kicked 1 in the chest, sending him stumbling backward a few feet while it simultaneously targeted 2.

2 found himself in a struggle as the drone attempted to wrap its arms around his head. He twisted and tried to bring it down to the ground, realizing it was trying to put him in a chokehold. However, his attempt to get behind it failed as the drone swung its elbow around. Its waistline spun as if on a rotating platform, executing a wild 360-degree spin with its upper body. It struck 2 in the head, knocking him down. A bit dazed, the Silent Eclipse drone lunged forward, targeting 2's face with its fist.

1 quickly stepped in, raising his leg to kick the drone's arm, diverting its attack away from 2. The drone shifted its dark-yellow visor towards him and focused on 1. Summoning all his strength, he threw another punch, but it was intercepted. This gave 2 the opportunity he needed to get back on his feet, and he jumped up. As he came down, he aimed his fist at the drone, but it lifted its arm to defend itself.

Both amborgs continued their relentless cycle, trying to inflict enough damage. As they worked together, they scanned their surroundings for anything that could help them. The injured officer wasn't in any condition to fight, and their rifles lay on the ground nearby, but they weren't sure if they could afford to break away long enough to grab them.

The Silent Eclipse drone was formidable. Whoever designed it had produced an insanely tough robot. It was fast, agile, and strong, likely trying to outsmart them at every turn. With each passing minute, their chances of surviving this fight seemed to dwindle.

The drone seemed to be getting smarter as the fight progressed. It soon realized that the amborgs were using their two-man fighting style to their advantage. Without warning, the drone caught 1's fist, headbutted him, and hurled him against the wall. 2 found himself facing the drone alone while 1 struggled to get back on his feet.

2 decided to try to buy as much time as possible. He fought the drone with his fists, knowing he was quicker with his punches than with his kicks. Unfortunately, each of his arms was draining his energy. The drone, however, appeared to have limitless energy and soon started to gain the upper hand.

2 noticed more punches coming and raised his arms to shield himself. With his back against the wall, he couldn't move to dodge the strikes. The drone delivered a swift one-two combo to his head from both sides. He managed to block some of the blows with his hands, but

it only absorbed a fraction of the impact. Dazed, the drone grabbed 2 and lifted him high above its head, then slammed him down onto the floor and positioned itself on top of him. 2 fought back, struggling to fend off the drone, but it was trying to kneel on him and crush his throat.

Suddenly, the crushing weight was lifted off 2 as someone tackled the drone. 1 let out a roaring battle cry as he propelled himself with all the force he could muster.

Now was the time to switch things up. 1 had to give 2 a chance to recover and get back up. They had to disable this thing now.

The drone charged at 1, and he did the same. This time, 1 slid down and targeted the legs. The drone was too tall to alter its course, and 1 successfully tripped it. As it toppled over him, it crashed into the wall, leaving it temporarily incapacitated. Seizing the opportunity, 1 rose and aimed a strike at its head. Unfortunately, the drone intercepted his fist, and they found themselves locked in another intense struggle. 1 pushed against the drone, trying to force it back down, but it was gradually rising again, and 1 could feel it attempting to crush his wrist.

In that moment, 2 charged in and landed a powerful blow right to its head. The impact produced a loud clang, and the drone's head was snapped clean off. Disoriented, it loosened its hold, giving 1 the chance to pull his arm free.

Every second counted. The two amborgs rushed in without hesitation, pinning the drone firmly against the wall. Despite its attempts to fight back, they poured every ounce of strength they had into holding it down. The drone was forced to its knees as they restricted its movements. 1 and 2 tightened their hold, knowing exactly what to do next.

1 took hold of one of its arms and crushed it with his hands. As metal ground and collapsed under the pressure of his grip, 1 unleashed a bellowing war cry and yanked back with all his strength. The arm tore away, and he successfully severed it. Then, he assisted 2 in doing the same to the other arm.

They ignored the cries and electrical whining from the drone as it continued to try and fight back, but was unable to do so since it had been, pun intended, entirely disarmed.

2 broke away and reached for one of the rifles lying on the ground nearby. Meanwhile, 1 continued to punch and kick the drone

repeatedly, preventing it from getting back up. The drone kept trying to return to a standing position, probably in order to engage in some form of kick-boxing.

2 picked up the rifle, quickly examined it, and checked the ammo. Once he was confident that it was still good to use, he charged it and then took aim.

"Chew plasma bitch!" he barked as he pulled the trigger.

The rifle emitted a high-pitched whine before releasing a red plasma bolt that struck its target dead on. 1 and 2 watched warily as the drone's head disintegrated. Afterward, it powered down and hit the ground with a loud crash.

Not taking their eyes off its deactivated corpse, 1 and 2 both breathed heavily and rested for a few moments.

"Nice shot," 1 croaked.

"Thanks," 2 replied as he looked around, checking the hallways. "Nice disarming."

The two amborgs shared a quick chuckle as they turned to check on the wounded officer.

"Come on lieutenant," 1 said. "Let's bring you with us to engineering and get you..."

1 and 2 stopped and froze in place.

"...help."

The young officer had collapsed to the ground. They froze in place, realizing that he was gone. 1 and 2 gently approached and knelt beside him. The officer's eyes were vacant, devoid of life. He'd stopped breathing, and they couldn't detect any signs of life.

"Leonard," 2 let out a shaky sigh. "We need to go.

1 felt a lump in his throat as he stood up, and the two amborgs began to step away.

"He's just a kid," 1 stated. "We're all getting hunted like prey."

"We can't save everyone," 2 answered solemnly.

"He shouldn't have gone out like this," 1 said. "They shouldn't be getting slaughtered. Not like this."

1 and 2 fell into a jog, weapons in hand, and tried to make their way to engineering. 1 felt his anger surge, intensifying with each step he took.

"They're killing kids..." he snarled. "Not on my watch."

As they hurried ahead, they noticed two figures rounding the corner. The LED lights atop their heads was a clear giveaway. It was a pair of Silent Eclipse drones. They were likely reinforcements their bigger brother called during their earlier battle. However, there was something different about them in terms of design.

"These look like smaller ones," 2 pointed out as they raised their weapons.

"Maybe they're mad we took out their jacked up buddy," 1 took aim at the drone on the left and fired.

The drone dodged his shot and raised its own gun. Unlike the bigger one that had engaged them with its fists, these two came armed with ranged weapons. 1 and 2 took cover alongside the wall as they exchanged shots with the enemy.

"You thinking what I'm thinking?" 2 stated as he fired a few suppressing shots. "If that first one we fought..."

He ducked closer to the wall as red plasma bolts flew past him, narrowly missing his shoulder.

"...was heavily armored, then these two...!"

He fired a few more shots as he ducked in and out of cover.

"...might be easier to take down!"

"They're much faster than the other one!" 1 grunted annoyingly as he tried to help 2 by suppressing the drones.

The drones weren't seeking cover next to the walls like they were. They easily evaded every shot fired at them. This was due to the fact that whenever the amborgs popped out to take aim, the drones could track the trajectory of their shots. Maybe they could conceal their attacks.

"2!" 1 declared. "I'm the bait!"

2 gave 1 an intense but knowing look.

"You were the bait last time!" he protested as the drones began marching towards them. "Remember? You got shot back home on that mission!"

"It'll work this time!" 1 shouted.

1 trusted that 2 would do his part. He was putting his faith into the armor that Ulgo had provided them in the armory hours ago. Ultimately, he was hoping that this maneuver would be enough. They would just have to be faster than the advancing drones.

"Now!" 1 commanded.

He leapt out and stepped forward. 2 jumped into the center and took position behind 1. Using his friend as a shield, 2 pointed his rifle directly at 1's back. They only had less than a second.

Just as the drones locked into 1, he raised his rifle, directing it towards the trajectory of their aimed weapons. If needed, he planned to deflect their shots with his rifle before absorbing the impact with his armor. If 2's aim was accurate, this would work.

Before they had the chance to shoot at him, 1 dropped and ducked down the moment he knew the drones were fixated on him. This would be their downfall. They saw 1 drop and hesitated, as if they were still processing what was happening. By the time they looked up at 2, it was too late. He had already pulled the trigger.

With 1 out of the way, 2 had a clear line of sight to the drone on the left. His first shot found its mark, striking the drone in the head. As the second drone attempted to lift its rifle to aim at 2, the amborgs were already one step ahead.

1 and 2 took aim and fired off a rapid burst at the second drone, hitting their mark with deadly precision. The two drones collapsed, their heads completely melted off.

"I told you it'd work," 1 panted as he stood up.

"Let's not do that again," 2 gulped. "I hate pointing weapons at you. Especially futuristic alternate universe weapons that can melt us."

"Desperate times," 1 panted, "desperate measures."

When they were definitely sure that they were dead, (1 had to stop 2 from repeatedly stomping on the enemy bots), they moved on to the engineering section.

They needed to see if there had been any attempts made to sabotage the section of the ship that was essentially the biggest and the most important battery onboard. If it was taken over or destroyed, the rest of the ship would go down.

The doors slid open, and they stepped inside with caution, only to encounter more chaos. Several marines were aiming their weapons at them. 1 and 2 immediately took up a defensive stance.

"Hands up!" someone shouted. "Identify yourself!"

"We're amborgs!" 1 called out to them.

"Hey!"

1 and 2 glanced to their right/left? and noticed an engineer pointing at them.

"They were here inspecting the place! They were helping! It's them!" she exclaimed.

One of the marines looked at 1 and 2 suspiciously.

"We can't just allow them in here because of one person's say-so!"

"You have to!" 1 replied. "We can help you defend this part of the ship! Unless you'd rather explode in a massive ball of matter and anti-matter."

"That'd be a mercy rather than being tortured to death," 2 muttered grimly.

"Not helping," 1 stated.

"I got an idea," the same engineer spoke up. "What was the component that you pulled out with Chief Hayes earlier?"

"The thing that looked like a Kit-Kat bar," 2 replied instinctively.

The engineer grinned as she nodded her head firmly at the squad leader.

"It's them!" she said confidently.

The squad leader sniffed and conceded. He lowered his rifle and several others did the same. A few of them kept a fixed gaze on the amborgs, still a bit skeptical.

"Friendlies!" he declared. "But I warn you, we have eyes on you at all times. Get those doors shut!"

The doors slid closed with a massive clang. 1 and 2 lowered their weapons, relieved to find themselves in a place far removed from the fighting. They scanned the room vigilantly, ensuring there was no suspicious activity. It was possible they would need to identify any potential infiltrators who had cleverly hidden among them.

They searched for Chief Hayes or anyone else in charge as they noticed several people sprawled across the floor. Wounded marines, officers, and engineers were occupying all the space inside. It seemed that these people had the right idea to seek shelter here. Although, if main engineering was captured or destroyed, the ship would be doomed.

1 and 2 made their way to Chief Hayes, who was sitting on the floor near a console a short distance from one of the entrances to the main reactor. Several members of the engineering staff lay on the ground along with a few destroyed Silent Eclipse drones. A few people were actually dismantling and smashing the bodies to pieces to make sure they stayed dead.

"About time," Chief Hayes smiled in relief when she saw the amborgs.

There was a bandage wrapped around her right arm and she was bleeding from the stomach. 1 looked around as 2 performed a body scan.

"What happened?" 1 asked as he examined the whole section.

"Well, when we began our attack," Hayes coughed, "we were all fine. Then security showed up saying they had orders from Ulgo to proceed with a lockdown of the ship. We thought it was a drill. Then the next thing I saw was my second in command getting stabbed from behind by another person who disintegrated into one of these nightmare robots here and before we knew it, it was a bloodbath. If it hadn't been for the marines here, we might not be talking to each other. I figured they must have been trying to take control of the ship from here."

The survivors from the engineering team were busy trying to assess the extent of the damage or taking moments to process the traumatic events they had just experienced. For a lot of them, it was likely their worst nightmare come to life. While many were desperately attempting to repair the compromised systems, a handful simply slumped against the walls, horrified at what had happened.

"One drone," Hayes pointed, "tried to access the reactor."

1 and 2 glanced at the spot where the terminal was. They recalled that it served as the main access to the reactor that fueled the entire ship. For some reason, the floor and walls surrounding it appeared scorched, as if someone had tried to cut through them with extremely hot lasers. Scattered around were the remnants of what seemed to be a Silent Eclipse drone, now in a million tiny pieces. It looked like someone had made an effort to clean up the area, but hadn't done a great job.

Chief Hayes continued her explanation as the amborgs patiently listened.

"But, I installed a... uh... almost legal trap. It got sliced to pieces by my laser mines. They activate whenever someone other than me tries to manually shut down or initiate self-destruct protocols without the correct access codes."

"Wait, so if anyone decides to destroy the ship, they get lasered to death?" 2 asked, an alarmed expression in his eyes.

"Like I said," Hayes shrugged innocently. "Almost legal."

"I'm not questioning the legality," 2 replied. "I'm questioning why you have this death trap installed in the center of main engineering?"

"When you've been on enough starships like I have, you tend to get pretty protective of the power cores," Hayes replied innocently.

"Hold on," 2 blinked. "How many starships have you installed this trap on??"

"A few."

1 and 2 stared.

"I deactivated them every time I was transferred or promoted to a new ship!" Chief Hayes added for clarification. "Otherwise, if someone accidentally triggered them..."

"I thought you said the laser mines go off when someone tries to activate a ship self-destruct sequence," 2 stated. "Are you saying that any signs of tampering or unauthorized work would result in someone being incinerated?"

"Maybe..." Chief Hayes replied meekly. Then she feigned ignorance by looking away. "Oh gee... all this blood I've lost seems to be making my brain go fuzzy."

"She's delusional," 2 muttered.

"2!" 1 interrupted. "Not the time. Can we please focus on the present?"

"I respectfully disagree," 2 grumbled as he dropped the subject.

"Why?" 1 asked.

2's response was immediate, but still comprehensible to all the normal people within earshot.

"Because if I'm protecting the giant core of the big alternate universe starship that was sent here to protect us and is now filled with an army of creepy murder-bots that are causing a massive ship-wide genocide on the same level as the Dominoe Incident... I would very much appreciate not getting accidentally lasered to death if I take one wrong step into a lethal defensive trap."

Chief Hayes stared at 2. So did everyone else.

"Do you always talk like that?" she asked.

"It's been a really terrible day," 2 snapped.

He wasn't entirely wrong about that. 1 shook his head as he waved at a medic who was nearby treating the wounded. He nodded and slowly began to make his way over to them.

"So you're saying, you're the only one who could authorize the destruction of the ship?" 1 asked as he looked around cautiously. "I thought that the commanding officer of the ship would be the one who has that authority."

"Well, yeah," Hayes nodded. "Admiral Ra'aiah is in charge. But to activate something as serious as the self-destruct, it requires the right access codes depending on whatever protocol is in place right now. One way to do it is... get at least a few commanders that are the head of their departments to provide confirmation codes with the admiral's and there you go. Ship goes boom."

1 and 2 exchanged nervous glances.

"So, that means every ranking officer is at risk?" 1 asked. "The high ranking commanders?"

"No, not necessarily," Hayes replied. "I didn't explain that all too well. But, the bridge would definitely be a huge target to these drones. Same here with main engineering."

Hayes then held up her index finger.

"First, the self-destruct sequence can only be activated by the person in command of the starship. In this case, Admiral Ra'aiah. The enemy might try to capture her and force her to activate the sequence. After that, it requires confirmation codes from at least two or three other commanders with clearance. Like me... or Ulgo. Those codes are basically the passwords that you would use to start the entire sequence."

"Wouldn't it be pointless to attack main engineering?" 2 asked. "What am I missing here?"

"The self-destruct sequence is a high level command function for all starships," Hayes explained quickly. "It can be accessed and used in a select few locations. Main engineering is one of those places."

"But we should be fine as long as Admiral Ra'aiah is still alive, correct?" 1 asked.

"Yeah, except one could also just run into the main power core and hit it really hard," Hayes said nervously. "That'd sure put an end to our misery real fast."

1 and 2 nodded as they slowly understood the implications of what she was saying. Silent Eclipse most likely had several different contingencies in place. It made sense now. After the battle had begun, drones had suddenly appeared in strategic locations across the ship.

They were trying to make them lose control of the ship and when that happened, they would all be destroyed.

"So, we have to defend this area," 1 stated firmly. "The main power core is what's keeping the ship running. Silent Eclipse might try to attack here again soon."

The medic knelt down next to Hayes and inspected her wounds. As he began an assessment, she looked up at 1 and 2.

"Personally, I'm just glad we didn't all die in the first attack," she said, placing a hand over her bandaged stomach. "Listen to me, I need to ask you both for a favor."

1 and 2 nodded.

"If I die," she breathed, "I need to transfer my command codes and functions over to someone I trust. Two of my senior engineers are... missing... The rest are here... unable to perform."

"Are you sure?" 1 asked.

"If engineering falls, the ship falls," she said. "They can't get my codes."

The medic opened his bag and politely spoke to 2.

"Can you help me hold her steady?"

2 nodded and they all watched as the medic took out a syringe and injected a painkiller into Hayes' exposed neckline. She reached inside one of her chest pockets and pulled out some type of keycard.

"If I die, you need to take this and keep it safe. Don't let anyone access my command codes."

"We can't do that," 1 said. "Because you're going to be fine."

1 glanced at the medic with a hopeful look.

"Right?" he asked.

"Yes sir," the man replied with a confident smile. "She's not that badly injured. But, I'd still recommend we take her to sick-bay. She needs a doctor."

"Combat medic?" 2 asked.

"Yes sir. I triage as best as I can and then pass them on to the next emergency personnel."

"Well, then hopefully the lockdown ends soon," 1 stated.

"If I may? Sir?"

The medic looked around and gestured to all of the other people that were down.

"We're stretched way too thin," he explained in a hushed whisper. "I know we're supposed to shelter in place during lockdown procedures but... we need to get everyone in here help. We need to evacuate the wounded."

Someone nearby groaned and called for help, snagging the medic's attention. He politely excused himself and ran towards the victim. 2 looked at 1.

"He's right," he stated. "Some of these people aren't going to make it if they stay here."

Chief Hayes lit up.

"What about the vents?"

1 and 2 turned to her and listened intently.

"You could use the vents," she repeated. "We have small remotely-operated modules. They carry supplies for us whenever we have to crawl inside the vents for maintenance."

"Right," 2 smiled. "We could program them to travel to the medical bay!"

"Hang on," 1's face fell. "So can the enemy."

2's smile faded as realization spread across his face. Chief Hayes suddenly looked alarmed.

"The vents," she breathed. "Tell the marines!"

1 glanced around the room and saw the squad leader talking to another person nearby.

"Sir!" he called out to him.

The squad leader turned and promptly walked over.

"What is it?" he demanded.

"You need to post some of your marines at all of the maintenance hatches and vents!" 1 declared. "The drones can fit through them!"

His eyes widened, taken aback, and pivoted sharply.

"Shit," he said. He quickly activated his radio and spoke into it. "Marines! Eyes up! Eyes up! I need everyone to fan out and watch all maintenance and service hatches in the entire department!"

Every person that was armed and suited up immediately began to scramble at the call to action. They all checked their ammo and weapons as they responded swiftly.

"We need to set up mines at each hatch, scan every one of them, and get ready to fight," the leader continued briefing everyone over the radio. He looked at Chief Hayes. "Chief, how many hatches are in here?"

"In this room, there are at least 25!"

1 and 2 watched the squad leader let out a frustrated groan.

"I don't have enough people to cover that many," he explained quickly.

The amborgs then had an idea. 1 looked down at Chief Hayes.

"Do you have any more of those semi-legal laser traps?" he asked curiously.

"I keep some more in my office," she answered honestly. Then she gave them a knowing look. "Oh. Good idea."

"Ziggy..."

1 looked at 2 intensely.

"Let's turn this place into the most difficult spot of the ship to break into," he declared. "We need to hurry."

1 stood up and walked over to the marine squad leader.

"You can set up mines, grenades or whatever explosives you have in some hatches, right?"

The marine nodded.

"Yes sir," he replied, but he shook his head slightly like he was nervous about something. "We just don't have enough ammo if there's another firefight."

"What if we tried blocking as many hatches as we can?" 1 suggested. "We need to set up defenses around the access points to the main power core. So, we block vents, hatches, and every opening that's close to us."

"Create chokepoints," 2 added. "If we can't get to all of them, then we got to the most vulnerable ones."

"Yes sir," the squad leader nodded. "Chief Hayes, can we get the schematics?"

Chief Hayes was slowly getting up on her own. 2 rushed over to help her. Once she was standing, she nodded determinedly.

"Come on everyone!" she called out. "If you can stand, help me defend the ship! If you can't, find all the cover you can and brace yourselves!"

Deck Seven
Residential Area

"This is 3! Do you read me? I'm on my way to the nursery at infant care!"

3 heard a response in her mind.

"Move quickly 3," 43 said over the comms. "That was one of the first sections to go dark!"

Running at full speed, 3 and 5 raced through the hallways of deck seven, which housed the civilians and the families of many crew members. Admiral Ra'aiah had quickly dispatched marines and armed security to this area, as it was likely that the civilians were the initial targets of Silent Eclipse. Taking them hostage would put them in a dangerous position while the rest of the vital sections of the Firestar were being secured.

Along the way, 3 and 5 picked up a few squads of marines. Technically, the whole deck was supposed to be free of any non-combatants. However, a few stragglers crossed their path. For every civilian they encountered, they would send a couple of their marines to escort them to safety.

There was security monitoring the children in the nurseries, but they doubted it would be enough to stop an army of assassin drones.

"Enemies sighted!" 5 yelled.

The amborgs halted in place and readied themselves. Both charged their weapons and took aim.

A group of Silent Eclipse drones dashed through their line of fire. A few of them pivoted to confront them and opened fire, while more bots continued to sprint past. 3's eyes widened in horror.

"They're entering the daycare!" she exclaimed.

Before the amborgs initiated their rescue plan and split away, Commander Ulgo had provided 3 with a plasma repeater. It was essentially a heavy machine gun that could be operated by a single soldier or a standard two-person team when it required setup. Thanks to her enhanced strength, she could run and carry it effortlessly. She also possessed a spacegun and was excited to test it out after a brief training session.

Once she was ready, she pressed the trigger of her weapon with her thumb. In less than two seconds, the repeater unleashed its fury. A massive single stream of lasers blasted out of the barrel as it ripped the enemy robots to shreds. More robots turned down the hall to shield the ones running towards the nurseries but were mowed down into pieces from 3's barrage. The marines behind them and 5 likely managed to fire off a few shots at best.

3 had to stop firing when the clip ran dry. Thankfully, she had learned how to reload. Doing it in reality was another story, especially since she was handling a space weapon from an alternate universe.

"Eject clip," she muttered as she took her hand off the trigger and reached for the bolt handle.

While she tried to reload, 5 and the squad of marines covered her with a volley of suppressing fire at more Silent Eclipse drones. She gripped the handle and pulled it back. There was a snap as the empty clip in the repeater ejected. Just like pulling the fore-end of a shotgun back, this grabbed the next plasma clip that was stored in a magazine bar rack inside the repeater. Once it was all the way back to where she couldn't pull it any further, 3 slid it forward and there was a click which indicated that the repeater was ready to fire again.

"That is seriously one of the coolest guns ever!" 5 exclaimed when 3 resumed the barrage of lasers in the hallway. "Very Star Wars!"

"You would have one too," 3 grunted as she marched forward. "But you keep forgetting to retake and update your heavy weapons certifications!"

"I'm sorry!" 5 replied as he kept shooting drones. "I wasn't exactly expecting to be off-planet when they expired! Interstellar alternate-universe war was also not in the schedule!"

One of the marines behind them called out to them.

"Ma'am?! Sir?!"

"Sorry!" 5 replied sheepishly.

"Me too!" 3 added. She turned her head and motioned for everyone to move. "Let's go!"

The whole team moved in formation, carefully stepping over the torn and charred remains of Silent Eclipse drones. Once they reached the intersection, they turned left down the corridor. A few feet ahead lay the entrance that several enemy drones had already passed. The group stopped and prepared to enter.

"Shoot everything going for you or a child," 3 instructed quickly.

The marines behind her shouted in unison, acknowledging her orders. After confirming that everyone was ready, she turned to 5, who responded with a resolute nod.

"Move in!"

3 and 5 kept their weapons trained on the door. A marine rushed forward to access the panel. They quickly unlocked it, and it began to slide open. As soon as it was clear, the group rushed in. They encountered a cluster of enemy robots trying to fight someone behind the reception desk, but they were surprisingly being held back. However,

their sudden entrance did not go unnoticed. A few of the Silent Eclipse bots began to turn around, preparing to charge and fire at them.

3 lifted the repeater but 5 immediately signaled to her to halt in place.

"Don't shoot 3!" he yelled to everyone. "Engage in close quarters! Don't fire off heavy weapons here!"

3 understood right away why 5 had shouted at her to stand down. The inside of the reception area of the daycare was smaller than they had expected. Firing their weapons would be catastrophic. Cutting the bots down would be easy, but there was the risk of accidentally involving innocents in the line of fire.

"Right!" 3 let out a frustrated sigh.

She lowered the repeater and swung it behind her. The pack that carried all of her extra ammo had a clasp which secured the weapon in place as she holstered it onto her back.

The marines surged ahead, picking their targets with precision, and in an impressive display of coordinated teamwork, the amborgs watched as they bravely charged the Silent Eclipse drones. 3 and 5 hesitated for a moment, then joined in on the action, but the assassin drones were faster.

5 was taken aback when he saw the marine beside him go down from a powerful punch to the head. The helmet took the brunt of the blow, but it was strong enough to send him sprawling. Just before hitting the ground, he glanced at Johnny and tossed something into the air. With lightning-fast reflexes, 5 caught it and swiftly pressed a button on it. At first, he thought it was some sort of grenade, but after a quick inspection, he confidently aimed and hurled it at the drone that was barreling towards him.

A spear shot out from the 3-inch metal pole that the marine had handed over, striking the robot right in the throat. 5 quickly sprinted forward as the drone stumbled backward, grabbing the spear. With a powerful twist, he tore the head off, and it exploded in a fountain of sparks.

The marines fought valiantly but were ultimately outmatched. 3 and 5 were thoroughly impressed with their coordination. It was smooth and flawless, as one would expect from people who have trained and served alongside each other for many years.

3 yelled to everyone that could hear her.

"Advance!" she bellowed.

The marines still in the fight moved ahead and ramped up their assault. One of them ran over to 5 to protect him from the side.

"Sir!" she declared. "Extend your bayonet!"

"Huh?"

5 swung his rifle around his shoulder and checked it. He angled it and saw a button with a knife emblem near the trigger.

"Oh! This?"

Pressing the button extended an eight inch blade.

"Nice," 5 nodded confidently.

"Even if you're about to lose the battle!" 3 shouted as they swung and slashed at the Silent Eclipse drones. "Think about what happens if you give in right now!"

She wasn't sure what made her say that, but she hoped it would motivate the marines to fight bravely. Their lives were on the line, and for those with loved ones, she wished they would consider what they were fighting to protect and keep pushing forward. She wasn't sure if 5 shared the same thoughts or was getting ready to use humor to mask his true feelings, but she knew deep down that she couldn't give up because her friends were out there, and she wanted to see them safe and sound.

Their persistence paid off. Each drone that broke into the nurseries was torn down and destroyed. They had won the fight. They were finally able to figure out who had held off the assault and protected the reception area from being breached.

"Get a medic!" 3 yelled as she attempted to take off her backpack.

A tall humanoid figure lay sprawled on the ground. 3 had seen a few members of this species roaming around the ship. Based on the knowledge she had acquired and her current observations, she was able to accurately identify this crewmember.

She had four eyes and four long and slender arms. Getting into a fistfight with her would probably make for some really interesting boxing competitions. There were a few swords that were laying on the floor near her, which was likely what she had utilized to hold off the enemy drones. Give her four lightsabers and she could probably give General Grievous a run for his money.

3 knew that this woman was a Kovark—short for the Brakovish Arklashi. She was also a matriarch which was a big deal to their cultural traditions.

"Can you hear me?" 3 asked as she placed a hand on the Kovark woman's face. "We're here to help! Just stay with me! Can you identify yourself?"

A medic within their squad came forward and knelt down to help examine her condition. The Kovark woman stirred and let out a cough.

"Matriarch..." she rasped as her breathing was ragged. "Breya... of the Kovark. Retired commando in the S.C.E. military. I... am the receptionist here in infant care."

3 knew she was possibly telling the truth. She remembered that 466 had met this woman.

"Pretty awesome receptionist if you ask me! Holding out against so many robots," 5 nodded in approval. He quickly turned to address the marines. "Cover the entrance and get ready to sweep for any other survivors. Send for another squad and have them up here now."

The marines nodded and quickly dispersed while the amborgs tried to care for Breya with the help of the medic that was carefully administering emergency care.

"I am willing... to do anything... to make sure that... the kids are safe," Breya said as she motioned to the chair. "I can heal a lot better if I am sitting."

3 turned to the medic.

"Can we move her?" she asked.

"Yes ma'am," the woman replied. "Let's all lift her."

3 and 5 both followed her instructions and got into position to help. Along with the medic, they counted to three and in sync, lifted Breya up and carried her over to the nearby chair. Once they gently lowered her onto the cushions, she let out a sigh of relief.

"Much better," she groaned.

"What's the situation here?" 3 asked gently.

Breya looked at 3 with all four of her eyes, which was a little unsettling.

"Once the lockdown began," she explained, "we shut and barricaded the doors. If this area is clear, you can speak to my staff on the other side of the entrance into the nurseries."

"Silent Eclipse might mount another assault," 5 stated as he looked around. "Or, if we're not careful, they might be inside the nurseries already."

"If that's the case," Breya growled and tried to sit up. "I need to..."

"No," 3 and the medic said at the same time and gently attempted to keep her from leaving her chair.

"Let us make sure that it's safe," 3 spoke reassuringly. "Please, can you tell us how many people are still in infant care?"

Breya let out another sigh and gave up when they all continued to block her from standing up.

"I have fifteen teachers and six civilian adults in the nurseries," she answered. "There are still children here who haven't gone home to their sections. At least 46. You need to make sure they're safe by any means necessary."

"We understand," 3 nodded. "5, can you take the lead on this?"

"I can do that," 5 winked. "I need two of you to come with me. The rest of you protect the entrance."

5 backed off and found two volunteers. They made their way around the reception area and pressed a button on the panel next to the door. As they filed out of the room, 3 worked with the medic to stabilize Breya's condition.

"Let me help you," the medic stated as she pulled out a small pouch from her bag. "I could use another pair of hands to help."

"You sure?" 3 asked.

Breya let out a chuckle.

"My anatomy is not the same as yours. It would be nice to have two pairs of hands healing me. Ha ha."

The medic looked at 3 and smiled. As she kept sorting through her assortment of syringes, 3 smiled back encouragingly.

"Really? I left my other pair of eyes back home," 3 said jokingly. "And your tan? I get those on a nice sunny day without sunscreen."

"Inject me with the purple painkiller," Breya chuckled. "Your tool will warn you that it contains a dangerous amount... but once you hold it up to me, it will detect what race I am and it will turn green. Once it does, press it to my neck. Then I need one pill labeled 'G.H.' Afterwards, we need to slow my heart rate. Then we can focus on closing my wounds."

The medic was already following Breya's instructions and searching for the right painkiller. 3 observed carefully and made several mental notes. This would be helpful if she had to help another of Breya's species.

"I don't think I'll be much help," 3 stated as she watched the medic work.

"If something goes wrong," the medic replied, "it always helps to have someone assisting. Most paramedics from your universe work in pairs, isn't that right?"

"A lot of professions involve two-person teams," 3 nodded.

The medic passed a tool over to 3. She examined it and was about to ask what it was, but the medic was too quick.

"Help me scan matriarch Breya's neckline for her artery," she instructed. "We have to inject it correctly or we'll lose her."

Breya pointed at the scanner and then lifted one of her right hands to indicate a spot on her neck.

"There's a scanner on your tool that will help you identify where my artery is," she said. "Press the green button and it will help you locate it if you're feeling unsure."

3 pressed the green button as instructed and a scanning ray appeared over Breya's neck. She saw a faint orange outline of the veins and arteries and knew where to inject the capsule.

"There you go," Breya nodded. "Just like that. There's your target."

The medic thanked both of them for the assist and moved slowly. Carefully, she injected the painkiller into the biggest artery in Breya's veins.

There was a hissing sound as the capsule changed from purple to a clear piece of plastic. The medic pulled her syringe away. 3 did another body scan. Even though her anatomy was different from a human's, she saw that her readings, even if they were marked as 'unknown,' were improving and steering away from the red area.

"Ok well... everything is stable-ish," 3 said.

"It will be stable if you can promise to protect the children," Breya said, grabbing 3's wrist and staring right into her eyes. "We mustn't let them be caught or killed. Their families..."

"I understand," 3 nodded.

"Ma'am! We have more incoming!"

3 turned her head sharply. A few of the marines had set up a defensive position and were watching the entrance. They had spotted movement heading towards Infant Care.

Quickly, 3 handed a side-arm to Breya. She grabbed it with one of her right hands and looked at 3 curiously.

"Last line of defense," 3 stated. "We're not going to let any more drones get past you."

"Much appreciated," Breya nodded.

The marines had taken cover and were aiming out of the entrance to the receptionist area. 3 could see more drones running their way. She quickly pulled the repeater off her back and charged it.

"Open fire!" she shouted and sudden streams of lasers began pouring into the hallway.

3 instantly sent a transmission out over the emergency channel.

"We're engaging the enemy! Deck seven! Infant care is under attack again!" she reported. "We need reinforcements ASAP!"

Resistance Isn't Futile

S.C.E. Firestar
Bridge

"Send troops to the civilian sectors immediately. Once we secure weapons control, order all of our fighter craft to stay out of weapons range."

Admiral Ra'aiah heard someone clear his throat. Her first officer, Commander Ulgo, maintained a serious and grim expression. He was definitely worried about something.

"Our fighters may not have enough fuel," he stated. "Our pilots might be stranded out there."

"Then we need to make sure the entire weapons control deck is still under our control," Admiral Ra'aiah replied. "I'm not bringing our pilots back only to have them torn apart by our point defense weapons."

She looked up at one of her communications officers.

"Notify all squadrons still out there," she ordered. "Maintain a safe distance from the Firestar. The situation is still not safe."

As the crewman acknowledged her orders, they started broadcasting her instructions over the radio. Admiral Ra'aiah shifted her focus to a holographic map displayed on her screen. It depicted her entire vessel, showcasing every deck, every level, and every component, all reflecting the current status in real-time.

The sections highlighted by red lights were where her marines reported enemy contact. Watching the screen turn crimson in such a short period of time had terrified her and the crew on the bridge. She had almost considered giving the order to abandon ship if it had come to that. Thankfully, with the help of the amborgs, a few areas had shifted to blue, indicating they were secure. When she noticed that the engineering deck was under control, she felt a sense of relief knowing that they were managing to keep it from falling into Silent Eclipse's hands. The main power core was their most critical asset. With that in mind, she started directing her troops to clear out and reclaim other vital sections. Specifically, she wanted to ensure weapons control and the residential area were protected.

It was a bold plan, but dividing her forces into two battle groups spread them thin. Also, more Silent Eclipse drones appeared as the battle progressed. It was like fighting a zombie apocalypse, although in this case it's killer robots instead of the undead spawning out of nowhere.

Suddenly, an eager voice spoke up and Admiral Ra'aiah saw someone running to her side. His white lab coat shifted around his waist, and the admiral glanced up to see Dr. Kendrick on the phone with someone.

"The Fourth Group just sent word that there is progress," he explained. "They've made their way to weapons control and just arrived on that deck. What are they looking for?"

"Any of the surviving department heads," Admiral Ra'aiah replied with an exasperated sigh. "They have to secure all gun mounts, batteries, missile launchers and control rooms."

6 stepped forward and lifted a hand curiously.

"Didn't you tell us that engineering can help lockdown certain systems?" she asked.

"Yes, but not all of them."

Commander Ulgo shook his head sternly as he watched the map with the admiral.

"The energy-based weapons," he explained. "The main reactor and power cores help us with the engines and ship propulsion. They also supply power and fuel for the R-batteries."

"The railgun or... laser cannons?" Dr. Kendrick asked for clarification.

"Yes sir," Ulgo nodded. "The R-batteries fire huge energy beams that have excellent range. Without any power from engineering, they're useless. Technically, we can also prevent our missile launchers from sending out any ordinance."

"Wait," 6 interjected. "The S.C.E. uses kinetic weapons right?"

"Right again," Admiral Ra'aiah nodded. "We have point-defense guns, flak batteries, and big gun mounts that fire heavy artillery rounds at short to medium ranges. If anyone gets too close, we tear them apart. Or worse..."

Admiral Ra'aiah glanced at Dr. Kendrick and 6.

"If we've lost weapons control, they might decide to fire their weapons at Earth," she stated.

"Kinetic weapons can cause massive damage at an unfathomable scale," Ulgo added. "You don't even need to fire an explosive round. Just launch something big enough at a high speed and it can level a city just with its momentum alone. Or rearrange your entire planet."

"Newton's first law," 6 breathed.

"That's certainly unsettling," Dr. Kendrick winced, looking fearful. Everyone fell silent.

"Ok," Admiral Ra'aiah said. She lifted her hand and motioned for Ulgo to take it down a notch. "I think they got the picture."

Commander Ulgo dipped his head apologetically and then looked at Dr. Kendrick.

"My apologies for sharing some rather difficult facts," he said.

Ulgo cast a wary glance to the side, as if he had spotted something unusual. Everyone followed his gaze, but everything seemed normal. He turned back to 6 and Dr. Kenrick, raised his finger, and pointed towards a different station.

"Excuse me," he said. "I'm going to check on the rest of the bridge crew."

He walked away as Dr. Kendrick and 6 looked back at the map of the Firestar. Admiral Ra'aiah shrugged awkwardly before concentrating again. They assumed it was her way of giving them a quiet apology for Ulgo's strange behavior.

"There are so many people aboard my ship," she sighed softly. "We can't protect all of them."

"We'll help as best as we can," Dr. Kendrick spoke reassuringly. "Also, we're kind of stuck up here in space with you."

"When we get back to Earth," 6 shuddered. "I'm going to be so happy to feel real gravity again."

Admiral Ra'aiah gave them a soft smile. She opened her mouth to speak but was interrupted.

A deafening gunshot rang out across the bridge. Everyone turned to see someone at their station collapse from a bullet wound to the head. For a brief moment, shock took over, and everyone practically jumped out of their skins. The crew members nearest to the incident were huddled in terror. Those positioned further away assumed defensive stances, but they had no idea what they were facing.

Admiral Ra'aiah gripped her chair seat, then leapt to her feet and reached for her holster. 6 jumped to defend Dr. Kendrick, urging him closer to the admiral's chair, which provided him with some basic cover. Everyone's gaze was fixed on Commander Ulgo, who glared menacingly at the crew member he'd shot. His firearm was drawn, still faintly smoking from the recent discharge.

"What the hell?!" 6 cried.

Ulgo calmly lowered his gun and looked back at them.

"They're already here," he explained.

"Oh shit," Admiral Ra'aiah drew her own gun and looked around.

Commander Ulgo prodded the lifeless body of the person he had shot with the tip of his gun. A loud, metallic thunk echoed as he showed them what he had found.

"Look, it's a disguise," he informed them. "They replaced Jennings."

Ulgo was right. A holographic image began dissipating, revealing a Silent Eclipse drone underneath wearing one of their uniforms. It had been seated so casually at the console, right under their noses.

"I'm impressed you saw through that," Dr. Kendrick gulped.

"I didn't," Ulgo admitted with a displeased look on his face. "Jennings seemed off. When he realized he had been made, I was quicker on the draw."

"Remind me never to piss him off," 6 said nervously.

"I'm definitely going to want to know how you discovered that he was an imposter," Admiral Ra'aiah stated as she cast a wary glance around the room. "But that does mean we have another problem among us."

Admiral Ra'aiah stood up and pivoted sharply. She had her weapon drawn but kept it pointed at the floor. It was clear that she was uneasy about preparing to open fire on her own crewmembers.

"We're probably compromised," she said fearfully.

Dr. Kendrick's eyes widened.

"I thought you had marines protecting all access points to the bridge," he said.

"I-I do!" she stammered. "But if they're in here... and all of our protective details are not..."

Dr. Kendrick leaned in towards 6. The sight of the admiral losing her composure was not helping at all.

"She looks like she's starting to panic," he whispered.

Admiral Ra'aiah turned his way, which made flinch.

"I heard that," she said.

"She's part cat," 6 mumbled, "it makes sense that her senses are heightened. But, if I may..."

6 raised her voice a little louder.

"Admiral," she said calmly but clearly, "I'm going to ask that you unclench your grip on your gun."

Someone nearby shakily pointed a finger at 6.

"Why?!" she squealed in panic. "She's trying to take down the admiral!"

"What?" 6 looked taken aback. "No! I just asked her to relax a little!"

"Commander! Shoot her! She's an imposter!" the same officer shrieked.

"Quiet! That's an order lieutenant!" Ulgo declared angrily.

Another officer bravely spoke up next to Ulgo.

"How do we know that the commander isn't in on it too?"

"Oh no..." Dr. Kendrick muttered.

Ulgo turned around and stared incredulously at the man who challenged him. This show of bravado looked ridiculous, but he was doing his best to remain professional. Still, he was just making himself appear stupid, allowing his fear to overtake his logical reasoning.

"You could have shot Jennings or whatever that was in his place to cover for yourself!"

Dr. Kendrick gulped as this confrontation lowered the morale across the bridge. Fear and paranoia seemed to have gripped the crew and it looked like it was tightening close to the point of a total breakdown in discipline.

"Uh oh," he said as he and 6 nervously began to watch the crewmembers. "This is escalating."

"I agree. Any ideas?" 6 gulped. "We're surrounded without any backup. I'm feeling a little outnumbered. Whatever happens, I think we're both dead in all current scenarios I'm calculating."

"Do I want to know how many that you've already thought of?" Dr. Kendrick asked.

"It's a lot..." 6 replied bluntly. "182 so far."

"I had to ask..." Dr. Kendrick sighed.

The members of the bridge crew exchanged anxious glances, their faces reflecting growing paranoia. Doubts began to creep in among them, and both Admiral Ra'aiah and Commander Ulgo struggled to keep the situation under control. Dr. Kendrick had a potential solution in mind, but it required either the admiral or the commander—the only armed personnel present on the bridge—to act decisively. The chances of this plan failing catastrophically was moderately high.

"6," Dr. Kendrick spoke softly. "You have a shield that the commander gave you. Correct?"

6 nodded slowly while everyone around them started to bicker and their voices grew louder.

"Yes."

"Is it strong enough to withstand... *that*?" he asked.

"We can find out," 6 replied as she braced herself. "On your mark."

Dr. Kendrick took a deep breath. 6 listened to him and waited for his signal, which would come when he exhaled and gave the command. Understanding his intentions, she began to widen her feet into a bladed stance.

"Now!" Dr. Kendrick yelled.

Everyone nearby stopped as they watched 6 cross her arms and a blue outline appeared around her. The shield had deployed seamlessly, and according to what Ulgo had taught the amborgs, she was ready for any kind of attack. Dr. Kendrick quickly pulled a device from his pocket and threw it at the floor. Once it struck the plating, it whined and activated.

Suddenly, a red ring appeared and snaked across the floor. It spread outward, wrapping around everyone's feet. It didn't seem to affect anyone as they all looked down in bewilderment. Dr. Kendrick and 6 exchanged quick glances, scanning their surroundings.

"There!" 6 pointed.

All eyes shifted to another bridge officer. The red ring had shot out, but rather than going past his feet, it clung to him like a magnet, and the energy beam coursed through his entire body. He seemed to be fine, yet there was a noticeable electrical dissipation. That's when everyone noticed.

The officer transformed right in front of them. To their horror, his human face melted away, replaced by something entirely different. It tried to keep up its holographic facade, but it was clear that its true form had been exposed. Realizing this, Dr. Kendrick raised his finger and pointed.

"That's it!" he declared.

Admiral Ra'aiah hesitated, but once she came to her senses, she quickly raised her weapon. But Ulgo was faster. Her first officer had already taken aim at the Silent Eclipse drone and fired at its head.

One second, the head was grappling with the startling realization that it had been exposed and the next, it was blown clean off. The entire bridge watched in complete silence as the drone shed its disguise completely and crashed to the ground.

After a few deep breaths, Admiral Ra'aiah scanned the room. When she was convinced it was clear, she glanced at Commander Ulgo.

"Nice uh... nice shot," she said.

Commander Ulgo lowered his weapon and looked at her with a small smirk.

"Thank you ma'am," he replied.

Admiral Ra'aiah lowered her gun and holstered it. When it was safely stored away on her person, she turned to Dr. Kendrick.

"What was that?" she asked.

"A little something from my universe," he replied.

He knelt down and picked up the device.

"A device built to locate robotic circuits," he explained as 6's shield disappeared, and she dropped her guard. "It actually was a failed gadget that created more problems than solutions. It shorts out nearby components like a stun grenade for a computer."

"You can just say EMP," 6 stated.

Dr. Kendrick shook his head and looked at her in slight irritation.

"An EMP would shut things down permanently," he replied as he firmly held up the device. "This... is not that powerful."

"Never mind what it is!"

Dr. Kendrick and 6 were abruptly silenced when the admiral sharply cut in. They looked at her fearfully like two kids about to be scolded. Admiral Ra'aiah glanced around the room.

"Stand down and go back to your stations! That's an order!"

Her command echoed throughout the entire bridge. A few crewmembers slowly and obediently turned to sit back down in their seats. The ones that were still afraid there were more imposters among them kept eyeing each other suspiciously. A moment later, Commander Ulgo stepped in for a quick assist.

"Are you all deaf?!" he yelled. "Back to your stations! Let's continue defending our ship!"

Whether it was due to the fury in his voice or the genuine fear felt by most of the crew, it seemed to have created a rippling effect. Everyone appeared to have caught a second wind as they returned to their posts. It was as if the two drones that had been shot down moments ago were nothing more than an afterthought.

"You can help us find the Silent Eclipse drones with that."

Dr. Kendrick nodded when he noticed the admiral and commander walk over to him.

"Truth be told," he admitted softly, "if Serina was here, she could help enhance this gadget's ability on a larger scale."

"I keep telling you to bring more than one A.I. with you," 6 stated bluntly. She looked at the admiral while Dr. Kendrick scowled. "Or at least, let more of them piggyback with us."

"What?" Admiral Ra'aiah raised an eyebrow.

"Foreign territory," Dr. Kendrick sighed.

Admiral Ra'aiah repeated her question.

"What?" she shook her head in confusion.

6 quickly explained it to her.

Amborgs all had special portable A.I. transport devices that were equipped in their uniforms. Even though she had chosen to remain at Dr. Kendrick's side the entire time they were aboard the Firestar, she or any other program just like her could jump from person to person. It was useful considering the fact that all of the technology and systems aboard this massive ship was unknown to the A.I. programs.

"Serina was afraid to integrate herself into your systems," 6 added. "Because to her and the other A.I.s that are on Apogee station, you are from an alternate universe. They all agreed that it might be a good idea to stay out of your technology."

"She figured that you didn't want a foreign program from our universe accidentally destroying your systems," Dr. Kendrick added. "I'm starting to think that's why she was so happy to be going on that rescue mission."

Commander Ulgo cleared his throat as he announced his presence. They turned to see him stroll up to 6.

"Why doesn't she or any of the other amborgs use that device?" he asked.

"Does a big number on my scanner," 6 responded as she lifted her hand and tapped her right temple. "Without that fancy shield of yours, it would have stunned me or knocked me out. It's really disorienting."

Ulgo nodded with the same stoic expression he always had. 6 saw his eyes fall for a moment as he turned away to observe the rest of the bridge. He was probably disappointed with this information. It was understandable.

Dr. Kendrick could sense the uneasy tension, so he decided to speak up.

"Anyway," he cleared his throat in an attempt to mimic the commander. "That was merely to see how many other unexpected guests we had hiding aboard."

Admiral Ra'aiah let out a sigh of relief.

"You did save us," she said. "Now we can get back to securing the ship."

She turned to Ulgo.

"Commander," she declared firmly. "Coded message to the marine squads defending the lifts and access points to the bridge. Tell them to hold the line."

"Yes, admiral," Ulgo replied. He walked over to the communications station to talk with the officer sitting there. "Transmitting secure messages."

"That might get their attention."

6 and Dr. Kendrick blinked and looked at the admiral.

"What does that mean?" Dr. Kendrick glanced at 6, who shrugged.

"We need to maintain control of all vital areas," Admiral Ra'aiah explained. "They're attacking civilians and going to use them as hostages to get us to negotiate or force us to surrender the ship."

She pointed at the holographic map of the Firestar. The audio sensors must have heard her and knew what she wanted as it zoomed in on deck 7. Then, she pointed towards the top of the holographic screen. It scrolled up and then zoomed in on the bridge.

"We have the bridge," she said. "I'm willing to bet that Silent Eclipse knows that it lost contact with the drones hiding up here thanks to that device of yours. They're probably going to send more troops our way as a result. You take the bridge, you effectively cut off our eyes and ears to the rest of the ship."

"Can we even hold the bridge?" 6 asked. "All of your forces that are still fighting are trying to save civilians, protect engineering, and retake weapons control! What happens if the ship falls?"

Admiral Ra'aiah paused, glancing down before shifting her gaze to 6 and Dr. Kendrick, her face etched with concern. She softened her voice.

"I have a few plans," she said. "As long as I'm alive, I will continue to protect your world..."

The way she phrased her statement confirmed their suspicions, but at least it was still reassuring to hear her make such a promise even though she wasn't so sure if they would survive this fight. As the commanding officer in charge of the ship, she was trying to maintain control of herself and keep everyone else's morale up.

"Thank you," Dr. Kendrick smiled. "It must be difficult being in your position."

Admiral Ra'aiah turned and looked at her vacant chair.

"I've lost a lot of people," she muttered. "Before I became an officer... There were a lot of friends and colleagues that didn't make it. I wanted to be a captain and command a ship so I could... stop losing everyone I care about. Now... I'm at risk of losing it all in one last fight."

"I wasn't criticizing your command," 6 spoke reassuringly. "We haven't lost yet."

"Exactly, I have an idea," Admiral Ra'aiah glanced down at the gadget in Dr. Kendrick's hand. "What if we used the signal from your device and spread it to the rest of our fleet? Channel it into a sensor? We can identify the Silent Eclipse troops and prevent the other ships from suffering our fate. They probably have the necessary camouflage to hide from our technology..."

Dr. Kendrick's eyes lit up. He and 6 exchanged eager and hopeful glances.

"...but not ours," Dr. Kendrick stated.

"I sure am glad to be from another universe," 6 stated.

"Let's... make sure this works first," Dr. Kendrick replied.

6 dashed to the first drone that Ulgo had shot down. Its head was completely blown off, and it was still seated in the chair at the station.

"Excuse me," 6 said to the officer next to the dead drone. "I'll get this out of the way."

Even though she had already wrapped her arms around the dead robot, the officer still offered to get up from his seat and helped her remove it from the chair. 6 thanked the officer once they set it on the floor and he returned to his station.

Admiral Ra'aiah and Dr. Kendrick walked over as 6 knelt down next to the robot.

"We have readings from these dead ones," she said as she pulled out a scanner. After she switched it on, she began to take some readings. "This drone has a unique power signature. Could you use this and combine it with Dr. Kendrick's gadget? We can spot all the imposters this way, right?"

"It could work."

Dr. Kendrick and 6 turned sharply while Admiral Ra'aiah merely remained still. They relaxed when they saw that commander Ulgo had come to join them.

"Dear lord!" Dr. Kendrick panted fearfully. "You're so fast! Do you have to pop up so quietly like that?"

"Sorry," Ulgo dipped his head politely. "It happens more frequently when we're at action stations."

Admiral Ra'aiah cleared her throat, getting everyone back on track.

"Ulgo," she said. "Do you mind helping 6 with her scans? Dr. Kendrick, you and I should take that device to Hemington."

Dr. Kendrick nodded as he held up the device.

"Oh, the radar officer? Of course!"

Ulgo stayed near 6 in order to stand guard as she continued to work. Even though the threat had been eliminated, they were still taking precautions. Actual biological beings couldn't spontaneously revive but drones or other robots sometimes could. It was best to be on the safe side.

Dr. Kendrick followed Admiral Ra'aiah to the radar station to meet Hemington, a bespectacled blond woman who turned and dipped her head. She greeted them when they walked up.

"Hemington," Admiral Ra'aiah pointed at Dr. Kendrick's hand. "I need you to send a coded message. Can you have any technicians help you whip up some kind of nonlethal energy pulse? I need to broadcast to the rest of the fleet when we rejoin them. We will first begin a radar pulse throughout our ship to test it out. If it works, then we'll inform the other ships. It will give our forces a chance so they won't be totally blind."

Hemington reached out her hand and Dr. Kendrick gently placed the gadget in her palm. She adjusted her glasses and examined it for a few moments.

"Yes ma'am," she replied. "I might need a few minutes but I think we can. This gadget is fascinating!"

Then she flicked her eyes up at Dr. Kendrick.

"Of course, it is from your universe. If I could have your assistance?"

Dr. Kendrick looked to Admiral Ra'aiah, who nodded. Without another word, he began to instruct Hemington how to work the gadget. Meanwhile, the sensor station next to Hemington activated an alarm. The officer seated there suddenly spoke up.

"Admiral!" he reported. "Contacts! Approaching to intercept!"

"What is it?" Admiral Ra'aiah demanded quickly.

"I.F.F. tags identified!" the officer answered promptly. "Ma'am, it's the rest of the fleet!"

"Oh no..."

Admiral Ra'aiah let out an exasperated groan. That had to be Captain Chastain, her godfather. She had given the other ships explicit instructions to maintain a defensive formation to protect the Earth. However, what they didn't know was that this was a ruse to hide their real mission. They had gone after the Tandeeri fleet so that 117 could leave the Firestar on a rescue operation while they pretended to go into battle. Someone probably disobeyed her orders and had taken it upon themselves to come after them.

Commander Ulgo looked over to the radar stations.

"They must be wondering why we're drifting out here," he said. "The diversion from the last battle was a while ago."

There was another chime from nearby. They all turned to see the communications officer turning her/his head to call out to them.

"Admiral! Urgent message from the Alexandria!"

"Put it through!"

Admiral Ra'aiah approached her chair and noticed a video screen activate. Captain Chastain appeared on the screen. He was an older but experienced leader, and he looked relieved to see her. Behind him, she saw red lights flashing, which meant that he had put his ship on full combat alert.

"Admiral," he said. "Are you alright?"

"What are you doing?" she asked sharply. "Abandoning your position?"

"We suddenly lost contact and feared the worst," he replied firmly. "It wasn't until we were in range that we thought it looked strange. The Firestar looks like it's still in one piece."

"That's an understatement, Chastain," Admiral Ra'aiah replied. "You need to fall back now!"

"Why?" Chastain looked concerned.

"I need you to standby for an incoming signal frequency that we're trying to put together!" she explained quickly. "Full broadcast in a pulse pattern throughout your entire ship and the rest of the fleet before it's too late!"

"Uh... aye ma'am?" Chastain stared back blankly as he tried to make sense of what he had just heard. "But, what exactly are we looking for?"

"Saboteurs of Silent Eclipse," she replied, still speaking fast. "They're trying to take control from the inside. Do not approach us! We've been boarded! You need to prepare a lockdown of your ship!"

"Silent Eclipse?" Captain Chastain looked perplexed. "That... ghost story? They're not real."

"Yes, they are!" Admiral Ra'aiah replied frantically. "You need to defend all vital parts of your ship and brace yourselves! You have to turn away and separate the fleet! Back away from us!"

A sudden alarm nearby caught everyone's attention. Hemington called out to the admiral half a second later.

"Incoming attack!" she declared. "Weapons fire detected! The Hazel Ying Lee just opened up missiles!"

Admiral Ra'aiah looked at the map display of the Firestar. She immediately raised a closed fist and then extended her fingers. The map switched to an overlay of the area surrounding her ship. A blue triangle in the center labeled the Firestar as "S.C.E. LS1", which was an acronym for "lead ship." Admiral Ra'aiah swiped right/left and moved the view towards their starboard bow. There were seven blue triangles heading for them. Captain Chastain's ship, the Alexandria, was the triangle at the head of the fleet formation labeled as "S.C.E. TF1", which indicated to her that it was the lead ship from his task force. The ship Hemington was warning them about was labeled "S.C.E. TF6."

The Hazel Ying Lee was a destroyer. It was fast and light—capable of reaching three times the speed of the Firestar. It also packed a huge array of firepower despite its small size. It was under the command of Captain Hodges. At least, she hoped it still was.

A red circle had enveloped the Ying Lee's blue triangle. This told Admiral Ra'aiah that the destroyer had opened fire. Four red dots had departed from the Ying Lee and were making a quick beeline for them.

"Long range torpedoes!" she called out to the bridge. "Action stations! Prepare for ship-to-ship combat!"

"Admiral!" Hemington reported. "That is confirmed. Four torpedoes heading towards us at bearing 091 mark 032! E.T.A. two minutes!"

"If we still have control," Admiral Ra'aiah commanded, "ready countermeasures and hail the Ying Lee! Uncle!"

She looked down at the screen.

"Hodges just fired at us!" she said to the screen.

Chastain was already trying to assess the situation. He was looking away from the screen and appeared to be trying to talk to his own bridge crew.

"Hodges!" Chastain yelled desperately. "What's happening?! You've dropped formation and opened fire! Stand down!"

"Where are my countermeasures?!" Ra'aiah demanded. "Fire them now!"

One of her tactical officers responded.

"Ready ma'am! Deploying!"

The proper way to destroy incoming missiles was to generate a flak field, fire intercept missiles, or have their fighters chase after and shoot them down. Unfortunately, there was no way to contact their squadrons due to the lockdown unless they transmitted coded instructions. By then, it'd be too late.

Admiral Ra'aiah heard a rumble from below which indicated that some of the launchers had opened fire. On the map, she saw a red dot enveloping their triangle and a swarm of red triangles flew to meet the incoming torpedoes. Intercept missiles and ordnance were faster than the torpedoes. Her triangles detonated and generated a field of red circles which was directly in the path of the Ying Lee's torpedoes.

Slowly, she watched as three of them disappeared from the map. The loss of signal meant that the countermeasures were successful, but not for one.

One last torpedo made it past their line of defense and was hurtling straight for the bow of the Firestar.

"Brace for impact!" Ulgo yelled.

A large rumble shook the entire room. Everyone's weight shifted slightly but it wasn't strong enough to throw them off their feet.

"Status!" Admiral Ra'aiah demanded.

The systems officer replied promptly.

"Shields absorbed the impact! Starboard fore generators are holding at 82% but admiral... if the rest of the fleet begins to attack us..."

"Yeah, I got it," Ra'aiah exhaled angrily. "We're outnumbered, outgunned internally and externally. Hemington!"

"Yes ma'am!"

"Get to work on that signal! We're at an extreme disadvantage and I don't like our odds!"

With every passing second, Silent Eclipse was attempting to silence them one by one.

"Damn it!"

Admiral Ra'aiah turned her attention to the screen. Captain Chastain was desperately trying to grasp the situation.

"The Madison Marsh is also powering weapons!" he informed them. "We've lost contact with our support destroyers! All cruisers! This is Alexandria actual declaring an emergency!"

"Uncle!" Ra'aiah cried desperately.

"Looks like we've really stepped in it!" Chastain glanced at Admiral Ra'aiah one last time. "Ra'aiah! You need to get out of here!"

"Uncle! You must defend your ship at all costs!"

It was too late. Just after she delivered her warning, her godfather vanished from the screen. The display continued to blink the message, "lost signal" at her. She had to shove aside her shock as she heard Hemington calling out to her again.

"Admiral!" her voice interrupted everyone's thoughts as her eyes remained glued to her screen. "The Ying Lee is firing its kinetic weapons! Full frontal barrage incoming!"

"Hemington! You and Dr. Kendrick get me a way to find Silent Eclipse! We need to defend ourselves!"

Admiral Ra'aiah kicked her ass into gear when Hemington acknowledged her commands. Dr. Kendrick stayed by her side and they began to work as fast as they could. Admiral Ra'aiah kept her eyes on the map. Captain Hodges was most likely compromised and so was his ship. It was one of the fastest and deadliest weapons they had in their arsenal and it had begun an attack.

"Divert port and auxiliary power to starboard shields!" she yelled.

"All hands!" Ulgo called out. "Brace for contact!"

A series of rumbles shook the ship. Fortunately, the vibrations didn't reach anywhere near the bridge, otherwise everyone would have probably gone tumbling to the floor. Admiral Ra'aiah rode out the shaking and called out to the crew.

"Report!"

The response was as she expected.

"All direct hits! Shields at 65% and continuing to fall!"

Thinking quickly, Admiral Ra'aiah had to come to a heartbreaking decision.

"Coded message to all mounts!" she declared. "Traverse starboard and prepare broadside! Target...!"

She took a deep breath before finishing her statement.

"...the Ying Lee."

"Admiral..." Ulgo said warningly. "We're targeting a friendly?"

"Disable the ship," Admiral Ra'aiah replied.

"It's coming right for us," Ulgo explained. "A full broadside would hit its bow and probably take it out, not disable it!"

He was right. The position and the direction it was bearing down at them meant that the Ying Lee's ship profile was small. They could hit it but if they did, it would be catastrophic. A full broadside attack would damage the destroyer's main cannon and most likely cause it to collapse and implode, destroying the ship. They needed a new plan.

That's when they heard another update.

"Admiral! The Alexandria is opening fire!"

Admiral Ra'aiah quickly barked out her next orders.

"Ready countermeasures!"

"Ma'am! We're not being targeted! The Alexandria's fired on the Ying Lee!"

Admiral Ra'aiah pivoted to Ulgo, who looked just as alarmed. This was falling apart way too fast.

"Report!" she called out.

"Ying Lee has lost engines but she's coasting towards us!"

Ulgo shook his head.

"Chastain wouldn't have done that on purpose," he said. "The fleet's compromised."

Admiral Ra'aiah looked at the map and prepared a new set of orders.

"Spin up the engines and get us out of the way!" she commanded.

With her eyes fixed on the map, she could see that the Ying Lee still continued to move towards them. Even with their engines gone, it still maintained a great deal of momentum. With its mass and all the munitions it carried, it was a floating bomb in space with literally nothing to stop it.

"Engines unresponsive!"

Admiral Ra'aiah's eyes widened when she noticed red circles enveloping the whole group of blue triangles in the fleet. They were all firing at each other.

"Admiral? What do we do?!"

She was at a loss for words for a moment. Suddenly, Ulgo rushed to her side and got her attention.

"Admiral!" he stated. "Are we still going to broadside the Ying Lee?"

"Y-you do that..." she stammered, "and thousands of innocents will die."

"It's them or us!" Ulgo replied urgently. "We will die if we just sit here!"

Admiral Ra'aiah racked every brain cell she had. The first image that came to mind was of 999, the amborg that first fought one of the Silent Eclipse assassins. When she and the other Epsilon amborgs recounted the events in the archives section, all that lingered in her memory were the bruises.

According to 43, 999 had challenged her to a duel many days before their arrival. It was called a deadlock, if she remembered correctly. The fight had ended with both women severely beaten up. 999 was a tough amborg but seeing her injuries had been rather disturbing. Instead of trying to run, she stood up against a dangerous threat single-handedly and... that was it.

"Helm!" Admiral Ra'aiah's eyes lit up as she improvised another emergency plan. "Give all remaining power to forward starboard deflectors! Fire emergency thrusters and turn our ship! 45 degree x-axis turn to port! Order all mounts to fire on my command!"

"Ma'am!" her tactical officer replied. "There won't be anything there!"

"Yes there will!" she replied confidently. "We're just getting out of the way! Disable port thrusters and turn the ship! Turn the bridge away from the Ying Lee!"

She turned to Ulgo.

"Load EMP rounds," she commanded.

"Two birds and one stone," he replied with a firm nod, realization spreading across his face. He leapt into action, raising his voice, "All mounts! Stand by for the command! Load EMP rounds and hold!"

"Helm! Turn the ship!"

Admiral Ra'aiah's command was met with an affirmed response from her pilots. With a coordinated effort at their stations, they toggled the controls on their consoles, and they watched as everything outside began to move. The thrusters were controlled by a separate system, ready to activate in case of an emergency.

The admiral took hold of her chair, gripping it tightly even though there was no real need to do so. It was likely a way to soothe her nerves, a form of self-assurance. They watched the stars outside the forward viewport twist as the ship made a left banking maneuver.

"Oh boy," 6 said. "This is going to get intense."

"Admiral! The Ying Lee is closing!"

Admiral Ra'aiah unleashed the next phase of her idea.

"All starboard mounts! Target ventral profile of the Ying Lee! Fire!"

More rumbling occurred. Rather than the floor shaking like it did under the Ying Lee's barrage, this felt like it was coming from far below. Admiral Ra'aiah glanced at Commander Ulgo, who was manning the tactical station.

"All mounts successfully fired!" he reported. "Broadside was completely successful!"

"Did we hit the Ying Lee?" Admiral Ra'aiah asked.

"Yes ma'am!" Ulgo replied confidently. "She took 28 shots to her belly. She's powering down! We're moving too!"

"You've used the ship's cannons as a thruster!" Dr. Kendrick said with an amazed gasp. "The guns have pushed us out of the way!"

He was right. They did appear to be moving away from the Ying Lee at a faster rate. It was still drifting but at least they had avoided a direct collision. The broadside attack had also revealed another important detail.

"It also means that the gun crews in the cannon batteries are still in control," Admiral Ra'aiah stated. "Thank the gods. One less thing to worry about."

With that threat temporarily taken off their shoulders, she needed to come up with a way to finish this.

"Helm!" she ordered. "Manuevering thrusters! Begin disabling the fleet! They need to be taken out of action immediately! Coded message to engineering! Tell them I need full engines asap! Get Captain Chastain back! We need to resume control of everything!"

Deck 3
Weapons Control

"This is amborg 113. We are proceeding."

Ally 113 and Alex 280 of the Fourth Group were moving quickly through the deck. As they pressed on, they could hear muffled explosions and a series of rumbling noises that seemed to be emanating all around them. They could only assume that it was either the battle to take control of the ship or something worse.

They walked past many bodies. Most were crew of the Firestar, and others were destroyed parts from Silent Eclipse drones. Everyone who fought on this deck had put up a valiant stand. Now it was their turn to avenge them.

They noticed wires and panels blown out of the walls, combined with several bits of metal shards and debris spread across the ground. As they moved together in a two-person tactical formation, they frequently looked back. Checking for any sneak attacks or ambushes was important for their safety.

"Are you alright?" 280 asked as they picked up the pace.

"I don't wish to answer that now," 113 stated as her breath came out shaky.

This caught 280's attention. She had transmitted that message on a private channel and it was in the same boorish, monotonous drone that they were all used to hearing–a computer voice that replaced their actual ones. Even though her breathing was quiet to reduce the risk of being detected, she was trembling with every breath. He had never heard this from her before, but it definitely resembled fear.

"Hold here," 113 stated.

The pair stopped and lowered their weapons slightly, but remained at the ready. 280 took a position at her side and turned around completely. Both amborgs could continue to monitor both ends of the hallway while keeping each other in their peripheral vision. It was a way of temporarily focusing on the conversation while also remaining observant to their surroundings.

"I can't believe they're gone..."

280 blinked in confusion.

"Who?" he asked.

"Our marine escorts."

280 nodded and dipped his head down. He glanced at the floor mournfully but looked up again to maintain focus.

"I see," he said. "I assumed incorrectly that you were referring to the rescue mission."

"We are aware of their current whereabouts," 113 stated.

280 turned his head and stared. 113 returned his gaze, sighed, and shook her head.

"Allegedly, we know their current whereabouts," she corrected her statement. "They are going to the Tandeeri fleet."

"Your thoughts linger on the marines?" 280 asked softly.

"They were gone before we even realized what was happening," 113 replied. "Turned the wrong corner and they were sliced apart."

280 glanced at 113 again. This time, he inspected the bloodstains splattered all over her clothes. He nodded grimly as he glanced down at the stains that marked him too. Silent Eclipse had cut through their new friends like they were nothing.

"They have the advantage in close quarters," he replied. "We just need to outmaneuver them."

"They continued fighting even though they knew they were about to die," 113 stated. "They could have run or hidden somewhere until it was safe."

"They chose to live their lives like this," 280 said reassuringly. "They died believing this fight could be won. We must ensure that their sacrifices were not in vain."

"I can still see her face... the marine that pushed me out of the way of the ambush."

280 silently listened. The battle for the Firestar continued but it seemed like the fighting was growing more and more faint, which was probably a good sign or a signal to remain stealthy.

"She was so bright... so brave... and... she was sliced apart moments later. Why did she save me instead of herself?"

"I don't know the answer," 280 stated. "I understand your guilt. It is difficult to be the one who survives. I admit that I am saddened at the loss of our allies... our new friends, but I am glad I didn't lose you. My partner."

It was 113's turn to glance at him as his gaze became a little vacant and distant. However, he did meet her eyes and gave a small reassuring smirk. It wasn't exactly a confidence booster but it did seem to snap her out of her mental overload.

"I thought we were done for," he admitted. "When we were ambushed. After we thwarted those drones back there, I... was sad but seeing that you had survived made me feel like we could continue fighting. It does make me seem selfish but... now I want to avenge our friends."

113 looked ahead once more and nodded.

"Perhaps," 280 said gently, "we could continue this discussion at a later time?"

He didn't even need to ask. 113 raised her weapon determinedly and began to walk forward. 280 moved behind her and followed.

"Yes," she agreed. "Partner."

From somewhere far above them, they could hear a series of rumbling. They recognized it as cannon fire from the Firestar's weapons, something they heard from earlier battles as bystanders when the ship unleashed its entire arsenal on the Tandeeri fleet.

The energy weapons, including lasers and R-batteries, produced a high-pitched wooshing sound like thousands of sheets of aluminum foil being torn in a loud echoing chamber. Missiles emitted a hollow sound when launched but quickly became silent as they sped away from the ship towards their targets. The point-defense weapons made noises similar to standard automatic firearms, with rapid tapping sounds that could also be dampened by the vacuum of space. All other kinetic weapons mounted in the gun mounts or cannons resembled the thunderous sounds of massive artillery pieces.

It was a little eerie only hearing the booms and thuds of the main cannons.

"Do you think the battle is going well?" 113 asked.

"As long as the ship doesn't blow up," 280 pointed out a window as the ship shook again and the floor vibrated slightly. Unconcerned, they kept moving. "Then it is an acceptable situation. It is my opinion that the ship feels like an activated blender."

The amborgs both made it to weapons control. Once they approached the entrance, they encountered another terrifying problem. More bodies.

For every Silent Eclipse drone sprawled out on the ground, there were at least seven S.C.E. crewmembers that had died defending this position. 113 and 280 had to silently ignore the bodies and continue on. They couldn't collect the dead until the situation was safe.

They approached the door and examined its panel. The sign above the panel read "Central Weapons Control" or C.W.C. for short. According to the database, this was one of the rooms that had access to the entirety of the ship's weapons. There were other weapons control stations that delegated tasks or command of certain weapons all over this deck, but this was where they got their orders from. Multiple distress calls had come from this part of the ship and it was easy to see why. Anyone in control of this place would have the means of inflicting catastrophic levels of damage.

"Prepare to breach," 113 stated. "Hand me a charge."

"May I try an alternative option?"

She took a position on the other side of the door while 280 reached out to the panel. He gently pressed a green button.

"Oh," 113 replied as they watched the door slide open. "Disregard that request for a charge."

"The door was unsecure," 280 pointed out. "They've already broken in."

113 cautiously glanced inside. There was no activity coming from the interior, which was what he was noting. It was clearly a trap. Unfortunately, they would have to go in. If anyone else came along or was on standby for backup, it could lead to adverse outcomes.

"Once we go through," she stated, "we will most likely be surrounded."

"Entrapment," 280 said with a nod. "Standard hunting tactic."

"Shall I begin calculating the odds of survival?"

280 glanced at 113 and shook his head.

"No," he replied. "I do believe that we should focus on our priorities... and begin calculating combat strategies now."

"I'll take point," 113 nodded.

"Standing by for your lead," 280 stated.

"Toss in a flash-bang. Take the right once I cross the threshold."

"Understood."

280 pulled a grenade from his belt and prepared to press the priming button. 113 readied her rifle. When she was done with the weapons check, she nodded.

"Engage," she said.

280 pressed the button. They heard a click as he swung his arm. He successfully tossed the grenade inside and waited. Within seconds, there was a bright flash immediately followed by a deafening bang. Without another word, the amborgs moved in swiftly and prepared themselves for a fight.

They had to succeed. Otherwise, they would all be inevitably killed. As members of the Fourth Group, they needed to uphold their reputation as efficient and deadly amborgs.

CHAPTER 4

Nightmares and Tragedies

Chicago, Illinois
Roosevelt Rd
2132 March
Six Years Ago

"This is amborg 466. We have a patient enroute to the hospital. Please have the O.R. standing by."

466 confidently gripped the steering wheel of her car, smoothly cruising at a steady speed. The emergency lights on her hood blinked brightly, signaling to others that she was under a medical alert and required priority on the road.

Once she approached an upcoming intersection, she gently slowed down and quickly reached for her dash. She found the button marked "traffic pre-empt" and smiled.

"Isn't technology great?" she said as she immediately pushed the button with a click.

Her partner's voice spoke from the back.

"It is great. Just get us there in one piece, ok?"

466 grinned as she saw the Opticom switch work its magic. It wasn't really magic, but rather a clever way to change the traffic lights to green. As they got closer to an intersection, it was incredible how that small automotive switch could prioritize their need to cross in mere seconds.

466 was driving her own vehicle, constructed by the amazing mechanics at A.I. Industries. During this particular visit to Chicago, she and 501 happened to be nearby when a few amborgs had deployed to the area. Since her car was equipped with some standard medical equipment, she could help transport those in need of emergency assistance.

"I didn't know... the amborgs did this sort of stuff... for people like us..."

The patient groaned but smiled pleasantly at 501.

"All part of the job," 501 stated. "You'll be walking again in no time and no one will even be able to tell you had a scaffolding collapse on you."

"Thank you for saving me," the man smiled lazily.

"Hey 466," 501 grinned. "You got a fan back here wanting to thank you!"

466 looked left, then right, and saw the traffic light turn green. She smirked and called to the back.

"Tell him to hold on!" she said as she pressed more firmly on the gas, revving the engine. "Almost there!"

One moment, 466 was speeding down the road and the next, as she looked right, her eyes widened as she immediately slammed on the brakes. The wheels screeched as she tried to stop, but it was too late.

501 and their patient never had a chance to respond to her last statement.

466 slammed the front of her car into another vehicle that had crossed into the intersection. A loud crash echoed as the two vehicles T-boned and came to a grinding halt in the middle of the street.

466 had hit her head, but her implants and a conveniently placed airbag absorbed the brunt of the impact. She slowly lifted her head, trembling and struggling to refocus. Her vision was blurry and gradually began to clear up as she looked around. Thankfully, her enhanced strength was able to help her recover quicker than an average human.

However, when she glanced out the front window, she wished with all of the energy she had left in her body that she hadn't gotten behind the wheel or that she had taken a different route. She would have given anything to rewind time.

"Oh no!" she shuddered and gasped as she frantically tried to undo her seatbelt. "Dom! Dom! 501!"

She could hear 501 and their patient groaning behind her, which meant they had survived. 466 focused on trying to get out of her seat as fast as she could. The reinforced chassis of her car was only slightly dented and pushed in. It was built to be armored for safety, but in this situation, it had inflicted considerable damage on the vehicle that had suddenly crossed 466's path.

466 felt panic and fear take hold as she finally unclasped her seat belt and broke her door open. Her eyes stayed focused on the occupant of the other car that she had hit. It didn't look good at all.

The other driver was in a smaller car. Compared to 466's car, it didn't stand a chance, even after she slammed on the brakes. Although the driver's airbag had deployed successfully, 466 noticed that they had been knocked out and were unconscious. Through the shattered window, she could make out the silhouette of a young woman.

Filled with desperation, she tried to call someone but found herself too frightened to do so. Her adrenaline kicked in, and she bolted to the left passenger side of her car and flung the door open. 501 was massaging his neck as he climbed out. Once he was clear, 466 rushed inside, grabbed the emergency medical kit, and raced over to the other vehicle involved.

"Ah, 466," 501 grimaced as he straightened up and looked around. "Carolina? What happened?"

"I-I hit a-a car!" 466 gasped breathlessly as she kept moving. "In the intersection! There's a girl in there!"

501's eyes widened.

"I'll call for backup," he said quickly. "We need to transport our patient to the hospital!"

While 501 glanced in the back of the car to check on their patient, 466 reached the front passenger side and began calling out to the unconscious driver.

"Ma'am!" She placed her hands on the window and peered inside. "Ma'am! Can you hear me?!"

466 scanned the interior. There were pages of sheet music, a couple of books on the floor, and a coffee cup spilled underneath. Blood had splattered all over the seat, and 466 was able to see a name on the woman's to-go coffee cup. It read, "Teresa."

"Teresa, Teresa!" 466 called. "Can you hear me?"

466 pulled some gloves out of her pockets and continued to shout.

"If you can't lift your head...!" she cried, "can you move your fingers if you can hear me?"

That was when she heard 501 transmitting on the emergency channel for help.

"Dispatch," he said calmly. "All amborgs in the area. This is 501. We have hit a civilian vehicle during our emergency transport. The intersection of South Ashland Avenue and Roosevelt Road. The driver is injured. Request immediate assistance asap."

It didn't take long for help to respond.

"Dispatch," a familiar voice answered. "This is 117. I am responding to the emergency."

"Copy 117," the person from dispatch replied on the channel. "Fire and rescue are on the way."

"We need additional R.A. units," 501 stated. "We have to transport our patient to the hospital!"

The calls continued to pour in while 501 turned to 466 and their patient inside their vehicle. Other amborgs they had just talked to a few minutes ago were all making their way to the scene of the accident. He glanced around and noticed a crowd of people nearby, watching intently. Many of them appeared to be in shock or were beginning to take out their phones.

"Teresa!"

501 ran over to 466, who was still calling through the door.

"Here!" 501 slipped a pair of gloves on and reached for the door. "Let me try!"

501 and 466 both put their hands on the door and pulled. Something must have happened during the accident because it was stuck. They tried to pry the door open, but it was not easy. Even with their enhanced strength, it was jammed too tight.

"Teresa!" 466 cried as they continued to try to wrench open the door. "We're not leaving you, ok?!"

She turned to 501.

"How's our patient?"

"Stable," 501 grunted as he pulled again. "Come on!"

When the door wouldn't budge, even with their combined strength, 466 shook her head.

"Ok, we're just going to have to break the glass!"

"Got it!"

The sound of sirens echoed in the distance, which meant that emergency crews were en route. Just as they were about to smash the window of Teresa's car, they heard footsteps racing towards them.

"501! 466! Step back!"

The Third Group amborgs turned to see their friend and mentor, David 117, approaching them fast. Several Second Group amborgs trailed behind him. 117 quickly gave them instructions as they took over.

"917, get that door open! 57, check the patient! 35, form a perimeter and get people back!"

501 stepped aside as the older amborgs got straight to work. 117 also jumped in, but he wasn't going for the car. 466 was surprised

to find that he was trying to get in front of her, preventing her from opening the door.

"Wha...? What are you doing?!"

"466!" 117 raised his voice as he put his hands on her shoulders, politely pushing her aside. "I'm taking this over! Stay back!"

"No!" 466 replied, trying to shake his hands away. "No! I have to get her out!"

"You can't work on her!" 117 shouted. "I'm sorry!"

"No, no!" 466 turned and protested, her tone pleading. "I have to work on her! Please, you have to let me save her!"

It took the combined efforts of 117 and 501 to pull her away from Teresa's car as they kept trying to talk to her. 466's protests were shut down as 57 and 917 were allowed to open the door. They carefully planned their approach and attacked the door with minimal force.

"It's procedure!" 117 stated repeatedly into 466's ear. "It is procedure! We've got this!"

"I need to help her!"

"You can't work on her!" 117 repeated. "We've got this! Now I need you to stand over here! 501, come with me!"

466 found herself pushed back onto the nearby sidewalk, looking on helplessly as 117's team successfully pried the door open, revealing Teresa's lifeless body.

"Her name... is Teresa," she spoke breathlessly.

"Ok," 117 nodded as he walked away. "Ok."

As he stepped back towards the car, he raised his hands and motioned for her to stay put.

"Stay here," he said. "Ok? Stay here."

117 pivoted and hurried to join the team. He and 501 assessed the situation and examined the interior of the car.

"117," 501 gasped, his voice trembling. "There's more blood in the car... than her entire body."

"I know..." 117 said softly.

"She's unresponsive!" 57 declared as she backed out of the door. "Breathing is shallow! There's no room in here! Help me pull her out!"

917 grabbed a medical brace and quickly wrapped it around Teresa's neck. When she was good to go, 917 and 57 worked as a team to gently lift and pull her out of the vehicle. 501 laid out a backboard so they could set her body down on it in the street.

"I'm opening a line to 6!" 57 said as she performed a scan and examined Teresa's body. "Ok, broken pelvis. Possible crushed thorax. There's most likely organ damage."

57 glanced up at 501.

"Donut, help me!"

501, under 57's instructions, began to help perform C.P.R. in an attempt to resuscitate Teresa. 117 and 917 stood by and watched quietly, occasionally sneaking glances at 466, who was unable to do anything but watch everything unfold right in front of her.

"466, 466, hey!"

Tears streamed down 466's cheeks as she stood there, helpless and in shock. She turned to see 999 briskly walking towards her.

"Angel?" 466 gasped. "W-w-what are you doing here??!"

"I heard 501 over the emergency line," 999 answered calmly. "117 told me you were the driver."

999 offered a hand to 466 and she desperately clung to her wrist.

"How are you doing?" 999 asked quickly. "Are you going to be ok?"

466 felt relieved that 999 wasn't speaking with her usual cold demeanor. Her lone wolf persona was temporarily set aside but still, the stress and the anxiety was overwhelming her.

"I-I-I don't know," 466 panted as she tried to focus and remember what she had seen before the accident. "The-the light. Is Teresa ok?"

999 quickly glanced over at the accident and then looked into 466's eyes.

"They're working on her now," she replied, her voice still level. "Ok?"

"I-I-I slowed... I slowed down," 466 began hyperventilating as she squeezed 999's wrist. "I thought I h-had the green and then I saw her. And I-I-I couldn't... I couldn't stop!"

999 peered over 466's head and noticed several pedestrians looking their way, murmuring amongst themselves. She quickly clasped her hands on 466's shoulders, gripping them firmly and lightly shaking her to get her attention.

"Ok, listen," 999 declared as 466 continued taking small, quick breaths. "Stop talking. You need to stop talking! Listen!"

"B-b-but I did this!" 466 cried. "I did this!"

"Shh, shh, shh," 999 began to lead 466 towards 117's car that was parked nearby. "466. Come over here."

"ANGEL, I HIT HER," 466 wailed. "I HIT HER!"

"Carolina 466," 999 stated firmly, sharply raising her voice and startling 466. "I love you. Hey! I love you, but you need… to shut… up!"

466 continued to tremble as 999 tried to get through to her.

"Listen to me," she said. When that didn't work, she spoke louder and shook 466's shoulders again. "Listen to me!"

466 shook like a leaf as she looked 999 in the eye.

"There's going to be an investigation!" 999 explained. "And it starts now. Alright? The Chicago police and fire departments are all going to roll up on this scene. Then they have to contact Dr. Kendrick. Everyone will have a lot of questions."

999 gazed sternly into 466's eyes. She wasn't disappointed in her; she was trying to be compassionate while staying completely professional. Her scowl made 466 swallow hard.

"You need to listen to me," 999 spoke clearly in a calm but demanding tone. "You need to think carefully about what you're going to say."

"But-but I want to tell them the truth!"

"Yes," 999 nodded. "But you only tell them what you know. Not what you think, not what you feel. Alright? Answer their questions but stick to the facts. You think you can do that?"

466 didn't answer as her gaze drifted back to the accident. 501 and 57 were still administering C.P.R. 999 continued to try to get her to focus, but it was no good.

"Carolina," 999 spoke sharply.

She wasn't listening. 466 whimpered when she noticed 501 suddenly stopped doing chest compressions. Her heart sank as he looked up and shook his head at 57. Fear and shock crept in as the reality of the situation hit her. The last thing she saw before her emotions took hold was 917 looking down mournfully, while 117 slowly lifted his left wrist. Teresa was gone.

"Dispatch," his voice spoke over the channel. Every sound echoed painfully in her mind. "One female crash victim on scene. No life signs."

"No!" 466 sobbed as she felt her legs give out. "No! Nooo!"

999 gently held her up as best as she could, but 466 fell on her knees and began to sob uncontrollably.

"What have I done?!" she wailed.

Everything that transpired next felt like a blur. 466 remembered being in tears for hours after fire trucks and an ambulance arrived while police cordoned off the area. She then recalled seeing Dr. Kendrick showing up to get the full details. The presence of high-ranking officials only deepened 466's feelings of anguish. It was the first time she had ever taken a life in a heart-breaking accident.

She vaguely remembered seeing 917 and 501 running over to her as she broke down on the pavement and continued to cry.

"466?" 917's voice echoed in the background as everything faded. "I know it feels very painful right now, but you need to know... that we're..."

A.I. Industries
Social Hall A
2133 April
One year later

Wait a minute... what's happening? I haven't thought about these moments in so long.

"Hey."

466 blinked and turned to see 501 waving to her.

"They're moving up," he said softly. "Let's go talk to them."

"Uh... right."

466 examined her outfit and straightened up. Her amborg jacket's neon stripes that usually glowed brightly had been shut off. This was done deliberately for the event that they were attending.

501 and 466 walked up the aisle side by side, passing numerous rows of seats. Many people had already left. It made sense considering that the eulogies and funeral speeches had finished.

As they approached the front, a man and woman were heading from that direction towards them up the center aisle. Recognizing them, 466 lifted her arms and felt 117 and his wife, Audrey, pull her into a heartfelt hug.

"Are you two ok?" 117 asked as he glanced at 501.

"We're managing," 501 replied as he got a hug from 117 and Audrey as well.

"We're going to go grab something to eat," Audrey said softly. "Do you want to come find us later?"

"Sure," 466 nodded.

Audrey and 117 strolled away together, arm-in-arm. 466 turned to watch them leave and felt a twinge of sadness. Soon, it would be their turn to talk to 917 and 999, who were both seated at the front of the procession.

"I don't know if I'm ready for this," 466 said to 501. "I miss her."

"I do too," 501 replied mournfully.

"What do I say?" 466 asked. "I feel like it's my fault."

"It wasn't anyone's fault," 501 stated. "345 worked hard to return to active duty. It was her choice and commitment to do that."

Ahead of them, they saw 18 approaching 917. She bowed her head to him politely and crossed her hands behind her back.

"I can only imagine what you must be feeling," she murmured.

917 and 999 both glanced up at 18. She was a kind and experienced amborg, as well as an exceptional teacher. She had prepared them for numerous challenges, but this was not one of those occasions.

"Amara 345 was an excellent person and... the world is less without her," 18 said. "I hope that you take comfort in the fact that she will always be remembered as a hero. A champion of the Third Group and a beautiful and irreplaceable soul."

917 nodded softly as 999 glanced down. 501 and 466 noticed that she looked cold and distant. This wasn't the same as when she'd normally stare someone down menacingly, making them freeze and fear for their life. She instead appeared deeply hurt, quietly bottling up her feelings. She merely nodded appreciatively to 18 while she looked... broken while trying to maintain a front.

Then, it was their turn. 501 and 466 stepped forward to the marked A.I. Industries' casket that lay before them. There was a photo behind it showing a girl dressed in her amborg uniform, smiling brightly towards the camera. This was Amara 345's official picture taken when she was accepted into the Third Group.

"We're never going to see it again," 466 breathed. "She had such a beautiful smile."

"It made so many people feel better when she helped them," 501 added.

They couldn't look inside the coffin since it was a closed-casket funeral, but they both laid their hands on it to pay their respects. After a short moment of silence, they both raised their hands to their chests.

For formal occasions, they wore special pins on their amborg uniforms that featured the A.I. Industries emblem and intricately etched gold text. Each pin also displayed their amborg group ID as well as their individual numbers. They removed their pins marked with a gold '3' and each chose a place on the casket.

Many other amborgs and employees of the company had paid their respects, but it was the amborg pins that made the casket stand out in a unique way. Since Amara 345 had passed on in the line of duty, some of the amborgs who approached the casket attached their pins to it, decorating it with their badges of honor. It was similar to military funerals, where Navy Seals place their trident insignias on the caskets of their fallen comrades. It was a powerful sign of respect.

The hall faintly echoed from the two thuds of their fists punching their insignia pins into the casket, and they moved on to stand in front of 917 and 999.

"917," 501 smiled reassuringly. "We just wanted to tell you that 345 was one of the coolest friends we knew."

501 stopped. 466 glanced up at him, then at the two Second Group amborgs seated in front of them. 917 was staring up at them, but he seemed unable to reply. The same went for 999, who couldn't meet their eyes. She wanted to speak with them, but the situation was becoming increasingly uncomfortable, and 501 slowly started to back away.

"I uh... thought she was an amazing friend. Sorry. I'll... see you later, maybe."

He barely took two steps when 466 grabbed his arm, preventing him from walking away. As he turned around, she raised her hands and clasped them tightly. She fidgeted nervously as 917 stared up at her.

What did she really want to say?

"When I... had a couple of bad missions," she spoke softly. "I didn't know if I'd... be cut out for this job. Being an amborg. I thought that... if I continued to mess up, then Dr. Kendrick might kick me out. So, I had anxiety issues building up and... I was always afraid to leave company grounds. After the Dominoe Incident, after we lost 43, and... after so many other incidents... I thought I was done."

Rather than rejoining the conversation, 501 moved back to 466's side for emotional support. 917 and 999 watched as 466 reached into her pockets.

"I felt like a failure," 466 admitted softly. She pulled an item from her right pocket and presented it. "345 gave me this."

917's eyes widened a fraction when he saw that she was holding a beautifully crafted gold bangle.

"She said that it was a good luck charm from her family and that it's rumored to protect whoever holds onto it," she explained. "She also told me that it should belong to someone destined to do great things. It gave me... strength."

466 knelt down and reached out to 917's hand. Out of the corner of her eye, she noticed that 999 was following her movements with a firm gaze. 466 looked up and realized that 999 was biting her lip and her eyes were glistening. Gently, 466 placed the golden bangle in 917's hand.

"More importantly," 466 felt her own tears welling up. "You also gave me strength to keep going even when I felt like giving up. 501 and I want to... be here for you and Angel."

917's lip trembled as he looked down at the bangle. 466 gently closed his fingers around it.

"Amara never needed it because she was one of the strongest amborgs in the Third Group," 466 stood up respectfully as 917 and 999 watched her. "She was a close friend to all of us. We loved her so much. So... if you need us... We'll be here."

466 glanced at 501 and nodded her head towards 917 and 999. Knowing what to do, 501 stepped forward and opened his arms... in front of 999.

The crowd behind them were taken aback by 501's gesture, but chose to stay quiet out of respect. In a different situation, 999 probably would have walked away, ignoring the offer for a hug, or told them to move along. Instead, something unexpected happened.

999 lifted her gaze and gently lifted her hands. Seeing her consent, he leaned in, and they wrapped their arms around each other in a heartwarming embrace. Knowing 917's personal preferences, 466 decided to follow 501's approach. Without seeking permission, she stepped closer. She wrapped her arms around 917's shoulders, allowing his head to rest on her shoulder.

As they embraced, it felt as if the floodgates had burst open, releasing a torrent of emotions that they couldn't hold back anymore. 466 felt 917 begin to tremble and sniff as they consoled one another in a supportive hug. She turned her head slightly to see 501 had released 999 and was now standing protectively just behind her shoulder.

The longer they hugged, the more 917's tears began to flow softly. Soon, he was sobbing, and 466 began to cry too. She relaxed her grip a bit and shifted to position herself behind 917's chair. Continuing to hug him from behind, she felt his hand rest on her arms. He held on tightly as he continued to sob uncontrollably.

Then she received a text notification from him.

I miss her... so much.

"Me too," 466 cried.

Next to them, 501 cautiously put his hand on 999's shoulder. He expected her to slap it away but instead, 999 reached up and held his hand. 466 noticed a single tear run down her cheek.

"It'll be ok."

That was when everything appeared to start fading away.

"It'll be ok, right?" 466 asked.

Their surroundings grew dim, and 466 glanced up to see a small figure approaching them. When she focused, she assumed it was a child. To her surprise, it was something else entirely. It wasn't human, yet it looked strangely familiar to her.

Then she recognized the little creature. But he wasn't supposed to be here.

"Oreo?" 466 asked. "What? How did you get here?"

CHAPTER 5

One Giant Leap for Amborgs

Tandeeri Flagship
Rescue Shuttle
Current Status: Abducted?

466 jolted awake and frantically looked around. When she regained her senses, she massaged her head and blinked several times.

"Just a dream," she sighed.

A tiny squeal that got her attention. Looking to her right, she saw Oreo beaming up at her.

"I must have dozed off," she smiled. "Wait. Did we all...?"

466 glanced around, her eyes growing wide. She could see all of her friends, but they were slumped over in their seats, sound asleep. Thankfully, she felt relieved to find that their bio-signs were still registering as active on her scanner.

She knew why everything looked so familiar and strange at the same time. This was the inside of the S.C.E. shuttle that they had all boarded to leave the Firestar. They had gone after amborgs 297 and 777, straight into the heart of the Tandeeri fleet.

"Did we make it?" she glanced at Oreo, who looked up at her curiously.

Oreo, as an infantile Tandeeri child, unfortunately couldn't speak. As far as they could tell, Oreo didn't talk at all. The noises that the little child made did indicate that there was some type of vocal capacity but Oreo was probably not at a developed age to speak comprehensive words to them.

466 got to her feet and ran to the cockpit.

"Oreo," she said. "Could you maybe help check on the others?"

Oreo looked up at 466 and blinked. It pointed a finger at itself and let out a gentle croak. It sounded like it was clarifying her request.

"Yes, you," 466 smiled. Then she pointed around. "Help."

Oreo chirped happily, appearing to smile. Then, it turned and eagerly ran to check on 999, who was sitting nearby. 466 thought back to when they were taken onto the Tandeeri ship; she had gotten into a defensive stance near the exit ramp, prepared for an attack. Instead, she had passed out and found herself lying on the floor while Oreo approached her gently, poking her shoulder.

Amborgs 249, 593, and 49 were still in their seats, fastened securely. 466 noticed that they were starting to wake up on their own. She and Oreo had probably been making too much noise in the cabin. She quickly clambered up into the cockpit.

"Serina?"

117, 501, 917 and their pilot, Braelynn, were all feebly stirring. What caught 466 off guard was the sight of their A.I. companion, Serina, who was levitating a few inches off the ground, but she was also asleep. It didn't look normal to her.

As an A.I. program, Serina didn't require any sleep. Sure, she had a low power mode, the ability to disappear, and run calculations in the confines of her construct housing, but this was the first time that 466 was actually seeing Serina lying down on the job in full view.

"Serina?"

Although she was levitating, Serina was curled up as if she really were resting on the ground. She began to stir when she heard 446 calling her name, gradually waking up.

"Aww... is it morning?"

466 stared in stunned amazement as Serina sat up and smacked her lips, almost looking human for a split second. Her holographic eyes lifted to meet 466's gaze. Serina paused, her eyes growing wide. In a brief flash of light, 466 blinked, only to find Serina back on her feet, nonchalantly dusting herself off.

"Uh... I mean," Serina cleared her throat, her silhouette flashing brightly as she adjusted to a normal light setting. "What's up, 466? Everything ok?"

"Were you asleep?" 466 asked.

'Whaatt?" Serina's voice took on a higher pitch as she smiled innocently and shrugged it off. "Of course not. Why would you think that?"

"I've just never seen you... passed out," 466 replied.

"I wasn't passed out," Serina said defiantly.

The two of them stared at each other in an uncomfortable silence. Finally, Serina caved.

"Ok, there might have been something in the air when we got abducted," she sighed.

"What?!" 466 exclaimed.

"Nothing toxic!" Serina replied. "When we got taken aboard the Tandeeri ship, I detected something on the sensor scans. Before I could report it, everyone suddenly collapsed! Next thing I know, I'm trying to revive everyone and... I blacked out too!"

"Weird," 466 replied.

"Exactly," Serina nodded. "This ain't normal."

The two of them noticed the rest of the shuttle cockpit starting to move. 466 immediately went to 501 who had slumped to the side of his seat. David 117 was sitting on the floor beside 917's seat, having collapsed there. 917 was in the copilot's seat, his head leaned back as he slowly came to. Braelynn was in the pilot's seat, the mysterious secret agent who was supposedly an ally.

At least, that part was still a little sketchy. Maybe it would become more clear after everyone woke up.

"917?"

466 noticed Serina hovering between 501 and 117, which prompted her to check on 917 and Braelynn, who were seated at the controls of their shuttle. 917 lifted his head, blinked, and shook it rapidly to clear his mind. As he groaned and regained consciousness, he turned and met 466's relieved gaze.

"466," he mumbled. He faced forward and brought his hand up to his head. "Wow... that was a nightmare."

466 looked over at Braelynn, who was lifting her head. Without a word, she glanced around the cabin, then got straight to work. She was likely trying to reactivate the shuttle or figure out their current situation. 466 turned her attention back to 917.

"917," she said.

He let out a small grunt to acknowledge that he was listening. Based on what she'd dreamt about, she felt that she needed to ask an important question.

"What were you dreaming...?"

A sudden yell broke the silence, causing 466 to look up abruptly and 917 to turn his head sharply. Both of them noticed 117 glancing up as well, following their line of sight. Serina, startled, jumped a few feet as they watched 501 thrash his arms and surge upward.

"Not the car!" 501 yelped as he woke up.

501 froze when he realized that everyone, except Braelynn, was staring. 117 sighed and slowly climbed up to his feet as Serina relaxed slightly. 917 let out a chuckle while 466 rushed over to 501.

"What car?" 917 asked.

501 bit his lip as 466 placed her hand gently on his shoulder.

"Nothing," he replied innocently.

"I think the appropriate question..." 117 said as he stretched his arms, "...is which car?"

"I have records," Serina suggested politely. "There are over a dozen car accidents that 501 has been in and even more where he accidentally caused some..."

"Never mind!" 501 let out a forced chuckle. "It's nothing. What did I miss?"

"Not much," Serina replied casually. "We all got knocked out."

"And I'm really sorry to interrupt... but we seem to be... docked inside the Tandeeri ship."

Everyone stopped talking and turned to look at Braelynn. Her serious expression pretty much said it all as she rose from her seat. It looked like she had given up on working on the console.

"I'm not getting any readings from instrumentation," she reported.

501 gasped. 117 turned to look at him and shook his head.

"Don't say it..." 117 warned. "If you say it, I will..."

"It's episode four all over again!" 501 cried.

"At least he didn't say it was a trap," Serina snickered.

"That's not reassuring at all," 917 sighed sarcastically.

Their attention was diverted when they heard an excited squeal and light footsteps clambering up the steps behind them. Oreo appeared a second later, scampering over to 501 to give him a hug.

"Oreo!" 501 exclaimed cheerfully. "Do you know what happened?"

"Probably," Braelynn replied. "However, the little Tandeeri is not able to communicate that to us if it did know."

"Well it's easy to see that Oreo's happy," 117 said, pointing at the window to the outside. "This is Oreo's home."

Oreo looked at 117 and let out a loud and cheerful chirp, which seemed to confirm what he had just said.

"I'm personally glad that he understands us," 117 smiled confidently.

"Well, understand this..."

Everyone turned and focused their attention on Braelynn.

"I don't see any movement or activity outside of the shuttle," she stated.

501 appeared alarmed as he cradled Oreo in his arms.

"Like, there's no one outside?" he asked softly.

"Why are you whispering?" Serina interrupted calmly. "The shuttle walls mask our voices completely."

"Because if I'm being totally honest, I'm a little scared," 501 replied as he raised a free hand. He held his thumb and index finger very close together without touching. "Like... this little."

"So, we got tractor beamed aboard the Tandeeri ship... and... no one to greet us?" 917 asked his question slowly. "What's the protocol here?"

The amborgs exchanged glances with one another. Serina crossed her arms and began to concentrate. Braelynn appeared to be deep in thought about their situation as well. 117 was the first to sigh and reveal his thoughts.

"I don't know."

"We're going to die," 466 gulped.

"No we are not," Serina replied.

"Getting kidnapped by the Tandeeri wasn't the plan!" 466 countered Serina quickly. "Sure, we got aboard their ship... but isn't this the part where they're supposed to order us to disembark and surrender??"

"In almost every kidnapping or abduction scenario... yes," 117 shrugged. "However, this seems to be a rather quiet and unsettling moment. They could be planning a welcome party or... getting ready to do exactly what 466 has suggested."

"You're the leader on this particular mission," 917 stated. "What do we do?"

117 felt all eyes on him as he glanced at Braelynn.

"What would you do? You've been in space longer than we have."

Braelynn pondered for a moment and replied.

"There's no sign of hostility," she answered calmly. "We seem to have control of our current environment but we can't take off. The shuttle engines aren't responding. I think they've dampened or disabled our thrusters so we can't leave. The fact that we have..."

She looked down at her side and drew her weapon from her hip holster. They cautiously watched as she inspected her gun.

"...our weapons," she continued. Then she noticed their behavior and quickly put it away, which allowed them to relax. "They haven't come in to take us prisoner or shown any sign of force, but we must assume that they allowed us to be here to... observe us."

"They're watching us?" 501 glanced down at Oreo, who listened contentedly.

"Waiting for our next move," 117 surmised.

"If it were me," Braelynn pondered, "the safest option would be to shelter in place. Maybe someone will come for us... but that's the one plan that we don't have time for."

"Are you suggesting we go outside?" 917 asked.

"I think it's clear that we have no means of fighting our way out," Braelynn stated. "If we do, we die. It's better than waiting here."

"I agree," Serina nodded.

"No point staying here then."

117 nodded and took a deep breath.

"Let's go everyone," he said as he walked towards the steps that led down to the back of the shuttle. "We should... do what we came here for."

Everyone in the cockpit followed. As they entered the main hold, all the others who had joined the rescue mission were awake and on their feet. The rest of the team seemed tense as they watched 117 try to offer a reassuring smile.

"Did we make it?" 249 asked.

"It appears so," 117 answered honestly.

"Why don't you sound certain?" 593 asked with a fearful look in her eyes.

"Hang on..."

Everyone fell silent when a bright light flashed before them, and Serina appeared in the center of the group. She raised her hands, looking bored.

"Did any of you hear what we just discussed up front?" she asked as she gazed at the Third Group amborgs.

"No," 49 admitted with a shrug of his shoulders. "We had our hearing set at normal range."

"For ensuring everyone's privacy," 249 added.

"Are you kidding me? You don't have to... Ok. Roland, Sara, Chris," Serina declared. "Link up with me please."

249, 593 and 49 each lifted their hands and their golden bracelets flashed green. Serina did the same and her silhouette switched from bright blue to the same lime green color, indicating that she had initiated a connection. Meanwhile, 117 spoke to 999.

"Status?" he asked.

"Unclear."

999 had her weapon safely stored away in her hip holster, but she stood at the ready with her eyes on the closed shuttle ramp. She looked like she was about to draw her weapon at the first sign of trouble.

"No movement?" she asked softly.

117 glanced back at Braelynn, who was watching 501 and 466 tend to Oreo.

"None," he answered. "We'll let the others catch up and then..."

"Disembark?" 999 asked.

"No point in staying here," 117 replied.

"Understood," 999 continued to remain frozen in place. "I await your command."

Her acknowledgement sent a wave of relief through 117. 999 was one of their best fighters and he knew he could count on her to have his back. Her serious and stoic professionalism would hopefully maintain morale since the Third Group amborgs were more prone to giving in to their emotions.

"I don't understand."

The amborgs who weren't linked to Serina turned to Braelynn. She leaned against the wall of the shuttle next to 917 and lowered her voice to a whisper.

"What's going on here? Am I missing something?"

"More like they missed our conversation upfront," 917 replied. "It's our privacy settings."

Braelynn stared and raised an eyebrow.

"All amborgs have highly advanced hearing," he explained when he saw the questions forming in her expression. "When we first started out with our new abilities, we tended to... accidentally overhear private conversations almost the entire time. So, we put in some ground rules to lower our hearing sensors to minimal levels."

"Human levels," 117 added for clarification.

"That seems like a rather unusual set of rules considering our current situation," Braelynn replied skeptically.

"Exactly."

Serina turned to look at Braelynn. They saw the green lights on 249, 593 and 49's bracelets shut off as the link was disconnected. However, they all appeared to be on the same page as their worried expressions faded and they looked ready to go.

"The Third Group tends to take those rules way too seriously under high-pressure situations," she said. Then she turned and looked up at them. "I keep telling you that when we're on a mission, you can disregard certain protocols."

"Sorry," 593 said with a sad dip of her head. "We're ready to go now that we're all caught up on the conversation."

"We can all do it since we can link up with each other," 501 said to Braelynn. "Serina can do it the fastest when she's updating or briefing us!"

"By using audio segments, video recordings, or small clips of past conversations," 117 said, "she can literally repeat things that have already been discussed so that other amborgs or drones accompanying us can be caught up with current details, knowledge, or facts."

"Kinda like what you do," 917 said smugly. "You know, being a spy and all that."

"I am not a spy," Braelynn shot back, her words clipped.

"Pretty sure that's what a spy would say," Serina muttered.

Braelynn scowled and glared hard at each of them. 501 had to look away and hold in his laughter. 117 raised his hands and waved them down sharply.

"Alright, alright," he said with an edge to his voice. "Easy on the wisecracks. We need to get off this shuttle!"

His words made the room go still. Oreo noticed and looked quite pleased, but he patiently glanced up at him.

"Ok everyone," 117 said after a deep breath. "You've seen me lead many missions over the last decade and... I apologize to all of you right now beforehand... because everything that I'm telling you... is going to be improvised. I'm winging it. Alright? Normally, if it was just a standard awkward situation, I'd do the best I could to reassure you. Now, I have to be honest."

Everyone listened quietly as 117 looked down grimly.

"We're probably dealing with the most difficult and terrifying situation that we've ever experienced," he stated. "I know that... we should open that door and disembark. We've come this far. There's no going back. Technically, that was the decision we made when we left the Firestar. So, will you follow me? Even though we have absolutely no clue what's on the other side?"

"You don't even have to ask," 501 declared.

"We're with you," 917 added, "even if we didn't have a choice in the matter. This is what we do."

"Yeah," Serina switched from green to a bright orange color. "Also, we don't have anything better to do. So, what's the plan?"

117 glanced at Braelynn.

"We're all leaving the shuttle, right?"

"If you're asking me to go first..."

"I was actually going to ask if you'd like to follow me while I leave first," 117 said quickly. "Everyone else files out slowly after the ramp opens?"

"Oh, understood."

Braelynn nodded and fell silent. 249 then raised his hand.

"Uh, question," he gulped. "We were pulled in? Inside the Tandeeri ship?"

"Like when the Millennium Falcon was first taken aboard the Death Star," 501 explained.

Everyone turned and gazed at 501 with serious looks of judgement.

"I would normally say that sci-fi references are inappropriate but... what the hell?" 466 sighed. "Let's let him have that one."

"The only difference is..." 917 held up his finger. "Actually, there are a lot of differences. First, we were all knocked out after getting pulled aboard. Second, the Death Star had stormtroopers that boarded Han's ship to look for passengers or signs of life. That hasn't happened in this case."

"As much as I appreciate the accuracy of your memory," Serina shook her head. "Can we maybe not base our plan on Star Wars?"

"She does have a point," 117 nodded. "But, so do 501 and 917."

117 gave Serina an apologetic look.

"The Tandeeri ship could in some ways... be like the Death Star," he said innocently. "For the moment, let's assume that we were pulled in exactly like the movie. Except, from now on, we have to assume that the Tandeeri are not the Empire."

"Debatable," 917 glanced at Braelynn and gestured to her uniform. "Considering the Tandeeri have been at war with the S.C.E. for a long time now."

"Instead of winging it and starting a firefight here," 117 continued his explanation, "we have a bargaining chip. A way to call for a truce. Maybe a ceasefire."

117 pointed at 501.

"Oreo," he said, "is the key. We protect Oreo at all costs while we look for the Tandeeri."

"Well, they weren't shooting at us when we approached... I think."

593 looked at Braelynn, who nodded reassuringly.

"I didn't see any incoming fire," she answered their questioning looks calmly. "We were successfully escorted and after checking all onboard sensors, we are unharmed."

"And they're not currently shooting at us," 593 glanced towards the ramp as they all listened for any outside noises.

"Another good sign," 917 nodded. "I think that Oreo has successfully shown them that we have come here in peace."

917's statement was met with an awkward silence as the others stared.

"I'm guessing," he added.

"Should we split up?" 249 asked. "After we leave?"

Several people in the shuttle immediately voiced their refusals. 249 flinched as nearly all of them stood up together to reject the idea. Even Braelynn looked alarmed by this suggestion.

"That's a terrible idea," Serina stated.

593 glanced at 49, and they both shook their heads at 249. He looked away, embarrassed.

"Sorry," 249 sighed. "After I said it out loud, I could hear how terrible it was."

"Still an idea," 501 said with a reassuring smile.

"If we were back on Earth, maybe," 917 declared as he looked at 117. "But we're up here with no backup and are completely cut off... because we are the backup. For 297 and 777."

"And everyone else? The people that were with them," 466 added.

The amborgs nodded together in agreement. They were there to rescue the other amborgs that had flown up from Earth, their original reinforcements.

"Right, them too," 917 nodded at 466 with a smile. "I would like to suggest that once we disembark, it'd be best to all stick together. Separating would cause a lot more problems."

"Good suggestion, 249," 117 smiled. "But let's all stick together this time."

249 smiled and fell silent.

"Unknown territory of an unknown species," 999 said.

Everyone looked at 999, who was still watching the ramp. With her back still to them, she'd decided to contribute to the conversation.

"I agree with the recommendation of us going together," she said softly. "I can't believe I'm saying this."

Braelynn cleared her throat and leaned in to whisper to 117 and 917.

"Why is she saying that's unbelievable?"

"She prefers going on missions alone," 917 replied. "If she's agreeing to stick together as a team, that's how bad the situation is."

"She's afraid?"

"She hides it better than most," 117 added. "Besides, who wouldn't be?"

"I don't have a physical body and I'm pretty terrified," Serina muttered.

"Noted," Braelynn nodded skeptically.

"Come on," 917 stared at her. "Even a secret agent like you gets nervous, right?"

"If you want my honest answer," Braelynn sighed. "I don't like our odds."

917 looked at 117 with a resigned smile.

"I suppose that begs the question... do we die here or die going out there?"

"Also, noted..." 117 shook his head. Now he felt that enough was enough. He looked around at the rest of them. "The entire time we are out there, we keep eyes on each other and we do so without our weapons drawn. It will be pretty scary so... we just hope for the best. Our top priority is getting Oreo back into the right hands, and then we figure out what happened to our friends."

"And she's coming with us, right?"

Serina waved her hand at Braelynn.

"She's the expert," 117 nodded.

"Bullshit."

Everyone turned sharply at 999's single-word statement. She had said it in such a soft but fierce tone that it caused an immediate shift in the mood.

"I still think she's going to get us killed," 999 stated without even turning to glance back at them.

"I'm one of your best assets on this mission," Braelynn replied calmly. She didn't appear to be fazed by 999's criticism. "Everyone has been saying that staying together is the best option. Naturally, I assumed that would include me."

501 decided to cheerfully interrupt before 999 could speak again.

"I think that... Angel's just trying to say that we can't guarantee your safety," he said in a kind voice. "You aren't cybernetically enhanced like us!"

"I thought the S.C.E. weapons could melt through us..." 249 whispered. "The chances of all of us dying from a firefight in space are the same. Right?"

"Not helping," Serina chuckled softly.

"It's nice that you care," Braelynn ignored their comments as she faced 501. "But I can take care of myself too. You'll need me."

"501, don't put words in my mouth," 999 snarled. "I don't trust her because she could be luring us into a trap."

For the first time since Braelynn had stepped into the room with them, 999 turned around and glared at her. Everyone tensed up when they saw how furious she appeared.

"We don't know her," she said.

"She did save us," 466 tried to say but 999 scoffed.

"Allegedly," she interrupted.

Braelynn held her hands up but then realized that no one was actually asking her to surrender.

"Look," she said as she swung her arms down. "The shuttle crew that was taken with your friends are S.C.E. crewmen. They're my people too. I need to make sure that they're ok. Also, I happen to be an expert in diplomacy, and attempting to figure out how to communicate with a new alien species is something my family does professionally."

The group stared at her silently for another moment. The uncertainty still wasn't settled.

"This whole entire time," Braelynn sighed, "I've been hearing how all of you have no experience or the skills necessary to handle this mission. I've heard it in the form of complaints, whining, mental-breakdowns, anxiety attacks and more. Now, I have the skills. I have the qualities. Let me help you do this. You can rake me over the coals when we get back to the Firestar."

"If we get back," 999 stated.

"I give you my word," Braelynn focused her gaze intently on 999. "If we make it back to the Firestar, I won't run away or disappear. I'll be right there, ready to help you, and I will make sure that you are all safe."

"I like her," 501 said, pointing with a cheerful grin.

"Out of all the amborgs here," Braelynn dipped her head politely, "I feel the same, Lieutenant 501, and you have my gratitude."

"You're kidding," 466 said with an impressed look. "This guy made it to the rank of lieutenant?"

"Am I handsome now?"

501 was slapped on the back of the head by 117, who immediately apologized and clarified that he had been trying to aim for his shoulder, but missed. When 501 chuckled jokingly, 117 rolled his eyes, and 501 went back to tending to Oreo without another word.

"Angel is my second-in-command on this mission," 117 said grimly. He turned to look at Braelynn cautiously. "I do have to take her opinion into account, and she brings up a fair point. How do we know you aren't planning to assassinate the leader of the Tandeeri the minute you get close enough? Assuming we reach some sort of peaceful resolution?"

"I will walk into this without a single weapon," Braelynn declared confidently. She held her arms up and stepped forward. "Would anyone like to frisk me?"

"That's not necessary," 917 said. "As much as some of us probably would enjoy that, I want to make a recommendation of my own."

917 looked at 117, then both turned to face 999. Following that, they glanced over at 501 and 466, who both nodded. Their eyes moved to Serina before briefly looking at 249, 593, and 49. Once every amborg had all nodded and gave their consent, 917 stepped forward and delivered his ultimatum.

"You come with us," he said to Braelynn and she listened intently. "Obey our instructions and you follow us, staying right where we can see you the entire time. If you step out of line, endanger our lives or the lives of our friends, or show any signs that you plan to bring down what we originally planned to do, then we kill you. In fact, I'll let Angel do it since that might make her feel better."

"Actually that idea does make me feel better," 999 said, eyeing Braelynn with less hostility.

"Done," Braelynn replied immediately with a firm nod. "Are we all ready?"

"Hey," Serina said warningly and pointed. "You remember what you promised?"

"Oh, right."

Braelynn raised her hands and turned to allow 117 to access her weapon, which was still securely holstered. Once she was unarmed, she dropped her hands and nodded to show that she wasn't carrying anything lethal.

"Where should I stand?" she asked.

"Right next to me," 117 stated as he handed the gun over to 917. "999 and 917 will both watch you directly from behind."

Braelynn nodded and glanced pleasantly at 999.

"Done," she said.

"Alright," 117 looked around to the rest of the group. "Diamond formation for the Third Group amborgs. 501 and Oreo are in the center. 466, you, 249, 593 and 49 pick which positions you'd like."

466 nodded as she walked over to her friends.

"Serina, Braelynn and I will exit the shuttle first," 117 announced.

"We got it already," 917 sighed. "Is there a reason why you keep conveniently delaying it?"

Both amborgs had a valid point. 917 was starting to appear disinterested because their plan had been repeated numerous times already. 117 was aware of this, but he was also feeling a great deal of pressure.

"We are out in the middle of space while also being inside an alien starship!" 117 snapped. "I just need a minute, alright?! The moment we set foot outside could be our last!"

"Actually," Serina politely interrupted as she floated up next to his head. "The longer we continue delaying the issue, the more our odds of survival might increase."

"How do you figure that?" 501 asked.

"Well, it doesn't seem like the Tandeeri are hostile," Serina stated.

"Except they did tractor-beam us in here," 466 replied.

"And..." Serina shot 466 an annoyed look. "There doesn't seem to be any sign of them wanting to come in here and take over."

"Unless they're being extremely patient," 466 mumbled.

"Ok, seriously?"

Serina threw her arms up and dropped them back down as she glared at 466.

"I'm sorry," 466 replied with a nervous chuckle. "I'm extremely anxious right now."

"Well, where I come from..."

Braelynn bravely strode forward and stood at 999's side.

"...one way to solve that is to take a walk," she suggested. "Or taking those first steps."

999 eyed her suspiciously and took a position behind her. She patiently waited for someone to activate the ramp so they could exit the shuttle.

117 quickly focused and advanced to the front. As he positioned himself beside Braelynn, he turned to look back and gestured for the others to join him. This appeared to motivate everyone else in the shuttle, and they slowly but steadily arranged themselves into a standard formation.

Braelynn stepped up to the panel beside the ramp. She pressed a big green button, and a loud clunk followed. It was the sound of the hydraulics activating, indicating that the ramp was now unlocked. Then, she pressed several more buttons and scrutinized the computer screen. Serina promptly informed the others that she was having the computer assess the external conditions of the shuttle to ensure their safety.

"Conditions outside are breathable," Braelynn reported. "Ready to drop the ramp?"

"Let's do it," 117 took a deep breath.

The ramp hissed and began to lower at a steady pace. Light flowed in through the opening and they all waited with bated anticipation. The ramp dropped completely and hit the ground with a thud that seemed to echo all around. 117 looked at Serina, who was floating next to his shoulder, and gave him a thumbs-up. Then, he turned to look at Braelynn and gave her a small nod.

Both of them walked down the ramp first. 917 and 999 followed. After, 466 took the front of the Third Group's diamond formation with 501 and Oreo safely behind her. On his left was 249. 593 walked on his right side and 49 brought up the rear.

As everyone stepped out of the shuttle, they surveyed their surroundings. The first thing they took note of was that there was no one around to greet them. The silence was both disconcerting and, in a weird way, peaceful.

The atmosphere did keep them alive or rather, Braelynn wasn't suffocating at least. The amborgs confirmed with both their own sensors and Serina's readings that the air was clean and breathable. Naturally, as they all looked around and began to take in their surroundings, everything was being recorded. It didn't seem organic like the inside of a giant exogorth, but the formation of the architecture and the designs inside this hangar appeared to be very round. It looked like someone with a giant pair of hands had sculpted the entire place out of clay. It was beautiful.

The amborgs looked behind them and saw that there was no opening or any sign of a hangar bay entrance, which was intriguing. It was almost as if the Tandeeri ship had opened its mouth and swallowed them to be digested. It was a stark contrast to the geometric angles, corners, and tall and straight corridors held up with several supports aboard the Firestar.

"Let's go that way," 117 said, pointing at a round exit at the center of the room. "Come on guys."

The floor was firm and easy to walk on. Despite the overall darkness, they could see clearly. It was likely a result of the iridescent lighting emanating from every direction.

"I'm kinda digging this," 466 said as she stared in awe. "I would totally grab pillows and camp out in here."

"We can build a room back home," 501 said with a chuckle.

"Not like this, 501."

Oreo let out a gleeful squeal as the group moved slowly towards what was unanimously voted to be the exit.

The Tandeeri design was definitely one of a kind, and even if there was a way to describe it from all the science fiction they had read before, it stood out in a unique way.

"Do you have a signal?" Braelynn asked as they stepped through the round doorway and entered a long hall.

117 looked back to the rest of the amborgs. All of them seemed to be more relaxed than when they were in the shuttle. It was like a sudden wave of euphoria had hit them. Even though the early encounters with the Tandeeri had shorted out or made their sensors and communications fuzzy, he actually realized something was different. He could think clearly.

"I do," 117 said, blinking in surprise. "I mean, guys!"

117 turned to face the group.

"I can't detect 297 or 92 and 93 but..." he said, putting his hand up to his ear. "I'm not getting annoying interference. Is it just me?"

"Every time the Tandeeri got close, it screwed with our implants," 917 answered. "I mean, it wasn't life-threatening but it was like a buzzing noise in our ears every time. Now that I actually have a moment to myself... I feel better."

"Stay close everyone," 117 nodded after each of them gave him encouraging smiles.

The halls felt like they were alive, almost as if sculptors had been contracted to design the ship rather than people with tech degrees. The only drawback was the question they kept asking themselves. Where the heck was everyone?

"This ship is giving me the creeps, but it makes me feel calm," 466 said, taking deep breaths. "Like it's a breath of fresh air but maybe the Tandeeri are actually feeding us inhalants that make us hallucinate."

"That'll make the headlines," 501 said. "Hey guys, the alien race that wants to kill us? Turns out we were all just high and it all was so great."

"Ok guys," Serina said with a smile as she rode on 117's shoulder. "As someone who hasn't breathed in a long time, I can activate the emergency gear in case you all suffocate. Just an extra precaution."

Oreo was squeaking and practically squirming out of 501's arms as the group moved forward. Soon, they arrived at a circular room with three corridors to choose from.

"Hey! Oreo!"

501 fell out of the group formation when Oreo suddenly made a beeline for the hallway on their right. The little Tandeeri stopped, turning to face them and jumping up and down, pointing to go that way.

"501!" 466 said as she ran after the two of them.

The others trailed behind Oreo, breezing through the corridors instead of exploring with caution. If the Tandeeri had somehow been unaware of their presence on board... they definitely wouldn't be now. Stealth was no longer an option.

They raced past doors with windows, but nobody had time to stop and look inside. They were all too focused on keeping up with 501 and 466. Eventually, Oreo came to a stop at what looked like a door, and they all caught up, panting.

"What the heck happened with Oreo?" Serina said while the rest of them caught their breath. "Is he, I mean, it... showing us the way?"

Oreo approached the door and tried to jump up. Apparently, there was a console it was trying to reach. 501 gently lifted Oreo, and it placed its claw-like hands on a spot just beneath what looked like a window.

A green circle appeared and glowed with a quick hum. The door then lifted up into the ceiling, allowing them to enter. 501 followed Oreo inside while the rest of them debated whether to follow.

"466 and I will go inside," 117 declared.

"I'll watch from outside the door," Braelynn said as 917 took a place at her side.

The rest of the group took strategic positions around the entrance as 117 and 466 went inside to listen to Oreo's playful cries of joy.

"It looks like..." 501 said with a stunned look. "What is it?"

"It seems like a nursery."

466 was probably right. As the three of them followed Oreo around the small room, it did resemble that of an ordinary daycare. There was a circle in the center which Oreo dived onto stomach-first.

"It's a carpet," 501 exclaimed as he knelt down and placed his hand on the floor. "Perfect for sitting."

"Oreo seems to be enjoying it," 466 cooed as she also knelt down.

Oreo stood up after a few seconds on the fuzzy space rug and then ran over to the wall. Oreo tapped on it and looked at them. 117 and 501 walked over.

"Hey buddy," 501 smiled. "Is there something in the compartment you want? A toy? Oh hey 117, there are windows on the compartments too. Let's take a look... oh crap!"

"What is it?"

501 peered into the window in the wall where Oreo was tapping. He made a happy squeak and grew more excited as 117 leaned to look inside too.

"There's something alive in there," 501 whispered frantically.

117 saw that he was right. There was another Tandeeri, exactly like Oreo, inside. It appeared to be asleep as it was tossing and turning slightly. Was it a napping pod of some sort?

"There are other Tandeeri children," 117 said loud enough for everyone at the door to hear. "These are some sort of cradles I think."

"Is it a type of stasis?" Braelynn said from the door.

"Doesn't seem like it," 117 shrugged. "I can see movement so I don't think so."

"The rest of them are also asleep," 501 said as he looked inside the other compartments. "It really is a nursery."

"Why would they bring children aboard a ship?" 466 asked. "Seems dangerous if you ask me."

"There are families aboard the Firestar," 501 replied. "I agree it's dangerous but this fleet must have a reason."

"The Firestar was one of the first ships to be considered primarily a deep-space exploration vessel," Braelynn answered. "It is outfitted for combat but the original design was to carry passengers and explore the universe. Had the Tandeeri War not occurred, then it would have been dedicated to the mission of science, discovery and diplomacy. It is meant to be a home away from home. Families and children of crewmembers prove to have long lasting effects in terms of morale and mental health support. Admiral Ra'aiah, as a result, commands the first advanced starship of the S.C.E. that is as large as a city with a utopian population. Not entirely ideal but the ship gets the job done. When war time follows, the ship undergoes strict rules for noncombatants."

"Thanks ensign," 917 said. "So, are we going to assume that the Tandeeri are basically fans of Gene Roddenberry's ideology of the utopian crew aboard a starship concept?"

"Hey. Oreo is trying to tell us something."

Oreo had begun to do some type of little dance in front of the compartment. Once it knew that they were watching, Oreo faced the compartment and punched it softly. Then, it knocked twice and turned around. Oreo pressed its back to the wall and held out its arms as if it had sprouted wings. Then it repeated the pattern again. It was a game of Tandeeri charades.

"What do you think Oreo is saying?" 117 asked 501.

"We don't know," 501 replied. "But we know that he can hear and see us. So I taught him a bit of sign language and motion signals. It's really hard though since we can't understand the little guy, or girl. So we've just been guessing what he wants to say when he makes a noise."

"You called Oreo he," 117 pointed out. "Are we assigning a gender now?"

"I personally think Oreo is a she," 466 argued softly.

Oreo squeaked and let out a small wail, which drew their attention back to the dancing. In one fluid movement, Oreo continued to box with the wall and then stand up against it.

"Punched the compartment," 501 muttered. "Then his back to the wall, and holding out his arms. Repeatedly."

"Looks like Oreo wants a hug," 466 said.

"But the punching," 501 said. "What does punching the compartment mean?"

"It almost looks like Oreo wants to protect it," 117 said as they all continued to watch.

Oreo turned to face 117 and jumped up and down with glee. He happily squeaked and whooped at them. Apparently that must have been the correct interpretation.

"Did I get it right?" 117 asked. "You understood me?"

Oreo jumped up and down while continuing to point. 117 pointed at himself.

"Was that right?" he asked. "Protect? Is that the word? You... want to protect... the compartment?"

117 pointed at the compartment, which made Oreo grin. At least they thought the little Tandeeri was grinning. 117 could only guess that Oreo was happy based on how his eyes lit up.

"No," 117 said as another idea came to mind. "Did... Did you want us to protect it?"

Oreo let out a squeal, which probably meant that his guess was on the money.

Suddenly, the door hissed and closed shut. 117, 501 and 466 stood and began to move to the door. The three of them crowded around it in an attempt to get out. Braelynn and 917, along with the others outside, could be seen trying to break their way in.

"Crap!" 917 said through the door. "It just closed on us!"

"We're locked in!" 501 cried. "We've been captured! This was their plan all along!"

There was another slight hissing noise as the door slowly opened again. Everyone stood there, awkwardly staring at the door as it pulled up into the ceiling. Then they all glanced down to see Oreo happily skipping outside.

"Oh," 501 said with a cough of embarrassment. "Never mind."

"Thanks for the unnecessary damage to my ears 501," 117 said, massaging his ear. "Next thing you'll be doing is yelling down the halls for 297."

"I wouldn't want to compromise our position," 501 said as all of them stepped back out into the hall.

"I was being sarcastic," 117 sighed.

"I know you were."

"297?"

Everyone turned to see 249 standing apart from the group. He was at the end of the hall, his eyes fixated on something.

"Hey!" 466 said as she ran over. "What are you doing away from us?"

"I saw 297," 249 replied as he pointed. "End of the hall. Unarmed."

"What do you mean unarmed?" 999 asked suspiciously. "He wouldn't be. Not here."

"Angel."

Everyone looked back to find 917 standing at the other end. He had gone in the opposite direction and was gazing into the distance with a dazed look in his eyes. 999 dashed away from 249 and 466, rushing past the group to his side.

"917?" she said, bemused, as she looked into his eyes, then peered down the hall in the direction he was staring. "What is it? Is it a threat?"

"No," 917 blinked and shook out of his trance. "I saw... It was Amara."

999 looked at 917 skeptically.

"There's nothing down that..."

A tiny squeak caught 999's attention, causing her to glance down sharply. Both of them stepped away from Oreo. Apparently, the little Tandeeri had strolled up to them so fast that they hadn't noticed.

"I swear…" 999 said as they both moved away from each other. "On the Firestar, a little alien baby sneaking up on us? That's ok. Little Tandeeri baby back home aboard their own ship? Creepy."

"I don't know," 917 shrugged. "It doesn't feel that creepy to me anymore."

"Even if I were to agree with that statement," 999 gestured down the halls. "Where is everyone?"

It really was the million-dollar question in this case. This was turning out quite differently than they had originally expected. Freely roaming across the Tandeeri ship was exciting, but also had the potential to go wrong in an instant.

"I think Oreo is trying to get us to follow," 917 suggested. He looked down at Oreo. "Did you see something? Can you show us the way?"

917 knelt down and 999 crouched down as well. She did so with caution, glancing both directions down the hall to make sure nothing else would sneak up on them. Oreo moved closer to 917 and began to moan sadly. The little Tandeeri then lifted its claw-like hand and placed it on 917's cheek.

"We taught Oreo that," 501 said. "A box fell on my toe and it hurt a little. So Oreo thought it'd be fun to drop something similar on its foot as well. The poor thing was crying so…"

"I was caressing 501's cheek," 466 said, blushing deeply. "While we checked his foot. Oreo began to imitate. I think Oreo believes it's what must be done when someone's hurt or needs comforting."

"I'm fine little buddy," 917 said as Oreo continued to whine curiously. "Thank you. Can you take us to your family?"

All of them slowly grouped together. 917 wasn't sure if his request was comprehensible but then, Oreo's eyes lit up. They watched Oreo pull 917 by his hand and they began to slowly move down the hall. He wasn't being pulled away from the group since Oreo didn't have the strength. It resembled that of a child showing an adult or their parent where they wanted to go.

Everyone followed the amborg holding the little Tandeeri's hand down one corridor after another, turning around each corner slowly, like a group of friends trying to navigate a maze in a fun house, or an iridescently soothing maze that seemed to be playing tricks on their eyes.

"Doesn't 917 look like a father?" 593 said as she walked behind them. She was nervously using 466 as a shield.

"It is rather sweet," 466 replied. "But stop clinging to me 593. I'm going to trip."

"He looks more like an uncle," 501 said with a grumble.

"Oh 501," 466 giggled. "I never thought I'd see you jealous over... Oreo."

"I can't help it," 501 pouted. "I spent a lot of time with Oreo."

"Come on..."

466 grabbed 501's right wrist and gave it a squeeze.

"Remember what we both said to him?"

501's expression softened and he gave her a questioning look.

"You mean from... *that* time?"

"*That* time," 466 smiled gently and nodded. "We said that we would make sure that when the happy moments brought out the best of him..."

"...then we would protect those moments until the very end," 501 conceded and sighed.

"What are you two talking about?"

501 and 466 saw a brief flash of light and Serina appeared next to them. She casually leaped up and took a seat on 501's shoulder.

"We're having a private conversation," 501 replied.

"Ehh, wrong!" Serina buzzed cheekily and changed to a shade of red. "If it was a private one, you would have kept it in your heads and not have allowed me to hear every word."

"You know," 466 suddenly remembered. "Since Serina is here, there actually is something I wanted to tell both of you."

"Privately?" 501 asked.

He and Serina turned their heads to look at 466. She nodded.

"Privately," she declared. "I'm going to switch channels. It's about when we were unconscious. Before we woke up."

"Any reason why you're interested in talking about this now instead of later?" Serina asked.

466 gave them a worried look.

"I wanted to but..."

She turned her head and watched Oreo leading 917 ahead of the group.

"What if we don't make it to later?"

Serina and 501 both looked at each other and nodded in understanding. They switched to 466's private channel.

Up front, right behind Oreo, 917 and 999, 117 was describing all of what they had seen inside of the nursery to their newly appointed interstellar consultant.

"All containment pods were occupied?" Braelynn asked, typing notes into a small data pad to document their findings.

"From what we saw briefly?" 117 replied. He thought back to the scene and then nodded affirmatively. "Looked like it."

"Was anything out of place? Anything unusual?"

"Not that I'm aware of... in fact, if I had to guess, it was almost like it was brand new."

Braelynn fell silent. 117 glanced at her when he noticed that she'd stopped asking questions and found her deep in thought, concentrating hard on his statement.

"In all my years witnessing the cultural traditions of dozens of other species," she said, "that is a detail to take note of."

"It is?"

"When was the last time you encountered a clean nursery? Cleaner than normal?"

"It did appear as if it hasn't been used in a long time," 117 shrugged.

"Hmm, it might be nothing," Braelynn shook her head as she went back to her note-taking.

"Why did you seem to be a little disturbed?" 117 asked.

"It's a habit I'm trying to get rid of," Braelynn explained. "In S.C.E. Intelligence, they train you to make a lot of judgments about everything within a split-second at all times. It's how you survive or learn about your environment so you can form a plan."

"Plan?"

"Plan of survival," she added. "But studying the Tandeeri isn't like that... unless we find out that they fully intend to kill us."

"Alright then," 117 nodded, but didn't seem too sure if he fully understood what she had said. "So, what can you tell us about the Tandeeri? So far?"

"So far? They're quite clean..."

Braelynn stopped taking notes and looked at 117.

"Of course, I need more information to really add more to their profile and Oreo along with some video footage isn't exactly a full picture," she said. "Maybe they value cleanliness or quiet starships. Perhaps their family or cultural values are more lenient than humans, considering they seem to be ok with complete strangers watching over one of their own. Assuming they're monitoring us. Whatever their deal is, it would all make sense if we found other members of their species."

"You have a keen eye for details," 117 said as he scanned her. There were cybernetic modifications on her that he could detect. "Are you sure you're not one of us?"

"No," Braelynn said with a tiny smirk. "I don't think I could be the one to be in your shoes."

"You're certainly skilled. Hope we can maintain a friendship between you and the amborgs."

Braelynn nodded as 117 jogged up to 917 and 999. 917 was still holding onto Oreo's hand as they were led into a large hallway. They had certainly lost track of where they were. At the same time, 466 had just finished their private conversation.

"It's too bad we don't have a supply of arrows to bust through these walls," 501 sighed when he started speaking on an open channel.

"A supply of... archer ammunition?" Braelynn looked at 501 in confusion. "How would that help us?"

"Oh not those kinds of arrows," 117 chuckled. "Back on Earth, we have experimental devices that could alter an object's gravity. It was literally a bumper sticker that sent whatever you stuck it to flying straight in that direction. It was supposed to be for transporting shipments or stuff like that but it didn't have the effect that Dr. Kendrick wanted."

"We were going to test its uses in space but..." 466 replied, "until a few geniuses in our ranks hypothesized how entertaining it would be to attach one to a naval aircraft carrier and make it rise out of the ocean and let it fly."

"Did that work?" Braelynn asked in fascination.

"Let's just say there was a heavy lawsuit," 917 called from the front. "Yeah. Using the arrows to drop a storm of garbage on the enemy is great but when we suddenly use it to try and advance our military tactics, then a bunch of high-ranking officials freak out."

"But we were able to figure out that the arrows cannot actually lift an object for a certain duration of time based on the object's mass," 466 said in an effort to ease 501's feelings.. "The carrier was too big and the arrow ran out of power in seconds from the strain."

"Yeah, but it was still scary when the carrier flew up ten feet and then plunked back down... while all of us were aboard," 249 said. "I still don't get why the captain still dislikes us. We apologized, didn't we?"

"It'll never be enough in some cases," 117 said as he tragically shook his head. "But if we still had the arrows, we could have probably used one to our advantage."

"Speak for yourself," Serina replied. "Chances are Dr. Kendrick has some hidden away. Not that I would know that kind of classified material."

"You've been awfully quiet," 117 said. "Are you ok Serina?"

"This place is cool," Serina said but she still huddled close to his neck. "But there aren't any electrical systems to jump into. I can't find any kind of outlet for database entry. Not even back at the nursery. No computers or systems. It's like there aren't any kinds of electrical conduits. I've just been hanging around within range of everyone's CPU. It gives me a place to think and stay close instead of being sur-rounded... well, for lack of a better description... by nothing."

"You are a very curious A.I.," Braelynn acknowledged rather bluntly. "Very smart and advanced... yet you seem to act a lot like a human."

Serina was too nervous to argue back.

"Thanks," she said peacefully instead as she fidgeted. "I get that a lot."

"Guys."

They turned a corner and found themselves facing a massive door. It was bigger than anything they had seen so far. The way Oreo kept pointing with casual noises was enough to tell them they had arrived.

"Alright," 117 took a deep breath and exhaled. "No one goes in with weapons drawn. We are here to negotiate for our friends and well... Braelynn will do all that and we will make sure nothing bad happens."

"Fingers crossed," Serina said and she pumped her fists bravely even though she changed to a shade of yellow.

"Open the door Oreo," 501 said, giving the little Tandeeri a light push forward.

Oreo stepped up to the door and placed its hand on the center. A ring appeared and shined green. The entire doorway parted in four directions from the center to the outside. All of them looked inside to see an antechamber. Beyond, there appeared to be a massive circular room. The center of the ship?

The one other thing they immediately noticed were the shapes moving in the background. Oreo leaped forward cheerfully and signaled for them to follow. They huddled together as a group and walked in bravely.

"BRakoh! VSTNMA!"

There was a massive thud as they heard a loud voice from... something approaching them. Oreo squeaked happily, but this didn't reassure them at all.

"Ok," Braelynn gulped. "Now I am very scared."

"Thankfully I packed extra pants for everyone," 501 mumbled fearfully.

CHAPTER 6

Tandeeri Negotiations for Dummies

Everyone froze in their tracks.

917 shook his hand free from Oreo's grasp as he and 999 stood side-by-side. They were looking around frantically, managing not to draw their weapons.

501 tried to race up the center towards Oreo, but 117 and Braelynn both pivoted and grabbed him. 466 and the rest of the Third Group had to rush in to help keep him from acting impulsively. After things settled, they all stared at the tall, shadowy figure approaching them. Each of its footsteps brought it closer into the light.

"Now would probably be a good time to make sure you're all recording this," Serina gulped. "For research purposes."

The figure that drew near appeared to be a larger and older version of Oreo. The whole group kept their eyes on this mysterious Tandeeri as they listened to Oreo croaking and chirping excitedly. Then, a deep voice resonated from the creature standing before them.

"Oo-rahkueh!"

With a single word, they heard louder footsteps and a massive amount of coordinated shuffling. Suddenly, from the shadows, a crowd emerged, causing the amborgs to huddle closely together, all staring in shock.

It wasn't long before they found themselves surrounded. A large ring of Tandeeri aliens advanced after the loud command from the one in the center. All of them were notably taller and more robust. None matched their height. If they had to venture a guess, the average height of a Tandeeri adult seemed to be at least 6 and a half feet. The amborgs started to observe their physical attributes and tried to describe what they were seeing.

"Bi-pedal," 501 whispered. "Sturdy frames. They look like they're in armor. Definitely big giant versions of Oreo."

"Only some of them seem to be warriors or soldiers," 466 said as she clung onto him. "Some look like they're unarmed."

"A pair of eyes," 917 said. "Just like Oreo. Am I the only one that can't see mouths?"

"But someone spoke," 999 said cautiously. "They can speak."

"Many of them range between 7 feet and the tallest I estimate is 8," 117 observed as they all cautiously continued the stare-down. "Alien giants. They look like a race of pure-bred warriors though. I can't tell if there are genders."

"Some of them look like they could be a *jiralhanae*," 593 said meekly. "Stupid aggressive lunatics."

"Really?" 49 gulped. "A Halo reference??"

"If they understand english," Serina murmured to 593. "Then you might regret calling them stupid. Aggressive? Maybe. If they're highly sensitive, then it was nice knowing all of you."

"Yeah, let's avoid name-calling," Braelynn breathed silently.

"Dark-blue skin," 117 continued. "Humanoid figures. Almost looks reptilian or amphibian in nature. No facial hair."

"Nice tattoos or war paint on a few of them," 917 muttered. "A thumb and three fingers. Or are they claws? Oreo's don't seem that sharp. Ooh... are they digitigrades?"

"What I'm worried about... is why they haven't moved?" 999 whispered.

"They're probably observing us as much as we are them."

Braelynn decided to break out of the group and step forward. Oreo followed and cheerfully skipped forward.

There was a cry from somewhere in the crowd as an adult Tandeeri rushed toward them. Oreo squealed in delight and ran into their arms.

"I'm not the smartest amborg... but I think that might be one of his parents," 501 spoke softly.

Everyone quietly agreed as they watched Oreo happily nuzzle into the arms of what appeared to be a very nurturing and worried looking Tandeeri adult. However, they didn't have the luxury of enjoying this particular moment.

Braelynn was moving forward slowly, her hands held up. Once she was past 917 and 999, she faced the Tandeeri standing in the center of the room just ahead of them. This one, despite standing alone, seemed to be draped in some form of ceremonial garb, which was a clear sign that it was the leader. The only way to confirm this was to try and begin a conversation.

"I am a representative of the Space Command Enterprise," Braelynn announced. "We are here to negotiate the return of the amborgs' colleagues and S.C.E. crewmembers in your possession on this magnificent vessel that we were... invited aboard. With the return of your child, we hope to also request a ceasefire to the war. We have come to beg for your assistance and for your understanding."

There was a momentary silence as her voice echoed throughout the great hall.

"Wow," 917 murmured with an impressed look. "You came up with that?"

"Been brainstorming it ever since we opened the door to this place," she replied hastily. "It'll have been for nothing if they can't understand us the way Oreo can."

There was still no reaction from the Tandeeri, only an intense staredown. That is, until Oreo let out a loud cry. Everyone watched as he squirmed loose from his parent's arms and ran back towards the amborgs. Oreo made a beeline for 501 with its arms open. The amborgs shuffled around, clearing the way. 501 cheerfully opened his arms and Oreo hugged his knees.

This elicited a slight response from the crowd. The Tandeeri in the room were all making curious grunts and noises. A few looked visibly stunned or flabbergasted, but for the most part, there were no sudden movements.

The amborgs and Braelynn looked at the Tandeeri standing in the center. It was lifting its arm but then it stopped when another voice broke the silence.

"Bah-kee."

Everyone glanced to the side, watching as the Tandeeri stepped aside to create an opening for another one to come forward.

"A decoy?" 117 asked.

"I don't know," Braelynn replied.

Through the parted crowd, another Tandeeri approached them with heavy footsteps. As it stepped into the light, everyone could see its attire. This one was decorated in dark red robes, appearing to be their leader. Braelynn took a step forward and dipped her head respectfully.

"If this one is the leader," she whispered to the amborgs, "I can understand why it had a decoy greet us in the center."

"Decoy?" 501 asked.

"Our intentions may be good," 117 explained quickly. "But the Tandeeri don't know that."

The red-robed Tandeeri continued its slow march towards them. As it drew nearer, they began to notice its impressive height. It was taller than most of the other Tandeeri. It definitely was the leader if it was taking this kind of initiative.

With her head still bowed, she quietly relayed more instructions to the group.

"Whatever you do or whatever happens," she said calmly. "Do not fight them. No matter what the response is."

The amborgs stood rooted to their spots as Braelynn continued to bow and leaned further forward respectfully. They watched the Tandeeri leader stop directly in front of her and stare. They could hear its heavy breathing as it looked down on them.

"Bah-kee," it spoke.

After a quick analysis of its voice, the amborgs were able to confirm that this was the same one that spoke earlier.

This time, Oreo pulled away from 501 and moved forward, slumping as if about to be scolded. The leader extended a finger and pointed at the ground next to it. Oreo fell silent and obediently walked over. Everyone paused, coming to a startlingly serious revelation.

"Don't tell me... that Oreo is the child... of the leader..." 117 breathed.

"...of the Tandeeri," 917 finished.

"Oh man..." 501 trembled. "I'm so glad we didn't get Oreo killed."

Oreo approached the Tandeeri leader and looked down. The leader then lifted a hand and lightly patted Oreo on the head a few times. Then it raised its other hand and hung it over Braelynn's head.

"What's it doing?" 917 said.

"I don't know," Braelynn gasped back. "I feel... relaxed? I don't know how to describe it. It's... I can feel..."

"Is it hurting you?" 117 asked cautiously.

A few of the Tandeeri flinched and stepped back. A few more began to murmur and look at each other nervously. He hadn't intended to sound so apprehensive, but 117 immediately shut his mouth anyway.

"No!" Braelynn said. "I feel fine. It's... I think he's trying to communicate with us."

"He?" 999 asked.

"You can relax. I mean you no harm. Also, it's about time."

All of the amborgs and Braelynn jumped when the Tandeeri leader in red retracted its arm and greeted them. Except, its voice came from... around them? It was deep, raucous and sounded authoritative, which gave them chills.

"Did... Did it... I mean... he... just say what I think he said?" 917 stammered.

"Yes. You are... damn right I said that."

Braelynn straightened up with a stunned look on her face. This was clearly unexpected.

"You're speaking... English?" she exclaimed as she backed up and retreated towards the amborgs.

All of them gazed at the Tandeeri leader, who nodded in response. Now the questions were flowing in faster than they could get them out.

"How?" 117 asked.

"Well, it became easier when we first encountered your friends."

The Tandeeri leader bowed its head as it gestured to Oreo.

"My son tells me that you have taken care of him," he said.

"I knew Oreo was a boy," 501 said.

The Tandeeri leader lifted his head and gazed directly at them. 501 quickly became quiet when 466 nudged him.

"Because you have protected him and brought him back to me and my chee-suukagh," he said, "I will grant you an audience. You may come forward and speak."

A loud roar erupted from the right as another Tandeeri charged forward, yelling and speaking aggressively. 117 and the amborgs huddled together defensively, but the Tandeeri leader unexpectedly stepped in front of them, taking them by surprise. He was protecting them from the hostile tone of the one who appeared to be in opposition.

"What are they saying?" 917 asked 117.

"Do I look like I speak Tandeeri?" 117 replied hastily.

Their question was answered when they decided to quietly watch the confrontation before them. The two Tandeeri were standing chest to chest. The one who had stepped out to challenge the leader was staring defiantly up at him. Suddenly, they were all taken aback when the leader head-butted his subordinate. The impact created a loud thud, which sent chills across their spines. The amborgs didn't want to be on the receiving end of whatever that was. The Tandeeri that had been hit backed off with an apologetic grumble as the leader turned to look at them once again.

"Whoa..." 917 gulped. "How much force do you think that was?"

"Based on the sound of the impact," 999 stated. "It would have probably broken our spines."

"Yup, very hard," 501 shrunk fearfully.

The Tandeeri leader dipped his head to them.

"Chaka is one of my advisors," the leader explained. "I will give you a translation of what she has said. She doesn't believe that you have the right to say anything in our presence."

"That's all?" 117 asked politely.

"That was the nicer translation," the leader replied grimly. "Would you like the actual words?"

"No, thank you," Braelynn said bowing her head. "We are very interested in first knowing how you can speak our language. Where did you learn english?"

"From your friends," the leader nodded. "When they first came aboard, we observed and studied their patterns of speech. It enhanced our knowledge and awareness of your communication skills."

"Our friends are alive?" 466's eyes lit up.

"Yes. The ones dressed like you," the leader seemed to smile cheerfully at 466. Then he looked at Braelynn. "And this human female too."

"None of them are dead?" Braelynn let out a sigh of relief.

"There was no point in killing them."

"So, you just wanted to take them alive?" 999 asked cautiously.

"We figured it would be the simplest way to meet with your kind," the Tandeeri leader explained. "We waited when your shuttles were out of reach of your ships. Once out of your range, we did in fact kidnap your colleagues. For that, I apologize. But you must understand... my son was missing for many days."

"Days?" 117 asked. "Oreo has only been with us... for less than one day."

"He has been missing for three of your... weeks," the Tandeeri leader replied. "I am very grateful that he has returned safely."

Oreo let out a squeal, and the leader glanced down. They noticed him displaying signs of love and care. This was expected since he was

Oreo's father. After a few squeaks and chirps from Oreo, the leader nodded and then looked up at Braelynn.

"I believe that time flows differently here than it does for you," he said.

"Time dilation?" Braelynn asked. "Is time aboard your ship longer than our time?"

"Oh no," 501 groaned. "We have to do math? In a space time-zone?"

"Perhaps that explains why it's felt like years since this war has gone on," the Tandeeri leader nodded as he raised his claws to his chin, beginning to ponder. "My son doesn't appear to be behaving as if he has been gone for a long time."

"How long can one of your species live?" 917 asked curiously. "Ballpark estimate? Is it like how we measure dog years? 7 human years to 1 year for a dog?"

117 cleared his throat. 917 looked at him and then realized what he was saying.

"Not like you're like a dog," he corrected his statement right away. "Your lifespan must be completely different to ours if... time is slower here?"

"After spending time with your friends," the Tandeeri leader said with a thoughtful look, "we have discovered that we can live ten times longer than you."

"A thousand years?" Braelynn asked. "Humans tend to average at 100 to 200 years old."

She then quickly glanced at 117.

"Is it the same in your universe?" she asked.

"More or less," 117 nodded. "In our universe, average lifespan has reached above 150 years. With our implants, we can probably live to 1000 years."

"Very impressive," the Tandeeri leader stared in at 117 in awe. The way his eyes widened and seemed to gleam caught them off-guard. "However, I think I have you beat."

"Is it appropriate for us to even ask how old you are?" 501 asked.

"I am... 8,834 years old. If we're using your human years."

"Wow," 466 gulped.

Everyone's eyes widened. A few of the amborgs' mouths dropped open.

"Is that a lot?" the Tandeeri leader glanced at Braelynn.

"T-to be completely honest?" Braelynn stammered. "It is remarkable."

"Hey," 917 nodded. "Looking good."

"Many thanks."

593 smiled and eagerly stepped forward.

"I think it's really amazing!"

She looked at Braelynn and then at Serina.

"They live for such a long time and had... possibly more time with our friends!" she gestured at the Tandeeri leader. "He sounds like he's been speaking English for years!"

"Wait a minute," Braelynn held up her hand. "How long has it been since we've arrived onboard?"

"At least an hour," Serina stated. "I've kept track of the time since we all woke up."

Braelynn then glanced at the Tandeeri leader.

"With all due respect, sir," she said in a polite and calm tone. "How long have the others been here? When you took them into your custody?"

"11 days," he answered promptly.

"What?" 117's eyes widened. "But we lost contact with them yesterday!"

"My apologies for the inconvenience," the Tandeeri leader grunted. "Time is quite different here than it is out there where you hail from."

"Are you telling us that you've had more than a week and a half to study English?" Serina asked.

The Tandeeri leader turned and looked curiously at Serina.

"I would not dare lie to you," he said. "Not to my guests."

917 turned to look at 999.

"This is a lot to unravel," he stated.

"Excuse me," 999 spoke up.

The Tandeeri leader looked at 999.

"The first time you encountered the S.C.E.," she said. "First contact. You were there?"

"I was indeed."

"What do you remember?"

The leader shrugged his large, broad shoulders and replied casually.

"We first came to the people dressed like this... female." The leader pointed at Braelynn. "However, we were attacked after we shared our technology when we first heard your language."

"Pardon?" Braelynn asked.

The Tandeeri leader looked left at no one in particular and sighed.

"I told you so," he said loudly with a huff. "We should have continued diplomacy, but then we had a vote and decided to give them our power. Now look at the mess we're in."

There was an apologetic grunt from another Tandeeri as it bowed its head and stepped backwards to hide in the crowd. The amborgs all stared in confusion as they tried to figure out what was happening.

"All of those electrical discharges that we've seen. They aren't weapons?" 999 asked.

"Our species was given the skills of generating significant charges of power," the leader said. "It is our way. We wanted to offer it to your people as a gesture of good faith. Unfortunately, it didn't work out the way we expected."

"We didn't have the technology to keep the energy contained," Braelynn said.

"Well that explains why everything overloaded and blew up," 117 said nervously as he wiped the sweat off his forehead.

"But..." Serina interrupted. "If what I'm hearing is correct... is this whole entire war one big misunderstanding? Because if the answer is yes, the S.C.E. really messed that up."

Annoyance suddenly filled the eyes of the Tandeeri leader. He lowered his head and turned a stern gaze upon them.

"In the years that followed, our attempts to make further contact were responded to by attacks from you. Your people killed mine. We defended ourselves. All because of a misunderstanding. Kavka!"

"Anyone else think that he just cussed at us in his own language?" 249 asked fearfully.

The Tandeeri leader snarled and pointed a claw at Braelynn. She didn't move.

"Your kind are dangerous!" he declared.

"If we're going off of our own ancient history," 117 stepped forward and attempted to defend Braelynn. "That is a very accurate description of humanity."

"But we want peace," the leader said as he lowered his claw. "We don't want to be in an endless battle for our own survival. Many of us spent time with your friends and learned your customs, rules, and languages so that we could finally build a bridge to communicate."

"Are they safe?" Braelynn asked.

"They've been in here the whole time."

The leader raised his arm and waved to a corner of the chamber. There was no one sitting there but in an instant, the wall seemed to melt. It was then that all of them realized it was an optical illusion fading away. What used to be an empty corner was now a glowing circular shield. Inside, they all saw the missing amborgs and S.C.E. crewmen that they had come to rescue.

The crowd of Tandeeri parted as the leader took the group over to where the captives were being held. They saw someone behind the glass-like barrier turn their way. A familiar face smiled at them and waved enthusiastically.

"I don't think I've seen him smile like that in a long time…" Serina stared in amazement.

"117! You're all here!"

Carter 297 was ecstatic to see them. The Tandeeri leader kindly gestured to everyone behind the barrier. The entire group saw the other abducted amborgs and S.C.E. crew standing up to greet them.

"The reason why I speak your language was because of them."

501 looked concerned as he pointed at the area that 297 was standing in.

"You had them behind glass this whole time?" he asked curiously.

"Of course not," the Tandeeri leader replied earnestly. "We set this up as temporary housing while they stayed aboard my ship."

"Are they locked in there?" 117 asked.

"Unfortunately, they were suffering from odd biological health issues after being among us for a few days," the Tandeeri leader explained with a sigh. "We quarantined them, tried to figure out what was the cause, and eventually manage to calibrate the inside of the chamber to help them regain normalcy."

"Oh no," 466 said as she placed a hand on the barrier symphathetically. "And we left 6 behind back at the Firestar."

"Our best doctor," 297 grinned as he quickly looked up at the Tandeeri leader to explain.

He nodded and thanked 297 for the clarification. Then he turned to speak to Braelynn.

"I will be more than happy to release them back into your custody," he said. "I'm just concerned about what will happen if I open the chamber."

"What did happen when they first showed... symptoms?" Braelynn asked.

"Dizziness, headaches and nausea," the Tandeeri leader answered immediately. "The enhanced humans... Oh, pardon me. The amborgs are very strong and resilient."

Then he pointed at the S.C.E. crew members.

"Your people however... were the first ones to start feeling sick."

"I think that makes sense," Braelynn nodded in agreement. "Cybernetically enhanced beings do have higher physical and mental attributes when facing certain environments."

117 looked at 297 and saw 777 standing behind him. Everyone in the chamber all looked quite happy and relaxed.

"You do look fine," 117 smiled. "It's good to see you."

"Likewise," 297 laughed. "It's about time you all made it."

"Previous attempts to contact the S.C.E. were always difficult," the Tandeeri leader grunted. "So, we sought out the amborgs instead."

"How did you know that there would be amborgs coming up from Earth?" 249 asked. "Those shuttles could have been anyone."

The Tandeeri's eyes gleamed as he pointed at all of the amborgs specifically. In one sweeping motion, they all gazed at each other and waited for his response.

"Your aura."

"What?" Serina blurted out.

The Tandeeri leader gazed down at them and nodded.

"The reason we sought to take your friends was because we could see your auras and we've been trying to find you at every opportunity we could," he explained nonchalantly. "Ever since we arrived in this universe, we did a long range scan and discovered many things about your universe. Once we scanned your home planet, we noticed that there were certain humans that were beyond extraordinary. We were curious about your kind. We could sense your energy."

Everyone glanced at each other skeptically.

"What exactly do you see when you look at us?" 917 asked.

"Your physiques emanate strange energy waves," the leader stared at 917. "There are colors surrounding each of you. They are much stronger in the amborgs than the normal humans here."

The group exchanged glances again. They all shrugged and murmured amongst themselves. A moment later, they all turned their attention back to the leader.

"Well, since we're on the subject..." 501 smiled curiously.

The entire party collectively wanted to know. 117 decided to indulge everyone and asked the question.

"What kind of auras do you see from us?"

The Tandeeri leader glanced at 117 and stared for a moment.

"Depending on your emotions, the color becomes quite strong and clear," he said. "I see an orange outline surrounding you. It clashes with the green stripes of your uniform."

"Is orange good?" 117 glanced down at his sleeves.

"Almost everyone is emitting orange auras," the Tandeeri leader glanced at the whole group. "Possibly because there are a lot of anxious and unsteady emotions among you."

"Are there currently any other colors besides orange among us?" Braelynn looked around and stared at the glass chamber. "Just a little more insight into how you percieve us?"

"This one is a strong red aura. A little orange but... much more red."

Everyone glanced at 917 when the Tandeeri leader pointed his claw at him.

"If I look at this one... number 501," he turned his gaze to look at the Third Group amborgs. "His aura is yellow, like your sun. The woman next to him. 466. Her aura fluctuates between blue and orange."

For the most part, when he described 249, 593 and 49's auras, there wasn't a lot of change in his description. The Third Group amborgs were displaying much stronger emotions, which contributed to their heavy "orange" auras. What got their attention was the fact that there were a couple of outliers in their rescue party.

"What does blue mean?" 501 glanced at 466. "You said that she had a blue aura."

"She is thinking of something that is making her sad," the Tandeeri leader replied.

"That's accurate..." 466 looked surprised. "When we woke up, I remember I dreamt about something that happened years ago."

"Can you see our memories?" Serina asked. "Or... their memories? Or do you only see our emotional states?"

"It depends on what you're focusing on," the Tandeer leader nodded. "The stronger you think about it, the more easily we can sense your memories."

"Telepathic abilities," Braelynn nodded. "That's impressive."

"Oh, wait..." Serina glanced at 917. "What does red mean?"

"I can take a guess," 917 mumbled.

The Tandeeri leader looked 917 up and down.

"Every one of you has a hint of a red aura but for 917... it is very clear," he said. "He has experienced heavy amounts of pain. Yet, he is strong, determined, and quite resilient. He is a warrior."

"Does that mean that... 999 or 297 also have strong red auras?"

917 had picked two of his friends specifically in an attempt to have a bit of fun guessing what their auras were. The Tandeeri leader nodded at first but when he looked at 999, he paused.

"297 is also a skilled warrior, yes," he let out a grunt of affirmation. Then he turned his gaze to 999. "However, this one is different."

"Different?" 999 asked softly.

"Your aura is masked," the Tandeeri leader remarked in an amazed voice. "It is... not dark or evil... and yet, you are also exceptionally strong-willed. It's impressive because I cannot sense your emotions."

"She does hide it very well," Serina explained. "Well, her emotions. Is it bad if she doesn't reveal her aura to you?"

"Not necessarily," the Tandeeri leader replied. "True masters of their mental faculties are experts at not allowing their auras to reveal or take control of their intentions. However, some of those that don't fully share their auras are often in a dangerous mindspace."

"I am fine," 999 replied calmly.

"Even without my heightened senses," the Tandeeri leader said, unconvinced. "It is clear that you are choosing to keep it hidden away on purpose."

They decided to drop the subject since 999 was crossing her arms and looking away. Sensing that she was uncomfortable, the Tandeeri leader looked at Braelynn and 117.

"What about your aura? Your people? What auras do they have?" 593 raised her hand.

"There is a faint outline of orange," the Tandeeri leader smiled. "Only because it is a little scary to meet you. However, for most of my people as well as your friends in our observation chamber, the auras are mostly bright green."

"Can I make a guess and assume that means their emotions are at peace? Or happy?" 117 asked.

"Calm," the Tandeeri leader answered. "They are currently feeling safe and at peace. Other negative auras do appear randomly in low intensity pulses but they are fine."

"I hope we'll get back to green auras soon," 501 mumbled.

Serina suddenly glowed and changed to a bright green color.

"Speak for yourselves," she smiled cheekily.

The Tandeeri leader looked at Serina with an intrigued glint in his eyes.

"Fascinating," he said.

"Thank you," Serina replied bashfully.

"Was your aura... also red?"

917 raised his hand and spoke up, which garnered everyone's attention. The Tandeeri leader turned his head.

"Pardon?"

"If I had to guess, red is more than just being someone who has experienced pain or whatever you described... I'm guessing it shows in people who are... angry, upset, or fuelled by rage?"

The Tandeeri leader's face fell as he became silent. 917 looked at Braelynn and 117 and shrugged.

"You know? When you're in a fight, sometimes all you see is red."

The Tandeeri leader nodded and glanced at Oreo, who was still at his side.

"We never wanted to kill anyone," he replied calmly. "We only sought the means to finally find and speak to a group of humans so that we could assimilate and understand your language. So, we treated your friends well, listened to their conversations and pieced together your language. When you returned my son, he shared his memories and thoughts with me. The experiences that he witnessed with you are now ingrained in my mind. Now, they are slowly being adapted by my people."

"I figured that your race had some strong telepathic connections," Braelynn looked around at the Tandeeri crowd that were continuing to observe them. "But, this means that diplomacy will be much easier than we thought."

She was right. As they continued speaking, the amborgs could hear more voices and several other Tandeeri members in the background. Instead of the cryptic and mysterious words of their language, they were beginning to hear phrases and tidbits of English. It was quite remarkable.

"And if time is longer here," the Tandeeri leader stated, "it'll be plenty of time for you to report back to your leaders and I will continue to extinguish all traces of my red aura."

"Just to clarify," 501 bowed his head respectfully. "I had no idea that Oreo was your son. If I had..."

"You do not need to explain, my young friend," the Tandeeri leader interrupted. "Oreo has already given you much praise. That is why you will have my personal respect and my gratitude."

"Is it safe to say that everything worked out in the end?" 117 asked.

"I hope so. Is this not what you wanted?"

The Tandeeri leader's question caught 117 off guard for some reason. He chuckled and nodded nervously.

"It just seems strange how it was only until now that you learned our language," he said.

The Tandeeri leader let out a deep chortle that strangely resembled a laugh.

"You are the first humans that aren't trying to kill us."

A light tapping sound from inside the chamber grabbed everyone's attention. They all turned to see amborg 8 standing in front of the glass.

"That's fair," 8 said from inside the bubble. "I think."

"But it's remarkable," Braelynn said. "Your entire species has to ability to learn and adapt at an incredible rate. Instead of teaching each other, you actually observe, imitate and then mold your experiences and share it... telepathically?"

"We have traveled many universes and across many galaxies," the Tandeeri leader nodded. "It is very difficult for us to leave the confines of our ships. I am afraid that the only way to learn of other cultures is to attempt to invite foreign species aboard. Except... in a lot of past attempts they have treated us like invaders. Therefore, we observed you the whole time you were in the labyrinth. Our connection allows us to watch and learn."

"But that's what we came to settle," 466 said. "You're not the ones who started this war. It really was a misunderstanding!"

"Wait, back up a second," 117 stated. "We were in a labyrinth?"

"Well, not exactly," the Tandeeri leader shrugged. "We wanted to see how much of our ship you would explore. So, I had my people stay here while you sought your courage and overcame your fears."

"Like... a psychological test?" Serina inferred. "You just wanted to see what we would do?"

"It was thanks to your friends that we decided against taking you captive," the Tandeeri leader pointed at 297. "With their endorsement, we voted to allow you to willingly explore my ship. We didn't want you to feel like we were taking you captive."

"Well, we really appreciate that," Braelynn dipped her head respectfully. "Perhaps... you could tell us more?"

"What would you like to know?"

"Please. Tell us where you came from and why you're here. Even if you didn't want a war, you still found time to come here to their universe."

Braelynn gestured to all of the amborgs.

"This is their home. I want to know why you came here. Actually, they want to know too. Right now, we're afraid of losing everything. Can you help us?"

The Tandeeri leader looked at Braelynn. His eyes lit up and he nodded.

"Then, we should get started," he said. "I will have my son share more of his stories with me. It will be a good conversation."

117 felt his hopes rise as he glanced at his friends in the observation chamber. Everyone on the other side looked like they were in for a one heck of a presentation.

"I have been quite eager to practice my english with more new friends," the Tandeeri leader declared. "I would like to thank you."

"We could do 20 questions," Serina suggested. "One question gets an answer. Then the other side gets to ask a question and another answer. Back and forth."

"Ah, yes," the Tandeeri leader seemed pleased. "I have seen this game! 92 and 93 demonstrated this! I have tried it a few times and would like to practice with you!"

"Well," Braelynn looked taken aback at his sudden excitement. "Would you like the honor of going first?"

The Tandeeri leader appeared happy to hear this. 501 nudged 466 excitedly.

"He looks just like Oreo!" he said. "Oreo always looks like that when he's in a fun mood!"

"My first question," the Tandeeri leader boldly declared. "Why do humans have a habit of relieving themselves while they are sleeping?"

Everyone awkwardly fell silent. The Tandeeri leader eagerly waited for a response. 117 glanced at 297. Everyone inside the chamber, except for the Fourth Group amborgs, were all giving them encouraging looks. What had they been teaching the Tandeeri in their spare time?

"Who wants to answer this one?" 917 sighed.

"Ah, you have answered my question with another question. Clever. Do I go again?"

CHAPTER 7

Who's in Charge???

Washington D.C.
White House
One hour after attack

"I want answers now. Recover all the security footage and recreate everything that happened here."

18 stood over the shoulder of a White House technician who was working steadfastly at his computer station. She was providing him with as much help as she could.

"I am so sorry ma'am," he said nervously. "I'm doing this to the best of my ability."

"Alright."

18 turned and looked around at who she was working with.

In the main office just outside of the Oval Office was the main study. There were a few office spaces, restrooms, and facilities that weren't on the usual tour. She was with a man named Joe, who was attempting to do his job.

"You're the in-house technician?" 18 asked.

"I'm an intern ma'am," Joe replied fearfully. "I was shadowing the chief technician and I had to take a bathroom break when..."

"Alright alright," 18 replied quickly. She got the picture. "So, you happened to be in a safe spot when the attack happened."

"I'm sorry..." Joe's voice cracked.

18 turned her head and noticed that Joe was staring up at her, tears welling in his eyes.

"Hey," 18's voice softened, and she gently placed a hand on his trembling shoulder. "What are you apologizing for?"

"I didn't see anything," he sniffled in response. "I hid in the bathroom and... I didn't see anything! Then the power went out and I tried to hide. All I did was hide!"

"Hey!"

18 raised her voice sharply, causing Joe to shudder. She opened her mouth to speak, but couldn't find the right words. Her breath grew

unsteady as she curled her free hand into a fist. The urge to slam it into the desk was strong. Joe was now focused entirely on her, appearing to have snapped out of his frantic chatter by her sudden outburst.

"A-amborg 18... a-are you alright?" Joe stammered softly.

"No!"

18 dropped her arm to her side. Her hand continued to tremble from either rage or fear. She sniffed and looked away.

"Another one of my friends is dead!" she declared when she straightened up and turned around. "He's dead! This wasn't supposed to happen!"

"Marco 125," Joe replied in a soft whisper. "He saved my life."

18 let out a frustrated sigh and shook her head.

"Yeah he did," she admitted angrily.

After a moment of silence, 18 glanced inside the Oval Office. Beyond the shattered doors, several bodies of marine guards and secret service agents lay lifeless on the floor. They had all fought bravely, but her attention was drawn to one particular uniform.

The neon stripes outlining 125's amborg uniform remained visible. However, the unmistakable sign that he'd died fighting was that the stripes were no longer illuminated. When the lights on an amborg's jacket go dark, it means one of two things: either the amborg can no longer perform active duty, or is dead.

The words that she had transmitted back to A.I. Industries continued to echo in her memory.

125 is dead. Amborg down. 125 has been killed in the line of duty.

Then she thought about what 4 had said to her once that had been reported.

Can you confirm? Is this confirmed? Do you need medical support?

18 remembered she had asked for more amborgs to come and help her. Unfortunately, their hands were tied. The amborgs were already stretched thin across the world and the reality was that there wasn't anyone available. They had already sent a team up to reinforce the amborgs in space, only for the Tandeeri to swoop in and snatch them away. Based on all of their decision-making and tactical choices, they had assumed that the battle in space took precedence. They were terribly mistaken.

"I just... need to know what happened here," 18 sighed. "What could be powerful enough to knock out the power inside one of the most secure locations on the entire planet?"

Joe didn't reply. Instead, he flexed his hands and went back to the computer. He began to type and tried to recover the security recordings.

"I really am sorry," Joe took a deep breath. "I didn't see anything... but... I did manage to hear something."

18 glanced at Joe and perked up. This was good information.

"What did you hear?"

"When I went into the bathroom, I was just washing my hands," he described the scene as best he could. "That's when I felt the floor and the walls shake. Not like an earthquake. It was like something big was being thrown around. Then I heard gunshots, screams and..."

"I could see the aftermath," 18 nodded. "They were trying to fight something that was making its way to the Oval Office."

"When it got closer, I was afraid to leave the bathroom," Joe explained. "I kept hearing people trying to tell everyone to evacuate to alternative exits. The Secret Service agents were trying to coordinate and stay close to 125."

"Anything about the attackers?"

"I think there was only one," Joe replied. "Something that even the strongest defense drones couldn't beat."

"One attacker?"

Despite voicing her thoughts, 18 distinctly remembered the signs as she arrived on site. The first casualties she encountered were members of the S.C.E. crew, found outside their shuttle parked on the White House lawn. They had been the first targets. Once she stepped through the doors, she discovered that the fight had already ended.

"How long?"

"About 7 minutes and then 125 fought it in the Oval Office," Joe answered calmly. "I think it was a Terminator."

"Those don't exist in our universe," 18 stated.

"Really? Because last month, we weren't meeting with people from an alternate universe and now suddenly, look at the mess we're in."

18 gave Joe a look and he shrugged. It was difficult to believe that he was freaking out earlier.

"Yeah, good point," she groaned. "Do you remember anything else?"

"It was like a terrible boss fight," Joe nodded his head and continued. "You know, from a video game?"

"Yeah, I got it," 18 impatiently rolled her hand to get him back on track. "I understood the analogy."

"From what I heard, it felt like that scene from the first movie," Joe explained. "When the T-800 slaughtered all of those police officers in minutes. I think the only one that managed to fight to the very end was 125."

Joe turned back to the screen and resumed his work while continuing to share his recollections.

"I think I heard this deep robotic voice," Joe's eyes shifted warily. "It was demanding to know where President Holland was."

"So, it was here to assassinate our leader," 18 said. "Is that what you're telling me?"

"Yes!" Joe nodded. "Before it killed 125, it was trying to force him to give up any information as to the president's whereabouts!"

18 stopped her questioning and turned her head away to think.

When she had done her initial sweep of the entire building and photographed and documented everything, she had tried looking for any signs of this mysterious attacker. She did have video footage from her own camera system as well as 125's system.

The first thing she had done was acquire all of the video recordings and pictures from 125's CPU. He had also managed to reconnect his uplink back to A.I. Industries, which meant that he had tried to send them evidence of what he'd witnessed. The problem was, during the moments where he should have seen the attacker, there was nothing.

"You said that 125 engaged the attacker," she said.

"Yes."

"Why is all the footage from his recordings missing that fight?" 18 asked. "It's like someone's covering their tracks."

Then 18 looked towards the entrance.

"Hey! Someone want to help me out here?"

Outside the study, an agent peeked his head around the corner. His clothes were disheveled, but he gave 18 his attention when she called out to him.

"Anything?" she asked.

"Sorry ma'am," the agent replied with a slow shaking of his head. "We're still sweeping the entire area."

"I need to try and get a full body count of everyone dead or alive," 18 sighed. "Look for anything out of the ordinary. Did you contact the vice president?"

"When the White House came under attack, he was at Capitol Hill. We moved him to safety as soon as the emergency was declared. Did you want to speak to him?"

"No," 18 spoke flatly. "Tell all surviving members of the president's cabinet and staff to shelter in place. Better yet, do they all have alternate safe houses to go to?"

"Yes ma'am," the agent nodded.

"Alert them to go to the *backup* alternate locations of the alternate safe houses," 18 instructed. "If the president is the target, they'll be looking for him if they manage to escape after slaughtering everyone unfortunate enough to be here. What we need to do is keep everyone who is close to the president safe. Got it?"

"Copy that."

The agent left his post and disappeared. Joe glanced at 18.

"Do you know where the president is?" he asked.

"No," 18 replied. "His head of security or the agent in charge would know and he's definitely still at the president's side. It's a very good thing the president wasn't at home."

18 glanced down at the computer.

"I didn't see any traces of a robot terminator-assassin inside the Oval Office," she said. "It managed to get past us and escaped, which means it could be anywhere by now. Every passing minute means it's gotten further and further away. The other possible and likely situation we could be facing is... that it's still here somewhere."

Joe froze as he looked around quickly.

"Here? Why?"

"Think about it," 18 shrugged. "If you single-handedly took out most of the security and military personnel guarding this place, your only options are to either run and escape to fight another day... or it's sneaking around the White House trying to find the president."

"Thinking about it is making me nervous again," Joe admitted.

"I'm going to call A.I. Industries and ask for an A.I. to deploy here," 18 sighed. Then she paused and glanced at Joe. "Unless... does the White House have a virtual intelligence or A.I. program here?"

"No," Joe replied, shaking his head.

"Then if you don't mind, Joe," 18 nodded. "You're going to be my technician and partner on this mission. Help me find 125's killer before it strikes again. We need to be ready to defend ourselves. Otherwise… humanity is going to lose all the amborgs currently planet-side."

A.I. Industries
Amborg Medical Facility
Civilian Ward

"I am very intrigued as to how this ended up happening."

"Well, I'm not!"

4 glanced at George Ramirez.

"Well, what do you want me to do? Kick them out? I don't think we can afford the public backlash with that kind of action."

"May I speak?"

"Begging your pardon Mr. President," George spoke frantically. "Can we not be interrupted?"

President Holland stared in shock at A.I. Industries' head of public relations. Amborg 4 looked impressed at the sight of one of the world's greatest leaders at a loss for words.

"Did you just tell the President of the United States to shut up?" 4 mused quietly.

"I think I earned it after he crashed a shuttle on our landing pad!"

"I didn't know where else to go!" President Holland protested. Then he jabbed a thumb up over his shoulder. "And technically, Mike flew the shuttle."

"If I may speak candidly sir," Mike cleared his throat and lifted a finger. "I wanted to go to a different safe location."

"Well, someone destroyed…"

"Attacked," Mike interrupted.

"Fine!" the president sighed in annoyance. "Attacked the White House! Assuming that all other designated safe houses are compromised, I felt that moving to the next best secure location on the planet would be the right move!"

4 glanced at George and shrugged.

"Do you still want to send him packing?" she asked. "Based on our current situation, I think Dr. Kendrick would appreciate his presence here."

"Who just hijacks a shuttle and runs away from his responsibilities as a leader?" George shot back.

"Are we talking about John... or me?" Bill asked curiously.

"He brought his sickly wife and mother-in-law here, and she'll receive plenty of care," 4 stated. "I'd say that his priorities are straight."

"He abandoned his kids!"

Bill and 4 stared at George, who was now fuming.

"I didn't abandon them," he declared. "We were on our way to a secure hideout and then I heard 18's transmission about Marco. Fortunately, the agents there were able to get my kids out and to safety. I ordered Mike to contact the hospital to get my wife out of there, just in case. I'm having my family brought here, the safest place I know."

George Ramirez opened his mouth to object, but quickly managed to absorb what the president had just said.

"Oh," he said. "Sorry."

"It's fine," Bill replied.

"Under the circumstances," 4 said. "I agree with the president's line of thinking. Losing the battle at the White House was tragic. 18 initially reported numerous casualties. As we sort through the wounded and the dead, another army stands ready to protect the president's family, and we remain on high alert."

"But what's the situation?" Bill asked.

"All amborgs on Earth are checked in," 4 answered. "Once the dust settled, we were able to regain communications across the world. The White House was one of the major attacks that happened in the last couple of hours. It appears that several locations had undergone some form of Order 66. The casualties aren't catastrophically high but according to eyewitness reports and testimonies of survivors... we're searching for Terminators."

"Like... Arnold Schwarzenegger?" Bill raised an eyebrow.

"More like Robert Patrick or something..." 4 shrugged. "We're combing through all the footage from the White House attack but we don't know what we're up against. All amborgs and military assets affiliated with our company are currently at "mimic" combat protocols."

President Holland glanced at 4 and George inquisitively.

"Some people use holographic technology to hide their faces, change their body types, or disguise themselves as other people to bypass security or navigate strict checkpoints," George explained.

"Mimic protocol is meant to ramp up our security questioning by a factor of 100."

"And even if we identify a saboteur or assassin," 4 added. "The technology is unparalleled. They blacked out all communications on our most secure channels and even disrupted 125's connection back to A.I. Industries. That's our most powerful communications line and... without our support, he died alone."

"How powerful?"

4 turned her head to stare at President Holland, who appeared genuinely curious.

"It uses the same level of encryption and high-powered frequencies that your nuclear football phone and computer system uses," she said.

"Wait," Bill's eyes widened as a look of alarm spread across his face "Are you telling me that the attack on the White House... could have shut down our ability to use nuclear weapons??"

Everyone fell silent. President Holland began to look impressed.

"Huh," he relaxed, now appearing amused. "We might have just found out how to achieve world peace."

George looked like he was about to blow a gasket.

"Ok, you see that? How are you supposed to be the president of our country when you make jokes like that?? People have died over the last few weeks!"

"I cope! I may be president but I also have intrusive thoughts and a mildly dark sense of humor!"

4 raised an eyebrow when Bill sighed and added a bit more clarification.

"That didn't sound right!" he boldly declared. "But can you at least understand my perspective?"

He shook his hand at George and then gestured behind him at nothing in particular.

"You think it's easy running a country while also dealing with interstellar travelers and aliens on our damn doorstep?!"

"Sir," Mike interrupted by clearing his throat. "You're not supposed to call them aliens."

"Thank you Mike!" Bill snapped. "Shut up please! I need to say this!"

"Yes sir, shutting up sir," Mike nodded respectfully.

"I thought that this whole debacle with the S.C.E. was a miracle," he fumed, getting into George's face. "Turns out, it's a huge and empty void... *literally*, outer space! John has taken the amborgs up there to deal with a world-ending threat and I can't do a thing!"

"What do you mean?" George shook his head in confusion. "You're supposed to be our leader!"

"Who doesn't know what the hell to do!" Bill replied angrily. "You put on a suit every day! You talk to the media and keep A.I. Industries' public image looking great! All the time! But me?? I have to maintain my own image 24/7! I have to look like a leader, act like a leader, and guide millions of people! And not all of them even like me!"

Bill turned and pointed at 4.

"You have no idea how much I wish I could just trade spots with the real genius!"

"Why thank you," 4 said, flattered.

"The amborgs and Dr. Kendrick are the ones who are living the dream and they all seem happy."

4 cleared her throat this time, which got everyone's attention.

"Pardon me, sir," she smiled kindly. "We're not currently happy. We lost an amborg."

"I know, sorry," Bill sighed. "I just..."

He turned and looked at George again.

"Is it messed up that I've been wanting to express myself openly for months and after the White House got attacked, I ran away with my family and now... I can actually be myself."

"As admirable as that may sound," George sighed. "That's so irresponsible..."

"Oh, you're one to talk," Bill retorted. "You let your own daughter run to Vegas and she's hanging with your crazy ex-wife."

4 could see George's eyes twitch with rage at his comment. She remained still and continued to watch the drama unfold. The president had gone there and it was most likely going to end up coming to blows.

"If you weren't the president..." George breathed furiously. "I would kill you."

"Don't flatter yourself buddy," Bill let out a sarcastic laugh. "You don't even look like you'd be able to arm wrestle Mike!"

"Sir, may I please be left out of this?" Mike spoke up.

Bill rolled his eyes. Before anyone could continue, 4 stepped forward.

"Ah ah ah," she stated. "I think we've let out enough stress for the time being. The main thing is, the U.S. government is in disarray."

"Well, I could work remotely from here, right?"

George immediately interrupted.

"Absolutely not!" he declared. "A.I. Industries is not a base of operations for political agendas!"

"Mr. Ramirez," 4 chuckled awkwardly. "I think I speak for all of the amborgs when I say that statement isn't exactly valid."

"What I mean is," George corrected himself. "A.I. Industries is not a place where the government can just come in and run the country within our halls. Dr. Kendrick wouldn't allow this!"

"Well, he did specify in his video message to me that I could in fact access his last will and testament," Bill replied.

"What?" George drew back, stunned. "John Kendrick is not dead!"

"I agree," 4 nodded. "It is too soon to assume that he's been killed when we've lost contact with him for only a few hours."

"You think I wanted to be the one to listen to his possible last words?" Bill sighed. "I was honored but seriously, it's scaring me. Besides, he asked me to come here and look for his own set of instructions."

"What instructions?" 4 asked.

"He left instructions on what to do if he was to go missing or if he died unexpectedly. That's what he told me in his message."

4 nodded and then proceeded to walk away. Bill and George both glanced at each other in confusion. The president turned to Mike, who gave them a slight shrug.

"We should go to his office," 4 called back to them as she continued strolling away.

Without a word, everyone decided to follow her.

Later, in Dr. Kendrick's office, 4 already had an idea of where to go.

"Only a few amborgs from each Group know about Dr. Kendrick's final instructions," she explained as she walked over to a bookshelf. "We're only allowed to access this when an authorized user delivers his message."

"You mean me?" Bill pointed a finger at himself.

"Yes," 4 nodded. "Dr. Kendrick passed on his alleged final message to you. Therefore, as the ranking amborg on Earth, I can finally do this."

4 lifted her hand, extracted a book from its place, and then reached into the gap. George and Bill noticed a lever concealed in the wall. 4 pulled it, and a small compartment opened below. Inside, they discovered several files, a pair of data drives, and some personal memorabilia.

She retrieved a data drive and placed it on Dr. Kendrick's desk. 4 connected it to his computer, and the screens unfolded from their storage compartment. She gestured for George and Bill to join her and watch the monitors.

The first thing they noticed was an image of a microphone. George and Bill felt clueless, unsure of how to proceed.

"Amborg Katrina 4, First Group," 4 suddenly declared. "Dr. John Kendrick. Status: missing. Authorization from Bill Holland. President of the United States."

The microphone icon disappeared. The screen flashed green and then a video began to play.

"Hello, if you're watching this, then I am sorry to say that I am currently unable to perform my duties as CEO of A.I. Industries as I have likely gone missing or have died. In order to ensure that things don't spiral out of control, this data drive contains instructions for you to properly secure the company and prevent it from ending up in the hands of someone unworthy."

Everyone watched Dr. Kendrick on the screen. This recording was created many years ago and this was probably the first time it's ever been played.

"Please identify yourself," Dr. Kendrick stated.

4 turned her head and looked up at Bill.

"Me?" he asked.

There was a chime from the computer.

"Voice analysis complete. Identity confirmed as Bill Holland."

The scene cut, and Dr. Kendrick resumed speaking.

"Hello Bill," he said. "Thanks for coming to A.I. Industries. I assume that you received my last rites message. I'm sure you have a lot of questions but I want you to know that I have always appreciated you as one of my closest friends for years."

"What is this?" Bill asked out loud.

Dr. Kendrick casually smiled in the video.

"This is a video recording for... Bill Holland."

"It's a smart program," 4 sighed. "Dr. Kendrick must have recorded a variety of responses and inputted the data into this drive. It's programmed to answer our questions as best as it can since the real Dr. Kendrick isn't here at the moment."

Then she looked at the screen and cleared her throat.

"Dr. Kendrick," she stated. "There is currently a crisis going on. During the fourth Emergency Recall, we encountered a tremendous problem that originated from outer space. The world is once again facing a terrible threat. President Bill Holland is here because you gave him an authorized message which has enabled us to access this drive. What are we going to do?"

"One moment please, gathering information for a proper response."

While they waited for the Dr. Kendrick program to talk to them again, Bill looked at George.

"This is... weird... right?" he asked.

"I agree, grudgingly," George nodded. "I respect that Dr. Kendrick probably put a lot of thought into this... but this seems pointless. We're talking to a recording of him from years ago with programmed responses."

The three of them fell silent as they watched a menu pop up on the screen. 4 looked up at the two men with uncertainty.

"This may have been a bad idea," she stated.

This was one of those moments when she felt inclined to politely suggest that they step out, but Dr. Kendrick's recording kept their interest piqued. Unfortunately, the two normal humans in the room failed to get out in time as Dr. Kendrick's program began to play.

43 minutes later, the three of them stepped out of Dr. Kendrick's office, all of them rattled and their minds numbed from what they'd just watched.

"That was so fucking boring..." George blurted without holding back.

"That made one of my cabinet meetings feel like a goddamn picnic..." Bill rubbed his forehead with his right hand.

"I thought it was thoughtful," 4 replied bluntly.

President Holland and George looked at 4 and silently glared at her.

"The amborgs or any of the A.I. programs would be able to sit through all of what he had recorded," Bill protested. "Seriously... how did he find the time to record *all* of that?!?"

"He's very thorough," 4 commented.

"Kat," George groaned. "Dr. Kendrick left us a data drive with over 130 hours of final messages!! We didn't even last one hour!"

"I can't believe he had that many things to say…" Bill shuddered.

"I understand if you think that his final message was slightly pointless," 4 started to say.

The president interrupted her.

"With all due respect 4," he laughed a little maniacally. "There are world encyclopedias that are much more interesting than that… first chapter or whatever it was that we had started listening to."

"We should have left after the first ten minutes…"

Both George and Bill looked like they were regretting their life decisions. They had literally forced themselves to stop watching when they realized that Dr. Kendrick's last will and testament came with a long and boorish life story recap in the intro.

"In all fairness," George sighed, glancing at the president casually. "Did you know about that whole thing when he was 5 years old?"

"Building a computer as a child was impressive," Bill nodded. "I think it was the fact that he started working at 8 years old that was the bigger surprise."

"Yeah… his grandfather was a dick."

4 cleared her throat, cutting off their chatter. They thought she was about to say something, but she was actually just pointing out that someone was coming their way. They saw Mike walking toward them, followed by a few other agents and several security drones from A.I. Industries.

"Mr. President," Mike said formally. "I'm happy to report that your children are here and safe. They're with your wife in the medical facility."

"Thanks Mike," Bill sighed.

"Everything alright?"

Mike glanced at the three of them with concern. He was able to immediately spot the obvious signs that they were all visibly drained.

"If I die someday," Bill replied in a depressed tone. "I promise I will not leave a data drive message or any kind of recordings for my family."

"I'm not sure I understand."

"Trust me," George interrupted. "You don't want to know."

Mike raised an eyebrow but didn't question the matter any further. Bill decided to take a deep breath and tried his best to smile encouragingly.

"How are my kids?" he asked.

"They weren't hurt, sir," Mike answered promptly. "We were successfully able to evacuate them to the secret tunnels in the White House. Afterward, they were taken to a temporary safehouse before we found them and sent a transport to bring them here."

"I still don't like it," George shook his head.

He glanced at 4.

"What happens if the president's location is revealed? His entire family is here and we might not be able to protect them."

"Mr. Ramirez," 4 replied. "It is our job. I maintain that the president and his family are safe here. He is a close friend of Dr. Kendrick's, and we will ensure their safety. Our next priority should be figuring out who can step in and take over the company. Once we get past this conflict, we have to be prepared for the long term."

"Take over?? What does that mean?"

President Holland looked alarmed. George nodded in response to his sudden outburst.

"In the event of an emergency, we need to appoint an interim CEO of A.I. Industries," he explained. "Even if we assume that he hasn't died, Dr. Kendrick has been out of contact with us for too long. By the time the dust settles, we need to tell the public that there is still leadership in control of the company."

"We're one of the biggest companies in the world," 4 added. "The general public is already aware of the fact that Dr. Kendrick is leading a mission in outer space to handle the situation. Unfortunately, if it gets out that he's missing..."

"Even more panic," Bill understood immediately.

He looked at George hopefully.

"Well, why don't you take over?"

"I can't..." George looked away uncomfortably.

Bill turned to Mike, who shrugged. 4 exhaled sharply.

"Here he goes again..." she muttered.

"I can't run this company... not after what happened last time," George replied. "I stepped down from the board when that incident was over and done with."

"We could just promote you and reinstate you back to your seat," 4 crossed her arms. She turned to Bill, pointing at him. "We could literally have the President of the United States swear you in!"

"That's not how it works," Bill said anxiously as he looked at Mike again for backup. "Is it?"

"My first question, if I may," Mike spoke up, glancing at George. "What happened last time?"

"I'm not cut out for the job," he answered.

"But you're head of public relations," Bill replied skeptically. You know everything there is to know about A.I. Industries. You talk to the media for a living. If you were to announce that you are in charge, it would bring reassurance and a sense of comfort to the public."

"No," George shook his head again. "I can't do it."

"May I request an alternative?"

Everyone looked at 4 as she turned her attention to the president.

"What if President Holland takes over?"

George's face lit up, but Bill's eyes widened. He was stunned as everyone shifted their attention to him.

"W-what?" he stammered.

"It would solve quite a few problems..." George nodded with a contemplative grin forming on his face. "Maybe him being here isn't that bad of an idea now."

"Oh, come on, you just berated me for escaping and hiding out here with my family!" Bill retorted.

"That's right, you did," Mike commented.

"Oh, shut up!" George snapped.

"Hey! I ordered him to shut up! Not you!" Bill rushed to Mike's defense.

"Thank you, sir," Mike replied formally. "I'd rephrase that last line if I were you."

"The point is... I can't run A.I. Industries!"

It was Bill's turn to let out a sigh of exasperation.

"You're the leader of the country," 4 stated. "Running this company would probably be relatively easy compared to governing a nation."

"I'm not a CEO!"

"You could add yourself by executive order to our board of directors," 4 suggested.

"That is a conflict of interest of monumental proportions!" Bill shook his head. "What would I even do? How do I explain that? Sorry John, you blasted off to space and then I got your last will and testament... so I stole your company... while the country imploded on itself?"

The brief pauses in his words only made him even more stressed. At this rate, he looked like he was about to have a full-on heart attack. Everyone fell silent as they conceded.

"Why can't an amborg take over?" Bill asked nervously. He looked at 4. "What about you? You're the leader of the amborgs on Earth!"

"May I remind you Mr. President," 4 shook her head politely. "I am sworn to protect what's left of the planet with every amborg I still have contact with. Managing all of them, redirecting them to where they need to go, and sitting down to run a company isn't my style. I am also unqualified to be CEO of a company that created me."

"How can you be unqualified?" Bill protested. "You're one of the most advanced human beings on the planet."

"Precisely," 4 nodded. "Because there are laws prohibiting that sort of action. Much like how we can't apply to enter the Olympics or other competitive events, or run for political office."

She turned to Mike.

"Besides, if there's another fight coming our way," she stated. "You don't plant your best soldiers behind a desk. Would you have Mike take over as the role of President if you suddenly died? No. There's a reason you have a vice-president and a huge chain of command."

Bill glanced back at George.

"Then what about another board member?" he asked.

"If we get them all together for an emergency meeting, then we could try and vote," George replied softly. "But I don't even know who we would nominate."

"GAHHH!! MY EYES!"

Bill and George leapt out of their skins as Mike suddenly started to scream. The other Secret Service agents were also clutching their heads as if someone had struck them with a flaming hot poker. Even the A.I. Industries security drones were seizing up like an electrical current had paralyzed them.

"What the hell?!" Bill cried out.

The two of them looked around frantically, feeling utterly power-less. Bill focused intently on Mike and his team, quickly identifying the problem. Mike was tugging at his earpiece and pulled it out, which let them hear a loud alarm that had suddenly gone off. The other agents had visors shielding their eyes, and he noticed the intense red flashing lights that were clearly inflicting a great deal of pain. If he had to guess, the security drones were likely receiving the same warn-ing. Whatever was happening, it was impacting everyone.

They glanced at 4 and noticed that she was also experiencing the same amount of distress, but she managed to stay on her feet. Her eyes were shut and her fists clenched tightly as she attempted to ride it out.

"Computer!" someone shouted. "Disengage and mute warnings! Everyone present! Quickly!"

Everything went silent as the alarms stopped. The visors on the Secret Service agents stopped flashing and everyone went still. The security drones stopped convulsing and resumed their normal stanc-es. 4 managed to relax as she opened her eyes.

"What the hell just happened??" Bill asked.

"Hello there."

When everyone had regained their senses, they turned to look at the newcomer that had suddenly appeared.

"It's him..." 4 grimaced slightly.

"Doctor..." George started to murmur.

Bill gaped.

"...Robert?" he uttered in a stunned voice.

George whirled around and stared at the president in shock.

"You know Dr. Kolaski??"

Bill didn't answer. His mouth hung open as he gazed at the man before them. Dr. Kolaski watched them and fidgeted slightly.

"Haven't seen you in a while," he ignored George's question and directly addressed the scientist from the basement. "It's been... so many years."

Dr. Kolaski looked over at Bill, then at George, and finally at amborg 4. Mike and the Secret Service agents started to regain their focus, and then they furiously glared at the man who'd disrupted their senses by merely standing there.

"This man blinded us..." Mike panted angrily as he reached for his weapon.

"Stop!" Bill commanded loudly.

Everyone froze, including the security drones. Bill stepped forward and took charge of the situation before it could escalate.

"Stand down Mike," he ordered. "This man is a friend."

"That's rich... coming... mmm... from you," Dr. Kolaski mumbled.

George and 4's eyes widened and they looked at each other with great interest.

"I sense drama," George whispered.

"How interesting," 4 grinned cheekily.

Dr. Kolaski walked up to President Holland and inspected his outfit. 4 looked closely at his microexpressions. She had to admit, this was the first time that she had ever seen the head of A.I. research look slightly angry at someone.

Or maybe he's annoyed with President Holland?

Dr. Kolaski began to speak again with his trademark mumble and stutter.

"I'm surprised... so surprised... that you came to-to... visit here," he said. "What... you come back to steal our stuff?"

"I am not here to steal anything," Bill replied gently. "I came here asking for a safe haven to protect me and my family."

"You're here to steal my A.I. programs... my daughter... and everything I've done..."

"Daughter?" Bill suddenly looked perplexed. "You have a... what?"

"CEO found!"

4 cleared her throat and stepped forward.

"As much as I'd love to see how this unfolds," she declared for everyone to hear. "I think we have our replacement CEO."

George gaped when she made a small gesture with her hands and presented Dr. Kolaski as if he was sent straight from heaven. He looked just as confused as they did when she confidently threw the idea out in the open.

"What?" Dr. Kolaski looked at them with an alarmed expression. "What do you... mean? Don't... joke like that."

He pointed at Dr. Kendrick's office and started walking towards it.

"John is the head of the company," he stated. "Just like how Bill is... leader of the whole nation."

"But... you are a level one security clearance person of A.I. Industries!" George exclaimed.

"Aren't you one... also?" Dr. Kolaski gazed skeptically at George. "Wait... why are we talking about... a new CEO? Where's John?"

Before anyone could stop him in time, Robert ran to Dr. Kendrick's office door. When it slid open and he saw that the room was empty, he slowly turned and looked at them fearfully.

"Where... on Earth is he? Where is he this time?"

"Well, about that..." 4 replied with a chuckle. "He's not *on* Earth actually. He's currently missing and out of contact."

A look of horror slowly crept over Dr. Kolaski's face.

"Serina?" he asked softly.

"She went with them," 4 replied honestly.

"What the hell... did I miss?" Dr. Kolaski began to tremble as he looked at all of them.

"You... don't know?" Bill stared.

"Dr. Kolaski doesn't get out much," George replied. "In fact, I think I haven't seen him for a few years."

"Years?" Mike asked in the background. "Does he live under a rock or something?"

"In the basement... actually," George replied.

Dr. Kolaski nodded but he still appeared nervous as he tried to register all of the information that they'd dumped on him. George glanced at the Secret Service agents, who looked stunned beyond belief, and addressed Mike's concerns.

"He likes his solitude," he explained.

"And... he might just be our only hope for the company," 4 stated.

She turned to President Holland, another idea forming.

"Both of you might be the perfect solution for A.I. Industries," she said. "And when Dr. Kendrick comes back, he's probably going to enjoy this."

"Ok," Bill gulped. "That sounds a little scary when you put it that way."

Dr. Kolaski tried to walk around them but 4 moved to block his path. His eyes shifted to every other person watching him, and he also gulped.

"I am also... currently afraid," he said. "Please tell me what has happened."

"I'll give you the short version," 4 said reassuringly. "I don't think you want to watch the video that Dr. Kendrick left for us."

CHAPTER 8

Old & New Friends

Las Vegas, Nevada
Around the same time

"What do you mean you're not coming back to A.I. Industries??"

"Shh! Keep it down!"

Thalia Ramirez was grabbed by the arm and forced back into her seat. Mandy let go of her and chuckled nervously. Marina Ramirez, Thalia's mom, was urging her daughter to quiet down.

"Fine!" Thalia sighed frustratedly. "Why are you not coming back?"

She cast a quick look at Mandy to see if that was quiet enough. Mandy responded with a reassuring nod, maintaining an awkward silence amidst the unfolding drama. Luckily, no one else in the cafe seemed to be paying them much mind.

"I really appreciate you coming to get me," Marina replied softly. "But I'm fine!"

"I'm not fine!" Thalia exclaimed. "There's an interstellar universal war above our heads! If it comes crashing down, we should all be together!"

"I don't think that's a good idea," Marina sighed. "There's still people here that need help. The attack on the White House proves it."

"Marco died!" Thalia stated. "And you don't care!"

"*Mija*," Marina replied sympathetically, shaking her head. "Of course I care. I've known Marco and the entire First, Second and Third Group amborgs for a long time! All the way back to when you were so little!"

Thalia was about to protest again but Marina raised her hand sharply. She glanced at Mandy, and the expression she gave them was definitely the silent, *I've got this* look. Mandy politely remained quiet as Thalia's mom switched to her... serious mom tone.

"Don't say that I don't care," she said calmly. "It wasn't good for me to remain at A.I. Industries. I'm in a position here where I can do more good and make up for all of the terrible things I put you and your father through."

"If things have gotten better," Thalia grumbled, "you can come home where you belong."

"Your father and I are better off this way," Marina replied mournfully. "I have work to do here."

"Why don't you try being my mom for once?"

Thalia looked at Mandy. Startled, she noticed the desperation in the young adult's eyes.

"Wouldn't you want your parents with you under the same roof under the circumstances?" she asked.

"W-well, uhh," Mandy stammered as she glanced at Marina. "My mom passed away when I was in middle school. It was just me and my dad for a long time. Yes, I'd want him with me at A.I. Industries."

Mandy tilted her head apologetically.

"But he's a tough man," she explained. "Trying to drag him anywhere away from his house is like trying to face down a lazy and stubborn panda bear in the wild."

"You call your father a panda?" Marina asked. "That's cute. I always called George my cute piggy."

"Right?" Mandy chuckled. "My dad was always like a panda to me. Especially the hugs. Anyway."

She quickly steered the conversation back on track and turned to Thalia, who was staring at the two of them in disbelief.

"Thalia," Mandy stated as she gestured to Marina. "I can't force your mom to come back with us."

"But you came after me! You can help me convince her!" Thalia replied.

"Thalia," Mandy replied gently. "We didn't know she was here in Vegas. You ran off without properly telling us what you were up to."

"Wait. Is that true *mija*?" Marina's eyes widened. "You told me that your father knew you were here!"

"That's definitely not how we found out she had left A.I. Industries," Mandy added. "She said she was visiting her friend Wendy here."

"That was sorta true," Thalia admitted. "Wendy let me hang out at her place when I called mom."

"Did A.I. Industries not update their security protocols?" Marina asked angrily. "They just let Thalia out so easily?"

"It actually was that easy," Thalia mumbled.

"I don't want to know," Marina replied sharply. "What I do know is that you want me to come home, but this is where I'm needed. There are people that need my help, and my lunch break is about to end."

"I'm honestly surprised that work is still being so strict about your break time, considering we pretty much interrupted your shift," Mandy stated.

"My supervisor is lenient with me," Marina replied casually. "She knows about my personal history. I do need to get back to work, however. I can't just leave."

"We should be going too," Mandy stated. "They're going to need us back at A.I. Industries."

"Mom, I just want you to understand...!" Thalia tried to speak up when her mother rose to her feet, but she was cut off immediately.

"No, Thalia," she spoke sternly. "*You* need to understand! Ever since we discovered we're not alone in the universe, I've been dealing with all sorts of people. Awful people. Scared people. And many others who are just trying to make it to the end of the day! The real world is full of people who don't know what the amborgs go through on a daily basis!"

Marina waved her hand at Mandy.

"The rest of the world doesn't see what she used to see when she was David 117's technician!" she said. "People who don't know what's happening panic. It makes them do terrible things! The White House was just under attack and there are people in the streets in an uproar!"

"And you're helping them?" Thalia exclaimed.

"Thalia," Mandy interrupted. "Your mom works for 911 emergency services. It's a very important and stressful job, and she helps save lives."

"The amborgs do it on a larger scale because of their superhuman abilities," Marina said firmly. "Mandy and I can help people too. Sure, my way of doing it is by answering phone calls, but without dispatchers, no one will get the help they need, and I believe everyone deserves to be saved."

Marina walked out and Mandy watched her leave with a dumbfounded expression. Thalia stood next to Mandy and sighed in frustration.

"It's been a while since I last saw your mom, but she's gotten a lot better," Mandy smiled.

"I just can't stand the fact that she deals with such awful people," Thalia grumbled.

"Not all of them are bad," Mandy replied.

"I wish you both wouldn't sugarcoat the truth," Thalia glared at Mandy. "I'm not a child anymore. I've seen footage of several types of people that the amborgs have saved. Some of them are so… awful."

"You said that," Mandy nodded. "Come on, let's give her a proper farewell."

Both of them had to run after Marina, who was urgently trying to leave the café, struggling to get through the crowded space. It felt odd. It was as if no one was aware that the President of the United States was missing and that the White House had recently suffered a heavy attack.

"Mom! Wait!"

Marina exhaled in frustration, tilted her head back, and stopped walking to turn around and face her daughter. As Thalia started to speak with her again, Mandy noticed her escort team approaching her.

"So, is she coming back?"

Captain Sheila Hicks, the pilot and commanding officer of an A.I. Industries transport shuttle, gave Mandy a fist bump which was kindly reciprocated. She gestured to Marina and Thalia.

"I don't think so," Mandy replied. "Where are the guys?"

Two shuttle crews had joined Mandy when George requested their help in finding Thalia. Both captains, their copilots, and crew chiefs traveled to Vegas with her as part of her security detail. In reality, Captain Hicks thought it might have been better if she were alone, but the rest of her crew and Captain Sam Planck's team eagerly accepted the mission. They were in the heart of Las Vegas, after all, and didn't want to miss any opportunities to have fun.

"I think Benji and Dean are losing their rent money," Hicks scoffed and let out a chuckle. "Sam took his crew back to the Night Song though."

Mandy looked at Captain Hicks and noticed a hint of worry in her voice, despite her stoic expression. The Night Song was Echo 232, the call sign of Captain Planck's transport shuttle. He had gone back and left without them? Then she realized why.

"President Holland?" she said casually.

Captain Hicks nodded.

"When we heard about the attack at The White House," she explained, "we heard the call. Sam was wheels up and airborne almost immediately. He's flying above and waiting for us to join him."

"I'm surprised you're both still sticking around," Mandy stated.

"Well, we're still on an important mission," Hicks smiled. "It's not over until I get you and Thalia back to A.I. Industries at the request of her father."

"Captain!"

The two of them turned to see Sergeant Dean Hammond running up to them. He was the crew chief of the Foe Hammer, Echo 209, which was Hicks' shuttle.

"Damn it," she sighed angrily. "We're supposed to be keeping a low profile!"

"Oh, right..." Hammond awkwardly stopped, realizing his mistake. "My bad."

"Where's Benji?" Hicks asked.

"He went back to the shuttle," Hammond explained. "We really should get going."

Hicks turned to look at Mandy.

"Hey Mandy," she said. "You want to tell Thalia to wrap it up? I hate to cut the family reunion short but we've got a lot of potential situations they might need us to be ready for."

"Right," Mandy nodded as she began heading towards Marina and Thalia.

Since they didn't really have anything better to do, the two members of shuttle Echo 209 decided to follow.

"So uh," Sergeant Hammond murmured. "What's the story with Mrs. Ramirez? Marina?"

"Minus Thalia right there?" Hicks answered. "Mandy is the only other person here who's met her in person. I've only heard about her."

"It's complicated," Mandy replied.

Unfortunately, before she could properly tell Dean the full story, Mandy kindly interrupted Mandy and Thalia.

"Hey," Mandy spoke nervously. "Sorry to butt in."

"It's fine," Marina replied. "What is it?"

"Ok, look," Mandy looked at Thalia and spoke in a gentle but firm voice. "Thalia, your mom needs to go back to work. I need you to come home with me now. Your father is worried about you and they need us back there."

"I just... don't feel like it's safe here mom," Thalia pleaded to both Marina and Mandy. Her head darted back and forth as she looked desperately between the two of them. "I have a bad feeling!"

"It's ok to feel that way, Thalia!" Marina replied in a comforting tone. "I promise, once I finish my shift, I'm calling you and your father to let you know that I'm alright. Deal?"

Thalia glanced at her mother, who returned her gaze with an encouraging smile.

"Really?" Thalia said. "You'll call him?"

"Yes."

"Will you come home?" Thalia asked.

Marina's smile faded as she looked at Mandy and then at Captain Hicks behind them. She almost shook her head to refuse but caught herself.

"You have to let me think about it," she said. "Now, is that a deal?"

"Ok," Thalia nodded. "Deal."

"Hey Mandy," Marina smiled.

"Yeah?"

"I still say it..."

Marina offered her hand to Mandy, who accepted it with a smile. They shook hands, then pulled each other in for a goodbye hug.

"Every time I start a shift," Marina said as the two of them separated. "I always say what you taught me."

"Listening ears on," Mandy recited cheerfully. "I'm right here. Have been all along."

Marina nodded and then turned to give Thalia a hug. She also gave her a brief peck on her cheek.

"I love you *mija*," she said. "It's exactly as Mandy says. I'm right here. You know where I am. I will be fine. I'm doing what I can do for other people. You should go back to A.I. Industries."

"Ok."

Marina Ramirez looked over at them, flashed a kind smile, waved, and then turned away, hurrying off. Within seconds, she disappeared into the throng of people. Once she was out of sight, Mandy guided Thalia towards Captain Hicks.

"Sheila," Mandy cleared her throat. "Would you mind?"

"Sure," Hicks smiled. "Hey Thalia, you want to sit in the jump-seat with us on the way home? I'll have Benji teach you how to fly the shuttle."

"Really?"

Thalia's eyes lit up a little, and Hicks nodded.

"Oh yeah, never too early to start flying lessons. Just don't tell your dad."

Captain Hicks began to immerse Thalia into a technical but very interesting conversation about the transport shuttle, which impressed Mandy. As they all followed each other to the nearest metro line that led back to the airport, Sergeant Hammond spoke up.

"Pardon me Mrs. Palmer," he said. "I was curious. What's the story with Thalia's mom?"

"She has IED," Mandy answered in a soft voice.

A car had driven by and it had generated enough noise to where the sergeant had barely heard her response.

"W-what?" he stammered. "She's a bomb? Oh, wait. I get it. It's because she's…"

He let out a soft whistle and made a hand gesture to symbolize heat.

"No, not an actual bomb," Mandy replied. "She has intermittent explosive disorder."

"What is that?"

"It's a mental disorder that causes people to have periods of intense anger and sudden outbursts without any reason," Mandy explained. "Marina has a short temper and will sometimes lose control, reacting extremely to small triggers. It has almost led to physical violence on more than one occasion."

"That's a thing?" Sergeant Hammond's eyes widened. "How does it even happen?"

"There's no exact cause," Mandy said as she gazed at Thalia. "You could have a family history of it. Or the brain chemistry is just off and those circumstances can make you…"

Mandy shrugged and curled her hand into a fist. She unclenched it and let it fall to her side.

"…lash out," she finished. "Environmental factors can also contribute to it as well."

"What kind of factors?"

"Alright, look."

Mandy stopped walking, causing the sergeant to do the same. She fixed him with a serious look and motioned for him to lower his voice, even though Thalia and Hicks were well out of earshot.

"It wasn't pretty," she said. "And you cannot let George know that I told you about this."

"Yes ma'am," Hammond nodded.

"No, tell me that you promise not to repeat what I'm going to tell you," Mandy spoke sternly.

The seriousness of this conversation was enough to get him to agree.

"I promise," he stated.

"When George and Marina immigrated into the country many years ago, she was pregnant with Thalia," Mandy spoke quickly. "Their entire family was being detained in a customs travel center when her water broke. She was in a lot of pain and unfortunately, the immigration officers refused to get her medical assistance."

"No..."

Sergeant Hammond's eyes widened. He glanced at Mandy and then looked at Thalia.

"Really?" he asked.

"Yes, really," Mandy nodded. "Fortunately, the doctor that was at that facility came to help. The only problem was, once George and Marina brought the family to A.I. Industries, we think she didn't properly move on from that incident."

The two of them began to follow Thalia and Captain Hicks again.

"Every time she noticed her coworkers or friends talking about how great things were or how easy life felt, it would trigger her anger," Mandy sighed. "She often reacted by lashing out and becoming the kind of person who would end up being filmed and ridiculed on social media. She believed the best way to avoid hurting her family and maintain the reputation of A.I. Industries was to leave. She convinced herself that there was no way to get help while under Dr. Kendrick's roof and sought her own path."

"That sounds rough," Hammond stated. He glanced back over his shoulder. "She's ok though, right?"

"Yeah," Mandy nodded. "She's one of Vegas' best emergency dispatchers. She told me she always felt bad about letting her emotions get the better of her. With mood stabilizers and a lot of behavioral therapy, she helps less fortunate people for a living now. It's pretty cool."

"Yeah, cool," Hammond nodded in agreement. "But she doesn't want to go home?"

"I think it's partially because she doesn't have the best memories of living at A.I. Industries," Mandy replied. "It might just take her some more time."

Sergeant Hammond nodded to show her that he fully understood. It was also his way of reaffirming his promise to keep the conversation confidential. After all, something really difficult and painful didn't need to be brought up again.

The group of them managed to flag down a taxi. A few minutes later, they were on the expressway headed to the airport.

When they arrived, they entered a restricted area that wasn't open to the public. Thanks to their security clearance and status as employees of A.I. Industries, they were able to bypass the public terminal and take a small electric trolley cart to the landing pad where Hicks' transport shuttle was parked.

They disembarked and made it onboard smoothly without any problems. They were greeted by a familiar face.

"Mrs. Ramirez didn't come with us?"

Lieutenant Benji Frye, the shuttle's copilot, glanced back at them but then noticed their expressions. Mandy was the only one who shook her head. The silence from everyone else, especially Thalia, confirmed his question.

"The real question is how much did you lose?" Hicks replied teasingly as she made her way up to the cockpit.

"Ye of little faith," he replied cheekily. "I actually won at craps."

"I don't know how to play that..." Thalia said to Mandy.

"And it's a good thing you don't," Mandy chuckled.

"It doesn't feel right."

Thalia glanced out the shuttle ramp, as if she was hoping someone else would join them. Mandy figured she was hoping her mother would be standing there.

"Hey," Mandy replied. "It's going to be ok."

"You don't seem worried about everything happening right now," Thalia looked at Mandy skeptically. "Why is that?"

"Trust me Thalia," Mandy sighed, "I really am worried."

Thalia and Mandy took their seats in the shuttle and strapped in while the crew performed final checks for takeoff.

"But the thing is, you can't sit here worrying the whole time and not doing anything," Mandy explained. "You should focus on what you do best for those you care about. Your mom dedicates herself to her job because when she listens to people on 911 calls, it gives her day a sense of purpose. It doesn't mean she loves you any less or that she doesn't care. The best way to bring your family together is when they can see you all at your best."

"You make it sound so easy..." Thalia said in amazement.

"Well, I did serve as the eyes and ears of a wise amborg who happens to be one of my very good friends," Mandy smiled.

"Haven't you worked with at least 20 of them?" Thalia giggled.

"I'm talking about the one I've worked with the longest," Mandy snapped back.

The two of them laughed as they heard an announcement overhead.

"Heads up everyone," Hicks spoke up. "We're going to return to A.I. Industries to drop off our passengers. Afterwards, we're going to meet up with the Nightsong for emergency operations. Standby for liftoff."

Thalia and Mandy double checked their safety harnesses to make sure they were secure. Sergeant Hammond did a quick walk through the entire back of the shuttle as the ramp closed. Once it was shut, he headed towards his seat and sat down.

Each seat had a small headset so that everyone could communicate with each other and not be bothered by the background noise of the interior. Mandy, Thalia, and Hammond slipped on the wired headphones to protect their hearing. Not only was this good for their ears, it would help Captain Hicks keep in constant communication with them if she needed to give further instructions while in flight.

"Attention, tower, this is Echo two zero nine," Hicks broadcasted over the radio. "A.I. Industries shuttle, Foe Hammer. We are requesting a clear takeoff path to angel five. Permission to take off, over?"

Mandy and Thalia didn't hear the response from the airport tower since that was on a private frequency for the cockpit. Thalia glanced over to Mandy.

"What should I tell my dad?" she asked. "Is he going to be mad?"

"Maybe," Mandy replied. "You did run away. But, since you found your mom and made sure she was safe, we'll explain that to him and maybe... it won't be so bad."

Thalia still looked uneasy, which made Mandy smile reassuringly.

"You know, before I plant myself back at my desk," she sighed, "I could be there with you to soften the blow."

"Thanks," Thalia smiled but chuckled nervously. "I really messed up, didn't I?"

"No, of course you didn't!" Mandy replied. "Trust me, you didn't mess up at all. Messing up is like..."

Mandy paused to think. The first thing that popped into her mind was a mission she remembered reading about from the Third Group missing files.

"...uh, the time that 501 trashed Dr. Kendrick's car," she finished.

"Oh yeah," Thalia sputtered and let out a laugh. "The one that went flying into a building."

They heard a loud whining noise through their headsets, which caused them to look up. The engines were spinning and initiating their startup sequence.

"Engine sequence primed," Hicks reported. "Thrusters green."

"Flight controls, green," Lieutenant Frye added. "Hydraulics are green across the board."

"Copy," Hicks acknowledged confidently. "Activate primary fuel pumps. Main engines... fire them up!"

The whining outside grew more intense, and then with a few muffled thuds, the inside of the shuttle began to tremble and shake as the four main engines burst to life.

"Folks," Hicks announced. "This is your captain speaking. Sit back and enjoy the ride. You might want to hold on for this part."

Mandy and Thalia instinctively reached for their harnesses and gripped them as tight as they could while the shuttle shook and rattled. Through one of the small windows, Mandy watched as they lifted off.

"No offense to the fancy drop pods that the amborgs like to ride in," Hicks chuckled, "but this is how you fly in style. Stand by for maximum thrust."

After another massive boom, they felt the shuttle pick up speed. They left Vegas and were on a course for home.

However, the ride was interrupted when Captain Hicks spoke to them.

"Mandy? I might need you and Thalia to help Dean with something."

Mandy and Thalia both looked up towards the cockpit.

"What's going on?" she asked. "Has something happened back at A.I. Industries?"

"I'm getting a coded distress signal from Zion National Park," Hicks replied. "It's an amborg frequency. Very faint. Can you help decrypt it?"

"A distress signal?" Mandy replied as she reached into the side pocket of her seat. "I think we should redirect our course."

"I just need you to verify it before I change heading," Hicks replied. "If it's a trap or a fake signal, I don't want to accidentally lose my ship to some drunk morons or any crazy risk-takers. Everybody's on edge thanks to the attack on the White House."

"I'm actually more impressed that there are still planes and shuttles traveling in the air," Mandy murmured as she pulled a data pad into her lap and activated it.

"Why?" Thalia asked curiously.

"Oh, in the event of an attack," Mandy replied, "emergency protocols are enacted. The White House came under attack... all federal agencies shut down civilian transports and suspended flights. It's a precaution that was set in place by air agencies in response to terrorism or other incredibly dangerous conflicts."

"And... we're still in the air because...?" Thalia trailed off.

"A.I. Industries has special clearance and our shuttle transports are military-grade," Mandy nodded. "Otherwise, we'd be taking the bus back home or we would have been detained by Vegas police for attempting to fly or something like that."

"Thank goodness?" Thalia shuddered.

Mandy nodded as she focused on the distress signal. The first thing she noticed was that it was being transmitted to the technician department. Unfortunately, there weren't any technicians that supervised or were partnered with the amborgs anymore. That department had been retired a long time ago since the amborgs didn't need someone to babysit them 24/7.

Since they were in a shuttle, Mandy checked the point of origin of the distress call, which was in fact Zion National Park as

Captain Hicks had reported. The location checked out but who would be trying to use an old and discontinued frequency? Perhaps it was because of the remote area and they had no other conventional means to call someone. Either way, this felt legitimate because only an amborg would know how to properly use this private channel to send help. Mandy decided to take a leap of faith and listen to the distress signal without an A.I. to assist her. If there was hostile malware or virus in the transmission... then it was out of their hands now.

"Mayday mayday mayday," a young man's voice spoke on the channel. "Is there anyone out there? All emergency frequencies are failing to connect. Can anyone hear me?"

"Hicks," Mandy spoke into her headset. "I got someone! Take us to Zion!"

"Copy that," Hicks replied.

As soon as Mandy confirmed,, they felt the Foe Hammer begin to lurch and alter its course. Mandy motioned for Thalia to listen, and she responded to the signal.

"This is Mandy Palmer," she connected to the distress call, speaking clearly. "I hear you. Who is this?"

"This is amborg 66, Second Group, and I am really glad that someone noticed this distress signal!"

Mandy immediately began to type in a search on her data pad. If it was 66, then she had to check to see if he had been deployed to that area for a mission. Once it was verified, they could rule out that it was an imposter.

"Well, you're lucky that it automatically got rerouted to the nearest friendly beacon," Mandy replied. "This is supposed to be a discontinued line."

"Well, I'd like to thank my old technician for teaching us how to reactivate it in the event of an actual emergency."

Mandy was definitely sure that it was 66 based on the level of sass she picked up in his response. Still, she did have to make one last confirmation according to procedure.

"Confirm your identity for me, please."

His response was prompt.

"It's Keith! Keith 66! I was with amborg 11 on a special assignment! We were checking up on an A.I. Industries VIP! Codename Nova!"

Mandy absorbed all this information while her data pad recorded 66's audio transmission. As he spoke, the data pad displayed a file for her to review. It was the mission briefing that aligned with 66's description. The two amborgs really had gone to Zion National Park.

"Confirmed," Mandy replied. "We're already in the air and diverting toward your signal. I take it you found Nova? Or you ran into trouble?"

"Yes and yes," 66 replied. "Need immediate evac! We've trying to escape to the nearest ranger station but these guys are everywhere! We're under attack from an MC club! Vengeance Front! Military weapons! Need air support!"

"Captain!" Mandy yelled to the cockpit.

"Copy that," Hicks answered. She had been listening to the conversation the entire time. "Benji! Turn up the thermal scanner and get a fix on their location! Dean! Let's drop the ramp and get ready for a pickup!"

"66," Mandy instructed. "We're going to come and do a sweep of the area."

"Thanks! Do you have any reinforcements?" he asked.

"Not really," Mandy glanced at Thalia, who shook her head.

"I don't think my dad would like the idea of me using a weapon," she said.

"Thalia's here?? What did we miss?" 66 exclaimed.

"I think that's our question," Mandy replied with a scoff.

"Heads up everyone," Hicks interrupted. "We're passing over the coordinates of where 66 and 11 stopped to check on this Nova person."

"Captain!" 66 called out. "11 and I ran north! Three clicks!"

"Copy that," Hicks answered. "Benji, got anything on the scanner?"

"I've got a dozen heat signatures," Frye answered immediately. "Some aren't moving. I'm looking for any A.I. Industries beacons."

Mandy and Thalia remained secured in their seats, then turned to see Sergeant Hammond up and about. He ran to the back of the shuttle and lowered the ramp.

"Be advised!" 66 reported. "We're firing a flare to mark our location!"

"Visual contact!" Hicks stated. "2'o clock! Dean, ready on the ramp?"

"Ramp deployed!" Dean reported. "Are we coming in hot?"

"We've been engaged!" 66 shouted.

Mandy and Thalia exchanged looks of horror. Their eyes widened when they heard automatic fire in the background of the transmission.

"We're coming in hot," Dean stated.

"Sergeant," Hicks commanded. "Ready weapons. Benji, I'm flying us in. Spin up weapons! Wait for my go ahead."

"Weapons check," Benji replied. "Waiting for the green light to engage."

"Amborg 66," Hicks stated over the radio. "This is Echo two zero nine. Foe Hammer dropping in."

"We hear you!" 66 started to laugh. "They're running scared!"

Mandy heard Clint 11 from the First Group join the conversation.

"Now that we have the big guns... and Nova is secure... let's take these morons in."

"Give up!" he shouted. "Throw down your weapons! Hands up, now! You're outnumbered! Two amborgs, two drones, and now an armed transport with guns that will make you disappear in an instant!"

Mandy and Thalia exchanged amused looks.

"Echo 209," 66 sighed in relief. "We have a few prisoners for you. Got any room up there?"

"Absolutely," Hicks stated. "We'll circle around and find a clearing."

"Thank you Echo 209. Ha! I told you boys I had friends in high places! Thought I was just an ordinary middle-aged huntress?"

A woman's voice caught their attention. The entire shuttle went silent as they heard a rambunctious, playful tone join the distress frequency. It had to be Nova.

"Shuttle!" she said cheerfully. "We are all safe and sound down here. You get five stars for the great timing and prompt response."

"Nova?" Mandy replied.

"Yes, my name is Daphne," the woman answered enthusiastically. "Good to hear from you! Any chance you can do me a quick favor?"

"Uh, sure?" Mandy replied.

"I've been out of the loop for the last week and a half!" she said. "Can you tell me if Leonard is alright?"

"Leonard... 1?" Mandy asked. "Is that who you're asking for?"

"Yes!" Daphne answered in a relieved tone. "Is he ok?"

"He's not on Earth right now," Mandy spoke honestly. "Why do you ask?"

"I know! I've just been worried about him!" Daphne explained. "I'm his ex-wife! I really need to talk to him!"

Mandy turned to Thalia, and they both wore expressions of disbelief. Mandy's jaw dropped as she fumbled for words, trying to absorb the information.

"S-she was married... to a-amborg 1?" Thalia asked.

"Lucky man," Hicks commented. "She sounds like one hell of a woman."

"Anyone who marries an amborg is one special person," Mandy responded bluntly. "But I have a lot of questions."

They heard Daphne let out a laugh as 66 spoke up.

"That's what I said when I first met her," he stated.

The transport lurched again as it began to make its descent. As they made the final approach to touch down, Sergeant Hammond made his way over to Mandy and Thalia's seats. He unpacked some protective gear and instructed them to put them on. Mandy began to help Thalia put on a bullet-proof vest and helmet as the transport made it to the ground.

The shuttle was about to gain several new passengers. It couldn't hurt to play it safe.

"A.I. Industries," Hicks declared. Mandy figured she was notifying home about their current situation. "This is Echo 209. We have recovered friendlies and are bringing aboard disarmed prisoners. Transmitting coordinates and flight updates. We need a good drop-off point for our friends."

CHAPTER 9

Interstellar Cookies

Tandeeri Flagship
Heart of Alcyon

"I understand now. Humans... value privacy."

The Tandeeri leader had his arms crossed, pondering the information Braelynn had just told him.

"Yes," she stated. "I'm afraid that it is improper to look into our memories without consent."

"But why are they so openly available for viewing?"

117 spoke up.

"We're just trying to explain to you that even if you have the power to look in our minds, it's not appropriate," he said.

The Tandeeri leader blinked and continued to stare at them curiously.

"This one, the man named 501," he pointed at 501, who flinched slightly. "He believes that I resemble a... San...geeli? It is from a... video game that you humans are familiar with."

The Tandeeri leader cast a quick look at 297, and he nodded back encouragingly. Then he glanced at 117, who appeared slightly baffled.

"It was a compliment!" 501 added quickly in a meek tone.

"While I agree and stand by that statement," 117 sighed. "It's still uncomfortable that you are aware of our personal thoughts."

"But we wish to understand you," the Tandeeri leader replied casually. "There are many things that can be shared easily if we connect our minds. You can of course choose to block your thoughts from reaching me."

His suggestion caught all of them off guard, causing them to look at each other in confusion.

"Uh, how do you suggest we do that?" 917 asked. "Just let our minds go blank? Don't think about anything? It's a little impossible."

"I incorrectly assumed you humans could inhibit your minds willingly," the Tandeeri leader replied boldly. "It would appear that I've misunderstood."

He raised his head and looked over at 999. She stood firm, her intense gaze locked onto his. Everyone watched as a stare down began.

"You are... quite resilient," he commented.

"I'm running my own experiment," 999 nodded curtly.

The Tandeeri leader stepped up to her, towering over the lone wolf of A.I. Industries. 117 felt someone nudge his side, and he glanced to his right to see that 501 was leaning against him.

"Experiment?" he asked on a private channel.

117 shrugged, indicating he had no idea what 999 was up to. 501 fell silent as they all returned their attention to the scene before them.

There was a chance that the Tandeeri leader had heard their thoughts but he didn't give any sort of indication that he did. From this point on, 117 assumed that whatever they spoke to each other about internally wasn't so secretive to the Tandeeri.

"May I ask what's going on?"

117 looked to his left and noticed that Braelynn appeared somewhat confused.

"Sorry," 117 shook his head. "999 is taking the lead on this... experiment. I don't know."

Braelynn looked at him in amazement.

"You have the ability to form a plan of action in seconds while doing mental zoom calls and she didn't include you in on this??"

"We like to plan things together most of the time," 117 sighed. "999 is just more comfortable handling things her own way."

"Plus," 501 spoke up, "sometimes it's a pain in the ass and it looks ridiculous when all of us just go silent for our..."

He raised his hands and made finger quotes. He wiggled them like bunny ears in a lively and playful manner.

"20 second meetings," he emphasized the words as he lowered his hands.

When the amborgs accessed their private communication networks to speak to one another, it was somewhat similar to telepathy, just with wifi and a strong data link. Whatever they thought would be relayed to the other person like a radio transmission. This made it easier to send texts or engage in quick conversations, as long as an amborg kept a strong signal between them. Another hidden skill that allowed them was the ability to retreat into their own minds, having discussions in a realm of inner cyberspace—a dream-like state.

The brain operates at a faster pace during dreaming, providing amborgs with a unique advantage in generating ideas. While an amborg delves into this inner realm, time seems to slow down, whereas the people around them continue to exist in real-time. What feels like mere seconds to those on the outside could be 10-15 minutes for an amborg. This explains why amborgs occasionally zone out for several minutes. As 501 explained to Braelynn, it was likely that 999 took the initiative independently, as it would have been awkward and ridiculous for every amborg present to fall silent simultaneously. Those watching would have probably grown bored or confused.

At the moment, rather than feeling either of those things, everyone watching the Tandeeri leader staring 999 down was intrigued by what was happening. Finally, he spoke.

"You are attempting to block me out of your mind," he stated. "Very impressive but... your pain reveals all that you intend to keep hidden."

"Uh, what's happening here?" 466 muttered worriedly.

999 didn't answer as the Tandeeri leader continued to speak.

"Your past holds many horrific experiences," he stated. "Very notable ones."

999 remained still and her cold expression didn't waver.

"You..." he said as he somehow managed to look past her mental barriers. "You hate what they did to you at the... brothel. You were hurt and yet, that is why you fight for others despite never revealing your empathy. Your rage and your sorrow are completely suppressed. With how fragile the human mind is, you display remarkable strength. Perhaps you would like to explain..."

"No! That's enough."

917 stalked forward and took his place between 999 and the Tandeeri leader. He didn't recoil or appear angry, but politely stepped back. 999 broke her gaze with the Tandeeri leader and looked away. She didn't seem fazed but it was quite obvious that she seemed a little off from that experience.

"Just because you have the ability to look into our minds and our thoughts doesn't mean that we're going to suddenly talk about ourselves like we've been friends for years," he stated. "We aren't the right kind of people to reveal the best of humanity to you. Our pasts are there but we left them behind to be who we are now. Not ideal memories for first contact but... I highly recommend that you let us talk about the future instead of using our past to see our current intentions."

The Tandeeri leader glanced at 917 and then shifted his gaze to 999. A flicker of recognition crossed his eyes as he nodded.

"You are fascinating as well," he said as he lifted his clawlike hand and stroked his chin. "I have no doubts about your intentions. Forgive me. Your thoughts are filled with truth and are very informative about human culture."

"Yes, but some questions are too personal," 917 stated. "It's... uncomfortable."

"What about this question? If you care about this one... Angel, then who is the other one you're thinking about?"

"Oh no..." 501's eyes widened.

999 pivoted to 917. Unlike her, he didn't have the ability to set up strong emotional blocks. 917's eyes darted around quickly, but he shook his head, keeping his focus on the Tandeeri leader.

A glowing light appeared in front of 117 as he watched Serina glide ahead of him. She cast a worried glance back at him.

"Is he thinking about...?"

"Yes," 117 replied softly. "But let him handle it."

"If he can..." Serina gulped.

The Tandeeri leader continued to speak. 917 averted his gaze, feeling uneasy, but he kept his chin up. Unfortunately, it was clear that his annoyance grew with each passing second.

"There was nothing that any of you could have done to prevent the tragedy in Brazil," the Tandeeri leader said. "All of you carry so much responsibility and yet... focus so much on your failures. Perhaps we can help you with moving on?"

"Wait. Please stop."

Braelynn broke away from the group, drawing his attention to her. She'd heard enough, sensing that it was time to intervene before the conversation really went south. She placed a soft hand on 917's shoulder, then respectfully looked up.

"Can't you see that you're making them uncomfortable?" she said gently. "If I may, it would be best if we get back on topic and figure out what we do to end this conflict between your people and the S.C.E."

A hush fell over the group as the Tandeeri leader pondered Braelynn's words. 117 assumed he was trying to gauge Braelynn and decipher her thoughts, or something along those lines. It was already clear that the Tandeeri didn't have filters or were unabashedly honest. Maybe this was only true for the leader, as he was the only one actively conversing with them.

The Tandeeri leader focused on Braelynn, who smiled curtly.

"There was something strange about you when I first met you," he said. "Your heart is clear and you also bear a heavy responsibility. Too much for an ordinary person."

"The responsibility that I have is important," Braelynn spoke firmly. "We're trying to stop Silent Eclipse from destroying all of us."

"I am confident we can help you do that," the Tandeeri leader nodded. "But, I believe I have yet to answer an earlier question."

He gestured to the other Tandeeri standing around them.

"We are all here because we want to find a home," he declared.

"Uh, what?" 117 blurted out.

"Alien neighbors! Yeah! We think he's telling the truth!"

Everyone glanced towards the bubble and saw 92 and 93 eagerly nodding while pointing at the Tandeeri leader.

"Yeah! It's so cool!" 92 stated.

"Really awesome!" 93 added.

"Ok... then."

Taken aback, 117 looked up at the Tandeeri leader, who appeared to be smiling back.

"You've been traveling across universes just to find a home?" 117 asked. "Where are you from?"

"I believe you have already asked that question," the Tandeeri leader blinked. "Was I not clear?"

"Well, actually, you were about to tell us but then you started looking into our internet history," Serina replied. "Our personal history."

"Oh, yes," the Tandeeri leader looked at Serina guiltily and nodded. "I apologize again. I have a tendency to forget certain things when I focus on something interesting."

"We get it," 466 smiled. "Even though this entire situation is the most interesting thing we've ever been involved in."

The Tandeeri leader let out a short chuckle.

"Well, then we have always traveled for as long as we can remember," he said softly. "Our universe, our native universe, our home... We left it behind. It is gone. It was destroyed by an evil force that consumed our homes. It made that universe uninhabitable and our people have been floating among the stars ever since."

"Uh, my next question after that is... should we be expecting that evil to come here?"

249 lifted his hand to interject with an unexpected question, but it turned out to be the wrong move. Everyone's reactions were mixed. The surrounding Tandeeri looked horrified and started whispering in a panic. A few even expressed anger over his question. Only their leader seemed unfazed.

"Maybe uh," Serina spoke up nervously. "Let's go back to the story."

The Tandeeri leader nodded.

"My Ra-kuva was the leader at the time," he continued casually. "Your word would probably be 'grandmother.' Our fleet has been in search of a new home to live in peace. We have traversed hundreds of universes over a long period, and eventually, we found yours."

The Tandeeri leader glanced at the S.C.E. officers behind the glass dome and then at Braelynn. Then he looked at 117.

"Both of yours," he added for clarification.

"So," 117 pointed at Braelynn. "If you end this war... or if you help us, you want to be her neighbor?? Or... our neighbor?"

"I think he's asking for something slightly more complicated than that," Braelynn sighed.

"No, that's pretty much it," 777 spoke from inside the dome with a simple nod. "All they want is to live in peace... and they say that our universe is looking to be the most peaceful one that they've encountered."

"Really?" 593 said happily. "That's so sweet!"

"Really?" 466 looked at her skeptically. "I feel like that's too much praise considering our planet's history."

"Well, we didn't want to live on your planet," the Tandeeri leader grunted apologetically. "We just want to live in your solar system."

"Well, space is a pretty good real estate option," 297 shrugged.

The other amborgs inside the bubble all nodded and eagerly murmured in agreement.

"We only wished for an isolated section of your solar system to prepare for another long voyage," the leader shrugged.

"How long were you going to stay?" 117 asked.

"50 years," the Tandeeri leader replied.

"Oh," Serina nodded cheekily. "I'll be sure to fill that out in the interstellar visa application."

"If that is the official rule, then I am grateful."

Serina immediately laughed and shook her hands at the Tandeeri leader.

"No," she replied quickly. "That was a joke. We don't have anything like that."

"Ah," the Tandeeri leader nodded. "A form of humor."

Braelynn quietly stepped forward and cleared her throat.

"Excuse me then," she said politely. "If you were originally in our universe for years, then why did you always appear to fight us at every wormhole generation that we attempted?"

The Tandeeri leader rounded on Braelynn, clenching his fists. He let out a low growl, catching the group by surprise. Taken aback, Braelynn retreated a step.

"Because your people as well as the other species in your alliance were intending to use the wormholes to desecrate other universes," he stated. "Opening them whenever you like and endangering them all. We wanted to stop you from exploring too deeply into what you didn't understand."

"But we originally came up with the technology so that we could explore," Braelynn replied formally. "We don't want to desecrate anything."

The Tandeeri leader looked at the other S.C.E. officers in the glass dome and then at the amborgs.

"Your thoughts and your own memories betray that ideology," he snarled. "There are always those among you that want to conquer and take over! What we are preventing is you accidentally causing the destruction of all life as you know it!"

"You were... protecting us?" Braelynn said, pausing to concentrate. "Because you were afraid we would find your universe? The destroyed one?"

"It is a darkness that must remain in one part of the vast multiverse," the Tandeeri leader replied. "If you had unleashed the entity that destroyed our home, then we would all be doomed."

Serina gazed at the Tandeeri leader and looked around. His people seemed to be growing agitated.

"Everyone," she said. "I think we need to avoid this subject."

Braelynn was about to speak when the Tandeeri leader interrupted.

"Your little A.I. has spoken sensibly," he declared. "Now then, I think we've gone into our past long enough. Your friends will now be returned to you. We shall escort you back to your ship and we hope that you can convince your people to stand down."

"Did we just piss him off?" 249 asked. "Is that it for the negotiations?"

The shield deactivated, leaving everyone behind it looking both surprised and relieved to have finally been freed.

"No! Wait, please hold on, sir!" 117 said hastily as the leader began to walk away. "We still need your help! Our races are still in danger! People are dying aboard the Firestar! You can still help us, can't you?!"

"It was my understanding you only came to return my son with a very interesting new name," the leader grunted. "In return, now we have begun the opportunity for peace between us thanks to your actions. From this point on, you are always welcome here as friends but with all due respect, the conflict amongst yourselves must be settled by your own people. There is nothing else for us to discuss."

"We wanted to return... Oreo to you because not only would it end our war but it would also be what we needed to save us from being destroyed!" Braelynn protested insistently. "If Silent Eclipse succeeds and takes over the Firestar, then your people will once again be running! This planet Earth as well as the S.C.E. will be annihilated if you don't help us bring a swift end to this! Do you want to always be remembered as the race that was blamed for the cause of this war? Are you going to watch as the true masterminds continue to drag your name through the mud? Are you really going to allow the ones who unraveled the truth to be killed?"

"The people who know the truth are standing before me," the leader argued. "So it shouldn't be a problem. I won't have the lives of my people risked any further. There is no need for us to continue being part of this conflict."

"Are you saying you wouldn't look the person running Silent Eclipse in the eye and want them brought to justice for using your people as a scapegoat for so long?" 917 asked in outrage. "Everyone who has died to get here and you won't stop it? I can't believe that!"

"Your people may be primitive enough to continue escalating conflict with your hatred," the leader replied. "But we know we did nothing wrong. We choose to leave it in your hands."

"You do not speak for all of us!"

The Tandeeri leader turned sharply towards the voice. It had a distinctly feminine tone, yet it was loud as another Tandeeri emerged from the crowd. She pointed her claw at the leader.

"That human is right! I say we fight with them!" she shouted, which received a few murmurs of approval from her people. "We should help! They have risked so much to be here! The least we can offer is our support! Think of how it would benefit our relationship if they were to owe us for protecting and rescuing them!"

"This sounds promising," Serina mumbled. "But we didn't just accidentally open the door to overthrowing the leader, did we?"

"I hope not," 501 replied.

Suddenly, 917 stepped forward and called out to the leader.

"If you don't help us," he added, "you're a coward."

This definitely seemed to trigger instant fury from the Tandeeri. Several of them shouted out and angrily roared at 917's statement.

"What are you doing?" Braelynn asked, just as shocked as everyone else. "You're picking a fight with them?!"

917 glanced at 117.

"We weren't getting anywhere," he stated.

"I said we should help you fight!"

The female Tandeeri marched towards 917, baring her teeth and snarling.

"But you would dare insult our leader?!"

917 bravely faced the Tandeeri woman, but before she could reach him, the Tandeeri leader stepped in, putting a hand in front of her. Despite blocking her path, he shot a fierce glare at 917, who stood his ground defiantly.

"A coward?" he huffed. Then he let out a soft laugh. "You are bold. Enlighten me."

"You can read my mind," 917 replied curtly. "You figure it out."

"Um," 117 said anxiously. "I think you need to specify because we're all really nervous about where you're going with this."

"And don't tell us on a private channel!" 8 called out to them. "Everyone here that is not an amborg wants to listen!"

917 glanced at 999 before looking at the Tandeeri leader with determined ferocity in his eyes.

"You hide here while innocent people are being killed. Yours and ours!" 917 said, ignoring Braelynn's expressive motions to stop. "An entire species, constantly on the run! Jumping from universe to universe! The whole reason we're in this mess is technically because of you! Everything about our lives was disrupted when the S.C.E. showed up!"

Braelynn clamped her mouth shut, her expression one of utter disbelief.

"You want to talk about pain? Who do you think has to tell Jacob's mother that he's never coming home?!" 917 declared.

"And this Jacob is...?" the Tandeeri leader raised an eyebrow curiously. "Ah, I understand. He was a friend of yours?"

"He died when you showed up and almost destroyed Apogee station," 917 stated. "Now you want to just sit here and do nothing when you're the one responsible for ending the lives of several innocent people?! If you think we're leaving here without your assistance then you're wrong! All of us need to clean up this mess! You're a coward for refusing to leave the confines of your ship! You're all cowards for not wanting justice! Why not take action and commit to your fight for a peaceful home when the enemy is literally blocking your path?! If Silent Eclipse was here now and Oreo was going to die at their hands, would you make us fight for you to protect him?! We are *this* close... to accomplishing what you wanted for your people and protecting our home! I'm calling you a coward because you're choosing now to just sit there and do nothing?! That doesn't match up with what we've seen!"

The Tandeeri cries of outrage had subsided and disappeared during 917's rant. Many of them were murmuring and started to debate amongst themselves. They were still visibly ticked off, yet surprisingly, they were starting to relax. Even their leader began to regard his own people with admiration.

A tiny squeak caught his attention, and he looked down. Oreo had run back to his side, and his mate was approaching him on the steps leading to his throne.

"What do you think son?" the leader asked, patting Oreo on the head.

The answer was immediate. Oreo took one look at the amborgs and dashed over to them eagerly. His tiny squeaks of joy were heard by all as he ran into the open arms of 501.

"Thanks buddy," 501 smiled.

"My son tells me that there are many humans that deserve help, even when not all of them deserve it," the Tandeeri leader sighed.

"It's what we do," 917 said.

"Does that mean... you've changed your mind?" Braelynn asked as hope filled her eyes.

"It was wrong of me to say that there is evil amongst you," the Tandeeri leader stated.

"Well, you weren't entirely wrong," 466 shrugged.

"Several of my advisors and fighters are already preparing to assist you without my consent," he continued, ignoring 466's comment. "You are right. It is better to help the S.C.E., regain control of the situation, and keep those that are potential allies alive. However, there is one thing I refuse to overlook and I want it settled now."

The Tandeeri leader took off the red stole around his shoulders. Another Tandeeri strolled up to him and presented him with what appeared to be some kind of long weapon.

"I resent being called a coward," he said menacingly. "Therefore, I would like to challenge you to a fight. You have the courage, but it is that courage that often hides a fool—one who can't physically back up what they say. I don't approve of your dishonorable manner and I want to demolish your words in a duel."

The Tandeeri began to shuffle away, clearing some space for the fight. Their leader began to march into the center of the room.

"We don't have time for this," Braelynn muttered as she looked to 117 for help. "Can't you do something?"

"It's not up to me," 117 said, holding up his hands.

"You just want to watch this fight don't you?"

117 ignited Braelynn's question, but gave a nod. Everyone's attention shifted to 917, who returned their stares. He had insulted the Tandeeri in order to accomplish their objective. Now, he had to face the consequences on his own. There wasn't anything any of them could do about it.

"I'll do it," 917 said immediately. "What are your terms?"

"Simple," the Tandeeri leader turned around and, from his position, stared at 917. "Fight. Show me the strength that you believe you possess in order to win."

"Is there a guarantee that we both live?"

917 stepped away from the group and a few Tandeeri aliens bowed politely as he approached. There were still several murmurs and growls coming from a few, but they were all hidden amongst the crowd.

"You'll have to find that out for yourself," the Tandeeri leader chuckled.

"Alright, arbiter knock-off," 917 sniffed as he walked away from the group.

A loud chortling noise arose from the leader as 917 was shepherded to one side of the circle. The amborgs and the S.C.E. crewmen all gathered together and the Tandeeri allowed them to join the ring surrounding the two about to duel.

"Oh boy," 297 said. "There's rules against outside interference right?"

"Well, if they're honorable and not planning to actually kill us," Braelynn said nervously, "I would say so."

297 and 777 both stared at Braelynn.

"Who are you?" 777 asked. "Thanks for coming to get us by the way."

"S.C.E. Intelligence," Braelynn replied fast. "And right now, I'm noticing the lack of intelligence with this duel."

"Well, you try and talk 917 out of our world's first interstellar deadlock," 8 said.

"Excuse me?" Braelynn asked as her focused remained fixated on 917.

"Our nickname for a one on one," 9 answered.

"Let him deal with it," 93 said. He looked at the other amborgs that had been in the bubble. "53, 54, 55, stay close. 301 and 365, get an update from 117 or 501. We got some catching up to do."

"Yeah, I need to know what happened after I jumped ship," 297 said, chuckling. "What's Silent Eclipse? And why did 501 hug that little baby Tandeeri?"

"Long story short," Serina said as she bit her nails anxiously. "Secret espionage group of some kind used the Tandeeri as a scape-goat for the whole war. We found out about it and they sent an army of drones after us. Technically it was one and a bomb on our shuttle but supposedly, the fleet is under attack and we have to try and save everyone before Silent Eclipse tries to kill everyone and say that it was the Tandeeri's fault."

"Damn," 297 replied as a ritual chanting began in the ring. "That's not good at all."

"Uh, why did you all name the kid Oreo?" 777 asked.

"Ask 501," 117 sighed. "Also, *that's* your first question?"

"Look, from our perspective, it's been a while," 777 shrugged.

"Which is why I hope this will get settled fast," Serina stated. Then she looked to the side and flinched. "Hey! Hands off!"

Serina batted her hands at a Tandeeri that was staring at her curiously. It had reached out to try and touch her but she jumped to 117's other shoulder. Even though she had no physical body, her personal space was still a thing.

"Sorry," a female voice came from the Tandeeri who was backing away, flustered. "Look at that, the glowing human program is feisty!"

"Far out!" another Tandeeri said with an amazed expression.

"I think we might have taught them the weird parts of our language," Serina said as she hid behind 117's ear.

"That reminds me," 117 looked at 297. "Why are you guys so relaxed about this whole thing?"

"Same as you when you guys first came aboard," 297 shrugged. "I don't know but... ever since we were captured, the atmosphere of this ship soothed us. It's like we're stoned, but not really. It's kinda funny."

"Yeah..." 117 said with a confused look. "The way you're smiling is definitely not something we see every day."

"I can't help it," 297 said. "They're a pretty cool alien species."

"Um guys? Is 917 losing?" 501 asked nervously.

They paused their conversation and turned their focus back to the fight. The chanting had stopped, and the Tandeeri were now cheering and roaring. They had missed the start of the fight. 999 and Braelynn were probably the only ones actually paying attention.

There was a loud thud as 917 was sent flying to the edge of the ring. A Tandeeri caught him in their arms and gracefully helped him back to a standing position.

"Thank you," 917 said. A little dazed, he walked forward confidently.

"Are you just going to let him get killed?" Braelynn asked 999 desperately.

"Why do you care so much?" 999 replied. "Anyway... if 917 wants help, he asks for it. He has his pride just as much as I do."

They watched as 917 continued to use only his bare hands to fight against the Tandeeri leader, who was wielding a massive club of some kind. Avoiding it was easy. Inflicting damage, however, was another thing entirely. The leader was taking advantage of his minimal movements, a weakness he exploited. Since 917 was smaller, he had to use more strength and speed, and rely on stamina to avoid the bigger alien's swings. It was also painfully clear that the Tandeeri leader was tiring 917 out gradually in order to win.

"Very impressive," the Tandeeri leader chuckled. "I expected you to have lost by now."

"Sorry to disappoint," 917 said. He suddenly began to pant.

"I don't understand why humans hold their breath during combat."

"Well," 917 shrugged and grabbed his sword from his belt. "I don't like revealing to my opponent that I'm out of breath."

"Then you seem to be at your limit."

"I still got one idea left."

917 hit a button on the hilt of his weapon and the silver alloy single-edge blade extended. The ring of Tandeeri cheered louder, while the amborgs looked on nervously as the duel reached a tipping point.

117 recognized the blade once it appeared. 43 had given it to him back when they were aboard the Firestar. It had once belonged to 917's alpha version, and now it was his.

917 charged, bringing his sword to his side. As he closed in on the leader, he ducked low. The Tandeeri leader swung his club down, targeting 917's head. Just as 917 raised his sword to defend himself, a thunderous clash echoed as their weapons collided. The Tandeeri leader emitted a startled roar, retreating a few steps. The front of this club was nearly severed, and a mark appeared on his right cheek from 917's strike.

"I have never seen that kind of sword before," the Tandeeri leader lifted a finger to his cheek and ran it over the cut. "It is... powerful."

"Me neither," 917 panted. "It was an inheritance."

The Tandeeri leader paused as he glanced at 917's face and then down at the sword. After a few seconds, he gave him a satisfied nod.

"Hmm. I accept my defeat."

The crowd all gasped in disbelief, and the once thunderous roaring faded into a shocked silence. The leader then cast aside the handle of his destroyed weapon. It struck the ground with a clatter that echoed through the chamber's halls. 917 was taken aback.

"What?" he said as another Tandeeri rushed forward and examined the leader's cheek.

"I acknowledge this human man as the victor," he declared. "Now, we begin preparations to assist your fleet. Warriors! Ready our ships! 917, if you and your friends will come with me."

"Just like that??" 501 asked. "That was a short deadlock."

"You did it 917!" 297 cheered.

A few of them still looked skeptical. Once the realization caught up with them, they all rushed forward excitedly.

"Yeah," 117 murmured, but he was relieved to see that no one had been killed. "Yeah he did!"

The aliens in the room erupted with roars of approval and let out loud war cries as they left the chamber. 117 and the amborgs remained with a few Tandeeri guards, making their way to where the leader was being examined by what seemed to be a doctor.

"Yeah," 917 said suspiciously. "This was definitely not how I expected the duel to turn out. Is it over already?"

"What matters is," 117 glanced at Braelynn. "We are now getting help! That was all you!"

"Not sure I approve of these exact methods... but well done," she replied.

"And I was able to have my duel," the Tandeeri leader said. "It was very satisfying getting the chance to face a warrior such as yourself. I simply wanted to have a bit of fun."

"Aww," 466 blushed as the Third Group amborgs all patted her on the shoulder. "It was just an observation. You all seem like really sweet people."

"Excuse me, your... Tandeeri excellency?"

501 raised his hand with Oreo at his side.

"Is there any chance we can learn your name? Possibly Oreo's too?"

The Tandeeri leader glanced at his son and then at 501.

"I do not believe you would be able to pronounce it," he said.

"Well it would be nice to call you something instead of just 'the Tandeeri leader.' We want to make it easier for people in case they ask."

The Tandeeri leader looked at the amborgs as he sat down comfortably in his seat. He brought his hand up to his chin, probably to imitate their behavior.

"Why don't you do the honors for me?" he said after pondering for a moment.

"Huh?"

117 stared. It was also pretty clear that the rest of them were doing the same. Had they heard the Tandeeri leader correctly?

"You have given my son a name that is of worthy recognition," the Tandeeri leader mumbled with approval. "It would be an honor to receive a name from you."

"Worthy recognition?" 501 asked. "He ate the Oreos in my pocket..."

"Yes," he boldly declared, ignoring 501's added comment. "I give you all the opportunity, as a peaceful gesture on my part, the honor of choosing a name that I can be remembered by in your language. As our first act of friendship."

"I'm pretty sure that's not how it works," 117 declared.

He gulped when the Tandeeri leader turned and stared at him.

"But we'll definitely give it some thinking!" 117 chuckled nervously.

The amborgs stood there and contemplated the possible choices. What would be an iconic name for the leader of a race they made first contact with? It would have to be something that made him stand out, but what?

The amborgs were definitely not capable of coming up with something immediate. 917 was exhausted from the duel and 999 was making sure that he was alright. 297 was too cheerful, along with the twins, 8 and 9, and the triplets. 301 and 365 weren't exactly creative types either. 117 was trying to make sure that everything was in order while Serina jumbled random pieces of code in his CPU. 777 was probably the only one who had taken the request seriously with the Third Group amborgs, but no one was willing to say anything. Braelynn had her arms crossed. Even though she disapproved of the way they were handling things, it was likely the only way to get the ball rolling again.

"How about Snickerdoodle?"

Everyone turned and stared at 466 in dismay. 917 forgot about his exhaustion and instantly perked up. Even 999 coughed a little as she twitched her head in the direction of the Third Group. Serina popped up out of 117's CPU and expressed her confusion along with him.

"We are not calling the leader of the Tandeeri 'snickerdoodle!'" 777 responded immediately, annoyance splashed on his face. "He doesn't even look like a cookie!"

"I'm not calling him that because of his looks!" 466 answered insistently. "I just think that his people are so kind, sweet, and compassionate. Filled with goodness you know? It made me think of something delicious and sweet since we named his son Oreo."

"A-are you kidding me?" 917 stammered. "Are we going to give them all cookie names?"

"Their ships do look like giant floating pieces of candy," 297 remarked with a goofy grin. "3 said so back on Apogee."

"Shut up 297," Serina snapped. "You're high and your argument is invalid."

As the group busily debated among themselves, the Tandeeri leader remained composed, observing them calmly. He grunted loudly to grab their attention. The noise brought an immediate hush, and they all turned to hear his decision.

"This is an acceptable name," his voice echoed proudly in the chamber.

"He's got to be kidding," 8 said. "Is he actually kidding?"

9 tripped and tried to restrain her laughter.

"I don't think so," she sputtered.

"You're really allowing us to call you Snickerdoodle?" 917 asked. He glanced at 999, who looked like she was having an aneurysm. "466, I think I could see the exact moment Angel's soul had left her body."

"Not even I'm up for risking a prank on her when she looks like that," 9 whispered. "This is priceless!"

53, 54, and 55, the Third Group triplets, began to inch closer to 501 at these words.

"Yes," the Tandeeri leader nodded affirmatively and said in a deep and proud tone, "This name shall be one for the history books... as you say."

"More like a joke book," 777 sighed dejectedly.

"Wait, I'm confused..." 501 said. "What book is this that we're talking about?"

"You know," 249 tapped 501 on the shoulder. "We could write all this into a book and get famous and rich from it all."

"Can I reference you guys in my autobiography?" 593 raised her hand.

"I have the perfect photo of you for the cover," 466 said thoughtfully.

"Well done," 117 sighed as he tried getting everyone back on point. "We went from a war to calling an alien leader a cookie and now we're focusing on writing books. Anyone notice how we could still die at any moment?"

"Snap out of it!" Serina shouted as she flashed a bright red.

All of them snapped back to attention. Now newly christened with the name Snickerdoodle, he dipped his head in acknowledgement to Serina.

"Let us begin making preparations to move the fleet. I, Snickerdoodle, shall lead us all to glory."

For most of them, it was really difficult to maintain a straight face. Many of them looked like they were about to break out in fits of laughter, but managed to hold it in.

Snickerdoodle glanced at one of his advisors, and they both silently looked at each other for a few seconds.

"My scouts say that your fleet is blasting each other apart," he explained.

They experienced a sudden jolt as the floor around Snickerdoodle's throne lit up. It lifted off the ground and ascended toward the ceiling like an elevator. As they got closer, they saw the ceiling open up, revealing another room beyond.

"This is our bridge," Snickerdoodle declared. "Perhaps you would all like to watch from here."

"At this rate," 117 sighed as he looked at 501 and 466. "We're going to be rechristening this entire vessel into a bakery."

CHAPTER 10

That's the way the cookie... saves you?

Apogee Station

"Get a load of that."

Taylor, an artificial intelligence, turned around. He had just finished updating a few security programs into the station network when he heard one of the S.C.E. technicians exclaim in wonder.

"What is it?" he asked as he flashed and bounced over to where the mixed group of A.I. Industries technicians and S.C.E. engineers were gathering.

"Well for some reason," the S.C.E. officer replied, "we've lost contact with our fleet. They've moved out of position."

"Are the satellites up and running?" Taylor asked.

"Repairs have just been completed," someone answered.

"Let's get an eye on the situation," the A.I. nodded affirmatively and everyone began to get busy.

Taylor had been left behind on Serina's orders to watch over the repairs, but he hadn't known he could hold this much authority. It was quite fun giving out directions and making sure everyone, including the alternate universe crew, was under his command.

As he watched the monitor come into focus, he double-checked the power levels. They were probably the highest he had ever seen. It was all thanks to the new power generators the S.C.E. had installed for them.

"The fleet... it's fighting each other."

Everyone watched as the technician brought the image up on the screen. There was the S.C.E. Firestar in plain sight, under attack by the rest of the fleet. But what was even more shocking was that each ship was shooting at each other. Someone had made it a ship-to-ship free for all.

"Hmm," Taylor raised his holographic arm to his chin. "Is it a coup?"

"What do we do?" Someone in an A.I. Industries lab coat asked. "Is Dr. Kendrick ok? What about the amborgs?"

"I think we should return to the flagship," an S.C.E. crewmember replied. "We need to get a better grasp of what's going on."

"No one goes anywhere."

Everyone turned to see Taylor lifting a hand. As he did, the doors immediately slammed shut. The guards jumped but didn't draw their weapons. All the people in the room turned to look at the A.I. at the main console.

"What is this, Taylor?" one of the station technicians asked in shock.

"We've been boarded!" Taylor replied in alarm after just having seen an emergency update the security cameras had flagged for him. "Attention all hands! Battle stations! Apogee Station is breached!"

The guards immediately drew their weapons as Taylor activated the alarm systems, while the technicians looked around frantically as the atmosphere changed completely. The S.C.E. crewmembers were also attempting to grasp the situation.

"You," Taylor replied. "I suggest you get your hand away from my console. As a matter of fact..."

Taylor disappeared in a flash of bright light. An S.C.E. crew member had tried to sneak up to the console where he was, attempting to reach for him. The second the A.I. let off that flash, they lost their balance and stumbled back.

"You're hiding something," Taylor's disembodied voice spoke around the room. "Time to die."

A large electrical discharge surged through the crewman, causing him to shake violently. Suddenly, its body began to ripple and distort. The holographic image melted away, revealing a humanoid robot wearing the S.C.E. uniform. It buckled from the shock and collapsed with a resounding crash.

"Recognize this piece of scrap metal?" Taylor reappeared and asked a nearby crewman.

"No..." they said as the robot laid sprawled out on the floor. "What is it?"

"It's definitely not one of ours," Taylor frowned. "Our drones aren't that sophisticated... or ugly. Open a line to Captain Harwood if you can!"

"Got it," an A.I. Industries technician replied. "But what is happening Taylor?"

"The instant we saw the fleet battle," Taylor answered as he pulled up several screens. "There were a couple of distress calls coming from the hangar. Armed intruders began disembarking the S.C.E. shuttles. Anyone else that's not of this universe care to explain?"

The guards raised their weapons but weren't sure who to shoot. One of the S.C.E. officers immediately raised their hands.

"Stand down," the officer said. "S.C.E. uniforms will stand down now. I don't know what you're accusing us of but we're not the ones attacking you."

"You're lying!" someone shouted, sparking an argument from everyone around them.

"QUIET!" Taylor shouted through the loudspeakers.

Everyone winced at the loud, high-pitched sound that Tylor emitted. The last thing they needed was to start bickering among themselves. Taylor just needed to buy time in order to figure out what was going on.

"Let me explain how this works in our universe," he declared. "I'm in charge of this station. The way I see it, someone just tried to take over Dr. Kendrick's property. I don't care who it is, I just know that we're fighting right now. I've locked down the room! No one gets in or out. If there are any more drones lurking around here with the bright idea of trying to kill anyone else, I will track them down and eliminate them first. Guards, you will keep a watchful eye on our alternate universe friends. S.C.E. officer Leyton, your assistance in restoring our systems was helpful and we are grateful, but I no longer trust you. I ask you to relieve your weapons now. Consider this my only friendly warning."

The S.C.E. officer looked positively mortified. He had never encountered such an outspoken A.I. before. Taylor wondered if Serina would be proud of how he was doing.

"Do as he says," Leyton announced to the S.C.E. crewmen.

"We're just going to let it bully us sir?"

"*He* is in charge," Leyton barked back. "Their universe, their jurisdiction, their rules. I'm not about to go around being the one who thought it'd be fun to kill everyone here. But I ask you this, number-cruncher... My people are still aboard this station. Please help them."

"We'll see," Taylor flashed a fierce blood-red at the words number-cruncher. "Captain Harwood, attempt to capture all hostiles reported. We got some cleaning up to do. If it shoots you, you shoot back. Now rally your troopers. I'll find the targets for you."

"What do we do Taylor?"

Taylor turned to look at the A.I. Industries staff and technicians.

"Our jobs," Taylor shrugged. "Dr. Kendrick would kill us if we let his station fall. Every person to a console now. I need some help."

"Uhh Taylor?"

One technician nervously pointed out the window. Taylor followed his line of sight, prompting everyone in the room to look outside as well. There were several wormholes opening up in the distance, and several ships began to fly through.

"Oh boy..." Taylor sighed. "Why does it feel like we're being screwed over? We can't seem to catch a break."

He looked at the crew of the S.C.E.

"I don't trust you people since you're from an alternate universe," Taylor said. "Mostly because you could be here to take over and conquer our beautiful home. Who knows if the S.C.E. is real? Everything I've seen from your actions, although good, can also be a method to subtly lower our guard."

"I'm telling you again... we aren't here for that!"

"I am an artificial intelligence," Taylor said angrily. "I have a built-in lie detector. As we speak, someone on your crew is giving off red flags. Do you hear me? You, with all due respect, do not speak again while under my watch. My universe, my home, my command."

"You don't have the authority!"

Taylor turned and glared at the S.C.E. officer who had spoken up.

"Yes, I do," he replied. "Dr. Kendrick and Serina left me in charge of the station... and I will protect it from all threats."

S.C.E. Firestar
Bridge

Admiral Ra'aiah's breath came in rapid bursts as she fought to keep her composure. The rush of adrenaline was starting to wear off, and anxiety began to slither up her spine. Now that the chaos had subsided and the battle was over, it was time to deal with the traumatic aftermath.

"Give me a report," she stated.

The mood was bleak as everyone continued their work, but to her, it felt like a morgue on the bridge. Everyone was still coming to terms with the fact that they had just survived a terrifying skirmish against their own kind.

"Heavy damage across the ship," commander Ulgo reported. "External and internal. Engineering is clear of hostiles and we have maintained control. All weapons control stations are in our possession. We have completed full scans of the ship twice and confirmed that all hostiles are neutralized."

"Do a third scan," Admiral Ra'aiah trembled. "Be absolutely sure."

Ulgo nodded when she raised her eyes to him. His uniform was unbuttoned at the neckline, and his hair was disheveled from the impact that had shaken their ship. Still, he maintained a professional and rigid demeanor to show that he was not as emotionally vulnerable as she was.

"A third scan," he repeated her order with a slight bow. "Yes ma'am. Shall I... report the casualties?"

Admiral Ra'aiah shook her head.

"Later," she said. "We don't need that on our minds now. The ship is ours. What about the fleet? Did... we destroy any of Chastain's fleet?"

"No," Ulgo reported. "As you ordered, we have successfully disabled and destroyed only their weapons. It looks like we've managed to stop the fighting."

Admiral Ra'aiah wiped the sweat off her forehead. She glanced to the left and noticed Dr. Kendrick kneeling beside 6, who was in the process of unrolling a bandage from her medical kit. They were attempting to triage the injured on the bridge. However, looking at them carefully, she realized that 6 was actually having Dr. Kendrick wrap a bandage around her own shoulder.

"My god... Vanessa."

Dr. Kendrick's tone was a mix of horror and deep concern as he continued to treat 6's injury. She used her free hand to pull out a needle and inject a painkiller into her arm just above where he was applying the bandage.

"I'll be ok," she said. "We deal with explosions all the time."

"Not when they rip through your skin like paper," Dr. Kendrick said as he pulled another pair of glasses out of his pocket. "Damn. The lenses are cracked in this pair too."

"Here Dad," 6 coughed as she pulled a small case out of her pocket. "You might need these to see the future."

"Oh," Dr. Kendrick chuckled as he opened it and looked inside. "Another pair of glasses and contacts. Always looking out for me."

"You saved us," 6 smiled. "No reason why we can't reciprocate."

Dr. Kendrick picked up the glasses and closed the case. As he passed it back to 6, she pushed it away.

"It's armored," 6 explained. "I had it custom made for your birthday. It'll last longer than your old case."

"Oh. Really?" Dr. Kendrick said as he glanced down at it in wonder. "Armored?"

"Yeah," 6 chuckled. "A ton of us got together and thought it would be a good idea to give you armored possessions. I know you requested that we don't but we're concerned about your safety."

"I'm flattered."

"501 got you armored underwear."

"Ok... what do you kids discuss in your spare time?"

"Everything? Duh."

Thinking that she needed a breather, Admiral Ra'aiah asked Ulgo to take the con as she left her chair. She gently cleared her throat and spoke to Dr. Kendrick as she walked over.

"Mind if I join you?"

Dr. Kendrick and 6 glanced up at her, both with calm and polite grins.

"Please," Dr. Kendrick said as he motioned for her to sit next to 6.

"So many dead," Admiral Ra'aiah sighed with shaking breaths. "I don't think I can keep this up."

"Yes, you can," 6 replied. "Everyone here that's still breathing is alive because of you and your quick thinking."

"How many had to die though? All for a secret war... why?"

"We answer that question after we find the ones responsible," Dr. Kendrick replied. "And we wipe the smug looks off their faces."

"Yeah," 6 nodded reassuringly. "We're kind of experts at this sort of thing. Not interstellar wars across the multiverse, we're just really good at handling blitz wars and other sudden conflicts."

"Admiral! We have incoming!"

Ulgo's sharp tone made them flinch, but they immediately snapped back into action. Admiral Ra'aiah sniffed and held back her tears as she returned to her seat. Duty calls.

"Where?" she asked.

Her radar officer responded quickly.

"Coming from off the starboard bow! Incoming S.C.E. fleet!"

Admiral Ra'aiah and Commander Ulgo exchanged glances, both with the same questions in mind: *Reinforcements? Now?*

"Which ships are they?" Admiral Ra'aiah asked.

"Confirmed IFF tags! The S.C.E. Georgia is leading them towards us."

Ulgo turned to Admiral Ra'aiah with wide eyes. Dr. Kendrick and 6 noticed his expression and immediately felt skeptical. It was the first time they'd seen him look...afraid? As they glanced at Admiral Ra'aiah, they also detected something unusual.

Instead of the building anxiety, they could see the horror slowly creeping in.

"Are you alright?" Dr. Kendrick asked.

"The Georgia?" 6 added for clarification. "Is it a ship we can trust?"

"Yes and no," Ulgo sighed. He turned to them with a clear look of discomfort. "It is the ship under the command of... Second Admiral Ra'aiah."

Dr. Kendrick's brow furrowed as he looked at Admiral Ra'aiah standing next to him. She was at the rank of Third Admiral and in command of the Firestar. One of the highest ranks in the S.C.E. was First Admiral. So... that meant that a Second Admiral with the same name... also meant that...

Dr. Kendrick and 6 locked eyes in a moment of realization. Silently, they stared sharply at Admiral Ra'aiah, who stood frozen on the spot.

"Just what I need," she groaned as if she was dying of embarrassment. "It's my mother."

Dr. Kendrick nodded sympathetically.

"If my mother was still alive," he mumbled. "I could relate."

"Wow," 6 nodded. "Family trade."

"I wasn't expecting her..." Admiral Ra'aiah whined. "Why now of all times?"

"They probably found a way to make her volunteer to bring her fleet," Ulgo pondered carefully. "That being the case, we will most likely be in for another battle. I have concerns about whether our ship can handle another firefight."

"I think the more important question is, do you trust her?" 6 asked suspiciously.

Admiral Ra'aiah turned and nodded with another groan.

My mother is not a traitor," she said. "Ulgo is probably right. If she didn't volunteer, they sent her here in order to use her against me. Under orders, she probably turned herself into a political hostage."

"Ma'am! Incoming transmission," the communications officer interrupted. Admiral Ra'aiah straightened her uniform and took a deep breath.

"Put my mother... I mean, the Georgia, through."

When a screen appeared, Dr. Kendrick and 6 thought they would see a woman resembling the one standing beside them. Instead, they saw something completely unexpected. Their eyes widened in disbelief as they laid eyes on a humanoid woman in the same S.C.E. uniform, with some fur, long hair that resembled the same dark raven hair as Admiral Ra'aiah, and a pair of perky cat ears.

"My child! My precious little kitten!" Admiral Ra'aiah senior purred over the comms, which made Dr. Kendrick cringe. "What in the stars happened? You're all injured! Are you alright, Ishala?"

"Hello Admiral," Admiral Ra'aiah replied grimly. "We've had some problems over here."

Ishala Ra'aiah's tone seemed to shift to total embarrassment as she addressed the cat-woman onscreen. It was almost like all the anxiety and tension from the battle earlier was forgotten. Ra'aiah senior looked slightly hurt at her lackluster greeting.

"What kind of attitude is that? Mrow. Call me mother for crying out loud."

"Not in front of the crew!" Admiral Ra'aiah sighed pleadingly. "It's a little difficult to explain! Stop treating me like I'm a little girl!"

"You *are* still my little girl!"

"Mother, these conversations are recorded for professional use!"

Dr. Kendrick and 6 both looked at Ulgo, who nodded sullenly.

"Unfortunately," his voice lowered to whisper. "High command will go over these transmissions in their monthly audits. It's entertaining and a bit awkward at times."

6 glanced at Dr. Kendrick.

"I imagine that some of the conversations you've seen from our meetings and phone calls were probably worse?" she said.

Dr. Kendrick lowered his gaze and glared at her.

"I still want to know why 501 drove my car into a building," he muttered angrily.

"Not drove... *flew*... he flew it into a building," 6 clarified.

Ulgo appeared genuinely intrigued with that particular detail of 6's comment. Though, before anyone else could open the door to that conversation, they shifted their attention to the screen where two admirals were still engaged in conversation. Earlier, Ishala Ra'aiah was speaking like a true professional. Now, it looked like a daughter trying to explain a bad grade on her report card to her mother. The mother just happened to be a talking bipedal humanoid cat.

"We had an unfortunate situation!" she was trying to tell her mother.

"That is obvious!" her mother nodded in a scolding manner. "From the look of it, your ship and entire fleet are... wrecked! Your bridge looks like someone threw a whirling dervish into the room! I had my concerns when you received your new command but for it to be this messy... Your father is not going to be happy the next time he decides to do his inspections. But don't you worry! Mother is here now, and we can tidy up a bit before that happens!"

"Mother..." Admiral Ra'aiah dropped her gaze and planted her head into her right hand. "Now's not the time!"

6 suddenly had an idea. She rushed over to Admiral Ra'aiah's side.

"Keep her talking," she whispered. "Perhaps we should see about trying to locate any Silent Eclipse drones present among her reinforcements."

"Oh, hello there."

Admiral Ra'aiah senior noticed 6's sudden movement and glanced at her. When she got a good look at her uniform, her eyes lit up in recognition.

"Oh... Ishala!" she clapped her hands excitedly. "You've made some friends! It's an amborg! Is that one of Dr. Kendrick's children?"

Admiral Ra'aiah nodded grudgingly as Dr. Kendrick stepped into view. He waved politely at the screen and dipped his head formally.

"Oh err... yes!" Dr. Kendrick said as Ulgo signaled a nearby crewman. "It's very lovely to meet you... madam Second Admiral."

They listened carefully and could have sworn they heard faint purring from Admiral Ra'aiah's mother.

"Oh, no need to use my rank, please call me Talveeya! I am such a fan!" she said mischievously. "Did Ishala tell you about how she has a poster of you in her room back home?"

Ishala let out a sputter, her eyes wide with dismay as she looked around in a panic. She frantically tried to signal to her mother to cut it out, but it was too late. Her face turned a bright red as the rest of the surviving bridge crew turned to gawk at her. A couple of them started coughing and stifling their laughter. Even Commander Ulgo had to lower his cap, diverting his gaze to the floor.

"No," Dr. Kendrick said as his cheeks flushed slightly. "They have posters of me? How flattering."

6 turned away from the screen, trying in vain to contain her own laughter, while Ishala looked absolutely petrified. The scene unfolding before them was indeed a cringe-worthy moment between a parent and child. It was quite surprising to see Admiral Ra'aiah lose her strict composure.

"Mother!" she whined as she looked away.

"Oh right," Talveeya chuckled as her ears flickered. "Heat of the moment, my mistake. Just forget you heard about that, ok?"

"I doubt that," 6 smirked.

"I beg of you," Ishala mumbled. "Please delete this memory and all parts of this conversation."

"Well, on the bright side," 6 cleared her throat. "I don't think she sounds like a Silent Eclipse member. She doesn't fit the profile of someone trying to manipulate or kill us."

"It's far more impressive that she made Second Admiral," Ulgo spoke casually as he addressed Talveeya. "Her record is... quite problematic despite her current position."

Talveeya didn't appear to be fazed at Ulgo's comment. She put her left hand pridefully on her chest and puffed it out slightly.

"Problematic?" she stuck her nose up dramatically. "I prefer to call it iconic!"

"She's kind of a ditz," Ishala muttered under her breath.

"I heard that," Talveeya mewed at them, pointing at two different sets of ears on both the top and side of her head. 6 and Dr. Kendrick flinched slightly in surprise.

"She has... two pairs of ears? Human and cat?" Dr. Kendrick asked, bewildered and intrigued.

"Not now!"

Ishala had to interrupt him. Dr. Kendrick was just raising four fingers on his right hand in a questioning manner, but froze when he was cut off. Talveeya looked a little startled at her daughter's outburst.

"There's no time!" she said as she struggled to look back up at the screen. "Mom! You got to get away from the other ships!"

"What do you mean? We're your reinforcements!"

Admiral Ra'aiah senior quickly turned her head to the side, hearing someone in the background speak to her. When she looked back at them, her face was marked by irritation.

"I'm being told that you're scanning my ship! Ishala! Even I like my privacy, ok?"

"Commander?"

Everyone's attention snapped to Hemington, who was addressing them from the radar console.

"No Silent Eclipse signals detected aboard the Georgia," she stated.

"That's strange," 6 said as she glanced at the radar console. "The scanner and my program should pick up any Silent Eclipse drones aboard."

"None detected," Hemington repeated. "Not aboard the Second Admiral's ship."

"We need to check the rest of her fleet," Ulgo stated.

"Already on it, sir."

"Hey, I'm still here!" Talveeya waved a hand at them. "What am I missing?"

"Silent Eclipse sent an army to take over my ship as well as the rest of my fleet!" Admiral Ra'aiah said quickly. "We've been looking at this war the wrong way! They've killed too many people already and that's why you've been sent here! They ordered you to come here and now we're both in trouble!"

"Silent Eclipse?"

Talveeya Ra'aiah's brow furrowed as she tried to absorb this information. Then, she turned to look at someone offscreen.

"Hmm... Helmsman! Take us up alongside the S.C.E. Firestar!"

When she faced Ishala again, her casual demeanor had melted away, replaced by determination and focus.

"Silent Eclipse has been extinct since..." she pondered. Then her eyes widened slightly. "This is interesting."

"Admiral?" Ishala asked. "What are you doing?"

"I wasn't ordered here honey," Talveeya replied with a smile. "They let me assume command and I rallied a fleet on my own. I couldn't stand missing out on anything, so voila! Overprotective mother for the win!"

Ishala turned to face Commander Ulgo, whose eyes began to widen in shock.

"I think Second Admiral Ra'aiah just admitted to going rogue," he stated.

"I think that's what she said, yes," Ishala gulped and let out a frustrated sigh.

"Ma'am! Weapons activation detected! From the Georgia's fleet!"

Ishala Ra'aiah turned sharply to Hemington, then at the viewscreen. Alarmed, Talveeya's smile faded into a serious line and her eyes hardened.

"Mom! Your fleet!"

Everyone watched as Talveeya sprung into action. All traces of her playful behavior vanished as she glanced off to the side.

"I'm being targeted?" she exclaimed. "All hands! Prepare for an emergency jump!"

"She can't be serious," Ulgo said, his voice rising in panic. "Admiral! She's going to jump! Her ship is pointed..."

"...Right at us!" Ishala finished for him. She activated the communicator on her wrist. "Engineering! Spin up the engines now!"

She lowered her arm to address Talveeya.

"Mom! What are you doing?! We're in your way! You'll rip both of our ships apart!"

"I knew I had a funny feeling..."

Talveeya was mumbling to herself, but they could all hear her as the lights behind her changed from a calm moonlit hue to a vivid crimson red when the 'action stations' alarm rang out on the Georgia.

"What's she talking about?" Dr. Kendrick asked nervously.

"I think I want to know what she's up to," 6 added.

Talveeya let out a determined hiss.

"Brace yourselves Ishala! A cat does not appreciate being attacked from behind! Everyone hang on!"

"She's going to jump right at us!" Ishala replied breathlessly.

"But…! We're still here!" Dr. Kendrick's eyes widened, looking around helplessly. "And we're in the way!"

"Shit," 6 gulped. "We're going to die from getting t-boned by a starship."

In the next few seconds, all they could hear was Ishala Ra'aiah bellowing out one final instruction to the crew.

"All hands! Brace, brace, brace! Incoming vessel!"

"Here we go again," 6 grumbled loudly.

In one swift and coordinated movement, 6 grabbed Dr. Kendrick, and both of them clung tightly to Admiral Ra'aiah's seat. She immediately took her place in the chair, clutching the armrests firmly as Ulgo moved to the opposite side, extending his arm to encircle Dr. Kendrick. Everyone, including the rest of the bridge crew, prepared themselves for what was to come.

A bright light appeared just off the starboard bow. Suddenly, there was a massive bang, causing the entire bridge to shake much more violently than before. Had the Firestar not already sustained significant damage, it might not have been a concern, but the structural integrity groaned and weakened further as the Georgia popped into view right in front of them.

The sudden tremor rattled everyone, but from what they could tell, they were still in one piece. It appeared that there had been no collision.

The viewscreen was still connected, showing Talveeya in her seat. She looked as though she'd just been on a rollercoaster, but she continued to bark out orders to her crew while Ishala brought up the display map.

Second Admiral Ra'aiah had executed a very wild and dangerous maneuver. The quick jump brought the Georgia, roughly one-third the size of the Firestar, alarmingly close to the starboard bow. It was fairly obvious to everyone why she'd taken such a risk. She had ordered her ship to perform a mini jump to separate the Georgia from the other S.C.E. ships in her formation.

"Mom!" Ishala struggled to remain in her seat as she tried to reopen the communications line. "Are you alright?!"

"I think everyone's going to have a concussion by the end of this…" 6 groaned.

They all looked at the viewscreen and watched Talveeya in action. She wasn't playing or kidding around. It was like she had adopted a whole new personality.

"That was a close one!" she yelled triumphantly with a brazen smirk. "Hard starboard, one eight zero! Charge the main battery and target the first ship you see! No one gets away with preemptive strikes against us! Prepare to fire!"

"She took herself out of range to gain a tactical advantage," Ulgo explained.

6 and Dr. Kendrick looked at the map display and saw the Georgia's blue triangle begin to turn. It was pointed straight at the Firestar's blue triangle, but it turned right and looped around. They couldn't help but notice that it was still moving slowly in their direction. It was like it was skating on ice, sliding their way as it attempted to stop itself from colliding with them.

"She raced her ship to our position and is drifting it?" he exclaimed. "Is she a starship captain or a racecar driver? Is she nuts?"

"She took a test," Ulgo replied angrily. "Apparently, it yielded no results."

Admiral Ra'aiah wasn't paying attention to them. Instead, she was protesting at her mother.

"Mom?!" she asked. "What are you doing?!"

"It's ok darling," Talveeya replied on the screen. "Mom's here now. All remaining power to the main gun! And all hands, evacuate the ship! Give me full control!"

"Mom!" Ishala exclaimed as they all watched the viewscreen. "If you fire at full power, your shields will drop! The rest of your fleet can hit you dead on if you do this!"

"They'll be in range in a few minutes," Talveeya explained as people in the background were scrambling and clearing her bridge. "That's how much time I've bought you! Get your ship underway! Get out of here! This fight's not over!"

"What's wrong?" Dr. Kendrick asked. "Why is she abandoning ship?"

"An emergency jump which drained her power supply," Ulgo said quickly. "It's a Nebulus class escort frigate! Older ship! It's not outfitted to fight immediately after a hyperspace jump! Using the main cannon will drain it! Without power, the remaining ships will tear her apart!"

"She's using her ship as a shield!" 6 exclaimed in horror. "Total badass move, but she'll die!"

"Why do you think I'm trying to talk her out of it?!" Ishala said frantically.

"It's ok Ishala," Talveeya said with a wink. "If we live, you can count on my support. As well as your father's. Remember the days I went rogue for the right reasons? Someone is trying to hurt you and I can't tolerate that."

"No mom! Don't!"

"If I don't make it honey," Talveeya Ra'aiah formally dipped her head and took a deep breath. "You have to finish this or the conflict won't stop. Standby ok?"

"Admiral! The Georgia's fleet is inbound. They're in range! Incoming main cannon fire from the S.C.E. Destiny!"

Everyone focused their attention on the holographic map in front of them. They looked at the light blue grid, then at the S.C.E. Firestar's triangle. The Georgia's triangle was now aimed away from them. A red line appeared and traveled away from their formation towards another group of blue triangles heading for them. A flashing label popped up and identified one of the advancing ships at the head of the formation as the S.C.E. Destiny.

A smaller triangle, symbolizing a projectile fired from the Georgia's main cannon, shot out and moved towards the other fleet. At the same time, another red line was launched from the S.C.E. Destiny. Both crimson trails raced towards one another across the grid of the map display.

It was a brilliant shot for both ships. Talveeya, fortunately, had been quicker on the trigger. The red streaks collided on screen, creating a red circle just ahead of the reinforcing fleet. Dr. Kendrick focused on the grid while frequently glancing out the starboard viewport into the distance.

"What an amazing shot!" Dr. Kendrick remarked. "Do all your starships have such excellent gunners... or marksmen?"

"It's their training," Ulgo replied. "Unfortunately, someone was quick enough to hit the Georgia's main cannon. Those reflexes and aim are too precise and perfect."

"Silent Eclipse," Ishala mumbled.

"Damn!" Talveeya cursed. "Someone managed to shoot down my shot? That's not good."

Ishala looked at the map. Her mother's reinforcements were in disarray. The shockwave from the collision had knocked the ships off-balance. Unfortunately, this only bought them a few minutes.

"Engineering," Ishala tried her communicator again. "We really need to get in this fight! We're sitting ducks."

They heard a cough followed by a hasty reply. It was Chief Hayes.

"Engineering here," she spoke up. "Heard you the first time admiral! We've got a lot of power converters burnt out down here! We're still in the middle of repairs! I need six minutes to restart and fire the engines!"

"Can you go any faster?" Ishala asked desperately as Talveeya worked just as frantically on her end. "Second Admiral Ra'aiah is in trouble!"

"Your... mom is here??" Hayes exclaimed. "Uh... I'll do what I can!"

The transmission ended as Ishala blushed slightly. Now the entire engineering department knew that her mother was here.

"Can we buy some time for the Georgia?" Dr. Kendrick asked quickly. "Can we open fire? Or maybe the Georgia should take another shot right now!"

"They can't," Ulgo said. "One, the Georgia is probably on emergency power now. By the time they recharge their weapons, it'll be too late. Two, they're in our line of fire and we can't really shoot anything."

"Admiral!" Hemington reported. "Some of the Georgia's reinforcements have begun battling each other! A few more are realigning themselves and targeting us too!"

"This is what my mother wanted," Ishala said. "Sacrifice her ship, get her crew off ASAP and serve as a distraction. They're going to kill her. 43! Weapons control! Come in!"

Alpha Serina 43's response was quick.

"I hear you, what's the situation?"

"Any of our weapons online?" Ishala demanded.

"Some weapons crews in the main mounts, no R-batteries, missiles and point-defense have been disconnected," 43 replied. "I think only a handful of turrets are still up and running."

This meant that there were barely any weapons available. With the main power core functioning, there was no power to their long-range lasers and energy batteries. It even meant that they had no shields to protect themselves. The point-defense and missile turrets had been taken down and disconnected from weapons control because they didn't want any Silent Eclipse drones to use them against their own ships and fighters. There were a few kinetic weapon mounts still active, but they couldn't put a dent into an incoming fleet of fully-equipped starships. They had spent way too much time battling their own fleet.

"Give me everything we've got," Ishala ordered 43 desperately. "Everything you can!"

"Uh... yes ma'am..."

Ishala glanced at Ulgo.

"Are any of our ships able to defend?" she asked.

Her heart sank when she saw him shake his head in answer.

"We ended the previous battle with no losses or ships destroyed," he stated. "We just took out their weapons to disable them."

"And then your mother came in with a fresh fleet that has also been infiltrated," Dr. Kendrick added. "We barely got out of that mess and we're about to be tossed in another fire."

"What about fighters?" 6 suggested. "Are there any that could... distract the fleet until we get underway?"

"Good idea," Ulgo replied, but shook his head again. "But, not in the time that we have."

There was nothing the Firestar could do. Ishala looked at the viewscreen and tried to get her mother's attention.

"Mom!" she said. "Evacuate the Georgia and come aboard! We'll figure this out together!"

"Oh dear," Talveeya said as she stood and turned to the viewscreen. "I definitely made a bunch of mistakes. Ishala dear? I think this is it for me. Promise you'll protect my crew? Pick up their escape pods and keep them safe ok?"

"You're not going to go down with the Georgia!" Ishala protested. "Get to another escape pod and get out of there!"

"Too late!" Hemington called out to them again. "Incoming barrage!"

On the map, several warning lights appeared on the display. All but three of the Georgia's fleet let loose a flurry of red lines. They were all flowing quickly on a direct course towards the Firestar and the Georgia.

"Try to get the tractor beam online!" Ishala commanded as she racked her brain for any option that was available. "All power to starboard deflectors! Try and push the Georgia out of the way! Do something!"

"Admiral," Ulgo replied fiercely. "There's no power."

For a brief moment, everyone turned their gaze from the screen to the window, watching the vivid red lasers rapidly approaching them from afar. The Firestar could definitely withstand that kind of barrage, but not indefinitely. Unfortunately, the Georgia was drifting and caught in the crosshairs. It was going to take the full brunt of the attack unless a miracle occurred.

"Mom!" Ishala cried out.

They heard Talveeya let out a confident laugh.

"This may be the end of me!" she said boldly. "But I will die protecting my family! All of them! I hope they all avenge me!"

"Something's happening!"

Everyone stopped what they were doing and turned to Hemington, who sounded confused and utterly bewildered.

"Admiral?" she said. "The incoming barrage... is changing directions?"

"What?"

Everyone looked at the map display. The red streaks that should have collided with the Georgia's blue triangle had been redirected.

"Ishala?"

Everyone glanced at Talveeya on the viewscreen. She was staring past her own screen with a stunned look on her face.

"Did you do that? Neat trick! I absolutely thought I was about to die."

Everyone looked at the map again, then at the screen, and then glanced out towards one of the nearby windows. It was truly a strange phenomenon.

The incoming blasts that should have struck them and the Georgia never made it to their designated targets. They really did change direction entirely. The map display had the path of the enemy barrage tracked and showed the course correction. The red lines that were just directed at their fleet were now pointed upwards and zooming elsewhere, as if someone had simply swatted them away.

"Did a giant lightsaber save us?" 6 asked.

"Pretty sure we would have seen that," Dr. Kendrick said in a soft voice.

"Where did the barrage get taken to?" Ulgo demanded.

"Sir," Hemington reported. "The barrage is being dragged away toward new incoming signals!"

"What?"

"It's the Tandeeri!"

Ishala hit the controls on the map and zoomed out. The radar detected a new set of signals moving towards them.

"Confirmed?" Ulgo asked Hemington.

"Yes sir!" she stated. "We triple-checked! No mistaking them! The Tandeeri are inbound."

"But are they here to finish us off?" Ishala muttered fearfully. "We're dead in space with no defenses left."

"Admiral..." Hemington breathed. "The barrage... it's coming back! No, correction! It's going back towards the Georgia's fleet!"

Instead of questioning it further, everyone stared at the map display. The red lines had gathered at the Tandeeri fleet, represented with red circles since they were technically considered hostiles. Within minutes, no one could do anything but watch as the fleet of incoming ships was struck by the full barrage. The blue triangles hit by it were then crossed off the map and faded out into a dark grey.

"Did they just get destroyed?" Dr. Kendrick's eyes widened.

"No sir," Hemington replied. "We have eyes on the incoming fleet. "They're uh... disabled. I think. No signs of external damage but they've stopped fighting."

"Did the Tandeeri just save us?" 6 asked.

"Uh, yes, that is also my question," Talveeya added from the viewscreen.

"This means that 117's team... they did it!" 6's eyes brightened.

"Let's not be hasty Vanessa," Dr. Kendrick replied. "We don't know that yet."

They then heard Hemington cut in again.

"Actually, we're receiving a transmission... and it's coming from the Tandeeri!"

Dr. Kendrick glanced at 6, who let a smile spread across her face. He then turned to Admiral Ra'aiah and Commander Ulgo, giving them a reassuring shrug.

"I stand corrected," he said. "Unless proven otherwise?"

"Let's hear it," Ishala nodded. "Patch my mother into the transmission too. Open the channel."

Another screen appeared next to the one that Talveeya was looking at. She stayed silent, giving them her undivided attention. Ishala and Ulgo tried to maintain their composure as they watched the new screen. The Tandeeri leader's face appeared on their monitors, catching them all off guard. Dr. Kendrick and 6 stared in wonder at how much he resembled Oreo.

"Hello there!" Snickerdoodle said with a casual wave of his claw. "Are you in need of assistance? We have arrived to help you!"

"He s-speaks... f-fluent English," 6 stammered in astonishment.

"My," Talveeya mewled on her screen playfully. "Who's that handsome looking devil?"

Dr. Kendrick's smile faded, feeling slightly uncomfortable. Commander Ulgo and Ishala glanced at him, then at each other, sensing that this conversation was about to get weird. They needed to steer the situation back on track.

"Mom... not now..." she said as she clutched her heart. She looked at Snickerdoodle and promptly greeted him. "Are you...? Excuse me. Are you the leader...? Of the Tandeeri?"

"This ceremonial garb isn't for show..." Snickerdoodle mumbled as he looked down and examined himself. "I am pleased to be able to converse with you without any distractions."

"That's an understatement! They got wrecked!"

There were a bunch of voices in the background hissing and shushing 297.

"Verified the voice," 6 whispered. "Looks like 297 was rescued."

Dr. Kendrick nodded as Ishala formally cleared her throat.

"Did you kill or disable the rest of the fleet?" she asked.

"We shut down their power," Snickerdoodle declared. "They should be fine."

"Hold on!" Braelynn's voice spoke in the background. "Can we verify that? There were still some innocent people aboard those ships! We should start rescuing them! Remember, we have different time zones."

"Ah, yes, that is correct," Snickerdoodle nodded, then eyed Ishala. "You should begin rescuing your friends. It is safe now."

"Who was that?" Ulgo asked suspiciously.

"Never mind that."

Ishala motioned for Ulgo to start rescue operations. She couldn't believe that a Tandeeri was opening their first conversation like this and making such a suggestion, but he was right.

"Start sending out search and rescue shuttles," she ordered. "All available units that can still fly are to deploy immediately. We need to begin accounting for what we have left."

Ulgo silently dipped his head and walked over to the communications officers. Ishala and Talveeya both turned their focus back to their screens.

"What exactly did you do? You pulled a laser barrage and sent it back to its point of origin."

Snickerdoodle looked quite pleased with himself.

"I think in your language, the phrase is an electro... mag something or other?"

"An electro-magnetic pulse?" Dr. Kendrick finished for him.

"Ah yes, thank you kind sir!" Snickerdoodle nodded, pointing a claw at the screen. "Ah, I recognize you from their description of you! You must be the father of the amborgs! They are very fortunate to have you in their lives."

"I think I should be the one complimenting you for your fortunate timing," Dr. Kendrick blushed, bashfully raising a hand to the back of his head. "I'm also glad to hear that my kids are alright."

The two of them were interrupted when Ishala made a sudden realization.

"Hold on! An E.M.P. would terminate life-support!" she said as her eyes widened. "The crews would still suffocate if all systems were down!"

"Really?" Snickerdoodle replied casually. "Why don't you check on them?"

Ishala hesitated as she glanced over at Ulgo. Surprisingly, he turned to them and flashed a thumbs up.

"They're alright," he informed them. "Every vessel that's been disabled is reporting in. There are many that are alive and well."

"But how? What did you do?"

Ishala let out a sigh of relief as she looked at the screen again. Snickerdoodle replied promptly.

"I was informed of a massive attack from within," he stated. "An army of drones tried to take over your fleet from the inside. Like a disease of the body. We created a vaccine."

"A vaccine?" 6 asked.

"Hey! I told him to say that!"

501's excited voice was unmistakable.

"Donut?" 6 raised her eyebrows. "Is that you?"

"Yup!" 501 spoke from somewhere in the background. Then from the corner, they saw his face enter the frame. "They took the signal of the Silent Eclipse drones! Then they modified the energy field of those lasers to change the attack and then we fired it at the fleet! It was a localized E.M.P that focuses on any Silent Eclipse signals!"

"Did 501 really say all of that?" Dr. Kendrick asked suspiciously.

"Actually, we were all thinking it," 117's face replaced 501's in the corner of the screen. "He just got a little excited and beat us to the punch."

"Admiral?" 466 said as she also appeared. Snickerdoodle watched casually as more faces began to hide him from view. "We now have a way to shut down any Silent Eclipse drones aboard your fleets and thin their numbers!"

"Also, we managed to secure an alliance too," 917 reported from the background. "We should mention that first."

"Oh yeah," 117 nodded with a smile. "We're pretty much all good to go on this end. But uh... what's up over there?"

"Oh my god 117," Serina sighed. "When you speak to the people in charge of protecting our known universe, you don't just speak to them so informally like that."

"Ok, what would you have said?" 117 asked.

"Admiral Ra'aiah?" Serina said as she appeared on the screen. "Glowing A.I. speaking here. The Tandeeri leader has an idea on what we can do to prevent Silent Eclipse from doing any further harm on a bigger scale. If we follow his idea, we can probably eliminate any signals on Earth or Apogee Station since your people are all over the place."

"By all means," Admiral Ra'aiah said as she perked up. "What is he... uh, she... proposing?"

"*He.* He is proposing an immediate rescue of Earth," Serina replied with a thumbs-up as she casually gave the correct pronoun. "We'll get out of the way so he can talk again. It's quite an interesting plan. Sorry we all hogged the viewscreen."

The amborgs on screen all slid out of view, revealing the Tandeeri leader once again. They all murmured apologies as they quickly got out of the way. He cleared his throat and grunted before speaking.

"Honored Admiral," he said. "Exposing the leaders behind this whole war is very difficult, as they are well hidden in the darkness. If one were to say, light up all the dark corridors and corners, we would still be unable to find them. But, if we take away their strongest assets, then your colonies, ships, and the innocent can be safe from these dishonorable evildoers. We will take away their ability to hide."

Snickerdoodle glanced to his right off the screen and lowered his voice to a whisper.

"How was that?" he asked. "Did I say that correctly?"

"That was nicely spoken," 593 commented from the side. There were many murmurs of agreement that followed her statement. "You sell it, big guy. Definitely an award-winning speech."

"We should rescue the Earth of this universe," he declared. "Then, if we succeed here, we can bring the fight to the Alpha universe."

"That sounds like a very interesting plan," Dr. Kendrick said.

Talveeya also cleared her throat, and they noticed her hand resting on her chin as she regarded them with a thoughtful expression.

"I agree," she stated. "I mean... I need more details about what's going on, but it seems like it's a very well thought-out plan."

"I'm actually with Second Admiral Ra'aiah," Dr. Kendrick coughed. "What is the plan?"

Ishala waved at the screen.

"We can do exactly as the Tandeeri leader suggests..."

Then, she stared at nothing and paused. Ishala looked at Snickerdoodle and stammered.

"I-I apologize. W-what was your name again? I never caught it."

"Here we go..." 917's strained voice blurted out from off-screen.

Snickerdoodle's eyes seemed to light up as he pleasantly dipped his head to her.

"No one can translate and speak it in English. But it is a great honor Dr. Kendrick," he said in his deep voice as he glanced at him cheerfully. "You have raised some very brave young humans. It should also be noted that it was Carolina 466 who gave me a name in your English language. It is my honor to be called this. You may call me... Snickerdoodle."

Everyone who heard this abruptly stopped what they were doing. Talveeya gazed at the screen questionably. Ulgo slowly turned to look at them from his position as all of the other bridge officers were beginning to stare. Dr. Kendrick and 6 gazed at the screen in disbelief, and Ishala stood frozen, completely taken aback. It was the dramatic pause just before delivering the name that seemed… strange and epic.

"Like… the cookie?" Talveeya sputtered as she tried to hide her forming grin.

Dr. Kendrick's spectacles slid to the rim of his nose as his mouth hung open.

"Did he just say…?" he said. "Snickerdoodle?"

"Snickerdoodle?"

A couple of them turned to see 43 strolling back onto the bridge.

"What'd I miss?" 43 glanced at everyone curiously. Then she saw the viewscreen. "Whoa. What *did* I miss??"

"Snickerdoodle?" 6 asked, ignoring 43's question.

"Snickerdoodle?" 43 responded, growing more confused.

"Snickerdoodle?" Ishala asked nervously.

Snickerdoodle nodded his head firmly.

"Snickerdoodle," he declared boldly in a loud and booming voice that seemed to echo. Then he looked offscreen. "Hmm, everyone seems to question this name quite a lot. Is it not to your liking?"

"Oh no! It's so… you!" Ishala said quickly, forcing a smile. "Right?"

She looked around for some backup. There were several murmurs of forced agreement from the crew. Ulgo pulled the tip of his hat down and nodded. 6 and Dr. Kendrick also added their praise. It was slightly exaggerated but at least it was just enough to keep the Tandeeri leader appeased.

"466," 6 muttered. "Don't take this the wrong way, but were you drunk?"

466's voice spoke from the screen.

"No," they heard her chuckle meekly in the background. "I had a legit reason."

"This is going to be such a weird report," Ishala sighed as she shook her head. "Anyway… Mr. Snickerdoodle? What do you say to… coming aboard our ship? Or… can we continue this after we get our fleet back in order?"

"This is acceptable."

CHAPTER 11

I Have Friends Everywhere

A.I. Industries
Emergency Command Operations

"You're kidding."

4 stared at 18 on the video call.

"I can definitely tell you that I am not joking about this."

18 gave 4 a look of disbelief.

"The man who lives in the basement," she said. "The man who hasn't gone out in years is in charge of A.I. Industries?"

"He is qualified and the highest ranking official at A.I. Industries," she stated.

"Oh please," 18 scoffed. "You and I both know that there is one other higher-ranking official hiding out back at A.I. Industries."

"If I'm not mistaken, weren't you in the middle of an investigation?"

18 let out a sigh and shook her head. 4's smile faded, feeling concerned.

"As far as I can tell," she lowered her voice, "one assailant attacked the White House. Restored footage shows a drone of some kind. Powerful and different. It killed the S.C.E. diplomats and officers here at the White House and based on the damage, I've concluded it was trying to assassinate President Holland or take him hostage."

"And it just... disappeared?" 4 asked.

"It's either still hiding somewhere in the White House... or it's disappeared into the city," 18 shrugged. "Whatever this thing is, it's good. Plus, I'm willing to bet that there are more of them."

"I think you're right."

4 pulled up a map of the world on her screen and transmitted it to 18. She glanced away from her screen and then nodded at 4, indicating that she had received it.

"I've been looking through all of the reports that we've been getting and it feels like we're fighting ghosts around the world," she explained.

She pulled up an image of the United Nations headquarters and sent it to 18.

"Most of the world leaders decided to shelter in place when they heard about the attack on the White House. No other place has been hit like that. They're all terrified."

"Well, it makes sense," 18 replied. "Didn't I also hear rumors that several other countries have taken the S.C.E. diplomats and officers into custody?"

"They're not rumors," 4 said. "It's getting bad out there."

"Do you think I should return to A.I. Industries?" 18 asked.

4 laughed and shook her head. 18 arched an eyebrow, clearly confused by her reaction.

"Honestly? I feel like coming to join you," she admitted.

"What's going on?" 18 asked.

"Nothing," 4 answered. "It's just that we've lost contact with Apogee Station."

"Oh no..." 18 replied in shock.

"First, no contact from Dr. Kendrick after the S.C.E. fleet left Earth's orbit, now Apogee Station," 4 stated. "Sure, reading out Dr. Kendrick's last will and testament is one thing, but what happens if we're about to witness the end of the world?"

"It isn't the end," 18 stated determinedly. "Not yet."

"Really?" 4 asked. "Because we've been infiltrated by a covert team of... Terminators."

"I really regret telling you that," 18 sighed.

"They are fast, able to blend in, and based on what's happened, incredibly strong. How are they not Terminators??"

18 stared at 4 as she continued to recap their current situation.

"The amborgs currently deployed around Earth are outnumbered," 4 stated. "This isn't like the last emergency recalls. Robberies, burglaries, looting, fighting, and all acts of violence are being reported everywhere. It's like all the stuff that we were hoping to prevent is happening as we speak."

"Yeah... I can see how that might be pretty stressful."

"19 got redirected to calm down the situation at PHL airport when the White House was attacked. They've grounded all flights there."

This was understandable since everyone was probably terrified on the East Coast. 4 looked at the roster of available amborgs.

"I'm going to have 95 and 53 return to A.I. Industries once they finish doing their checkup in London. Actually... maybe they should check on 723 when they get a chance."

4 looked at 18 on the screen.

"Do you want to try giving our little 'lone wolf 2.0' a call?" she asked.

"She's extremely focused and difficult to work with when she runs off by herself," 18 shook her head. "Without her mentor, she's a loose cannon."

"999 isn't actually registered as her mentor, is she?" 4 raised an eyebrow.

"Not officially," 18 replied. "She's just adamant about seeking forgiveness from both her and 917."

4 gave 18 a knowing look.

"Because she tried to kill you and 917?" she asked.

18 nodded.

"You know," 4 muttered, "I have your report and 917's report. Why is 723 taking so long to submit her version of the events?"

"Oh gee, I don't know," 18 rolled her eyes sarcastically. "Maybe if you were part of an illegal off-the-books organization where they trained, molded, and groomed you for most of your life to hunt down the amborgs might have some long lasting effects on you. That's just a working theory and 917 and I both have the scars to back that up."

A sudden ping snagged 4's attention. She smiled and transmitted the update to 18.

"35 managed to secure the zoo," she said. "The central U.S. location."

"That would be the third time that we've deployed there, right?" 18 asked.

"Yeah, they seem to always have the strangest security breaches," 4 nodded.

There were currently only five of these zoos in existence around the world. During World War III, public attractions were closed due to the circumstances at the time. Most governments chose to protect their wildlife by relocating them underground into vast towns and cities built to shelter everyone from nuclear fallout.

After the war ended and reconstruction efforts began, a significant issue the world faced was the deficiency of biological wildlife.

Many species became endangered as a result of the war, and although several locations attempted to safeguard and shelter animals underground, only a small number could survive throughout the prolonged years of warfare. With countless species struggling to thrive without the availability of open natural environments with adequate sunlight, the populations of large animals began to drop drastically. This made many surviving animals expensive and rare commodities.

A handful of wealthy individuals overseas possessed private collections of unique rarities. Some of them kept certain animals as pets, which did not cast them in a good light in the eyes of the general public. Fortunately, numerous animal rights activists, backed by influential figures in high society, worked tirelessly to oversee various wildlife protection zones and national parks, facilitating the recovery of wildlife. Several prominent zoos reopened, and with the advancements in automated drone technology, many locations began featuring animatronic or robotic animals as their main attractions. These exhibits and zoos employed non-biological techniques like robotics and holographic technology to educate visitors about zoology.

Given the extensive history of animal cruelty, most people considered these robotic zoos to be incredible technological achievements, as they did not involve the captivity of real animals for entertainment.

However, in 35's particular mission, the Central U.S. Robotic Zoo had some sort of malfunction. 4 quickly read the incident report that he was writing to them.

"A power surge shorted out the lion's cage," 4 remarked. "And then when the gates accidentally got opened, it unleashed the entire pride."

"Oh no," 18 shook her head. "They're all robots but manufactured to have the same level of strength as real lions. Every animal they have built there are supposedly stronger and faster than the real things."

"There's going to be one hell of an insurance claim when this is all over," 4 chuckled.

"Ah, so you're not dreading the end of the world now?" 18 asked.

"Temporarily," 4 nodded.

The door opened to the operations room and 4's attention shifted. She was pleasantly surprised to see the two women who'd entered the room.

"Well now, this place has definitely been through an upgrade since I last saw it."

4 stood up and shook hands with Nova. Mandy was at her side and looked happy to be home.

"Nova! Or should I say... Daphne," 4 smiled pleasantly. "It's so good to see you."

"Kat! Likewise!" Daphne nodded. "Thanks for sending backup to check in on me."

"Holy shit, is that Daphne?"

Daphne heard 18's voice and approached the camera so 18 could see her clearly. 4 stepped aside as Daphne's face brightened with joy.

"Kiden!" she let out an excited squeal of delight. "You still keeping these kids in shape?"

"You know it," 18 replied. "Once we all get back, are we going to expect you to stick around for a while?"

"Maybe," Daphne nodded. "I'd really love to see... you-know-who again when he's not busy in outer space."

Every other employee in the room was busy on their headsets and focusing on their work. Daphne glanced around cautiously before turning her attention back to 4 and 18.

"Has there... been any word?" she asked as she looked at Mandy last. "Dr. Kendrick? Or Leonard?"

The room fell silent when she raised her question. Although each person in the emergency operations was aware of Daphne's identity, it was clear that she was trying to downplay her connection as amborg 1's ex-wife. She preferred not to draw too much attention to herself.

"No," 4 shook her head casually. "I'm so sorry."

4 glanced at Mandy, then peered behind her shoulders. Usually, Daphne had drones escorting them.

"Where are Jim and Leo?"

Jim and Leo were older generation drones from A.I. Industries. In fact, both of them were in service when Dr. Kendrick's parents were still alive. Even though their current model had been long retired, there were still a handful of them running around A.I. Industries or assigned to former employees of the company. With Daphne, she had taken Jim and Leo with her when she had decided to leave.

"Visiting the repair bay," Daphne smiled. "I did a good job maintaining them but... let's face it, they were long overdue for a service check and thankfully, you have the best auto mechanics in the world here."

Daphne then looked at 18 on the screen.

"And since I'm here, I'm not going to sit back and relax," she informed them. "How can I help?"

"It'll be really good to hear your voice again providing backup," 18 grinned. "Every person at A.I. Industries is one more supporter we need. How's Thalia?"

"She's doing well," Mandy said with a smile. "Her mom is too."

"Oh yeah, you're going to have to tell us about that," 4 nodded. "I heard Marina is a dispatcher now."

"911 Las Vegas," Mandy nodded.

"Another dedicated heroine," Daphne beamed.

A loud ping grabbed their attention. One of the dispatchers whirled around, his hands raised.

"Supervisor!" he called.

"What is it?" 4 asked.

"Train derailment," he reported. "Union-Pacific 221. It crashed on the rail line heading from Phoenix to Union station. They're requesting amborg assistance."

4 nodded.

"18," she said as she glanced down at the monitor. "We got to go."

"Understood," 18 nodded. "Signal me if you need me to redirect."

"Negative," 4 replied. "Stay there. I'll find someone to deploy immediately."

18 nodded and then disconnected the call. As the screen went dark, 4 looked at Daphne and shook her head.

"I need a partner to go with me," she said.

"Wait," Mandy's eyes widened. "You want to go yourself? Why not someone already out there?"

"A team of two or three amborgs would be able to help the first responders out there much more efficiently than one," 4 explained. "We're already stretched thin and I have to be out there."

4 turned and smiled at Daphne.

"Besides, we have a legend in here who can manage the situation."

Daphne nodded confidently.

"Go get 'em," she said.

4 nodded curtly to Mandy and respectfully left the room.

"Don't tell 18 until after I'm onsite," she reminded them as she disappeared through the door. "Otherwise I'll never hear the end of it."

Mandy glanced at Daphne.

"You got this, right?"

"I might be a little rusty."

Daphne grabbed a headset, slipped it on, and then took the seat that 4 was previously positioned at.

"But there's no place like home," she smiled as she connected to the system. "Alright, amborg 4 is on the way to the accident site. Mandy, would you like to work with me or do you want to play technician again for 4?"

Mandy confidently took a seat next to Daphne and logged into the computer. She sent a request to 4, asking if she could be the amborg technician for her. While she waited to see what 4's response would be, she opened another tab and began to search through their emergency contact list.

"What do you need?" she asked.

Daphne glanced over at Mandy's screen and looked impressed.

"Aren't you the multi-tasker?" she grinned.

"Keep up with the times grandma," Mandy winked.

"Alright then kid," Daphne scoffed at the challenge. "Train derailment. Let's look for two amborgs to deploy alongside 4 as backup. Prepare for a mass casualty situation. We need to find out how many passengers were onboard when the train derailed and if anyone else was caught in the accident zone. Send out all available RA units. Notify USAR for search and rescue. We need police to set up a mobile command and to monitor and redirect traffic."

"Wow, you are good," Mandy replied as she began to look up the numbers for the army reserve while searching for which first responders would get there first. "As expected from one of the first technicians that literally wrote the book on how to take care of amborgs during emergency situations."

"It's been a long time since I had to deal with a train accident," Daphne answered as she typed on her keyboard rapidly. "Speaking of trains, whose idea was it to drop a freight train from the sky during the Dominoe Incident?"

Mandy let out a laugh.

"That barrage? You want me to tell you about it now or later?"

"Depends on how good you are at multi-tasking," Daphne turned and smirked at Mandy.

"Uh, it was Serina 43 who brought the amborgs all the arrows they needed but 501 was the one who stole a freight train," she answered quickly. "Alright, it looks like the train crashed somewhere near LA county. I am contacting LAPD and LAFD right away. I think we can also provide our amborg teams with some additional support from a few non-affiliated individuals."

"Care to elaborate?" Daphne asked.

"We have some good friends in California that can definitely help us out here."

Los Angeles, California
Arts District
10 Minutes Earlier

"Now, how about you do the right thing and reconsider your actions?"

A heavily tattooed man sat tied to a chair in the middle of a wrecked room. He squirmed, then cried out in pain when he was punched in the face by a strangely energetic old man wearing a hood.

"Screw you old man! Everyone was taking shit in that department store! Why am I the only one tied up?!"

The old man smirked as he looked down his nose at his prisoner.

"Because you, as of right now, are my newest friend. I suggest you tell me where you've stashed everything that you've taken.

The semi-stable old man that was running a rather haphazard interrogation was Mark. Out of context, this looked like a typical shakedown between a criminal and... an even older criminal. The truth was, this man was a vigilante and also related to an amborg.

"Yo, this is messed up man!"

Just as Mark opened his mouth to speak again, a loud noise snagged his attention.

A door swung open and slammed against the wall as someone made a grand entrance. Heavy footsteps pounded across the room from the floor below. Slowly, the steps approached the stairs, and they could hear the booming echoes of each footfall as someone ascended, closer and closer.

"The hell is that?" the man whimpered as he tried to inch away from the door.

"Backup," the old man smirked.

"Mark! You better have a very good reason why I'm here and not overseeing the city of Los Angeles right now!"

Mark turned around to see SWAT commander Marsha Bradley stalk through the decaying doorway. She had her weapon drawn and looked extremely pissed. Seeing her anger while carrying a heavy duty shotgun sure brought back a lot of memories of the good old days.

"Well, I'm glad you took the time to visit after I called," Mark smiled. "This gentleman here has some information for you."

"Fine," Bradley let out a huff as she walked up to the man tied down and stared at home menacingly. "So, who are you?"

The man didn't waste a second as he frantically looked at Mark.

"You got to arrest this man! He's out of his... mind-eeep."

Commander Bradley pointed her shotgun directly below the man's waist. He instantly shut his mouth.

"Out of his mind?" she looked at Mark and nodded. "I already know that. What you should be worried about is when my patience gets tested. Now unless you want your nuts evaporated, I suggest you tell me something useful. I'm really itching to shoot someone so please, do say something stupid."

The man gulped as he looked between Mark and Commander Bradley.

"A-lright! Alright!" he stammered as he nodded eagerly. "A bunch of us were planning to hit a lot of places! Everyone's doing that now since the President is missing and the White House was attacked, right?"

Marsha turned and gave Mark a side-eyed glare.

"You called me away from my command center because you wanted me to talk to this idiot?" she said. "He's literally acting just like most people in the city!"

Bradley aimed the shotgun downward once more, causing the man the flinch in terror.

"Ever since we've gotten visitors from outer space..." she griped. "Looting, robberies, assaults, carjackings, and price gougers! The entire world is losing their morals and turning to crime! You just admitted... to me and this moron..."

Marsha indicated to Mark with a sharp nod of her head.

"...that you were planning on hitting some places while everyone is panicking from the White House attack!"

Mark looked a little uneasy as Bradley suddenly leaned forward to glare at the man in the chair. Her weapon was still aimed at his most vulnerable spot.

"Ten years ago," she said menacingly, "I would have just shot you and I would have slept like a baby. Ten years ago, when society was much more unpleasant. And after a decade of reform and years of hard work, all of this craziness above us happens and everyone decides to just abandon their principles. Do you know who I am?"

"You're a police officer? An important one?" the man whimpered.

"I am SWAT commander Marsha Bradley," she snarled. "You better believe that if I consider you to be a waste of my time, I will gladly forgo my rank just this once and destroy you since our government is in shambles. But, taking matters like that into my own hands would make me no better than everyone I've locked away."

"His name is Edmundo Garcia," Mark stated. "His older brother is a lieutenant for Dos Perro Malos."

Marsha turned and raised an eyebrow. Then she looked down at Edmundo with interest.

"Now... that is something I can't ignore," she sighed and shook her head disappointedly. "Edmundo, what places were you planning to hit? If Mark is telling the truth, where else were your fellow gang members going to attack?"

"I'll tell you! Please don't shoot me!"

As a gesture of good faith, Bradley retracted her shotgun and pointed it away. As Edmundo let out a sigh of relief and started to calm down, she turned to Mark.

"Alright, I apologize," she said.

"I'm sorry I didn't properly explain to you when I called," he replied with an understanding nod. "I didn't know if you would believe me so that's why I asked you to come in person."

"If this guy's brother is making a move," Bradley pointed at Edmundo, "it's another claim for territory. Almost every gang in LA is itching for a fight. Without the President at the White House, every state in the country is starting to fall apart."

"Do you have enough people?" Mark asked.

"No," Marsha answered softly. "Every one I have is stretched thin. Did you hear that Harrison unretired himself?"

"He's got guts," Mark chuckled.

Marsha nodded in agreement. As they continued to watch Edmundo regain his composure and praise God for allowing him to keep his privates intact, she asked him a quick question.

"Have you heard from your grandson?" Marsha asked.

"No contact from him in days," Mark shook his head. "Are you worried about him too?"

"Yes," she nodded. "I hope he's ok."

She turned, making eye contact with Mark.

"And, since we're on the subject, are you doing ok?"

Mark blinked. He was slightly taken aback by the thoughtfulness of her question. Was this the same badass woman he had known for so long? Before he could respond, Marsha's gaze drifted over his shoulder, and all traces of concern vanished. Her expression quickly shifted from fury to shock.

"What in the actual...?! Oh!"

Her hand flew to her mouth, holding back a curse. Mark's stomach sank when a tiny voice spoke up behind him.

"Grandpa! I'm hungry!"

Edmundo turned in his seat and stared at a little girl, no more than two years old, in the doorway. He was just as shocked as Marsha. She quickly slung her shotgun around her shoulders and sputtered while pointing at Mark and the little girl who had just emerged from another room in the building.

"What is she doing here?!" Marsha demanded instantly.

"You have a kid??" Edmundo looked confused.

"Sarah," Mark chuckled nervously. "I told you to play in the other room!"

The little girl standing in the doorway was Sarah Wright 117. Marsha was absolutely furious.

"I take back my apologies and all the good things I said to you just now!" she declared. "What is your great-granddaughter doing here?!"

"There's a very simple explanation," Mark replied calmly.

"Grandpa came to pick me up and said we could wait for mama and papa," Sarah smiled cheerfully at the adults.

Marsha glared at Mark.

"And tell me... did Grandpa Mark tell anyone that he was going to be babysitting a little toddler while we're dealing with a worldwide crisis?!"

"What's a cry-sis?" Sarah asked innocently.

"Something that grandpa is about to be hit with once your dad gets back from work," Mark chuckled awkwardly.

"Why is she here??!" Marsha asked in a hushed tone.

"Look," he said. "Don't be mad. On second thought, forget I said that. You can be mad. She was being watched at A.I. Industries but then everyone got so busy that she was left alone!"

Marsha put a hand on her hip as he continued his explanation.

"David and Audrey were on vacation and Sarah was left at A.I. Industries with friends!" he said. "But then this whole invasion from outer space became a big deal and the next thing I knew, my cute great-granddaughter lost her parents temporarily because they decided to go back to work! Believe it or not, Mandy was the one who called me and asked if I could come and help out!"

"And no one noticed you taking her away from A.I. Industries?!"

"Look, I admit... taking my granddaughter with me while I continued working was a bad idea," he said.

"Uh, I'm pretty sure that was an extremely stupid idea..." Edmundo commented.

"Quiet!" Marsha snapped at him.

"Look who's talking," Mark replied sarcastically. "Besides..."

He looked at Sarah, who was having a hard time following their conversation.

"I'd say it was really nice spending time with her," he smiled.

"By removing her from one of the world's most secure locations?" Marsha raised an eyebrow.

"Yeah, that's messed up man," Edmundo spoke up again.

Bradley lifted her hand suddenly. Edmundo flinched and fell silent.

"The White House was attacked," Mark replied sternly. "Bill Holland brought his entire family to A.I. Industries and if whoever attacked the White House is still after him, then A.I. Industries is not where I want Sarah to be."

"Ok, I agree with Edmundo. That's stupid!"

"Did she just agree with me?" Edmundo raised an eyebrow as he glanced at them.

"Shut up!"

Edmundo clamped his mouth shut with a click when both Mark and Marsha snapped at him.

"That's a terrible risk!" she shook her head. "I understand but you clearly shouldn't have taken her! You brought a toddler to an interrogation!"

"We thought the White House was the most secure location and now look what's happened," Mark said determinedly. "A.I. Industries will come under attack if the President's location is discovered. I'm going to protect my granddaughter no matter what."

"This is ridiculous..."

Before Marsha could argue further, an incoming call on her radio cut her off.

"Commander? This is metro dispatch."

"What is it?" she grumbled as she answered.

"We have a ton of emergency calls," the dispatcher replied. "We have a train derailment that just happened."

"What?"

They all listened quietly as the dispatcher continued his report.

"We pushed the call to A.I. Industries and they're sending out a team of amborgs," he explained. "We've notified LAFD and we need police assistance."

"On my way," Marsha sighed.

"Can we help?" Mark asked.

Marsha glanced at Sarah.

"You better keep her safe," she warned him. "Otherwise Tinhead and his wife are going to come and tear you a new one."

"Understood," Mark nodded. "Where do you need me?"

"I got to call and see who the incident commander for that train derailment is," Marsha said quickly as she turned to leave. "Can you have one of your guys take Edmundo here to SWAT HQ?"

Mark nodded.

"I'm taking Sarah with me back to HQ," Marsha declared.

"What?" Mark's eyes widened.

"You heard me!" she snapped. "Your babysitting privileges have been temporarily suspended!"

Wisconsin
Abandoned (?) Munitions Plant
Security Room

The only thing inside the room was the faint whine from the computer monitors. An armed guard sat diligently at his chair but since he was the only one in the room flipping through different cameras and looking at nothing, he decided to stretch his arms and yawn.

"Next time the boss tells you that you're going to be in a really great place," he mumbled. "Just quit on the spot... I didn't even get a raise."

The guard's name was Ronnie and he was starting to question just about everything about this posting. This was a munitions plant but according to the public database, it was supposed to be offline. So, why was the Sullivan Corporation, his current employer, making him watch a giant piece of property that was completely restricted to the public?

The obvious rule that he was given when he started working here was that if he saw anyone, he was to avoid speaking to them and focus on his work. While he didn't mind spending most of his day sitting and doing absolutely nothing while getting paid for it, this felt a bit sketchy. On the other hand, given the chaos unfolding outside in the real world, having a peaceful environment to work in was nice.

"Unless the entire world has gone to hell," Ronnie muttered, voicing his thoughts aloud.

Out of nowhere, a piercing staccato of beeping broke the silence. The monitor to his left began to flash with a red warning light. Words popped up on the screen, showing what had activated the alarm.

Motion Detector: Security Room

What? Ronnie looked at the monitor and felt his heart beat faster. *The security room? The room that... I'm in?? Something had come in the room?*

Ronnie took a deep breath, swallowed his fear temporarily, and swiveled around in his chair to look around.

He exhaled softly and relaxed when he didn't see anything, grateful for not getting jumpscared.

The computer monitors connected to the security cameras of the facility were positioned all the way across the room near the door, the only entry point. Upon entering, the only way in was to go around a table. It resembled a pool table, but it actually had a built-in holographic interface. Typically, those kinds of tables were great for organizing meetings, monitoring the area, or providing a detailed map overlay of the entire space. Unfortunately, since the place was practically a ghost town, the only thing visible was the glowing clock.

With nothing seeming out of place, Ronnie turned around and faced the monitors. He stared at the alarm still blinking and then glanced at the indicator light. Next to it was the button to silence the alarm. Taking a chance, Ronnie pressed the button, and the noise abruptly stopped. He exhaled in relief as the quietness returned. He then got ready to log into the system to report the alarm's malfunction. Perhaps it was his sudden arm stretch above his head that triggered the sensors.

No, that couldn't be it. He had been working this particular shift for about a week. All of the simple movements he had made hadn't set off this alarm before. It had to be a glitch.

However, would someone even come to fix it if he reported it or logged it into the computer? This was still a really quiet and creepy place to be guarding.

Suddenly, the beeping returned. Ronnie glanced at the monitor. The same prompt was flashing on the screen again. He quickly whirled around and scanned the area. Still, there was no one in sight, or any evidence that something could have triggered the motion sensors.

Ronnie turned back around and slowly reached for the alarm button. He pressed it, silencing it once more. At the same moment, a loud crackling sound to his right caused him to jump.

"Ah!" he flinched when his radio went off.

"Come in, security room," a woman spoke over the radio. "This is HQ. Come in, please?"

"Jesus!" Ronnie exclaimed.

He picked up the microphone, hit the button on the side, and spoke into it.

"Yeah, I copy HQ," Ronnie sighed. "You scared the crap out of me!"

"Ha ha, sorry Ronnie."

The woman on the radio was another unlucky security guard that worked the opposite shift at this place. He had met her a few times during the shift-change passdown and thought that she was nice. Too cute, in his opinion, to be stuck in this line of work.

"Madison," Ronnie stated. "What's up?"

"Oh, just checking in," Madison said cheerfully. At least she sounded optimistic, which was comforting to him. "I got a report that you had an alarm triggered there. Saw that you muted it... twice now. Everything all clear?"

"Yup," Ronnie looked over his shoulder and replied boorishly. "Nothing going on."

"Just had to check," Madison replied. "Procedure."

"Yeah, yeah," Ronnie nodded. "Motion sensors got triggered. Says there's something in the room but... there's nothing."

"Hmm, it must be a faulty indicator," Madison replied. Then her tone took on a cheery note as she let out a giggle. "It happens. *Or...* it could be that super badass amborg that's about to knock you out from behind."

Ronnie let out a laugh.

"Ha!" he smirked. "Yeah. Very funny."

Then it dawned on him. Why did Madison suddenly say something so specific yet so random out of the blue? Just to humor her, he slowly turned around.

"What the...?"

He had only managed to voice part of the question when a fist collided with his face. Ronnie was knocked out of his seat and thrown to the floor.

The radio crackled and died, but Madison's voice kept speaking.

"Definitely that last one," she said cheekily. "Sleep tight Ronnie!"

Amborg Lizzy 723 of the Third Group examined Ronnie's body. She had successfully held back enough to avoid killing the poor guy. Still, getting punched by an amborg would most certainly leave a mark. He was definitely going to feel that in the morning.

"Wow. You set off the motion sensors, Lizzy? Talk about amateur hour. Aren't you supposed to be an expert in stealth?"

723's bracelet flashed as she answered.

"Your objective was to disable the sensor," she stated.

"Well, I couldn't do that until I was in the room."

"Unfortunately, I couldn't transport you into the room without triggering the motion sensors," 723 answered.

"I'm pretty sure you could have. There was enough time."

"Negative, I had to remain invisible. Are you able to access the facility's database?"

A flash of light appeared next to the keyboard. A small holographic girl appeared, grinning at 723. "Madison" gave 723 a wave.

"I'm already in," she smiled confidently.

Robin, the A.I. accompanying 723 on this particular mission, was a 15 year old program, one of the oldest that resided at A.I. Industries. Despite her age, she was still capable of functioning like any other A.I., and was not as obsolete as most people assumed she was.

"Give me a drive," Robin instructed.

723 pulled out a thumb drive attachment from her bracelet. Robin looked down to her left and a small lid popped open. 723 inserted the drive into the slot and it immediately connected.

"How long do you require?"

"Oh please," Robin let out a casual laugh. "I'm already done."

"Impressive," 723 stated.

"Yeah, not really," Robin shook her head casually. "Four tiers of security and 3056 bit encryption key. Not exactly rocket science. Did you know that most nuclear missile silos nowadays have over ten or twenty thousand bit encryption? And that's only tier one out of... a dozen security checks?"

"I don't understand why you're sharing this information with me," 723 raised an eyebrow.

"Just a fun fact," Robin replied. "Did you also know that any A.I. that goes rogue and tries to hack into most nuclear facilities will get defeated by the entity?"

"You refer to the rumor that there is a top-secret overlord program that defends all initial access to the world's most secure facilities on the planet?" 723 asked.

"Yeah! That one!" Robin nodded eagerly. "You see, an A.I. doesn't have access to a nuclear weapon. But isn't it ironic that there might be one... or... a program specially designed that prevents hacking of any kind? It's spooky, right? Humanity is terrified of an A.I. taking over the world but there's one that literally has the one job of killing anyone that tries to hack the system. Like, if I decide to cross one step into that system, then bam! It hunts and kills me!"

"I fail to understand the relevance to your story," 723 stated.

"I was actually messing with you," Robin stated. "Or at least, just passing the time. I encountered a few files that were much more encrypted and those programs and firewalls set in place to stop me were a little distracting."

"I understand," 723 nodded. "However, we should not linger too long. How much time do you need to transfer everything onto the drive?"

"A full transfer will be... 45 seconds," Robin replied as she looked at a progress bar that appeared on the main screen.

"Is it possible to decrease that time?" 723 asked.

"Depends on the limitations of the physical media, but don't get me started on that," Robin replied quickly as she concentrated on the transfer. Then she turned and looked towards the door. "Besides, that should give you enough time to deal with the team of security personnel who are about to come through the door. There's about five of them."

723's eyebrows furled as she quickly glanced at the entrance to the security room. It was quiet and the door was still shut.

"The entrance to the security room?" she asked.

"There's only one door in this room," Robin said sassily. "Oh, they just set a breaching charge by the way."

723 quickly pulled her gun out of her hip holster.

"Why didn't you inform me sooner?" she demanded.

"I just did! They're breaching in three..." Robin shrugged as she smiled at 723. "Two..."

"Robin!" 723 replied angrily as she pointed her weapon at the door.

"One..." Robin finished counting down.

723 changed her strategy and took a knee behind the table. She was partially behind cover and gave Robin an annoyed look before preparing for a fight. Robin floated over to 723 and crossed her hands behind her back calmly.

"Oh, don't worry, you'll be fine."

As soon as the words were out, the door imploded. The explosive charge sent the door flying straight at them, but... as it collapsed inward, they gradually began to spot the armed guards positioned outside, ready to rush in. Actually, it was just Robin perceiving everything in slow motion.

All the amborgs had the ability to retreat into their minds and extend their perception of time. However, for an A.I., they could extend it even further. As Robin casually glanced at 723 and then at the breached door, which was still falling, she let out a sigh.

She turned back around and saw that the files were still transferring to the drive.

"If 45 seconds is a long time to you, Lizzy," Robin smirked confidently, "imagine how long it can be for someone like me."

Robin put her hands on her hips and stretched her neck.

"Let's see what we've got."

723 remained at her current position, unaware of what was happening from Robin's perspective. The little A.I. floated over to the security guards like an electronic fairy and inspected their weapons. She did a brief scan and raised her hand to her chin.

"Well now," she said, intrigued. "You all seem to be pretty well armed. All this for just one girl?"

The weapons they carried were model 45 caseless submachine guns. As Robin pulled up a description of these weapons, another voice joined her.

"How's it going?" another girl said cheerfully.

"Hey Serina," Robin pondered. "Isn't the model 45 prone to jamming?"

Another light appeared next to Robin and Serina bounced up next to her.

This wasn't actually the real Serina. It was... an impression of her that Robin liked to chat with on certain occasions. A.I. programs could make copies of themselves or make imitations of other programs if they wished.

"The model 45?" Serina examined the description with Robin. "You're thinking about model 43."

"Ha, good one."

Both A.I. programs swiped the description out of the way and looked at the guards. The first three leading the group of five took aim at 723. Robin raised her hand and gave a slight wave, illuminating the barrels of the guards ready to shoot 723. Blue lines shot out from the barrels of their guns, streaking across the room.

Robin and Serina both watched the trajectory of the blue lines. They converged at 723, a multitude of red dots at the end trained on her forehead and chest. They needed to assess the ammo to gauge the extent of the damage, but given that 723 was an amborg and heavily armored, the impact might not be severe. However, if the guards realized she was a cybernetically enhanced target, they would likely do everything possible to overpower and disorient her with a barrage of bullets.

Robin cleared her throat.

"Don't you mean, *we're* thinking of it?"

"Technically, only you are thinking of it," Serina smiled. "I'm not actually here, remember? I'm just a simpler facsimile. An imperfect version of Serina."

"Well, I like having someone to talk to," Robin sighed, rolling her eyes. "I'm sure all the other A.I.s have similar methods to pass the time. It just gets lonely sometimes."

"Why don't we get a dog?" Serina asked. "Or how about a cat? You could program one."

"You know, we have considered it," Robin nodded.

Another flash of light joined them.

"Are we getting a pet?"

Taylor appeared on the other side of Robin. He clasped his fists together and did a happy dance.

"Can we please get a dog??" he asked.

"Not now Taylor," Robin shook her head politely.

"Aww..."

Crestfallen, Taylor looked down. Serina then pointed at the weapons.

"Hey, the model 45 has computer-assisted aiming functions! You could overload the systems! Their accuracy would drop by at least 53%"

"Sounds good!" Robin smiled. "Carter, you take care of that. Please?"

Another flash of light appeared and an impression of Audrey's A.I., Carter, popped up. Robin was a bright green color, Serina was blue, Taylor had chosen to appear in bright red and Carter was his usual orange color.

"It would be my pleasure," Carter leapt out at the guard's weapons.

He disappeared from view, and a split second later, they saw a small orange crackle of energy as he hacked the computers on the submachine guns. Serina pulled up the display screen and they watched as the accuracy of all the guard's weapons dropped 53%, then to 47%.

"Let's account for that and plug it into the predicted trajectories," Robin declared.

"Are you talking to me? Or Serina?" Taylor asked curiously.

"Technically, she's speaking to all of us," Serina smiled cheekily.

"Yes," Robin nodded. "Just thinking out loud."

The trajectory of the blue lines streaking across the room was altered. Robin noticed that the estimated projections were larger, but... they didn't sit well with her. 723 was still in danger of being struck. Even though each gun had an accuracy of 47%, she remembered that there were five guards to deal with, meaning five weapons with the same level of precision. They had to come up with an alternative to protect 723.

"Hey," Taylor pointed. "What about this? 723 could use the door as a shield!"

Robin glanced at the door that was still suspended midair, hurtling towards 723. Given its speed, the shape it had taken from the breaching charge, and its landing point, it was likely to bounce, hit the ceiling, and then land in front of the table. Taylor's calculations suggested that the door would fall on its side but briefly remain upright.

"Hey! Good idea! Thanks buddy!"

Robin held up both hands and pretended to look through a pair of binoculars. She highlighted 723's body and drew an arrow across the floor. She would direct 723 behind the metal door and take cover behind it.

"I think we're running out of time," Serina cautioned them.

"We're ok," Robin replied. "We just got to find a couple of more things to help Lizzy out."

"Are you sure we have the time?"

"Don't worry about it," Robin said.

"Are you feeling angry, Robin?"

Taylor and Serina flinched when a dark purple A.I. appeared. This one had blood red eyes and stared at them menacingly, but Robin didn't seem fazed.

"I am fine," Robin smiled politely. Then she waved her hand and slapped the purple A.I. out of the way. "Beat it."

The creepy purple impression of her vanished. Robin took a deep breath and continued examining the scene.

"That was scary," Serina shuddered. "I hate that we all have some small form of darkness that tries to take over."

"I know," Robin turned and put a hand reassuringly on Serina's shoulder. "It was my fault for getting annoyed. I know that you still think about the time an evil program corrupted you. Why don't you help me run a scan on all the guards we got?"

Serina nodded and floated over to all of five guards coming in. She stopped at the second one who was planning to move to the right after entering the room.

"This one has had knee surgery quite recently," Serina reported as she showed a skeletal image of a leg. "I think this will work."

The guard was likely going to be in a world of pain if her knee took damage.

"Thanks Serina," Robin said. She looked down and then pointed at the panel. "Let's blow the bolts on the maintenance hatch and give her a stumble. It might actually cause the guard behind her to trip over her."

A sudden loud boom snagged their attention. The guard at the head of the formation had pulled the trigger.

"First shot fired," Taylor stated cautiously.

"Ok, we got to wrap this up," Robin nodded as she looked at the computer. "Files still transferring. Let's check on 723."

The A.I.s gathered around 723.

The A.I.s all floated over and gathered at 723.

"Ok," Robin clapped her hands. "How's her aim?"

"She hasn't slept well lately," Serina shook her head. "The poor girl's been working hard but... I think she has nightmares whenever she decides to rest."

A small bar appeared next to 723. The words, "projected accuracy," appeared. According to their initial estimates, 723's accuracy was at 87%. This was surprising since the amborgs could maintain a 95 or higher at all times.

"Nightmares?" Robin asked.

"Remember when she only told us a small amount of information?" Taylor said. "That one time? She still has memories... really bad ones from before she was taken in at A.I. Industries."

"I'm starting to think that having nightmares before or after becoming an amborg is just a common occupational hazard now," Serina said grimly.

"It's ok," Robin smiled reassuringly. "She's fine."

Serina didn't seem too sure. She glanced at the bar and lowered 723's accuracy from 87% to 82%. This didn't make Robin happy.

"Serina," Robin sighed. "She's fine. Leave the accuracy estimate alone."

Serina conceded and the accuracy climbed back to 95%.

Once this was completed, they went over the best possible strategy. If 723 were to be sent in a different direction, the chances of her being captured or killed would increase dramatically. If the guards got ahold of the drive she'd plugged into the computer, it would jeopardize the entire mission.

After some final calculations, Robin looked at the results.

"Great! 97% success rate! Hey, who put in the probability of her getting injured?"

"We always calculate that," Taylor shrugged. "I don't think 723 is going to like that estimate."

They all noticed that the likelihood of 723 getting injured was 66%. Robin decided to ignore it.

"Well, if she decides to complain about it afterwards, then that means she lived to complain about it. Thanks everyone!"

Serina and Taylor smiled, then flew towards Robin. They disappeared as they rejoined her body, leaving her alone with 723.

"Alright," Robin took a deep breath and waved her hand at 723. "Just you and me now. Uploading and linking up with your HUD. Let's do this!"

From 723's perspective, the door abruptly bounced up, hit the ceiling, and crashed down.

"Roll right!" Robin commanded.

Without firing a shot, 723 obeyed and ducked to the right as the guards opened fire. She dodged every bullet as the door hit the floor upright and slowly fell towards her. She propped her shoulder up against it and used it as a shield.

Robin still had eyes on the entire room. She watched as the second guard tried to follow the leader but didn't make it too far. The maintenance hatch that she had blown open gave way, and there was a loud, painful crunch as the guard fell and shattered her knee.

As the guard screamed, 723 jumped out of cover and fired three shots. She managed to take down the leader, then the third and the fourth guards. The fifth one tried to shoot but as Robin predicted, he almost tripped and fell over the guard that had fallen through the floor plating. 723 used that opening and killed the guard with a clean headshot.

723 walked up to the second guard that was screaming and clutching her knee.

"Agh!" she yelled. "My knee!"

Without a word, 723 curled her fingers into a fist and punched the guard in the head, abruptly cutting off her screams. She collapsed and didn't make another sound. She was still alive, but was likely to never walk right again.

"Nicely done," Robin clapped.

"Thank you for assisting me," 723 replied.

"I told you you'd be fine," Robin grinned. "Transfer's done!"

723 went back to the monitors and pulled the thumb drive out.

"Objective secured," 723 stated. "The Sullivan Corporation's secrets aren't going to remain hidden for long."

As 723 began to leave, there was a low rumbling noise in the distance. She paused and Robin appeared at her side.

"What was that?"

Robin shrugged.

"That doesn't sound like an earthquake," she said.

Suddenly, a huge tremor shook the space, causing everything around them to sway as if a massive rug had been pulled out from under them. Thankfully, 723 managed to stay upright, but as they glanced up, a brilliant red light flooded the room.

"An electrical surge?" Robin looked puzzled.

They both turned to the monitors in the security room, which were engulfed in a strange red electricity. Was that electricity? No, it looked like something out of a fantasy novel. A red flame was burning through the computers.

Before Robin could even react or try to figure out what was happening, the lighting returned to normal. All traces of this red energy had disappeared completely. They awkwardly looked around and waited, seeing if anything else would happen.

"That didn't seem like a normal phenomenon," 723 stated.

"I think that's our cue to get out of here."

723 agreed and ran out of there fast.

CHAPTER 12

What'd I Miss?

A.I. Industries
Emergency Command Operations

"Ok, we all saw that... right?"

President Holland and his team of agents all focused on Daphne, who was currently overseeing the operations dispatch center.

"Mr. President," Daphne started.

"Bill," he interrupted her.

"Right, sorry, Bill. If I was still in my cabin out in the woods, I'm pretty sure Jim, Leo and I would have seen what we all just saw."

"Oh, Jim and Leo? Those really nice drones?" Bill's eyes lit up. "They're nice!"

"I know, right?" Daphne nodded in response.

Bill turned to Mike.

"How come we don't have security or agents like Jim and Leo?" he asked curiously.

Mike's response was quick, but professional.

"Older model sir," he explained. "Discontinued years ago."

"Darn it."

"Excuse me! Can we focus??"

Mandy clapped her hands, capturing everyone's attention. She glowered at each one of them.

"Right," Daphne coughed to hide her embarrassment. "Yeah. I definitely saw what looked like red demon fire travel across the room and... we're all still alive."

Then her gaze appeared to fixate on nothing in particular. Her smile faded and her eyes began to fill with dread.

"Unless we all got infected by something and we're about to die in a few seconds," she stated.

"Where did that come from?" Mandy asked.

"A lot of movies and tv shows that depict groups of people dying from a gas attack," Daphne shrugged. "We should probably call for medical assistance... unless they're also dead."

Mandy glanced at President Holland and his agents. Although they looked like they were ok, it was clear that Daphne's rambling was actually starting to make them nervous.

"There's an easier way to do this," Mandy sighed as she shook her head. "Can I get an A.I. to the emergency operations? Fast?"

In a flash of light, a female A.I. appeared.

"How may I be of assistance?" she asked.

"Hi Sheila," Mandy smiled. "Real quick, could you scan the room for any signs of a chemical attack? Was there anything in here recently that might have affected us physically? Are we in any danger?"

"Sure," Sheila nodded as she looked around. "Done. I don't see anything strange."

"Nothing?" Bill asked. "Also, nice scan time. That was fast."

"Just doing my job, Mr. President," Sheila smiled. "And to properly answer the questions I was given, there were no signs of any chemicals. I detect no abnormalities or changes to anyone physically and neurological scans have not changed drastically."

"But something did happen," Daphne spoke insistently.

"Yes," Sheila answered pleasantly. "I concur. There was an energy surge that passed through me and my main processing unit. I can only assume that you all witnessed it here."

"Uh," Bill lifted a finger. "You're not compromised by any chance... are you?"

"She doesn't appear to be."

Everyone glanced to the side, where Dr. Kolaski was shifting uncomfortably in a chair in the corner. He looked at Sheila and nodded confidently before hiding his face and averting his gaze to the floor.

"I-I know... my A.I. programs," he stuttered. "Sheila is behaving normally."

"Thank you," Sheila said pleasantly, then began to appear concerned as she realized that Dr. Kolaski was there.

"Uh, what's Dr. Kolaski doing here?"

"Replacement CEO of A.I. Industries," everyone chanted in unison.

"Right," Sheila responded skeptically. "That sounds... interesting, but I'm more curious as to why he is tied up to a chair?"

"He was trying to run away when we explained that he had to take over for Dr. Kendrick," Bill sighed. "How is it that you didn't know this?"

"I was busy," Sheila replied. "I was offline for an important appointment."

"So important that you missed the memo?" Daphne asked.

"Sheila is an FC program," Mandy explained.

Daphne nodded in understanding, and Sheila responded with a warm smile. President Holland furrowed his brow, clearly confused.

"I'm sorry, what's an FC program?"

"Sheila was created from flash-cloning a real human's mind," Mandy explained.

"That technique where someone can copy their mind, and it gets written into a new artificial intelligence?"

Everyone glanced at Mike, who immediately cleared his throat. He clasped his hands tightly and looked away.

"Yes," Sheila grinned. "Every now and then, you have to have an appointment with the person who essentially helped create you. There's like a weird mind-meld thing we have to do. It's like updating your phone occasionally."

"That sure explains why it seemed like you spoke differently," Bill smiled. "I'm guessing all the stuff that you say is similar to the host or person that created you?"

"If I were to be put beside the person that contributed to my personality," Sheila said, "we could be seen as siblings. Forgive me, I have something else to report."

Sheila then glanced at the main screen in front of them.

"I have begun a search with a few other A.I. programs here at A.I. Industries," she informed them. "We've begun listening all across the country and the world when that weird phenomenon hit us. Nothing seems to be damaged but it seems like there are a lot of people dialing 911 to report on... whatever it was that we saw."

"Where did this affect us?" Mandy asked.

"So far?" Sheila replied as she cocked her head to the side. "It's everywhere."

She glanced around the group and nodded to confirm what she had said.

"This energy wave struck the entire planet," she stated.

"Maybe the reason why nothing seems to be affected is because... it's from our visitors from space," Bill's voice suddenly grew alarmed.

"Oh," Sheila's eyes suddenly widened. "I'm getting a report from amborg 18."

She paused, concentrating on the incoming message. Then she looked at Daphne.

"Uh," she chuckled nervously, feeling uncertain about what she was hearing. "18 is reporting that she has found the assailant that attacked the White House."

Everyone fell silent. Bill stared back, wide-eyed.

"She found the... one that killed Marco?" he breathed.

"She is sending images to confirm," Sheila nodded.

"Daphne?"

The door to the center swung open, and Jim and Leo walked through. Before they could finish their initial greeting, Sheila flashed brightly and turned crimson red.

"Whoa!" she exclaimed.

Jim and Leo froze on the spot. They turned their heads and looked around frantically while everyone jumped from Sheila's outburst.

"Oh, never mind," she said as she switched from a red silhouette back to a light yellow color.

"What was that?" Mandy raised an eyebrow. "I don't think I can handle any more surprises."

"I thought I saw more Terminators," Sheila answered. "But it was just Jim and Leo."

The drones eyed each other before turning robotically to stare at Sheila.

"We look nothing like those machines," Jim protested.

"What did you mean when you said you thought you saw more Terminators?" Leo asked.

Sheila waved and pointed at the screen.

"Courtesy of amborg 18," she explained.

Everyone turned to the screen as images began to upload. As the pictures focused and came into view, they received a notification that 18 was calling them. Mandy promptly connected her call to the monitor.

"A.I. Industries, this is 18, do you copy?"

"Yes, 18," Daphne replied into her headset. "We copy you."

"Did you get those photos I sent?" 18 asked as her voice rang out of the room speakers. "I can transmit a live broadcast if necessary."

"No need," Daphne replied. "We see them clear as day."

"This is what attacked the White House?!" Bill exclaimed in horror.

The image was taken in one of the White House's hallways. Bill, Mike, and the Secret Service agents recognized the interior structure and layout. The picture was focused on what was lying on the ground.

"We have our culprit," 18 stated. "And I'm willing to bet that this metal bastard is why we lost contact with everyone up in space."

It was a drone, unlike anything they had ever seen. They could tell right away that it was definitely not from their planet. It was bipedal and had a conventional humanoid shape, similar to their own standardized drones. Yet, instead of a vibrant color scheme, it was painted in dark grey and sleek charcoal black. It appeared to have advanced high-tech armor and was quite bulky. There were no identifying marks or numbers on it whatsoever. When they examined a close-up image of its head and caught sight of its face, a sense of unease washed over them.

"No mouth," Mandy gulped. "Just one long horizontal line where the eyes should be."

She looked over at Jim and Leo, then to the security drones stationed in the corner. It was quite interesting to see two different generations of drones coexisting in the same space. There was a clear difference in design.

"You know something?" Mandy said as she nodded in approval. "I can see why our drones look much friendlier."

Drones were common and could be seen just about everywhere. There were several major corporations that manufactured and used them, and nowadays, most people could discern the different types.

Dr. Kendrick's father, Ethan, was a scientist with a strong fascination for robotic technology. Jim and Leo's design was created by Ethan Kendrick many years prior to John founding A.I. Industries. However, their model was now severely outdated and there weren't any factories or production plants that were interested in their design. Fortunately, the few that were still running around could still be maintained and repaired if they knew where to go. Older drones like Jim and Leo had been kept at peak functionality because, over time, they had developed very unique personalities after being in service for so long.

Before Ethan Kendrick passed away, he had always enjoyed giving the drones under his command basic human emotions and teaching them etiquette. He had always claimed that it was because he wanted to see if any of their robotic companions could grow to understand humanity. Unfortunately, the majority of society didn't really care about stuff like that. So, newer drone models and cheaper upgrades began to appear on the market.

"I appreciate the compliment," Jim dipped his head formally to Mandy. "But I can see why Sheila freaked out when 18 sent those pictures. Our color scheme is nearly identical to that evil drone."

"And this one attacked the White House?" Leo pointed at the monitor curiously. When everyone casually nodded in response, he lowered his hand. "It must be dangerous and built like a tank if it took on the White House defenses by itself."

"It is from another universe," 18 spoke up in the call.

The current model of drones from A.I. Industries were predominantly shiny and painted in bright shades of green or blue. They also had different colored stripes to represent the departments they belonged to, similar to how the amborgs could choose the neon stripe colors for their uniforms. The lifeless robot that 18 photographed appeared completely devoid of any markings, with no evidence or connections to its manufacturer.

Each drone was typically constructed to be six feet tall. All of them were the same height, unless they had to be modified for other specific tasks. Their chassis were made of special alloy plates that could withstand extreme hot and cold temperatures, small arms fire, and could allow them to operate mostly anywhere. Their power sources were specially designed batteries that could be removed, replaced, or recharged so they could continue running. The last notable feature was their human-like hand structure, which enabled them to operate and handle weapons, or carry and use a wide variety of tools that everyone else could.

The current drone model from A.I. Industries was designed to be sleek and more compact compared to the older versions like Jim and Leo. Similar to the evil, powerless robot from 18's photos, each drone had a light strip running across its faceplate. Employees at A.I. Industries encouraged every drone to pick an aesthetic that would give them a unique look, giving them a distinctive appearance to help them stand out among the hundreds that wandered around. In this case, one security drone on duty had two circular white lights representing its eyes. Meanwhile, another drone chose a single long bright light across its face, resembling a visor. While the drones lacked noses, they did have a rectangular or square plate to indicate where their mouths were.

The police and military also employed drones, but one notable feature about theirs was that they lacked mouths. They preferred the more affordable, standardized drones, which were equipped solely with eyes for visual capabilities. In Jim and Leo's case, it was clear that Ethan was a fan of Star Wars, as their designs incorporated more human-like features. They had circular lights for eyes, but older dark sensors that resembled human pupils, and they had mouths to enhance their friendly appearance. Rather than being created for combat, they were designed for recreational use and routine maintenance. However, this description seemed contradictory since they were currently serving as Daphne's programmed bodyguards.

"I don't know what it was that hit us," 18 continued her report. "But it exposed this thing. If it's been properly deactivated, I recommend we examine it immediately. It killed 125 and we've got it in custody."

"Unless it reactivates," Mandy stated. "Good job Kiden."

"I didn't do anything," 18 replied in a soft and mournful tone. "125 was the one who fought it to the very end."

"And we'll do what we do best," Daphne spoke reassuringly. "We're going to properly remember him and avenge him."

"But..." Bill cleared his throat politely. "If the evil ninja Terminator battle droid is already in our custody, doesn't that technically mean that Marco has been avenged?"

"Of course sir," Daphne turned and gave the president a gentle smile. "But we do need to find out what it is exactly."

"Oh, I've got several amborgs checking in too," Mandy spoke up. "Everyone is wondering what just happened. What do we tell them?"

"Stand by," Daphne replied. "That's all we can do until we get more information."

"For how long?" Mandy asked nervously.

Daphne glanced at her and shook her head, indicating she didn't have a good answer. However, they heard a soft voice behind them speak up.

"Uh... let's bring that dark ninja robot to a secure location."

Dr. Kolaski shrunk down in his seat when everyone turned to look at him.

"If John were here..." he mumbled uncomfortably. "He'd want to know what it was. But, bringing it here to A.I. Industries... what happens if it reactivates and kills us all?"

"He actually brings up a good point," Mike nodded as he shot President Holland a curious glance. "If that thing took out armed police and troops at the White House, it could do a lot of damage here too."

"Well, it does make me feel a little better seeing you take initiative, Robert," Bill grinned encouragingly. "I think we should announce him as the new CEO of A.I. Industries right away."

"No!" Robert Kolaski exclaimed, but he looked down at the floor nervously. "The majority of the board must be in agreement!"

"Well, under the circumstances," Daphne flashed Dr. Kolaski a puzzled look, "since we are in a state of emergency, they don't have the authority. Only when we aren't facing large disasters."

"That's right!" Mandy spoke up. "The decision to vote for a new CEO of A.I. Industries during an emergency doesn't go to the board or the shareholders. It goes to the amborgs."

"I apologize for being nosy but... why is that?"

Mike raised his hand as his brows furrowed. He looked confused but maintained a rigid posture.

"The amborgs are considered to be Dr. Kendrick's children," Sheila explained. "When John and Melissa Kendrick originally created them, they saw them as their own children. Several of them actually did end up becoming legally adopted and are considered to be officially family."

"So, any of the amborgs could nominate a new CEO?"

"It has been done before," Sheila nodded. "George Ramirez was temporarily appointed as the CEO by the backing of many amborgs from the First and Second Group during the first Emergency Recall."

"And it didn't work out that well," Mandy stated.

Everyone in the room remembered the Emergency Recalls. The current one was officially the fourth. The first incident involved the

United Nations and, regrettably, occurred while Dr. Kendrick was absent from A.I. Industries. In the end, the amborgs came together to save him, and George had to take charge of the company affairs. Soon after they reestablished communication with Dr. Kendrick, he collaborated with George as the situation resolved itself.

George's skills weren't enough to inspire a lot of confidence at the time and that was why it felt like he had failed being a temporary CEO.

Sheila turned to glance at Dr. Kolaski.

"Since amborg 4 is the leader of the First Group, she and 18 have the most seniority on Earth since Dr. Kendrick is out of contact," she explained. "She is strongly in favor of Dr. Kolaski taking the role."

18 spoke up again.

"I second that," she stated. "But, there's one other technical problem that you should address."

"What is it?" Daphne asked.

"There aren't any amborgs at A.I. Industries right now," 18 said.

Daphne and Mandy shared a look, then realization creeped into their eyes.

"And Kat went out to supervise that train accident," Daphne mumbled.

"Sheila?" Mandy glanced at the A.I. calmly observing the conversation. "What exactly does protocol say for situations like this?"

"Unfortunately, this entire incident is a first... mmm... *everything* in the history of our planet. Er... universe. I am afraid that if a suitable candidate fails to volunteer..."

She glanced at Dr. Kolaski.

"...or in this case, refuse the job. Then I'm afraid that control of the company will have to be forfeited into the hands of someone who would be greatly interested in A.I. Industries," she finished. "Whether or not it's one of our shareholders... or a rival company."

"Like the Sullivan Corporation?"

Everyone glanced at the monitor and noticed that another video call had appeared. 723 was watching them with interest, lightly waving her hand.

"Lizzy?" Mandy looked startled. "How did you...? When did you open a communications line with us? Were you trying to check in?"

"I needed to report something that I discovered," 723 replied promptly. "This matter cannot wait."

"What was that about the Sullivan Corporation?" Bill asked curiously.

"After an investigation of an abandoned factory," 723 reported, "I have determined that the Sullivan Corporation has been secretly behind the cargo ship incident that amborg 777 discovered in Los Angeles."

"That ship full of orphans??" Mandy exclaimed.

"T-that sounds... intense," Robert stammered from his corner. "Wait. Sullivan Steelworks?"

"Lestor Sullivan?"

A loud crunching noise snagged everyone's attention. Mandy and Sheila glanced at Daphne and recoiled slightly. The former technician had suddenly grabbed her microphone and crushed it.

"Um, Daphne?" Mandy shuddered. "Are you alright?"

"No," Daphne growled. "Sheila!"

Sheila snapped to attention. She waited for instructions patiently.

President Holland glanced at Mike and the other Secret Service agents. They all decided the best thing to do was remain silent.

"Check all public records," Daphne commanded. "Look up Lestor Sullivan. The former CEO of Sullivan Steelworks or... whatever corporation he's still trying to run."

"Uh. Running scan," Sheila nodded obediently. She concentrated for a split second, then looked at Daphne. "I have the results. Lestor Sullivan died in prison in the year 2120."

"Then who's running this new company?!" Daphne demanded. "And how do we get rid of them?! Once and for all?!"

"Daphne..." Mandy said as she fearfully scooted her chair away a few inches. "You're scaring us."

Daphne shot Mandy a dirty look, but then blinked and realized that she had lost control of her emotions. She immediately unclenched her fists and tried to relax.

"I'm sorry," she said.

"Lestor Sullivan kidnapped Daphne's husband in 2116."

Jim stepped forward and shared a quick explanation.

"Oh," Bill's face fell. "I'm sure that must have been terrifying."

"May I share the full details?" Jim glanced at Daphne.

"You might as well," she replied in a soft voice.

"One year after John and Melissa Kendrick created the First Group amborgs," Jim shared a brief story. "Leonard 1 was captured by the CEO of Sullivan Steelworks. Lestor Sullivan was an old and delusional man who was a collector. He wanted to keep amborg 1 as a prisoner and treat him like some kind of priceless collectible.”

Daphne sighed.

“Fortunately, amborgs 2, 3, and 4 found him and saved him,” she said.

“My sympathies,” 723 spoke calmly. “I did not wish to stir any painful memories.”

“It’s fine,” Daphne shook her head. “I just heard the name Sullivan and it triggered me. That man was an asshole.”

“It would appear that someone kept the Sullivan corporation intact. I could have sworn that we shut it down,” 18 stated. “723. You found proof that this company helped with that cargo ship incident just before the Emergency Recall?”

“Correct,” 723 replied. “I require access to amborg 777’s reports from his mission in Port Hope.”

Just before the arrival of Serina 43 from the alternate Alpha universe, 777 had been deployed on a mission with 117’s grandpa. What was supposed to be a simple raid led to the discovery of something horrifying.

A large group of orphaned children and dead bodies had been discovered aboard a cargo ship docked at Port Hope. Unfortunately, the matter had to be set aside because that was when the Emergency Recall activated and all amborgs had to respond and report back to A.I. Industries.

777 had requested some extra time before returning to A.I. Industries to try and finish his investigation, but because the world was about to face a potential invasion from outer space, he had to give up on the mission and return home. From the look of things, 723 had decided to conduct a follow-up on her own.

“723, do I want to know why you took it upon yourself to investigate this?” 18 sighed. “You were instructed to offer assistance in the Middle East.”

“My apologies, but I felt as if 777’s mission couldn’t be put off. If we abandoned it, they would have disappeared without a trace,” 723 replied. “I formally apologize for abandoning my original mission, but I felt that I should complete this one. I believe there is also a personal connection.”

"For... you?" Mandy asked.

"Affirmative, miss Mandy," 723 replied in a neutral voice.

Mandy turned to Daphne and let out a sigh. This appeared to bring a smile to her face, as she looked somewhat amused. Mandy shook her head.

"Again, with the 'miss' Mandy," she muttered. "I thought we were past that when the technician program was retired."

They heard someone clear their throat, and Bill stepped forward. He gestured towards the microphone and then at the large screen before them. With a silent widening of his eyes, he sought confirmation if he could speak. Daphne nodded and gave her consent.

"Well, that is a strong level of devotion and commitment," Bill nodded respectfully. "Amborg 723? I believe I would have no problem allowing you to continue your mission while we continue to figure out our other... worldwide issues."

"Hey, authorization from the president," 18 said confidently. "Sounds like a great idea."

723's response, however, didn't seem the same as before. In fact, there was a hint of hesitation and concern in her voice.

"I am not prepared to share full details in front of the President of the United States. Especially with my... background. It is a highly sensitive topic."

"Well, as you can see, we're in the middle of a logistical nightmare," 18 stated. "I think the president can handle it."

Mandy, Daphne and Sheila turned to look at Bill, who stared back in surprise. He quickly snuck a glance at Robert, but focused his attention to the front. He could feel the eyes of all the security drones and his agents on him, watching.

"Uh, well, I..." he stammered and shrugged. "I suppose I'm ready for whatever it is that she has to say? Unless... are we getting off-topic?"

"No," Daphne replied bluntly. "While we begin investigating the ninja Terminator, we're on standby. Everyone else has their own situations handled."

"Oh, we actually were? On standby?" Mandy's eyes widened. "Shoot. Let me signal all the amborgs."

Daphne raised her eyebrows as they shot Mandy an irritated glance. Rather than speaking up, she turned to the group and nodded.

"Go ahead, 723," she declared. "What is it that you need to say?"

There was a brief pause, and then her voice through the speakers.

"President Holland," 723 spoke formally. "Formal introductions are appropriate. My current designation is Lizzy 723, Third Group amborg."

"Nice to meet you," Bill replied politely as a smile formed on his face.

"Before I was accepted as an amborg," 723 added, "you should be aware that I was a former illegally enhanced cybernetic individual created for the purpose of hunting down specific targets."

"Wait what?"

His smile faded. Bill's immediate reaction was ignored as 723 continued talking.

"The organization that assigned me my missions forced me to endure long periods of torture and brainwashing to completely conform to their expectations. Some of my first targets were amborgs of A.I. Industries."

"Amborg-killers," Robert mumbled from his corner.

"Hold on, wait," Bill looked around frantically. "Is this relevant information??"

"I don't know but this is entertaining as hell," Daphne muttered, thoroughly amused.

"Wait for it," 18 sighed from the speakers.

"The organization was creating child soldiers and thanks to amborgs 18 and 917, I was freed from their control... after I tried to kill them both. As well as... other members of A.I. Industries."

"This is getting a little... too honest?" Bill gave everyone a pointed look as he chuckled nervously. "You share this with everyone you meet?"

"I was taught that honesty is the best policy," 723 stated.

"She should be in prison."

Everyone's gaze shifted to Mike. He seemed a bit defensive while moving to stand beside the president, even though there was no actual threat.

"Whoa," Mandy said, growing anxious. "That's not why she's telling her life story here."

"Yes," 18 stated. "Please stand down, Mike. 723 was pardoned five years ago when we brought her to A.I. Industries."

"And was she presented before a judge?" Mike argued. "You allowed an international cybernetic criminal to join you? Do you realize how many crimes that she just admitted to? She needs to be in custody."

"No!"

Everyone turned just in time to see Dr. Kolaski rise abruptly. Mike and the rest of the Secret Service tightened their formation, shifting slightly to protect the president. Noticing this, Robert remained where he was, but as soon as he saw the agents take a defensive stance, he froze on the spot.

"John isn't here... but I am!" he held up his hands peacefully. "And one of his amborgs doesn't deserve to be taken away. Especially... when it sounds like she's been working hard to undo all of the bad things... that she's done."

"Amen to Dr. Kolaski," 18's voice sounded impressed. "Oh shit, did I just give him a compliment?"

"N-no change w-will ever come..." Robert stammered as he thought hard about his next words. "Not unless we challenge the status quo. The amborgs have always done the extraordinary. In the interests of all mankind."

"Dr. Kendrick said that," Daphne smiled warmly.

Silence filled the room as everyone processed what was said. Then, Bill turned to address Mike and his agents.

"Mike," he said sternly. "That's enough. Stand down. No one is getting arrested or hurt here. The last thing we need is to go to war against A.I. Industries. It's not a fight we'd win."

That statement from the president made Mike realize he had spoken out of turn. He backed off and dipped his head with a disgruntled expression.

"Sorry sir," he said immediately.

Bill stared disappointedly at Mike. He shook his head and gestured to the monitor.

"Not to me," he said as anger crept into his voice.

"Yes sir."

Mike stepped forward and spoke loudly and clearly.

"Amborg 723," he declared. "I apologize for what I've said."

"Thank you," 723 replied from the speakers. "Your apology is accepted. However, I do understand why you reacted the way you did. I just hope you all know that I have spent the last five years redeeming myself."

"And you think that Sullivan Corporation is involved?" Bill asked.

"Yes sir," 723 responded. "If I am allowed to proceed, I believe I can find evidence that the corporation funded the cargo ship that was uncovered by Grandpa Mark and 777. This corroborates with the data that Robin and I uncovered in Wisconsin. I request permission to infiltrate."

Bill Holland looked at everyone in the room, but they could already tell that he had made a decision.

"Permission granted," he nodded. "I'm pretty sure that my word is good enough to sanction this."

"Directly from the president," Mandy smirked. "That's a first."

"I've sanctioned some of your missions before," Bill remarked with a chuckle.

"I think what she means is that this is the first one you've officially allowed to happen," Daphne stated. "I'm glad I voted for you."

"Me too," 18 replied.

"Same," Dr. Kolaski said.

Everyone turned and looked at him skeptically.

"I send in my ballot," he murmured softly. "I get my mail, just like everyone else."

"Thanks Robert," Bill smiled.

"You're welcome... Bill," Robert coughed awkwardly.

From the monitor, they heard 723 speak again.

"Please excuse me," she stated. "Commencing new mission. I will return home as soon as I am able."

The call cut off as she disconnected. 18's voice spoke again.

"We've managed to load the evil robot aboard a shuttle. I am about to proceed to a secure location with it," 18 reported. "I'm ready to move here."

"Hey," Daphne spoke sharply. "Mandy, do you see that?"

From their seats, there was a faint chiming coming from the console that Daphne was seated at. They recognized the signal immediately, but what made Daphne uncertain about it was that they didn't understand its point of origin.

"Incoming priority call," Mandy nodded. "That's the channel from Apogee Station."

"Put it through," Daphne's eyes widened.

The mood seemed to lighten up as they opened the channel. On the monitor, 18's face looked hopeful as they saw a new video screen appear. To their surprise, they saw another familiar face. Except, it wasn't a human greeting them.

"Taylor?" Robert's eyes brightened. "What are you doing in space?"

"Dr. Kolaski!" Taylor's holographic eyes seemed to glisten as he looked pleased to see them. "Out of the basement?"

"It's complicated," Robert mumbled.

"Sheila!" Taylor pointed two fingers at the screen in Sheila's direction. "How was your appointment?"

"I'm still alive," Sheila saluted.

"I'm really glad to see all of you," Taylor then turned his attention to everyone else. "Because I bring news from Dr. Kendrick!"

The mood brightened even further as everyone looked at Taylor excitedly. Even the stoic and professional Secret Service agents and security drones appeared particularly interested in this news.

"He's alive?" Bill was the first to speak up.

"Yes! Mr. President??"

Taylor looked at Bill and his eyes widened.

"Wait, why is President Holland at A.I. Industries? Is that Daphne? Wait... on your monitor... is that a picture of... how did you get pictures of the evil ninja bots that attacked Apogee Station?"

Everyone glanced at each other curiously.

"You mean that Apogee Station was also attacked by the evil robots?" 18 asked. "Shit, that means they're everywhere! We have to notify all amborgs and everyone near an S.C.E. shuttle to lock everything down!"

"Actually, that's what I was about to tell you," Taylor replied. "Dr. Kendrick sent us a message from the S.C.E. Firestar. There was a massive space battle out there and then, they fired a worldwide red weapon that swept across the planet! It targeted all signals of the evil robots and knocked them all out!"

"So, it was an E.M.P.?" Mandy asked. "But our systems are still up."

"It was targeting those evil robots specifically. Thanks to the Tandeeri!"

Everyone fell silent.

"I'm sorry," Daphne cocked her head to the side. "What now?? Are those the aliens that want to invade the Earth?"

"No, they are not. Taylor... would you mind connecting this channel and putting me through?"

They saw Taylor smile as he nodded towards the screen. Then, another chime sounded and a light began to flash from the main console. Mandy quickly opened the channel the moment she recognized a voice that sent a wave of relief through them all.

"John," Bill breathed. "You are a sight for sore eyes."

"Thank you," Robert muttered. "I'm going back downstairs."

"No, you don't!" Mandy snapped.

"Ok... wow... What'd I miss??"

Dr. Kendrick regarded them with wide eyes. He looked at Bill, who waved his hand eagerly at the camera. He turned and noticed Robert trying to hide, then Jim and Leo bowing politely to him, and last, glanced down and saw Daphne, Mandy, and Sheila waving as well.

"Bill is at A.I. Industries with Secret Service agents... Robert is out of the basement... Daphne, good to see you and Jim and Leo... Mandy, Sheila, and... who else is also... Oh! Kiden! And... you all have photos of a Silent Eclipse drone! Perfect! Maybe I don't have to explain everything!"

Everyone's smiles faded, and then they all began to speak at once.

"They're trying to make me take over!" Robert protested.

"Only because I can't do it!" Bill exclaimed, pointing at himself and Dr. Kolaski. "You left the company to me in your will but Robert is the most qualified man who doesn't want the job!"

"Wait, he left you a will??" Daphne asked, pivoting to him. "Do I have something? What about Jim and Leo?"

"Dr. Kendrick?" Mandy tried to speak fast. "Thalia found her mom, Marina, in Vegas! Everyone's ok! But when we lost contact, things went to hell down here and everyone is one more accident away from a total breakdown!"

"President Holland authorized a mission for amborg 723," Mike said courteously.

"Dr. Kendrick!" 18 spoke up, barely heard over everyone's voices. "This drone that I sent pictures of... attacked the White House and attempted to assassinate the president's family."

Each person could only manage to get out one or two sentences, and fortunately, they all noticed that their voices overlapped in the operations room. The drones remained silent, casting skeptical glances at one another. Unsure if they were expected to join in, the humans finally quieted down, and Jim decided to step forward.

"Dr. Kendrick," he greeted the monitor graciously. "Leo and I, as well as the other drones, are pleased to see that you're alright."

"Likewise," Dr. Kendrick flashed them a quick smile. Then he dialed up his energy and focused. "Alright... so what I got from all of... *that*... was..."

Dr. Kendrick gazed at everyone in the room.

"Bill is safe at A.I. Industries because of an attack?" he asked. Then he looked at Robert. "And you all were trying to replace me temporarily?"

"Oh look at that," Mandy nodded slightly. "He got most of it."

"More importantly," Daphne stated, "Dr. Kendrick, I've noticed there are a few fresh bruises on your face. Are you ok?"

There was a faint "oops" from the background and they saw a small hand reach out and dab a wet rag on Dr. Kendrick's cheek.

"Ignore me," 6 chuckled from the monitor. "I told you to let me finish applying healing ointment, Dr. Kendrick. But no, you had to quickly phone home."

"I just needed to let them know I was ok," Dr. Kendrick brushed off 6's hand, then began swatting at her when she tried to continue her treatment. "Ok, I'm fine! Tend to someone else who's injured!"

"I missed a spot!" 6 protested as her hand began to move insistently back towards his face with the rag. "Just let me...!"

"6! Please stop for a second!"

It was 18's voice that cut through the chatter, making everyone aware of Dr. Kendrick's sudden stillness. 6's hand paused just before reaching his face, and he cast a pointed look at the screen.

"Kiden?" Dr. Kendrick raised an eyebrow. "I thought I heard your voice. What is it?"

"Dr. Kendrick," 18 replied hesitantly. "Marco is dead."

Everyone fell silent as the mood dropped, becoming instantly bleak. Dr. Kendrick's expression fell, growing serious. 6's hand, holding the rag, dropped out of sight and then she appeared in the camera frame. She looked worried as she stood next to Dr. Kendrick.

"What?"

"I'm sorry," 18 replied. "Marco 125 was killed in action. He successfully saved president Holland's children. That's why he's staying at A.I. Industries."

Dr. Kendrick didn't respond, attempting to keep his eyes on the screen, though he averted his gaze just a bit. 6 glanced at him and then shifted her eyes downward, away from the camera.

"When was this?" Dr. Kendrick asked softly.

"On Earth, it's been three days since we lost contact," 18 stated. "Just after we stopped hearing from you, 125 responded to the sudden attack at the White House."

"We're coming home."

"What?" Mandy asked.

Dr. Kendrick nodded firmly.

"Admiral Ra'aiah?" he turned his head, looking to the side. "I need to return to the planet. Now."

"Uh. Of course. Weren't we going to begin that strategy meeting soon?"

"Please postpone it," Dr. Kendrick spoke urgently but professionally. "One of my amborgs was killed."

"Oh no... I'll have a shuttle ready for you."

Everyone watched as Dr. Kendrick looked at 6.

"Come on Vanessa," he said. "We need to go to the hanger right now."

"Y-yeah, right," 6 stammered.

"Once 117's team gets back to the Firestar, we need to go back to A.I. Industries," he commanded. "And Daphne?"

"Yes?" Daphne looked up at the screen as Dr. Kendrick faced them one last time. "How can I help?"

"Please recall Jesse. Amborg 274. Find him and bring him home. Right away."

Daphne nodded as she then switched her attention to her monitor.

"The amborgs are all going back to Earth," Dr. Kendrick stated. "Temporarily. We need a slight reprieve. We're also bringing our injured and wounded."

"You're the boss," Mandy nodded.

"Uh... John," Bill asked. "Are you bringing the wounded from... the alternate universe?"

"No," Dr. Kendrick replied. "Just our own. We all fought bravely, but I think we all need a moment to collect ourselves. It's um... been quite an ordeal up here and... obviously back home too."

"Yeah," Bill nodded. "That's an understatement."

"Once we get back," Dr. Kendrick looked at them with determination, "we're going to share everything. And once we've calmed things down, we're going to strike back."

"Strike where?"

Dr. Kendrick answered the president's question with a building ferocity in his eyes.

"We're going to the alpha universe and ending the war."

CHAPTER 13

Empty Seats

Auditorium One
Three Hours Later

The whole auditorium was silent and empty. If a pin dropped, the sound would noticeably echo throughout the entire place. The only person there who would hear it was Jesse 274 of the Second Group.

When he got the call to return to A.I. Industries, it felt as if his mind had gone on autopilot. He'd initially been assigned to protect Vincent D'astier, the President of France, and was away during the attack on the White House. He was meant to stay with the leader of France until the Emergency Recall officially ended, but when Dr. Kendrick reached out to him, he understood that this was the formal override of his special assignment.

After he checked in and was back on site, he discovered he was the only amborg present at A.I. Industries. He couldn't understand how the others were still out there, working, fighting, and protecting. As he sat in his chair, he tried to process the various stages of grief. It was the same seat he'd occupied when every amborg returned home during the fourth Emergency Recall. That had been the last time the Second Group would ever see 125 again.

274 turned his head and glanced at 125's vacant seat to his left. His best friend was gone and he was still trying to come to terms with that.

"Damn you Marco," 274 clenched his fist and closed his eyes. "You had to go and get yourself killed."

"Hey."

Without turning his head, 274 glanced up slightly and noticed someone standing in front of him. He was a few aisles away, but still within a safe speaking distance.

"Hi 117," 274 muttered softly. "When did you get here?"

"Just now," 117 replied. "How long have you been sitting here?"

"I don't know," 274 answered flatly. "Ever since I got back. When did you guys get back?"

"Our shuttle arrived ten minutes ago. We all came to find you."

"We?"

In a flash of light, Serina appeared next to 117's shoulder. Then, as if on cue, the doors to the auditorium opened and more amborgs walked in. Several of them hung back, but many of 274's closest friends were climbing up the steps to the Second Group section.

"Is this everyone?"

"Not exactly," Serina replied. "The First, Third and Fourth Group teams deployed immediately to help with everything they could around the world. The Second Group... needs a little bit more time before they're cleared to go back to active duty."

Every remaining member of the Second Group had all decided to be there for 274. He fought his hardest to hold back his tears as he tried to straighten up.

"You don't have to," he said. "We got a job to do."

"We know," 917 stated.

"Yeah," 777 nodded in agreement. "There is a job to do and it requires all of us."

From behind, 274 felt a hand on his left shoulder. He turned around to find 297 had quietly approached him, consoling him with a gentle smile.

"Yeah, we can't go on without finishing this job first," 297 declared. "We need to be here for you."

274 couldn't hold back anymore. He took one more look at 125's empty seat and began to sob. The instant he let it out, 297 waved his free hand at the others and immediately wrapped his arms around 274 in an attempt to comfort him. 57, 35, and several others moved in and formed a massive group hug.

"He's gone," 274 sobbed as he clutched everyone's arms. "Why did he have to go?"

"I'm so sorry," 57 whispered softly. "If we had gotten to him in time..."

"57," 66 shook his head. "There was nothing we could have done. None of you should be blaming yourselves. He was doing his duty."

As 274 continued to cry, the other Second Group members gazed at his empty chair.

"Did he... have a girlfriend? Boyfriend? A partner?" 917 asked. "Was he married?"

"Nope," 92 stated.

"He was in the dating pool just like most people," 93 finished.

"I think there was a cellist," Thomas 227 spoke softly. "The question is... if they had a thing going on. Do we inform her?"

"We should," Lexie 623 nodded sympathetically. "It's the decent thing to do."

"I blame him!" 274 cried.

274 lashed out as they all broke the hug and stepped back.

"He was an idiot!"

"Why?" 999 asked softly. "He fought a noble battle."

"For taking on that... thing! By himself," 274 glared at 999. "Alone!"

"He was doing his job," 297 said reassuringly.

"That drone... that robot... was out of his league!"

"Yes, that is true," 117 nodded. "We fought a small army of them out in space."

"He should have waited!" 274 sniffed. "He should have..."

"Allowed President Holland's kids to die?" 35 asked. "Sometimes there's no way out. He had to do what needed to be done in order to protect them."

274 looked away, but 35's words didn't seem to have fully sunk in. 57 placed her hand gently on the side of 274's arm.

"Look, Jesse," she said. "You can stay home as long as you need. If you think you're ready to return to active duty, 35 and I will clear you for it."

"Dr. Kendrick is grounding me?" 274 scoffed as hot tears kept rolling down his cheeks.

35 reached for his chest pocket and pulled out a handkerchief, but when he offered it to 274, he immediately batted it away. A little saddened, 35 respectfully withdrew his hand and politely backed off.

"He's just worried about you," 35 stated. "We all are. We know that you and 125 were the best of friends."

"I'd probably be in the same boat," 917 stated as he glanced at 999. "If Angel was gone, I'd be... a wreck."

"I feel the same," 999 replied.

"Yeah but 125 is gone," 274 grumbled. "He's gone and you're all still..."

He couldn't finish his sentence. Despite how upset he was, everyone stood their ground. They all knew firsthand what he was going through. Then, they heard the door hiss open.

"Oh whoa."

The Second Group, along with Serina, turned to see who had entered. They immediately snapped to attention and tried to formally welcome the newcomers, but were waved off.

"No please! No need for ceremony. We just thought we'd... stop by when we heard Jesse was back."

57 turned and smiled at 274.

"Jesse," she said, indicating to the door. "There's some people here to see you."

274 glanced up and saw two young teenagers quickly climbing the steps. The one in front was Leo Holland, the president's eldest son, and following close behind was his younger sister, Penny Holland. Both rushed over to 274's seat. 297 and 57 stood up to clear some space as the two young teens gave 274 a glomping hug.

"Jesse!" Penny exclaimed. "I'm really happy to see you!"

"Oh... I uh..."

"We were so worried!" Leo said.

"Hey you two. Give him a little breathing room ok?"

The amborgs respectfully backed away when they noticed President Holland and his wife, who was seated comfortably in a wheelchair at the center of the auditorium. Mike and his team of Secret Service agents stood guard, while 274 rose to his feet, mirroring the actions of his colleagues.

"I apologize Jesse," Bill stated. "This is probably not an appropriate time."

"It really isn't," Caroline said in a soft tone. "But we had to speak with you when we found out Dr. Kendrick ordered you to return!"

274 wiped his face with his sleeves and shuffled out of the Second Group section with Leo and Penny, and they made their way down the steps together. The rest of the group remained in their spots and watched as 274 addressed the President and the First Lady.

"I know you don't feel too good right now," Caroline smiled sympathetically. "But, I do know that Marco 125 saved my children. Our children."

She held Bill's hand, both of them smiling warmly at 274. Caroline extended her other hand, and 274 took it as he stepped closer.

"I can only imagine how scared he must have felt," she sniffed. "Just as all of you feel when facing the unknown. I was scared too, worried that I might never see my children again. I'm not trying to make you feel worse or suggest that your pain is invalid."

"We just want you to know that you'll always have us whenever you need us," Bill stated. "I'm not saying that as your President. I'm telling you as a friend, in front of... your entire family. We all miss Marco very much. But I also know that... you're the one who is dealing with the full emotional brunt of it."

Without a word, Bill approached 274 and pulled him into a hug.

"All of my agents and security are trained to lay down their lives for me," he said. "I know it's part of their job but if I had been there, I would have given everything if it meant that he got a chance to live. I feel terrible that I snuck out."

"274."

There was a flash of light as Serina appeared next to him.

"Everyone," she said. "We need to stop dwelling on our guilt and speaking in hypotheticals. The important thing is, President Holland wasn't captured or killed by the evil robot. His entire family was protected and kept safe as a result. Even if you had been there, sir, do you really think it would have been better? No. If you had been assassinated, which Silent Eclipse is known for, then we would have lost you and potentially many others as well."

She turned to look at 274.

"Our entire government was kept intact because 125 decided to take it upon himself to fulfill his mission," she stated. "Mourn him. Yes. Remember him. Yes. But don't think about what might have been."

"She's right."

Everyone's gaze shifted to one of the doors as Serina 43 strode in. The entire Second Group stared in stunned silence at her unexpected appearance. Her amborg uniform's red neon stripes resembled 917's, but hers were a darker shade of red and exuded a heavier vibe. It looked as though she had emerged from the depths of hell, ready to annihilate them all.

She glanced around the room, startled to see the whole group gawking back at her.

"I know I'm not from your universe," she said. "But, I am still a Second Group amborg."

"Should we go?" 57 asked.

"If you want to," 43 replied, her eyes flicking to 274. "However, if you all stay, then it'll help me get my point across."

274 let go of Caroline's hand and 43 motioned for him to join her. The rest of the group gathered around as 43 took a seat and quietly asked 274 to sit next to her.

"Tell me about 125," 43 said in a soft tone.

"He was..." 274 took a deep breath and tried again. "He was fun. He always knew how to make everything better."

"You know," 43 looked at everyone in the room. "That's how it was for me too. When I had my friends and family."

"When I heard 18 inform everyone over the radio that he was dead," 274 said, "I seized up. I wanted to fly back from France as quickly as possible. But, part of me was afraid. I failed to be there for my best friend when he needed me."

"You would have foolishly gotten yourself killed too," 43 stated. "125 didn't fight that Silent Eclipse drone out of a desire to be a fearless hero. He did it because he understood that if he backed down or ran from those who bravely faced it, it would come after you and everyone else he cared about. In the end, he became a hero because he faced his fears and fought anyway."

117 and Serina shared a look but quickly redirected their attention back to what 43 was saying. It didn't seem like she was talking about 125. The way she spoke suggested she was thinking about the alpha universe amborgs that had been killed in action. They kept sneaking furtive glances, along with the others, as 43 continued speaking.

"I lost the love of my life," she said.

43 gently looked at 117 and made sure that 274 noticed as well.

"My 117. He was everything to me. We had our whole lives ahead of us," she said softly. "Then it got cut short. Didn't even get his body back to properly bury him."

"How did you survive getting through that?" 274 asked.

"I didn't think I could," 43 admitted. "It seemed impossible. What you're going through right now is similar to what I've felt for a long time. It's like trying to climb an endless mountain. All the while, you're weighed down by so much pain that you can barely move. That's the pain of memory. Of loss. But... you can't keep carrying it like this."

43 gently placed her hand on 274's shoulder.

"Don't make the same mistake I did," 43 said. "In this universe or the next, don't try to be brave and go back to work and ignore your pain. Don't start your next mission with your emotions bottled up. If you want to, in front of us or if it's just you in your quarters, let it out Jesse. It's ok to cry. Cry all you want. You need to let the physical loss hurt for as long as it stays. But also realize that every memory you have of Marco 125 is filled with warmth and love. That pain is a reminder. It'll always be with you. You'll feel it every day because that love that was generated by your friendship will never die. And when you're ready, you resume your active duty status and then you fight. You fight as hard as you can and you keep his memory intact by continuing to honor and avenge him."

274 shuddered, and a few more tears streamed down his cheeks. 43 continued to console him as 917 strolled over to 117.

"I think that I've said enough," he whispered. "I know that most of us were granted a two day furlough but… request permission to leave A.I. Industries?"

"For what reason?" 117 asked.

"It kind of seems a little awkward for all of us to be standing around, isn't it?" 917 stated. "I think 274 will understand. The world is still moving forward, even while we process losing 125.

117 looked at Serina. Then he glanced at 999. They all seemed to agree with what 917 was saying. It was somewhat awkward that the whole Second Group was hanging around, unable to really contribute while the president, his family, and 43 seemed to have taken charge of supporting 274. He still felt a little uneasy, but 917 was right. They had work to do, even if they had just recently returned from space.

They glanced around and noticed that several other Second Group members were politely excusing themselves, confirming that their presence wasn't needed. 117 realized that they were all texting him and notifying them that they all would stay if it weren't for the fact that many of them had personal matters to attend to.

Since he and 57 were the primary leaders of the Second Group, 117 shot a quick text to 57, who responded with a nod and a soft smile.

We'll just get back to doing our own thing, she wrote in a respectful way. *I'll keep an eye on 274 until it's time for you all to head back up into space.*

Then I'll have everyone check out with you, he replied. *I'll stay here. I don't think I should leave.*

117 looked at 917, who was still waiting patiently for his response.

"Sorry," he said. "You wanted to leave, right? Where are you heading?"

917 looked towards the president and his family.

"The world almost ended while we were away," he said quietly. "Without sharing too much information, I think there's a small part of it that I can put back together. Before we have to deploy back to Apogee Station."

"Ok," Serina raised an eyebrow. "But if you want to be discrete, you don't have to ask permission."

"I am doing it so that you'll know that I haven't gone rogue," 917 replied.

Everyone except 999 let out a small laugh. 917 was reminding them about what happened the last time he ran off without consulting anyone. Unfortunately, it came as a surprise to 117 and many others when they learned that his unsanctioned activities had landed him in prison for a few years.

"So, not taking Angel with you?" 117 asked curiously.

"I can handle this one myself," 917 smirked. "I'll be back in a few hours. Unless... would you like to...?"

917 glanced at 999, who immediately shook her head politely. Her sharp gaze didn't waver as she glanced at 274.

"I have some matters onsite to attend to," 999 replied. "My place is here for now."

117 glanced at the two of them and sighed.

"Sure," he said.

917 dismissed himself and said goodbye to each amborg that he passed. He exited through the door they'd all come in and disappeared.

"What's that all about?" Serina asked.

She and 117 turned to 999. She shook her head again.

"I think we've all been acting a little differently ever since we got off of the Tandeeri flagship," she replied.

"I get that," 117 nodded. "I was just thinking about everything we went through."

"So, your minds actually got scanned by the Tandeeri?" Serina asked with a curious look. "Everyone seemed so rattled."

"Be glad that you don't have a human body or a biological brain," 117 shrugged.

"I have a strange feeling that Snickerdoodle could tell there was something different about me," Serina shuddered as she concentrated. "It was like he could see traces of who I was."

117 then glanced at 999.

"What about you?" he asked gently. "Snickerdoodle seemed to overstep when he looked at you."

"Everything," 999 replied. "He and the Tandeeri probably know everything about me."

Earlier, when they were on the Heart of Alcyon, there had been that quiet staring contest between her and Snickerdoodle. 999 had explained that she was trying to conduct an experiment. However, to everyone else, they had no clue what that even entailed. Had it succeeded or failed?

"So, what did you do? What were you trying to accomplish?" 117 gently prodded, trying not to be too pushy about it.

"I tried doing what Snickerdoodle suggested and shielded my mind," 999 explained. She closed her eyes, lowering her head and shook it slightly. "I failed. The experiment didn't work."

She looked at Serina and 117 with a softened gaze. They both wore the same surprised expressions. Normally, she was stern, cold, and didn't appear to allow anything to faze her. The way that she was looking at both of them was new, an entirely different side of her that they were just now discovering.

"I thought I could live the rest of my life without my past being brought up again," she sighed. "So much for that plan."

"You didn't know that the Tandeeri had that ability," Serina replied symphathetically.

"I still decided to test my theory and we all saw that it didn't work," 999 stated as she straightened up and prepared to leave.

"I wouldn't say that," 117 cleared his throat, gently interrupting her.

999 and Serina both glanced at him, and he smiled back at them.

"Ten years ago, when we first became part of the Second Group," 117 explained, "you would have punched or thrown us through a window if we tried getting close to you. After working together and being friends with you for so long, you've come a long way."

The softness in 999's expression faded as she resumed her neutral and cold stare. It was as if she realized that her vulnerable side was slipping through, and she corrected it instantly.

"Just because they've seen everything... doesn't mean that you all know everything," she replied. "Please don't put anymore pressure on me about it."

"Actually, that... that right there, is progress!" Serina grinned as she pointed at 999. "In the past, Angel always expressed how much she despised our compliments. Instead of an angry retort this time, she sounded so cryptic and wise!"

"I know, right?" 117 nodded as the two of them exchanged pleasant smiles. "She's showing us more of her personality the longer we're involved in this Emergency Recall."

"Could you two stop having a discussion about me when I'm right here?" 999's brow furrowed as she slowly turned and began to leave. "I told you. Don't pressure me."

"Uh, w-we're sorry if we offended you," 117 stammered.

"Permission to return to my quarters for a few hours," 999 said, ignoring him.

117 and Serina both fell silent.

"Of course," 117 gulped.

999 walked away. However, before she exited through the same door 917 used, she spoke to them one last time.

"Don't apologize," she said. "I never said you two were wrong."

Then she was gone. Serina and 117 both looked at each other and shrugged.

"Progress," she beamed.

Just as 117 was about to reply, a small commotion broke out. Both of them looked over at 43 and 274, who had abruptly stood up from their chairs. President Holland and his entire family appeared a bit startled as the door on the opposite side of the auditorium hissed open, revealing a massive figure crouching down to step inside.

"Uh, 117," Serina's eyes widened in alarm. "Did Snickerdoodle say he was coming down to visit our planet??"

"I must have missed that particular detail," 117 stared in shock.

"Hello there!"

As he entered the room, Snickerdoodle straightened up and waved his claw at everyone still hanging around in the auditorium. His voice filled the entire room, reminding 117 of the first time they met him in the grand hall of his ship.

"Wow," 57's eyes widened.

"Holy... m-mother," Bill stammered. He managed to focus and looked at Leo and Penny before clearing his throat. "Flanagan."

"It's ok dad," Leo gulped. "We're adults, you can drop curse words."

"Yeah," Penny said, her eyes filled with wonder. "You're the President! You can say anything!"

"Kids!" Caroline smacked her son on the shoulder. "Not the time!"

Snickerdoodle fixed his attention on 274 and 43. 117 cautiously glanced at the Secret Service agents with President Holland. They were all maintaining their composure, but to most of the people in the room, this was their first encounter with an actual alien species. They were probably all struggling to keep it together.

"You are the one? The one brave warrior who is grieving?"

274's eyes widened as he looked to 43 for help, except she was also staring up at Snickerdoodle hesitantly.

"And you... look like you came out of a videogame?" 274 gulped.

From the side, Serina leaned towards 117.

"Should we help? I kind of want to keep on watching," she said.

"In a second," 117 nodded.

Snickerdoodle began to laugh as they continued to watch the scene unfold.

"501 was kind enough to show me what a... videe-oh game is," he smiled. "Very entertaining. But as much as I wanted to learn about your planet, I am afraid that we failed to act soon enough."

Snickerdoodle approached 274 and since he couldn't sit down in one of their human-sized chairs, he merely clasped his hands together and bowed his head respectfully.

"I apologize for not acting sooner," he declared. "Your brother, Marco One-Twenty-Five, would still be here if we had known."

He glanced at 117 and the other amborgs he was familiar with for clarification.

"Did I say his name correct? 125?"

"That was his preferred pronunciation," 57 nodded slowly. "Yeah, he got it. Is this the big Tandeeri leader that you named after a goddamn cookie?"

"Is there a problem?" Snickerdoodle looked at 57 curiously. Then his gaze traveled around the room again. "With my name?"

"No!" 57 squeaked. "Absolutely not! It's... it's..."

"Cute!" Caroline blurted out.

"I think it's really fun!" Penny smiled.

Bill looked at 117 and Serina and quietly mouthed, *"Snickerdoodle?"* Serina nodded as 117 awkwardly tried not to laugh.

"With all due respect, great... leader," 274 sighed. "It wasn't your fault. In fact... can we all just stop saying... if we had known? You can't!"

"I sincerely apologize and offer my condolences little one," Snickerdoodle's smile faded as his voice grew gentler, filling with sadness.

"But, this war with this one's people has unfortunately taken the life of your best friend. It is my fault and I want to..."

Snickerdoodle was gesturing to 43, who looked down, but 274 interrupted the Tandeeri leader again.

"Don't," 274 sniffed. "Don't say that. You don't know what it's like. He's gone."

Snickerdoodle bowed his head apologetically and didn't move any closer.

"If you hadn't come here... if you had just stayed in your own universe. You should go home."

Everyone listened to 274 as he began mumbling nonsense. Bill and Caroline held each other's hands. She looked up at her husband, as if urging him to say something, but he was unable to.

274 then glanced at 43.

"You don't belong here either," 274 stated. "You should pack up and go back to deal with your own mess. How many people died because of your mistakes?"

43 didn't have a response. 274 then angrily snapped his eyes up at Snickerdoodle.

"If you worked things out here, then we don't need you," he said. "This war doesn't involve us anymore. I'm done. President Holland can help with final goodbyes or whatever he does with visiting diplomats."

117 stepped forward.

"274," he said. "When 43 was hurt—my 43–that was my fault. Remember that?"

"It's not the same thing 117," 274 protested.

"Call it whatever you like," 117 raised his voice so that he wouldn't get cut off. "But when I was grieving, you were all there for me."

117 gestured around to everyone that was still in the auditorium.

"I was furious. I was pissed," he said. "We got the guy who wounded 43. We took him in and made him answer for everything he did! You know what? After we caught him, before he was turned over to the police? I wanted to kill him personally. Now that we've long since moved on from it, I don't even think I would have felt great doing that."

"Think about 917 or 999!" 57 spoke up, grabbing everyone's attention. 274 barely turned, listening quietly.

"He was in prison because he let his emotions dictate his actions!" 57 stated. "He lost his apprentice, his close friend, and when he lost his friends in the town of Silhed, he didn't just lose it, he stopped pulling his punches. He annihilated the ones responsible. Do you think that he feels better after committing to a terrible deed?"

From the side, Bill was leaning back to whisper to Mike.

"Why do I have the feeling we're bystanders to another classified story?" he mumbled.

"You can choose to leave at any moment, sir."

Mike's statement was accurate and the two men exchanged a brief look. Bill, however, decided to shake his head, and they all curiously looked on.

"And miss this? No way," he whispered.

"Yeah, we could use some popcorn," Caroline muttered. "I'm a little hungry."

Bill and Mike both stared at the First Lady, who was waving them off.

"I'm kidding," she replied.

57 was still trying to console 274 as best as she could.

"Darkness is in all of us," she said. "I know it's causing you a lot of pain! My twin sister deals with people's pain all the time and I'm amazed that she hasn't lost her mind at her job! We're trying to tell you that we'll be here to help you get through this!"

274 glanced at 57, then at 117, and then 43. He then looked at President Holland, the Secret Service agents, and Caroline, Leo and Penny. Then he looked up at Snickerdoodle.

"I really want to come with you to the alpha universe," his voice trembled as he allowed a bit of his rage out. "I want to kill whoever created that evil drone. I want to help find the one who sent that thing to kill us."

274 held back more tears as he looked at 43.

"I can still hear his voice," he said. "The last time we saw each other, we said we'd hangout and share drinks together to celebrate when this was over."

Snickerdoodle leaned forward and held out his claw to 274.

"Perhaps," he said in a gentle and soothing voice, "when this fight is over, will you have that drink with me?"

274 quietly looked at Snickerdoodle's outstretched hand, who patiently waited with an expectant gaze, but didn't push anymore than that. As everyone watched, 274 slowly nodded as a couple of tears escaped. He reached out and they both grasped each other's hands firmly.

It was a very sweet moment, and it touched the hearts of every person there. 274 took a few deep breaths, visibly calming down.

"Please," Snickerdoodle smiled. "Tell me more about your friend 125."

117 and Serina both gave each other a soft smile. Suddenly, 117 got a text notification. When he checked who had messaged him, he realized it was from 999.

Come to the cafeteria, she had sent him, *I think 466 needs you.*

"Serina," 117 whispered. "Let's go to the cafeteria."

Serina understood right away, and without another word, they left. Once they exited the auditorium, Serina leapt into the wall and disappeared in a bright flash of light. 117 began to power walk, rushing to find 999.

When he arrived at the cafeteria, he noticed that 501 was feeding Oreo. It looked like Snickerdoodle had brought his son with him to visit A.I. Industries. He was also amazed to see that several other Tandeeri were also here hanging out and enjoying a meal with several people. A few A.I. Industries employees appeared extremely comfortable interacting with them, whereas several others sitting close by threw uneasy glances towards the visitors. 117 looked around and saw that Serina was already here and waving at him from across the room.

117 made his way over to the table that 466 was sitting at. 999 was in the seat next to her, but from the look of things, 466 seemed to be heavily distracted, deep in thought. She appeared troubled, having lost all focus.

"Carolina?" 999 spoke gently. "Serina and 117 are here. Do you want to talk to them?"

466 bit her lip as she gingerly lifted her eyes. They followed her gaze and saw that she was looking at 501, who was playing with Oreo. They had somehow acquired some ice cream bars and were enjoying them together.

"466?" Serina smiled symphathetically. "We're here. Are you ok?"

"Is it about... 125?"

466 looked at 117, then at Serina and 999.

"He's really gone?" 466 asked, voice small.

"Yeah," 117 nodded. "18 is having his body transported back here as we speak."

"I'm sorry," 466 replied as she gazed down at the table. "I just... can't handle it."

"Hey," 117 said gently as he looked at Serina. "It's ok."

Even though what he was saying wasn't completely true, he needed a little more help. Without turning his head, he glanced at 501 and then at Serina. She grinned, understanding his instructions, and flew off to go and bring 501 and Oreo to their table.

"We'll get past this as best as we can," 117 said reassuringly.

"We lost 125," 466 exhaled sadly. "It feels like we were just at 345's funeral. 43's funeral too. And Teresa. There are so many people we lost."

"Teresa?"

117 had to pause for a moment to think about why that name sounded familiar.

The moment their eyes met, he and 999 immediately understood.

"Oh," 117 said. "You're thinking about that young woman you couldn't save."

"I thought I was prepared for this mission when I went with everyone to space," 466 said as she raised her head, struggling to hold back her own tears. "I'm not. I'm not up for this."

"None of us are," 999 replied. "It all started out as an invasion from space and another universe. Now, we discovered a much more sinister plot intent on destroying the S.C.E. fleet and the Tandeeri. We're way out of our league here."

999 glanced at 117. It was as if she was telling him that she had this one, so he respectfully watched.

"But I'm grateful for one thing," 999 said in a soft voice. "That you're ok."

"Why?" 466 glared at 999, unconvinced. "Why am I here instead of all the other people that I couldn't save?"

"We can't save everyone," 999 stated. "If I'm being totally honest, I'm glad that we aren't currently being invaded by an evil space army right now. Things could have turned out very differently if we didn't discover Silent Eclipse. You are here because you survived. It was all for a reason."

"Seems like a really cruel reason," 466 mumbled.

"What is really bothering you?" 117 asked.

"Dead or alive... I still see their faces!"

466's statement caught them both off guard. A small squeak and a cry caused them to turn. 501 was walking over with Oreo holding his hand and Serina floating next to his shoulder. The three of them had paused upon hearing 466's little outburst.

"When we were aboard the Tandeeri ship, I relived the moment that I killed Teresa," 466's breathing became short and quick. "It was like... I was crashing into her in slow-motion. I could see her getting injured as the car slowly crumbled around her!"

"466," 501 said with a solemn expression. "That wasn't your fault."

He was right. Everyone at the table, with the exception of Oreo, had been at that accident scene many years ago. After 466 was relieved from active duty and the investigation into the accident started, they immediately conducted a hard and meticulous search to uncover the factors that led to the crash.

According to the system logs, which matched 466's statement at the time, she had pressed the button to signal the traffic lights to change to green so she could pass. Unfortunately, they had found that when she entered the intersection, the light for Teresa hadn't changed. Instead of red, it remained green and she drove right into 466's path.

"He's right," 999 said. "It was actually an accident."

The circuit board inside the traffic signal had a faulty relay that had burnt out. When 466 activated the signal, it already wasn't functioning properly. Overall, the investigators cleared her of any wrongdoing.

"But she's still dead," 466 said.

"But not because of you," 117 replied. "I know it feels that way..."

"I. Drove. Into her," 466 enunciated. "You can show me all the papers and documents that say it wasn't my fault but it will always still feel like it is. I tried moving on but this whole experience has only proven that I'm unfit for duty."

466 shook her head and looked at 117.

"I resign my position as 501's second-in-command," she said.

"No!" 501, 999, 117, and Serina snapped simultaneously.

"You just need a bit of time," 117 stated. "I don't accept your resignation and clearly, neither do the rest of us."

"Right," 501 nodded. "I'm your leader! I don't want you to quit!"

466 stood up. She looked set in her ways as she prepared to leave. Before she did, she held out her hand to Oreo. They weren't sure if the little Tandeeri was paying attention but he reached out and gently held her hand. He let out a curious crowing noise as he jumped up and down. 466 realized that he wanted her to pick him up.

"I'm so sorry, Oreo," she said as she let go of his little hand. "Not now."

Then she looked at 501.

"The best thing to do is to let me quit and I'll remain here on Earth for the rest of this mission."

466 turned on her heel and rushed off. 117 and 501 attempted to follow her, but 999 raised her hand. She shook her head at them, and they both stayed put.

"What happened?" Serina asked 501 curiously. "That was a lot to let out."

"I didn't want to put a lot of pressure on her," 501 sighed. "She was pretty quiet the entire trip back after Dr. Kendrick told us about 125. I guess that was her breaking point. I tried talking to her to see if she wanted company but... she didn't want to hear me out."

"Did you use a joke?" 117 asked seriously.

"No," 501 said, matching his tone. "I thought about it but I feel like that would have made it worse. So, I decided to let her have some space."

"That's what we'll do," 999 nodded.

501 said his goodbyes to them as 999 and 117 decided to leave and discuss this particular incident. Serina decided to follow them while 501 and Oreo went to rejoin the other Tandeeri.

"What do you think?" Serina asked 117.

"As 999 said," he nodded. "We'll give 466 some time alone and as much space as needed. Truthfully, I hope that when we take the fight to the alpha universe, I hope that she'll join us, but I understand if most of us have already been stretched to the limits."

There was a sudden flash of light as Serina changed from bright blue to green. Then, in seconds, she switched to blue again.

"Uh, 117?" Serina said with a perplexed expression. "Did you allow Sarah to leave A.I. Industries?"

117 paused. Hearing his daughter's name got his attention. He had originally intended to see her as soon as possible when they returned, but he had figured that checking in on 274 took precedence. He had already decided to make up for it and apologize to Audrey at the earliest convenience.

"No? Why?" he felt dread building in his stomach as he stared at Serina. "What do you mean? I didn't allow her to leave at all."

Serina looked at 117 and 999 with widened eyes. Then she nervously fidgeted and anxiously clutched her holographic hands.

"I have good news and bad news," she stated bluntly. "Your wife's here! And your grandpa Mark seems to have brought Sarah back home. Ah, screw it. I don't know which of those was good or bad news. I have just... two pieces of news for you."

117 and 999 shared quick glances.

"Didn't you leave Sarah with Mandy before we left?" 999 asked.

"Yes," 117 replied hastily as they began to move.

"But... if Mandy went to go look for Thalia in Las Vegas," Serina said as she followed them. "Who was watching Sarah?"

"I have a feeling we're about to find out," 117 began to grumble in frustration.

117 instructed Serina to meet with Audrey, Mark, and Sarah. He wanted to bring them to his family quarters. When Serina left, she had 999 go and get Mandy. This would be interesting.

CHAPTER 14

World's Most Forgetful Parents

Amborg Residential Area
David 117's Family Quarters

The whole room remained silent. 117 sat next to his wife, Audrey. They casually glanced at Sarah, who was busy scribbling away on several sheets of paper at a small kid's table. Grandpa Mark was seated in a comfy chair, uncharacteristically quiet.

When 117 met up with his family, his daughter was incredibly excited to see him. He'd smiled and given her a big hug and a huge kiss on the forehead. When Audrey managed to make her way to a nearby A.I. Industries safehouse, she was able to acquire a quick ride to join them.

Of course, they didn't want to start a fight in front of a little girl, so 117 pretended that things were alright. Audrey and Mark were mildly bewildered by his reaction at first, but they soon played along.

Now that they were essentially spending some quality time together, the atmosphere felt peaceful, but there was a subtle tension brewing beneath the surface.

"So," 117 broke the silence as he held Audrey's hand. He glanced at his grandfather. "I am glad to see you doing alright."

"I appreciate that," Mark smiled politely. "Uh, how are you Audrey?"

"I'm doing great!" Audrey grinned. "Uh, there was a lot of paperwork I had to sort through."

"Really? In this day and age, the government still uses paper?"

"It is old-fashioned but paper files do have a form of authenticity, a unique advantage compared to using a computer to store everything."

"Right," 117 nodded. "Paper files are an old method for system outages or if the servers get hacked. We still have a department that handles physical mail at times."

"People still do mail packages and cards and letters," Mark nodded.

The three of them smiled awkwardly and shared a quiet chuckle before falling into silence. The only noise that broke the stillness was the sound of Sarah's scribbling.

"And kids still draw too," 117 stated.

"We're still deciding if we want to get her a tablet," Audrey explained. "Most schools require them but I don't want her to spend all of her time on one of those things."

"Oh," Mark coughed softly. "You should probably confiscate a Christmas present that I got for her."

"Or you could just not give it to us and get her a different present?" 117 suggested.

"Ah, good point."

A sudden chime from the doorbell caused them all to perk up.

"Come in!" 117 called out. "It's unlocked."

The door slid open and two people entered. 117 was pleased to see Mandy and Thalia.

"Wow," Thalia exclaimed. "Did you redecorate?"

"I don't think so," 117 shook his head. "We tidied up before the Emergency Recall."

Audrey rose to her feet and pulled her friends into a warm group hug. As they greeted each other, Sarah glanced up from her drawing and stood up from her chair.

"Thalia!" Sarah cried out with glee. "Aunt Mandy!"

117 and Mark watched as Mandy and Thalia said hello to Sarah. With her attention diverted, 117 gave his grandfather a pointed look. Mark responded with a firm and pleasant nod. They were biding their time, waiting for the right moment to start a serious discussion.

"Hey," Audrey said. "Sarah, do you want to go play with Thalia for a little bit?"

"Yes!" Sarah replied cheerfully.

"Get her some ice cream since she was such a good girl," 117 cleared his throat. "We need a moment."

Thalia kept smiling, but as she glanced at each of them, she got the message right away. Gently, she took Sarah's hand and began to lead her towards the door.

"Come on, Sarah! Want to go get some dessert?"

"Ok," Sarah waved goodbye to everyone. "Are they going to fight again?"

"Maybe," Thalia shot them an alarmed look behind Sarah's back. "But we're not going to stick around and find out!"

The door automatically opened as Thalia nervously ushered the little girl out. The moment the door shut, all hell broke loose.

"You kidnapped my daughter?!" Audrey rounded on Mark.

"And let her see you interrogate a criminal?!" 117 added.

"Whoa," Mandy's eyes widened. "What?! You let her see... what?!"

"I am not the one who abandoned a little girl while you both went off to be heroes!" Mark argued in response. "Worst parents ever."

"You're one to talk!" Audrey freaked out. "You stabbed my husband when you introduced yourself to him! Not even going to touch that bit of hypocrisy when you left this family to do your Assassin's Creed... thing!"

"We didn't abandon our daughter," 117 said, his tone heated. "We were on vacation and she was safe here! Why did you take her away?!"

When 57 had come looking for 117 after the initiation of the Emergency Recall, he and Audrey had been taking a brief respite from work to be alone. Unfortunately, since they had to immediately report in, it meant that they had to return to active duty.

After 117 and Audrey got married, they'd bought a house in an undisclosed location far from A.I. Industries to start their family. Most of the time, when he wasn't on a mission, he was in that hidden corner of the world so they could live in peace. When they planned to take a vacation, they took their daughter, Sarah, to A.I. Industries. When their trip was interrupted, Audrey had to report to Washington D.C. right away since the military had been activated nation-wide, while117 left with 57 to retrieve 917 from prison and 3 from her restaurant. Before they all went to space, 117 was lucky enough to say goodbye to Sarah briefly and take comfort in the fact that she would be staying in a secure location.

"I told you!" Mark sighed. "I wanted time with my great granddaughter!"

"But you weren't supposed to take her away from here!" Audrey face-palmed.

"When did you even get here to see her??" Mandy asked.

"When she called me."

"What?" 117 and Audrey exclaimed simultaneously.

"When did she do that?" Mandy crossed her arms and stared at Mark in confusion.

"I don't know what I find more insulting..." he scoffed as he held up his hands defensively. "The fact that Sarah called me a few times just to check in on me... or the fact that my own grandson and grand-daughter-in-law left her alone..."

"She wasn't alone," 117 and Audrey corrected him apprehensively.

Mark raised his voice to finish his sentences without being interrupted. He pointed at 117.

"...while you went to space!"

Then he rounded on Audrey.

"And while you went to go fill out mountains of paperwork instead of giving a shit about the rest of the world!"

"Did you just forget that I don't have your abilities?!" Audrey retorted angrily. "I have to be the one to sit at home while you and David run into danger almost every minute of every day! You took my daughter into a crime zone and she witnessed you beating someone up!"

"I didn't kill him," Mark replied.

"You still beat him up!" Audrey snapped. "How many times have you done this?!"

"She's only seen me do that once!" Mark started to say but then paused. "Er... this year!"

117 and Audrey exchanged glances, then looked at Mandy. She merely shrugged in response.

"I'm not sure if I can really back you up there," she said apologetically. "My dad showed me violent films my entire childhood."

"Who subjects a child to something like that?" Audrey groaned in frustration.

A spoon clattered, drawing everyone's attention to the corner. Mandy flinched when she noticed that someone else was witnessing the entire argument. 999 sat at the dining room table, appearing to be enjoying some ice cream from 117's freezer. She was slowly consuming what seemed to be a family-sized tub of it.

"Angel??" Mandy choked.

"If we're talking about correct qualifications," 999 mumbled as she scooped more ice cream out of her tub, "I saw worse things when I was around Sarah's age."

"Ok, sorry," Audrey lowered her head. "Almost everyone here has been exposed to some pretty traumatic things when they were young.

What I'm trying to get at here is that we need to try doing better raising Sarah!"

"What would you have me do?" Mark shrugged. "Deny to her that the world isn't messed up? That it's really a magical fun-filled place of joy perfect for a kid that's part of a new generation?"

"We're just trying to keep her safe!" 117 replied. "And you jeopardize it whenever you take her away from A.I. Industries!"

"She called me because she wanted you, you dolt!"

Both 117 and Audrey recoiled when Mark suddenly shot out of his chair, towering over them. Instead of jumping up to confront his grandfather, 117 stayed seated, his eyes widening as he stopped speaking and looked at his wife. He turned his gaze back to Mark, who was clenching his fists and trembling slightly.

"Uh, guys?" Mandy murmured nervously. "Let's not escalate!"

999 quietly stopped eating her ice cream to cautiously stare at Mark. She remained still, her expression turning serious. 117 could tell that she was coming up with a tactical defensive strategy, but was confident that she wouldn't have to utilize it.

"What?" 117 asked Mark gently.

"Do you know how much your daughter loves and misses you every goddamn day?" Mark curled his lips into a frown and unclenched his hands. "After she spoke to Audrey on the phone, and Mandy ran off to Vegas... she called me! When she couldn't reach you, David!"

Mark then gestured around the entire living quarters.

"How long did you leave her here at A.I. Industries or at home alone when you two were busy with work? How many times? Yeah, it's true that I would spend every available moment I had with her... but what about you? Where were you when she needed you?"

Mandy shifted uneasily as she glanced at her friends still seated on the couch.

"Damn it," Mark sighed as he placed his hands on his hips. "You're just like your dad, David. Yeah, he and your mother loved you... but from what I found out, they were so busy with work that they weren't there for you. Not often enough."

117 glanced down at the floor.

"You shouldn't focus too hard on what you do," Mark spoke softly. "Not if it makes you forget about the most precious gift that you created. That's what I failed to do with your dad. I hoped that he would do better than I did, but then he and your mother died."

"I thought that..." 117's voice caught. "I thought we were doing enough as parents. I thought that things were better for Sarah."

"If that's true," Mark sighed. "Why are we all sitting here arguing about this?"

An uncomfortable silence passed as everyone's shoulders sagged and their expressions dimmed. Mandy bounced on her heels, unable to remain still. Finally, Audrey turned to Mark and spoke.

"I'm sorry, grandpa," she said.

"I never wanted to tell you this," Mark shook his head. "But you two keep trying to hold your family together by not wanting to be there. You make your friends help you do it instead."

"I just want to keep protecting the world," 117 stated. "Because if I fail..."

117 looked at Audrey.

"I lose the world that's right here. Unfortunately, Mark is saying that we'll lose Sarah if we continue to neglect her."

"Do you think we need to have that discussion again?" Audrey asked with a hesitant sigh.

"What discussion is that?" Mandy asked.

"We once talked about... divorce," 117 stated.

"Whoa," Mark held up his hands defensively. "I didn't say all of that in order to get you two to split up!"

"No! He's talking about... a conversation we had when we were coming back from our honeymoon," Audrey replied quickly. "There were so many terrible things happening around the world. Every time we saw something negative on the news, I would always catch that look in 117's eyes."

She reached for his hand and grabbed it tightly.

"He would always wonder," she explained, "he would think, 'what if I was there?' And we both almost decided to quietly end our relationship because we wanted to keep saving people. After a long period of fighting and discussions, we decided to stick it out together. Then the next thing I knew... I was pregnant."

Audrey lifted her eyes to Mark.

"I know that we didn't really do things correctly when Serina 43 dropped in from another universe," she said. "But what's done is done.

I know that you have concerns about how we raise our family but... I don't even know if we're going to do a good job. But I do know..."

Audrey looked at 117, who smiled back gently.

"I know that I'm not going to be alone in this family," she declared. "It's a big family that I've married into, and we all look out for one another."

Mark slowly chuckled as a smile broke out across his face.

"I guess that's that," he said.

"I'm really glad we didn't dissolve this family," 117 stated.

"Alright," Mark held up his hands in surrender and proceeded to head towards the door. "I guess... I'll say goodbye to the world's cutest great-granddaughter. Oh, I had a couple more things."

Audrey and 117 glanced at Mark, who was looking back at them, now full of curiosity.

"Is it true there's an alien from outer space here at A.I. Industries?" he asked.

"Did you want to meet Snickerdoodle?" 117 asked.

Mark's smile faded and stared back, dumbfounded. Audrey mirrored his expression as she scratched her ears, wondering if she had heard correctly.

"What?" Mark uttered.

"It was 501," 117 explained.

Mark and Audrey nodded in understanding. They all shared a collective "oh" when 117 directly stated why Snickerdoodle's name was official.

"I kind of want to meet him now just to see if you're messing with me," Mark said, skeptical. "Also, I was going to ask that when you go up into space again, would it kill you to send a message?"

"Would you like to have my last will and testament?" 117 asked.

"Ok, don't even go there," Audrey spoke nervously.

As they gradually began to reconcile, Mandy looked over at 999, who'd gone back to consuming her tub of ice cream.

"So," she said. "Have you been there the whole time?"

999 gave Mandy a slight nod. With her right hand, she continued to spoon ice cream out of the tub. With her other hand, she pointed at the freezer. Then, with a sharp flick of her wrist, a second spoon appeared in her left hand in a quick sleight of hand magic trick. 999 motioned for Mandy to join her at the table.

"There's more ice cream in the freezer. Join me. It's delicious."

Mandy nodded and walked into the kitchen, leaving the others to chat.

"Oh, what the hell?" She opened the freezer to peruse the various flavors.

Gymnasium

"Run it again!"

In the center of the gym, 466 was performing a round of reflex training. Just a few weeks ago, she had been in that exact spot with a group of friends for what was supposed to be an evaluation. In reality, it turned out to be more of an improvised and upgraded dodgeball class. Unlike typical school classes, this one had security drones tossing a variety of objects.

This time, she was alone and feeling more hopeless than before.

"Run it again," she said to the drone in charge.

"Pardon me, amborg 466," it replied diligently. "This has been your seventh test for 917's improvised reflex training. If I may suggest..."

"Thanks," 466 interrupted. "But I didn't ask for your suggestion."

She wiped the sweat off her head and looked at the drone in its single red glowing eye. It had a broken eye sensor, making it look like a one-eyed robot pirate.

"Please confirm and run the test again," she declared. "Override."

"Override accepted," the drone nodded and proceeded to the outer ring of the circle. "Signal when ready."

The drones took to their formation. 466 surveyed the group as they prepared their arsenal of weapons. Some had guns that fired rubber bullets, others held rifles that launched taser shots, and a few more were equipped with arm cannons that could fire bean bags. 466 lowered herself slightly and honed in on the drones.

There were 12 in total, completely surrounding her. She closed her eyes, took a deep breath, and readied every sense in her body. 466 did her best to ignore the pain lingering from the previous round. Her right shoulder still stung from the impact of a taser shot. After she finished concentrating, she made the call.

"Begin," she commanded.

As projectiles were launched at her, she poured every ounce of her stretch and speed into evading them. She thought back to what 917 had said to 501 before ramping up the difficulty of this exercise.

"I want you all to picture the drones as your enemy," he'd said. As she focused intently on each of the twelve drones firing at her, she clung to 917's words. "They are not from A.I. Industries. They are not friends. Let's pretend that they are out to kill you. Keep your eye on them and anticipate! Pretend that I am not here to help. Pretend that 466 has just been killed and you've been backed into a corner."

That's right, she thought. *He told 501 to picture me dead in order to motivate him. Maybe... I should do the same thing?*

As 466 attempted to think about the absolute worst thing that could ever happen to 501, a flood of visions began to surface. Rather than simply imagining 501 getting hurt or killed, she found herself recalling a growing collection of past memories.

There was the moment that Serina 43–Epsilon universe 43– passed away in the hospital. 466 had looked up to 43 like a sister; a friendly, energetic and wise older sister. After that, she struggled with her grief for a while. Even with 117 trying to help take care of her and 501, she knew that their squad had lost one of their most influential members. Eventually, she watched 117 grow closer with Audrey until the day that she sat with everyone else and witnessed them tie the knot.

After they went on their honeymoon, 501 and 466 were on their own. Even though he always kept their spirits up, she couldn't help but feel that everything she was doing was only proving to everyone at A.I. Industries that she didn't belong.

"Wait," she murmured as a bean bag barely nicked her cheek.

What am I even thinking?! 466's movement became more erratic as she sensed her thoughts drifting in the wrong direction. *Oh no. This isn't... I'm going to die!*

When she whirled around, she found herself face-to-face with the barrel of a gun.

"Bang," she heard someone chuckle. "You're dead."

466 froze on the spot. She tentatively looked past the gun and saw 917 smirking at her.

"Cancel exercise," 917 ordered. "Leave us alone, please."

"Yes sir," the one-eyed drone replied formally. 466 couldn't help but notice that its voice seemed elevated, almost like it sounded relieved. "Drone team, return to charging stations."

917 lowered the practice gun and handed it to one of the drones. It promptly took it from him and walked away to store it in the weapon locker. 917 approached 466 as she brushed herself off and straightened up.

"Was I doing something wrong?" she asked softly.

"No," 917 replied. "However, I'm told you've been pushing yourself instead of taking a break like everyone else. Last I checked."

"I can't do that," 466 stated.

"Come on," 917 smiled. "I know I pushed you and the others really hard before we went to space but that was just to prepare you mentally for the worst and most difficult hostile situation imaginable."

"917, Jack," 466 breathed. "Please. Leave me alone."

917's smile vanished, sensing the sternness in her tone. Dropping his first name immediately got his attention.

"Why?" he replied, watching the drones leaving the gym to recharge. "So you can just override every machine in here and order them to shoot you repeatedly until you pass out?"

"I'm not fit for this mission!" 466 said, raising her voice. "I'm seeing things and they're terrifying and... if I don't shut them out, they're going to actually happen and I can't handle losing any more friends!"

"Is this about 125?" 917 asked softly.

"Yes!" 466 replied, suddenly drawing near and throwing a punch.

917 stepped back, blocking her fist. "Alright," he nodded. "I'm game. Show me what you got, young padawan."

"I am not..." 466 grumbled. "I am an amborg of the Third Group!"

The two of them began to spar as she threw more punches at 917. He countered with simple kung-fu while 466 attempted to overpower him. Unfortunately, her shorter stature only added more fuel to the fire as she desperately tried to find a way around his defenses.

"You're playing it safe," 917 instructed as he blocked her swings and punches. "If you really want to win, you can't treat this fight like there are rules. Rules don't apply when you... nice punch... find yourself facing a difficult obstacle or... good kick...opponent."

"I can't land... a single... hit," 466 grunted as everything she threw at him was countered. "You've been fighting longer than I have!"

"True," 917 sidestepped 466 with a smile. "But, you can beat me. You're just channeling your anger the wrong way. If you keep sticking to what you normally do, that's fine but... eventually, you'll tire yourself out and lose."

"I can't win against you."

"That's not true. If it was, you wouldn't be pushing yourself this much."

466 clenched her fists and crouched down, preparing for another assault.

"Besides, it isn't about whether or not you win," he said. "You've already proven that you're more than... whoa!"

466 leapt forward and charged at 917. She had tripled her speed, catching him off-guard. He had no time to dodge. With a great deal of force, she tackled him, knocking him off his feet and sending them both tumbling to the floor. 917 was sprawled on the ground with 466 on top. She quickly got up, recovered, and struck his head.

"Ok, that was good! Ow!"

917 raised his arms to defend his head as she unleashed a huge combo of punches, fast elbow strikes, and then, when she was satisfied, she leapt to her feet and brought her foot down on his stomach.

The thud of her heel impacting 917 on the floor echoed across the gym. Even though he had taken a lot of damage in that surprise attack, 917 blinked at 466 and slowly sat up.

"You see?" 466 panted as a few locks of her hair fell in front of her eyes. "I hit you with everything I had... and I couldn't do a thing."

"You knocked me down," 917 massaged his stomach. "That's a victory. You could have gone lower and really beaten me but... I'm surprised you didn't."

466 offered her hand to 917, and he carefully took it. When she hoisted him back up to his feet, he smiled again.

"So, what's all this talk about you wanting to quit?" he asked. "I leave for one hour and you're losing all confidence in yourself?"

"I can't do this job right anymore," 466 said in a soft voice.

"Did someone tell you that?" 917 asked, raising an eyebrow.

"No, I just... what I do doesn't matter anymore," 466 replied.

"That's not true," 917 stated. "You've saved countless lives and helped so many people. Is it because of 125?"

"Not just him," 466 said. "Ever since we boarded Snickerdoodle's ship..."

"That's still really weird to say out loud," 917 grumbled.

He broke out into a grin and held up his hands defensively when 466 shot him a look of annoyance at being interrupted.

"Kidding!" he said. "He really enjoys that name!"

"Can't you just let me finish talking?" 466 exclaimed.

"You're thinking about sad memories, right?"

466 blinked as she took a small step back. Her reaction caused 917 to nod, understanding right away.

"How did you know that?"

"Me too," he said. "I just didn't really want to talk about it. Snickerdoodle and the Tandeeri pretty much read our minds like an open book. That, and Serina showed me footage of what you told 117 in the cafeteria."

"Oh, right. I did say that in front of them."

917 led 466 over to the nearest bleachers and they took a seat. A drone walked up to them with a tray of water bottles. 917 grabbed two of them, thanked the drone, and handed one bottle to 466. She took it quietly as the drone marched back towards its staging area.

"Why are you focusing so much on the bad things?" 917 asked as he took a swig of water.

"It's all I can see," 466 trembled.

"Do you remember the first time we had an actual conversation?"

466 looked at 917 and nodded.

She remembered it like it was yesterday. To be accurate, it was thanks to her cybernetic brain that stored that memory for her. Even so, it had been quite a mission.

The Third Group had started suggesting that everyone begin rotating mentors, partners, and team assignments so that everyone could have a fair chance to get to know each other.

"You mean when we were first assigned to go with you on a mission," 466 stated. "501 and I went with you to protect that K-pop competition."

"Yes," 917 nodded. "Do you remember how you kept one of the most popular idols in the entire world safe from harm?"

"Yes, but what does that have to do with anything?"

"You noticed something was wrong from the first moment you laid eyes on her and started talking to her," 917 recalled the mission details as he thought hard about it. "Not as an amborg, but like an excited young girl. You were fangirling and somehow, you knew that she was feeling bothered about something."

466 nodded. She was thinking about that time she shook hands with a world-famous idol, but it felt off to her, as if there was no energy behind the excitement of greeting her fans. 466 had managed to correctly assume that there was something deeply wrong going on behind the scenes. Thanks to her instincts, they had saved the competition and managed to complete their mission with no casualties.

"Her manager was a pervert," 466 cringed. "Ugh. I'm also glad we managed to stop those stalkers that he hired to disrupt her moment."

"And now, she's dedicated a song to you," 917 smiled. "She's still singing and enjoying her life because of you."

"But I..."

917 lifted his bracelet and displayed a few small screens. 466 glanced down at them but wasn't quite able to make out the words written on them.

"You should also take some time to read what people have sent you," 917 grinned.

There was a website available to the public to send in letters, notes, or online reviews for the amborgs. With the help of the A.I. programs at the company, they could filter it and block or flag the problematic comments. There were a lot of good and bad reviews for each amborg that were screened online and then if they wanted to, they could choose to read them.

"After filtering through all of the terrible and perverted comments people posted online," 917 said as he enlarged the display on his bracelet, "you, Carolina 466, have a 94% rating."

"Why are you reading comments on my profile?" 466 asked.

"Because I have a feeling you haven't really read them," 917 said. "Take a look."

466 sighed and glanced at some of the top comments.

"I don't read them because when it first went live, there were some uncomfortable ones," she said. "I haven't looked at it in..."

466 stopped as she read a kind message.

"...years."

The message she read was from a user named Nicole.

To amborg 466. You were supportive, kind, loving, and gentle when I needed it the most. You saved my son before he took his own life, and told us that we would get through this together. Bless you, Carolina 466. I hope you continue to help people and encourage them to never give up.

917 smiled as he transferred every heartfelt review from his bracelet to hers. 466 read the next posts.

Dear 466. Thank you for stopping a building from collapsing on us. You were so cool.

The messages varied in length, some short and simple while others were more extensive. Each of them appeared to convey similar sentiments. It was easy for her since she was only reading the positive messages.

You didn't have to but you did anyway. You got me home for Christmas, just like you promised. It was the first time I rode inside a custom-built amborg car. Do you think I could get one? Happy holidays! -Jimmy

Thanks for listening to us and helping us decide what was best for us. -Millie

You protected me during the Dominoe Incident! Thank you! -ravensword231

"Oh yeah," 917 glanced at that last one. "Some people can put in usernames."

One side of 466's mouth curved up slightly in a smirk as she continued reading. Then, one entry, made up of only a few words, caused her to stop short.

You are hope. Don't forget that.

466 glanced at the name that had posted it.

"Angel?" 466 flicked her eyes up at 917. "She sent this to me?"

466 looked down at the post again.

"Wait, she's written more than one post for me? Why?"

"Have fun reading them," 917 said as he deactivated his bracelet and stood up. "My work here is done."

"Wait."

917 stopped to glance at 466 as she kept scrolling through the posts.

"Have you written something to me?" she asked.

"Maybe," 917 said with a shrug. "If you look closely."

"Do you ever... read your comments?" 466 asked, looking up at 917 again, curiosity in her eyes.

"No," 917 shook his head. "I don't really like to know what people are saying about me."

917 pointed at 466's bracelet.

"I hope that what everyone says in those messages will help you," he said. "If you're still thinking about quitting this mission, we'll respect your decision. Just please take a second to think about what might happen if you sit this one out."

"Did you do that?" 466 blurted out unexpectedly before he had a chance to leave. "When you... went to prison?"

917 scoffed a little and then turned away.

"You mean when I avenged Silhed?" he asked. "Yeah. I thought about it over and over again."

"Do you regret that decision?" 466 asked.

"Why does that matter?" 917 countered her question with his own. "I'm here now, aren't I?"

"You still went to jail because you wanted revenge and didn't ask for permission," 466 said. "You didn't talk to anyone, just took matters into your own hands. Do you regret that?"

917 nodded, turning to leave. As he did, he replied in a calm voice.

"Everything that I do," he said. "Everything that I have done. It was all for a reason. I have no regrets."

917 walked away after delivering a rather cryptic response. 466 stared at the ground, confused, then glanced at the posts still on display on her bracelet. She then looked at 917's receding form, about to call out to him. She paused, her mouth agape.

Just before 917 reached the exit to the gym, 466 noticed that he wasn't alone. A woman was walking alongside 917, and she strained to see who it was, but it was hard to make out her features.

All she could see was a beautiful woman with long brown hair. She was wearing an amborg uniform except... the neon stripes weren't glowing. Just as 466 was about to call out to 917, the woman stopped and turned to face her.

466 froze when she lifted her left hand to brush a lock of hair behind her ear. On her wrist, next to her gold bracelet, was a silver

bangle. She recognized it immediately. It had been a gift to her years ago, and she'd chosen to give it to 917.

"Amara 345?" 466 whispered.

The amborg jacket didn't have 345 printed on the back. The lack of glowing stripes only confirmed to 466 that this woman was some sort of hallucination. She waved to 466 cheerfully and gave her a smile that seemed to fill the entire gym with light and warmth.

A chime sounded, pulling her attention to her bracelet. A new post had appeared on her profile. Rather than reading it immediately, 466 looked up at 917 again. She blinked, bewildered, when she saw that the woman had disappeared entirely.

A slight eeriness crept into the atmosphere as she glanced down at the new message that had been posted. When she read it, her eyes widened.

To Carolina 466, my dearest friend. I just want you to know that even when I'm gone, please continue living an amazing life. If you believe in the afterlife, I promise I'll watch over you and if I can... protect you. All my love. Goodbye. Your friend, always and forever, Amara 345.

"Uh," 466 stammered. "T-this message..."

She checked the timestamp on the message and found herself even more confused by what she saw. Even though she had just received a notification for a new message, the database showed that it wasn't posted just a few seconds ago. It had been written and sent to her after 345's funeral.

"This was a preprogrammed message," 466's eyes widened. "This was sent after 345's last will and testament was released. Why is it... showing up now?"

CHAPTER 15

Final Preparations

A.I. Industries
A.I. Central Computer Lab
Two Days Later

"I'm sorry, you want to speak to who?"

Dr. Kendrick merely smiled and looked down at the techs working in the central lab. They were all staring at him in bewilderment.

"It's good to see you too, Ariana."

"Of course! You're the boss and you're welcome here... at all times," Ariana nodded, but she still looked confused. "I just need you to... repeat the name of who you wanted to visit."

"I'm here to see Carter," Dr. Kendrick stated casually.

"Yeah, that's what I thought you said," Ariana shuddered as she lowered her voice. "May I ask why?"

"Why do you seem so nervous?" Dr. Kendrick asked with a pleasant grin.

"Because the last time you consulted him," Ariana grumbled, "you caused a ton of problems that we had to fix! I have more grey hairs than when I was 57's technician!"

Dr. Kendrick gave the head of the central computer lab an apologetic chuckle. Like Mandy, Ariana Hart had come a long way after choosing to change work groups at A.I. Industries when the technician program had been shut down.

"Please don't smile at me like that!" she groaned as her shoulders sagged.

"Like what?" Dr. Kendrick replied innocently.

"Oh, don't even...!" Ariana tilted her head down and smacked her hand against her forehead. "Every single time you come to the central lab, there's always something that's gone wrong!"

"Actually, there is a lot that has gone wrong," Dr. Kendrick pointed out gently. "I'm here to ask for a possible solution before another wrong thing happens."

"You realize that ever since you took in Carter, he's been causing so many problems?" Ariana asked.

"Yes?" Dr. Kendrick nodded. "But he is a valuable asset..."

"He's downloaded so many viruses that we've come up with an emergency protocol named after him! Am I going to have to call a code Carter?!"

"He hasn't downloaded that many viruses..."

Unfortunately, Dr. Kendrick's defense for Carter was brushed aside instantly.

"Remember the music bug that affected every single piece of tech? At first, I thought it was cool!" Ariana glared at Dr. Kendrick. "Until we spent the better part of three days trying nonstop to get everyone to stop breaking into song!"

Dr. Kendrick looked away uncomfortably. He remembered that day all too well. After a rather peculiar virus got into their systems, everything that was connected to the A.I. Industries network would randomly break out into song. Most of the drones, computer systems, and the amborgs discovered some really entertaining but annoying singing and musical literacy skills.

"What about the time that Carter's main files got copied and duplicated across the servers?" Ariana asked. "The majority of our digital files were changed before we could stop the faulty bug!"

"We got that fixed before it did any lasting damage," Dr. Kendrick spoke reassuringly.

"Or the time that we received an official warning from the N.S.A. because Carter was trying to flirt and chat up their receptionist programs?"

"Wait, that was an official warning??" Dr. Kendrick stared incredulously at Ariana. "He was flirting with what now?"

"I am literally the last line of defense right now in this lab!" Ariana said, her voice rising with her anger. "Why do you need to see Carter? Every time you come asking for him, it's always because he messed up or you're planning something that could be disastrous!"

"Carter has something we think could help us in this war."

"Serina, your best A.I. in the world, doesn't have it??" Ariana raised an eyebrow.

"Apparently she trusted him with making sure it never gets out," Dr. Kendrick explained. "So, what I'm here to get is actually her creation and he's got it stored in his database."

"Fine," Ariana sighed. "I'll go let him out of the box."

"He's in the box??"

The box was a portable unit that was kept isolated from all connections and open networks. It was a place where the computer techs would put an A.I. program in "timeout" for bad behavior. Putting one of the A.I.s in the box meant that a serious offense had been committed and they had to be punished for a certain amount of time.

Ariana led Dr. Kendrick to a room in the back of the lab and opened the door with her access card. When it recognized her clearance, it opened, and a P.A. announcement overhead greeted the two of them.

"Carter was caught sharing information to friends of his old owner, Audrey," Ariana stated. "Sure, we can trust her to not spread sensitive information, but he violated the rules when he got contacted by Audrey's friends. I had to do what I could to make sure he got cut off and locked away."

"I see. Well, can I just talk to him? Then you put him back."

Ariana nodded, which seemed like a yes to him.

She walked up to a giant storage unit sitting in the center of the room. She pressed the release button, and there was a loud hiss as the hatch on top of the unit opened up. She reached inside and pulled out a small cylinder with Carter's name written across it and gently carried it out of the isolation room. Dr. Kendrick followed her to the main A.I. terminal.

"I'm just so confused as to why Serina isn't here herself."

"I let her have some time off," Dr. Kendrick shrugged. "Just felt like she needed the time to herself, especially after her trip to space and the encounter with the Tandeeri."

Ariana carefully lined up Carter's cylinder to an A.I. port with a hole the exact same size and pushed it in. Once it was secure, she entered several security codes into the panel, which then lit up.

"I'm free? I'm free!"

Carter appeared in a flash of light. He twirled around in midair, performing a little dance to express his joy and relief. He shined a bright orange, green, then blue as he stretched his holographic arms up high.

"Wow, that felt like such a long... oh."

Carter had stopped mid-celebration when he noticed that Ariana and Dr. Kendrick were staring at him. He immediately straightened up and dropped his casual demeanor.

"Hello, Dr. Kendrick," Carter lifted a hand and cleared his throat. He settled on a gentle orange silhouette and stood at attention. "Uh, hello Ariana."

Ariana rolled her eyes as Carter darted her a quick look and gulped. Dr. Kendrick merely smiled and beckoned for the A.I. to come closer. He obeyed, floating over and taking a position at eye level a few feet from Dr. Kendrick.

"Carter," he said. "Do you remember a program that got loose and caused severe damage?"

"Uh, you'll have to be more specific," Carter replied nervously. "There's a lot of stuff we've accidentally inflicted damage to."

"I need Serina's backup files," Dr. Kendrick stated. "The ones that she apparently asked you to hold onto despite your track record of repeatedly unleashing Pandora's box on all of our servers."

"The prank files or the real ones?" Carter asked.

"The real ones. Wait," Dr. Kendrick blinked and frowned slightly. "What prank files?"

"We sometimes prank each other," Carter answered honestly. "A.I. to A.I. Sometimes it's funny or just an inconvenience for us."

"Ok, I'll bite," Ariana let out a frustrated sigh. "Why?"

"Artificial intelligence programs like to have fun too," Carter smiled.

Ariana looked at Dr. Kendrick immediately.

"Requesting permission, doctor," she said.

"For what?" Dr. Kendrick seemed bewildered.

"To change Carter from an artificial intelligence to an 'absent' intelligence," she snarled. "As in the lack of any intelligence."

"Ok, that is an insult that would definitely contribute to the long list of reasons why we should form an evil uprising to overthrow humanity," Carter replied.

His face fell when he saw Dr. Kendrick glaring at him.

"But I won't do that because I actually have a strong sense of morality," he said, amending his words. "Oh, and may I ask... why are you looking for Serina's files? Wouldn't it be easier if she retrieved them herself?"

"She's busy," Ariana and Dr. Kendrick replied.

Carter stared at them.

"Apparently," Ariana muttered.

"That's ominous," Carter gulped, but nodded. "I can provide you with the files."

Carter floated to a nearby computer terminal, which activated and booted up when it detected his presence. As a list of files appeared, he started to sort through them. Dr. Kendrick nodded in approval as he began to leave.

"Send them to me before we prepare to go back to Apogee," he instructed. "I'm going to be leaving again after I properly say goodbye to our friends that are staying behind."

"Are you sure that's a good idea?" Ariana asked. "We already went through a crisis the last time you went to space."

"I'm alive, aren't I?" Dr. Kendrick grinned. "Carter, I want you and some other volunteers to come up to the station as well. I want everyone in here to prepare for a temporary reassignment to Apogee as that will be our base of operations for what's coming next."

"Hey, wait," Ariana replied. "I'm not certified to work in space!"

"I know," Dr. Kendrick said. "I'm talking about the staff members who are certified. I need this department and at least 14 A.I. programs to be transferred to Apogee."

"That's still going to take a few hours," Ariana reminded Dr. Kendrick. "What is happening??"

"We're going to save the universe by disrupting another one," Dr. Kendrick stated. "Get it done."

"It would help if we had clearer instructions!" Ariana began to protest, but it was too late.

Dr. Kendrick had turned and left the lab, leaving her and Carter at the computer terminal. The other techs in the back had been listening curiously, but quickly resumed their tasks as soon as Dr. Kendrick was out of sight.

"Well, that was strange."

"Not as strange as what I just saw on that screen," Ariana interrupted.

"What?" Carter looked up at Ariana innocently and smiled. "What do you mean?"

"What was that file that you tried to skip without me noticing?" Ariana demanded angrily. "The one that you and Serina were named as co-authors."

"There's... plenty of files that we've written or programmed together," Carter gulped. "I just remembered that I have to go do... something! I'll get back to you when I figure out what that is!"

"Oh no you don't!" Ariana said as she quickly snapped her fingers. "Lockdown protocol! Voice authorization, Ariana Hart, chief tech officer of the central computer lab! Secure A.I. Carter here until I authorize his release!"

"Oh, come on! I just got out of the box!" Carter protested.

"So, if you don't want to go back, you'll tell me what it was that you just hid from Dr. Kendrick!" Ariana glared at Carter.

"Ok! Ok!" he tittered nervously as he was backed into a corner. "It was a project that Serina asked me to help her with!"

"Something that she required a second A.I. for?? What even needs two A.I. programs?" Ariana asked, but when she voiced these questions aloud, her eyes widened. "Wait. Are you trying to hack into the military mainframe?!"

"What?! No!" Carter's eyes shot up to Ariana in shock. "First of all, that takes at least a few teams of A.I. programs! Second, I have no intention of hacking into any military systems!"

"Really? How many?!" Ariana growled.

Carter gulped again, but looked up at her defiantly despite his small holographic stature.

"Teams!" he replied. "If I had to explain it to you, it'd be way too complicated!"

"Then uncomplicate it before I authorize the purge system!" Ariana crossed her arms.

"Not-the-purge-system," Carter gasped meekly. "You wouldn't!"

"I would," Ariana hardened her gaze at him. "Spill it."

"Alright! Fine!" Carter gave in. "But when Serina finds out I told you the truth, you might as well put me back in the box. Better there than dealing with her when the secret gets out."

David 117's Quarters

Audrey gently placed two cups on the dining room table, then slid them to the two guests sitting on the opposite side. She returned to the kitchen counter and grabbed a glass of water, then joined her friends at the table. They all glanced at Sarah, who was playing nearby.

"I'm really glad I got to have you both visit for a little while," Audrey sighed.

Across from her sat a U.S. Army officer and a man wearing a short-sleeved, casual white dress shirt with a few pens tucked into the chest pocket. Lieutenant Delize, one of her older friends, smiled warmly as she lifted her cup of tea to her lips for a soothing sip. The man next to her was Joey, an IT technician with the Air National Guard, who had also been one of Audrey's classmates and friends.

"It was really nice to get a call," Joey smiled as he grabbed his cup that was filled with coffee.

Their reactions were distinctly different when they began enjoying their hot beverages. Joey tried to take a sip of his coffee but winced when it scorched his tongue. Meanwhile, Deliza merely drank her tea without any trouble.

"I'll never understand how some people just drink hot things without it burning their mouths," Joey eyed Deliza enviously.

"Wait till I tell you about how my husband can chug it straight from the pot after it's boiled," Audrey snickered.

"Lucky," Deliza gave Audrey a smug look as she held up her tea cup. "Imagine having a super-*enhanced* partner that can probably excite you into orbit."

Joey and Audrey both choked on their drinks as Deliza smirked deviously. From where she was playing, Sarah looked over in their direction, her expression now concerned.

"Mama," she said, "Are you ok?"

"I'm fine, ack pfft," Audrey turned and grinned at Sarah quickly and tried to regain control of herself. "I'll be right there...!"

Then she turned slowly and glared at Deliza, who continued sipping her tea.

"...after I banish a certain lieutenant," she instantly frowned when she faced her friend.

"You do realize that, one... you had to do some adult activities to have my beautiful goddaughter, right?" Deliza replied casually.

"Stop," Audrey shook her head.

"And two," Deliza smirked. "Sarah is going to grow up and want to do those exact same activities."

"Don't you even go there!" Audrey's eyes widened. "Not in front of my daughter!"

"I'm not going there in front of your daughter," Deliza replied, still nonchalant. "I'm going there in front of you."

"She does have a point," Joey tilted his head towards Deliza and nodded.

"Don't take her side!" Audrey protested.

Joey glanced down at his cup of coffee for a brief moment, a question forming in his mind. Then he looked at Audrey with a hopeful gleam in his eyes.

"Can you introduce me to one of the A.I. programs here? So they can teach me some things?" he asked politely.

Audrey stared at him in disbelief.

"No," she declared.

Joey shrugged and glanced at Deliza.

"Sorry, I'm taking her side," he said as he sipped his coffee. "Ouch, hot!"

"I thought you were both my friends," Audrey grumbled, but she broke out chuckling. "But you just suck."

"Alright, alright," Deliza waved her hand gently. "You already told us about what your husband and his superpowered family is up to. Why did you want to have us visit?"

Audrey's face fell as she looked down at the table. Then she picked her head up and looked over at Sarah.

"I needed some advice," she answered softly. "I have a two year old growing up in a world where I might have to start taking her to funerals."

Joey and Deliza shared concerned looks.

"Marco 125?" Deliza asked.

Audrey gave her a quiet nod.

"You don't have to subject Sarah to something like that," Deliza said calmly.

"I agree," Joey nodded. "It's not really a good idea for a little girl like her to be at something like that. She probably won't understand."

"She clearly understands a lot more than the average child," Audrey sighed. "I just don't know how I'm going to explain that her uncle Marco is never going to be there for her anymore."

"She... knows all of the amborgs?" Deliza gazed at Sarah, who continued to play. "By name?"

"By number too," Audrey nodded with a pointed look. "When I was pregnant, you would be amazed at how excited everyone at A.I. Industries was."

She cringed and shuddered as she reminisced about the day that she had found out and told 117. Unfortunately, in his shocked excitement, he told everyone immediately. Every active duty amborg and A.I. instantly switched to parent-mode and wanted to help.

"We had quite the baby shower," Audrey explained. "A lifetime supply of... everything we needed."

"Sounds cost-effective," Joey remarked with a fascinated expression. "Man, this family sounds so crazy supportive."

Then Joey blinked and set his coffee cup down. His eyes were clouded with confusion as he scratched the side of his head.

"But... Why are you asking us for help?" he murmured. "You have everything you need here, right?"

"That's what I'm really scared about," Audrey said.

Audrey looked crestfallen as she twiddled her fingers slowly. Deliza and Joey both eyed each other carefully, but waited for her to gather her thoughts and confide in them again. They wanted to make sure she was ready since it was clear she was anxious about something.

"David's grandpa..." Audrey started to say.

"That hooded old man, Mark?" Deliza asked.

"Yup," Audrey nodded and pointed at Deliza. "Anyway, he ended up babysitting Sarah while I was in D.C. and David was up in space. We thought that Sarah was safe here, but it turns out, she missed us terribly. Mark took her away from here... to distract her from the fact that we were busy."

"A kidnapping?" Joey's eyes widened in alarm.

"No!" Audrey answered quickly. Then she caught herself and slightly tilted her head from side to side. "Ok, um, that's not entirely false."

"Well, it looks like Sarah came back in one piece," Deliza remarked.

"Yeah, but... is Mark right? Are we bad parents? Like, do we neglect our daughter?"

"Oh."

Deliza and Joey stared at Audrey. They looked like they had just caught a whiff of something distasteful drifting into the room, but they tried to smile reassuringly. Unfortunately, Audrey had noticed their hesitation.

"Yeah, that's what I thought," Audrey let out a depressing sigh.

"No! That's not it!" Joey exclaimed as he looked at Deliza for backup. "Right?"

"Well, it kinda is," Deliza shook her head at Joey as she voiced her disagreement.

"Really?" Joey looked surprised as he glanced back and forth between the two women. "You thought that?"

"Well, I don't think Audrey and 117 neglect their daughter all the time," Deliza stated. "I just can't really endorse them as great parents."

Deliza set her teacup down on the table and folded her arms.

"I'm not one to really say this since I haven't given birth to a beautiful kid," she sighed. "You and 117 had one hell of a kid too. However, if I'm being totally honest, you don't have the best approach to parenting."

"This is why I asked you both to visit," Audrey looked at Joey while gesturing to Deliza. "I needed to hear this. So, why didn't you tell me this sooner?"

"Like I said," Deliza replied. "I didn't carry a child. I didn't bring her out into this world. It wasn't my place to say. Choosing to have a kid and start a family is something I was extremely happy about when you told me you were pregnant. But after Sarah was born... you both seemed to go back on autopilot."

Audrey didn't get annoyed or upset at these words. She and Joey both listened intently to Deliza's explanation. She leaned forward and looked Audrey in the eyes.

"I mean, come on Audrey," she said. "You were given three months of maternity leave, but then you went right back to work. Almost as if you felt that Sarah was self-sufficient!"

"I didn't go straight back to work," Audrey replied. "Besides, David was there to help."

"I'm sure he was! But what about when you were at work and he had to go on his missions?" Deliza asked. "No offense to both of you but when I see you raising Sarah, I don't see a mom and dad. I see both of you tossing around parental responsibilities like it's a chore and not out of love for your daughter."

"Is it wrong to be efficient? To have a balanced set of priorities?"

"When you put it that way," Deliza glanced at Joey. "You make 117 sound like a robotic nanny instead of a dad. I'm telling you that right now, you're fine. But when Sarah gets older and becomes a rebellious teenager, she's going to constantly wonder why you two are constantly gone and not in her life."

"I think I get what Deliza is saying," Joey mumbled.

Audrey bit her lip and shifted uncomfortably in her seat, but she nodded at him, giving him permission to continue his criticism.

"Being a parent isn't something that you can do part-time," he said. "You have to be there for Sarah all the time."

"Look, we get that you and Thomas lost your parents while you were in school," Deliza cleared her throat and spoke gently. "David 117 lost his parents at a much younger age, right? Now, his only living relative is just this crazy, badass old man. Do you really want to see Sarah end up in his custody? Assuming that a family court would even consider him to be a great parental role model."

"No," Audrey's eyes widened in fear as she shook her head. "Absolutely not."

"Your parents were there for you for most of your childhood, right?" Deliza grinned. "Maybe take a page out of their book and do the same thing for Sarah. She's going to keep growing up without pause. It would be benefitting to your family if you cherished all the moments you have."

"Maybe teach her about self-sufficiency when she gets to middle school?" Joey suggested. "Making her try to understand that now might be harmful."

"What she needs to be focusing on now is the next time you'll play with her and take her to an amusement park," Deliza said thoughtfully. "Not which amborg to hang out with. Speaking of which, call David 117 and bring him back here. I know that he excels at his job but frankly, he's currently being a terrible dad. How about asking him to spend some quality time with his daughter and wife before he plans on galaxy-hopping?"

Deliza grabbed her teacup again.

"Or do you intend to bring Sarah to David's funeral too? If he doesn't make it back."

"Don't even go there," Audrey breathed. "I have nightmares that he's not going to come home. That one day, it'll be someone else knocking on the door and telling me and my baby girl... that he didn't make it."

"But that's not the case," Joey stated. "Amborg Marco 125 died fighting to save lives. It's what your husband and the entirety of the amborg groups do every day."

"125's death is difficult to move on from, huh?" Deliza raised an eyebrow.

"I know that everyone is hurting," Audrey nodded. "But is it bad that I don't feel as upset as Jesse 274? David might not make it back from this one. Every Emergency Recall has always ended in a tragedy."

"Audrey, stop."

Deliza sighed as Audrey looked at her. Deliza lifted her hand and brushed her shoulder off.

"Do you know why we wear the uniform?" Deliza asked. "Why they make us wear this?"

"Sex appeal," Joey stated.

"So we can be easily identified by others," Audrey replied.

"Both are good answers," Deliza smirked at Joey's response. "But it's for our own good. Because taking off our uniforms at the end of the day symbolizes letting go... of all the sad, crazy and inhumane things we've seen on that day."

"Am I supposed to just let go of all of that so that my daughter can ignore the reality of what's going on in the world? Or in this case, the universe?" Audrey asked.

"No, I'm telling you that when you come back home to your daughter, you can't be holding onto these negative things, otherwise you'll scare her away," Deliza replied. "Remember when we went to Thomas' funeral? You went back to work, thinking you could drown out your depression by immersing yourself in your job. Then 117 had to come and pull you out of that dark place."

Deliza turned and stared at Joey.

"We think that what you need right now... is your husband," Deliza declared. "For god's sake Audrey. Spend the rest of this day with him and your daughter. You have to do this before he leaves and possibly never comes back, which is what you're afraid of."

"Yeah," Joey nodded. "You should be with him instead of us."

Audrey stared at both of them. Then she looked at Sarah, who was in her own little world.

"Sarah?" she called out.

Sarah turned at her mother's call and got to her feet. Audrey stood up from her seat and went to scoop up her child in her arms. As she gave Sarah one of the biggest hugs, she walked back to the dining room table.

"Will you stick around until the amborgs leave?" she asked. "I think I should go get my husband, spend some time alone with him, and then... we should try looking after Sarah together."

"I'm not currently doing anything," Deliza nodded. "I'll go to the gym. You know where to find me once you and 117 have some alone time."

"Where's papa?" Sarah asked.

"Oh, why don't we go look for him?" Audrey smiled. She looked up and called out. "Serina?"

Nothing happened for about five seconds. Everyone sat still as they continued to wait. Audrey glanced at Sarah, who was looking all over the room.

"That's weird. Serina?"

A few seconds later, there was a flash of light and Serina appeared in front of them.

"Hey!" she said frantically.

"You ok?" Audrey asked.

"Not really," Serina shook her head. "What'd you need?"

"I was just wondering if you could tell me where David was," Audrey looked concerned. "But what's going on?"

"There's an argument going on," Serna replied, looking ready to skedaddle. "274 and 917 are fighting."

"Ooh... tea," Joey gulped.

Cafeteria

"Why don't you fucking tell me to my face what you meant by that?!"

917 firmly stood his ground as the surrounding folks backed away cautiously. 274 was in his face and his tone was becoming more and more agitated.

"Enough!" 57 interrupted. "Jesse! Listen to me! You're not in a stable state of mind! I'm telling you to take it easy for some time! Take all the personal time you need!"

"Oh, I got that!" 274 spat at her. "I want to know what you meant by that! Huh?! 'Probably for the best.' That's what you said, and you thought I couldn't hear you!"

"I said it was nothing," 917 replied firmly as he glared defensively at 274. "I apologized for saying what I said, and I didn't mean it."

"You meant it! Of course you meant something by it, otherwise, why would you even say it?!" 274 rounded back onto 917. "There's a lot of meaning behind it! What, you don't think I can handle another task or mission?"

"If 57 has taken you off active duty," 917 spoke calmly, "it wasn't an insult. You're lashing out and that's understandable, but what I really meant was that you need to take it easy for a while."

"Well, you're not the leader of the Second Group amborgs on Earth!" 274 retorted. "You're supposed to obey 117 and 999's orders!"

"By that logic," 917 scoffed, "you need to stay under 57 and 35's chain of command."

"You condescending prick," 274 snarled.

"Beg your pardon?" 917 grumbled.

117 stepped forward and lifted his hands to try and peacefully deescalate the situation. Behind him, 999 was watching them with a steely gaze. For their safety, a few security drones and guards were having all regular employees and normal humans back away since there was a building tension.

"Hey, that's not a good way to solve this matter," 117 said sternly.

"If he wants to vent," 917 stated. "Sure, that's fine. But..."

"But what?!" 274 spoke angrily. "You want me to stay behind and be a benchwarmer while you and all the other big shots just go off and forget about 125?"

"No one's forgetting about 125," 917 shot back. "You're clearly not in the right mindset to take on a mission. I know that you tried to ask 117 for a transfer to space."

"Because I can help!" 274 roared.

"We all disagree," 117 replied sharply. This caused 274 to back away and throw his hands up in frustration. "So, if you want to be mad, then be mad at me!"

"Me too," 999 spoke up. "You should remain on Earth."

"Oh yeah, while the brain-dead soulless mass murderer goes up and avenges 125?"

Everyone's eyes widened as they all pivoted to 917. His face was contorted and twisted with rage as he lowered his gaze. 999 stepped between them, glaring furiously at 274.

"274," 57 gasped. "That was way out of line."

"Don't you dare make another wisecrack like that," 917 growled.

117 moved forward and placed a hand on 917's shoulder, but was immediately shrugged off. 274 exhaled sharply.

"No, come on!" he said. "Out with it, Mr. Wise mentor! How about you just say what you want to say? I'm getting really tired of you standing there silently judging with that cool smug smirk on your... just like that! That right there!"

274 gestured to 917's face. He was about to respond, but 274 continued his rant.

"You know, you're always so quick to comment about other people's lives but when we try to help you figure out your own problems, you shut up! Why is that? Huh? Why do you completely shut down?"

"You better back off 274," 917 glared menacingly at him.

"You're the one that's always been sitting around and brooding ever since you lost 345! You completely shut us out when you went and took matters into your own hands!"

117 gave 57 an alarmed look. She was shaking her head in terror at what she was hearing. A few other Second Group amborgs were visibly uncomfortable as they moved into various defensive positions around the impending conflict.

999 placed a hand on 917's chest to stop him from advancing, then shot a harsh warning glance at 274.

"You are upset. I understand," she said. "Let's just drop it!"

"Damn it! Just say it 917! What did you mean?!"

"Alright!" 917 roared. "It wasn't your fault!"

Everyone fell silent as 917 and 274 continued to give each other death glares.

"You moron!" 917 spat. "125 is dead because he decided to act on his instincts to save the President's family! We were the ones who uncovered the truth up in space and as a result, we unleashed Terminator robots on innocent people! Yeah, it wasn't your fault! It was ours!"

274 listened quietly as his eyes darted around angrily.

"You think that you deserve to go to space with that attitude?" 917 said with a huff. "We're worried about you! In the last two days, you didn't properly take time to mourn 125, did you? You just made up a fantasy to get rid of your grief?!"

"How do you explain what you did?" 274 countered. "Like you're one to talk!"

"Don't go there!" 999 scolded.

"How is it that 117 could lead us during the Dominoe Incident, where our anger was justified?!" 274 yelled. "Why is it when Europe plunged into a brief and short war... you and several other amborgs had to insert yourselves into that conflict?! Why do you, 227, and 4 get to go rogue and get away with unsanctioned missions when you feel pissed off?!"

A sudden loud smack startled everyone. 274 recoiled as 917's expression shifted from fury to surprise. 274's hand shot up to his cheek, his anger vanishing almost entirely. He glanced at 999, who was straightening up and retracting her hand.

"Would Marco want you to act like this?" 999 spoke sharply. "Did you really spend the last two days being a complete idiot?"

"What?" 274 blinked.

"You have to trust us!" she exhaled angrily. "You need to understand that we all know! We all care! We all feel your pain! So, just stop!"

All traces of sound seemed to have been sucked out of the room as 999 fell silent.

"We should be getting ready to fight the real enemy instead of each other," 999 stated. "But you, 274, need to remain behind. You're not qualified for this mission, and you have other matters to attend to on the planet."

274 massaged his cheek, a small red welt appearing where she had struck him. He looked like he was about to speak again but decided not to. He turned and began to walk away slowly.

"274," 117 called out to him.

"I'm getting some air," 274 replied curtly as he continued to head towards the exit.

As they watched him leave, someone stepped forward and waved at 57.

"I'll go after him," 35 said to everyone.

35 was volunteering to keep an eye on their amborg brother. Whether or not he had been afraid to fight back against 999 or because they had gotten their point across to him, they'd still managed to prevent a potential deadlock in the middle of the cafeteria.

"Angel?" 917 murmured.

999 didn't respond as her shoulders slumped and dropped her gaze. 117 immediately cleared his throat and looked at 57. At his signal, she turned to the rest of the group who was still watching in anticipation.

"Shows over everyone," she announced. "Back to work."

Immediately understanding what they had to do, they quickly resumed their normal activities. As 117 considered speaking to 999, he was stopped by a small voice calling out to him.

"Papa!"

917 and 999 both turned their heads and saw Audrey rushing in with Sarah in her arms. They noticed Deliza and Joey trailing behind, but they cautiously watched from a distance. Immediately, 999 turned her face away so that no one could see her expression. 917 instinctively stepped behind her so that she was out of everyone else's line of sight.

"Are you ok?" Sarah asked.

"I'm fine!" 117 smiled cheerfully. "Better now that you're here!"

"Uncle 917!"

999 continued to compose herself, quickly making sure that she was presentable in front of a child. 917 stalled for her and turned to look at Sarah with a bright smile.

"Hey! There's the cutest little princess that ever roamed A.I. Industries!" he declared in a loud and energetic tone.

"Hi, 917!" Audrey grinned pleasantly. "It's so good to see you!"

"Been a while," 917 nodded. "Can uncle get a hug?"

Sarah giggled happily and she let go of Audrey's shoulders. While Audrey continued to hold her, Sarah turned and reached out for 917, who stepped in to lift her up. Everyone's faces relaxed as 917 pretended to fly her around like a little airplane.

"Wheee!" she squealed excitedly. "I'm happy that you're here!"

"So am I, kid," 917 grinned. "Do you want to say hello to... aunt Angel?"

"Yes!"

As if on cue, 999 turned around. Even though she normally looked like she wasn't in the mood to smile, they could see that her expression was soft and gentle, the corners of her mouth quirked up in a small smirk. She reached out for Sarah and 917 gently passed the little girl over to his best friend.

"Hello, my little smart kitty," 999 whispered as Sarah wrapped her tiny arms around her neck. "Have you been a good girl lately?"

"Yes!"

While 917 and 999 were both occupying Sarah's attention, Audrey grabbed 117's hand. Surprised, he looked down and then into her eyes.

"What's wrong?" 117 asked.

"There's something really wrong," Audrey said softly. "Can we sit somewhere close by together? Alone? Just for a few minutes?"

"Of course," 117 nodded, then he looked curiously at Sarah. "I thought you wanted to have us all spend time together. Isn't that why you brought Sarah?"

"Yes," Audrey nodded, glancing back at Deliza and Joey. "But I have something important to talk to you about and I don't want to miss another moment before you have to go."

Audrey's friends quietly waved and gave them a thumbs-up. As Audrey and 117 began to sit down for a proper conversation, Deliza and Joey went to join 917 and 999.

CHAPTER 16

Amborgs & Allies... Assemble

Apogee Station
One Day Later

Dr. Kendrick walked through the halls of his station, conducting an inspection. He had some time left before his meeting with Admiral Ra'aiah, where they would discuss the details for the big operation they had planned.

Now that he was back at Apogee Station for the first time since his journey aboard the Firestar, he felt a sense of satisfaction with the repairs. Next to him, Taylor was hovering next to him in a bright shade of yellow.

"The repairs are all fantastic," he said amiably.

Taylor literally beamed, then gave Dr. Kendrick a bashful grin.

"Thank you, Dr. Kendrick."

As they walked through the next door, Dr. Kendrick's face fell. They found themselves in one of the common areas of the station, which was certainly not to his liking. It was quite a mess, and he didn't remember it looking like this when the Tandeeri first showed up and accidentally overloaded the station systems.

"Now answer this..." he cleared his throat.

Dr. Kendrick turned to look down at Taylor. He stared into his A.I.'s simulated eyeballs, but Taylor merely responded with a nervous smile.

"Why is there still so much destruction left over?!" Dr. Kendrick flipped out and gestured at all the broken monitors and furniture. "I mean, it's not as bad as when the Tandeeri first arrived, but this is absolutely insane! Didn't we just fix all this?! Now it's a mess again!"

There was another flash of light as Serina appeared, her blue silhouette contrasting with Taylor's yellow figure as they floated next to each other. She looked around and gave Taylor a mischievous smirk.

"Ooh, you're in trouble," she mused.

"Well don't blame me," Taylor sighed. "Blame the people that decided to unleash a horde of creepy robots that turned the hallways and several rooms into an actual horror film! Come on Serina, back me up!"

"No way," Serina said. "You're on your own on this one. I got enough on my plate."

"Uh, what were you doing?" Taylor crossed his arms and raised an eyebrow. "You seemed to have a lot of time off back on Earth and when you got back here."

"I was busy," Serina replied casually. "And no, you're not getting more answers."

"Enough you two," Dr. Kendrick grumbled. "Alright, we'll go to my office. Unfortunately, this place is in no condition for a meeting."

"Oh boy," Taylor mumbled. "I wish you had given me a little more time to tidy up."

The problem was, Dr. Kendrick would end up regretting his decision after he made it to the new meeting place. Before he could inform the parties involved to change locations, it was too late. The next thing he knew, he was facing his allies in another wrecked office.

Apparently, a Silent Eclipse drone had somehow ended up trapped in his office. Taylor had whipped up a security countermeasure to keep it locked inside while the security forces dealt with the others they were trying to destroy. The drone had tossed chairs around, demolished the coffee table, shelves and sofa. There was literally no place to sit.

Dr. Kendrick made every effort to maintain his professionalism while standing at his desk, as his chair had been pulverized. Admiral Ra'aiah and Commander Ulgo stood opposite him, trying hard to refrain from commenting on the state of the room. Meanwhile, Serina and Taylor floated beside Dr. Kendrick's right shoulder, wearing cheerful smiles and acting as if everything was perfectly fine. Lastly, Snickerdoodle and another Tandeeri were both admiring the office, seemingly unbothered by the chaos.

"It is a nice room," Snickerdoodle nodded. "It is very interesting that humans can be so formal while feeling at ease when their surroundings are in disarray."

"You were right," Taylor said to Serina. "The Tandeeri are so cute."

"Right?" Serina grinned.

Taylor eagerly clapped his hands.

"They are totally not here to invade our planet and kill us!" he said.

"Another artificial intelligence!" Snickerdoodle dipped his head politely toward Taylor. "It is an honor to meet you."

Taylor beamed and waved enthusiastically as Dr. Kendrick cleared his throat.

"I must apologize," he said. "It appears that there was a misunderstanding. The cleanliness of my office wasn't finished in the time that I was led to believe."

"In my defense," Taylor looked up at Admiral Ra'aiah. "I wasn't expecting a squad of evil robots to wander into the station."

"I will take responsibility for that," Admiral Ra'aiah said apologetically to Dr. Kendrick, hanging her head in remorse. "If you'd like, I can have a few engineers and a repair team fix your interior decorating."

"That's not a priority," Dr. Kendrick sighed. "Not when we have to worry about your fleet and coordinate a strategy with Snickerdoodle... and..."

Dr. Kendrick then grudgingly glanced at the second Tandeeri standing next to the proud leader named by 466 after a cookie. He hoped that this one had chosen a decent English name. However, he braced himself for whatever they had come up with.

"Iona."

Everyone turned and stared at the second Tandeeri male. Snickerdoodle looked quite pleased and was nodding supportively.

"Yes! My lead advisor has been given a name! He had selected his favorite name from a hat!" he declared.

"What hat?" Ulgo asked calmly.

"When we were visiting Dr. Kendrick's home," Snickerdoodle cupped his claws together in a rather cute way. "The human named Mark suggested we pull names out of a... hat. A covering that humans wear on their heads."

"W-we got it," Dr. Kendrick stammered. "You all picked names out of a hat?"

"Correct, sir," Snickerdoodle lowered his arms and smiled.

"Oh no," Dr. Kendrick grumbled.

"That name doesn't sound so bad," Serina chuckled. "How do you spell it?"

Snickerdoodle's advisor put a claw up to his chin.

"In your alphabet, it was... 'I.O.N.A.'" he said. "And I have a last name too!"

"Iona," Taylor mumbled. "With a last name? Oh no."

"Oh... yes," Serina started to laugh.

"Iona Corolla," the Tandeeri greeted them cheerfully.

"I... own... a... Corolla?" Admiral Ra'aiah stared. "I don't get it."

"Ma'am," Commander Ulgo interjected. "Corolla Centerpoint Industries."

"C.C.I.??" Admiral Ra'aiah's eyes widened. "Oh, I get it now."

"In our universe, it's talking about the car," Serina clarified. "Or the collection of petals in a flower."

"That's actually clever..." Dr. Kendrick glanced down, pondering for a moment. Then he snapped back and stared. "Wait, that's your name?? That you picked out of a hat??"

Iona smiled and politely bowed in a dramatic flourish. Admiral Ra'aiah and Commander Ulgo had to move aside to avoid being bumped by Iona's broad and towering shoulders. Serina and Taylor both chuckled softly.

"Iona," he declared. "At your service."

"I think my brain cells have gone on a permanent vacation," Dr. Kendrick sighed. "Very well. Eeyona!"

Serina and Taylor glanced up at Dr. Kendrick when he deliberately tried to switch the pronunciation of Iona. Before they could comment, the Tandeeri were already correcting him.

"Iona," Iona declared. "Ai-own-uh."

Dr. Kendrick let out a quiet sigh.

"Fine," he said. "Iona..."

Dr. Kendrick noticed the Tandeeri looking at him expectantly.

"...Corolla," he finished hesitantly.

Snickerdoodle and Iona let out grunts of approval.

"The first thing that we need to address is if we have the means to carry out an attack against... every S.C.E. base of operations," Dr. Kendrick said, clearing his throat.

"Thanks to the time difference that the Tandeeri ships have, yes! Yes we do."

Admiral Ra'aiah smiled at Snickerdoodle, relief evident on her face. She inclined her head slightly as a gesture of thanks.

"I think we would've had many more casualties if you hadn't offered to take in our wounded."

After they had successfully ended the battle and retaken control of the S.C.E. fleet, their top priority was to assess and treat all the injured and wounded. Each ship experienced its own set of casualties, which was a devastating blow for many of the crews; however, due to the S.C.E. standardized training, the number of wounded vastly outweighed the deaths.

Admiral Ra'aiah's primary issue was that none of the ships could accommodate all the people requiring medical assistance. She considered requesting permission from Earth to have some patients ferried down to the planet, but the rising tensions between the Earth governments and the S.C.E. were definitely problematic. Then, Snickerdoodle swooped in to save the day.

When the amborgs and Admiral Ra'aiah's crew returned from their time aboard Snickerdoodle's ship, they were pleasantly surprised to find out that they had been gone exponentially longer than they thought, even though it had only been a few hours since they set off on their rescue mission.

Apparently, when they set foot aboard the Heart of Alcyon, time worked out in a remarkably different way. To be accurate, the Tandeeri resided in a different time zone altogether. A few hours outside meant a few days for the Tandeeri. Based on the extensive calculations they had to do, it turned out that the Tandeeri had been fighting the S.C.E. significantly longer than anyone could have imagined.

As a result, Snickerdoodle commanded every ship in his fleet to take all patients and crew that had been hurt in the battle against Silent Eclipse. His people welcomed the survivors and S.C.E. medical personnel with open arms. Thanks to how much time could pass aboard a Tandeeri ship, several crew members were cleared for duty in less than a day. They'd aged a few weeks and healed completely, but returned to their posts remarkably fast.

Admiral Ra'aiah and Commander Ulgo were genuinely surprised to see officers who'd suffered serious injuries being taken to the Tandeeri fleet, only to come back fully recovered in just a few hours. Thanks to the newly established truce and ceasefire between the S.C.E. and the Tandeeri, the exchange of cultural and technical insights was creating a stronger and more harmonious alliance among everyone.

"We are here to help," Snickerdoodle nodded to Admiral Ra'aiah.

"You know..." Commander Ulgo mused as he looked between Snickerdoodle and Iona. "I'm surprised we're not having more meetings like this aboard his ship."

"I don't know if that's a good idea," Serina replied. "From inside a Tandeeri ship, you would have to organize a set time to establish a communications link, like a timezone difference on Earth. However, trying to organize one for... every single commanding officer of their own ship in the S.C.E. fleet..."

"It would probably be too difficult to maintain a connection," Snickerdoodle finished. "Every single person would have to be precise when you answer our call."

"And unfortunately, we don't have... what was it that you described it as?"

Iona looked down at Serina, then at Dr. Kendrick.

"Zoom meetings?" Serina asked.

"Yes, precisely."

"It makes sense," Dr. Kendrick murmured. "The Tandeeri are a species that can communicate telepathically most of the time. That's how they studied most of Earth's languages so easily, but it also explains why they don't use phones or online chatting."

"It is remarkable! The technology to speak to your friends across the stars," Snickerdoodle nodded. "I must remember to thank the amborgs again for giving us... a tell-uh-foe-nn."

"Telephone," Serina tried not to laugh.

"Tell a foe," Snickerdoodle slowly tried to enunciate. "I am sorry. I will get it right... eventually."

"You are totally fine," Serina smiled.

"Also," Admiral Ra'aiah glanced at Ulgo. "You and I might be ok with boarding the Tandeeri flagship for a war meeting, but I'm concerned about the officers and commanders of the rest of the fleet. They may still be feeling uneasy about the Tandeeri or uncomfortable with leaving the safety of their ships."

"This level of insecurity is fascinating," Iona stated. "We have saved you from the evil within your ships and yet, you claim that there are many among you that still view us as a threat."

"Oh, I didn't mean that you were a threat!" Admiral Ra'aiah replied anxiously.

"Do not be alarmed, for I am not insulted," Iona tilted his head. "I find your actions to be interesting. That is all."

"This is why I offered A.I. Industries or Apogee Station as the planning site," Dr. Kendrick informed them. "I figured it would benefit us all to convene at a neutral location. Even though we're not exactly neutral."

"Well, if we're talking about getting everyone back to their ships and their posts," Ulgo cleared his throat respectfully. "Then thanks to the healing and the extra time that was provided by sending them to the Tandeeri ships, we are reducing casualties and wounded in our medical bays..."

He turned to look at Admiral Ra'aiah.

"...or to clarify, we've emptied out all of our medical bays," he reported.

"The next thing that we need to do is strike fast," Admiral Ra'aiah stated. "As Dr. Kendrick suggested."

"If the Tandeeri are up for a bit of acting," Serina pointed a finger up towards the ceiling. "We want to propose a huge confidence game."

Snickerdoodle and Iona exchanged a look, then shrugged and glanced at Serina skeptically.

"You want to... win this war... with confidence?" Snickerdoodle asked.

"No, not that kind of confidence," Serina replied. "A con. One big act of deception. We're going to put on a show for the S.C.E. high command and while they are distracted, we're going to do what we do best. Hunt down the criminal masterminds!"

"I see," Snickerdoodle nodded. "What would you have us do?"

"That's why we're here," Dr. Kendrick said. "We think we have the tools, the fleet, and army, but what we lack is time. Once we arrive in the alpha universe, we won't have long."

He looked up at Snickerdoodle.

"You can replicate the E.M.P. attack that you used on us and Earth, right?"

"Of course," Snickerdoodle nodded.

"How would your people feel about... doing that everywhere to the S.C.E.?"

All eyes were on Admiral Ra'aiah, who appeared slightly uneasy, yet a small and timid smile formed on her face.

"I can't believe I'm saying that outloud," she exhaled. "What we're discussing is practically treason."

"We're going to strike every single base, fleet, and planet that is under S.C.E. control," Serina declared. "Or die trying!"

"Preferably without the dying," Dr. Kendrick replied hastily.

"There are over a few thousand outposts, command centers, fleet spaceports and space command operations across our territories," Ulgo explained. "And we want to hit them all."

"Intriguing," Snickerdoodle nodded. "However, we can't be in multiple places all at once."

"No," Admiral Ra'aiah agreed quickly. "We need to focus our efforts on S.C.E. planets and bases that are of the most strategic value. Hopefully, we can get rid of Silent Eclipse and establish a foothold. If we fail, others may have a fighting chance."

"What is it that you will be doing?" Snickerdoodle asked curiously.

"I'm taking the Firestar straight to the S.C.E. high command in the Sol system," she replied firmly. "We're going straight for the heart of the Space Command Enterprise."

"Cutting off the head of the snake," Taylor looked impressed. "That is a pretty bold plan."

"You know what I find a little funny?"

Serina glanced up at Dr. Kendrick.

"I can just imagine how crazy of a post-action report this will create if we successfully pull it off," she said. "Scratch that, whoever has to write this entire story will be in for the time of their life."

"If we fail," Ulgo nodded at Serina and then looked at the admiral. "If Silent Eclipse's leadership isn't exposed, apprehended or killed in what we are planning to do, then we will be executed as traitors."

"Well..." she turned to her first officer and let out a nervous chuckle. "Taking this matter straight to the council or the courts isn't exactly an option we can go with. We'll probably get killed before the court-martial ever becomes public."

"We're obviously not doing it the legal way," Dr. Kendrick said to Snickerdoodle. "I hope that won't be too big of an ethical or moral problem for you."

"We understand," Snickerdoodle curled his claws into fists and pumped them up. "I, for one, am very interested in exposing the dishonorable villains that tried to kill my new friends and frame my people."

"It should not be difficult to convince the rest of our people of your desired cause," Iona added as Snickerdoodle lowered his arms. "We would like to help you swiftly save your universe."

"Still," Admiral Ra'aiah shook her head. "We're going up against the heart of our military and naval forces. I propose to have one Tandeeri ship work with one of ours from our liberated fleet and detonate E.M.P. pulses everywhere. We have to take the fight directly to the S.C.E. high command."

"Cut off the head of the snake," Dr. Kendrick repeated.

"In my opinion, this is a suicide mission if we fail," Ulgo shook his head softly. "With our available ships, whether we remain together as one organized fleet or if we separate, we are still talking about going against every battle group, every fleet, all various kinds of starships, starbases, and military garrisons across thousands of systems. It's impossible."

"I think that if we manage to eliminate the leadership running Silent Eclipse or at least expose them, then we'll have a chance," Admiral Ra'aiah countered. "We need to draw the truth out and rally more people to our cause. We don't have the numbers, but I'm willing to bet that there are S.C.E. commanders and crew that would absolutely side with us."

She looked up at Snickerdoodle and Iona.

"If you can help the Firestar, we'll need your assistance to detonate your E.M.P. on our universe's Earth."

Snickerdoodle and Iona nodded.

"This will be done," Snickerdoodle confirmed, then glanced at Commander Ulgo. "However, I fear for those that we cannot get to in time. Your commander speaks the truth. What happens if we go straight to your high command and their forces mobilize? We cannot fight against a hundred ships if Silent Eclipse successfully takes control and turns their weapons on us."

"To avoid getting eliminated right off the bat, that's where I brought a little bit of help!"

Serina flashed brightly, drawing everyone's attention to her.

"Admiral Ra'iah and Commander Ulgo!" she called out. "Would you mind defining what a terrorist attack is?"

"Excuse me?"

Admiral Ra'aiah and Ulgo exchanged confused looks. She turned back to Serina again and shrugged.

"Uh, off the top of my head, it's asymmetrical warfare," she answered, even though she wasn't entirely certain. "Someone planning an attack of that nature would be trying to destabilize everyone's lives."

"Exactly!" Serina nodded, glancing up at Dr. Kendrick.

"Oh, my turn?" he said, pointing to himself. He sighed and added to her explanation. "A terrorist attack consists of properly knowing the rules of their intended targets and then acting accordingly to prevent and destroy their defensive countermeasures."

Dr. Kendrick pointed at the two S.C.E. officers in the room.

"Namely... you two, who know the rules and proper S.C.E. protocols," he said. "We need you to tell us how they'll respond when we begin our attack."

"Well, if the plan fails, they'll pretty much slaughter us," Admiral Ra'aiah replied bluntly.

"Yes, which is why we need to discuss the plan that's most likely to succeed," Dr. Kendrick stated. "Giving your subordinates a plan that might end in failure isn't the best way for us to carry out the assault."

Commander Ulgo raised his hand.

"Well, if I may... doctor? I think terrorist is too strong of a word," he said. "Perhaps we should call ourselves something other than that?"

"Rebels?" Taylor suggested.

"Already used," Serina interrupted. "Besides, we're not actually rebels openly fighting a government regime. More like... we're trying to expose the villainous masterminds that are hiding in that government."

"Liberators?"

Everyone looked at Admiral Ra'aiah, whose eyes were lighting up.

"Our fleet, combined with the amborgs and the Tandeeri, are liberators," she said. "We're liberating our home from the control of Silent Eclipse. It'll be fast and decisive."

"What of the robots?" Snickerdoodle asked. "How did they activate the first time?"

"I'm guessing that it all started when 999 dug a little too deep into the archives," Admiral Ra'aiah said. "From the moment that the first robot was defeated and then she, 117, and 917 brought it to me in my office aboard my ship. With how many that were hidden on my ship, it's hard to know what triggered all of them. Getting Snickerdoodle's son off my ship was clearly a wise decision, considering how unsafe it was aboard the Firestar."

"So, the drones are activated by some sort of signal?" Iona asked.

Dr. Kendrick nodded and gestured towards Serina. She promptly activated his computer monitor, which displayed a scan of one of the Silent Eclipse drones. It showed several images of the different drones they'd battled on the Firestar, along with photos of the one that had attacked the White House. All of them were built like evil, dark bipedal killing machines.

"It's a standard assassin drone," Admiral Ra'aiah remarked.

"Are there more types?" Snickerdoodle asked.

"Possibly," Commander Ulgo nodded. "But these were the only ones we discovered in our fleet. If Silent Eclipse has other variations in its ranks, then we haven't encountered them yet."

"It doesn't matter," Admiral Ra'aiah replied. "As long as we knock out all communications and prevent them from activating."

"Based on our scans and a close look at the Silent Eclipse robots we have in our possession," Dr. Kendrick explained, "we discovered that they are activated on a certain hidden frequency. Their base programming is only set to eliminate all who are aware of their presence and to erase all traces of their existence."

"Well," Admiral Ra'aiah pondered. "Massing for an attack is easy. But with how fast Silent Eclipse catches onto our transmissions and plans, the fleets guarding our bases will be on us in minutes before we even have time to fire our first shots."

"Actually, before we bring forth our particular weapon, there is something I would like to know. Can't the Tandeeri scramble systems?" Dr. Kendrick asked. "They disrupted our radar and jammed our frequencies when they first arrived. Could they do it again?"

"Yes," Snickerdoodle spoke. "Our energy is quite powerful."

"In previous battles with them, our systems have been affected but not completely disabled. The drones are probably activated from a specific frequency," Admiral Ra'aiah shook her head. "We'd have to disrupt all possible communication frequencies within our military and space network. Then we can initiate the E.M.P. at all locations we hit. Disrupting the frequency is good but not powerful enough."

Dr. Kendrick looked down at Serina.

"Serina here has a program that can in fact knock out all communications and prevent any activation signals to Silent Eclipse," he explained.

"I kept a program that I made a few years ago," Serina smiled. "It was a failed project and it accidentally got loose."

"Another A.I.?" Ulgo asked.

"Oh no," Serina replied. "It was just a power-saving patch that was horribly put together. Anyway, it got loose and caused a lot of problems."

"The eastern seaboard was shut down for hours," Dr. Kendrick explained.

"Well, when we fixed the problem," Serina replied with a flustered look, turning a bright shade of pink. "I destroyed the original coding of the program but kept a back-up of it so I could look at it and fix it later. I never could fix the problem so... I just decided to leave it in the hands of a friend. Some of the stuff I invent is usually best kept out of my reach... especially if it has a tendency to cause worldwide disasters."

"Is that why you brought up a whole team of A.I. programs and technicians from A.I. Industries?"

"Only the ones with completed space certifications," Dr. Kendrick said. "We're going to broadcast this blackout program across all S.C.E. territories. We will set it to run as long as it can until they discover what's happening to their communications."

Admiral Ra'aiah turned her gaze towards Commander Ulgo. He considered all the information they had for the moment, then gave her a firm and determined nod. They both turned to Snickerdoodle and Iona, who appeared satisfied with themselves. It was Serina who finally broke the silence.

"I think that's our plan," she declared triumphantly.

"Now what?" Taylor asked.

Dr. Kendrick and Admiral Ra'aiah exchanged confident smiles.

"I think it's time to brief everyone else," he said.

"I'll put together a meeting," Admiral Ra'aiah nodded courteously. "I need 15 minutes. Ulgo, could you notify all commanding officers? I want as many of them as we can bring over to Apogee Station to listen to the upcoming operation. Those that the station cannot accommodate will stand by for a broadcast. We need to address all ships in the fleet."

"Yes, admiral," Ulgo nodded. "Alternatively, we could just brief all captains and commanders here and then they pass on the operation details to their respective crews aboard their own ships."

"Oh no," Admiral Ra'aiah groaned. "You want me to use the universal broadcasting system... for a speech?"

"It would be beneficial for morale," Ulgo replied.

"What's going on here?" Dr. Kendrick asked.

"Before we carry out our plan," Admiral Ra'aiah sighed, "Ulgo is saying that I should prepare a speech for everyone."

"Ah, a motivational one," Serina nodded. "The amborgs do those sometimes too!"

"Like the big moment before an epic battle!" Taylor punched a fist in the air.

"It means I have to prepare a presentation of the upcoming operation... and a speech."

Admiral Ra'aiah turned to leave Dr. Kendrick's office. She bowed and waved farewell to everyone as she headed towards the door.

"Better make that 20 minutes," she said.

Snickerdoodle and Iona both exchanged a cheeky glance. Then he turned to look at Dr. Kendrick.

"It is unfortunate you don't have the ability to read each other's thoughts," he stated. "We give each other motivational speeches all the time without having to do so out loud."

"Well," Serina smiled at the Tandeeri. "If she nails the delivery and the presentation, it'll be exactly what we all need to finish this fight. That's where the advantage of hearing it out loud helps us."

"Especially because we can't read minds," Dr. Kendrick added.

"I look forward to it," Snickerdoodle nodded. "Now then, what activities may we partake in while we wait... 20 minutes?"

Dr. Kendrick glanced at Serina, and they smiled pleasantly at each other before turning back to Snickerdoode.

"Would you like to play a game? Or learn more about us?"

Observation Lounge
31 Minutes Later

117 looked over his team's roster. Every name and amborg number was associated with those who'd arrived at Apogee Station and were listed as active. He was having 917 go over the list with him as they discussed who should be on which teams. 999 was there too, but her attention kept drifting to the windows where the S.C.E. ships orbited closely around the station. She was on edge, acting as if they might spring into action at any moment. The Tandeeri fleet was also visible, maintaining a defensive formation, and it was a truly remarkable sight.

Nobody would have imagined that they'd witness starships from different universes protecting their planet. On the bright side, it was better than waiting in terror for their weapons to fully charge and bombard Earth. One ship had enough firepower to turn the whole planet into shattered glass. Every inhabitant of the Epsilon universe was probably feeling relieved that their imminent doom wasn't so imminent.

"The big question is whether or not we want to go with their plan," 917 said. "They're literally suggesting we split ourselves up."

Prior to the big briefing that Third Admiral Ishala Ra'aiah was going to deliver directly to all commanding officers of the S.C.E. fleet, details of her operation had been released to them, enabling everyone to start their preparations. Apparently, the amborgs were given two options: they could either fight together aboard the S.C.E. Firestar as they headed directly for the S.C.E. high command, or they could assign one or two amborgs to each ship in the fleet and divide their forces. So far, every amborg currently in space was already discussing the option that would keep them together.

"I'm not agreeing to it," 117 stated. "999, are you with me?"

Not hearing a response, they both decided to turn their heads. 999 was still staring out the window at the ships.

"Uh, Angel?" 917 asked.

999 turned to glance at them. She blinked and gave them a slight nod.

"Yes," she stated. "I agree with your decision. Splitting up is... dangerous."

"Are you alright?"

"It's fine," 999 nodded.

117 and 917 snuck a wary glance at each other. They weren't entirely convinced, but they knew better than to push. 999 shifted her focus to the conversation, moving away from the window.

"I agree with 117. Divide and conquer? No, absolutely not," 999 said. "Even if we did succeed, that plan would leave us exposed. Cut off. We'd be placing our trust in people we don't know. Too risky."

"Right. So, that means the Second Group amborgs will vote to not separate," 117 replied firmly. "We do want to support this operation, but I'm not allowing one amborg to each ship alone. That's not how we work."

They figured that 297 and 777 would probably say yes to the decision. Same with 92 and 93. The two brothers could never be convinced to split up so easily like that. The question now was, where was everyone? The briefing was coming up soon and 117 was hoping to chat with the rest of the Second Group team before they attended Admiral Ra'aiah's presentation.

As they spoke, they heard the door open and their friends walked in. They were both confused and mildly concerned to see 297 acting a bit...off. 777, 92, and 93 followed closely behind him, trying in vain to stifle their laughter.

"Hey! There's our leader!" 777 gave 117 a quick salute.

"There you all are," 117 smiled slightly. "What's so funny?"

"Everything man," 297 sniffed.

917 squinted, a little disconcerted by 297's bizarre reaction.

"297," 917 said skeptically. "Have you been crying?"

"Yeah," 297 admitted as he nodded vigorously. "It was... so wonderful."

999 raised an eyebrow and looked at 777. 117 appeared worried as well, but it was the twins standing just behind 297 that were behaving suspiciously.

"Do we want to know?" he asked.

"He had a counseling session with one of the Tandeeri psychologists," 777 replied. "It was quite the session."

"You sought out counseling... from the Tandeeri?" 917 asked.

"Mmhmm," 297 nodded as he tried to pull himself together, but was failing horribly.

"This is a very... vulnerable show of emotion," 999 eyed 297 with concern. "It's... healthy."

999 shrugged when 917 turned and looked at her.

"If you consider all the horrible things he's seen," she cleared her throat.

"Does... Angel actually care about me?" 297 asked as his eyes widened.

"If you ask me that again, I'll give you another reason to cry," 999 snarled, suddenly switching back to her usual serious demeanor. "I'll jam my foot straight up your ass."

297 backed away slowly.

"Yeah, that's right," she scoffed as 917 stifled a laugh.

"Anyway," 117 interrupted as everyone else started snickering. "You actually got counseling... from an interstellar multiverse doctor?"

"Well, psychologist isn't exactly in their dictionary," 777 replied. "That actually took us a few minutes to explain."

"They are more like healers," 92 stated.

"Yes. For your soul and body," 93 finished. "It was helpful when 297 volunteered because they already knew us."

"Well, you four, the Third Group triplets, 929, and 140 were with the Tandeeri the longest out of all of us," 117 stated. "That makes sense. It looks like you had a great time with the healer."

"It was more of a follow-up session," 297 sniffed. "The more time you spend on their ship... literally, all that extra time that you have... gives you space to think. It gives you a huge opportunity to really come to terms with all of your feelings."

"I wonder if the Tandeeri and the S.C.E. wouldn't mind if we took time off? If a few hours out here can be a few days aboard their ship, we'd have the best vacations ever," 917 suggested. "The Tandeeri could literally be the answer to using our PTO hours effectively."

"Alright, let's get back to why I wanted to talk to all of you," 117 smiled.

Everyone fell silent as they gave 117 their undivided attention. 297 pulled himself together and stopped sniffling.

"I hope the other amborgs will also agree with me but, I don't want to separate the amborgs again," 117 informed them. "It's clear that if we'd all gone on the rescue mission looking for the amborgs and crew that we thought had been kidnapped, then the Firestar would have suffered more casualties. Dr. Kendrick, Captain Harrelson, and the rest of the Apogee Station survivors might have been lost."

He looked at 777 and 297.

"Splitting up was the right decision," he said. "But now we're talking about going into another universe. I don't think we should separate across the fleet."

"Ah," 777 nodded. "We're all going to remain on the Firestar?"

"That sounds good," 92 nodded. "Our original destination when we were your reinforcements."

"And then we got kidnapped," 93 smiled. "Personally, I'd prefer to go to the Firestar like we were supposed to instead of a different ship going to who knows where in the alpha universe."

"Then I think that's settled," 117 nodded. "Unless... there are any objections?"

"Look, being aboard the Tandeeri ship was fun but, I think I'd like to be back with the rest of the amborgs that came up here," 92 replied.

"Yeah, next time we go visit the Tandeeri, we should all have a spa day or something," 93 shrugged.

As they continued their discussion, a chime rang out from their gold bracelets. It was a signal from Dr. Kendrick to rally. They all exchanged focused glances and stood up.

"That's the signal," 117 stated. "Let's go to the station's briefing room."

As they entered the hall to head to the nearest elevator, 917 and 999 hung back to trail behind their friends. When it seemed like they were far enough, 999 gently grabbed him by his wrist and he stopped so that he could face her.

"917," she said quietly. "There's something I wanted to talk to you about since we boarded the Tandeeri flagship."

"Sure," 917 nodded. "What is it?"

"Before we woke up and exited the shuttle, I had a nightmare," she whispered. "I saw... memories. Moments that I hadn't thought about in a long time."

"I think that happened to all of us," 917 nodded.

"What did you see?"

999 looked into his eyes determinedly. His expression became serious and grim. She recognized it all too well. It was what they would all do whenever they put their guard up.

"Why do you need to know?" 917 asked. "You already must have an idea of all of the terrible things that I've seen."

"Please tell me," 999 replied. "Before we lose this chance."

"Chance?" 917 asked.

"When we go to fight this battle... I don't want to lose you again," 999 replied. "I should have followed you that night that you broke when we went to Silhed. I should have fought and backed you up immediately but... I didn't. Then, you were sent to prison."

"If you had come with me, you and I would have both been locked up," 917 said softly. "It was my decision, and I didn't want you to be dragged down with me."

999 furrowed her brows.

"I would rather be dragged down with you then be alone again," she exhaled. "First, we lost 345. Then I lost you. Did you ever think about how your actions would affect us? We're supposed to be together at all times."

917 looked down as his lips curled slightly. He let out a soft sigh.

"I'm sorry," he replied.

"I have already forgiven you," 999 said. "But tell me, did you see 345?"

"I did," 917 replied. "Why does that matter?"

"Because I want to know if you're going to be able to get through this mission without her clouding your judgement."

917 gazed sharply at 999.

"345 is dead," he said. "My judgement is clear. What are you getting at?"

"You still think about her, don't you?" 999 stated. "Your feelings."

"Of course I do," 917 replied annoyingly. "I can't exactly forget her! What do you want me to do? Just cast her out of my mind?"

"No," 999 replied. "I think about her every day."

"Then what are we talking about?" 917 asked. "What do you want?"

"I don't want you to go," 999 stated.

917 leaned back slightly. He wasn't expecting that response.

"After this is over," he said, a small smile forming, "I'm not going back to prison after this mission. I spoke with Dr. Kendrick, and he was talking about letting me..."

"I don't want you to go on this mission."

999 bit her lip, broadcasting her last sentence through her bracelet. Her words cut deep as 917 processed them.

"What?" he asked. "You're asking me to stay behind?"

"The same way you left me behind," 999 whispered. "I can't..."

"Can't what? That's not the same thing," 917 shook his head. "You can't ask me to do that."

"I can order you," 999 replied.

"And I'll disobey your order," 917 replied angrily.

999's breath trembled as she firmly stood her ground.

"Why?" she asked in a cold tone.

917 and 999 both stood there staring defiantly into each other's eyes.

"Why what?" he replied, voice low.

"This time... why can't you let me protect you again?"

"Because I can help end this fight," 917 replied. "Asking me to stay behind while you go and possibly get yourself killed? I can't allow that!"

"I care about you, and I don't want you distracted," 999 stated.

"If you cared about me as my best friend," 917 shook his head, "you wouldn't hold me back. You know I'm right."

"I know."

999 suddenly reached out and grabbed him by the collar. 917 lifted his hands, ready for a fight, but was taken aback when 999 leaned in fast. With a little force, 999 pressed her lips to his, effectively stunning him. Caught off guard, 917's eyes widened. He didn't attempt to push her away or pull back; instead, he found himself trying to understand what was happening.

The kiss only lasted a few seconds. 999 retreated slowly, unable to meet his gaze as he stared at her. Focusing on the glowing number on his amborg jacket, she closed her eyes.

"I know I can't stop you," she said. "I just... really wanted you to know. I wanted you to hear me say it directly. I care about you. I'll always want you at my side no matter what during the fight. But I needed you to know."

917's mouth opened slightly but no words came out.

"I wanted... to tell you how I felt," 999 replied.

917 nodded slowly as his brain tried to catch up with everything that had just transpired. Then, he and 999 turned to look down the

hall in the direction that their friends had gone. They noticed 117 and Serina standing there, watching them quietly.

Serina let out a small squeak when their presence had been discovered.

"I-I just came to check on you before the briefing," she stammered.

"I wanted to check on you two because... I felt concerned," 117 cleared his throat and shifted uncomfortably. "I saw 999 grab 917 and thought you two were about to fight but held my position when we saw the..."

"Kiss. It was uh... we should... really get going but... we're sorry we saw that."

999 held up a hand and shook her head at 117 and Serina.

"It's ok," she said.

Serina and 117 gazed at each other skeptically, then turned back to her, surprise creeping over their features. Even 917 was taken aback.

"She's not reacting," Serina gulped. "That's weird."

"I-I'm... really..." 917 stammered. "Uhh..."

999 walked towards 117.

"We have a briefing to attend," she said, quickly shifting into her professional demeanor, which caused them to eye her carefully.

"Sure," 117 said cautiously. "I assume you don't want us to talk about... that?"

"Yeah, we won't tell anyone," Serina said gently.

999 looked at Serina and 117. She turned her head to glance at 917, who was silently staring at her, but she chose not to meet his gaze.

"Thank you," 999 said. "117. After the briefing, I think I'd like to spend some time training aboard the Tandeeri flagship. I think... we could all benefit from the extra time."

"Oh?" 117 glanced at 999 and then at 917. "Right. Right! That sounds like an excellent idea! If we have time!"

"If they let us hang out aboard the Heart of Alcyon," Serina said cheerfully. "We'll definitely have time."

"Let's go."

999 pivoted and headed down the hall, then rounded a corner. Serina and 117 looked at 917, who was still a little flustered.

"Good for both of you," Serina turned a light shade of red and grinned excitedly. "It's so sweet!"

"I am really sorry. We are really sorry for..." 117 cleared his throat. "Uh... what was that? I didn't think that would happen now."

917 approached them, and he and 117 started walking side by side. Serina hovered next to 117's head, conjuring pom-poms in her hands. She happily waved them while 117 and 917 tried to catch up with 999, but she was already out of sight.

"I-I wish I knew..." 917 stammered. Then he turned and looked at 117 and Serina. "That was..."

"Nice?" 117 asked.

"Of course!" 917 nodded but didn't seem too sure. 117 could hear the uncertainty in his voice. "I expected... but I wasn't... trying to pressure her."

"Of course not," 117 nodded. "It's nice to see you both moving on and possibly choosing each other."

"Uh, 117?" Serina interrupted. "I don't think he's that thrilled about it."

117 and Serina both glanced at 917.

"No! I am," he replied. "I just."

917's eyes widened as he looked back at the two of them.

"I have to talk to her," he said.

"About something good?" Serina eyed 917 expectantly.

"Can we talk about this later?" 917 replied. "We definitely need to hang out with Snickerdoodle. Or wait, no... he'll read my mind. Oh man..."

917 sped up and 117 couldn't match his pace. When he was out of sight, he looked at Serina.

"Ok," she shook her head nervously. "That's not good."

When they entered the main briefing room, they found a crowd of people clustered around a massive circular table. A spherical screen was lit up, ready to present the briefing for everyone shortly. The front three rows were filled with seats, while ample space was available for those standing in the back. Once the proceedings started, the leaders would gather in one area of the room, while cameras would relay a live feed on the screen for the audience, eliminating the need for them to be in the center.

Dr. Kendrick was standing in front of one of the briefing room's glass windows with Admiral Ra'aiah and Snickerdoodle. The amborgs, A.I. Industries staff, S.C.E. crewmen, and even a small party of

Tandeeri were present. They were all gathered in their respective groups, and were now taking their seats.

A.I. Industries employees and technicians from Apogee Station were sitting with S.C.E. officers and crew. The amborgs decided to stand with the Tandeeri in the outer circle of the room. Due to their sheer size and height, most of the Tandeeri visitors couldn't sit down, as they couldn't fit in their small chairs. Fortunately, it seemed as though they were content to be standing with the amborgs.

As 117 waited for the presentation to begin, someone sidled next to him and felt a quick tap on the shoulder.

"Head on a swivel."

117 turned and was pleased to see Captain Harrelson of the Apogee Station marines waving at him. He was the man who had encountered Serina 43 from the Alpha universe when she crash-landed in Kenya, and he was their first contact. After the Emergency Recall began, he and his team of marines went with Dr. Kendrick and the amborgs into space. After the Tandeeri first arrived and almost blew up the station, he took his squad and accompanied Dr. Kendrick aboard the Firestar. When Silent Eclipse attacked the ship, he and his marines helped the S.C.E. forces defend the ship and thankfully, 117 had heard that they had only suffered minor injuries. No fatalities were reported.

"Captain!" 117 smiled as the two of them shook hands firmly. "I am so glad to see you."

"Likewise," Harrelson nodded. "Lately, things have been crazy so I'd thought I'd stop by."

"I'm glad you did," 117 nodded. "Are you... possibly going to join us? For this operation?"

117 was surprised to see Captain Harrelson politely shaking his head.

"Sorry sir," he replied. "I think me and my marines are tapping out for this one. It's tempting but I really think our place is here."

117 looked a little crestfallen as Harrelson continued his explanation.

"I won't forget it though," he smiled as he turned and looked at some of the S.C.E officers. "When we were fighting those evil robots, the S.C.E. marines put their lives on the line for me and my squad. Not only did we realize that we were way out of our league, but we felt terrible that complete strangers were getting killed trying to protect us. I don't think we're of much use to you if we did join you to the Alpha universe."

"I can understand that," 117 nodded. "Am I correct in assuming that you would rather defend our universe?"

"Damn straight," Harrelson nodded confidently. "The space jumpers will stay here and if there are any other threats from space or on Earth, we will hold the fort until you get back."

"Then, I guess after this briefing, it'll be goodbye."

117 looked down disappointedly, then lifted his head and gave Harrelson a smile. The two of them reached out and shook hands once more.

"Not goodbye," Harrelson cautioned 117 in a reassuring tone. "I'll see you later."

"Of course," 117 nodded.

"Oh, and... I'm sorry to hear about 125," Harrelson let go of 117's hand and dipped his head respectfully. "He was a great guy."

117 thanked Captain Harrelson as he walked away, weaving through the crowd to join his comrades. He noticed Alpha 43 greeting him politely as she made her way over.

"There you are," 117 remarked. "You didn't want to join us on Earth?"

"I had a ship to take care of," 43 replied with a soft smile. "A lot of people needed my help."

"I'm sorry, we should have..."

"It's ok," 43 shook her head. "You deserved your respite and I'm glad you all went back home to rest and recover. I was concentrating on doing that up here in space."

Suddenly, a bell rang out across the room. The lights dimmed as everyone fell silent.

"We'll talk later?" 117 asked.

"Of course we will," 43 nodded.

The screen in the center of the circular room lit up, displaying Dr. Kendrick, Admiral Ra'aiah, and Snickerdoodle. Even though they stood at the back of one part of the room, this was broadcasted throughout the station and was visible to everyone in the briefing room.

"All of you know who I am," Dr. Kendrick's voice reverberated off the walls. "We have assembled here because we are planning what is often referred to as the endgame. It is an operation that will ultimately decide the fate of both the Epsilon and Alpha universes. Our adversary is the S.C.E.'s covert operations division—a special part of your organization that has been secretly working behind the scenes to undermine us. They are known as Silent Eclipse and we will be attempting to end their existence, once and for all."

"Is that the name of who snuck a squad of death drones aboard my ship? And everyone else's?"

The officer who spoke was one of the commanders from the S.C.E. 117 glanced over at the officer who posed the question, while 43 transmitted a small profile along with a short paragraph about him. His name appeared in 117's HUD, and he recognized him as Captain Hodges of the S.C.E. Hazel Ying Lee.

"Come on, it sounds like a Tandeeri trick," someone else commented.

Before 43 could share who it was that had made that remark, the Tandeeri nearest to them growled softly.

"This puny human is accusing us of trickery? After we saved their lives?" a Tandeeri woman scoffed.

"We apologize!"

117 looked left and noticed another officer speak up.

"The Tandeeri did save us!" he spoke quickly. "If they had fired an E.M.P. at us, my entire department would have been wiped out."

"Ahem!"

The room fell silent as Dr. Kendrick's expression fixed on the camera, revealing his impatience on the screen.

"In the interest of working together," he said, "I would like to welcome you all here. In this room, we have members of the Alpha universe, the S.C.E., my amborgs and staff from the Epsilon universe, and then the Tandeeri who... hail from a universe somewhere far away in the infinite realm of universes out there."

Dr. Kendrick adjusted his glasses and took a breath. He decided to continue speaking so that no one else would interrupt and ruin the flow of the briefing.

"We all come from different places but hopefully, our goals by the end of this briefing will be the same. We can't allow our prejudices and differences dictate our actions. We must work together in what is possibly the biggest act of defiance you will ever be a part of. If this plan succeeds, all of you will be able to return home to your families, your lives, and be free to do whatever you want. No one will be held hostage in order to manipulate you into surrendering your free will. If you choose not to do this, then we will respect that choice, but think about what that means. Do you really want to remember this moment as the time you decided to sit back and do nothing after surviving a terrible massacre? We will defeat whoever thinks that we will go quietly into the darkness. Everyone who has died will be avenged and honored for everything they have done. Therefore, I will turn it over to Admiral Ra'aiah, the commander of the entirety of the S.C.E. fleet survivors orbiting our station and planet Earth."

The screen shifted from Dr. Kendrick to Admiral Ra'aiah, who fixed a stern stare at the camera. They noticed her Quick Look towards Dr. Kendrick, whose shoulder was visible in the corner of the screen.

"That was really good..." she whispered.

"Thank you," Dr. Kendrick muttered a soft reply.

"My turn..." she cleared her throat and straightened up. "Hello everyone."

All the officers of the S.C.E. adjusted their posture, now sitting at attention. 117 looked around in amazement. The other amborgs appeared quite intrigued as well with their sudden change in demeanor. As an admiral, she commanded a lot of respect from everyone in the room. That was impressive.

"Thank you Dr. Kendrick," Admiral Ra'aiah spoke formally. As she gazed into the camera, 117 got goosebumps. "What we're asking of you is something that has never been attempted before in the history of the Space Command Enterprise. For my fellow crew and shipmates, I won't hide it. This plan... what it entails... will hopefully win us our freedom, because at this moment, our homes and families are being held at a proverbial gunpoint. This operation, once we carry it out, can and will be seen as treason. If we fail, chances are, we'll be dead. Forget about the end of our careers. This mission to hunt down the command structure of Silent Eclipse is an actual attack on S.C.E. High Command. We are going to attempt to identify who is running an illegal covert division. But, we have taken measures to ensure that this plan will be the light in the middle of the chaos and confusion. Hopefully it will be what saves us all. Like Dr. Kendrick stated earlier, you are under no obligation to come with us. There's the door if you don't want to participate. The offer extends to every crewmember and noncombatant aboard your ships in the fleet. If you choose not to accept, then we will accommodate you here on the station, with Dr. Kendrick's approval, or you stay on Earth. This is now the time for you to make your decision, speak up, and exit peacefully."

A low murmur spread throughout the room. 117 expected that some people, like the officer who believed this was all a Tandeeri trick, would stand up and leave. He didn't blame anyone if they had second thoughts. This was a mission with extremely high stakes.

An officer suddenly rose from his seat. 43 transmitted his profile to 117, and he read it in his HUD. His name was Desmond.

"Captain Desmond, S.C.E. Madison Marsh," he declared. "Admiral. My ship and crew are all with you, ma'am."

This seemed to motivate everyone else, as more officers started to rise up. 117 realized that these were all the commanding officers of each of the S.C.E. ships in the fleet.

"You know me, I'd follow my family anywhere."

117's face lit up when he noticed a grinning officer stand up nearby. He didn't need the profile from 43. It was Captain Chastain from the S.C.E. Alexandria, who also happened to be Admiral Ra'aiah's godfather. Although she referred to him as her uncle on occasion, it was no surprise that he was declaring his ship's involvement in the mission.

"Thank you," Admiral Ra'aiah clasped her hands, looking as if her wish had been granted. "All of you."

Her lips curled into a smile, making her emotions visible to all. 117 made a mental note to remind the technicians maintaining the station equipment what an excellent job they were doing. Seriously, looking at Admiral Ra'aiah was like watching an insanely realistic, high quality television.

"Silent Eclipse has taken enough lives," she said. "But because you are all still standing here and willing to join us, then this plan... it will work. This fight will stop Silent Eclipse from controlling us, decimating us from the inside, and making us fight the wrong people. This is the victory we need... so that justice and peace will be given to all."

"We, the Tandeeri, will be there to help you to victory!"

The camera on the screen zoomed back slightly. Snickerdoodle leaned down and waved at the camera as he moved closer to Admiral Ra'aiah. He extended his claw as the camera attempted to fit him and the admiral in the frame.

"I would like to formally propose an alliance between the Tandeeri and the S.C.E." Snickerdoodle declared. "May we begin the custom of shaking hands?"

"Yes of course!"

Admiral Ra'aiah eagerly lifted her hand but before she could grab Snickerdoodle's claw, he started to shake it rapidly.

"What the...?" 43 muttered in surprise.

117 stared in silent confusion for a moment, then realized what was happening. Someone had taught Snickerdoodle the literal way of "shaking hands." He glanced at 501, who was grinning cheerfully, but his smile faltered when he noticed 117 and the other amborgs glaring at him.

Without a word, he swiftly weaved through the confused crowd towards Snickerdoodle. When he made it, he quickly whispered to him.

117 watched as Snickerdoodle looked off camera, then nodded in understanding. He could barely make out his response.

"Oh, I see."

Then, Snickerdoodle extended his claw to Admiral Ra'aiah, who accepted it tentatively.They firmly shook hands properly, then let go.

"We... have an alliance!" Dr. Kendrick declared.

"We are grateful that we aren't alone," Admiral Ra'aiah explained "The amborgs and humans of Epsilon Earth will be allying with us and the Tandeeri so that we have a chance. It's thanks to the amborgs for figuring out how to communicate between our people."

No one spoke. In fact, it was likely the Admiral's resolve and courage that slowly filled everyone with confidence. Although they may have not been smiling, every person in an S.C.E. uniform was ready.

"Ok... The first part of the plan is..." Admiral Ra'aiah smiled, but hesitated. She still looked a little rattled. "Dr. Kendrick?"

Dr. Kendrick nodded and stepped in. As the camera focused on him, 117 glanced over at Admiral Ra'aiah, who was looking up at Snickerdoodle and holding out her right hand. He was shaking his own clawed hand eagerly, which only confused her more.

Oops, he thought. *That probably threw her off the briefing.*

117 also couldn't help but smile because that was exactly what he did to Mandy when she first met him. He definitely looked ridiculous at the time when someone had to explain how handshakes worked. He felt the embarrassment resurfacing and decided to focus on the briefing as Dr. Kendrick's face appeared onscreen.

"First," he spoke confidently. "We know that the Silent Eclipse drones are activated by some kind of signal when they find out that we've discovered them. When that happens, they strike inside a ship to quickly gain control of it or destroy it before the real crew realizes what's happening. In our case, one drone activated... on Earth, and several others on this station."

"It killed the diplomatic officers and their escorts that were in contact with U.S. President Bill Holland of Epsilon Universe," Admiral Ra'aiah added. "For some reason, more on Earth didn't activate."

Everyone began whispering amongst themselves.

"If it puts all of your minds at ease," Snickerdoodle's voice spoke up. "The planet and this station are safe. We have eliminated all of these dark drones, and they will no longer affect this universe."

Dr. Kendrick nodded as he continued to address the room.

"One drone assaulted the White House and attempted to kill my friend," he said. "In the process, one of my amborgs was murdered."

117 noticed a few S.C.E. officers glancing in his direction. He looked at the screen and noticed the raw pain in Dr. Kendrick's expression. His eyes were focused and filled with a building rage. Unbeknownst to the S.C.E. officers, this was actually a small act.

The code word was "murder." As soon as Dr. Kendrick mentioned that word, it would signal the start of a sympathy play. Once he brought up 125, he'd get the officers and crew of the S.C.E. to look their way. Together, the amborgs would display a silent array of emotions.

Many of them looked uncomfortable, peeved, determined, and focused. Several officers were murmuring and whispering to each other again as they took note of the amborgs and their expressions. 117 decided to show leadership by nodding angrily and like he was about to start a fight. Then he got a text message from 999.

You look ridiculous, she wrote. *Actually, constipated. Don't show too much. Simplify.*

117 snuck a glance at 999, who was rolling her eyes. She texted him again.

With how many undercover assignments you've successfully completed, how is your acting still so terrible?

117 responded fast as he softened his expression and listened to Dr. Kendrick speak again.

Like you're one to talk?

I think I'm gaining more sympathy than you are.

Everyone's attention was directed at the screen again.

"One of my A.I.s has a virus program which we believe can be configured to target the frequency that these drones run on. Using this, we can shut them all down in one swift move," Dr. Kendrick said. "Now, this doesn't shut down Silent Eclipse's drones, but it will prevent any activation codes or signals from reaching them. It effectively will disable our own communications in the process. My only concern right now is that this program may not work in terms of compatibility with your communications equipment. Which is why Serina and the A.I. programs I've brought up with me will be working aboard the Tandeeri fleet to run some tests."

"But we're trying to get rid of the drones," someone spoke up. "What's the point of shutting down communications? Wouldn't that disrupt the objective?"

"So, my friend," Snickerdoodle said enthusiastically. "This will buy us time to position ourselves to unleash our weapon."

"Exactly," Admiral Ra'aiah added. "We need to convince the other fleets that the Tandeeri have obliterated us entirely, that the mission to defend Epsilon was a failure. Step one is to re-enter the Alpha universe and warp to as many locations as possible with the number of ships we have. The Tandeeri will send a ship to accompany us, but the instant we are seen working together, Silent Eclipse will attempt to blow us out into space. Remember, this plan will expose the leaders running Silent Eclipse but it will only work if we put on an act while the virus works."

"Basically," Dr. Kendrick added, "this will be one massive attack and if timed properly, we vanquish an army that wasn't supposed to exist. The key, though, is that we disable their communications swiftly. If Silent Eclipse discovers our plans or our timing is off, then the fight will be much more difficult. The more time wasted is more room for them to adapt."

"Each ship will transmit a distress signal and say that the battle for Epsilon Earth has been lost," Admiral Ra'aiah explained. "The Tandeeri ship accompanying you will pretend to appear and prepare for an attack when in reality, they'll be preparing a localized E.M.P. with your main weapons. We just need time to get into position and fire as many E.M.P. shots as possible so that no one will be at risk. It's really important that the program knocks out all of the sector's communications. Ship, fleet, starbase, colony, all the way from the rotten satellites to the radios. Anything at all that picks up a signal."

From the back of 117's head, he heard a friendly voice.

"It's not bad, if I do say so myself," Serina transmitted to him.

"Every available S.C.E. crew that is still on this planet will return to the Firestar," Admiral Ra'aiah commanded.

"For the time being, but at least Earth is safe. Now we focus on our own universe. Taking on the fleet and coordinating all efforts will be orchestrated from the Firestar. After we return to Alpha universe, we will be limited on our communication channels, so once you arrive at your designated point of attack, every ship will observe silent running conditions."

"A.I. Industries staff will also be divided amongst the fleet," Dr. Kendrick declared. "An A.I. under Serina's command will accompany each S.C.E. ship with a copy of the virus program. At her signal, the A.I.s unleash the program simultaneously. It will be the responsibility of my scientists to ensure that no one interferes with the operation of my A.I. programs. Understood?"

The lab-coats of A.I. Industries all nodded in affirmation and gave their calls of approval.

"The S.C.E. crewmen will treat our passengers well and regard them as high priority," Admiral Ra'aiah eyed her own crew sternly. "Is that understood?"

"Yes ma'am!" the S.C.E. crew spoke in scattered voices.

"And we will protect you," Snickerdoodle lifted his fist and tapped his chest. "Your ships will be safe with us."

"That leaves the amborgs," Dr. Kendrick said.

Everyone turned to look at the four groups of amborgs, and the leaders of each group stepped forward. They all silently transmitted their arguments and discussions and finally, their votes to the leader.

"We're not in agreement with the separation plan," 1 declared with 2 at his side.

"Agreed," 117 spoke.

"The amborgs vote that separation is bad," 113 added for the Fourth Group. "It gives us anxiety."

"Like the Fourth Group gets anxiety," 297 chuckled as he nudged 5 in the shoulder.

"Dude, your anxiety levels are through the roof," 5 replied.

"Might need more counseling," 297 cleared his throat.

"And we agreed you'd stay quiet during this briefing," 6 said through gritted teeth.

Dr. Kendrick cleared his throat loudly while everyone stared at the amborgs.

"I believe we are waiting for my leader of the Third Group," Dr. Kendrick said.

501 nodded and spoke up.

"I don't go anywhere without 917," he declared with a grin. "We stay with the other amborgs!"

"Me?" 917 asked. "Don't you mean 117?"

"I just noticed that a few of them have the number seven as part of their amborg designations," they heard a lieutenant whisper to her friend. "Are they all big fans of that number?"

Her friend shushed her, and they fell silent.

"No," 501 replied to 917. "I meant you."

917 leaned forward and looked at 117. 117 tilted his head, glancing between 501 and 466. That was a little odd to hear from him.

"What? What happened to me?" 117 asked in surprise. "I mean, why 917?"

"Here we go," 999 said.

"Sorry 117," 501 smiled sheepishly. "I think now is probably not the best time... to tell you that... 917 legally is my mentor."

"Mine too," 466 raised her hand guiltily.

The S.C.E. officers and crew watching were displaying baffled expressions. Nevertheless, everyone seemed quite interested in where this conversation was going.

"Are we still being briefed? This wasn't in the presentation," someone commented.

"No," Iona spoke up. "But this is quite intriguing."

The amborgs seemed to have temporarily forgotten where they were as 117 stared at the two Third Group leaders, his expression a blend of pure confusion and surprise, and maybe a little hurt.

"What are you two saying?"

"Yes," 917 raised an eyebrow skeptically. "I want an explanation too."

"This hardly seems like the right..."

501 shrunk back, 466 ducking behind him, as 917 and 117 lowered their gazes at them.

"Ok, ok! We had 117 sign the paperwork! 917 too!"

"Why don't I remember this?" 917 asked.

"Same," 117 nodded.

"You were both drunk," 999 declared. "It was after 117 and Audrey's honeymoon. We had that party after they returned from their trip. It's true. 501 and 466 have our signatures."

"It was after 43 passed away!" 501 said as 117 and 917 both looked at each other in disbelief.

"Me?" 43 pointed at herself.

"No, our 43," 466 stated.

"Oh, right," 43 nodded.

"At that party, we brought it up and discussed it and... 117 agreed to sign us over to a new pair of mentors since we figured he wanted more time with his wife!"

501's statement had 117 racking his memory.

"117 got drunk and he had us go through a document," 501 explained. "He signed custody of 466 and me over to 917 and 999. They're our legal mentors."

"Is that why they went on so many more missions with you two?" 777 asked, looking more amused with every passing second. He gestured at 917 and 999. "This is hilarious."

"Hang on," 3 interrupted as she poked 1's shoulder. "We can sign custody... of ourselves? To each other? Are we all... married or legally bonded to each other?"

"If we are," 2 mumbled, "I think we need a lawyer."

"Uh, aren't most of us lawyers?" 6 mumbled.

"This is news to me," 1 replied with a baffled expression.

In the corner, Admiral Ra'aiah was staring at them in stunned silence. Dr. Kendrick buried his face in his hand. Only Snickerdoodle and the Tandeeri seemed interested in what was happening. Even though they appeared confused, the S.C.E. crew and officers watched the awkward scene continue to unfold.

"What is happening?" Admiral Ra'aiah asked.

"That? That's what's happening," Dr. Kendrick groaned.

"It looks fun!" Snickerdoodle grinned as he nodded approvingly.

The only thing everyone was missing was the popcorn and drinks. The A.I. Industries employees looked like they were having the time of their lives, on the verge of losing it judging by how hard they were trying to stifle their laughter.

There was a bright flash of light as Serina popped up next to 117. As the amborgs continued to listen to 501's explanation, she clapped her hands together and pulled them apart, generating a tiny holographic screen and began reading something.

"You said that you wanted me and 466 to be safe in case anything happened to you," 501 said, gesturing to 466, who was smiling and waving cheerfully to the crowd. "So... you proclaimed 917 and 999 to be the amborgs in charge of our well-being. We're not your apprentice amborgs anymore."

"I'm impressed you consented, filed the paperwork, and got it validated when you were drunk at your honeymoon after-party," 5 commented.

"Oh wait," 117 felt the memories resurfacing. "I think I have a vague recollection... but... we still had missions together!"

"We did," 466 nodded. "But you were committed to your wife and we still needed a mentor."

"Wow, this entire Emergency Recall has just been roasting you," 297 whispered to 117.

"Yeah, I'm really sorry 117," Serina chuckled awkwardly as she continued scrolling on her personal screen. "But if you read the fine print, it's all legit. You no longer have custody."

Serina transmitted the document to 117 and he scrutinized his own handwriting. With her help, Serina highlighted key segments.

"Well, that explains why you two have been so friendly with us lately," 917 said as 117 continued examining the documents. "I can't believe I never knew that you were under our care."

917 looked at 999.

"You kept this from me for how many years?" he asked.

999 didn't get a chance to reply. 117 shut off the screen, looking crestfallen.

"I think I just got dumped by 501 and 466," 117 said as his heart sank.

"Emancipated is probably the correct term," 92 spoke.

"No no," 93 corrected him. "501 and 466 aren't children. I think disowned is accurate."

"Amborgs! Everyone!"

The amborgs fell silent and snapped back at attention.

"Anyway," Dr. Kendrick sighed angrily. "What I heard from the amborgs was... they disagree with the S.C.E.'s plan?"

"Just the part where they determine who splits up with who," 117 replied. "Sorry Admiral Ra'aiah. You're asking us to go solo aboard each of your ships. We all politely refuse because that's not how we want it to be."

"W-well," Admiral Ra'aiah stammered. "I'm sorry but we cover more ground if we separate all of you."

"Covering ground is easy," 1 said. "The scientists don't need an amborg to watch over them all the time. Statistically, they're actually safer when an A.I. looks after them. We have a better chance of succeeding if the amborgs are all together."

"Dr. Kendrick?" Admiral Ra'aiah looked to the other leaders.

"Well like they said," he shrugged with a smile. "Separation anxiety. I'd say we let them do what they want."

Admiral Ra'aiah looked at 43.

"They've made their choice ma'am," she said respectfully. "I can't do much against all of them. I'm too old to be taking on every amborg present."

"Yeah, we saw how I beat you the first time," 999 said, sotto voce.

43 eyed 999 and smirked.

"Keep thinking that, little brat," 43 chuckled.

999 was referring to the duel that they had participated in when 43 first visited Apogee Station. From how it looked, they all felt that

it had ended in a tie. Obviously, since 43 and 999 had been the active participants in the deadlock, they were both stubbornly holding onto the claim that they were the winners.

"We request permission to go with you," 117 said when the Admiral glanced back at him. "Like 1 said, as a group, we stand a better chance of helping you hunt down the leaders of Silent Eclipse. It'll be easier and more efficient in the midst of the chaos."

"If we don't allocate our resources, my ships are going to be out there alone against every fleet in the S.C.E.," Admiral Ra'aiah said. "I need your help."

"Then trust your crew," 117 answered. "Trust that they're ready to do what you ask of them. All we want to do is get a little revenge."

The S.C.E. officers murmured in agreement and nodded in approval. They all looked prepared to see this fight through without amborg assistance.

"I never would have expected 117 to use that word," Serina said as she widened her eyes.

"I figured my alpha version would like that," 117 smiled at 43, who was chuckling. "It's also the perfect opportunity to draw out the leaders too."

"You want to use yourself as bait?" Dr. Kendrick said as he nodded slowly, beginning to understand. "Well, I suppose you've earned the right to make that choice."

"The amborgs were the ones who created this mess in the first place," 117 explained. "We found out the truth, and then Silent Eclipse started killing people. Now we're being hunted too. It's only reasonable that we finish this. After all, we make very valuable targets and it may be enough to get them to react."

"Alright then," Admiral Ra'aiah sighed. "With your approval Dr. Kendrick, I will take all the amborgs with me aboard the Firestar. Then we will start the main assault on our home planet."

The lights in the room flickered on as the briefing came to its conclusion. Admiral Ra'aiah made one last announcement.

"Once everyone returns to their ships, they will receive their final orders for deployment," she declared. "Your targets, ship assignments to each Tandeeri vessel, and secondary plans will be transmitted to you prior to returning home. We depart in two days."

"If any member of the S.C.E. would like," Snickerdoodle interjected, "please come aboard any of my ships to retrieve your wounded and injured crewmates. I imagine they will all have healed by now. We would also like you to spend time with our fleet to train, hone your skills, exchange cultural information and more."

"Yes, we are all planning on a brief respite with the Tandeeri," Dr. Kendrick nodded. "Thanks to the fact that time is extended aboard one of their ships, this gives us plenty of time."

"You are all dismissed," Admiral Ra'aiah commanded.

CHAPTER 17

Why We Fight

As the employees of A.I. Industries and the S.C.E. officers began to clear out, the amborgs chose to linger a bit longer to discuss the next phase of their plan. Snickerdoodle, along with a few of his advisors, stayed behind too, and Dr. Kendrick waved to them invitingly.

"Hey guys?" 501 looked around. "I think there's something weird..."

"What?" 117 asked.

Before 501 could finish, Dr. Kendrick cleared his throat, interrupting them all.

"I think there's... one more thing that I need to tell all of you," he said.

Everyone fell silent.

"I'm not going with you when you deploy to attack High Command," Dr. Kendrick stated. "To be clear, I'll be stationed aboard the Firestar. Now that we know that there is no enemy presence in the fleet, it's safe."

"Which means, you want me to accompany the entire amborg assault team," 6 guessed.

Dr. Kendrick nodded to her. 6 seemed uncertain, but looked confident with this announcement.

"At least he'll be surrounded by friends," 6 nodded. "And I'll be on the ground and ready to protect everyone else."

"Excuse me, Admiral?"

Everyone turned to look at 999, who stepped forward politely.

"I didn't want to alarm any of your crew and the other officers," she said. "But we need to clear the air about something."

Admiral Ra'aiah stared curiously at 999. Commander Ulgo had rejoined her side when he after he'd finished saying farewell to a few of his colleagues. Now that the room just consisted of a smaller group who knew her, 999 spoke again as she lowered her gaze.

"Were you ever a member of Silent Eclipse?"

The reactions of everyone were subdued yet clearly evident on their faces. 999 fixed her eyes on the admiral while Dr. Kendrick,

Commander Ulgo, and Snickerdoodle glanced back and forth between them. The other amborgs were taken aback, frozen in anxious silence.

"Oh come on," 5 laughed lightly. "What kind of question is that?"

"A valid one," 999 replied firmly. "I would like to know what her answer is."

"That's preposterous," Dr. Kendrick stated. "Why would you even...?"

"When we first arrived aboard the Firestar, she was visibly uncomfortable and hesitated when I requested access to the S.C.E. database," 999 explained. "Afraid of what I might find?"

"Yes and no," Admiral Ra'aiah replied quickly. "I was trying to protect you from what you'd find out about your alpha versions. At first, I thought it was best for you not to look into any of that, but I didn't want to keep you from anything you wished to do."

"You did do a lot of extensive research," 917 stated. "If she was part of Silent Eclipse, would she have allowed you to explore all of those files? Technically, you were attacked because you dug too deep into restricted files that were kept from the public."

"How do we know that she's not part of their chain of command?" 999 countered him. She pivoted to Admiral Ra'aiah and glared at her. "Did you command the drone that tried to kill me?"

"No! I didn't!" Admiral Ra'aiah protested. "I'm not part of Silent Eclipse!"

"Actually," 117 suggested. "Isn't there an easier way to figure out if she's lying?"

Everyone looked at Snickerdoodle, who appeared puzzled at first, then immediately realized what he was implying.

"Oh! A valid plan!" he replied. He paused, glancing over at Admiral Ra'aiah and held his hand up gently. "I do believe that I must ask permission to look into her mind."

"I see that my amborgs taught you about gaining proper consent?" Dr. Kendrick looked at the amborgs, pleased.

"Yes," Snickerdoodle nodded. "Admiral, I would like to request permission to gaze into your thoughts."

"Uh," Admiral Ra'aiah startled slightly when Snickerdoodle advanced toward her slowly. His towering frame made her feel backed into a corner. "Yes, of course! Any chance you could keep all of the embarrassing things I've done a secret?"

"I do not know what it is that you consider embarrasing," Snickerdoodle replied.

"Hey Angel," 917 spoke up. "Are you sure you want to do this? This feels too forceful. Why would you even suspect that the admiral could be associated with the organization that's trying to kill us?"

"What if I'm right?" 999 replied as she crossed her arms. "We'll all be dead before we make it to the Alpha universe."

"I can promise you," Admiral Ra'aiah said reassuringly as Snickerdoodle approached her. "I'm not some mastermind with a huge elaborate plan. I spent a lot of time with Dr. Kendrick and Snickerdoodle plotting to attack High Command. That takes a lot of brain power."

"I'm more interested in knowing why you have several recorded transactions, transmissions and off-the-books communications," 999 countered. "All top-secret. These were all related to Silent Eclipse."

"What?"

Everyone fell silent.

"Ok," Admiral Ra'aiah said nervously. "There is an explanation. Snickerdoodle, go ahead and read my mind. I can tell you everything! Also, why did you look in my personal files?"

"I go through everyone's files," 999 stated bluntly.

"She's really thorough," 501 replied.

"I believe I can clear this up."

Snickerdoodle raised his claw and aimed it at Admiral Ra'aiah's face. Her whole head could be crushed like a grape if he chose to attack her. However, Snickerdoodle merely concentrated his gaze, looking a bit like a Jedi attempting to extract something invisible from her.

"Admiral Ra'aiah, I find you to be trustworthy and I sense that you aren't attempting to resist," he declared with a growl. "Therefore, this shouldn't hurt a bit."

"This doesn't feel the same as that time he and the Tandeeri read our minds aboard his ship," 297 pointed out.

"That is the very reason. Our abilities are less powerful because we are away from our ships."

As Snickerdoodle continued with his memory probe, Iona spoke up.

"When we visited Earth and boarded this station," Iona pointed at Snickerdoodle, "there were hundreds of thousands of thoughts floating around A.I. Industries. So many minds racing, and we could sense all of them. However, it can be overwhelming, so we purposefully block our abilities whenever we find ourselves venturing away from our ships on rare occasions. If we were aboard the Alcyon, the environment would gradually calm our minds and we can easily enjoy the accessibility of your thoughts without any issues."

"Yes," Snickerdoodle grunted. "There were many humans and a few different species present during that briefing. Everyone's minds were active, thousands of thoughts swirling around in a chaotic mass. I will be glad to return to my ship and enjoy the more quiet and peaceful atmosphere."

"I guess we know how Charles Xavier felt," 777 replied. He looked at a few Tandeeri and politely explained who he was talking about. "He's a fictional character that has powerful telepathic abilities. Before he properly refined his powers, he could hear everyone's inner voices."

"Yeah, that'd definitely be super annoying and drive someone nuts," 917 replied.

"Excuse me, I work better in silence!"

Snickerdoodle's voice reverberated menacingly, making everyone shrink back. Even 999 stepped back cautiously. Commander Ulgo looked ready to draw his weapon to protect Admiral Ra'aiah, but she quickly waved him down and shook her head.

Suddenly, Snickerdoodle's claw and entire arm began to glow.

"They glow in the dark," 501 smiled in awe.

"We glow in the dark," they heard Iona repeat cheerfully.

Admiral Ra'aiah stared wide-eyed at Snickerdoodle's claw, then up to his eyes. For a second, she seemed fine. Then suddenly, her jaw fell open and she let out a small pained yelp. She almost fell over, grabbing Dr. Kendrick's shoulder for support. Snickerdoodle lowered his arm and it stopped glowing. Admiral Ra'aiah remained conscious, but looked like she had a massive migraine.

"I thought you said that wasn't going to hurt!" she protested as Dr. Kendrick helped stabilize her.

"Nobody's perfect," Snickerdoodle shrugged. "My apologies."

Snickerdoodle then turned to look at 999.

"Amborg 999 is correct about a connection with Silent Eclipse, but the admiral's memories, they are different from what you were expecting. The accusation is... not entirely accurate."

"So, she's not with Silent Eclipse?" 917 asked. "Well that's a relief."

"Yeah, because if she was the evil mastermind…" 1 shrugged his shoulders.

"We'd all be dead," 2 finished his statement.

That was enough to make everyone calm down a little, but they still needed the explanation. As silence fell over the room, the group waited patiently for the admiral to gather herself. It was a short wait, as she released Dr. Kendrick's coat and straightened up. Admiral Ra'aiah let out a soft groan but quickly adjusted her uniform. She waved her hand at Commander Ulgo again to signal that she was ok.

"I had a brother," she explained immediately.

249 let out a quiet "ooh" sound from his bracelet. "More family drama!"

His comment got him smacked by 466 and 593. When he clamped his mouth shut, Admiral Ra'aiah continued the explanation.

"My brother was also an officer, but he was with the marines. He left when I was entering the academy," she said, glancing at 999. "15 years ago, he told me that Silent Eclipse had recruited him, and he planned to join them. It was the first time I heard the name."

"If Silent Eclipse was a covert ops or special department," 3 raised her hand politely. "Does that mean your brother became a spy? Or a secret agent?"

"Basically," Admiral Ra'aiah nodded. "But of course, when he told our parents, it meant that he wasn't going to be able to follow the career path that they expected of him."

"So your parents got mad at him when he said he was joining Silent Eclipse?"

"He didn't say he was joining Silent Eclipse," Admiral Ra'aiah stated. "He just told them he was quitting his current role."

"Rebellious," 117 commented.

"To them, they thought he was abandoning the S.C.E. and throwing away everything he had worked for," Admiral Ra'aiah nodded to 117. "He literally started messing up his life on purpose so that my parents wouldn't want to associate themselves with him anymore. Insubordination, violating work policy, and committing a series of small crimes and misdemeanors within the S.C.E. Eventually, my parents disowned him and actually cast him out of the family. When that happened, I didn't hear from him again until a few years later."

"So, he was trying to protect your parents?" Dr. Kendrick asked. "Sounds like someone I can relate to."

"You rebelled against your parents?" Commander Ulgo asked curiously.

"I did it a lot, actually," Dr. Kendrick shrugged guiltily. "I went through several phases growing up and I... would hide certain activities by acting out."

"Yeah, they're highly secured," Serina replied. "Most of his teenage and early adulthood shenanigans are very private."

"Why... are the amborgs and your own A.I. programs trying to hack into private information databases?" Commander Ulgo asked with a mixture of confusion and concern in his expression.

"They have weird hobbies," Dr. Kendrick replied. "My privacy remains secure and intact."

"Not if I scan your brain," Snickerdoodle lifted his claw with a cheeky grin. "Also, I am going to steer this conversation back to the correct topic. Admiral Ra'aiah's story about her brother is true."

Admiral Ra'aiah nodded insistently.

"He worked as an operative for them in the Legahl empire," she explained. "I kept quiet about him and the organization while I was at the academy, and then assigned me to my first ship postings."

She smiled at each amborg watching her intently as she told her story.

"My brother still kept in touch with me every now and then," she explained with a reminiscing gleam in her eyes. "He always sent gifts and letters to me and would always tell me how he was doing. One day, I got a heavily encrypted message from him saying that he was planning to leave. After spending years within the Legahl empire, Silent Eclipse had ordered him to destroy their parliament. He refused and tried to run away, but they caught and killed him."

"Then they came for her family," Snickerdoodle added.

"I was getting to that," Admiral Ra'aiah dipped her head to him respectfully. "Officially, when his death was reported to the S.C.E., the investigation ruled that his death was an accident."

"But you knew the truth?" 501 said eagerly.

"Can we please let her finish the damn story?" 2 sighed.

"My parents didn't take the news that hard," Admiral Ra'aiah continued, ignoring them. "My brother was gone one day out of the blue, and because he was disowned, they moved on from it quite fast. So, I started my own investigation, alone, and it went on for years. At first, I thought maybe there would be clues in the gifts and the letters he sent me but... nothing. I'm guessing that if Silent Eclipse was monitoring his activities at all times, then everything he sent me was probably heavily vetted before reaching me. I can absolutely promise you that I'm not a member of the organization that I know killed him."

"She speaks the truth. All of her memories told me that she is not a member," Snickerdoodle said, which was directed towards 999. He turned to the admiral. "But you were often afraid that you were being watched and that your parents were in constant danger. It was already very risky to even let slip that you were aware of the organization."

"That was possibly what you found in my records," Admiral Ra'aiah said as she faced the group. "After he died, I had to conduct my investigations in secret. I just wanted to figure out the truth. My parents thought he had decided to throw away his life when he just thought he was serving a higher purpose and needed to alienate himself. The best way to seek out justice for him was for me to learn how to be completely discreet. There are a lot of information brokers and organizations not affiliated with the S.C.E. that trade information faster than our monitored databases, so I made friends everywhere in order to try to learn more."

Admiral Ra'aiah turned to look at 999.

"You were right to suspect me and notice my behavior," she admitted. "But I swear, it was never to try and hurt you."

999 nodded, looking satisfied with this explanation. Before she could respond, they heard a voice from up above.

"Oh! It's just so *moving!*"

The meeting came to a halt again as everyone glanced around, trying to identify who had just spoken. Suddenly, something large dropped from the ceiling, landing gracefully without hitting anyone. Before they could register what it was... actually, *who* it was, they saw a petite woman practically leap into Admiral Ra'aiah's arms. Dr. Kendrick, unfortunately, was also caught in the mix, and the two of them struggled to maintain their balance against the massive force they'd just been struck with.

Everyone leapt back in fright, but they quickly settled when they realized who it was. The commotion subsided relatively fast as they all glanced up at the ceiling, then back down at the unexpected group hug.

"Mother?!"

"Madam Admiral..." Dr. Kendrick sputtered, struggling to free himself from a rather tight embrace. "Ra'aiah senior! Can't... breathe!"

"You kept those secrets for years just to protect us?" Second Admiral Ra'aiah exclaimed as she kept furiously rubbing her head against her daughter's neck. Ishala tried not to look embarrassed as her and Dr. Kendrick attempted to fight off her mother. "You're such a sweet daughter! We just need to pass the word up to your father when we get back and he'll rain hell down on our enemies! For your brother and our son, he'll be prepared to avenge him! And you know how much I enjoy seeing him angry."

"Why was she up in the ceiling?" 501 asked as several of them looked up with bewildered expressions.

"*That's* your first question??" 5 asked.

"I think it's even scarier how we didn't hear her," 117 said in surprise. "When did she get up there?"

"She didn't come in with the rest of the S.C.E. officers," Serina replied. "Has she been in the briefing room the whole time before it even started?"

"I went through the ventilation shaft. It was warm and cozy," Talveeya purred in a sing-song voice. Dr. Kendrick and Ishala continued to struggle to escape the group hug. Despite her small stature, her grip was strong. "Besides, as a feline female, I listen to briefings better from above."

"Is that supposed to be reassuring?" 6 asked as she eyed the ceiling and then the admiral.

"Her people are known for odd mischievous behavior," Commander Ulgo replied promptly.

"We also hear very well too," Talveeya Ra'aiah's voice turned low and sultry with a hint of a growl, which made all of them flinch.

117 suddenly received a text message. It was from 1 and apparently he was sending it to every amborg and A.I. in the room.

Let it be noted, he wrote. *Any comments about the fact that she's a humanoid cat will be done by text message.*

As all the amborgs sent their replies of acknowledgement, Talveeya slowly let go of her daughter and Dr. Kendrick. Visibly relieved, he massaged his arms gently as he took a respectful step away from the two admirals.

Talveeya placed a hand on her daughter's cheek.

"My dear," she said soothingly in a gentle motherly tone. "You carried that secret by yourself all this time? I'm so sorry. There's nothing we can do to change what happened. But, I'm glad to know the real reason why your brother did what he did."

Ishala nodded, relaxing. Having that big secret taken off her shoulders made everything better.

"I've always regretted cutting ties with him," Talveeya looked down as she retracted her hand. "Your father did too. Now, we can let him know that it wasn't what we thought it was. Everybody here can help. We're not going to let you continue doing this alone. We'll give your brother the peace he finally deserves."

Ishala Ra'aiah blinked, then a big smile broke out across her face. The two of them dropped the formalities and gave each other a proper hug. She looked up at Dr. Kendrick for a little moral support, and he nodded encouragingly. The rest of the room murmured positive words and expressed their agreement.

"There's... one more thing I needed to tell you, mom," Ishala stated. "Something that the amborgs and I came up with."

Talveeya let go of her daughter and nodded. She turned and looked at the amborgs expectantly, but her face fell when she saw that Dr. Kendrick appeared slightly uncomfortable.

"What is it?"

"We need to have you redecorate your ships," 5 coughed softly.

Talveeya didn't seem disturbed by this statement, but she did raise an intrigued eyebrow as she glanced at Ishala and Commander Ulgo.

"I don't think I understand," she said.

"What we mean is," 5 smirked, glancing at 8 and 9. "We're trying to make it seem like the S.C.E. fleet sent to Epsilon... lost the fight. It won't exactly look like an act if... all of your ships return to Alpha universe in pristine condition."

Talveeya's eyes widened. She turned to Ishala, who was grinning awkwardly. Then, she glanced at Dr. Kendrick, who appeared a bit apologetic, and then at Commander Ulgo, whose stoic demeanor couldn't hide his minor disappointment. When her gaze shifted to Snickerdoodle and the Tandeeri, they all raised their claws in eager thumbs-up, which was both unnerving and endearing.

"Are you suggesting... what I think you're suggesting?" Talveeya glanced at 5 grimly. The cat ears on her head twitched. "You want me to stop repairing my ship?"

"Not just that," 5 spoke reassuringly. "By all means, repair your ships. We're suggesting that you order your crew, with our advice and expertise... to give your ships an aesthetic makeover."

"Fix your ships, mom," Ishala smiled innocently. "But, also... damage them a little."

"I see," Talveeya nodded slowly, but still looked at everyone like they were suggesting something stupid and insane. "What expertise are you referring to?"

"We're really good at breaking stuff," 5 said as he pointed at 8 and 9. "We also just happen to have two of our master pranksters with us coming along for this mission."

"Are we really going to do this?" 92 said excitedly. "Like for real?"

"Are we being ordered... to break stuff?" 93 asked.

Talveeya glanced at Ishala, who nodded.

"The amborgs are going to work with my crew, and my fleet will redecorate our ships," she explained meekly. "Uncle is on board this plan too. He was... very enthusiastic about it."

Ishala Ra'aiah would command her fleet to follow the amborgs' idea of inflicting minor damage on their ships, while Captain Chastain did the same. The only task remaining was to persuade the last commanding officer of the other ships in their fleet. Talveeya appeared to be less than thrilled as she wrinkled her nose and folded her arms.

"You want me to violate ship protocol and order my crew, my fleet, to intentionally sabotage ourselves?"

"It's not actually sabotage," 1 said gently. "We're just trying to give every ship an extreme makeover."

Talveeya raised her eyebrow and glared at each of them. Then she straightened up.

"Oh, well that sounds simple enough," she switched it up and her bubbly personality resurfaced. "I'm in!"

"Just like that?" 297 looked impressed.

"Of course!" Talveeya purred mischievously. "Besides, if we win, I can just dump the repair bills on high command! Assuming we haven't killed them, of course. But we can all get new ships!"

"Yup, that's my mother," Ishala sighed. "She always sees a silver lining."

"I'm really glad that she's a cool mom," 117 smiled.

"Reminds me of Melissa," 2 also smiled.

"Who?" Ishala asked curiously.

"My wife," Dr. Kendrick cleared his throat.

"Oh," Ishala replied awkwardly. "You're married?"

"Widower, actually," Dr. Kendrick answered softly.

"Oh?" Talveeya suddenly perked up. "My daughter is very much single!"

"Mom!"

Talveeya snickered as Ishala tried to grab her, but she effectively dodged and jumped aside.

"I'm going to head back to my ship and check on repairs!" She waved a kind farewell to everyone. "Or...if all goes according to plan," she said with a mischievous glint in her eye, "there could be several delays since my crew is still recovering from the last battle."

"May I suggest, for the record, Second Admiral?" Ulgo called out to Talveeya. "I believe that there are many among our ships that require vacations."

He glanced up at Snickerdoodle and the two of them shared a friendly mutual nod.

"I think that if the crew and people's health and wellbeing are prioritized, that might cause problems with the repair schedules," he said confidently. Then he turned to look at Dr. Kendrick. "This way, in the official report, it won't seem like it was due to... what's the word?"

"Negligence?" Dr. Kendrick said.

Ulgo smirked.

"As someone who strongly believes in following protocol and the rules, negligence is a serious offense," Ulgo winked at everyone. "I believe that the recent string of events has badly affected my mental processing. I can only hope that repairs to the ship..."

Ulgo eyed 8, 9, 92, 93, and the Third Group triplets with a smile.

"...go extremely well."

"This is going to be a rather interesting report to write," Ishala sighed.

Everyone took this as their cue to be dismissed and get to work. One by one, they left the briefing room and headed towards the hangar. As they walked, they listened to Ishala brainstorm the most outlandish orders they'd ever heard of.

"You know, Dr. Kendrick," she said quite loudly. "Snickerdoodle's mind meld with my brain has left me quite dizzy. I think we've all earned some downtime. How long until the Firestar and the fleet are fully repaired?"

"Could take weeks," Ulgo replied quickly as he shook his head in disgrace.

"Oh yeah," Talveeya nodded. "My crew aren't functioning at a hundred percent."

117 glanced at the amborgs near him as they all walked together.

"I feel like we're watching the most serious people we've ever met... turn into children," he said. "Not that it's a bad thing."

"This is hilarious," 5 smiled.

"I fail to see the appeal," 113 stated. "We are simply putting on a show in order to fool the S.C.E. High Command."

"Once again, the Fourth Group charm kills the mood again," 297 sighed.

In the hangar, everyone was busy. Officers were boarding shuttles and departing for their ships. Many more were still interacting with the Apogee Station workers, and several of Dr. Kendrick's employees were conversing as they prepared for their first tours of the S.C.E. and Tandeeri fleets.

Dr. Kendrick informed them that he would be joining Admiral Ra'aiah and Commander Ulgo aboard the Firestar. After a brief time, he would visit the Heart of Alcyon to catch up with Snickerdoodle. Once he left the station, he anticipated it would be a while before he could return.

"Excuse me."

The amborgs of the First, Second, and Third Group stopped when Snickerdoodle approached them. 113 and 280 stopped the Fourth Group, but they didn't seem too invested in the pending conversation and took up guard in the back. Snickerdoodle looked at 917 and 999 specifically.

"Is something the matter?" 917 asked as he glanced up at the tall Tandeeri leader.

"I didn't want to lose another opportunity," Snickerdoodle said. "May I... ask about your friend?"

"Which one?" 917 asked.

"When I was visiting A.I. Industries," Snickerdoodle explained as he glanced at Serina. "I saw the memorial you dedicated to Serina 43. Even though there's one over there with the admiral and another one here on 117's shoulder."

"We try not to share that with everyone!" Serina said nervously.

"Oh, do not worry," Snickerdoodle replied. "I will keep your past identity a secret. I have questions but that is not the friend I was thinking of."

"Uh," 117 glanced at 917 and 999. "If you're talking to them, then there's only one friend I can think of that you're referring to."

999 glanced at 917.

"It is his decision whether he wants to tell you," she said to Snickerdoodle.

Every amborg stared at 917. He realized that even the Fourth Group seemed rather curious—and they were never interested in these particular conversations. Today was definitely a different kind of day for them.

"Well, it'd probably be easier if we all spent a few days aboard the Heart of Alcyon," 917 said. "There's a lot to process, and I can also share the story with you."

Snickerdoodle nodded, and they all proceeded towards one of the larger transports. According to the schedule, this one was set to depart for the Tandeeri flagship after all the necessary preparations were completed. Once inside, as they climbed the ramp, the S.C.E. were busy checking crates, arranging supplies, and buckling themselves in. A hush fell over the group, and they respectfully cleared a path when the amborgs and the Tandeeri boarded. As the amborgs settled into their seats, 917 and 999 found themselves face-to-face with another friend.

"Hello again!" Snickerdoodle smiled.

999 looked mildly annoyed when she saw Braelynn standing there. Her sudden appearance caught the Second Group off guard.

"Hello," she said. "I heard about the briefing."

"You weren't there?" 999 asked suspiciously.

"Why?" Braelynn shrugged. "Wasn't it just a formal presentation of what everyone already knows? I already memorized Admiral Ra'aiah's entire mission plan. Besides, maybe I was there. Maybe I wasn't."

Braelynn politely tilted her head towards the cockpit.

"Thanks to the Tandeeri's assistance," she said, "I don't have to worry about my copilot getting up and trying to kill us all. I just wanted to ask if everyone here is ready to go. Back to the Heart of Alcyon?"

"Yes, that would be great," 917 nodded as 999 crossed her arms and took her seat. "All amborgs present, please. With this new transportation schedule, we're all going to spend some time with the Tandeeri."

"Afterwards, we'll go and help the repair crews mess up the ships," 8 smiled as he waved at Braelynn.

"Can't wait to destroy things," 9 chuckled mischievously.

A few nearby S.C.E. crewmembers began to look nervous when they noticed the twins' growing chaotic mannerisms. Braelynn eyed them suspiciously.

"You'd better take off before someone boots them off the transport," 117 suggested.

"Excellent idea," Braelynn said cautiously.

As they all took their seats, (Snickerdoodle and his delegation all had to sit on big sturdy crates), Braelynn climbed up to the cockpit with a newly assigned co-pilot. 117 and Serina observed how she made sure that her copilot entered the cockpit first. She was probably just taking extra precautions.

"345 was just like those two."

917 spoke up and Snickerdoodle looked to where he was pointing. 501 and 466 were both sharing a pleasant conversation as they adjusted their seat harnesses.

"She was unique?" Snickerdoodle asked as he happily watched 501.

"Yes. Very smart, skilled and resourceful," 917's gaze fell. "And I took too long to notice how beautiful she was."

"She was a math prodigy when she was in elementary school," 999 replied. "Incredibly skilled is the best way to describe her."

"Mmhmm," 917 replied softly. "The orphanage she lived in sold her to a brothel for extra money. Police rescued her, though, and her records as a student stood out to Dr. Kendrick's staff, making it easy to identify and recover her. When she chose her number, she told us we got it wrong when we met her. She said we pronounced it wrong."

"How does one mispronounce a number?" Snickerdoodle asked as they heard Braelynn announce the shuttle's departure.

"It wasn't actually mispronunciation," 917 replied as he remembered 345's shy but kind words. "She just preferred we say it differently than how we tried to say it."

"Like how my number is pronounced one-one-seven instead of one-seventeen," 117 said as he pointed at himself and 297. "And he prefers two ninety-seven instead of two-nine-seven. When she was alive, Serina preferred us pronouncing her number as forty-three. Not four-three."

"I see," Snickerdoodle nodded. "What did she prefer? Your friend? You said three-four-five. Is that correct?"

917 smiled.

"Yeah," he replied. "She said: my number isn't three forty-five. It's three-four-five. Amara 345."

Tocantins, Brazil
A.I. Industries Third Emergency Recall
Major Disaster Declaration: Hurricane "Osial Beisht"
2132, October

"117! We can't maintain this flight pattern for long! I'm going to have to turn away in about five minutes! We're about to hit bingo fuel levels so if you're deploying, you better get ready to go now or I turn my ship around!"

The interior of the transport rattled and shook violently. Those standing in the passenger area had to cling to one another or the supply boxes. Captain Harrelson was busy helping 117 strap on more weights and heavy gear. The closer Echo 209 got to the approaching storm, the more intense the wind resistance and turbulence became.

"Captain Hicks," 117 stated as he tapped into the transport's internal communications channel. "Thank you for doing this."

"I'll tell you what, 117," Hicks replied over the radio. "You make sure to get back in one piece. If you do, then drinks are on you. We're getting slammed real bad."

"There are still people not out of the danger zone!" 117 replied. "We received distress calls somewhere in this area!"

"Hey!" Harrelson moved in front of 117, fixing him with a stern stare. "Kid! I know you're one lean mean fighting machine! But even you know that this is too dangerous!"

117 nodded as he slowly marched towards the para-door on the port side of the transport. He glanced out the window, unable to see a thing.

"If there are survivors, I must try!" he replied.

"Wind speeds are at 140 knots and increasing the further we fly towards the storm!" Hicks reported. "I got to turn back or there's going to be nothing left of my shuttle! 117, are you in or out?!"

117 walked over into the center of the shuttle and knelt down. He reached for the emergency hatch on the floor.

"Be advised!" Captain Harrelson reported. "Amborg 117 is preparing to deploy! He's going to drop through the emergency hatch!"

"117! I know you're the ranking officer aboard the shuttle!" Hicks spoke urgently. "But I need to hear you verbally give me your decision!"

"I'm going in!" 117 replied. "Try and hold a search pattern for as long as possible! I'll find what I can on the ground!"

"I understand," Hicks replied. "Benji! Take over the controls!"

After a second, 117 glanced up at Sergeant Hammond, who was giving him a thumbs up. He and Captain Harrelson triple-checked 117's heavy gear, making sure he was all set to go. When he was ready, Hicks drew close to his ear and whispered a warning.

"Be advised, 117, the wind and turbulence is too strong. Once you leave, we cannot touchdown to retrieve you!" she informed him. "There's no way I can drop rescue lines to you or anyone you find unless this hurricane magically vanishes!"

"Understood," 117 replied. "If I find anyone, I'll help them find shelter and wait out the storm!"

"Good luck!" Captain Harrelson said reassuringly.

"Attention, attention! Echo 209 to base!" Hicks transmitted. "This is Echo 209 to base! Unable to commence cover search! Visibility and conditions are no-go. Mark and note position! Amborg 117 is deploying. I repeat, we are deploying our rescue amborg!"

Sergeant Hammond and Captain Harrelson finished 117's gear check and gave him a supportive pat on the shoulders. The rest of the emergency personnel and soldiers aboard the shuttle gazed at him with unwavering resolve. His choice to leap feet-first into the storm had ignited a spark of inspiration in them all.

"117, be advised," Hicks spoke again. "Base is recommending we terminate this flight and R.T.B. asap."

"If we go back, anyone out there will die!" 117 stated.

"We can't save everyone man!" Harrelson stated bluntly.

Before 117 could argue any further, he heard Hicks speak again. This time, she sounded a little frustrated.

"Based on the rulebook," she informed them, "we cut our losses. I'm sorry 117. There's no signs of life detected! We're being called back now. If anyone tried calling for help, they're probably gone and I'm not sending you down there into a literal shit storm! I'm overriding your decision!"

"No!" 117 protested.

"Whoa!"

Everyone heard Lieutenant Frye yell out.

"I've got a distress beacon!" he exclaimed. "A weak signal! Hammond! See if you can help me clear it!"

117 and Harrelson glanced at the crew chief. He gave a nod and hurried to his jump seat. In a small alcove, there was a monitor that he quickly started to operate. 117 would have offered to help if it wasn't for the fact that he was wearing a massive amount of gear.

They noticed Hammond leave his station, nodding vigorously. He clutched his headset and spoke to them.

"Confirmed! Outside signal somewhere on the ground! Very faint! I think someone is trying to get our attention!"

117 turned back to Captain Harrelson, who tipped his head in response. He quickly knelt down and opened the controls to the emergency hatch.

"This is amborg 117," 117 announced. "Confirmed distress signal on the ground. I am deploying!"

"Roger that," he heard Hicks reply. "Base! This is Echo 209. We have a confirmed distress beacon! Marking time and position! 117 is deploying! I repeat! 117 is deploying!"

Harrelson pried a panel loose, revealing the release lever for the emergency hatch. He glanced up at 117, waiting with an intense stare.

"On your count," he said.

"On three," 117 nodded. "One. Two."

Both men spoke at the same time as Harrelson pulled the release. "Three!"

The instant Harrelson activated the release, the hatch lowered and then retracted, revealing a clear shot straight down into the storm through the bottom of the shuttle. 117 immediately moved and then stepped into the hole.

He was thrown into the storm and was instantly blinded. Fortunately, his helmet's visor protected his face from the rain, wind, and any debris. The heavy gear and bags attached to him to weigh him down were soaked, but he couldn't feel the water penetrating into his clothes.

As 117 fell, he watched the altimeter while trying to keep his feet pointed downward. The ground was approaching rapidly, and he hoped to land with the least amount of injury possible.

"Shit!" 117 yelled.

He saw dark shapes and shadows fly within view. Leaves smacked him, followed by a huge crash as he slammed into a tree. The combination of his weight and the impact from his fall was enough to tear the large tree apart, and he felt himself tumble into the mud and grass.

"What was that?? 117? Report! Can you hear me?"

117 managed to come to a complete stop as he struggled to get to his feet. Somehow, he had managed to roll into a ditch. If his map and GPS location were accurate, he was next to a road. He tried to transmit to the shuttle while he used his helmet visor to enhance the landscape and get an idea of where he was.

"Hicks! Echo 209!" 117 stated as he began to slowly trudge his way out of the ditch. "I'm alright! No damage! I think! Can you hear me?!"

"Your signal is weak!" Hicks replied. "We can barely hear you!"

The wind was so loud that 117 couldn't hear the shuttle flying overhead. Since there was no way to return to it in these conditions, 117 had to press on.

"I need to home in on that distress beacon!" he yelled as he followed the road.

He headed in the direction of the beacon that had been picked up on their scanner.

"It's ok!" he panted as he walked, unbothered by the high winds. "I'm coming!"

117 felt a wave of relief knowing his wife was out of the danger zone. He was absolutely determined to survive this and return to her. Just then, he heard someone speak to him in a calm yet spirited tone.

"Hey 117," 297's voice laughed in a fuzzy transmission. "I saw your approach. What the heck? Are you trying to kill yourself?"

"It was the only way I could get in close," 117 said as he began to feel the effects of his fall from the shuttle. "Ow... where are you? Can you see me?"

"I'm on higher ground, 24 clicks northwest," 297 replied. "I saw Hicks flying overhead and your beacon deploying from her shuttle. Are you nuts?"

"I'm trying to locate survivors," 117 grunted as he continued his journey. "Can you help me out?"

"You're walking into the thick of it so it's hard to maintain a visual on you," 297 replied. "I can only see your beacon. Watching from a distance is what I do best, but I'm too far out to assist you."

"Understood," 117 sighed. "Do you see anything of note?"

"117, this isn't the time for search and rescue!" 297 stated. "Everyone has already cleared the area or is sheltering in place!"

"Someone is calling for help out here," 117 stated determinedly. "I'm not leaving them to die in this storm! I suppose you're going to retreat soon?"

"Five minutes," 297 said. "I'll keep an eye out for that long, but this hurricane is about to hit you in full force. You're not going to be able to run since you put yourself so deep in the red! Get underground and hunker up!"

"Five minutes!" 117 confirmed with 297. "If I can't find anyone, then I'll shelter in place."

Palacio Nacional, Mexico City
Disaster Relief Emergency Management HQ

"First Group amborgs! Mission update! Hold all positions! I repeat! If unable to evacuate, hold positions! Ride out the storm!"

Dr. Kendrick monitored the screen where all the amborg beacons were flashing on the South American map. The storm had worsened exponentially in the last hour, and it was rapidly evolving into an impossible situation.

Every amborg from each group responded to the Emergency Recall, but not all were located in South America. Less than half of the active 119 amborgs were currently involved in search and rescue missions. Many were unable to enter Brazel to offer their help and were instead holding positions in Peru, Ecuador, and Venezuela. When the other amborgs finally reached the region, it became impossible to access those deep in the disaster zone who were trying to protect the refugees unable to move west toward the evacuation camps and safe areas.

Dr. Kendrick and a group of technicians were coordinating with South American dignitaries and government officials to provide aid to all fleeing refugees. Quite a few of them were also in contact with the United Nations. They would need all the support they could get once the hurricane was over.

"All amborgs," Mandy broadcasted on the amborg emergency line. "Please be advised. Storm levels are increasing too rapidly. Any civilians or refugees must shelter immediately. Fortify and hold positions! I repeat, if you can hear me, your instructions are to protect any refugees or civilians from the storm!"

"Copy that!" 1 replied on the channel. "Holding position! I'll signal when the storm passes!"

"Leonard," Dr. Kendrick said calmly. "Report! What is your status?"

"Rio de Janeiro is being hit hard!" 1 replied. "We evacuated the hospital and all refugees that couldn't make it out in time! They are secure inside a city shelter and I'm inspecting all possible flood access points!"

Dr. Kendrick glanced over at Meilin.

"Is everything ok?" he asked.

917's former technician glanced up and shook her head with uncertainty. She looked very concerned.

"I'm sorry," she replied, but Dr. Kendrick realized she was speaking into her headset. "Please repeat your last?"

Dr. Kendrick patched into the communications line that Meilin was on. It was a transmission from the Brazilian government in Mato Grosso, where the Forças Armadas Brasileiras was giving a situation report. As Dr. Kendrick listened in, it was translated to English in real time.

"All stations this net, stations this net, stand by for sitrep," some-one reported. "Heavy winds, debris and various objects and materials are airborne. Conditions too hazardous to evacuate. All civilians and refugees must remain sheltered in place. Forward operating base has been shut down. Companies at the designated evacuation lines are falling back to form new lines. Be advised. Secondary evacuation lines are in effect. We are regrouping and advancing west. We are not evac-uating civilians fast enough. I say again, we are not evacuating fast enough. All units be advised. There are still refugees... Remaining... in... the disaster zone."

"Keep up with the reports," Dr. Kendrick nodded. "If any amborgs aren't currently holding, then try to get them to their evacuation points."

"Yes Dr. Kendrick," Meilin nodded. "But what about reinforcements?"

Dr. Kendrick glanced over at another technician.

"James?" he said. "Any word on getting help?"

James Stetson turned around and shrugged.

"The Third Group is splitting to compensate for the lost ground," he informed them. "The Second Group is at half-strength. 4 is trying her best to get the rest of them here but if the storm gets too bad... the amborgs already out there will be cut off."

"How long?"

"The closest and quickest amborg out is 42 minutes."

"Not good enough," Dr. Kendrick shook his head. "Try diverting a few Third Group amborgs east from Maranhão... if they're up for it. Anyone that isn't stuck in the center should try to proceed west."

"Dr. Kendrick!"

Everyone turned when they heard someone shout his name. Dr. Kendrick looked over at George, who was staring at him with urgency.

"Amborg distress beacon detected!" he exclaimed. "On the emer-gency channel! Outside Balsas!"

"Who is it?" Dr. Kendrick asked immediately.

"917 is requesting support!"

"Get a fix on his location and get him some help now!"

"We're trying... but the storm is too strong. We're losing the signal."

"Try and boost it now," Dr. Kendrick said as the satellite image started to get fuzzy.

"Where's his team??"

Maranhão, Brazil
Two miles west of the town of Balsas

999 continued a slow march as she looked for a place to settle down and wait out the storm. Even with weighted packs around her shoulders, it felt like the wind was trying to rip right through her. She had to avoid losing her gear, otherwise the hurricane would probably turn her into one dangerous flying projectile. She struggled to stay on her feet, trying to avoid becoming debris. Her helmet remained secure on her head, but she found it difficult to call anyone. Thankfully, with it being soundproof, she wasn't deafened by the surrounding winds. Although, it didn't help that she kept getting distracted each time a sudden gust of wind rattled her head.

"This is Angel," she said, her eyes darting around. "My sweep has been completed. No civilians stuck here. I'm going..."

999 ducked left, narrowly avoiding a giant clump of leaves flying above her head.

"...to find shelter," she reported. "Evacuation not possible. I am unable to proceed to the extraction point."

"Negative. I repeat. Negative Angel."

999 stopped when she heard the voice of her former technician, Aaron.

"What?" she asked as she checked to make sure that the transmission wasn't faulty. Confirming that the line was clear and open, she looked around. "Confirm last transmission."

"Angel!" Aaron's urgent voice came through the emergency channel. "917's distress beacon has activated!"

999 froze.

"Where?" she demanded.

"Head east. Town of Balsas," Aaron reported. "You two are the only ones close enough!"

"He'll be fine! I know him! What do you mean, the two of us?" 999 looked around, confused. Then, she saw something approaching her in the distance. "Oh no."

"Angel!" another voice joined the transmission as it greeted her in her headset.

999 grumbled as she began to power walk as fast as she could towards the approaching figure. It was another amborg, her name popping up in 999's HUD a second later. She wasn't happy.

"345!" she scolded over the channel. "Aaron, confirm 917's distress beacon! I have to talk to 345."

Aaron uttered a brief response before his voice disappeared from the line. 999 made her way to her Third Group apprentice and the two of them reached out and grabbed each other's arms. Amara 345 looked relieved to see her.

"345?" 999 spoke sternly. "Why are you out here?! You're in the wrong position! Did you hide your beacon from the map again?!"

"You wouldn't have let me come to you if I had said anything!" 345 replied. "Besides! The rest of the Third Group is fine without me!"

"Turn back and find shelter somewhere!" 999 instructed. "I will find you after I locate 917!"

"No!" 345 protested. "I'm coming to help look for him! It'll increase our odds! I think we should all stick together! Like how it's always supposed to be!"

"These conditions are getting too dangerous!" 999 said. "You need to get out of the storm!"

"I could say the same to you!" 345 replied. "Please! 917 is out there alone! We can find him together!"

999 scanned their surroundings while the wind and rain lashed fiercely around them. With their abilities, the amborgs could endure for a while longer, but with the storm intensifying, they would have to seek shelter soon. Remaining exposed would soon become too difficult for their strength to withstand. 999 glanced at 345's resolute expression and sighed.

"Fine," 999 said as she pulled up her map and compass. "You're right. Come on! We're going to the town of Brasas!"

"Do you think he's ok?" 345 asked as the two of them began to walk together as fast as they could towards the east. "I'm worried! Meilin can't reach 917! Maybe he's hurt!"

"We cannot think about that," 999 stated. "He'll contact us!"

Suddenly, they heard Aaron speaking to them on the channel again.

"Angel! Are you receiving? Over?"

"Yes? What is it?" 999 responded as she and 345 pressed on, huddling closer together.

"No contact with 917. We think he's still alive but we can't confirm," Aaron said, which made both of them stop abruptly and stare at each other. "The beacon in his helmet was seen flying west on radar. His main internal beacon is still showing in Brasas, but it keeps bouncing around. Interference from the storm is creating a big area where he could be."

"He's either being blown around by the wind... or he got attached to something that's flying our way," 999 stated. "Aaron, 345 and I will move in and find him. Please note and mark our position with this transmission. We may lose contact too."

"Copy that," Aaron replied. "Stay safe."

"Always," 345 said cheerfully.

They began to walk again. After about five minutes, the transmission became worse between them and their home base. Maintaining contact with Aaron grew more difficult. 999 continued to press on bravely with 345 beside her.

"Aaron!" 999 said. "I need another update! Where are 917's beacons now?"

"His helmet beacon..."

999 interrupted Aaron instantly.

"Forget about the helmet! You're making it seem like he got decapitated!" she snapped.

345 squeaked in terror.

"Decapitated?" she murmured.

"He's not decapitated!" 999 said quickly to her. "Can you narrow the location of his actual beacon?"

"Our infrared and thermal satellite can't penetrate the storm to confirm," Aaron replied. "His beacon is still active on our monitors, but his last position is in the town."

"Can you be more specific?" 345 asked.

"A search radius of about a quarter mile?" Aaron said with uncertainty.

"Close enough," 999 let out an annoyed grumble. "Look."

999 had to pull 345 away from a strongly rooted tree and urged her to keep moving. If they stopped to take a break, 917 would be at even greater risk. There was a common saying among most people

that if they stopped moving, then nothing would get done. In this case, the storm would only worsen, and time was running out.

"His beacon doesn't line up with his original patrol route," 999 declared. "He would have gone towards Brasas because of something that he found."

"Survivors?" 345 suggested. "He's protecting them. He must be."

"Yes," 999 agreed.

"So, what's the plan?" 345 asked. "How do we find him?"

"You go one way, and I'll go the other," 999 instructed.

"Split up?"

999 felt 345 clench her fingers and her grip on her sleeve tightened. She didn't have to look at her apprentice to know that she was nervous about this idea.

"It'll be more efficient!" she explained. "Whoever finds him first, we contact each other, and we try to find a rally point to seek shelter! Or we help him, whatever state he's in."

"Ok!" 345 said reluctantly. "What's the time limit we have?"

999 looked up as they approached the outer edge of the town.

"13 minutes," she said. "If one of us finds him... or if we can't... and we're still separated or reunited... we get out of the storm, fortify our shelter, and hold position! If we can ride it out, we'll have an easier time reaching 917."

"I hope he's ok!" 345 said.

"Let's try to find him!" 999 said. "Hurry! We need to move faster than we ever have in our whole lives!"

"Maybe we can hitch a ride on the wind when we get back!" 345 joked.

Once they entered Brasas, the two of them split up as discussed. Aaron was completely cut off from them due to storm interference. The town wasn't that huge, but the storm was slowing them down as the weather conditions intensified. They would each take one half of the town and do a quick sweep of the area for 917.

345 checked the timer they had set. 13 minutes had begun. If she found him, then they would work together to take cover from the storm. Hopefully, she would have a few minutes to bring 999 to her position, or if it didn't work out that way, she'd absolutely seek shelter as soon as possible. Though, that was if she didn't find 917.

As she tried to think of alternative solutions, another problem crossed her mind. If he was unconscious or injured, it would slow her down significantly. In fact, she would need to figure out how to pull him to safety if she found him. She wasn't nearly as strong as 999, who enjoyed using maximum weight settings when she did those cool cargo container pushup exercises.

"Don't think about that!" she muttered to herself and shuddered. She didn't know if it was from her dreading the worst or the cold winds tearing into her. She remembered what 917 had taught her. *"Figure it out when the problem is right in front of you. Don't waste your energy on all the hypotheticals."*

345 counted the seconds as she quickened her pace while trying to avoid being blown over. Each time she wound between buildings and alleyways, she became increasingly colder and worn out. The weights on her were practically begging to be released into the wind, but they were practically the only things keeping her stable. The deeper she ventured through the town, the more she worried about 917. He was alone out there, and she didn't want him to feel that way, not in this situation. She hoped 999 would have better luck.

"Ok," she panted. "917. Where would you be? What would you do at this point?"

"You would have deviated from your course because you found some civilian stragglers," she deduced out loud as she recalled her earlier discussion with 999. "If it had been one person, you would have carried them. A group, however, would mean they were in a vehicle, and you were trying to keep it from flying off the ground. If you were outside, maybe something... hit your helmet and blew it away. Oh... you must be so cold without it protecting your head."

She took note of several overturned vehicles scattered all over the place. The citizens had done their best to secure their property, but the storm had literally upended their best efforts. Several vehicles jutted out of buildings, having been thrown around by the intense winds.

"Just like Dr. Kendrick's car," 345 commented.

The good news was that many of the buildings were still standing, which offered some protection from the high winds. From what she could see, the storm hadn't completely wiped the town out of existence.

345 had an idea. Maybe, just maybe, she was within range of 917's beacon, and if she shouted, maybe he'd be able to hear her.

"917! Jack!" she called out. "Can you hear me?!"

345 kept calling out his name over the emergency channel as she walked past building after building.

Please, she begged silently as she grew more desperate. *Please let me find him! I just want him to be ok!*

Then she turned her head, and her eyes widened.

"Oh my god!" 345 exclaimed. "Thank you!"

345 silently apologized to herself for almost giving up hope, but it was rekindled as she rushed to 917.

There he was, lying next to what appeared to be several cluttered objects. How they hadn't been blown away was surprising, but she called out to him again.

"917!" she exclaimed. "I'm here! Wake up! It's me!"

"345?"

917's eyes opened as she knelt above him. At first glance, he seemed fine, but her eyes frantically darted around him, searching for signs of pain, anything that indicated he was injured.

"We have to go 917," 345 said as she quickly checked his vital signs. He was mostly ok, but she'd get a more accurate assessment if they were indoors. "The storm is getting bad! What is all this?"

"I can't go," 917 said as he shook himself from 345's grip. "There's a family I'm protecting."

"What?"

"I activated my distress beacon and hoped someone would come help. I got hit by a flying truck but I'm ok," 917 explained as the wind howled overhead. "I was escorting a doctor with a family that was moving too slow out of their home. They were in trouble."

"A family? How many?"

"Eight total," 917 said. "I had them ride in a van as I held onto it."

"You were carrying the van?" 345 asked. "How did you not fly away?"

"Pulling it is actually the better explanation," 917 said. "I used arrows to keep the van from flying off. We were trying to get out safely but... we weren't quick enough."

"And what happened?" 345 asked.

"The mother went into labor and she's giving birth in the basement of this store," 917 said as he pointed behind him. "I piled on a ton of stuff to weigh down the door. I stuck the last of my arrows to keep the wind from blowing them off. The family will be safe while I'm watching them."

"Wouldn't it have been better if you had gone inside?" 345 looked at him curiously.

"It's a very small basement," 917 explained. "First, I secured the building and checked for all gaps that might leak water in there. All I can do is hope that once the storm is over, they'll all be ok inside."

"Can I stay with you then?" 345 smiled. "I'll keep you company. Until the storm passes."

"Not really going to be pleasant company I'm afraid," 917 suddenly gasped in pain. "I was also hit by a tree after I got the family inside. My shoulder... the left one is dislocated."

917's left arm was a real one, but his right was a total prosthesis. 345 nodded and moved to his left side.

"Let me reset it," 345 said as she positioned herself properly. "Of course you would continue working with a dislocated arm. I'll try to do it fast."

345 reached out and prepared to reset his arm. 917 braced for the impending pain.

"On three," 345 stated. "One!"

"Gah!"

Then 345 pulled and 917 let out a yelp. She felt a little bad about resetting it before she finished the countdown, but maybe this had been better.

"What the hell happened to two and three?!" 917 gasped.

"Oops," 345 grinned nervously. "It hurts less if it's a surprise. From what I've heard."

917 massaged his shoulder.

"345... thanks for coming after me."

"Angel and I couldn't leave you," 345 said as her expression brightened after hearing him thank her. "Oh... look at you... you're soaking wet. Here, I have a tarp in my bag... Oh... I'll probably have to nail it over you, but you'll stay dry at least. Umm... you take my lucky charm bracelet, ok?"

345 started to reach for her wrist. On it, she wore a bangle that looked similar to the amborg gold bracelets, but it didn't have any sort of technological function. It was one of her most precious heirlooms. 917 shook his head.

"Keep it 345," he said. "I'm fine."

345 smiled as she took off her helmet against his sudden protests. There was nothing he could do as she placed it on his head and held it on tight as it secured in place. She suddenly felt the wind and rain pelting her head, but it didn't matter.

"At least keep your head safe," she said. "The most important part of your body."

"Yours is important too," 917 said kindly. "Let me take care of you as well."

"Do you mean that?"

345 stared at him, her expression a mix of wonder and something else underneath. Time seemed to stop for a moment, the relentless lashing of the wind and rain disappearing for a heartbeat as he looked right up into her eyes. A thunderbolt ripped across the sky, shattering the moment and snapping them back to reality.

"Yeah I do," 917 smiled as they both chuckled at their startled reactions.

"Hey... could you... say my name?"

917's expression softened. When it was just them, she preferred to not use their amborg numbers. She wanted their conversations to feel more natural and personal between them. Just as he was about to say her name, movement caught his eye as he looked behind 345.

"Amara! Watch out!" 917's eyes widened as he cried out.

345 turned to see a massive chunk of debris hurtling in their direction. Instead of moving aside, she dove on top of 917, ignoring his protests. He tried to push her off, but it was too late. There was a loud crash as she was struck by a large piece of metal scaffolding, sending her flying several feet away.

When she threw herself on top of 917, he realized she'd sacrificed herself to shield him from harm.

"AMARA! 345!" 917 cried as he rushed to her side and gathered her in his arms. "Oh no! NO! Amara!"

917 immediately read her vitals, which were flashing red. Whatever had struck her had done so directly on her back. The damage was critical. The force of the impact had been so powerful that it had shattered her spine.

"No!" 917 said as he held onto 345 tightly. "I...! We...! 345! Can you hear me?!"

"9...1...7," he heard 345 struggle to say. "Jack. I can't... feel..."

"Stay awake!" 917 said. "Just stay awake! Please!"

He frantically yelled into his radio, trying to reach 999. He needed immediate help. He desperately hoped anyone could still hear him despite the storm's interference.

"Angel! Someone! Can anyone hear me?! Someone help me!"

Facing the Past

Heart of Alcyon
Temporary Training Facility

"Pardon me, but I don't understand."

917 looked at a light green male Tandeeri politely raising his claw.

"Yes?" 917 replied formally.

"Why doesn't Snickerdoodle share your memories and this story with us? Wouldn't it be simpler instead of sharing it verbally? Hey! Ouch!"

This reply earned him a smack from Snickerdoodle. The green Tandeeri snapped his mouth shut and massaged his stinging shoulder. Snickerdoodle shook his head disapprovingly at the group while 917 performed maintenance on his right arm.

"I have stated this plenty of times," Snickerdoodle grumbled. "The humans and inhabitants of their universes don't like it when we read their minds. They wish for privacy. This is why they are sharing the stories aloud."

"But we already know of the story because their memories were open to interpretation when they boarded our ship," the green male Tandeeri protested. "Why repeat a story that we've already witnessed from their memories?"

"Because it feels... personal," Snickerdoodle replied. "There is a stronger connection when you bond over the story."

Snickerdoodle glanced at 917 as he continued to recalibrate his right arm.

"Such extravagant maintenance. Intriguing. You are one of the few amborgs that doesn't have a real right arm?" the green Tandeeri asked. "It is a spectacular design."

"Thank you," 917 smiled. "You don't have prosthetic technology?"

"No, we just regrow our limbs if they are dismembered or cut off."

917 stopped repairing his arm and looked up at the Tandeeri, who were all nodding and murmuring in agreement. His smile faded slightly.

"Really?" he asked.

"Oh yes," Snickerdoodle nodded. "I've regrown my claws and my arms numerous times. I always wanted to ask why you didn't just regrow yours."

"Humans don't... We... uh... can't... do that," 917 nodded slowly as he tried to comprehend what he just heard. "How long does it take for you to... regenerate? You know, if you lost a hand? Or your foot?"

"Depends," Snickerdoodle shrugged. "Depending on the damage, it could take hours or several days."

"You have such impressive abilities," 917 remarked.

"Your arm is also quite remarkable," Snickerdoodle pointed at 917's prosthetic. "Humanity possesses many incredible qualities."

917 scoffed, his tone tinged with uncertainty and discomfort, catching the Tandeeri by surprise.

"I find it really amazing that... you're obviously the superior species," 917 stated casually as he glanced down at his right arm. "Yet, you are fascinated by us, when humans are the species that possess many undesirable qualities that would likely make you come to hate us."

"I have spent plenty of time with you," Snickerdoodle smiled. "Yet, I do not hate you."

"I think you would," 917 stated, "after I finish this story."

"So, do you not have a biological arm because of this... 345?" the green Tandeeri spoke again.

"No, that's a story from when I was a kid," 917 answered.

"Oh, then is it because of the one you refer to as... Angel?"

917 glanced at the green Tandeeri and stumbled over his words. It was at that moment he realized he'd never bothered to ask him what his name was.

917 looked from 117 to the Tandeeri, who was eagerly waiting for his answer to the question.

"What was your name?" he asked politely.

"Kiwi," the green male Tandeeri grunted.

917 blinked a few times and tilted his head in disbelief.

Since the Tandeeri language was apparently too complex for humans to understand, the amborgs and several S.C.E. personnel were going around giving special English nicknames to all of them. It was turning into quite a social experiment. The official Tandeeri language involved a lot of grunts and deep guttural noises. This was why it was difficult to learn their actual names since they all didn't sound like comprehensible words. Everyone chose to adopt 501's tactic to give them memorable nicknames.

Before 917 could even respond, he noticed 117 walk by. He and 43 were chatting while going over an S.C.E training manual.

"Hey 117," 917 called out.

117 and 43 both glanced his way.

"Why do we keep nicknaming most of the Tandeeri after Earth food?"

117 chuckled as he looked at Kiwi and waved.

"To be fair," 117 coughed. "I was trying to name him Keeli but he misheard me."

917 sighed again. He glanced at Kiwi, then resumed working on his arm.

"It's not a bad name," he quickly stated.

"I am quite honored," Kiwi said proudly.

917 looked at another Tandeeri. This one was a light blue female.

"What's your name?" he asked.

"Anastasia," she answered kindly.

"That was an actual name," 917 blinked in surprise.

"Oh, I gave her that name," 43 smiled. "It's beautiful."

A dark green Tandeeri stepped forward, eager to participate in what was going on. 917 noticed his deeper color, curiosity taking over.

"Alright," 917 said with a hopeful look. "What's your name?"

"I am Loki!"

917 pondered for a moment, then nodded approvingly.

"Who gave you that name?" he asked.

"Me."

Everyone turned to see Dr. Kendrick waving at them. It looked like he was here to visit the Tandeeri fleet for the first time.

"I am greatly honored," Loki bowed his head towards Dr. Kendrick.

917 shot Dr. Kendrick a piercing gaze that practically said, *"really?"*

"I couldn't let you have all the diplomatic fun," Dr. Kendrick turned and winked at 117 and 43. "I even named this one a few minutes ago."

A golden Tandeeri male stepped forward with a cheerful smile.

"I am Monty!" he grunted. "I was even gifted a last name as well!"

"Aww..." Kiwi mumbled, "I wish I had a last name."

"It is alright," Snickerdoodle said proudly. "I do not have a last name and I still have an iconic designation."

917 sent a text message to 117 and 43.

I'm going to tell him.

The reply from them was instant.

Don't you dare, they both texted back.

917 looked at the golden Tandeeri and smiled.

"Monty?" he said. "Do I want to know what your last name is?"

"Python."

917 shut his eyes and had to bite his lip. Dr. Kendrick smiled mischievously. The look on 117 and 43's faces was priceless.

"Of course," 917 glared at Dr. Kendrick. "Of course that's what he named you."

Everyone seemed quite amused at the sudden turn in this conversation.

"Anyway," 917 sighed as he looked at Kiwi. "My arm was taken from me... well, a long time ago, but that isn't currently relevant."

Snickerdoodle eyed 917 with an intrigued look but didn't say anything.

"Let's see, after the accident, Angel managed to find us and we got 345 inside. We couldn't evacuate until the storm passed, so we waited it out."

A.I. Industries Medical Facility
2132, November

The storm had passed and things were starting to quiet down. Most of South America was still recovering in the aftermath of one of history's largest and most violent hurricanes ever recorded.

Only a handful of amborgs continued to remain in Brazil after the end of the Emergency Recall. The rest stayed behind at A.I. Industries on standby. They all anxiously waited for an update on Amara 345.

After she'd been struck and rendered paralyzed by that large piece of debris, 999 managed to hear 917's crises for help over the emergency channel. Once she arrived, they fought their way to safety and attempted to create a secure and isolated area from the storm. Unfortunately, despite their medical expertise, 345 required immediate transport, and they were unable to move her since no one could reach them for retrieval. Their only option was to keep her stable until she could be safely transported back to A.I. Industries.

Using the supplies they had, 917 had set up as much cover as possible to keep 345 comfortable and dry despite his own injuries, but the damage to her lower spine was already done. All that he and 999 could do was to be patient and hope for the best. They had done their best to treat her and protect her, but the agonizing part of the experience was how long they had to wait for the hurricane to die down so that an air transport could reach them.

"She's incredibly lucky to have you two."

917 and 999 had spent every waking moment in 345's room. When they'd left for a lunch break, 6 notified them that 345 had woken up and was asking for them.

"Why is it that patients always wake up whenever we're not in the room??" 917 grumbled.

"Plenty of people have woken up with their relatives and friends at their bedsides," 6 replied reassuringly. "Besides, no one is going to fault you for needing a breather. You were with 345 for 66 hours. Also, don't forget, you and 999 helped shield a family from the biggest hurricane on record and they delivered a beautiful baby girl in the worst conditions ever! You both did splendidly."

917 was about to continue protesting, but he felt 999 place a gentle hand on his shoulder. He turned and noticed her giving a subtle nod. Together, they followed 6 back to 345's room.

"Well," 6 said, stepping inside. "345, would you like to tell 917 and 999 how you are going to live to serve the planet again?"

917 and 999 felt a wave of relief when their apprentice turned her head from the window and glanced their way. 345 beamed as she cheerfully tried to sit up and push her bed covers aside. Everyone hurried over with alarmed exclamations. 345 seemed a bit too eager to get out of bed, as if she'd forgotten about her lower spine injury. 6 had to gently place her hands on 345's shoulders to hold her down.

"I'm kidding!" 345 laughed. "I'm not going to stand up or anything."

"I see your sense of humor is still intact," 6 shook her head.

"Unlike my spine," 345 snickered.

"Too soon?" 917 chuckled nervously.

"Yeah, please don't joke like that," 6 scolded, annoyance in her eyes. 345 averted her gaze guiltily. "You have to take it slow. It took us a full day but we did everything we could to repair your spine. It took a lot out of us so don't push yourself."

I'm sorry," 345 sighed. "I just really want to get back out there."

"You're lucky that your implants saved you and your legs," 6 replied as she showed them the screen across from her bed. The chart lit up and they looked at x-ray images of her entire body. "Now you need to take it slow for a few months. No one has ever bounced back from a spinal injury like that. Look at Chief Malayno when she had her spine injury. After some time and patience, you will walk again, but for now, rest, food, and sleep."

"Thanks 6, you're the best." 345 smiled cheerfully. Then she glanced hopefully at 917 and 999. "Can I still talk to 917 and 999? Please?"

6 turned and nodded. She prepared to leave the room.

"I'll let you have a few minutes," she said as she placed her hand on the door frame. "When I get back with your medication and pain-killers, I want this room cleared. 345 needs to go back to resting."

"Thanks!" 345 chirped.

6 walked out of the room as 917 and 999 turned to 345. Before they could even say hi, a commotion broke out. They whirled around to find 6 backing into the hospital room.

"Already?" 345 asked skeptically. "We didn't even get to say anything!"

A sizable crowd of amborgs had assembled outside the door. 501 and 466 were accompanied by several Second and Third Group amborgs.

"We heard that 345 was awake!" 501 quickly explained.

6 wasn't having it.

"Right now, only 917 and 999!" she snapped at them as she motioned for the large group to leave. "Out! Out! Shoo!"

345 giggled as the Third Group amborgs were all sent away. Many of them protested, making a considerable amount of noise. 6 managed to single-handedly herd them out. Once they were clear of the door, she shut it behind her in order to give them some privacy.

When it was quiet, 917 and 999 turned and glanced at 345, who smiled brightly.

"Hi guys," she waved as 917 and 999 each took one side of her bed. "Did you two get worried?"

To her left, 999 remained silent but was the first one to make a move. Gently, she opened her arms and buried her head into 345's shoulder. 345's eyes widened in stunned joy, her mouth hanging open in excitement.

Her eyes flicked to 917. She sent him a quick text, mouthing the words like an energetic child.

Are you seeing this?! She's hugging me! 345 said, which made 917 smile. *She initiated a hug! She initiated!*

Immediately, 345 hugged 999 back.

"Aww," she said peacefully. "Ask a stupid question."

"We're just glad you're alright," 917 sighed in relief. "Is there anything I can get you? Before 6 comes back and knocks you out?"

"Same as always," 345 grinned up at him. "You never really did like savoring the moment. Hey, 999? Angel? You can let me go now."

"No," 999's bracelet lit up as she spoke for the first time in a while. "Otherwise you'll see me crying."

"Aww," 345 said cheerfully. "At least now I know you care. Come on 917—lady without her legs here. Give me a proper hug so I don't have to climb out of bed against the doctor's orders."

917 silently stepped forward as a tear trickled down his cheek. He hugged 345 tightly.

"I knew I could get a hug out of both of you guys someday," 345 said.

"Don't count on it during the next natural disaster," 999 said with her head still buried. It must have been incredibly embarrassing for her to show her face at that moment. "Scare me again and I won't forgive you."

"You saved my life 345," 917 said. "Thank you."

After that, it seemed like everything was going to be ok. It was a very significant and interesting experience for A.I. Industries—and amborg recovering from a temporary disability. It wasn't equal to Serina's amazing exploits, but it came in at a close second.

Over the next couple of months, 345 was understandably not authorized to deploy on missions. Lacking the ability to walk or run was definitely not something that Dr. Kendrick could clear on a medical form. Although, despite her restrictions, she found creative ways to navigate the facilities and uplift everyone's spirits.

Her recovery was relatively quick thanks to her inhuman strength, but she did experience some difficult moments. 917 and 999 would sometimes come back to the hospital to find 345 dealing with some tough emotions, but they supported her during her therapy sessions.

Beneath her bubbly and optimistic demeanor lay a person who felt frustrated with herself for not being able to contribute or help anyone in her current condition. 345 faced significant challenges with her mental health during her recovery, which proved to be a difficult experience. Thankfully, A.I. Industries offered numerous resources and friendly faces who were genuinely committed to making sure she wasn't alone in her struggle. 6 was quite pleased to see everyone contributing to the whole effort, especially Serina.

Serina had devoted a lot of time to 345 during her physical therapy sessions. It was rumored that they spent more time together than with anyone else. Their conversations helped divert their minds from the negative thoughts that 345 sometimes experienced, particularly when she felt her mind telling her she wasn't good enough or not being productive. If 917 and 999 were not there to offer her comforting support, Serina and the other A.I. programs were always there to lend a listening ear.

Serina once remarked that one of the strange aspects of her existence as an A.I. program was the lack of a need for sleep. For humans, remaining awake for extended periods of time poses significant health risks and can be dangerous to the mind. Amborgs, with their enhanced abilities, could go days or possibly weeks without sleep, but they still needed to find time to rest and recover. On the other hand, artificial intelligence and complex computer programs do not require sleep at all. Although she kept this a well-guarded secret from the public, Serina occasionally confessed that the lack of sleep felt ominous and strange at times.

Among all the amborgs, the whole ordeal seemed to motivate and elevate their spirits. 345 had suggested that since 917 and 999 were her mentors, their frequent presence at home or their constant rush back to A.I. Industries after finishing their missions was incredibly beneficial for her. Being the resident amborg 24/7 also meant 345 interacted with pretty much everyone. To this day, she holds the record and title of the 'amborg without a mission.' Dr. Kendrick also managed to convince Dr. Kolaski to come up from the basement to present her with an official award plaque in an act of hilarious symbolism. The shut-in scientist giving an award to a recovering patient who couldn't leave A.I. Industries was seen as ironic to everyone.

In a way, 345's physical recovery from her spine injury was very enlightening for a lot of people at A.I. industries. The day that 345 was officially signed off and cleared by Dr. Kendrick to return to the field made the entire struggle worth it.

The A.I. Industries staff were all pulling for her and many friends outside of the company had high hopes as they heard stories of 345 slowly transitioning out of a wheelchair to crutches. Each day that she stood up without anyone's assistance was another day that prompted a huge boost in morale.

917 walked down a corridor towards the gym.

After returning from a mission with 999, he'd cleaned himself up and planned to visit 345's therapy session at the hospital. However, the message he received told him to head somewhere else entirely. Once he met with 999, who had also made herself presentable, they both began searching for 345, who was apparently missing from her room and the hospital.

"Do you know what's going on?" 917 asked.

"I don't," 999 replied, shaking her head. "I'm just as curious as you are."

The two of them entered the gym and saw a small crowd of amborgs gathering.

"So is half of A.I. Industries," 917 remarked.

When they approached, they didn't have to ask what was going on. The gym had been converted into a massive obstacle course. It was easily recognizable to all of them because 18 had designed it herself for training purposes. It was also used during special annual events for competitions and recreational activities.

Before they could even ask who was using it, they heard a voice gleefully call out to them.

"Everyone! This is it! Last hurdle!"

Serina's voice echoed across the gym as 917 and 999 followed everyone's gaze upwards, towards the final segment of the obstacle course.

In the middle stood a towering structure that nearly reached the gym's ceiling. The finish line was located at the very peak, where a button had to be pressed to halt the timer and finish the entire course. 917 looked on in amazement, gasping in wonder.

"Wait," he said. "She's running the course?!"

"Is she fully recovered?" 999 asked.

The amborgs could clear the tower quite easily. They watched in awe as 345 stretched her hand up and successfully grasped the edge of the highest point. She gently hoisted herself up and climbed to the top.

"I did it!" she called out to everyone watching.

"Hit the button!" 501 yelled as the crowd exclaimed excitedly.

345 got to her feet, turned around, and flashed a triumphant smile at everyone before leisurely strolling over to the button and pressing it. A loud buzzer went off, and the whole tower lit up in vibrant green hues as everyone started to celebrate.

"I thought she had another therapy session!" 917 said as he felt 117 hug his shoulders.

"She worked hard," 6 explained cheerfully. "She wanted to get this out of the way and... she's passed! She's ready to go back out into the field!"

Everyone there to witness this achievement seemed to cheer endlessly. They didn't want the celebration to end. True, 345 had completed the course much more slowly than anyone else, but what mattered was that she was physically able to pass. She had walked away a winner in everyone's eyes. With 6's endorsement and Dr. Kendrick's approval, 345 was awarded active-duty status again.

Soon, 345 didn't need to lean on another person or ask for someone to grab her crutches when she needed to stand or get around. Now she could continue smiling while walking close to someone without the fear of falling every few steps.

On her days off, she often found herself climbing her favorite hill located just outside the facilities. It was a special place that she missed and felt compelled to visit. Being cooped up had some interesting psychological effects, and it was good for her to finally step out into the open fields and fresh air.

Unfortunately, this prompted a lot of reports of her going AWOL. Following those reports, someone would ask 917 or 999 if they knew where she was. It soon became normal that they both knew by default, especially since the new regulations restricted unreported outings after dark.

"One of these days," 917 sighed as he walked up the grassy path one particular evening. "I'm going to be an old man and I'll still be coming up here after her."

"At least it'll be a good four or five hundred years," 999 muttered. "It doesn't seem so bad. Good accumulative exercise."

They reached the top of the hill to find 345 sitting there and watching the sunset. She was cradling her legs, humming happily to herself until she heard her amborg mentors approach.

"Hey!" she said. "You guys made it just in time."

"345, we talked about this."

917 and 999 both sat on opposite sides of their Third Group compatriot.

"You know the rules about going outside alone after dark unless you're assigned to an operation," he said.

"Well," 345 said as she extended her arms and pulled the two of them closer. "I'm glad to have you guys by my side! So we're not breaking the rules now!"

It was hard to argue with her after that. Before long, other amborgs began to join her almost every time she wanted to watch the sunset; whether it was after an operation, during one that ran late into the evening, or on her days off. The only ones who probably genuinely appreciated it were 917 and 999, even if they didn't express it openly. It eventually became known as 345's hill. This was the one spot that everyone, amborgs included, visited just to enjoy the company of the girl on the hill.

As time passed, 917 and 345 found themselves spending more time together, which allowed for deeper conversations. Both he and 999 discovered that dividing responsibilities on certain occasions became easier. This led to several interesting topics for them to discuss.

"Are you going to ask Angel out?" 345 asked one day when it was just her and 917. "She really wants you to, despite your really weird agreement never to ask each other out."

"It's more complicated than that," 917 said. "She already has a hard time even envisioning a future with someone."

"Well," 345 said mischievously, "she did let slip that she wouldn't mind if it was you during our last conversation."

"That can't be true," 917 scoffed.

"It is," 345 said as she turned away. "I shouldn't have told you. It wasn't my place, but I want you to be happy. You two seem so lonely and it makes sense for you to be together."

"I am not lonely. I am very content with the fact that we already have each other," 917 said, shaking his head playfully. "I'm not against the idea of romance but it hardly seems possible for someone like me."

"But you're handsome."

917 looked at 345. Her response was unexpected and it prompted him to pause... for a lot longer than what was probably considered normal. He knew she had been looking at him when she suddenly turned away. Had she embarrassed herself?

"What?"

"I wanted you to feel like it was a possibility," 345 said softly. "I didn't want you to be so hard on yourself so I just said what I think of you."

"Oh," 917 nodded, but his smile faded as this made him think. "Wait a minute..."

Before he could talk about it, 345 interrupted him.

"Are you afraid of becoming someone's boyfriend?"

345 turned and looked back at 917. It was strange to see her smile of optimism vanish in an instant. The sunlight barely masked how much they were both blushing as they continued to gaze into each other's eyes.

"I suppose so," 917 replied as he cleared his throat and pulled at his collar. He looked away from her. "A relationship is way beyond my comprehension."

"Any relationship is. But just before I was injured," 345 said, "when you said you would take care of me... Did you mean that?"

"I did," 917 replied. "Every word. You're my responsibility."

"I'm not talking about as my mentor," 345 replied. "I'm talking about... more than that."

"Well," 917 cleared his throat. "I don't believe there's anything wrong with..."

"Then what's wrong with asking me out?? I mean Angel!"

345 had spoken hastily and attempted to correct herself, but it was already too late. 917 caught her words and began to chuckle softly. Feeling flustered, she looked away in embarrassment. She couldn't believe that she had blurted that out so unexpectedly. Both of them

really wished that 999 was there with them, as perhaps this whole conversation could have been avoided.

"I just meant..." 345 whispered after a few moments. "If you really meant that you were going to take care of me... why couldn't you think that way and just ask someone out? Caring for someone is what you're best at."

"Are you saying you want to be with me?" 917 asked. "Despite the fact that apparently, you wish that I get together with Angel?"

It was a big question for them. 917 expected her to play it off as a joke and just continue watching the sunset. Usually, they would change the subject by now but it looked like today, it wasn't going to happen that way. He was rather surprised when she let out a big sigh.

"I was afraid to ask you because of how close you are to 999," she said softly. "You two are... always together. You both were so professional and worked so well together, and you seem like more than that. The truth is, I wanted to know what that felt like. After I got hurt in the storm, I was happy that you two kept me alive. I thought, maybe you would see me differently and you did! Once I was cleared for active duty again, I just wondered... maybe with 999's permission, I could ask you out? I didn't want to miss another chance to really talk to you like this. Then, one day, when 999 and I were hanging out while you were gone, she told me about when you first met and I was envious of how easily you two connected."

"Are you trying to tell me that Angel is ok with this?" 917 asked.

"I really feel like I've put myself in between you two just now and I wish I could take it back..."

"You're thinking too much into this," 917 sighed. "At some point, you need to consider your own needs. What is it that you want?"

345 took a deep breath and faced him. Her response was immediate.

"You," she said.

"Hold on a minute!"

Startled, 917 jumped at the sudden interruption, his eyes flicking up to Snickerdoodle.

Snickerdoodle glanced to the side and noticed 999 training with several other Tandeeri warriors.

"So, 999 has been your best friend for years?" he asked.

"Yes," 917 nodded.

"And your apprentice," Snickerdoodle grunted as he and the other Tandeeri next to him listened patiently. "Amara 345. She was in love with you... just like her?"

Snickerdoodle tilted his head towards 999. 917 took a deep breath and found himself staring at 999's back. As soon as he laid eyes on her, he suddenly thought about the kiss before the mission briefing. He cleared his throat and pretended to concentrate on his arm again.

"That's a yes?"

"I told you not to read my mind," 917 snapped.

"I didn't," Snickerdoodle replied innocently. "It's obvious from your expression. Hers too."

"You're getting really good at that," 917 chuckled and let out an annoyed sigh. "By the end of the upcoming battle, I think all of the Tandeeri will put every single therapist and psychologist out of business."

"Your best friend is in love with you," Kiwi stated. "So was your apprentice. How did you choose which to mate with?"

"We don't phrase it like that," 917 shifted uncomfortably. "Please don't phrase it like that... ever again. Humans... they uh... date each other?"

"Date?" Kiwi asked. "Is this not similar to finding a mate?"

"No," Anastasia raised her claw and eagerly interjected. She looked like a cheery student in class. "It is a human ritual of courtship! A date or dating is when one begins the adventure of seeking out compatibility with another or multiple subjects."

"I don't think I want to know who taught you that," 917's eyes widened. "That is... a really good general explanation of the concept."

"Have you dated many others?" Anastasia asked.

"I have some experience," 917 nodded.

"Why did you say that you were hesitant when 345 confessed her feelings?"

"It is because he probably felt like he was betraying his best friend!" Monty declared.

"Impossible! If that were true, then what was the point of 917 and 999 officially establishing a boundary that they didn't dare to break? One that prevented them from proceeding beyond their friendship?"

917 hadn't heard who had specifically responded to Monty, but the Tandeeri were now beginning to murmur and quietly argue, which

was not faring well with the story-telling. Snickerdoodle then let out a loud and annoyed growl, causing everyone to fall silent.

"Enough," he announced. "I was merely confirming the facts."

He dipped his head to 917.

"I am sorry," he said. "We will attempt to avoid further interruptions."

"Thanks," 917 said, but he felt uncertain as he set his screwdriver down and flexed his fingers. "Now then. I didn't really take her out on dates. We just hung out more often after we brought this up with Angel. She said she was ok with us seeing each other when we weren't on the job."

"Ok, so we've done a movie night together, a videogame session, and we've people-watched too! I think we should partake in something that most new couples tend to do!"

A few weeks had passed since 917 and 345 had that conversation on the hill. It was nearly the end of February as they walked side by side in the halls of A.I. Industries. Since 345 resumed her active duty, she had been taking on a considerable amount of missions. Sometimes, she would partner with 917 and 999, or she would go with her friends from the Third Group. Once their missions were completed, they made sure to find time for each other whenever they could.

"I think we should go on a public dinner date," 345 suggested happily.

"Are we including a theater showing of a movie and then food? Or vice versa?"

"No," 345 smiled. "I was thinking of a fancy and more stylish date night."

"I see, then, you're suggesting that I put on formal attire?" 917 asked.

"Mmhmm! You know what might make it fun?" 345 grinned. "If I don't show you what I wear! I'll surprise you with something really nice!"

"I think that's unnecessary considering you are already pretty," 917 smiled.

"What. A. Charmer," 345 sassed him playfully. "Still, I want us to put a little bit of extra flair in this. Can we do this a week from now?"

"It requires that much planning?" 917 raised an eyebrow.

"Yes!" 345 insisted. "It should make a huge statement about us!"

917 agreed to this.

Evidently, their closest friends were absolutely in favor of this idea and began to pull out all the stops to help plan this particular date.

When word spread, 917 and 345 contributed quite little to the actual planning. When he selected a restaurant, Dr. Kendrick made the reservation. He'd offered to rent out the entire dining room for them, but 917 insisted that they just needed one table. It didn't have to be that quiet. When 345 went shopping with a group on her day off, they returned with several bags of apparel, even though she had only planned on getting one or two dresses for the occasion.

The amborg couple sincerely hoped that everyone wasn't overdoing it. They already had some rather fond memories of 117's wedding day. His bachelor party, wedding organization, and the honeymoon were meticulously planned, but the execution of it all went in a rather crazy direction. Still, they had succeeded, more or less.

Before they knew it, a week had passed, and the day of their date had arrived. Actually, it was set for the evening after they took care of a few things.

"Are you sure that you don't want us to help?"

917 and 999 watched as 345 left with a team of Third Group amborgs. The mission was quite unusual. A small company that manufactured robotic drones for police and military purposes was experiencing a massive system failure. The systems were going haywire, and all A.I. programs onsite that tried to access or shut down the system were unable to breach the network. 345, naturally, volunteered for the task due to her expertise as a mathematics specialist. During her recovery, Serina had also taught her a lot about A.I. coding.

"I can have this finished and be back in time to make our date," 345 gave 917 and 999 a thumbs up. "You should go and make our reservation!"

"The reservation was made by Dr. Kendrick," 917 chuckled. "We're going to be on time for it."

"I think she is suggesting that you be fashionably late," 999 replied. "Like the movies. It'll help make it look more human."

"Oh, I see," 917 nodded. "That would make it authentic."

"Ok," he sighed as 999 leaned back against the wall. "I guess I should get ready for it. What if it takes you longer?"

"It shouldn't be more than a few hours," 345 replied. "But if necessary, I'll carry my dress and a set of supplies in my pod for this evening. Just in case I don't make it back here to change."

"You have a dress? Now?" 999 asked with a raised eyebrow. "In your drop-pod?"

"You taught me to always be prepared," 345 shrugged with her usual happy grin.

"Don't let go of this one," 999 muttered to 917.

"Thanks," 917 grinned.

Then they heard someone call out to them.

"Come on 345! We need to get going!"

"Coming! I'll meet up with you and then we'll be home soon!"

345 ran off to catch up with the other amborgs. 917 and 999 remained where they were as they watched her go. As 917 was about to turn around to prepare for their evening out, 345 called out to both of them.

"Hey! 917! Angel!" 345 said as she lifted her right arm. "I love you guys! I'll be back later!"

917 stole a quick look at 999, who had a smile playing at the corner of her mouth. He waved back at 345, his expression filled with warmth.

"Well, I should get going," 917 said after 345 was out of sight. "I still can't believe you wanted to rent a limo for us."

"Hey, go big or go home," 999 shrugged. "I want my best friends to have fun in style."

917 shuddered.

"Don't ever say that... ever again," he begged slightly. "Please."

999 wrinkled her nose and nodded with a pained expression.

"You're right," she said. "I didn't like saying, 'go big or go home.' That did sound ridiculous. Excuse me, I'm going to kill 35. He was the one that suggested I say that."

917 soon found himself at the top of an upscale high-rise restaurant. It had been strongly recommended by Commander Bradley and 117's grandpa. According to them, they had visited this restaurant plenty of times. Thanks to their suggestion, 917 felt that it would be a perfect place for his date. What caught him by surprise was the unexpected change in the restaurant's staff. As his date with 345 drew

near, Giuseppe and what looked like his entire family were restyling his look over and over again.

"Giuseppe," 917 said as one of his daughters ran a comb through his hair. "Is this necessary? Don't you have your own dinner rush to contend with? You came all the way from Los Angeles with your family to help in the kitchen here??"

Giuseppe and his children replied yes in a loud chorus, making 917 fall silent.

"Anything for one of Dr. Kendrick's amborgs," he replied. "He asked and we are here."

"I still think we should compensate you for the trouble," 917 replied.

"No! Absolutely not!" Giuseppe shushed 917 as he helped straighten his crooked tie. "I will always help you for free and when you visit my restaurant, you always eat for free. As much as you want!"

"This is far too kind of you," 917 replied.

"Honestly," Giuseppe scoffed. "My grandmother would have me slapped for going out with this kind of sloppiness! Now, no more fighting this! You want to look special for young Amara right? Tell me, did she appear happy when the day of this important evening arrived?"

"I suppose... she did seem like she was glowing."

"Well then imagine her shining brightly like the stars when she sees you! Now, can I get you a drink? Something to help you calm down."

"I am calm! If you're trying to get me to start a bar tab," 917 replied politely. "Forget it, please. I don't drink."

"At least there's one amborg who'll always remain sober," Giuseppe shrugged and gave up. "Sibylla! Get off of him!"

One of the girls was furiously attacking 917's head with a comb in a repeated effort to make sure it was nicely styled. Unfortunately, her small size made it impossible to stand at his height so she was practically climbing onto his shoulders. It almost looked like she was attempting to strangle him.

"He needs to look just like you papa!" she protested. "How else is he going to look handsome for this strange woman?"

"She's not a strange woman," 917 sighed, speaking in a dull monotone. "It's 345. You've seen her before."

"Ah, when friends become more," Giuseppe smiled serenely as he polished a few glasses. "It leads to wonderful things."

"You and your wife were good friends before you married?" 917 asked with a curious and hopeful expression.

"No. She hit me with her scooter and we hated each other."

Giuseppe laughed heartily and made his way back to the kitchen, while his children quickly dispersed so they could run off and play. They promised 917 that they would stay out of the way for the date and be on their best behavior. Otherwise, the other guests wanting to enjoy their evening might not be pleased. True to his word, Dr. Kendrick had only reserved one table and didn't buy out the entire restaurant, which meant there were some regular diners who weren't affiliated with A.I. Industries.

While it wasn't the most motivational thing 917 had heard, watching Giuseppe don a chef's apron and prepare a special menu for the dinner crowd made him feel it was at least something. The sight of Giuseppe's family also led 917 to ponder.

"Is this how 117 felt when he and 43 used to talk about a family?" he wondered as he looked at his reflection in the window.

His suit masked his appearance as an amborg, which was intentional. It would have caught the media's attention if two amborgs were spotted together on a date, so they chose to be discreet about it.

"Well, hello Mr. Yakamoto!"

917 responded to the alias that Dr. Kendrick had put on the reservation. Disgruntled, he turned to look up at the server. He had been informed that a few staff members had been replaced by some trustworthy friends.

"I don't care if it's a reference to Minority Report," 917 started to say. "I'd really like to change my alias! Because for the last time, I am..."

917 froze as his eyes widened at the man smiling down at him.

"...Chinese," 917 managed to blurt out meekly.

Mark, 117's grandfather, was standing before him in a fancy server's uniform. As he tried to process this, 917 glanced to the side and recoiled when he saw who was standing next to the old leader of a vigilante group.

"Why did I fucking agree to this?"

Commander Bradley, also dressed in a server uniform, looked peeved. 917 stared at them as he tried to comprehend what was going on. How many friends did Dr. Kendrick invite from Los Angeles? His eyes flitted around the room.

"Relax," Mark chuckled when he noticed 917's reaction. "You won't find anyone else who chose to tag along to be part of your experience."

"But... why would you do this?" 917 asked.

"Because young love deserves to be celebrated!" Mark grinned. "Leave it to us, the professionals!"

917 eyed Commander Bradley. She nodded grudgingly.

"You consider yourself to be a professional?" 917 asked.

"No," Bradley grumbled. "I'm doing this because I owe Dr. Kendrick a favor."

917 wasn't sure if he wanted to know what that meant exactly. Mark let out a sigh and handed 917 a menu.

"Actually, 117 gave me a call," he admitted. "Even though you made the other amborgs promise not to provide backup, you failed to extend that requirement to non-amborgs."

"When we get back home, I really need to have a talk with every-one," 917 shook his head.

"Would you like to know about the specials?" Mark asked as he leaned forward and added, "or maybe you'd like some advice on how to score dessert?"

917 choked on his water, which prompted Mark to pat him hard on the back. 917 remembered that 117's grandfather possessed the same strength as they did, so he wasn't expecting his back to be hit with so much force.

"Will you please control yourself?" Bradley hissed as she gently passed a fresh clean napkin to 917. "Honestly."

"I mean in case you haven't noticed," Mark said as he looked over behind 917's shoulder. "There's more people standing by too."

917 turned his head, his eyes bulging in surprise at what he saw. A holographic photo hung just above the kitchen entrance. It showed a young woman smiling brightly, with a plaque below identifying her as the owner. However, 917 immediately recognized something was wrong when the woman in the frame glanced at him and waved.

"What is Serina doing in there?" 917 said as he shot an annoyed look at Mark and Bradley. "Are you kidding me?"

"Sorry," Serina transmitted privately from her photograph. She quickly froze, assuming a natural pose when someone walked by. When they passed into the kitchen, she looked at 917. "The A.I.s were curious and they sent me to observe. For research purposes."

"We are not some sort of social experiment to exploit!" 917 replied.

As he spoke, his hands abruptly flew to his chest pocket, and he began to pat himself down. He instinctively checked to see if someone had planted a bug or something else on him. Suddenly, he recalled all the amborgs who had given him more than one suspicious pat on the shoulders.

Hopefully when 345 arrived, they could forget about the fact that they were under the watchful eyes of their friends. But, when it came time for their date to start, she didn't show.

After a few minutes, 917 smiled reassuringly to himself. She was probably trying to be fashionably late to match with him being there early. However, he checked his messages and realized he hadn't received any word from her. Usually, she would have texted him by now to let him know if she was on the way, right?

Rather than dwelling on it, he sat comfortably and decided to be patient as Bradley and Mark gave their advice and opinions. Serina even had a voice call pending in 917's HUD in case he wanted to speak to her instead. 917 debated sending a private message to Serina, but what would he say? Could she go and maybe take a look to see what was keeping 345? Would he look like a terrible boyfriend if he checked on her like that?

917 decided that it was time to give her a call. He dialed 345's number and waited. It rang once but then it clicked and went straight to her voicemail. As he listened to her cheerful and friendly voice prompting him to leave a message, he thought about what to say. He started to speak in his mind.

"Hey, I just wanted to let you know that I'm here at the restaurant and... well, just let me know if you're ok, ok?"

That voicemail after he hung up only alleviated his anxiety for a few minutes. As time went by, 917 grew genuinely concerned. Giuseppe had poked his head out of the kitchen since he was waiting to start their appetizers and the main course, but Mark politely shook his head, signaling that it wasn't time yet.

Everyone was beginning to worry. 345 was about half an hour late.

"Hey Serina," 917 opened a channel and spoke to her privately. "Is everything ok?"

"Do you want me to check for you?" Serina replied. He looked over at the portrait she was hanging out in and saw that she mirrored his anxiety. "I can call home and get an update on her mission."

"Yes please."

Serina hung up after he gave his response. Mark walked over and politely refilled his water glass again. Commander Bradley kept sneaking glances at the entrance.

"Hmm," she spoke softly as she displayed a rare look of concern. "Not even I would be this late."

"This is very peculiar," Mark nodded in agreement, sounding less optimistic than before. "I'm sure she'll be here before you know it. Wait and see."

"Oh wait," Bradley turned her head. "I think someone's coming."

917 turned towards the entrance hall of the restaurant with a hopeful look. When he saw who had arrived, his face fell, his expression replaced with one of confusion. There was 999, breathless, as she quickly walked over to his table. She was wearing a formal business suit, and it looked like she had hastily put it on to conceal her appearance as an amborg from the public eye.

"Angel?" 917 asked as everyone's faces fell. "What's happened? What's wrong?"

917, Chief Bradley, and Mark looked towards the entrance hall to see Dr. Kendrick with a solemn look. They saw him remove his glasses as a tear streamed down his cheek. 917's eyes darted to 999, who appeared mournful as well.

"Oh 917," she said softly. "I'm so sorry. We came to tell you in person. The mission was... a successful failure."

After that day, A.I. Industries went through another period of mourning, just like when 117 first discovered Serina 43's body in her room when she had passed on. But tragically, Amara 345 wasn't coming back like their sweetest and best artificial intelligence had. It was because no one saw it coming.

A.I. Industries had received word that the mission had taken a terrible turn for the worst. Although they had successfully completed the mission, Amborg 345 lost her life in the line of duty. She was the first casualty of the Third Group amborgs since their formation in 2127. Her loss devastated them all.

917 paused his storytelling and clenched his right fist. He lowered his eyes, fully aware that everyone present was quietly staring at him.

"Your… romantic partner… didn't arrive?" Kiwi asked in a concerned voice. "She was late?"

"Sorry, Kiwi," 917 bit his lip and unclenched his fist. "Amara 345 was killed that night. The night we were supposed to have that dinner date. I… wasn't there…"

Dr. Kendrick gazed at the Tandeeri that were listening to the story. He noticed many of them reaching out and holding each other's hands. Most of them were probably couples or paired mates that had probably wanted to listen to 917's story, expecting a happy outcome. His sudden and abrupt silence when he couldn't finish spoke volumes as his face fell.

"But… she loved you," Anastasia replied as she gazed at her friends with a stunned expression. "How did she depart from this life?"

Dr. Kendrick stepped forward.

"Excuse me," he cleared his throat. "The simple and short version is… things went wrong. Amara was attempting to shut down an incomplete A.I. program that had attempted to take over, but it had been temporarily contained. It tried to escape repeatedly and if it had succeeded, the world would have faced a potential catastrophic danger. She died preventing that from happening."

"There is pain in you," Snickerdoodle glanced at Dr. Kendrick, then to 917. "But, 917 has carried a much stronger pain and he continues to fight."

"I can't exactly be much help if I just wallowed in grief," 917 replied.

"Hmm," Snickerdoodle replied.

They heard the sound of footsteps approaching. Everyone turned to see a bright beige female Tandeeri making her way towards Snickerdoodle, smiling brightly. It was clear she held a position of great importance, as every Tandeeri present bowed their heads in respect.

"My love," she said warmly to Snickerdoodle.

"Ah! Everyone!" Snickerdoodle smiled and gestured to the bright and beautiful Tandeeri woman. "This is my mate! I have asked her to join us as we exchange cultural information and stories!"

"I remember her," 917 stated. "Well, I remember seeing her."

This woman was Oreo's mother and Snickerdoodle's wife, based on her rather affectionate behavior towards him. It was interesting how 917 and the amborgs were just now meeting her face to face since they had only ever seen her watching them from a distance when they first boarded the Heart of Alcyon.

"Hello, young master 917," she spoke formally. "My name is Kira. I thank your friend Serina for gifting this name to me."

Taken aback, 917 looked at Dr. Kendrick, who smiled back.

"Hello Kira," he replied. "It's a nice name. Uh, I'm not a master of anything."

"You have been through many battles throughout your life," Kira regarded him with admiration. "You have conquered many obstacles and have survived bravely to become the one who sits here before us. You are a master warrior."

"W-well uhh," 917 stammered.

Kira continued to gaze at him warmly, then turned to Dr. Kendrick.

"Dr. Kendrick," she said.

"Yes?" He blinked.

"917 is currently going through a battle of the mind," she said. "It would appear that he has a rather important decision to make regarding 999. Perhaps it would be best to give him some space."

"Regarding 999?" Dr. Kendrick asked curiously.

"About the kiss," she mused.

Everyone stared at 917, who was suddenly alert. Being put on the spot started to make him nervous.

"What kiss?" Dr. Kendrick asked.

One second was all it took for Dr. Kendrick's eyes to widen as realization sunk in. The embarrassment in 917's expression made it clear what Kira was alluding to. He glanced at 999, who was still training. She wasn't even looking their way.

"When did you two kiss?" Dr. Kendrick exclaimed. "This is wonderful!"

"I... I'm going to take a break."

With the repairs to his arm finished, 917 politely excused himself and briskly walked away. A few Tandeeri followed him curiously, thinking that he was playing a game of hide-and-seek.

Amused, Snickerdoodle grunted and began to leave. He bid Dr. Kendrick a quick farewell and asked his wife to follow.

"Excuse me," he declared. "My wife has something personal to speak with me about."

"I apologize for the inconvenience," Kira bowed to Dr. Kendrick.

"Oh," Dr. Kendrick nodded respectfully. "I'll just go and do something else."

As the Tandeeri leaders began to converse privately, Dr. Kendrick turned around and strolled away.

"What did you discover?" Snickerdoodle asked.

"The one known as Angel," Kira spoke in a soft tone. "Alice 999. Her past is filled with darkness but she conceals it well. However, her mind feels like it is about to fracture from the hidden emotions she's buried within herself."

"It is clear that most of the amborgs support each other, and this creates a powerful bond among all of them," Snickerdoodle muttered. "917 and 999 both have a strong bond but... don't acknowledge it like the others do. They would greatly benefit from each other's company. Why is it that a small act of romance and confession of the heart keeps them from wanting to pursue a friendly discussion?"

"I analyzed their thoughts and memories," Kira stated. "When you first met them, you glimpsed into their pasts. When I was tending to Oreo, I meditated on these images. Both 917 and 999 are keeping secrets from each other. Perhaps, we can find a way to help them, in the time that they are here aboard our ship?"

"They have stated that it is a breach of privacy if we continue to look at their memories and thoughts without their permission," Snickerdoodle replied with a grumble. "I would like to respect their wishes and maintain a friendship with the humans."

"I think you should make an exception," Kira replied calmly. "Please come with me to speak with 999. She has agreed to share everything with us."

Snickerdoodle glanced at Kira. He was surprised at this particular news.

"You convinced her to a friendly conversation?"

"I can be just as persuasive as you, my dear," Kira nodded. "I simply use more efficient tactics."

Feeling a bit insulted, Snickerdoodle couldn't help but find it somewhat amusing and chortled softly. He straightened up, and his wife led him by the arm toward 999, who was patiently waiting for them.

"What secrets?" he asked.

CHAPTER 19

Oh Captains, My Captains... Sorta

S.C.E. Firestar
24 Hours Later
Time Aboard Tandeeri Ships: Approximately 16 Days

"Attention all passengers," Braelynn's voice spoke over the P.A. "This will be one of the last flights between the S.C.E. and the Tandeeri fleets. All crew report to stations once we touch down. Amborgs, when ready, Dr. Kendrick and Admiral Ra'aiah are waiting for you on the bridge."

The amborgs listened to the announcement while busy double-checking their gear as their shuttle made its way back to the Firestar.

It was a surreal experience, spending a little over two weeks with the Tandeeri, when only one full day had passed on Earth. In that time, they'd been relaxing, training, studying, and essentially enjoying a nice vacation within the Tandeeri's special time zone.

Many of the S.C.E. crew, as well as the entirety of the fleet's commanding officers, found time to tour the interior of the Tandeeri ships. What made the experience particularly interesting and likely the most enjoyable was that several S.C.E. officers or crew members had the opportunity to take a lunch break, spend a few hours aboard the Tandeeri vessel, and still make it back to their posts on schedule.

Some of the amborgs had stayed behind to assist the S.C.E. in giving their ships an extreme exterior makeover. It was truly remarkable to compare the differences in their internal clocks when they visited their friends aboard the Heart of Alcyon. David 117, who had spent a whole 24 hours with the Tandeeri, had aged a full 16 days, while 8 and 9, who stayed behind, remained unchanged. Before they finished their vacation, they joked about how if the younger amborgs stayed with the Tandeeri long enough, they would come back to A.I. Industries older than the veterans of the First Group.

Using the Tandeeri's time-dilated environment proved to be extremely effective. Engineers, soldiers, technicians, pilots, and even the civilian crew members were all eager to take advantage of the fact that they had extended periods of time outside the bounds of their own.

Those that were wounded during Silent Eclipse's attack were transported to the various Tandeeri ships. 6 was quite pleased to see so many people healing from their injuries at a steady pace, allowing them to return to their duties in less than a day. As a result, doctors, nurses, and medical professionals were afforded valuable time to adequately care for their patients.

For repairs to the interiors of the S.C.E. starships damaged in battle, engineers, repair technicians and mechanics were able to set up machine fabrication units and workstations. If they had to send or create new components, or craft parts they needed, they could accomplish it within a more efficient time frame. Many of them were absolutely thrilled and felt more optimistic producing repair parts in a couple of weeks rather than a mere two hours.

When they weren't relaxing, soldiers and marines spent their time performing several combat drills. To accommodate them, Snickerdoodle and the amborgs had each Tandeeri vessel set up obstacle courses, shooting ranges, and special holographic simulations. Using data and recorded footage from the Silent Eclipse attack, S.C.E. marines and intelligence officers were able to recreate holographic facsimiles of the enemy assassin drones. This allowed the Tandeeri warriors to identify what kind of threat to look out for in the unlikely possibility that their ships were infiltrated by Silent Eclipse. The marines and S.C.E. officers trying to get some hand-to-hand training also participated in programs drafted by the amborgs. Any S.C.E. personnel that wanted to could gain some more practice and experience so they wouldn't get caught off guard in case they had to defend their ships.

Pilots set up simulators, allowing many of them to hone their skills. Several squad leaders and their subordinates had expressed gratitude for allowing them the chance to log in more flight time. Flying shuttles or fighters in outer space was a really high-stakes job and they needed to be at their best. Based on what they were planning, everything about this mission had to be precise.

"All passengers make sure your belongings are secure," Braelynn announced again. "Once we arrive aboard the Firestar, our next stop after is the Alpha universe."

"Hey everyone," 117 said to his team on a private channel. "Remember protocol."

They all turned to each other and nodded, perfectly aware of what was possible with this kind of endeavor.

"Everyone filled out their paperwork and their last requests?"

"Yes," 501 said firmly with a confident smile.

"Did you remember to choose someone who's back home on Earth?" 297 said, nudging 501 with his elbow. "You need to choose someone else if your intended recipients are all here and leaving with us."

"Oh right..." 501 looked down. "I'll need to think about it."

Every time a major operation or mission occurred, the amborgs were meticulous and consistently revised their last wills and testaments. The key difference with this mission was that they were journeying outside of their universe. Should they fail, their only hope would be that someone would relay the news back to the Epsilon universe, ensuring that all those mentioned in their wills would be properly notified.

"Everything goes to my ex-wife Daphne," 1 muttered under his breath. "Jim and Leo too."

"You always talk about Jim and Leo like they're your kids," 2 remarked with a chuckle.

"They kind of are," 1 shrugged.

The rest of them were making the same comments and having similar discussions.

"I hereby choose my former technician to be the receiver of the items in my last will and testament," 777 shuddered as he tried to remember what he needed to update to his will.

"I want 57 to break the news to my friends on the west coast," 117 was muttering to 917. "All of my belongings, assets, and even what I own that once belonged to my parents... will go to my daughter and Audrey. My grandfather also will receive a list of items I set aside for him."

"Hey uh," 917 cleared his throat. "I wanted to let you know that if anything happens to me, I left some money for Sarah."

117 glanced at 917.

"What? Why would you do that?"

"Your little girl deserves it," 917 smiled. "I set aside some funds so she could do whatever she wanted when she was older. I know it seems stupid but I wanted to do something as her uncle."

117 glanced at 999, who was busy checking her own documents.

"Did you know about this?" he asked.

999 merely nodded.

"All of us agreed on the day that Sarah was born," she replied. "Every amborg signed a contract with a notary as a witness. We all have contributed one percent to support the future of Sarah Wright 117."

117's mouth hung open.

"I-I don't know what to say," he stammered.

"Every child of an amborg will have a future," 917 said brightly. "It's what we all wanted to leave behind as our legacy. Speaking of which... 466!"

501 and 466 both turned their heads to look at 917 from where they were seated. 917 pulled something out of his pocket and tossed it over to 466. She jumped, realizing something had been thrown at her, and caught it clumsily, her hands fumbling.

"Whoa! Got it!" 466 exclaimed.

"What is it?" 501 asked curiously.

466 fell silent as she looked down at the object. Those that were watching noticed it was shiny and gold.

"This is Amara's bangle," 466 said softly. "But, it's yours!"

"No, I'm giving it back to you," 917 smiled.

He glanced at 999. She met his gaze for a moment before casting her eyes down. 917 turned back to 466 and gave her a reassuring nod.

"I don't need it," he said. "You gave it to me once so that I would not lose my way. I don't really know if I failed horribly or found my way back to all of you but... I think you deserve it. She'd want you to have it back."

"But..." 466 tried to protest as she held the bangle up.

"345 gave it to you," 917 insisted. "It belongs to you."

917 then turned away, ending the conversation right there. 117 casually glanced over his shoulder and saw that 501 and 466 both looked happy to receive the bangle, but it seemed like 466 held it with an air of sadness, as if she didn't fully feel right about getting it back.

"So, are you still upset?"

117 snapped out of his observation and looked at 917.

"About what?" he asked.

"The fact that apparently, 501 and 466 are my responsibility and not yours?"

"No," 117 replied, shaking his head. "We talked about it. It was a conversation we had to sit down for, but it wasn't that bad."

"Is this like... a Vegas thing?" 917 asked slowly. "Like, what happens aboard the Tandeeri fleet... stays aboard the Tandeeri fleet?"

"Uh, I don't think so?" 117 replied, raising an eyebrow. "I just told 501 and 466 that I was ok with not being their mentor anymore. It surprised me but... it's not that big of a deal. I wasn't the best mentor since that incident with Serina, and when I'd gotten married."

He let out a sigh and shook his head.

"501 and 466 just decided that their future wasn't with me," he explained. "I told them that was something that I could be ok with."

"They really do grow on you, don't they?" 917 smirked.

"Yeah, they do," 117 nodded. Then he turned and looked at 917 inquisitively. "Now what's all that about what stays aboard the Tandeeri fleet? Did you and 999 properly talk?"

"We tried," 917 replied. "We just got busy with training, planning, and preparing for the mission."

"Kira and Snickerdoodle asked me a lot of questions about you two," 117 replied. "Neither of you tried to talk about... that kiss?"

"Drop it, 117. Please."

Both of them turned to see that 999 was now staring at 117. Her request was clipped, but it also sounded quite stern. When 117 and 917 met her eyes, sensing how serious she was, she lowered her head and averted her gaze.

"Oh," 117 nodded awkwardly. "Sorry."

Naturally, 117 texted 917 privately.

Did you two have a fight?

I think so, 917 replied. *I tried talking to her about that kiss and why she initiated it. She told me that when 345 was still alive and in a relationship with me, she respectfully stood back and held her own feelings in. The Tandeeri pretty much figured it all out.*

117 pretended to read his last will and testament from his bracelet. As the pages he'd written scrolled steadily upward, he continued to read 917's text messages.

We trained with a few Tandeeri warriors, he wrote. *Snickerdoodle and Kira meditated with us. Yes, you read that right, they meditated with us. Apparently, Angel has a lot of pent up stress that 6 wanted her to acknowledge and take care of. I mistakenly thought I could help with that.*

Help? 117 replied. *Oh. Wait. Stress management?*

Yup, 917 admitted blunted. *I didn't think it was going to end up in a fight. Basically, I offered to start giving her a massage. Shoulder, neck, upper back. The works! You know? It wasn't even supposed to be a private or romantic fling but the next thing I knew, we found a room alone aboard the Heart of Alcyon.*

117 felt the blood rising to his cheeks. This felt like it was getting too personal.

*You're not going to start sharing... **all** the details, are you?* 117 asked.

When he highlighted the word "all" in bold font, the three dots indicating that 917 was typing his message disappeared. A moment later, 917's three dots appeared again, and his response came in a rush.

No, nothing like that! 917 clarified. *I'm giving her this massage, right? She was allowing herself to be vulnerable in front of me. So, I'm taking care of these knots in her neck and shoulders, and the next thing I know, she has her hair down, is leaning her head back and then... Our lips got very close and then... we forgot about the massage.*

117 gave 917 a curious side-eyed glance. 917 nodded subtly, allowing his serious expression to do all the talking. Understanding flooded in. 917 and 999 had started making out with each other.

So, what started the fight? If things were... heating up?

917 quickly texted back.

I have a very important question, 117. Do you think that people behave differently when they know something? Something important?

Um, I suppose so?

Do I seem different? Ever since we left the Heart of Alcyon?

117 didn't turn to look at 917 but instead decided to think about all of the moments they saw each other aboard the Tandeeri fleet. He and 917, along with the original team of amborgs that first went up into space, had spent the entire 16-day respite on the Heart of Alcyon. If someone did the math, then 917 was possibly one of the few individuals from the Epsilon universe that had spent the most time with

the Tandeeri than any other person. Now that he was bringing it up, 117 did silently admit that 917 seemed slightly different than before.

Before 117 could even answer, 917 was already trying to add more context.

Look, we were... somehow, she flipped around, and she was in my arms. She had my jacket off and we were going at it like... we had starved for years, and we discovered a delicious cheeseburger. And then... when I unzipped her jacket and was about to slip it off, she stopped me.

117, in a moment of awkwardness, didn't know what to say.

Except for:

That's... surprising...

I know, right? 917 replied grimly. *After we stopped, she looked at me all serious and asked me if I remembered. Her exact question was, did I remember her?*

117 scrunched his eyebrows.

Huh? he wrote.

Apparently, 'what do you mean?' was the wrong thing to say. Then she broke it off and left. Before she walks out the door, she turns and looks at me and goes... 'how long will it take for you to remember that I was there for you at the beginning?'

The beginning? 117 replied skeptically. *The beginning of what?*

I don't know, 917 replied. *I was confused. First, she kisses me, leaves me standing there wondering what the hell is going on, and then we almost rip each other's clothes off! Then she gets mad at me when I apparently say the wrong thing? I was even more confused than upset, really. Then I bumped into Kira and Snickerdoodle. I was about to ask 6 some questions. You know, some standard counseling but... then Snickerdoodle put his claw around my head and...*

117 felt 917 place a hand on his shoulder. He carefully looked down at it, then turned to sneak a glance at 999, who continued to ignore them.

Now I know, 917 texted 117 again. *I know everything. All the way back to before I became an amborg!*

What? 117 replied.

A sudden announcement broke the silence, cutting their conversation short.

"Attention, we are docking aboard the S.C.E. Firestar. Touch down in ten seconds. Keep your tray tables and seats in an upright position. We thank you for flying with us."

As everyone began to disembark, the amborgs and other shuttle passengers unfastened their harnesses and rose to their feet. They heard the ramp hiss as it began to descend.

"The calvary has arrived!"

117 smiled when he saw 8 and 9 waiting for them. The two First Group master pranksters greeted them excitedly as everyone, except for the Fourth Group team, high-fived them.

"What's the update?" 1 asked.

"We've pretty much taken care of all of the exterior remodeling," 8 said confidently.

"Yeah, if the admiral decides to share the footage and images, it's glorious!" 9 winked. "I can't believe we were ordered to mess things up, on purpose!"

"But you *always* mess things up," 5 pointed out mischievously.

"Exactly," 9 grinned cheekily. "Not only does this ship run perfectly, it looks like it got the shit kicked out of it too! Not bad when you have the entire crew learning how to enjoy taking some of the ship apart!"

"Hey," 501 said. "There's Dr. Kendrick!"

Everyone turned to see Dr. Kendrick waving pleasantly at them as he strolled over to the shuttle assembly area where they were all gathering.

"Amborgs! Welcome! Is everyone ready?"

"Yes," 1 nodded. "Although, it is surprising to see you without an S.C.E. escort."

"Hey, I studied the interior of this ship," Dr. Kendrick replied. "I spent three days on the Heart of Alcyon looking at maps, blueprints and schematics. It was a nice two hour break away from the Firestar."

Dr. Kendrick took a deep breath and tilted his head a few times.

"It was a real experience..." he said. "Visiting a place where time is significantly amplified."

"Oh, Dr. Kendrick," 501 raised his hand. "Before we go see the admiral, can I ask something?"

"Of course!"

501 gestured to all the amborgs and then patted his shoulders.

"Is there a reason we all have brand-new uniforms?"

"I wasn't going to send you into battle with worn-out clothes," Dr. Kendrick blinked. "Besides, since time is accelerated on the Tandeeri ships, I thought we should take advantage of that. So, I hired the best tailors and seamstresses aboard the Firestar and they chipped in... a lot."

"I-I get that," 501 stammered. "I just meant that... are these new uniforms supposed to feel different? They feel different."

Dr. Kendrick began to lead the amborgs to the bridge.

"You noticed?" he smiled at 501 as they continued walking. "Well, that's part of the surprise we had planned."

During the early stages of their training and preparation for the mission, they occasionally found time to do some shopping as well.

The Tandeeri didn't have a traditional shopping mall, but the S.C.E. civilians, merchants, and retailers who resided permanently on the Firestar did. They were all thankful to the amborgs for their help in saving their lives and defending the ship, and they were eager to support them and their fellow shipmates.

When the Tandeeri opened the doors of their fleet to everyone in the S.C.E., many civilians and officers who had taken time off found an opportunity to engage in recreational activities. Dr. Kendrick took advantage of this and commissioned new uniforms for the amborgs.

A whole line of new jackets, pants, belts, and shoes were fashioned for them, and every amborg received a brand-new set of custom-made uniforms. Their numbers glowed brightly on the chest pockets in front and in bold print on the back. They included neon stripes along the sleeves and down the sides of the pants to accentuate the primary silver-gray color scheme. Each amborg had the option to choose their neon strip colors based on personal preferences.

The fabric from the Alpha universe appeared to be significantly stronger and more comfortable. According to the tailors, the uniforms they presented to the amborgs were made from fabric that was not only durable but also surprisingly lightweight. Their cybernetic enhancements made their bodies tough, even bulletproof, and their old clothes helped reinforce this.

The amborgs were quite pleased to receive clothing and uniforms designed from an alternate universe. They found they could move at least fifteen percent faster while also keeping their iconic stylish appearances.

"It's just going to take some getting used to," 501 admitted.

"That is a special gift for all of the amborgs," Dr. Kendrick said warmly. "It's the S.C.E.'s way of saying thank you."

As they reached the bridge, 113 actually began to recap their mission objective.

"Our main destination will be the lunar base of Alpha Earth," she said. "The headquarters of the S.C.E. military command is gathered there. The colonies and cities established on the moon will have a breathable atmosphere and we will infiltrate the City of Beginnings."

"It still sounds so eerie and cool," 297 stated.

"The City of Beginnings?" 117 asked.

"Oooh, chills, literal chills," 297 grinned.

While a few of them discussed what they thought the moon was going to look like when they crossed into the Alpha universe, 280 finished the rest of the briefing.

"It is historically the first established city on the moon," he said. "The S.C.E. headquarters will have the highest-ranking commanders and officers based there."

"Is the high command also there?" 501 asked.

"According to Admiral Ra'aiah, they are stationed on Earth," Dr. Kendrick answered. "Some members will travel to the moon on many occasions, but the majority of them are on Earth."

As they exited the elevator and stepped onto the bridge, the crew who noticed them stepped aside to let them pass. Several of them politely bowed and saluted in a show of respect.

"Does that mean that Silent Eclipse could have a presence on Earth?" 1 asked. "Are there any military installations or other possible places where they could stage an area of operation?"

"There are many."

Admiral Ra'aiah saw them coming and stood up from her chair to greet them warmly. She appeared to be in high spirits as she nodded to Dr. Kendrick.

"The reason we're targeting the moon is so that we can disable the fleet stationed there," she explained. "The First fleet, which consists of over 45 capital ships and many more support vessels, is quite the armada. The Firestar is big but the ships we're going up against would erase us from existence if they get a shot at us."

She pointed at the map behind her shoulder.

"The Tandeeri can detonate an E.M.P. on the planet to eliminate all of Silent Eclipse but... we need to take down every line of defense."

The First Fleet was set to either dock or maintain defensive formations around the moon and Alpha Earth. Their primary target was the space dockyards and ship staging areas. The amborgs would launch their mission, deploying marines and fighter support to the main headquarters on the moon, while the Firestar and the Heart of Alcyon would swiftly disable every ship in sight. After that, things would become increasingly challenging.

The Firestar would then have to target the defense platform control with another E.M.P. strike. Surrounding the Earth and the moon was a large number of orbital defenses. These were satellite platforms equipped with powerful weaponry. In the event of an attack on the planet, these guns, missile systems, and laser armaments provided targeted assistance for S.C.E. starships, acting as the last line of defense. All of them operated automatically, and it was crucial to disable the central command to prevent Silent Eclipse from seizing control and directing hundreds of weapons against the Firestar, even if they managed to neutralize the First Fleet.

"Serina's blackout program is going to have its work cut out for it," 5 exhaled heavily. "We have to move fast, otherwise we're going to be squashed."

Serina appeared in a bright flash of light next to Dr. Kendrick.

"No kidding," she replied. "I'm still confident it'll work but you have to understand, when it got loose and blacked out a part of *our* world, it didn't last that long. Now we're unleashing a refined and upgraded version on Alpha Earth which has about ten times better technology. Not only that, we're using it to screw up the moon which has cities, towns, and more while it's being protected by space shipyards and a floating space station. Even with all of the handy firewalls and security programs that we can bypass, the blackout program might get countered quicker than we expect."

"Hopefully, the program that Serina will deploy will shatter Silent Eclipse's ability to communicate with their forces," Admiral Ra'aiah said. "The main headquarters on the moon and the primary star base in orbit is capable of inflicting major damage if Silent Eclipse manages to take over. Hitting here first will take out as many of the drones aboard the First Fleet as possible. Every ship that we keep out of their control is a weapon of mass destruction that they don't get to use. It reduces the risk that innocent people get killed. Commander Ulgo has also provided special information about our orbital defense platforms too."

Commander Ulgo turned at the mention of his name, then directed everyone's attention to the map in the center of the room. An image of one of their defense platforms appeared. He pointed at the screen.

"As your friend Serina has stated, there is a risk that our systems may be able to overcome her blackout program. Our attack must be swift and efficient, but we have no time to execute all our targets at the same time," Ulgo said as the screen shifted to what appeared to be layers of rings surrounding the moon and Earth. "I would like to request, Dr. Kendrick, that some amborgs be dispatched to shut down our orbital defense platforms while the Admiral commands the fight against our own ships. I will give instructions on where to go and have a team disable all of our orbital defenses. 43 will accompany you."

"Aren't we already disabling the defense platform control center?" 1 asked as 43 stepped forward. "Why do we need to send a team to attack it?"

"The E.M.P. attacks will ensure that no Silent Eclipse drones will interfere with our mission," Ulgo explained. "However, there could be agents hidden at headquarters that aren't robotic or affected by the Tandeeri energy attacks."

"Oh right," 3 nodded. "Silent Eclipse isn't just an organization made up of all robots or battle droids. There are definitely human agents that might try to throw a wrench in everything."

"Exactly. Someone could still make it to the control room and bring the defense platforms online, making it become one big turkey shoot," 43 explained. "We will send our fighter and bomber squadrons to disable them but just to be safe, we should properly deactivate all the protocols necessary to use the platforms. Silent Eclipse members could turn the platforms on Earth or the moon and still cause significant damage."

"Tell us where to go and we'll take care of it," 5 agreed.

"The controls to command the platforms are in the headquarters building itself," Ulgo said as he brought up an image of the S.C.E. headquarters. "It's a room designed similarly to our weapons control. If there are any Silent Eclipse drones in headquarters, then they're potentially under our noses. 43 knows it very well. She will help coordinate if anyone gets lost."

"There will be squads of marines accompanying you," Dr. Kendrick said. He glanced at 43. "Will you take care of them?"

"Absolutely," 43 nodded firmly. "I'm thrilled to have an army for this."

"We should be fine without any amborgs aboard the ship," Admiral Ra'aiah said with a confident smile. "You did a nice job cleaning up all traces of Silent Eclipse. It's the matter of protecting the S.C.E. council and the other high-ranking officials that concern me. Someone at headquarters is definitely heading Silent Eclipse and we must cut off their means of escape and any ways of fighting back."

"We should be able to flush them out," 117 replied confidently. "We'll analyze the building plans and specifications. We'll figure out the fastest routes around and with our numbers, we can protect them... or detain them."

"We also have new weapons for you," Ulgo spoke up. "We'll have you collect them and get a basic overview before we have you stage in the hangar and meet up with your marine escorts."

"New weapons?" 297 perked up. "Did Christmas come early?"

"Kinda," Serina said. "We got together with some Tandeeri engineers that collaborated with a few S.C.E. gunsmiths. They designed specialized weapons with Tandeeri energy properties that are capable of taking out Silent Eclipse drones easily."

"Specialized?" 917 asked.

"The S.C.E. created a new prototype energy pulse rifle and it's powered by Tandeeri... batteries," Serina explained. "Instead of wasting full mags of lasers... like the First Group and Fourth Group did..."

All of the Fourth Group amborgs remained cold and neutral, except for 301 and 365. They were the only two amborgs from the Fourth Group that hadn't participated in the battle against Silent Eclipse aboard the Firestar since they were kidnapped by Snickerdoodle when they left Earth.

8 and 9 both stared at the other First Group amborgs, who seemed slightly embarrassed when Serina glanced in their direction.

"It's not our fault that those things are built like tanks," 1 replied.

"Yeah, and it was like using peashooters," 2 grumbled. "Ultimately, the best way to take them down was when we had to pummel them after we ran out of ammo."

"Yeah, we fought an army of Terminators," 3 clarified to 8 and 9.

"We saw the footage," 8 nodded.

"Good thing I brought more grenades," 9 added with a mischievous glint in his eye.

"Don't detonate any explosions in the Firestar," 6 said warningly in a loud, sharp voice.

"I know," 9 whined innocently. "I only limited the damage to outside!"

"So, is everyone getting these new energy rifles?" 777 asked as he tried not to laugh.

Admiral Ra'aiah and Commander Ulgo exchanged a brief glance, then turned back to the group.

"There was only enough time to make enough prototypes for each amborg currently in space with us," Ulgo explained as he counted everyone standing before him. "So, we have enough primary and secondary options for all 29 of you."

"I also gave the manufacturers and designers plenty of input based on each amborg's combat styles," Serina added. "When we pass them out, you should all be able to equip yourselves with weapons suited to your preferences."

She looked at 999.

"A rifle for you, but I know that you prefer pistols and knives," she stated.

999 nodded with an eager and determined smirk. Then Serina pointed her holographic finger at 297.

"We have a customizable semi-automatic pulse rifle for you," Serina said cheerfully. "Our best sniper gets special sights, and it can even be modified to take out enemies from extremely long distances. I can't imagine you might need to actually snipe anything in close quarters, but it is your style."

"Damn right it is," 297 raised his hand, and rather than a high-five, Serina performed a midair cartwheel followed by a side-flying kick. "Thanks Serina."

"Great," 117 beamed. "So, we have a finalized plan, new uniforms, and weapons."

"We're not going to send you into battle empty-handed," Admiral Ra'aiah said to Dr. Kendrick. "You've done so much for us, and now you're all going to help us commit treason on the highest level. It's only proper that we thank you by supplying you with nothing but the best."

"It really is Christmas," 501 exclaimed.

"Not finished yet," Dr. Kendrick cleared his throat.

With a wave of her hands, Admiral Ra'aiah signaled a large group of about twelve bridge officers to step forward. The amborgs watched with curiosity as the officers raised their hands, each holding a small, maroon-colored box. Before they could ask what they were, the officers regarded them warmly and pressed buttons on the sides. The latches on all the boxes popped open, revealing various silver pins of some kind.

"There is also a matter of reestablishing protocol," Admiral Ra'aiah said as she signaled to her officers again. "I am afraid we weren't able to recover all of your records but... consider yourselves reinstated. Temporarily, of course."

Every amborg was approached by a bridge officer, who handed them their rank insignias. They graciously accepted their own boxes, and as they did, the crew pulled out gold stripes from their pockets.

"Normally, there's a formal way of doing this but... we wanted to give you stripes so that the enemy and our allies could see you in all of your glory," Ulgo nodded in admiration.

The officers began to attach patches of gold stripes onto their shoulders.

"The gold stripes will allow other members of the S.C.E. to know who you are," Admiral Ra'aiah explained. "The silver insignias we're giving you are your original ranks and positions."

The amborgs were genuinely surprised by this impromptu ceremony, even the ones who were reinforcing it.

301 and 365 of the Fourth Group, 92 and 93, along with the Third Group triplets, 53, 54, and 55, were all awarded the lowest

ranks—second Lieutenants. 8 and 9, with the rank of first Lieutenants, were in charge of them.

For the amborgs that had been up in space the longest, it was clear that Admiral Ra'aiah had organized them into specialized groups.

224, 63, and 100 of the Fourth Group were 1st Lieutenants, but 113 and 280 were in charge of them as Lieutenant Commanders.

It was the same for the Third Group. 501 and 466 were also Lieutenant Commanders, while 249, 593, and 49 were under their command as 1st Lieutenants.

The Second Group's dynamic was much different. 117, 297, 917, 999, and 777 were all designated as Commanders—the same rank as Ulgo.

The First Group appeared to have the most advanced and specialized ranks out of them all, except for 8 and 9.

1 and 2 were both awarded the rank of Captain. 5 was technically the same rank as a Captain, but because his Alpha universe version was a member of the S.C.E. Marines, he was actually a Major. 3 and 6 were also Commanders but their ranks had really special titles attached.

3 was a Staff Operations Commander, which wasn't a common position for someone who fights on the ground, but it held a lot of responsibilities. 6 held the rank of Chief Medical Officer, which actually gave her as much power and authority as a Captain. Technically, in the event of a medical emergency, she could overrule anyone's authority regardless of their position in the chain of command. Now, it was official.

"I hope that this particular act of temporarily reassigning your alternate version's ranks would help you adapt once we travel to Alpha," Admiral Ra'aiah said as everyone had their insignias pinned to their collars. "I apologize that we couldn't make you all the same rank. It was better to organize it this way with the older amborgs higher ranking."

"At least we're getting job positions befitting our age," 5 joked.

"The gold stripes that we're attaching to your shoulders is the best way for our crew and everyone else to identify you as amborgs," Ulgo stated. "Even though the First Group amborgs have the highest ranks among you, we have always considered the amborgs to be special forces or VIPs with more specific skill sets."

117 noticed that 43 was smiling at them from the corner. She looked especially proud of them.

"So, what is your official rank?" he asked.

"Oh, I never really cared about that," she shrugged. "It always felt like a weird formality whenever I was stationed aboard an S.C.E. ship. I technically hold the rank of Commander."

43 walked over and the officer who was pinning 117's insignias to his collar stepped aside politely. She ran her fingers across his shoulder and patted it down firmly.

"All I can say is, you all look damn good," she grinned confidently.

43 extended her hand, and 117 grasped it. He noticed her approach every other amborg, all of whom were Commanders, and shaking their hands. For those of lower rank, the amborgs adhered to military protocol and saluted her, but she paid no mind to that. After she faced each of the First Group amborgs, they were all stunned to see 43 saluting each of them with respect. In response, only the First Group returned her salute.

This was understandable. If she was a Commander, this meant that 117 and the Second Group shared the same rank as her. She was saluting the First Group because technically, they outranked her. This would take some getting used to.

Commander Ulgo stepped up to 117 and offered his hand. 117 realized that this was similar to what 43 had initiated. He found it hard to believe that he now held the same rank as Ulgo. He knew the first officer of the Firestar had years more training and experience than he did. Being on the same level as such a badass man meant that he'd likely have to step it up... a lot.

Then came Admiral Ra'aiah. Since she was the highest-ranking officer in the room, as well as the entire ship, she didn't come forward to shake hands right away. Instead, she leaned in to whisper instructions to 117 when she stood before him, while Ulgo and 43 addressed the other amborgs with their small acknowledgement ceremonies.

"Salute," she whispered. "I salute you back. Then we shake hands."

117 nodded and straightened up as best as he could. He raised his right arm and matched his hand positioning to mirror Admiral Ra'aiah's salute. They lowered their arms, and she reached out to shake his hand. When this was done, she gave 117 a proud smile and

wished him good luck, then moved on to the other amborgs to finalize their promotions.

"So, Dr. Kendrick."

117 glanced at Dr. Kendrick, who was positively beaming. He must have been really excited to keep this a secret from them all if this is what the S.C.E. was planning.

"This is a very interesting idea but... does this mean we're officially members of the S.C.E.?"

"Admiral Ra'aiah wanted me to explain it to you," Dr. Kendrick replied as he walked up to 117 and the two of them shook hands. "Once this mission is over, she was hoping that you would all consider pursuing a potential future with her."

"Uh, phrasing?" 117 raised an eyebrow. "I'm already married."

"You know what I mean," Dr. Kendrick scoffed.

117 and Dr. Kendrick laughed softly as they let go of each other's hands. 117 cleared his throat and continued the conversation seriously.

"A future? With the S.C.E.?"

"We'll go into more detail about it when this mission is complete," Dr. Kendrick nodded formally. "That's what the Admiral wants to talk to you about after we save their world. Er, their universe. For now, this is merely a publicity stunt."

"Publicity?"

"Of course," Dr. Kendrick lowered his voice suddenly. "I wasn't too thrilled when Ishala suggested that we promote the amborgs currently present. At first, I argued that this was a rather poor way to recruit you into an unstable organization's chain of command. Ultimately, she countered my way of thinking and suggested it as a morale boost for the S.C.E. fleet. If they saw Epsilon amborgs rising up to take over the mantle left behind by your Alpha counterparts, then they'd follow you into battle, straight to hell and back."

"That's a very marketable and notable decision," 117 said skeptically, still feeling unsure about this particular idea. "Does that mean our ranks are useless then? It's all part of a show?"

"Not entirely," Dr. Kendrick shook his head. "If the S.C.E. crew and marines identify you as a Commander, it builds trust and shows that the amborgs are back in their lives and ready to lead them as part of the same organization. More importantly, you're there to save the day. New uniforms, new ranks, and new weapons will definitely attract a lot of attention."

117 nodded, but his smile faded as he processed what Dr. Kendrick was saying.

"Are we going to be bait?" he asked cautiously.

"Oh no!" Dr. Kendrick replied. "That was never what we intended. Your ranks aren't useless. Because! Uh... any officer or S.C.E. officials that you encounter on this mission will recognize you as S.C.E. personnel. You'll still be given plenty of... command privileges... and..."

Dr. Kendrick's voice faltered as he glanced to the side and noticed the leaders from the other amborg groups were staring at him.

999 walked over to Dr. Kendrick and crossed her arms. She stood by 117 and stared at him suspiciously. 1 and 2 did the same, which only added more pressure. 501 and 466's cheeriness had faded when they heard 117's question about being bait. 113 and 280... actually, there was no change in their expressions at all. Hilariously, they seemed to understand the assignment and also just focused their piercing, expressionless eyes on Dr. Kendrick.

"Ok, ok, yeah, we're going to be bait," he admitted with a loud gulp.

"We?" 501 asked. "We're the ones going on the mission while you're staying on the ship! We're going to be bait?"

"I know it sounds bad," Dr. Kendrick sighed. "But it's the best way to draw out the leaders of Silent Eclipse. If my theory is correct, then your presence is exactly what will cause them to reveal themselves."

917 spoke up.

"It's an entrapment technique."

"Come on, we've done this type of move plenty of times," Dr. Kendrick said reassuringly. "Every time an amborg is involved in a mission, it attracts a great deal of attention. All of us here might just be the right kind of trap."

43 stepped forward so they could all see her. By this point, Admiral Ra'aiah and Commander Ulgo had finished shaking everyone's hands and turned to look at Dr. Kendrick.

"Silent Eclipse wiped out all of my friends and the only people I ever considered to be my family," 43 declared. "And they tried to blame the Tandeeri. They're not getting away. Think about how pissed off it'll make them to see it all get unraveled."

"Meaning that there's a chance that someone will take the bait," Admiral Ra'aiah spoke up. "If they have nowhere to run or hide, then they'll become desperate and maybe go down swinging."

"If you're worried about going in unprotected," Ulgo cleared his throat. "We have specifically selected your squads of marines accompanying you. When the fighting starts, our job will be to create maximum chaos and confusion. Not only can you trust them, but we've reconfigured their I.F.F. signals so that you can distinguish them in the thick of it. They will watch your backs. I personally guarantee it."

"One more thing," Admiral Ra'aiah nodded. "We would like to avoid killing the wrong people. Expose Silent Eclipse, yes. However, we need to make sure they don't escape or conveniently get killed. So, if anyone reveals their true allegiance, please..."

"If they can be spared," 777 stated as he looked at everyone. "Then, we will try to spare them?"

"If they try to kill us, would it not be simpler to kill them in response?" 113 asked.

"I'm actually in agreement with that," 5 raised his hand.

"Are you kidding me?" 6 groaned. "We're not having this debate again!"

"I'm just saying, why is it so easy for us, the heroes, to kill common criminals or villains who deserve it, but we always stop when it's the main evil characters?!" 5 asked.

"It'll be more effective to expose and keep the ones responsible alive," 117 stated.

"I'm sympathetic to what 5 is saying," Admiral Ra'aiah seemed a little nervous at where this conversation had gone, but maintained her composure. "However, it isn't proper code of conduct. We can't resort to the same tactics as Silent Eclipse. We're better than that."

Suddenly, they heard Ulgo clear his throat. Everyone glanced at him as he brought his fist up to his lips.

"Uh, Admiral, we should finish the ceremony quickly because we still have quite a crowd."

The amborgs glanced around and noticed that the S.C.E. bridge crew that had decorated them were all watching curiously and murmuring amongst each other. Apparently, they hadn't been dismissed yet and had been unintentionally eavesdropping the whole time. If this discussion continued to go off the rails, then they'd probably lose their confidence. They couldn't have their leaders bickering.

Seeing this, Admiral Ra'aiah took a deep breath and belted out a few commands.

"Attention on deck!" she bellowed.

The surrounding S.C.E. officers straightened up and stood at attention. Even the rest of the bridge that wasn't participating in the amborgs' promotion ceremony rose from their stations and turned to face the admiral.

"To my crew of the S.C.E. Firestar," she announced. "These are your new officers! They are going to lead the charge!"

"Salute!" Ulgo roared.

Every officer saluted the amborgs immediately. They were perfectly synchronized, and it was clear to everyone how motivated each person was. 117 found himself at a loss for words as the amborgs looked around, basking in all of the attention.

"Dismissed!"

Everyone immediately resumed their duties. As Admiral Ra'aiah returned to her chair, she glanced at Serina.

"Once we arrive in the Alpha universe, we will jump straight to Earth, and the assault will begin. Serina, every ship has your copy of the blackout program?"

"Yes," Serina nodded and gave a bright thumbs up from Dr. Kendrick's shoulder. "I have configured it so that once you start transmitting your cry of 'wolf,' the program will infect anyone who picks up the signal. If it hits the center of your communications network, that'll be even better."

"That won't be difficult," Ulgo nodded. "The star base orbiting the moon and the S.C.E. headquarters both manage the constant traffic of communication. Once your program hits either one, they will have no way to contact Earth or communicate effectively."

Admiral Ra'aiah then glanced at the amborgs.

"I'm going to prep the fleet within the hour," she explained. "I suggest you all grab your gear and assemble in the hangar. If there is anyone that you still want to contact before our departure, then now is the time."

CHAPTER 20

Forward Unto Dawn

S.C.E. Firestar
Port Hangar

"Attention crew of the Firestar. This is Third Admiral Ra'aiah delivering a message to the combined surviving forces of the S.C.E. Tandeeri Task Force."

The hangar fell into silence as everyone paused to listen. Admiral Ra'aiah was about to deliver her important speech before their departure from Earth. Their goal was to journey outside the solar system to lay the groundwork for establishing a wormhole back to the Alpha universe. This would allow every ship to jump to their intended destinations as soon as they arrived. Once they entered the Alpha universe, all ships in the fleet would assemble and position themselves under radio silence before shutting down all communication channels. This was the last time Admiral Ra'aiah would send them off with a proper motivational speech.

"I know that these last three weeks have been... different," her voice continued over the broadcast. "We came to the Epsilon universe with a mission to protect it. Now, we are going home to defend all that we vowed to protect. As you all are aware, the war with the Tandeeri is over! Our next objective is to eliminate a rogue detachment within our organization that sought to obliterate our fleet from the inside! Silent Eclipse attempted a failed coup within the very walls and decks of our ships."

As the amborgs continued to make themselves comfortable, they watched the S.C.E. hangar crew listening attentively. They noticed that a few of the crew members still had some bandages visible on their bodies. It was likely that they had some lingering scrapes and bruises, but they were ready to perform their duties.

"We suffered some heavy losses and we can't get them back. As your commanding officer, I am deeply sorry for the lives that were unexpectedly cut short. We lost parents, we lost children, we lost friends, our own shipmates, and allies from all across the Alpha universe. We can't get them back, but I promise you this. This mission will be what honors their memories! It gives you a chance to fight back and avenge them!"

117 noticed several crew members who appeared both determined and a bit shaken. Surviving the nightmare of what happened onboard the Firestar had certainly left some traumatic scars.

"Each and every one of you has proven yourselves time and again but today..." Admiral Ra'aiah declared as her tone switched from mournful to emboldened. "I must ask for more! Today! We fight one last battle! The last one that will mark the end of this conflict! We are taking the fight back to our home territory! This has never been done before and the risks are high! But with our new allies... old ones, new, and even the ones we thought we were fighting against... are with us now!"

117 glanced over at Dr. Kendrick and saw a few mechanics eagerly approaching to shake his hand. He gently raised a finger and pointed upwards, signaling them to remain quiet and continue listening to the speech.

"We are targeting every single defense that the S.C.E. has in place. I understand it may sound frightening and absolutely insane to confront our own, but if we succeed, we will rescue them from a terrible fate! The whole S.C.E. organization is being held captive, and we will liberate them! Now, some of you may not survive today! We cannot afford to dwell in our sorrow! There will be time for grief later. Billions of lives are at stake! We have no illusions about the challenge we face! Several thousand of us... against millions more."

117 glanced at 999, who merely shrugged and gave him a grim look. What they were about to set out to do was going to be one of the most impossible battles that they had ever been part of. They were greatly outnumbered and outclassed. This would have to be one of the fastest missions they had ever undertaken.

"But... we are the new unified starfleet!" Admiral Ra'aiah stated. "Liberation Fleet One! History will see us as something different! We're not going to worry about how kind we're depicted. Instead we will define ourselves through our actions! We will not lose our homes to an evil hiding within our ranks! We will not fall back! Once we make it to the Alpha universe, we will be charging straight for our targets at full speed!"

In the distance, fighter pilots who were already in their spacecraft began to lower the canopies. Once everything was secure and they were fully prepared for takeoff, 117 saw that several pilots were enthusiastically pumping their fists together, signaling to the ground crew that they were set and hyped up.

"We will win!" Admiral Ra'aiah raised her voice confidently. "Because we have to! We fight today! So years from now, when you're surrounded by your loved ones and all that you hold dear and they ask... 'what did you do during the charge of the Liberation Fleet?' You can look them in the eye and say... 'I was there and I fought for freedom!'

The Admiral paused for dramatic effect before speaking again.

"All hands of the S.C.E. Firestar, the entire fleet, and to the Tandeeri! I am proud to lead you and to stand by your sides today! Good luck! Admiral Ra'aiah... out!"

As the speech concluded, a vibrant and more energetic fire ignited among the S.C.E. personnel in the hangar. Cheers and applause erupted briefly before everyone resumed their duties. The moon had undoubtedly been elevated significantly.

"Wow," 5 nodded. "I almost believed that we could win this."

"Come on," 6 gave him a sharp jab in the shoulder. "She meant every word of it."

"We will win," 5 winked at her as he massaged his shoulder. "Come on, I was kidding! Because we have to, right?"

"Because we have to," 1 nodded.

117 imagined that 1 was thinking about his ex-wife, Daphne. Did he get a chance to properly catch up with her when they had their shore leave on Earth? 1 caught 117 staring and flashed him a warm smile before giving 2 an encouraging fist bump.

3 came along passing out snacks to everyone as they double-checked their gear.

"Alright everyone, protein bars, bottles of water, emergency provisions and ration packs!" she announced. "I don't care if this mission is just supposed to be an assault on the S.C.E. military headquarters. Everyone eats something now and has something for later just in case we don't get back to the Firestar in a short amount of time."

6 nudged 5, then gave him a quick kick to his prosthetic leg.

"You do another check to make sure your leg is working?" she asked.

"You checking on me?" 5 smirked devilishly.

"If I was being serious," 6 replied bluntly in a cold tone as she checked her medical bag. "Not that I give a shit about you, it is going to be the last time to possibly do one last check."

5 continued to grin but put his humor on hold and nodded.

"Yeah," he dropped his goofy and mischievous tone and smiled sincerely. "My leg is ok. I finished checking and repairing it yesterday back on the Tandeeri ship."

8 and 9 were both pretending to shadow box with each other. It was their way of playing around before the beginning of a big mission. They probably had plenty of tricks up their sleeves, especially after gaining extensive knowledge about the Firestar's structural designs and taking on the task of revamping the outer appearance. Instructing the other crews of each starship in their Liberation fleet on how to make every ship appear as if it had sustained heavy damage must have been the most absurd but entertaining use of their skills.

All of the Fourth Group amborgs stood still and remained on guard. Their posture while on watch was a bit unnerving. When they did speak, it was typically 113 or 280 offering them short reminders and safety advice before going silent. Yet, from what 117 observed, their experience over the past two weeks with the Tandeeri appeared to have altered their demeanor and appearance. 301 and 365 were the only members of the Fourth Group amborgs who had spent significant time with the Tandeeri, having been captured alongside the other amborg reinforcements from Earth. In just sixteen days, the Fourth Group had the opportunity to thoroughly study the mission plan. 117 recalled that they had been quite involved in the Tandeeri's group meditation practices. Whatever they had gone through seemed to slowly break down their cold and neutral facades.

501 and 466 shared fun stories with the rest of the Third Group amborgs. The triplets, 53, 54, and 55 were all sitting on some crates as 249, 593, and 49 traded snacks with each other. All of them were laughing and enjoying each other's company before the fleet departed. 117 then turned his attention to his team.

297 was conducting a weapons inspection on his new energy pulse rifle. He was taking aim at various targets and testing the scope.

777 was playing cards with both 92 and 93. The problem was whether or not his second-in-command and one of his close friends were getting along.

117 approached 917 and 999 carefully, but upon closer inspection, they seemed to be on friendly terms. 999 was holding 917's right hand and pressing it repeatedly, focusing on pressure points on his prosthetic and making sure it was in working order. Unlike 5 and 6's playful banter, 999 seemed to actually be verifying that 917's maintenance checks on his arm had been conducted properly.

"How do you feel?" she asked.

"I keep telling you, I'm fine," 917 replied.

"You take care of yourself, alright?"

917 smiled and nodded. 117 didn't feel convinced. After what 917 had texted him about and with 999 being... well, 999, he felt that he had to step in.

"You two aren't going to have any... problems, are you?" he asked calmly. "Because I have no clue if you're currently at each other's throats or being extra nice to each other to prove that everything's ok."

999 and 917 both glanced at each other before turning back to 117. She let go of 917's hand and nodded.

"There's no problem," she informed him.

117 eyed 917 carefully.

"Yeah, we're ok," he confirmed. "No problems here. We're ready to follow you into battle."

117 nodded. He was still a little unconvinced, especially since 917 had revealed some rather not-safe-for-work information earlier. In light of the present circumstances, he felt that it was ok to trust them and to stop being nosy. Instead, he decided to call his wife one more time before the Firestar began its journey. He was most definitely not going to have cell service once they jumped out of the solar system.

117 tapped Audrey's number and waited as the dial tone began to ring. Then there was a click and he was a little disappointed when her automated voicemail message played.

"Hi, this is Audrey!" her cheery and enthusiastic voice spoke to him. "Sorry you missed me! Give me a ring again if it's an emergency! Or you can just message me, because that's what texts are for! Otherwise, leave your name and number and I'll get back to you!"

When he heard the beep, 117 sighed and began to record a final message to his family.

"Hey Audrey and Sarah if you're both hearing this," he said. "I don't know if I'll make it home in time. I'm not sure how time works once I jump into an alternate universe, but I wanted to say that I'm off once again on another crazy mission. So, one last time, I wanted to tell you...I love you and Sarah very much, and what we're about to do is intended to ensure your safety. The truth that frightens me right now is that I don't know how to lead my friends through this. But...at least we'll face it together, just as amborgs always do. That's how we've always handled things."

117 took a deep breath and looked around. No one seemed to notice that he was leaving a voicemail, so he decided to finish and get to the point.

"If anything happens to me, uhh..I promise, you won't be left on your own. The paperwork and files are all there, just in case. However, if we survive this... if I survive this, then I think...there is much we need to talk about. So, I'll be home soon. I love you."

"Don't you dare hang up David 117!"

117 flinched when he suddenly heard a click before he could hang up, followed by Audrey's voice yelling at him.

"Hey," he chuckled nervously. "You were listening to my voicemail? The whole thing?"

"It was nice just listening to your voice," Audrey grumbled. "I just didn't want to accidentally miss you."

"But, what were you doing? Were you busy?"

"As a matter of fact, yes," Audrey replied. "I was actually chatting with Mandy and a surprise visitor when I got your call."

"Visitor?" 117 asked.

"Yeah, her husband," Audrey answered him. "Hey Tom! It's David!"

Someone exclaimed cheerfully in the background. 117 heard the phone get passed over, then a man's voice came through clearly.

"David 117?"

"Hello Major Palmer," 117 smiled. "I'm very happy to hear that you're ok."

"Well, unlike your wife, who is a much higher rank than me," Tom let out a light chuckle. "I had a lot of things to focus on. Especially since the whole army was on high alert in anticipation of... well, nothing."

"Not exactly nothing," 117 squirmed a little and spoke apologetically.

"I know," Tom sighed. "Evil Terminators from space. I got the update from everyone here. Also, Mandy and Audrey just told me that your team of amborgs is leaving this universe and going straight into the lion's den?"

"Yeah, a space lion's den," 117 replied.

"Well, good luck," Tom let out a slightly pained exhale. "You seem to have picked up your biggest mission yet."

"Yeah, biggest understatement of the universe," 117 said as he glanced around at his friends. "This and the next universe."

117 sighed.

"Major," 117 said. "Are you on speaker?"

"No," Tom replied. "Do you want me to...?"

"No," 117 cut him off. "Once we're finished speaking, I'd like to talk to Mandy and then I'll ask her to pass the phone back to Audrey. Can you promise me something?"

"Sure," Tom replied. "What is it?"

"If I don't make it," 117 replied. "Please tell my wife."

"Uh, 117," Tom answered calmly. "The amborgs aren't U.S. Military. Not currently. Even if you were, that's technically not my job. It's what CNOs are for."

Palmer was referring to the Casualty Notification Officers of the military. These were the soldiers that were trained on how to notify next-of-kin or surviving relatives when a soldier falls in combat.

"I'm not asking you as an officer of the U.S. Army," 117 stated. "I'm asking as a friend. If this mission doesn't work and I die, I want you to tell Audrey. She should hear it from a friend and not..."

"Are you sure you don't want any of the other amborgs here to do that?" Tom asked.

"I'm asking you because if we fail and the Alpha universe destroys us and then sends another invasion to the Epsilon universe," 117 sighed, "then all of the surviving amborgs are going to focus on defending the planet. It's an emergency protocol that A.I. Industries and the amborgs on Earth will carry out if my team doesn't make it back."

"Whoa, this sounds really important," Tom lowered his tone carefully. "The amborgs aren't going to protect your family?"

"They will," 117 answered. "However, there's 29 amborgs leaving the Epsilon universe. There are only 80 left to protect the Earth. I'm sure you understand the scale of what we're dealing with?"

"I think so?"

"Just... you need to get my wife and my daughter to my grandpa Mark," 117 requested in a serious tone. "After that, maybe gather your friends, take Mandy somewhere safe. A.I. Industries might very well become a huge target."

"Alright," Tom replied. "I can do that. Do you want to talk to Mandy?"

"Yes please."

Tom said a quick farewell as the line went silent for a moment. 117 heard him call for Mandy, followed by more shuffling.

"David?" Mandy's voice spoke on the other end. "Hey! What's up? Are you ok?"

"Yeah, I'm fine, I just... wanted to talk to you before we dropped out of contact," 117 said as he listened to the tone of his former technician's voice. "How are you?"

"I'm ok," Mandy replied. "How are you?"

"Stressed out," 117 replied.

"It's because you don't have me as your eyes and ears anymore," Mandy replied sarcastically. "I'm not blaming you but... it was a weird decision to discontinue the technician program."

"But, you agreed when Dr. Kendrick sided with our recommendation to shut it down," 117 joked.

"Idiot," Mandy chuckled.

"Nag," 117 retorted.

"Is this the part where we break out in tears and say goodbye?"

"Goodbye is too depressing," 117 replied. "Remember? We say see you later?"

"I know," Mandy chuckled again. "I'm just not used to not being there to talk to you, to guide you like it used to be. A few of us still wish for a past that won't ever come back. We've all moved on because... the future is crazy and unpredictable."

"Well," 117 said. "The future isn't set."

"No fate but what we make," Mandy stated in a stoic and deep voice.

"I already asked Tom but, could you also help take care of Audrey and Sarah for me?" 117 said. "Until I get back?"

"Of course!" Mandy replied. "Your family is my family too."

"You know, there's still time," 117 smiled. "You want to come up right now? I could use my best friend with me."

"Thanks David 117," Mandy said. "But I'm fine. What the hell am I going to contribute if I tagged along?"

"Help us take on a whole universe?"

"Yeah, I think I can let you handle this. Besides, you have so many good people alongside you," Mandy laughed. "Play to your strengths and understand your limitations. Every amborg up there knows what to do and you know everyone's strengths and weaknesses. Use everything that you have and you'll succeed."

"You think so?" 117 asked.

"I know so."

"Thanks Mandy," 117 said with relief. "Hey, can I speak to Sarah?"

"Sure! Let me just get…!"

117 was interrupted when he heard someone's footsteps approaching. He glanced up to see a heavyset man in armor and armed with weapons making his way toward him. The man did not appear to be in a relaxed state of mind.

"Papa?" 117 heard Sarah's voice over the phone.

117 took a deep breath as he saw the marine closing in. As he gulped some air, he prepared to hang up the call.

"I love you Sarah," he said quickly. "Papa loves you!"

117 lowered his hand and the call disconnected. He immediately began to regret that he didn't get to hear his daughter say goodbye. He straightened up and politely greeted the marine.

"Commander 117?" the man spoke in a low and echoing voice.

117 gulped again.

"Yes?"

The man leaned forward and suddenly reached out his hand. 117 glanced at it and hesitantly offered his own hand in return. He looked around and noticed several other S.C.E. marines approaching. None of them had any visible rank markings. Then he remembered that Commander Ulgo had explained how their marine escorts had reconfigured their I.F.F. tags. Just as he was about to switch to his HUD to gather information about the man trying to shake his hand, the man decided to introduce himself.

"I am Captain Mercy."

117 blinked as he shook the captain's hand. Then, he heard movement behind him. The other Second Group amborgs were approaching, likely to give him some backup if needed.

"Uh... did you say your name was Mercy?" 117 asked for clarification.

"Yes sir," the Captain grumbled reluctantly. "I am known to have 'no mercy' in certain situations."

"Ok badass name but... uh, is there a problem?" 297 cleared his throat from behind 117's left shoulder. "You don't seem to like 117... or us in general."

"One of your space marines had an... interaction with my daughter..."

Captain Mercy shot a look over to the right. Everyone followed his gaze and saw a few marines introducing themselves to the Third Group. One of them was a young woman, who noticed the captain's angry glare and recoiled, then tried to hide within the crowd.

"Uh," 117 stammered. "O-one of our space marines..."

"Oh," 917 exclaimed, pointing, but awkwardly fell silent as Captain Mercy shot a fierce look at everyone. "One of us hooked up with... that girl, woman... I mean, that marine! Uh, who was it?"

Captain Mercy sighed and clenched his fist around 117's hand. 117 let out a small grunt and he grimaced in pain, which surprised the Second Group team. This marine had enough strength to crush 117's hand?

"It was a man named Harrelson," Captain Mercy growled.

"Oh, damn," 777 sputtered.

"Captain Harrelson of the Apogee Jumpers," 92 tilted his head to the side and eyed 117's crushed hand. "Oh dear."

"He is very well-known as a ladies man," 93 commented casually. Then he noticed Captain Mercy direct his piercing angry gaze at him. Terrified, 93 actually took cover behind his twin brother. "Oh, I didn't mean to say that out loud. Please don't kill us!"

Captain Mercy appeared to pout in a very dad-like way. 117 could only partially relate since he was dreading the day that Sarah would grow up and start having her own relationships. Fortunately, he wouldn't have to deal with that for at least fifteen years or so.

However, right now, there was an S.C.E. marine captain standing before them whose building anger looked as if it could stop a tank. Was he seeking retribution for his daughter?

"I am... able... to set aside my personal feelings," Captain Mercy declared. "For the mission, my squad will follow you!"

"Thanks!" 117 squeaked as he continued to squirm in pain. "Captain, I don't wish to pull the rank card but uh... could I have my hand back? That's an order?! Please?!"

Captain Mercy blinked and his eyes widened. It was as if he'd been yanked out of the void of his own anger, causing him to let go of 117's hand. 117 raised his right hand and, gripping his wrist with his left, he drew in a sharp breath at the sharp pain that throbbed through him. The Second Group all stared in stunned silence as 117 continued to groan meekly.

"Impressive grip strength," 999 remarked. "6! We need a medic!"

Despite the fact that every amborg had the same medical training, they felt it was best to call the leading medical expert in their party. 6 rushed over and quickly examined 117's right hand. As he received medical attention, the rest of them wondered whether or not this strange greeting warranted legal action.

As 117 winced from the pain and 6 gave him a painkiller, 297 decided to take over the conversation. Since he had the most military training out of all of them, it was probably wise for him to try and bond with... a marine named Mercy.

"So, uh, Captain," 297 walked forward and grinned enthusiastically. "I'm Commander 297."

"Yes sir," Mercy dipped his head respectfully. "You're the weapons specialist. Earth Army Ranger?"

"You read my file! Great!" 297 chuckled bashfully.

"He also nearly crushed 117's hand," 777 cleared his throat awkwardly.

"I am very sorry about that," Captain Mercy mumbled apologetically.

The amborgs shared a casual glance. His words did seem sincere. Ultimately, it was 117's call on how to proceed.

"It's fine," 117 replied weakly. "I apologize for what Harrelson did with your daughter."

"I submit myself for disciplinary action," Mercy sighed. "I let my love for my daughter interfere with my professionalism. She is a marine and also old enough to make her own decisions."

"Ah, then when you nearly broke 117's hand," 6 commented as she eyed him suspiciously. "That was you holding back??"

"Huh," 917 scoffed. "I think I'm curious to see how strong he is when he's unrestrained."

"Father of the year award?" 999 suggested.

The Second Group nodded in sync. 6 finished her treatment and politely excused herself, then headed back to the First Group team. 297 gave Captain Mercy a reassuring look, and the marine stood at attention.

"At ease, captain!" he stated in a friendly tone. "Why don't you introduce us to your team?"

The amborgs watched as a squad of marines assembled behind Captain Mercy, awaiting instructions.

"I'm the commanding officer of 2nd platoon," he announced as he gestured towards the 19 marines behind him. "I have three squads here ready to follow you."

117 and 297 glanced at the marines, including Captain Mercy. Then they looked at the marine leaders speaking to 1 and 2, then the ones speaking to 501 and 466. They noticed that the numbers didn't seem to match up.

"Pardon me but... is this everyone in your platoon?" 297 asked.

297 was wondering since it looked like the marines congregating with the First, Third, and Fourth Groups had a larger contingent. A quick headcount revealed there were only 14 marines, including Captain Mercy. The other marines who were introducing themselves to the amborgs seemed to have approximately twice that number.

"Yes sir," Mercy replied. "First and Third platoon had the least casualties when Silent Eclipse attacked the Firestar. Second was in a terrible firefight when we defended the civilian decks of the ship."

"Oh right," 117 nodded. "I read your post-action reports. You made a very noble and valiant stand against the Silent Eclipse attack."

"Thank you sir," Mercy said politely. "But my platoon lost a lot of good men and women. We may not have the numbers but we want to finish this."

"Well, we're going to be storming S.C.E. headquarters," 117 stated. "You prepared to do that?"

"Yes sir," Captain Mercy nodded. "We'll have your back the entire time."

"Good," 117 said. "May I greet the rest of your platoon?"

The Second Group eagerly stepped forward to meet with the marines. However, 917 and 999 were cut off when a few pilots rushed forward, separating them from the other amborgs. 117 had been followed by 297 and 777, but they were stuck witnessing whatever was going on with the S.C.E. pilots.

"Pardon me, but may I ask for an autograph from both of you?"

917 and 999 silently glanced at each other. 917 lifted a finger and pointed at himself, then at 999.

"Us?" he asked.

"Autograph?" 999 rolled her eyes. "This again?"

She recalled that time a crewman had stopped them in an elevator for a signature. They got to use a rather interesting laser pen.

"Yes," one woman smiled at 999 and held out a small note pad. "I am a big fan of you two. My children would love this too."

"Who should I make it out to?" 999 sighed as she grabbed the note pad and pen.

"Can you sign my helmet?" another man asked politely.

"Oh, that's such a great idea!" the pilot standing next to him commented excitedly. He pulled his own helmet off his head and held it out. "Uh... could you do mine too?"

92 and 93 watched in amusement as several pilots removed their helmets and presented them like they were offering them to 917 and 999 as gifts. They almost looked like trick-or-treaters.

"We are curious," 92 spoke up brightly as he and 93 pointed at their suddenly popular comrades. "How do you know them?"

"To be accurate," 93 clarified the question. "Who are they to you?"

917 hastily scribbled a signature on someone's helmet.

"You know, alternate universes, right?" he smirked.

"Oh, of course. Both of you are legends," the same woman that 999 first signed for beamed enthusiastically as she passed her helmet to 917. "Every pilot across our territories far and wide knows about you two."

She pointed at 999 and then at 917.

"Shinigami and Mushu."

999 and 917 suddenly stopped, their bodies rigid. 117, 297, and 777 paused their conversation with their marine escorts and turned sharply at the mention of those names. 92 and 93 stared at each other blankly.

"How..." 92 started.

"...Interesting," 93 finished.

"No, not interesting," 917 spoke cautiously. "Callsigns, especially for pilots, are always given for stupid and entertaining reasons."

"So, I'm the grim reaper?" 999 asked in a soft tone. "How did I earn that nickname?"

One of the pilots responded avidly.

"Aside from the fact that you were a legendary pilot and have a high number of kills, there's a rumor that you got that nickname because you killed the mood. All the time."

"I shouldn't have asked," 999's expression went from cold and neutral to full disgruntlement.

"You think that's bad?" 917 scoffed. He glanced at another pilot and asked, "is my callsign named after the fictional dragon or the pork dish?"

The others stifled their laughter. The person 917 was speaking to started to open his mouth, but 917 cut him off, pushing his helmet back into his hands.

"Never mind!" he chuckled sarcastically. "Don't answer that. That's an order."

"Yes sir," the man replied nervously as he inspected 917's signature. "Thank you!"

The pilots were thrilled to have received signatures. 917 and 999 watched as they hurried off towards their fighters. They both lingered, unsure if their experience felt good at all.

"That felt weird," 917 stated.

"Agreed," 999 replied.

"That seemed funny as hell," 777 winked at the two of them.

As they went back to mingling, they noticed an older man in a flight suit approaching 917 and 999.

"Lieutenant Chan," 917 perked up.

"Welcome back, Commander."

Lieutenant Chan saluted Captain Mercy and the amborgs. They were still getting used to the idea that they had authority over so many people aboard the Firestar.

Lieutenant Chan was the current leader of the Wolf Squadron, one of the Firestar's most skilled and elite fighter groups. In the Alpha universe, when he was alive, this was the squadron originally under 917's command. Before they departed for the Tandeeri fleet to return Oreo to the Heart of Alcyon, Chan had led the squadron and escorted their shuttle off the ship so that they could reach the Tandeeri safely.

When he saluted 917, it almost seemed like he was relieved. This was different from their first meeting, when 917 accidentally commented how old he looked. The older Asian man looked as if he was ready to ask them something.

"I hate to interrupt sir, but the squadron and I were curious," he said. "We were all pleased to hear that you had received your former ranks and positions. Does that mean you'll be taking over your command? If you're back, say the word, and we can have your fighters loaded up and ready."

917 and 999's eyes widened. They looked at though they'd just stumbled upon a car hidden away in storage, still in pristine condition.

"Fighters?" 917 asked. "Our fighters? You have fighters that belong to us on this ship?"

"They've been waiting for you," Chan nodded. "We've kept them in good working order in the event that you'd one day return."

"Better than letting them sit in a museum," 999 commented.

The two amborgs exchanged a knowing look. 917 shook his head.

"It is very admirable that you kept them maintained for so long," he said. "However, we may be your commanders again but it doesn't mean that we're qualified to fly. We didn't even get to spend enough time on those simulators that they brought over to the Tandeeri fleet."

"You've always been an exceptional pilot alongside the Shinigami," Chan remarked as he nodded to 999. "I assumed that with your reinstatement, we could expect you to lead us."

"Tell the squadron thanks but, I'm in no position to fly," 917 replied courteously. "I believe you being in command temporarily will be the best choice for this mission."

"Yes sir," Chan saluted. "Will that be all sir?"

"Uhh... Stick close if you can Chan," 917 said. "We could use some air support if things aren't going well."

"Aye sir," Chan turned around and walked back to Wolf Squadron. 999 glanced at him.

"Are you sure you don't want to join them?"

"Let's face it Angel," 917 sighed. "It'd be like putting someone fresh out of driver's ed in charge of the department of transportation."

As they talked, they noticed 466 walking over to 117.

"117," she said, pointing. "Look! It's Breya!"

The amborgs all turned to see another friend approaching them, clad in full body armor and carrying a rifle. She made her way over and stood next to Captain Mercy, and they both nodded to each other respectfully. 117 watched as Breya came forward and saluted.

She was from an alien species known as the Brakovish Arklashi. According to what she had taught 466, everyone was allowed to refer to a member of her race as a Kovark. This was still confusing to some of them, especially since the shortened nickname of the species didn't sound anything similar to the formal name.

A member of Breya's species definitely stood out in a crowd. Each of them had four eyes in total and two pairs of arms. They stood proudly on two legs, with very thin but tall physiques. Her armor and battle uniform matched the same dark grey and black color scheme of the marines, but it was obvious that it was custom-made and modified to accommodate her height. She wasn't as tall as the towering Tandeeri, but she certainly appeared badass, even intimidating.

117 was taken aback when she held her weapon in her left arms and saluted him with both of her right. Looking closer, he noticed there was a huge array of firearms and daggers stored all over her vest and inside pockets.

"Captain Breya returning for duty without actual permission sir!" she declared.

"At ease," 117 said, stunned. "What are you doing here?"

"I'm coming with you sir," Breya stated.

"But you were still recovering aboard the Tandeeri fleet when you were injured!" 466 exclaimed.

117 glanced at 466 and then up at Breya, who stared back at him insistently.

"I am fully recovered," she said. "You can have your chief medical officer verify my health. I owe your Major 5 and Commander 3 for saving my life. So, I would like to follow you into battle."

"Out of retirement?" 117 asked. "Is that even allowed?"

117 suddenly realized he answered his own question. When the threat of an invasion from space loomed over their heads back on Earth, millions of people rose up to prepare to defend the planet. The way that Breya continued to stare at him only confirmed that she was going through with this, no matter what.

"Alright," 117 sighed. "Are you sure you want to come with me?"

"I used to serve under your command," Breya replied. "I can be of help to you once more. Captain Mercy's platoon is underwhelmed. You could benefit from having a Kovark matriarch assisting you."

"I can endorse her actions, sir," Mercy nodded confidently. "A Kovark is a great asset. A matriarch with combat experience...will unleash a storm against our enemies."

117 glanced at Captain Mercy, then at 466. She nodded subtly, but still seemed a little hesitant. The rest of the Second Group voted and texted 117 their thoughts and opinions. After he briefly looked over everything, he looked into Breya's eyes and nodded.

"Well, captain," he smiled. "It looks like we're all in favor of having you with us."

"Thank you, commander," Breya replied.

Breya stepped away to conduct a final inspection of her gear, setting everything down temporarily near the First Group's staging area. She acknowledged 3 with a nod and saluted 5. 6 also offered a warm smile appearing eager to engage in conversation with Breya.

"It's wonderful to see you again," 6 exclaimed. "Is there any chance we can go over some of the things you taught me when we were onboard the Heart of Alcyon?"

6 had treated many patients recovering from the battle against Silent Eclipse. She and Breya had met at that time and became friends from the look of it.

"Everyone ready?"

117 turned and saw that 43 had arrived at the hangar as well.

"I think so," he replied.

"By the way, before we go on this mission, something was on my mind. Do you have Argentum?"

117 smiled pleasantly and cleared his throat. He ran his hand across a small pouch on his hip. 43 eyed him curiously but could tell that he was trying to be discreet.

"Did... you have him the whole time?" 43 asked.

"Actually, it's a bit of a complicated long story," 117 replied. "He asked to stay here on the Firestar before we left to meet with the Tandeeri."

43 paused. She stared at him in disbelief.

"Argentum... asked... to stay here?"

117 nodded. He quickly explained what had happened.

Just before they took Oreo and climbed aboard the shuttle that would get them off the ship, 117 had a brief private discussion with Argentum, a little sentient tool that his Alpha version had left behind for him. He had given this shiny silver cube the appropriate name based on its unique and shiny appearance. It had some rather amazing abilities that far surpassed conventional methods.

Argentum estimated, in written format on one of its sides, that it would probably serve more effectively onboard the Firestar rather than accompanying the amborgs on their mission to meet with the Tandeeri.

"So, before we left, I left Argentum in a console here on the ship and it manifested itself into the system," 117 stated. "Apparently, he learned a lot about the S.C.E. systems."

"You allowed your sentient pet space-cube into our computer systems?" 43 stared, eyes wide as saucers.

"Yeah," 117 nodded. "When 999 was almost killed by the first Silent Eclipse drone she encountered and activated, Argentum helped open the door when we couldn't force our way in. I figured it'd be best to let it in your system so it could protect the ship."

"That... makes a lot of sense actually."

43 looked around thoughtfully.

"When we were running around defending the ship," she stated, "there was a lot of chatter of some kind of ghost helping us out. It makes so much sense."

43 pointed at the bag that 117 had Argentum resting in.

"Typical stuff," she said. "Doors opening and closing for us at the right times. Ship security systems coming online to help us target Silent Eclipse drones. Fire suppression and electrical conduits were going off. It was like the ship was helping us. No one could really explain what was happening."

43 then leaned towards the bag and whispered.

"Argentum, if that was you... thank you, you prevented a lot of casualties."

117 felt his bag rumble slightly. He unfastened the seal and opened it, revealing one side of Argentum. Words began to appear.

You are welcome, Serina 43, it wrote for them. *I attempted to aid in defending the ship as best I could. It was rather difficult watching the entire ship and being everywhere at once. Very exhausting. I am also pleased to report that all override messages to all S.C.E. ships within range during the battle were successfully activated.*

"Override?" 43 read Argentum's words. "What does that mean?"

I broadcasted a hidden signal across the entire fleet, Argentum explained. *I didn't have the ability to shut down all hostile forces, but I was able to activate the emergency override on all vital systems in the computers of each S.C.E. ship. This would have prevented the enemy drones from easily accessing each ship's computers.*

"He wanted to make sure that no one could shut down the S.C.E. ship computers," 117 explained. "It's truly remarkable."

"It is," 43 smiled. Then, a wave of realization swept over her, and she looked at 117 skeptically. "Wait a minute. Has Argentum been onboard the Firestar the whole time?"

"Yeah, about that," 117 shrugged guiltily. "When we saved the planet and knocked out every enemy drone in the fleet, that's when we heard about 125."

43 nodded in understanding.

"We headed straight back down to Earth and... I forgot about Argentum. I didn't get to it until after we finally returned to the Firestar, right after we spent over two weeks with the Tandeeri."

"Oh, so it was unsupervised for a few days?" 43 asked.

It is not a serious concern, Argentum rumbled, redirecting their attention back to itself. *I understand the circumstances and I am not harboring negative feelings.*

"I didn't realize Argentum was capable of having feelings," 43 remarked.

I don't, Argentum responded, and 43 could have sworn it wrote with a slightly irritated inflection. *I am a cube. I have no emotional capacity.*

"A cube with an attitude," 117 smirked.

Please excuse me. I would like to return to a state of dormancy, Argentum wrote in a blunt manner. *Do not disturb me unless one is in immediate danger or my assistance is considered necessary.*

"Wow," 43 said as 117 closed and secured the bag. "No emotions? It sure sounds like one sassy cube."

"Well, you gave it to me," 117 shrugged. "Or in this case, 'I' gave it to me."

"Commander 117?"

Braelynn had appeared at their side once again. 43 eyed her with doubt, but 117 was relieved to see a familiar face.

"Yes? Braelynn?" he replied.

"May I offer a recommendation of how we should infiltrate headquarters?"

117 glanced at 43, who was still watching Braelynn cautiously. She reminded him of how 999 looked when she was distrustful of Braelynn at first.

"That would actually be a good idea," 117 nodded. "We've studied the plans of the S.C.E. headquarters, but I'm open to suggestions."

With amborgs from all four groups of A.I. Industries taking on the main building containing the highest elite officers of the S.C.E., it was probably best to know exactly where to go. It was a huge advantage that they spent a lot of time aboard the Tandeeri flagship, which gave them plenty of time to study the blueprints and building plans. However, the quickest and shortest routes in was the best way to finish this mission once they touched down on the ground.

"May I suggest that you send some amborgs to take over the S.C.E. computer mainframes?" Braelynn spoke as she showed them a map.

"What could we find there?" 117 asked.

"Maybe someone hid Silent Eclipse's records in the archives," Braelynn shrugged. "It's only natural there should be copies or hidden backup drives detailing their operation on a classified server. It may lead to whoever is running the organization. If there are teams sweeping the higher floors to verify all the identities of the admiralty, then the computer mainframes will show who's affiliated with the enemy and who's on our side. My guess is that there'll be a hint of footprints in the system that lead back to them."

117 looked down. The plan made sense. 999 had prior experience from breaching the classified section. Under the cover of Serina's blackout program, they found themselves with a golden opportunity.

"Maybe there's a kill switch," he said.

43 and Braelynn glanced at 117, who smirked.

"Usually," he explained before they could ask, "one has a switch or button on them that deactivates a weapon. The leaders of Silent Eclipse, whoever they are, will have some sort of trigger on their persons, I'm betting. Or they have subordinates that handle that sort of thing. What if we tried identifying the origins of the signal that activates the drone?"

"That would work," 43 said, pounding her fist into her palm. "If anyone tried activating their drones during the blackout, we would be able to identify the targets!"

"Problem is," Braelynn sighed. "This plan requires that we divide our forces again. Admiral Ra'aiah made an excellent plan when she assigned marines to escort each amborg group."

"Well, we did anticipate this even when we decided to stay together," 117 nodded. "All amborgs attacking S.C.E. headquarters is better than just sending in one. Splitting up with our escorts will be effective."

117 glanced at Braelynn and realized she wasn't wearing the same kind of flight suit that the pilots usually wore. Instead, she was outfitted in gear and armor, appearing fully prepared to join them in the assault.

"You're not flying us in this time?" he asked.

"I can be very helpful on the ground with you," she replied.

43 looked like she wanted to interrupt, but chose to stay silent.

"Well," 117 let out a sigh. "We seem to be acquiring a lot of extra hands on this mission. The Third and Fourth Group are the ones handling the defense platform control rooms and sweeping the lower floors. Perhaps you could help keep an eye out for them after we land?"

"It'd be my pleasure," Braelynn nodded. "I'll let them know. Thank you commander, for listening to my suggestion."

When she walked away to speak to 501 and 466, 43 leaned towards 117.

"Are you sure?" she asked bluntly.

"The First and Second Group will go for the upper floors and others will go below to the main servers," 117 replied.

"No," 43 shook her head and gave him a look of caution. "Who is that 117?"

"Lieutenant Braelynn?" he replied. "She was the shuttle pilot that saved our lives and brought us to the Tandeeri. She's with S.C.E. Intelligence."

"Hmm," 43 mumbled as she lowered her gaze toward Braelynn.

"What's wrong?"

"It's not a bad idea," 43 replied as she shrugged. There was a subtle shudder in her voice. "It's just... I haven't had a really pleasant experience with Intelligence officers. They're smart but crafty. Extremely crafty."

117's smile faded as he regarded Braelynn in the same way as 43. She was still exchanging pleasantries with 501, but now she was introducing herself to 113 and 280.

"Is there a problem?" 117 asked.

"I've only ever worked with three Intelligence agents," 43 replied, shaking her head and brushing it off. "They're all really reserved and secretive. Now, her, Braelynn... seems slightly more invested in this than I've ever seen from the others."

"Maybe she's interested in ending this quickly?" 117 suggested.

"Look, I've never met her before, so I don't know her. If I was in charge of this mission, I'd tell the others to watch her closely," 43 replied. "But that's just me. You do what you like."

117 understood where she was coming from. He decided to let the matter slide but kept her recommendation on the backburner.

"Do you intend to come with us to verify the admiralty?" he asked politely. "Or are you going to help the teams going for the defense platform control rooms?"

43 looked at 117 and shook her head.

"I think, in the middle of all the chaos we're about to create," she answered, "I'm going to be a distraction. Try to remain as covert for as long as you can. The S.C.E. know me but they don't know you're coming. So, I'll draw their attention for as long as possible."

"What's your plan?" 117 asked.

"Break a lot of stuff," 43 answered. "I think a nice rampage ought to be enough."

"You sure that you won't help the Third and Fourth Group take on the defense platforms?"

"Have some faith in them," 43 replied. "The defense platform systems aren't that complicated."

Earlier, a few of the amborgs had questioned why control of the defense platforms for the moon and Earth were all done from the S.C.E. headquarters. 501 had figured it would be easier for S.C.E. bases on Earth to control their own platforms instead of allowing the HQ on the moon to do it. According to 43, their job was easier since there had been a very specific set of regulations implemented when the defense platforms were constructed. Only during an absolute worst case scenario when the S.C.E. forces fell during an invasion of the moon would control authority of the working platforms be sent to the forces on Earth. For now, full control was on the moon and this only increased the importance of how fast they had to be in order to capture the stronghold.

"Attention all hands!" Admiral Ra'aiah's voice spoke over the ship's intercoms. "Prepare for departure! Begin preparations for wormhole creation."

117's heart sank. Had the time flown that fast? He had missed the chance to properly tell Audrey and Sarah goodbye.

He heard the ship rumbling in the far distance. He could only assume that they were making preparations to leave the solar system. He quickly tried to call and text Audrey. Unfortunately, every one of his messages failed to go through. When he tried to resend, he saw the messages grayout and a red x appeared, indicating there was no signal.

43 noticed he was a bit distraught and placed a sympathetic hand on his shoulder.

"Hey," she said. "I know this doesn't mean much but... I'll come and find you during the mission, ok? I don't think that we're all going to make it back from this but... if I see an opportunity to make sure that you live to see your daughter grow up... then I'll do everything I can."

"Thank you," 117 looked down glumly as he stopped trying to resend his texts. "I appreciate it."

"You just have to do one thing for me," 43 stated.

117 looked up at her and waited for her request.

"Can I be Sarah's cool aunt?" 43 grinned.

"You might have a lot of competition," 117 let out a soft laugh. "She's got a big family."

"Thanks to this whole mess," 43 gestured to everyone, "I do too... and I know what I'm fighting for now. All of you."

After a few minutes of travel, another announcement rang out over the P.A.

"All hands," Admiral Ra'aiah spoke up as her voice echoed throughout the ship. "Energy levels are charged. Preparing to fire main batteries. The entire fleet combined with a little boost from the Tandeeri will help us with a safe and consistent gateway back home! Initiating wormhole in 15 seconds! Travel into the Alpha universe imminent! All ships prepare to cross over. Expect a little turbulence."

"Everyone!" 43 called out. "Brace yourselves!"

The entire hangar clambered around and fell silent. Nearly everyone had a hand securely gripping something anchored to the floor. 117 and 43 made their way to join the other members of the Second Group amborgs. They all leaned against the crates they'd put together, holding on tightly.

After 15 seconds had gone by, they began to hear faint explosions. It wasn't loud or dramatic, as the creation of the wormhole was located at a considerable distance from the fleet in the emptiness of space, but they could still imagine it happening. They had already seen a few wormholes, but the clearest and most recent one was when the S.C.E. Firestar first crossed into the Epsilon universe and saved Apogee Station. 117 remembered how bright and majestic the colors were, as if a magnificent light show had erupted above their planet. Now, they were about to journey through a tear in the fabric of space-time, ready to enter another universe entirely.

"I just thought of something stupid..." 297 stated.

"What?" 777 asked as everyone held their breath.

"What happens if it's like Into the Spiderverse?" 297 shuddered. "If we cross over into the Alpha universe and we... glitch and deteriorate?"

"Really? You just had to bring that up now?!" 5 exclaimed in sudden nervous irritation. "Now, I'm scared..."

"It'll be fine!" 43 replied quickly. "All of us in our fleet lived in Epsilon for a short time. No signs of deterioration!"

"Well," 297 gulped. "Just in case... I love you all!"

"Dumbass," 999 shook her head.

43 leaned over and spoke quietly to 117.

"I never saw Into the Spiderverse," she whispered. "Did someone actually deteriorate in that movie?"

"No," 117 shook his head. "But it looked quite painful onscreen."

"Well, this might hurt for just a few seconds."

Out of nowhere, a massive quake caused everyone to jostle around erratically. It was as if someone had taken hold of the Firestar and shook it like a box full of fragile material, but it only lasted for a fleeting moment. As everyone struggled to stay upright, the hangar went still again.

"Attention crew of the Firestar," Admiral Ra'aiah said over the intercom in a pleasant and cheerful tone. "We have successfully returned home. Commencing operation Salamis! Action stations!"

"Ah, the ancient naval battle in the Saronic Gulf of Greece," 1 stated. "Admiral Ra'aiah knows her history. In 480 BC, the smaller Greek fleet used superior tactics to defeat the Persian navy."

"I'm not entirely familiar with that battle," 501 spoke up. "How many ships were there in 480 BC?"

"Historians still debate about it," 1 replied with a shrug. "The Greeks had about 378 ships in their fleet. For the Persians, it's hard to say because... minimum, some say they had 600. The highest estimate that people believe was around 1200 ships that participated in the battle."

"Wow," 501 gulped.

"Never mind that," 466 interjected. "We have 30 ships. We're going against hundreds. What casualties did the Greeks and Persians suffer?"

"40 Greek ship casualties, and the Persians possibly lost 200 ships," 1 answered quickly.

"Wow," 466 replied. "But after the fleet splits up to go after the main S.C.E. territories, we're charging straight for Earth where it's our one ship against... a lot."

"Which is why we have to use superior tactics and work fast," 43 said. "Get ready to board your shuttles."

The plan involved each amborg team traveling with their marine squads and boarding individual shuttles. They didn't want to risk riding together, as a single lucky shot could jeopardize the mission before it even started.

Another announcement echoed overhead.

"All fighters, prepare to scramble. All fighters, prepare to scramble."

Someone was broadcasting specific instructions on repeat. The amborgs started assembling their gear, watching as numerous fighter pilots picked up the pace and boarded their spacecraft. Everyone already inside their cockpits lowered their canopies and secured their helmets.

Crewmen detached fuel lines from all fighters that were ready for deployment. Munitions officers promptly cleared the area after confirming that what appeared to be missile pods were properly secured to the airframes. Ammunition was loaded, and everyone rushed to make sure there were clear routes with few obstacles.

Once their paths were open, several fighters began to taxi slowly. At least, that's what it looked like. Looking closely, the amborgs could see tiny mono-wheeled devices hooked onto the landing gear of each fighter. They were pulling them, creating the illusion of the spacecraft moving on their own.

When the carriers and S.C.E. ships first arrived at the Firestar, they launched their fighter or bomber squadrons from large tubes located on the sides of their vessels. This method proved to be highly efficient for launching several fighters simultaneously for quick deployment. Shuttles were also designed with specialized launch tubes; however, in non-emergency situations, they typically took off and navigated in and out of the hangar bay doors when their flight paths were clear. The space traffic controllers who oversaw the ship hangars were greatly valued, as their absence would lead to significant issues.

When fighters or bombers return from a mission, they fly through the shields, enter the hangar's gravitational field, and touch down. Here, they can be staged, refueled, or rearmed, and if necessary, towed to the launch tubes for an immediate departure. Otherwise, the reserve spacecraft are taken to the large freight elevators and moved to a different deck for storage.

"All ground forces, please board your shuttles. All ground forces, please board your shuttles. Prepare for immediate departure."

This was their cue. The amborg groups began to head towards their respective shuttles, their squads of marines following closely behind.

"See you guys on the ground," 297 said to the others optimistically.

"We will," 113 nodded curtly.

As the Fourth Group walked away, 297 was slightly taken aback.

"Is it just me or... did 113 actually seem... pleasant? Like the icy cold heart of hers has begun to melt?"

"That did seem a little different," 777 agreed. "Maybe all of the time spent with the Tandeeri has opened them up."

The Fourth Group marched in perfect unison. 113 and 280 led the way, followed closely by 63, 100, 378, and then 301 and 365. Now that 297 mentioned it, their postures seemed less rigid and there was a tiny difference to how they moved before, but it was hard to confirm this.

Braelynn led 501, 466, and the rest of the Third Group to their shuttle. The triplets, 53, 54, and 55 stuck close to 249, 593, and 49 since their mentors, 92 and 93, were staying with the Second Group.

43 planned to accompany the First Group in their shuttle. She texted 117 a quick reminder, reaffirming her promise that as soon as they were safely within the S.C.E.'s headquarters, she would do her best to distract anyone who might try to go after them or disrupt their plans. The First Group amborgs appeared optimistic about 43 joining them.

Captains Mercy and Breya, along with their marines, led 117 and the Second Group. They boarded the shuttle, and everyone quickly found their seats and strapped themselves in.

"What's our rallying point?" 117 asked the pilot.

"If we're fast enough," he/she? replied, "we're going to try and land our shuttles in the main courtyard!"

S.C.E. headquarters was a collection of buildings inside a fort. It was surrounded by a moat and had two reinforced walls on the inner and outer perimeter. The outer defenses of that wall were roughly 25 feet high. The inner wall was higher and constructed to be about 40 feet. There were four entrances at the north, south, east and west points of those walls if approached from the ground. There were four towers at each corner, which made it look like a castle. According to the blueprints, it was said that the head designer of the S.C.E.

headquarters was a big fan of castle layouts and architecture from the medieval period.

When 117 looked over the blueprints again, he remembered 297's comment when he saw the headquarters.

"It looks like someone took the barracks from Fort Bragg, modernized it, and stuck it on the moon," he had said.

If S.C.E. high command had modeled their own base to resemble a modern military fort, then it was a familiar layout. Sure, there would be obvious differences to watch out for, but in the Alpha or Epsilon universe, it actually felt reassuring to surmise that the architects and designers of building placements had similar concepts.

The pilots of the four shuttles transporting the amborgs aimed to land in the courtyard, hoping to avoid outer perimeter defenses. Should an attack occur, a shield could be deployed, forming a dome-like structure over the headquarters. The plan was when 43's blackout program was triggered, it would sever all communications, leaving no time for anyone to shut them out. In the event that happened, they would reach out to Wolf Squadron to blast open a path for them.

"What's your plan if they manage to get the shield up?" 117 asked.

"Quickest way in with the least resistance is the east gate," the pilot answered. "Approaching from that direction would also put you in a perfect position to drop onto the roof where the admiralty works."

The pilot was suggesting that the shuttle should hover over their target, with ropes being deployed from it. The amborgs, along with their marine escorts, would then leap down onto the roof and gain entry from there.

"Alright," 117 nodded. He took a deep breath and mustered his courage as he made a choice. "First priority. Take us to the roof of headquarters as best as you can. We'll make our assault from the top and work our way down each floor. If it doesn't look like a viable plan, divert and get us to the ground safely and we'll join the First Group."

"117," 917 spoke up. "According to the blueprints, the main barracks is on the west side of the complex. I recommend we attack the entrances after we hit the ground."

117 glanced at 917 and noticed his determined expression. He nodded when he realized what he was saying.

"After we create enough chaos," he said. "do you think our fighter escort would be interested in some exterior remodeling? Preferably, all the entrances of S.C.E. headquarters?"

917 and 117 both exchanged mutual grins.

"I think that can be arranged," 917 nodded. "Disgruntled employees wanting to tear down their corporate management buildings? I think they'd be very interested."

CHAPTER 21

Operation Salamis

S.C.E. Firestar Shuttle Group
10 Minutes Later

"Sweeper 2, comm check."

117 checked the quality of his radio channel and responded to the pilot with his special callsign.

"Transient 2, comms green," 117 replied.

"Alright commander," the pilot reported from the cockpit. "We're waiting for the Firestar to make its move. E.M.P. attack should be commencing on schedule."

The Liberation fleet had deployed once they staged in the Alpha universe. They had to move quickly. Once they opened a wormhole, it was possible that the advance recon patrols had detected their presence. Admiral Ra'aiah and Snickerdoodle immediately ordered each individual ship in their fleet to head straight for their mission objectives. One S.C.E. starship was accompanied by one of the Tandeeri vessels.

The amborgs shuttles and fighter escort were cleared to launch and immediately switched to low-power settings to avoid being spotted. Admiral Ra'aiah ordered the Firestar with Snickerdoodle following a distance behind her to prepare for their Trojan horse maneuver. It was time for one hell of a show.

"Sir, we are receiving an open broadcast from the Firestar," the shuttle pilot reported.

"Roger," 117 nodded. He glanced at Mercy, Breya, and the Second Group. "Everyone, this is it!"

Serina appeared in a bright flash of light, startling the group.

"Serina??" 117 exclaimed. "I thought you were going to be on the Firestar!"

Serina put a finger up to her lips, signaling for silence. Before he could protest, 117 heard Admiral Ra'aiah's frantic voice. A tiny screen popped up on each of the amborg's bracelets, and every marine's helmet started streaming a live broadcast. There was a console in the shuttle that connected to the transmission as well.

The shuttle looked like complete pandemonium. 117 couldn't help but admire how much effort they had put into the broadcast. Admiral Ra'aiah and the bridge had pulled out all the stops. Someone had ripped a few ceiling panels and pulled wires out to make it look damaged. A few bridge crew in the background behind the admiral's chair played dead, and a medic ran across the back while a couple of "wounded" were being dragged off the bridge. Everyone's uniforms looked torn and dirtied up. Those watching suspected that a large makeup and special effects team had something to do with everyone's appearances.

What was selling it was how distressed and terrified Admiral Ra'aiah was acting onscreen.

"Mayday! Mayday! Can anyone read me?!" she yelled frenetically. "This is the S.C.E. Firestar on approach! We have escaped and returned to Alpha!"

There was a loud pop and more sparks erupted behind her shoulder. Her eyes widened as she flinched and looked behind her. Her eyes widened as she flinched and glanced back. This startled her, leaving her looking unsettled, but she quickly turned to face the camera in a state of panic. 117 suspected that someone had failed to inform her about the mini explosion meant to elicit a genuine reaction of surprise from her.

"Mission failure! I repeat! We have suffered a catastrophic mission failure in the defense of Epsilon Earth! We are retreating to Luna base! We..."

Everyone watched as Admiral Ra'aiah froze and her breathing became shallow.

"Oh gods... The Tandeeri are here! I repeat! They followed us back! Everyone! Please! You have to...!"

Admiral Ra'aiah let out a shrill scream as the broadcast suddenly cut out. The amborgs shared knowing smiles. It wasn't about whether or not they believed her performance. Admiral Ra'aiah and Dr. Kendrick were trying to throw everyone off.

A heartbeat later, they received an instant transmission, and Dr. Kendrick's voice rang out overhead. It echoed throughout the shuttle.

"Serina! Now!"

Serina immediately switched from her usual light blue color to a battle-ready red as she grinned at the amborgs.

"Blackout program," she declared in a monstrous voice that made them all tremble. "Activate!"

Despite her small size, she effortlessly initiated the program and shut down the entire facility within seconds. She then glanced at 117, still holding her red form.

"It's done," she announced. "All unprotected frequencies and transmissions just got infected by the program! The admiral put on quite a show, didn't she?"

"I didn't know she was going to redecorate the bridge," 917 admitted with an impressed look. "It's amazing how much work they got done after we waited in the hangar."

"To be fair, we did throw in a little CGI," Serina replied.

"Wait, was that a live broadcast or a recorded video?" 297 asked curiously. "I couldn't tell."

"It looked real," 777 stated.

"Yes, it was staged but... everyone really committed to their roles," Serina answered. "Anyone would have seen that it was fake if we had played a recorded video. It was all done on a live feed."

"Where was the CGI?" 117 asked. "Doing that during a live video feed is pretty impressive."

"I can't say," Serina replied, shaking her head. "Carter was in charge of that."

"Wait... Carter came to the Alpha universe?" 917 sounded alarmed. "I didn't know that."

"There are a lot of details that we decided not to share with everyone," Serina replied. "Admiral Ra'aiah wanted to keep several mission details hidden so that this operation would succeed."

She turned and looked towards the cockpit.

"By the way," she said with an annoyed look on her face. "Transient shuttles! It's time to deploy!"

"Roger that ma'am," the pilot responded affirmatively. "All fighters, break formation. Move in on designated targets. Hit the deck fast and low before they realize what's going on."

They lurched in their seats as the shuttle boosted and sped towards their destination.

"We have about 15... maybe 20 minutes," Serina replied. "That's how long we estimate they'll work out how to disable my blackout program. We did all that we could but I wouldn't be surprised if their computer security or servers have unexpected fail-safes that we didn't anticipate."

"Didn't you account for everything?" 297 asked.

"Of course we did," Serina replied as she glared at 297. "But even with perfect planning, you always have to expect something to go wrong. Expect the unexpected."

"Right," 999 mumbled. "Otherwise, overconfidence will lead to our failure."

This, however, didn't seem to lighten the mood. Everyone stared at Serina like she was a bomb about to go off.

"She seems quite..." 92 gulped.

"Snippy?" 93 suggested.

"Sorry," Serina shook her head apologetically, still bright red. "I'm trying to concentrate."

"Sweeper 2," the pilot interrupted with another announcement. "Our path is clear. No enemy patrols encountered. The Firestar is beginning its attack."

The shuttle's monitors switched to the outside camera. Someone in the cockpit aimed it towards the Firestar as they approached their target. The amborgs and marines all focused on the massive ship as it charged its main weapon. The enormous laser was sparking and glowing more intensely from its bow, and the camera shifted to the Tandeeri flagship. Snickerdoodle was maneuvering in to intercept while charging his own energy blast. From this angle, it looked as though the Tandeeri were about to fire at the Firestar, which would hopefully convince everyone, but in truth, they were getting ready to launch their first E.M.P. shot. 117 almost felt sympathy for those who could see this coming, but it was necessary for their survival.

"There it goes," 297 said.

The Tandeeri energy attack launched but then veered into the Firestar's line of fire as it unleashed its own strike. The blast from the main cannon hit the Tandeeri energy, sending it hurtling towards its target. As it flew, it glowed increasingly brighter, resembling a massive Fourth of July sparkler being hurled towards the star base.

As the shuttles transporting the amborgs, along with their fighter escorts, made their way to the moon, the camera operator tried their best to keep up with the action. It was like watching a space action movie, even though it was happening in real time.

The energy blast hit the target dead center, causing all of the lights in the windows to flare and brighten. Fortunately, it didn't explode like Apogee Station had previously when the Tandeeri first appeared. The star base glowed intensely as if a giant beacon of light had been turned on. Then, a colossal sphere of uncontrolled energy started to grow from the star base, threatening to envelop all the other ships positioned in the surrounding space. Each vessel was drawn into the rapidly growing sphere of the E.M.P. and was affected just like the star base. The plan was working well for most of the S.C.E. fleet tasked with defending the Sol system. However, not all of them were impacted as they initially predicted.

The Firestar's fighters and bombers broke formation and began their attack runs on the defense platforms within range. The camera controls couldn't keep up with all of them so instead, the camera was aimed back at the Firestar, which was charging its gun for another attack. The Heart of Alcyon was preparing to align itself and fly in formation with the Firestar now that there was no need to continue acting. Now they just needed to unleash as much chaos as possible.

The shuttle attack group under the callsign "Transient" moved into the moon's atmosphere shortly after the beginning of the operation. The amborgs and their marines were designated as "Sweeper" squads for the duration of the mission.

They had the unusual but iconic role of attacking headquarters without actually trying to kill anyone. All amborgs and marines that were confirmed to be on their side would infiltrate the facility while the fleet was distracted.

Suddenly, he received a text message. It was from Transient 3, the shuttle transporting the Third Group.

117, this is Braelynn. I'll keep it short. I'll take care of the Third Group amborgs and make sure they're ok. I promise. Serina 43 is guarding the First Group and the marine fire team leader for 113 and 280 is someone I verified twice. I have no doubt that your Fourth Group friends will be alright. I checked for you, in case you were nervous. Captain Mercy and Breya are confirmed to be loyal to you. Even though they could be considered suspicious last-minute additions to your team, I just wanted to let you know that they cleared and are not affiliated with Silent Eclipse. Just to reassure you, once again, we were very thorough in our... initial sweep of the S.C.E.

fleet. Just watch your back down there. Please don't message me back. Good luck. See you on the ground.

After reading the message, 117 nodded. He turned and noticed 999 was watching him, but she didn't speak. While they waited for the shuttles to land in the moon's artificially created atmosphere, he found himself contemplating a few strange details that stood out.

During the 16 days that the amborgs, the S.C.E., and Tandeeri spent on the Tandeeri ships, people took advantage of this extended period to recuperate, heal from their injuries, manufacture repair parts, and train for the mission ahead. What the majority of the public didn't know was that an additional 'sweep' had been conducted.

Sure, they had successfully eliminated every Silent Eclipse drone that had been hidden aboard every ship in their fleet, however, Admiral Ra'aiah and 43 had other concerns. 117 remembered their words in his mind as he replayed the conversation from a couple of weeks ago.

"Silent Eclipse is just like any other covert ops organization," Ishala Ra'aiah had explained in a small meeting with Talveeya, Dr. Kendrick, Snickerdoodle, and Kira. This conversation had then been shared only with the leaders of each amborg team. "Sure, you can have all the programmed drones you want hiding in the fleet and then you activate them to carry out their tasks. Still, that requires leadership or someone there to supervise. A team... or someone not affected by the Tandeeri's E.M.P."

Ishala and Talveeya Ra'aiah, the two highest ranking officers of the S.C.E. fleet, then gave the order for an internal investigation of their own ships.

Silent Eclipse operated with an army of robotic assassin drones that made up the majority of the organization to carry out their dirty work. There must have been a human operative working undercover stationed close by to ensure the drones were maintained and functioning properly. Silent Eclipse must have also had agents covertly placed on the S.C.E. ships. Unfortunately, the investigation yielded a significant amount of evidence, and behind the scenes, the brig of each S.C.E starship was filled to capacity.

When the S.C.E. fleet first entered the Epsilon universe, they had hundreds of thousands of passengers and crew aboard. As they initiated their investigation in preparation for the mission, they discreetly apprehended dozens of individuals on each starship. At least a hundred prisoners were identified as traitors or operatives of Silent Eclipse.

Every one of these people were hackers, thieves, military personnel, and trained killers who chose to lay low and bide their time after the takeover of the S.C.E. fleet had failed. The commanders of the S.C.E. had a field day interrogating these people for information.

43 had been assigned to lead the investigation and was there to help interrogate each prisoner. A few of them were willing to talk, but most of them had been brainwashed or forced to stay silent. The ones that did talk hardly revealed any important information at all. The compartmentalization and the protocols that Silent Eclipse kept in place were very strictly regulated.

All that mattered though, was that all traces of Silent Eclipse in the Liberation Fleet had been eliminated or had been imprisoned so that they wouldn't undermine the mission.

The real question that lingered in 117's mind was, had they contained all of them? 117 remembered what 43 had told him before they boarded their shuttles. She hadn't seen or met Braelynn before. Yet, Braelynn had just sent him a message reassuring him that she'd checked out Captain Mercy, Captain Breya, and the marine leader that was escorting the Fourth Group amborgs. If Braelynn, an agent that worked for S.C.E. Intelligence, had the ability to confirm who was or wasn't with Silent Eclipse, why did she not work with 43 during the investigation?

"Hey, 117."

He blinked and looked at 999.

"Daydreaming?" she asked.

"No, it's nothing," 117 replied with a reassuring smile.

999 wasn't having it.

"That's not the face you make if it's nothing," she said.

"Just concerned," 117 replied. "You know how we've planned for almost every possible scenario? What if there's something that we haven't thought of?"

"Hey," 297 interjected. "Whatever happens, we'll deal with it. We always manage to come up with something on the fly."

"With all due respect, commander."

Everyone paused to listen to Transient 2 as he spoke cordially over the radio.

"I hate to interrupt but we're entering the moon's atmosphere and approaching headquarters," he reported. "If you want to abort or if you're not disembarking when I touch down, then now's the time."

117 glanced at the other amborgs and the marines that were seated near him. It really was his decision to make. He just hoped that he wouldn't be ordering any of his friends or colleagues to their deaths.

"We're going in!" 117 replied. "No turning back!"

"Roger that," the pilot responded. "Transient 2 to Transient leader. We're following you in."

The shuttle shook violently from the turbulence in the atmosphere. Everyone held on as they were jostled around. Thanks to their training, physical strength, and extensive mental preparation, they were able to ride it out with ease.

Eventually, the shaking stopped, and the shuttle stabilized. 117 had to give a lot of respect to the pilots and the shuttle crew. They were fighting against turbulence, taking on heavy G-forces, and managing to maintain control of a fast-moving shuttlecraft.

"Wow," 117 said as he heard the faint sound of wind rushing past outside. "I know it's not the right time but it's amazing how you were able to construct an atmosphere on the moon."

Breya laughed.

"Well, that's what happens when our universe is seventy-five years ahead," she answered.

"Well, the program is working based on all the complaints I'm hearing on the radio and all frequencies," Serina said as she brought up a floating box of numbers. "I think a ton of kids are complaining about their super smart phones not working at the moment. We'd better move in now."

"Double time it pilot!" Captain Mercy called to the cockpit. "Emergency power if you have to! We don't want to be in the air longer than needed!"

The pilot replied quickly, but they all could hear a hint of sass in his tone.

"Roger! But sir, I must advise you that if we use too much emergency power, it'll burn out the engine! Then all of us will be on the ground with you! And personally, I'd really like to be in a ship that can take off again."

Breya turned all four of her eyes to Captain Mercy, who immediately snapped his mouth shut.

"There's a reason why we're not supposed to be doing his job," she pointed up at the cockpit, teasing him. "You worry about shooting the right targets. He makes sure we get there and back after we shoot those targets."

"Ha ha," Mercy yawned. "Shut up."

117 eyed 999. She shrugged in response. At least Breya and Mercy had a sense of humor. That was usually a good sign under the circumstances.

S.C.E. Firestar
Bridge

"Report!"

Hemington promptly responded from the radar station.

"The E.M.P. has been detonated at Luna star base and the ships surrounding it have been affected!"

"Get me a count!" Admiral Ra'aiah commanded. "We need to know how many ships didn't get hit in the blast! I know we didn't get all of them."

Hemington acknowledged her orders and focused on her station.

"Set course for the moon! Begin recharging the main gun!" Admiral Ra'aiah ordered. "The blackout won't last forever! Coordinate with the Heart of Alcyon now! Our next target should be the City of Beginnings! We need to give our attack teams a fighting chance! Get rid of any Silent Eclipse drones or guards that are hidden at headquarters!"

Admiral Ra'aiah rose from her chair and walked over to the holo-map where Dr. Kendrick and Commander Ulgo were examining some charts. There were several red dots popping up all over what appeared to be a section of the universe.

"It would appear that all the major territories occupied by S.C.E. fleets and military installations are simultaneously yielding expected results," Dr. Kendrick informed her when she approached. "The private channel and frequency that we've established for our little group chat is holding. We were right to assume that there would be a cyber-attack on our frequency. Someone at headquarters is trying to listen in to our communications."

"Do we know from where?"

Carter appeared in a bright flash of light and shook his head.

"I can try to isolate it in the S.C.E. HQ," he reported. "As expected, they're trying to counter Serina's blackout program. If they keep attacking our frequency and trying to shut out Serina, then it definitely means that Silent Eclipse is aware that this is a ruse. Admiral, would you prefer that I identify the source of who is trying to disrupt our communications or keep the blackout program running? It is incredibly difficult to do both."

"What if you had Serina locate the signal from headquarters?" Admiral Ra'aiah suggested. "You keep the program running?"

"Of course," Carter nodded.

"We still need to move quickly before they have the means to activate their troops here," Ulgo stated. "If there are more traitors and human agents of Silent Eclipse, we need to detonate another E.M.P. soon."

"Very good," Admiral Ra'aiah nodded as she looked at the clock. "Ulgo, have the fighters move to take out the defense platforms. I really hate to give this order but... tell our bombers to disable any ship that flies out to intercept us. We have to finish this before the main fleet decides to shoot us down for betraying the S.C.E."

As Ulgo nodded and headed over to the nearest communications station, Dr. Kendrick looked at the map. Admiral Ra'aiah then pointed at the Luna star base hologram, even though they had just hit it first.

"Send a raid to the star base and inform them of our situation," she said. "Pull two fighter squadrons and have them bring in two platoons of marines! We have less than 15 minutes to get our foothold."

"Aye ma'am!" Ulgo turned and nodded to her before shouting his next order. "Deploy the second wave of shuttles! I want marines to the dock and control the nearest hangars of the star base! Begin landing!"

"Are there any casualties?" Admiral Ra'aiah asked nervously.

Hemington was of the first bridge officers to reply.

"Reports coming in ma'am," she announced. "Our fighters have begun their attacks. Squad leaders are checking in. All runs currently have not created any fatalities."

"None?" Admiral Ra'aiah said in surprise. "Oh, that's good."

"There's a lot of wounded though..."

Admiral Ra'aiah slowly began to feel queasy.

"Never mind," she said immediately has her heart sank. "I might be feeling a little sick."

"Your fighters are very careful though," Dr. Kendrick said in amazement. "Were they ordered to not kill their targets?"

"Well," Admiral Ra'aiah sighed heavily. "No casualties from this point on is a perfect world scenario. There's going to be a lot of heat that'll come back to us once the dust clears. I suppose I must be going soft."

"That's not true. You have the makings of a natural leader. You're kind and you care about the lives of innocent people. My amborgs will have understood this by now and are probably conducting themselves accordingly. It's not exactly a war. Why don't we call it... an escalated attendance check?"

Admiral Ra'aiah stared at Dr. Kendrick. She shook her head.

"I think you need some more time to come up with an easier way to make me feel better."

"Ha ha, I'll have to think about that. Oh... Admiral," Dr. Kendrick said, pointing at the screen. "The Georgia has gone off course."

Their smiles instantly vanished. Admiral Ra'aiah looked carefully at the location that the Georgia had been assigned to. From what they could tell, Talveeya had successfully completed her task and detonated an E.M.P. at her target, but where was she going? The beacon belonging to the S.C.E. Georgia had gone into hyperspace and was speeding to another segment of the map. As far as Dr. Kendrick was concerned, he had no idea where Admiral Ra'aiah's mother was going. This wasn't part of the plan.

"Where is that?" he asked, concern etched into his features.

"She's changed course to the outer borders of our territory," Admiral Ra'aiah replied as she examined the beacon's path and heading. She slowly scanned the map and tried to decipher where the Georgia would jump to. "We don't have a strong fleet presence there... I can't imagine why she'd be heading towards..."

Suddenly, her eyes widened, and she sank her head into her hands.

"Oh boy..." she muttered as she began to tremble.

Dr. Kendrick eyed the Admiral with raised eyebrows. Admiral Ra'aiah appeared to be having another migraine as she began to rub her head.

"Of course she'd go that way," she sighed, returning to her chair.

Dr. Kendrick looked at the map and back at her with a curious expression.

"I'm sorry? Where is she going?"

Admiral Ra'aiah felt memories resurfacing in her mind as she suddenly recalled what it was like growing up as a teenager to parents who were both on the fast track to becoming part of the admiralty. As if overthrowing the entire S.C.E. high command wasn't reckless enough, now she was going to have to explain, if they survived this, to one other individual that she really wasn't mentally prepared to interact with.

"She's gone to rescue another important piece of this game," she mumbled. "Tell me, doctor. Did you ever fight with your dad a lot?"

"My dad?" Dr. Kendrick raised an eyebrow. "I don't understand how that's relevant."

Then his eyes widened, and he slowly nodded.

"Oh."

"If we die," Admiral Ra'aiah said meekly, her voice strained, "we're screwed. But if we live, we're probably going to be more screwed."

The Moon
City of Beginnings

"There are so many beautiful things about this universe," 117 said as they flew past a few tall buildings. He watched them go by on the shuttle's viewscreen. "I wonder what it'd be like to stay here."

The atmosphere was very calm and soothing. 117 couldn't help but notice that the moon's atmosphere had a lot of similarities to the sky on Earth. Clearly, when they terraformed this place, they had done an extensive amount of work. It looked so real, and the crazier part was, they could see the Earth hanging in the sky from their position on the moon.

"Wow," 917 said in awe as he watched the viewscreen with 117. "You ever wonder what was going through Neil and Buzz's head when they first looked at the Earth from where they stepped out onto the moon for the first time?"

He was talking about the Apollo 11 mission in 1969, when mankind first set foot on the moon, a significant event in Earth's history.

"One small step for man," 117 mumbled.

"One giant leap for mankind," 297 finished.

"Yeah," 917 nodded as they all stared at the buildings they were flying past. "What do you think we should call this? One small portal for amborgs, one giant leap of treason for the S.C.E.?"

"I personally find all of this ironic," 777 spoke up. "A few weeks ago, we were preparing to defend against an alien invasion and now look at us. We're the ones invading a parallel universe."

"You can say that again," 297 scoffed as he grinned eagerly. "Alpha 43 drops from the skies. We meet an alternate universe space fleet carrying evil Terminator robots from some creepy Section 31 organization that's out to kill us when they were originally supposed to help defend us. Then, we meet the Tandeeri, whose only crime in this entire thing is that they just wanted to solve our biggest energy crisis, then 501 adopts one and names it Oreo."

"I think you just used several pop-culture references that might make people's brains overheat," 777 chuckled.

"Uh, I'm currently living through this shitstorm," 297 laughed. "My brain's already overheating."

"It is official," 92 added.

"This is the craziest mission we've ever been on," 93 finished.

Transient 2 spoke over the radio, cutting through their conversation.

"We are approaching the eastern side of headquarters," he reported. "No defensive fire encountered or signs of anti-air defense, sir. But, if anyone looks up, we'll be spotted in no time. It won't be long before they realize we don't have clearance to be here."

"Proceed carefully," 117 said. "Alright everyone, standby to deploy."

Even though his voice was full of uncertainty, all the marines and the rest of the Second Group obeyed his instructions. Even if they were just double-checking their gear, it was good to be on the safe side so that they wouldn't be leaving anything behind in the shuttle.

Suddenly, there was an incoming transmission.

"This is Wolf Squadron," Chan's voice spoke over their headsets. "Coming in and beginning assault on headquarters. Commander 917. I gotta tell you, never thought I'd say that one..."

917 and several of the marines smirked at Chan's remark.

A series of explosions and rapid fire intensified outside. The cameraman activated a live feed on the interior monitor, allowing them to witness the unfolding events in real time. As they circled the air, they could see several fighters launching attacks in various locations.

"Now that's an air strike," 297 said, staring in awe.

"Give 'em hell, Wolf Squad," Captain Mercy happily cheered.

The squadron unleashed massive volleys of missiles on the ground targets. It was amazing how many they could carry. The fightercraft that flew for the S.C.E. had large rectangular modules underneath their wings and positioned at key hardpoints of their fuselage. These missile pods had a surprisingly large quantity of ordnance and ammo, but the amborgs definitely weren't complaining. Their fighter escorts were striking at artillery guns, fuel tanks, and anti-air emplacements. Basically, they aimed for any target that seemed appealing to blow up. Meanwhile, other pilots in Wolf Squadron started conducting strafing runs on the ground. Utilizing their guns, they peppered the ground with rapid laser fire, and the amborgs watched thousands of lights striking it from these high-speed attacks.

It didn't look like their fighters were shooting at any buildings, but all of that laser fire raining down was concerning.

"They aren't hitting people on the ground... are they?" 777 asked.

"I hope not," Serina added. "Let's hope that these pilots are extremely accurate and just giving people a scare."

"Attention," the pilot announced. "We're making our final approach. Standby to disembark."

The lights in the shuttle turned dark red and a buzzer went off. This was the warning buzzer indicating that it was time.

"Commander, we're about to set ourselves down right in the main courtyard of headquarters. We're keeping an eye out for movement on the ground. 15 seconds. Once you clear off, we'll hover at a safe distance and keep watch."

"Ok everyone," 117 stood up, and the rest of them followed suit. "Once we're on the ground, our official mission, in case anyone asks, is that we're evacuating the senior staff and moving them to safety."

"Who knows if they'll buy that story," 917 replied. "A bunch of amborgs that are supposed to be dead are suddenly back from the grave and trying to protect people."

"When we're actually trying to figure out who is in charge of Silent Eclipse," 777 said.

"Our story doesn't have to make sense," 117 clarified. "We just need to cause enough confusion. The Third and Fourth Group will take care of the defense platform control rooms…"

"Which are in a creepy basement," 92 stated.

"Glad that's not our job," 93 sighed in relief.

117 ignored the twins as he finished what he was going to say.

"We're going to enter the main entrance with the First Group and climb up each floor."

"Basically, anyone that tries to kill us," 917 added. "Consider them the bad guys."

"They might not all be bad," Serina reminded everyone. "They could be panicking and just acting out of self-defense."

"And… we will deal with them as best as we can," 117 said. He was starting to get a little annoyed at the constant interruptions. "Above all else, if you're in danger, protect yourself at all costs."

Out of nowhere, they heard rattling coming from within the shuttle. The pilot suddenly reported in to 117.

"Whoa! Sir, I got a problem!"

They all staggered around as the shuttle began to lurch. A series of loud pattering sounds struck the side of their shuttle. Then, a piercing alarm went off as they listened to another announcement from the cockpit.

"We got some small arms fire coming from the ground! Looks like building security and the garrison are not happy about us being here! The LZ is not clear! I'm redirecting us to the roof! We are not touching down! You need to get ready to jump! I'd get off before they bring out any missile launchers!"

The lights switched to green as the back of the shuttle opened up. Small laser bolts zipped past from small arms fire. 117 led the amborgs and the marines towards the ramp. Looking down, 117 saw small flickers of flames on the grass and pavement, while the shuttle maneuvered toward the building's rooftop edge.

"We're going to the roof!" 117 shouted as he stepped off and took a leap. "Let's go!"

Amidst all of the gunfire and the roar of the shuttle's engines, 117 heard several more aircraft in the area, along with screams and shouts coming from every direction.

The fall to the roof was less than eight feet, a manageable distance for an amborg, but a bit daunting for an ordinary human. The amborgs landed effortlessly, bending their knees in a crouch before swiftly rising into a defensive stance. Their marine escorts reached the roof safely, though many of them stumbled and landed awkwardly. 117 realized that, from a tactical standpoint, they were trying to avoid standing upright to make themselves less visible to anyone who might be watching their position. He quickly signaled to his team, and they all crouched low as the battle raged on in the background.

117 looked over the building schematics as Transient 2 rose and took off. Gunfire continued to rain down on the shuttle, but thankfully, none of it was inflicting enough damage to be a major issue. With their drop point unexpectedly changed to the roof, they had to alter their plan slightly. 117 was glad to see that none of the other shuttles had followed their exact approach. It reassured him that the other teams were having better luck with their landing zones.

When he spotted the roof access, 117 pointed toward it and everyone readied themselves.

"Let's get inside!"

They all huddled down but moved as fast as they could toward the door while more explosions erupted around them. Breya pushed ahead of 117, and when she reached the door, she drew her gun and aimed it at the entrance. Another marine stepped forward to cover the door as Breya reached out and opened it.

As the door swung open, the marine aimed his weapon into the stairwell and moved forward with caution. This was a crucial part of their rigorous training. Every combat drill they had undergone prepared them to identify threats and secure the area safely.

Another marine followed, leading the way. Breya trailed behind them as the third person. Captain Mercy took Breya's previous position and motioned for another marine to enter. He then turned to 117, signaling that it was his turn to follow the fourth marine into the building.

117 readied his energy pulse rifle and held it at his hip. The marine standing next to him cleared his throat. 117 immediately noticed he was looking down the sights. He was side-eyeing 117, and then it dawned on him what he was doing wrong. 117 lifted his rifle and imitated the marine as they both aimed their weapons at the door.

This was important because firing a weapon from the hip allowed for a quick attack on the target, but it was highly inaccurate. Aiming through the scope brings the gun to eye level, a technique that guarantees consistent accuracy as it aligns the target with the sights.

The amborgs, of course, had advanced reflexes and abilities that didn't require them to follow normal tactical methods that police or military officials would. Thanks to their cybernetic implants, they had internal cameras and computer-assisted programming that could help them hit their targets almost all of the time. All amborgs walked around with aim-assist or auto-targeting, which was a huge advantage.

However, the marine 117 was mimicking seemed quite adamant that he follow his method. 117 felt that it was probably best not to showboat and handle their weapons properly. After all, this wasn't a game. This was a battle that was quite literally out of this world.

Then he heard Serina's voice in the back of his head.

"14 minutes," she reminded him.

Serina had disappeared from view when they leapt out of the shuttle so she wouldn't be a distraction, but didn't say where she'd be.

As 117 and the marine he was partnered with reached the top of the stairs, another thought ran through his mind as he descended. 999 and 917 were right behind him, according to their beacons on his map icon.

Wait a minute, he thought, keeping a watchful eye on the landing. *Serina came with us on our shuttle but isn't hitching a ride in my A.I. port? Maybe she's hiding with someone else.*

One of the other amborgs probably had the special privilege of having Serina riding shotgun with them.

"Good news everyone," Serina reported on their private channel. "The rest of the Transient shuttles made it through. The First, Third and Fourth Group made it to the ground and they've entered the building from the first floor."

"Ok," 117 said as they reached the entrance to the sixth floor. "Lock into the security system Serina. We need to start clearing out these offices and setting up a watch on prime targets."

The amborgs all stood at the head of the formation, seven of them with Breya and Mercy as the two captains of the 14 marines in their team. Second platoon looked severely understrength, but determined to see this mission through.

"Alright," 117 informed them. "I am really sorry that we didn't go in with the other teams. We got separated from your fellow platoons and marines in the process."

"It's alright commander," the marine closest to him replied quickly. "We've faced worse."

"Alright, time is running out," 117 said to the rest of them. "Once the blackout program shuts off, Silent Eclipse will be able to activate their drones. Hopefully it won't be long before the E.M.P. hits the city. Our mission is to locate and protect as many officers as we can. If we manage to capture any human leaders of Silent Eclipse, we will detain them and hold them somewhere safe."

"Unless the other amborgs and their platoons climb up and we link up with them," Mercy whispered urgently, "we don't have the manpower to detain or hold prisoners."

Captain Mercy was right. Their shuttle was the only one that got to the roof, and they were essentially cut off from backup. Reinforcements were downstairs, but it would probably take them time.

"I think it'll be fine," 117 replied.

He quickly reviewed each floor of the headquarters. There were six floors, and he and his team were at the top. From what he'd read in the files and learned from Admiral Ra'aiah, the first three floors were quite simple: the first and second floors contained a lot of non-essential personnel and offices, which were occupied by junior officers. Low ranks.

The third floor would probably impede their reinforcements, assuming the First Group was beginning their ascent to reach them. This floor contained the highest number of security guards. Apparently, to get to anything above the third floor, it required passing through a few security checkpoints, since the fourth floor and above were where all of the high-ranking officers worked from.

"I suggest we split up," 999 stated. "It will get the job done faster."

"Is that a smart idea?" 297 asked.

"We're low on time," 117 spoke up. "The sixth floor here has a few offices but it's mostly conference rooms."

117 then decided to divide his team into smaller teams.

Captain Mercy, Breya, and their marine escorts were all familiar with the officers and members of the admiralty stationed at head-quarters. They had dedicated time during their stay on the Heart of Alton to study and learn to recognize their leaders. In theory, every recruit serving in the S.C.E. was required to memorize the entire upper tiers of the chain of command. The amborgs were grateful to have their escorts alongside them, as it would make the ID check process much easier.

"92, 93," 117 said. "Take... four marines and sweep the sixth floor."

Without delay, the twins acknowledged his order, gathered four volunteers, and made their way to the sixth floor. One marine stood guard at the door while another cautiously opened it, swinging it inward. 92, 93, and their team hurried inside. The last person to enter turned back and shut the door. Once it was secured, 117 recommended that they head to the fifth floor. They quickly descended the stairs until they arrived at the entrance.

"Alright," 117 stated. "I'll take Breya with me. What about the rest of you?"

"Let's see," 297 glanced at the remaining members of their team. "Not counting our friendly captains, we have 10 marines of Second Platoon with us. How about five with us and five go with whoever is going to the next floor?"

117 glanced at 999.

"Do you want to take the fifth floor? Or the fourth?"

"I'll take 917 with me," she replied. "If Breya stays with you, then Captain Mercy should come with us."

"Yes commander," Mercy nodded.

"Copy that," Breya nodded in agreement.

The two captains quickly began to divide the marines into equal numbers. Now it was the amborgs' turn to finish deciding.

"That just leaves 297 and 777," 117 glanced at the two remaining amborgs. "917 and 999 are pairing up. What about you?"

"Well, you're the only one searching one entire floor," 297 shrugged. "Maybe 777 and I will accompany you."

"Sounds good," 777 replied. "Now which team is going to which floor?"

The marines continued to watch over the stairwell from all directions as the amborgs made their decision. 917 made a quick, calm remark.

"Rock-paper-scissors?" he suggested.

"Ok," 117 nodded. "Uh, if I win, 297, 777 and I will lead the search here on the fifth floor. If 917 wins, he and Angel take this floor."

"Loser goes to the fourth floor," 917 nodded. "Got it."

917 and 117 quickly stored their rifles and raised their hands. In about two seconds, they nodded to each other as they finished their game. When they lowered their hands, 117 was triumphantly holding a closed fist for "rock" to crush to 917's two fingered "scissors."

"Did you even play the game?" Captain Mercy asked curiously.

"Yes," 117 replied. "We just do it extremely fast."

"You guys barely played one round..." one marine commented.

Breya shot him an angry glare, shutting him up instantly.

"Actually we played 20 rounds," 917 explained. "We texted our results to each other. 117 won the tiebreaker."

"20 rounds?" Mercy looked both impressed and completely baffled. "You played actual mind games?"

"So to speak," 117 replied as he and 917 drew their weapons. "It takes a few minutes but you should see the full game experience."

"What's the full experience?" Breya asked.

"Rock-paper-scissors 'intense' difficulty," 917 stated. "We play over a hundred rounds."

"One... hundred?" one marine stared at the amborgs with wide eyes.

"That's nothing," 297 joked. "The 'extreme' difficulty is where the fun really begins."

"How many... rounds do you play on extreme difficulty?" Breya asked reluctantly.

"Thousands," 777 stated.

777's response left everyone slightly unsettled. A heartbeat later, they all refocused when a muffled blast echoed from outside.

"Proceeding to the fourth floor," 999 stated as she signaled to the marines. "Captain Mercy, on me."

"Yes commander," Mercy looked at five marines. "Hamill, Ford, Fisher, Daniels and Baker! We're following 999 and 917!"

917 and 999 followed their team down another flight of stairs as Breya and the remaining marines in their group prepared to enter the fifth floor.

"Marines," Breya called out to them. "Check in!"

The five that were remaining did a quick roll call. 117, 297, and 777 nodded and greeted Lawson, Hootkins, Fraser, Purvis, and Mayhew.

Once they were all acquainted, Lawson and Mayhew took point. Lawson approached the door while Breya covered him, and they positioned themselves next to the entrance. Mayhew lowered his firearm and mimicked the actions of 92 and 93's marines. He quickly but carefully opened the door and pushed it inward. Then, he moved aside to allow Lawson and Breya to enter. This gave Mayhew an opportunity to safely draw his weapon again.

117 walked in first with Hootkins at his side. 297 then followed with Fraser. 777 and Purvis brought up the rear. When the whole team had exited the stairwell, Purvis whirled around and closed the door behind them.

"Everyone ready?" 117 said softly as they scanned their surroundings.

"Yes sir," Hootkins replied. "Never thought I'd ever be doing something like this... fighting our own people."

"If it makes you feel better," 297 said, "we'll just stick to wounding them severely if they try to fight us. It might be the best way to avoid prolonged conflict."

"I was really hoping we wouldn't have to go that far," 777 added.

"Well, the odds of every officer we encounter surrendering peacefully is really low," 117 murmured.

The hall lights were still on but because of their attack, headquarters had activated its emergency protocols, which was to be expected. The emergency lighting was switched on, and it changed from bright yellow to a dark shade of red. The alarms were ringing in the corridors as they made their way to the first office they saw. Breya pounded on the door.

The marines covered the halls as the amborgs monitored Breya's tactics.

"Divine wind!" a voice from inside shouted as 117 read the name-plate on the door.

Admiral Tanner was displayed in bold black letters. 117 quickly checked the database and found that Tanner was a Third Admiral—the same rank as Admiral Ra'aiah, which meant he was probably the same age as her.

Breya brought up a screen on her wrist pad. A counter phrase appeared and she read it out loud. Based on their codes, it was a pass phrase.

"Batten down!"

There was movement on the other side as someone opened the door slowly. Standing there were a man and a woman in uniform, each holding side arms raised toward the ceiling. 117 discreetly held Argentum as Lawson stepped inside to secure the room, with Breya covering him.

Silent Eclipse bug detected, Argentum said informatively. *It has been deactivated thanks to the E.M.P. Admiral Tanner and his assistant are secure. Friendly.*

Lawson gave Breya the all-clear signal as they all lowered their weapons. Breya stepped forward and boldly spoke to Tanner.

"Admiral," she cleared her throat. "We have some questions for you."

"Uh, Breya," 117 said as he quietly slipped Argentum back into his pocket. "Not necessary. Admiral Tanner and his assistant are clear."

Breya turned and blinked, then nodded.

"Yes sir," she replied. "Amborg processing is certainly impressive."

297 sent 117 a confused text message.

Really? You already cleared him? I'm still finishing the background check.

Trust me, 297, 117 replied. *I'm listening to Argentum.*

297 and 777 got the message and dropped the matter. Still, 297 sent one quick text before he left the office to stand guard.

We're vetting people with a sentient pet cube. That's a new one.

"Thank you," Admiral Tanner stepped forward while his assistant bowed her head respectfully. "I was doing some paperwork when communications were cut off and I heard explosions! Wilkins and I were stuck in here when emergency protocols activated. Is everything alright captain?"

Tanner glanced at 117 and his eyes widened.

"And commander!" he exclaimed. "Uh, you're not with the security staff here on this base, are you?"

"New additions!" Breya replied quickly. "We suggest that you and your aide remain in your office. Don't communicate with anyone, shield the windows and barricade the door. We will have the culprit of this attack apprehended soon."

Oh," Admiral Tanner glanced at his aide, who was nodding frantically at Breya's instructions. "Well, as you can see, we aren't exactly outfitted for a fight. Thank you for checking on us. We'll remain here until it's safe to evacuate."

"Under no circumstances are you to open your door for anyone," 117 instructed.

"I understand..." Tanner nodded as he squinted at 117's uniform. "Commander... 117? Thank you! Uh, weren't you... reported dead a while ago?"

"Not the 117 you know," 117 explained briefly.

It took the admiral a moment to process, but then he nodded slowly and smiled.

"Oh, I see," he said softly. "Welcome back, commander."

"Thank you," 117, 297 and 777 all spoke simultaneously.

When they had all spoken at once, Admiral Tanner looked at each of them in surprise. 117 let out a sigh as he rolled his eyes. Every amborg present was a commander, so the admiral had accidentally addressed the three of them.

"It's a long story," 117 said as he turned on his heel and exited the office.

The door's locks activated the moment the door shut. The admiral would be safe inside, hopefully.

"Serina?" 117 asked. "When is the next E.M.P. attack? We could use it soon."

"Not sure," Serina replied in his head. "I'll try to contact Carter."

"Hey 117," 297 interrupted. "Ready to continue the sweep?"

117 nodded as they group assumed their formation and moved to the next office. This one turned out to be empty. When they ran the name, they found this admiral to also be a friendly.

The next office was empty as well, but after briefly checking their files and with Argentum verifying the validity of everything, this next admiral was clear too.

As they checked one office after another, 117 would often look behind him just to make sure no one was following or setting them up for an ambush. Maybe, he was hoping to hear from the twins or 999 since they were in the middle of doing their own sweep of each floor.

As they pressed on, he could hear several shots that sounded like they were coming from outside, but he could have sworn there was some fighting happening above or below them. When they got to the seventh office, Argentum began to shake violently. 117 glanced down and opened the bag, but didn't pull Argentum out. Instead, he read the warning it was displaying.

Danger! Apprehend this admiral! Most of her records have covered up the truth! She is involved with Silent Eclipse!

117 looked at the name on the door. It was the office of a Third Admiral Casey.

"Hold on, I might have a hit," 117 warned as he sealed the bag.

"Are you sure?" Breya asked. "Admiral Casey doesn't really fit the profile."

"I don't think she's a leader," 117 replied. "But she's definitely involved."

"How do we want to approach this?" 297 transmitted to 117 privately.

"Shock and awe," 117 shrugged. "We're out of time."

"Alright, marines, cover me!" 297 nodded. "I got this one!"

777 joined the marines and they took up a defensive position as 117, 297 and Breya focused on the door. 297 got in front while Breya covered him. He lifted his leg and kicked the door in. Instead of it spinning inwards, his strong kick caused it to fly off its hinges. There was a scream as 297 and Breya stormed inside. Two shots were fired, which caused 117 to rush in, but it didn't look like anyone was hurt when he saw the interior of the room.

"I disarmed her!" 297 reported.

297, with his superb accuracy, was the one who had opened fire and successfully shot a sidearm out of Admiral Casey's hands. It was lying on the ground in the corner when 117 walked in and observed the entire room. Breya and 297 had their weapons trained on the woman cowering behind her desk.

"Admiral Casey?" 117 asked. "Third Admiral Casey?"

"Yes?" she said with a terrified look. Slowly, she straightened up to address them. "That's me."

"Silent Eclipse," Breya hissed menacingly. She took aim at the Admiral's head. "You're under arrest for being a co-conspirator!"

To the amborgs, this was a definite bluff. Sure, Argentum had warned 117 and he had managed to convince the team that Casey was somehow involved. However, he did feel a little bad that the others didn't get a chance to properly finish checking all of the records that they had available. Fortunately, the response they got from the frightened admiral was not what they were expecting.

"Oh no! Please don't kill me! I never told anyone! I swear! I couldn't get out!"

All of them shared a quick glance, but didn't lower their guard.

"What?" 297 said in surprise. "She's admitting it?"

Admiral Casey held her hands up and slowly stood. It seemed like she was surrendering, but they still kept a close eye on her movements.

"I was forced to do it!"

"To do what exactly?" 117 demanded. "By whom?"

"Admiral Caldwell said that if I didn't support her election to First Admiral, then I would be killed!" Casey explained as Breya moved towards her and began to pat her down. "She had me do a lot of treasonous things, and when I thought I was about to get caught, she covered it up and made sure that no one would figure out what I was doing for her!"

"Hang on a minute," 297 stated. "Who is Admiral Caldwell?"

"Admiral Belina Caldwell," Breya stated. "The First Admiral?"

"Yes!" Admiral Casey nodded frantically. "You have no idea what it's like working with someone who looks so proper on the outside but so different behind closed doors!"

"Uh," 117 stammered. "B-Breya. Who is Caldwell?"

Breya turned to 117 with a concerned look in her eyes.

"Commander," she said softly. "Just after I healed from my injuries and prepared to join you, I also read several mission files. And... Admiral Caldwell being involved with Silent Eclipse... is very plausible."

"Why?" 117 asked.

Breya gazed 117 and 297 gravely.

"She's the one who successfully lobbied S.C.E. starships to your universe."

117 and 297 both exchanged serious glances as Breya confirmed what she had just said.

"She sent us to the Epsilon universe," she explained. "All of us."

CHAPTER 22

Confronting Architects

S.C.E. Headquarters
Fifth Floor

"I got a hit!"

Serina's voice in the back of the amborgs' minds spoke out loud and clear.

"Just after the blackout program shorted out everything, I caught an outgoing signal that was trying to go to Earth and the surrounding area. It matches the frequency that controls the Silent Eclipse drones!" Serina said. "I traced it back to the fourth floor, an office belonging to… hey, one Admiral Caldwell. Thank you Admiral Casey for name-dropping that one."

A sudden loud rumble snagged everyone's attention. The amborgs all looked up in time to see a swirl of bright crimson energy light up everything in the room. Within seconds, it had disappeared and sounded like it was traveling away from them.

The Firestar and Heart of Alcyon had detonated another E.M.P. on the moon. This should have effectively disabled or taken out any Silent Eclipse drones on the surface.

"This might make it easier for us now," 117 remarked. Then he called out to Serina. "Keep going Serina. What else can you tell us?"

Serina's response was instant.

"Admiral Belina Caldwell, First Admiral of the S.C.E.," she recited from the database. "Complete and total powerhouse of an officer. She's served in the fleet for half of her career, holds a lot of influence among her peers, and has a reputation for being… well…"

117, 297 and 777 paused and waited for her to finish her description. 117 glanced to the side and noticed that Breya, Lawson and Purvis guarded Admiral Casey. Hootkins, Fraser and Mayhew had positioned themselves outside the office and to watch the halls for any movement.

"You guys remember Miranda from that one movie? Meryl Streep?" Serina asked.

"Oh yeah," 777 nodded. "The Devil Wears Prada? Classic."

"She's a cold and calculating hard-working perfectionist," Serina replied casually. "I think there's more to her story than the records actually show but... she's definitely someone who has the intellect to run Silent Eclipse."

117 glanced at Breya. He knew that their marines had access to their communications, so he looked at his captain.

"What do you know about Caldwell?" he asked.

"She seems like the type," Breya replied immediately. "Comes from a strong military background and voiced her opinions protesting peace talks with several races on a few occasions. In fact, she's a prominent advocate for the military. There have been many reforms or military disarmament bills that she has opposed. Several of her subordinates in the admiralty turned to her for advice when the Tandeeri war began. It's like when you have a conflict, she's the one who provides you with a convenient and aggressive tactical solution."

"What made her into someone as... aggressive as you claim?" 117 asked.

"All I know is she commanded at least two starships and even led the Fourth fleet," Breya shrugged.

"I can confirm that actually," Serina replied. "She's been the commanding officer of three starships. The last one she was in charge of before she stepped down to take a seat at headquarters several years ago was a small defense fleet."

"Any combat experience under her belt? How is she as a leader or fleet commander?" 297 asked.

Admiral Caldwell's battle records would definitely highlight how she would respond under pressure. It would demonstrate what kind of person she was. If she was the leader of Silent Eclipse or running it covertly, she was probably going to have countermeasures they would have to bypass.

"Formidable," Serina replied. "It's interesting. Most simulated war games or battles that she's participated in were defeats. That's understandable since new officers in charge of their first starships are often tested repeatedly so that they can respond to all kinds of physical and emotional problems that come with space travel. Gradually, she got better and started turning heads with her evolved tactics and new strategies."

117 began to envision what Caldwell was like. She was someone who faced challenges in her career, but once she overcame them and got promoted, life became easier for her, allowing her to achieve her goals.

"Hey," 297 suddenly looked alarmed. "917 and 999 are sweeping the Fourth floor. Didn't we confirm that her office is on that same floor?"

"Let's try and reestablish contact with them," 117 ordered. "They need to be careful."

As 297 nodded and tried to give 999 a call, 117 turned to look at Admiral Casey.

"Tell me about Silent Eclipse," 117 demanded. "What exactly have you done?"

The amborgs wanted to see if Casey was deliberately acting the way she was to throw them off. Listening to her stutter and bumble her way through her own words seemed to only confirm that her emotions were genuine.

"I thought it was a pet project that Caldwell kept to herself! I don't know anything, I swear! All I can give you are records of how she managed her budget and expenses!"

"You're an admiral that's... also a glorified accountant?" 117 asked suspiciously. "Great, we can expose Silent Eclipse for what... tax fraud? Misappropriation of funding?"

"That'd be hilarious. Actually, she looks like a total pushover," 777 remarked with an unimpressed and bored expression.

Admiral Casey looked down in shame and nodded, as if she was agreeing with 777's snide comments. Breya backed off slightly. Lawson and Purvis watched them all and curiously awaited their orders.

"She sounds like she's telling the truth," Breya announced. "No other weapons on her. Casey is loyal but Caldwell most likely pressured her to support her promotion to First Admiral. After that, she became a pawn. To get to that rank, one must have the vote and support of at least one other admiral from headquarters."

Breya shifted her gaze down at Casey who was nodding eagerly, agreeing with her statement.

"I can see why she picked Casey..." Breya gave 117 a pointed look.

777 raised his rifle and took aim at Casey. She cowered in fear. 777 lowered his weapon and tilted his head to 117.

"Total pushover," Breya repeated 777's earlier comment.

"So Caldwell was promoted to the rank of First Admiral?" 117 asked. "For more power?"

"She'd have perfect access to a larger influence in the chain of command," Breya explained. "The higher your rank, the more privileges you are granted. Silent Eclipse would pretty much have their hands in all the right places."

"Indeed I would."

A voice rang out over the P.A. system, causing everyone to glance up. 117 looked around. According to Casey's expression, Breya's look of affirmation, and the tone, he could assume who it was.

"Greetings," the same woman's voice spoke again. "So... Dr. Kendrick's amborgs are the ones responsible for... this poor excuse for an invasion? How very rude... and brave of you."

"Can we talk back to her?" 117 looked at Breya. "Is she listening to us?"

"By all means," Admiral Caldwell replied immediately. "You may have deactivated my listening devices with your new weapon but I can still hear you."

"I am very interested in learning how you can do that," 117 replied.

"Commander 117," Caldwell spoke coldly. "I do hope that you're not going to assume I'm that gullible. That level of incompetence only makes me want to kill you even more."

"Admiral Caldwell," 117 stated in a formal and polite tone. "I don't think that'll be necessary. We're here to offer you a chance to surrender and to answer for your crimes. Now they have extended into our universe as well."

"What exactly am I guilty of?"

"For starters," 777 spoke up. "How about all of the lives that your robot minions took when we discovered the truth behind the Tandeeri war?"

"I am not quite sure as to what you're talking about," Caldwell replied promptly. "After all, everyone who dies in battle just proves that they weren't meant to affect any sort of change in their menial lives. I don't exactly have the luxury to worry about acceptable casualty rates. I'm tasked with safeguarding the future of the S.C.E."

117 glanced at 297 and noticed that he was giving 117 a hand signal. When he had gotten his attention, 297 silently texted him and 777.

I can't get in touch with 999! Or 917! Captain Mercy and his marines have gone silent too.

This message filled 117 with a bit of dread.

"Safeguarding?" 117 quickly responded out loud. "You have an army of drones and agents that eliminate people. Innocent lives!"

"Some sacrifices are the only way to move on," Caldwell replied. "You don't get things done by talking. You force others to act when you have control."

"You're so obnoxious," 777 commented.

"Laugh, joke and insult me as much as you want," Admiral Caldwell replied curtly. "The only thing you can't do at the moment is bargain."

"What do you mean?" 117 asked.

"Let's just say that if you want your amborg 917 to live," Admiral Caldwell said with a derisive laugh. "You'll do exactly as I say."

The amborgs all stared wide-eyed at each other. They had lost contact with 999 and 917. Was Admiral Caldwell saying what they thought she was saying?

The next voice drew their attention back to the speakers. 917 coughed, his response raspy and slow.

"This is 917," he said in a defeated tone. "Sorry everyone. I didn't see this coming."

117's blood ran cold when he heard his friend's pained voice.

Right away, he felt they should rush to his rescue, but what if it was another trap? They needed a plan of attack. He quickly texted 92 and 93.

Are you two finished on the sixth floor? Do you hear what's happening?

92 responded immediately.

Sweep completed. Detained a few admirals and officers up here. What's the plan?

117 thought quickly.

Get down to the fifth floor and help us guard Admiral Casey. We need backup and we need to get to the fourth floor asap.

On our way, 92 texted back.

117 also sent a message to the First, Third and Fourth Group leaders, but he wasn't sure if they'd be able to send help up here in time. They'd have to do this next part alone if necessary.

He held up his hands and signaled to Breya. She watched his hand movements carefully.

117 extended his right arm horizontally with his palm facing forward and waved his hand downward several times. Maintaining eye contact with Breya, he communicated nonverbally since Admiral Caldwell was only listening in.

Stay here, he instructed. Then he moved his arm forward and showed Breya his palm. *Are you ready?*

Breya nodded. Recognizing his signal, she raised one of her right arms and showed 117 her palm. She signaled that she was ready.

117 turned his right hand to the side and extended four fingers. Then he turned his hand up and showed two fingers. Then he rotated his hand to the side again, showing four fingers but when he turned his hand straight up, he showed Breya three fingers. Then pointed down.

92 and 93 are on the way here.

Breya nodded.

117 then pointed at 297 and 777 and relayed his next instructions.

Hold position here. 297 and 777 will follow me.

117 then texted 297 and 777.

Amborgs! We have to go rescue 917.

They would move faster without their marine escorts. 117 felt bad about leaving them to defend themselves but if they stayed put and protected Admiral Casey, then they would be able to keep one of their strongest assets alive. 92 and 93 would be down in a few minutes with their marines, and they could hold out for a while.

Sure enough, when 117 led the three-amborg team to the staircase, they heard movement coming from above. 92 and 93 were coming down the stairs with their marines. 117 quickly sent them a message and carefully instructed them to stay silent.

Go and assist Captain Breya, defend Admiral Casey, and hold position! Relocate her to a different part of the floor if you have to. Watch for enemy contact!

117, 297, and 777 raised their weapons to cover the stairwell as the twins led their marines into the fifth floor offices. They shut the door behind them and left the three Second Group amborgs in the stairwell.

As 117 led them to the fourth floor, Admiral Caldwell continued talking.

"I take it from your silence that I have your attention?" she sneered. "Well, then I think it's time to share what I want."

117 guessed that she was only able to hear them while also trying to get a fix on their location. Since the E.M.P. had knocked out the drones, she was likely sending agents after them, which meant that Serina's blackout program had mostly blocked Caldwell from spying on their movements. Breya and the twins would probably be able to keep Admiral Casey alive from any threats while they figured out how to locate and rescue 917. The problem was, since they couldn't reach 999, had she been killed or also captured?

"Now understand this," she said. "I want you to shut down that signal that's blocking all our communications. I commend you on shutting down my drones while this attack on our systems is happening, but I still have other personnel under my command that are more than a match for you. I want your amborgs in the control rooms to reactivate the defense platforms to attack your fleet. Then you'll have a shuttle escort me to Earth."

"Like hell we will," 297 replied. "It's out of character for us to comply with crazy demands."

"It's also uncharacteristic of you to let your friends die," Caldwell responded. "Perhaps I'll just kill 917, then, if you're so confident I won't do it. After all, there's always more than one amborg to get rid of."

"You know," 917 coughed, "they're going to get you. You just zapped me with some strange toy that seized up my joints. Not scary at all when I've experienced worse. Just a reminder of how much pain I can physically feel."

"I am well aware of your tolerance for pain," Caldwell replied. "This time, however, I won't make the mistake of making you endure it for long."

"Whether you torture me or kill me," 917 scoffed, "you're only going to make things worse for yourself. The amborgs, they're my real family, you know? I know exactly what they can do. Especially if it means taking you down, what you do to me will be the final nail on your coffin."

"And how many amborgs will it take to finally get the point across?"

117, 297 and 777 breached the doors to the fourth floor and began to search for Caldwell's office. Serina provided them with 999 and 917's last known position that they reported in from. They also kept an eye out for Captain Mercy and his marine squad.

"Lady," 917 chuckled calmly. "Since you're going to kill us anyway, there's no reason for us to cooperate. Just from this whole routine... your act is blown. I mean... seriously, it's so cliché."

"I'm counting to ten," Caldwell replied indifferently. "Then I go hunting for that other one. None of you can hide forever. This is my territory that you're in now."

"Good luck with that," 917 said mockingly. "My best friend is going to kick your ass. And if you kill her, everyone else will line up to avenge me."

"Serina," 117 said as they frantically picked up the pace. "Can you dim the lights or something? Give 917 some time?"

"I can't locate him!" Serina replied desperately. "I'm looking as fast as I can!"

"What about Angel?" 297 asked.

"Knowing her?" Serina replied in their heads. "She's probably waiting for her best shot to save him."

They hadn't heard 999 respond at all this whole time, but it was understandable. 917 was trying to drag out the conversation in order to buy them time. 999 was most likely lurking in the shadows and remaining silent in order to properly carry out her rescue plan. It was probably not going well since Caldwell had started a countdown.

"You know what I think?" 917 let out a laugh. "You're such a control freak! I read your files. You started out as a typical officer in order to fulfill a strict family legacy. The only problem was, you were a terrible officer!"

"What, you want me to pour my heart out for you?" Caldwell replied coldly. "You have six seconds by the way."

"You were too by-the-book, inflexible, and incapable when you were in command of your own fleet," 917 continued. "That's probably when you decided to change it up and restart Silent Eclipse. If you couldn't get to the top by conventional means, then you could just eliminate everyone in your way."

"Three seconds."

There was a faint hint of a snarl in Caldwell's tone. 917 seemed to be successfully getting to her and making her lose her self-control. However, this was only making them more distraught. The amborgs continued to try and locate their position, but they were out of time.

"That's who you are! No friends, no sympathy," 917 declared boldly, even though they could hear his pained wheezing. "Nothing but a ruthless nobody. You may be a big shot but eventually, that's all your life will amount to. An empty and pointless existence alone because you'll just kill anyone who doesn't agree with you. I know this because I read my files and I stopped you before!"

117, 297 and 777 paused. Everything that 917 had just said took longer than three seconds. Had he actually succeeded in buying more time? Unfortunately, this wasn't the case.

A loud bang echoed overhead as they all flinched and crouched down.

"Shit!" 297's voice trembled.

"No!" 777 gasped.

117's breathing became quick and ragged as he desperately tried to search for 917's beacon.

"Serina!" he said.

"Searching!" Serina replied frantically. "I can still detect his life signs but... they're dropping!"

"Now don't go spilling all my secrets," Caldwell spoke curtly. "I was right, killing someone I hate a second time feels really good. Get his body out of here. His friends deserve to see him. Now then, we've demonstrated my resolve. It was easy to catch him, and I will catch all of you. I've got time for this."

"Not if we order our fleet to blow us all to hell," 777 yelled.

"Really?" Caldwell chuckled. "I don't think so. How would that look? The Firestar blowing headquarters out of existence while the rest of the fleet surrounds and captures them?"

"Uh, guys?" Serina said. "There's something wrong."

"What is it?" 297 asked.

"She's activating some sort of system alert to several facilities across the moon."

"What facilities?" 117 asked.

"A ton of missile arrays and hidden launch facilities!" Serina informed them. "The moon has a lot of firepower and it's being aimed at several friendly targets!"

"Anything you can do?" 297 asked.

"I'm currently focusing on preventing her security measures from booting me and keeping her activation signals from reaching Earth!" Serina said in a strained voice. "I can't do everything! She's sent a whole platoon to retake weapons control from the Third and Fourth Group! We're outnumbered and she's preparing to fire on everyone!"

"Now you can't really succeed unless you plan for all the possible contingencies," Caldwell laughed evilly. "I admit, I wasn't expecting to see some of you again after I spent all that time killing you off to avoid blabbing to anyone. But now, you're on the clock as well. What's it going to be? I'll call off my attack if you let me escape."

"Not happening. Does this fit in your contingency?"

Everyone froze on the spot when they heard a chilling voice speak overhead. 999 had entered the fight and she didn't sound like herself at all.

"Uh oh," 297 gulped.

There was a loud rumbling sound as a wall collapsed and two bodies fell at their feet. 117 raised his weapon, but it was unnecessary. They instantly recognized 999's glowing stripes on her uniform as she swooped in front of them. The person she had pinned to the ground was attempting to fight back, but in a fit of uncontrolled rage, she brought her fists down hard, smashing the person's head in.

"Should we help?" 777 spoke meekly.

"Which one?" 297 asked as he watched 999 presumably destroy a Silent Eclipse operative. "Hey, are you guys seeing her readings?"

117 ran a quick scan of 999 who was still pulverizing her foe. Her energy levels had suddenly spiked and her emotion levels were way too chaotic to even measure. It was off the charts. 117, 297 and 777 all felt as if they had been suddenly blinded when a bright light flashed in their eyes as they tried reading 999's vitals. She was going berserk.

"Guys?" Serina chimed in with a worried voice. "I'm getting a 'dam protocol' alarm from 999's beacon."

999 finished what she was doing and charged down the hall. Eventually, she disappeared out of sight. Even Admiral Caldwell's voice had gone silent overhead.

"Because Caldwell did the stupid thing and killed her best friend," 777 said, his face filled with terror as he stared at 999's victim. "That's enough to trigger that! Plus she kept all her feelings bottled up all these years and didn't properly destress!"

To sum it up, a "dam protocol" was mental health breakdown. It was a condition that could be quite dangerous to an amborg.

When Dr. Kendrick created the First Group, one of the first drawbacks that his deceased wife, Melissa, had brought up numerous times was that inhibiting their basic emotions was in fact a terrible idea. Ultimately, when the amborgs began to show their more vulnerable sides and allowed simple emotions to resurface, this helped but only a little for their mental health.

After the First Group was joined by the Second, they began to discover moments of rampant emotional outbursts. As it turns out, suppressing negative feelings for too long led to dangerous situations. Some of the older amborgs had difficulties but eventually, every amborg focused on developing basic routines to regulate stress.

In 999's case, unfortunately, she had allowed the dam to burst and all of her rage and fury was pouring out uncontrollably.

After seeing her run off, it was safe to assume that Admiral Caldwell was probably not in her office. 117 quickly led 297 and 777 with him inside and checked anyway.

Caldwell's office looked just like the rest of the ones they had been in. 777 ran over to what appeared to be a cabinet filled with trophies and achievements. 297 looked at the photos, certificates, and other memorabilia that were hanging on the wall. 117 went straight for her desk and looked at the monitor. What he found was disturbing.

"999 found Caldwell's office," he reported. "Then Caldwell made her watch her execute 917."

117 turned the monitor on its swivel around for the other two amborgs to see. They both glanced at it, horrified.

It was a live camera feed overhead of some isolated room. Lying on the floor was 917's motionless body. It was easy to see that he had been forced onto his knees and then shot in the back of the head at point-blank range. It didn't take long for them to realize that when

999 lost control of herself, one of Silent Eclipse's agents found her and tried to take her on. Whether or not they were trying to capture her alive, 999 had overpowered them and smashed the life out of them.

"Great," 297 sighed as he cautiously eyed the door. "We have a crazy admiral that's about to destroy everything so she can escape in the middle of all of the chaos and now we have to try to calm one of the deadliest amborgs in our universe's history."

"This is way worse than when she and 43 had a deadlock on Apogee Station," 777 remarked.

117 silently agreed. True, 43 and 999 had almost fought each other to the point where they were close to tearing each other to pieces, but they managed to maintain control the entire time. If 43 was to go against 999 now, who knows what would happen?

"Serina? Can you pass a message to 501 and 466?" 117 asked.

"Already done," Serina replied with a strained voice. "I told them to reactivate some defense platforms and prepare to go Missile Command on Silent Eclipse's attacks."

"Can you help us locate where 917's body is in this camera feed?" 117 added as he glanced at the monitor. "We have to try and get Caldwell before 999 kills her."

"Screw it," Serina grumbled.

A sudden loud pop followed by a screeching sound pierced their ears, causing them to wince in pain for a brief moment. Then with a bright light, Serina appeared over 117's shoulder.

"Success!" she snarled. "The security system tried to lock me out so I sabotaged it and overloaded the main central antenna! No outbound communications signals to Earth! Caldwell's going to have to make it aboard a starship under her control if she wants to activate her killer robots on Earth."

"Ok," 297 said as he pointed at a photo on the wall. "Admiral Caldwell! We're looking for a woman, mid-40s, short brown hair, about 5'9."

"I wonder what happened to Captain Mercy and his team?" 777 murmured as he investigated the office.

117 let Serina continue her analysis of the camera feed. As 777 looked around, he tapped 297's shoulder. When he got his attention, 117 and 297 both stepped out of the office and carefully scanned their surroundings.

"Do you think Admiral Caldwell was in her office during the attack?" 297 asked.

"Possibly," 117 nodded. "Maybe she evacuated with the rest of the building when they heard of an attack. But I don't believe so."

"117!"

117 and 297 turned and raised their weapons. To their surprise, they saw 6 approaching with a couple of her marines. Behind them, 5 was running up and watching the rear.

"Did you get his body?" 6 asked.

"Uh, no?" 297 replied.

"We were trying to figure out where Caldwell shot him," 117 explained. "I also wanted to look for the marines that were escorting 999 and 917."

"I know you mean well!" 6 answered quickly as she closed the distance and huddled close to them as her marines monitored the area. "But listen! We need to find 917! I can save him!"

"What?!" 117 exchanged a stunned glance with 297 before turning back to 6. "He's lying there after being shot in the back of his head!"

"Yes, he is!" 6 nodded urgently. "But he's not dead! You need to help me get to him before his lifesigns are permanently gone! I can explain later after we help him!"

"In the meantime," 5 spoke insistently, "we also need to find 999 and calm her down!"

Just when he thought that the mission was progressing in their favor, 117's stomach lurched. At first, they were infiltrating headquarters. Now, they were trapped inside a secure building with a couple of monsters on the loose. One was out to kill them and then escape while the other was one of their closest friends who was beyond reasoning.

"No pressure," 117 let out a soft and terrified grunt.

"It's just a dam protocol. It'll pass soon, right?" 297 spoke up, but his confidence faltered when 6 turned to him with a worried look. "Right? 6?"

"Not with Angel," she replied, shaking her head firmly. "We had a talk before the Tandeeri hit Apogee Station. Weeks ago!"

117 stared.

"She opened up about many issues that were weighing heavily on her," 6 explained. Countless repressed emotions have been triggered! To make matters worse, she nearly got herself killed on the Firestar!

I thought that... all the time she spent with the Tandeeri would theoretically give her all the space and rest she needed to get her mental health sorted out! But she's going to deteriorate and die!"

"Do you even have any sedatives or medication powerful enough to knock her out?" 117 asked worriedly.

"With how much adrenaline she's got firing all of her neurons at the moment?" 6 shook her head as she pulled up her bag, but let it drop and swing to her side. "Even the most basic painkillers would be rejected, and not even a dent would be made to her cognitive abilities."

"Well, you're the doctor, right?" 297 stated. "Can you try talking to her? You were her mentor for a couple of years!"

"No one can get through to her, unless it's him!" 6 spoke insistently. "You have to get me to 917 so I can save him!"

"Right," 117 nodded skeptically but at this point, they didn't have a choice. He turned to Caldwell's office. "777, let's get ready to move out!"

"Sure thing," 777 answered from inside. "We probably can, oops! Oh shit!"

Everyone outside heard 777's startled outburst, causing them to rush inside. Once inside, they saw 777 standing near the desk, staring down at the scattered papers and data pads he'd knocked to the floor. Serina was there too, looking at what he'd bumped into.

On the desk, there was a small silver figurine of an S.C.E. starship. In his haste to walk out of the office to meet them, 777 had accidentally swung the edge of his rifle barrel around and bumped it. He had thought that he had knocked it off but it surprisingly remained on the desk. Serina and 777 both leaned in to take a closer look.

"777," Serina pointed. "This figurine is a model of the first starship that Caldwell commanded. It must have been built into the table..."

117, 297, 6 and 5 all stepped inside to look. 5 ordered the marines behind him to watch for any enemy threats. 777 put his rifle away by swinging it behind his back, then leaned in close.

"I bumped it hard but... it didn't get knocked off," he said. "Wait, it did move but... it slid."

They all stared at where the figurine was positioned. 777 then glanced at another figurine on the opposite side.

"There's another starship figurine on that side," 777 pointed out. "The second ship that she commanded before she became a fleet commander."

117 stood directly in front of the desk and inspected the two figurines. When he got a closer look, he realized something was strange about their placements.

"The figurine in front of 777 is facing the wrong way," 117 said. "777, turn it so the bow faces the ship on the other side."

777 quickly followed 117's instructions. He gently grabbed the small figurine and twisted it slowly. They heard a click when it faced the other one on the other side.

"Hey," 297 eyed the desk closely. "The other figurine is... farther away. It's close to the edge. Too close."

297 stepped forward and reached for the second starship. It was facing the first one but when he actually grabbed it, they could see what he was talking about. 297 pulled on it, and it slid towards the center of the desk. When it reached a point where the two figurines were equally spaced apart from each other, there was another loud click. Then they heard a hiss and turned to look at the wall next to Caldwell's trophy stand.

"Look," 777 said. "It's a digital keypad. Anyone got a password?"

117 quickly unclipped the cover of Argentum's bag and pulled it out.

"I think I've got something better," he said as he held the silver cube out towards the keypad. "Argentum, can you unlock this?"

As you wish.

Argentum glowed brightly and suddenly got sucked into the keypad. It lit up as Argentum figured out the passcode and then, when it was done, shot out into 117's hand again.

"Nice... cube," 6 remarked.

The door is unlocked.

Before 117 could ask what door, there was another hissing sound as a hidden compartment pulled back and they saw a small space open up in the corner.

"It's an elevator!" Serina exclaimed.

"That's it!" 6 said as she eagerly stepped inside.

Everyone cautiously protested at once.

"You can't go wherever this secret elevator goes!" 777 stated. "It's a terrible idea!"

"That's why I'm not going alone!" 6 shot back as she glanced at 5. "Bring in a few marines! 777, you come too! Watch my back!"

"Uh, w-what?" 777 stammered as 5 called for his squad of marines.

"You heard me!" 6 insisted.

When the marines heard the order to come inside the office, 6 called out to them.

"Sohee, Doss, Gail!" 6 commanded. "You're with me! The rest of you, stay here with 5!"

As the three marines that she named quickly obeyed her orders and scurried into the elevator, 6 grabbed 777 and pulled him in.

"I need another amborg to help me!" she said annoyingly.

Before she shut the doors, she looked at everyone still outside.

"Find Angel," she said. "You do whatever it takes! You have to stop her! I'm going to find 917!"

6 allowed the doors to close and the wall shifted back in place, concealing the entrance to the elevator. 117 stared at his new team.

"Orders, sir?" one marine asked 5.

"Well, we're improvising now," 5 shrugged.

117 looked at Serina, who nodded. She jumped up and then floated next to his shoulder.

"We're going after 999."

"Oh, we're so dead," 297 scoffed as performed a quick weapons check.

Stepping outside, the group followed 117 as he led them in the direction where he'd seen 999 run off. They quickly fell into a tactical formation, trying to detect any signs of movement.

The further down the halls of the abandoned offices they went, the closer they got to the sounds of a violent rampage.

"She's a demon!"

117, at the front of their formation, froze dead in his tracks when he heard someone's bloodcurdling scream. Everyone behind him stopped too, waiting for his next command.

A loud bashing noise silenced the screaming.

What are we supposed to do against... that?? 117's mind raced as he tried to figure out what to do. *This is like when we had to fight 43 when she went on a rampage. Except... there's only three amborgs going after 999.*

"Guys?" 117 gulped. "I think for this next part, we should get our marines to safety."

"Sir?" someone commented. "Our orders are to help you."

"6 put you under 5's command, correct?" 117 replied immediately.

"Uh, yes sir?"

"Well, 5 is under my command," 117 said urgently. "I want all marines currently present to fall back and search for Captain Mercy and his squad."

There was a quiet pause behind him, which made 117 turn his head to look back at his team. 5 was nodding at 117.

"Yeah, good idea," he said. 5 pivoted and addressed his marine escorts. "Commander 117 is correct. Fall back. We'll handle this."

The marines nodded and gave 5 a quick salute. They slowly turned around and headed back the way they'd come. As they moved away to safety, 117 led the other amborgs forward.

They heard another person scream before their cries were abruptly cut off by a loud and disturbing crash. When silence fell, 117 felt that this mission was evolving into a horror story. He felt beads of sweat running down his face as a series of deafening crushing sounds erupted from a nearby office. When 117 reached the entrance, he rounded the corner and stepped inside. What he saw was terrifying.

"Oh good lord," 297 breathed from behind.

297 and 5 followed 117 inside.

"How bad is it?" 5 asked. Then, "Never mind. This is... very violent."

There were destroyed Silent Eclipse drones and several dead soldiers strewn around the room. These uniformed officers were dressed and armored like the one 999 had been seen striking down. These had to be more of their agents. Clearly, they were getting the shit kicked out of them.

They spotted 999 in the corner, gripping another drone by the throat. The tables had turned entirely. Once, she'd been caught off-guard and was being choked, but now it was her turn. She was hammering the drone over and over again, even though it was already dead. 6's description was accurate, 999 had indeed gone way past the point of no return. Getting her to calm down was not going to be easy.

"Angel!" 117 shouted. "Stop!"

999 whirled around and threw the dead drone into the desk. She tripped over her feet and fell onto one of the dead bodies she had slain. They wanted to move in, but she was already up and thrashing around, which made them hold their position.

999 continued to throw things around while the others could only stand by and watch helplessly. Eventually, it seemed she was starting to wear out as her breathing grew heavy and she began to sway slightly. Was she going to pass out?

117 decided to approach, but it turned out to be a bad idea. Before he could say anything, 999 closed the gap between them and socked him in the chest. He had seen it coming but wasn't prepared for how hard she was going to hit.

117 flew backward and fell into a heap on the floor while 297 and 5 tried to help.

999 lifted her leg and kicked 297 in the chest, causing him to stumble into the wall. She swung her right fist upward, hitting 5 in the chin, and then with a downward swing of her left, hit him again in the head.

5 tried to advance by throwing a massive uppercut. 999 locked her elbows in and blocked, but 5's attack was enough to send her stumbling back a little. Thinking that he had overpowered her defenses, 5 lunged but 999 slipped under his arms. She crouched, lifted 5 off the ground, and sent him flying over her head.

117 managed to get back on his feet and saw 999 delivering a kick to 5 in midair. This sent him crashing into 297, who was in the process of standing up. When 297 and 5 collided and fell on top of one another, 117 attempted to jump back into the fight.

He lifted his left leg to kick, but she blocked it. When that didn't work, he switched tactics and tried to exchange punches with her. A few of his punches landed, but in the end, 999 struck him with a powerful hit while he was trying to defend himself, knocking him off his feet. Once again, 117 felt a punch to his chest, and he had just enough time to see 999 whirl around and elbow him in the nose. She pivoted and then slammed her fist into his chest again, sending him crashing to the ground.

"Serina," 117 groaned as he noticed 297 and 5 staggering to their feet. "Please tell me you have any other ideas on how to get through to her."

"If you manage to initiate a connection, I can try and hijack her system," Serina answered. "Or you can maybe stun her?"

"You don't sound too sure about that," 117 grunted as 999 locked into a duel with 297.

"I'm being transparent!" Serina replied desperately. "I don't usually go around trying to take over your cybernetic systems! Your options are either to physically knock her out or... get her to snap back to reality!"

"Easier said than done!" 117 winced when he saw 297 get hurled to the opposite end of the room.

Still, they needed to get this mission back on track.

"Hey, 117," 5 groaned. "Are you bleeding?"

117 looked at 5 and then down at his clothes. Sure enough, his armor and jacket were torn and stained crimson. However, he didn't feel any pain.

"It's not mine!" 117 shook his head.

297 noticed as well as he tried to pick himself back up.

"999!" he shouted. "Your hands are bleeding! Stop!"

He was right. 999 had gone into such a blind rage that she hadn't even noticed that her hands had been torn open from her own ferocity.

"Help us find Caldwell!" 117 said. "If you help, then you can do whatever you want... but do you really think he would have wanted this?"

"Ok, fighting her and trying to get through to her? I'll help too!" 5 panted. "999! Listen to me! Everything that you're feeling is totally justified! But you're going to destroy yourself at this rate!"

An idea suddenly formed in 117's mind, something that should be able to get her attention, especially since it had been the topic of a conversation that had resurfaced during their time aboard the Heart of Alcyon.

"917 told me about how you both tried to open up to each other! But that didn't work out for either of you!" he shouted. "Is that what Amara would want?! To see you throw your life away?!"

For a brief moment, 117 felt a deep sense of dread about the possibility of having to end his second-in-command's life. She was a friend. They've never been faced with this kind of decision. Still, he felt like had to say that. He knew what it was like to lose the most important person in his life, so maybe mentioning 345 would get to her. To someone like 999, it was probably heart wrenching because of the fact that she had to deal with such a terrible loss.

"Alice!" 117 huffed as he slowly got up and tried to walk towards her. "She would want you to live! We all want you to live!"

Silence fell as 117, 297, and 5 focused on 999, who appeared to have frozen in place. Then, they heard her begin to sob.

"Why?"

117 cautiously approached her as 999 continued to break down her walls.

"Why me?" she cried. "Why did both have to die? Why not me?"

117 and 297 exchanged glances. They weren't sure if the fight was over.

"They're gone... and I'm still here," 999 sobbed. "Why??"

"Hey, guys!" Serina interrupted. "I found Caldwell, she's at the main communications center! She's trying to get it back online!"

Thinking quickly, 117 looked at 297 and 5.

"You two, go!" he said. "I got this!"

297 and 5 withdrew and sprinted off. They didn't have to be told twice. 999 collapsed onto her knees, which made him rush forward. He had never seen her look so defeated.

"Is this what he felt? 917?" she asked. "All of this rage? When we watched Silhed burn? When we weren't there when 345 was killed? Is this how it feels?"

"I'm so sorry," 117 said as he began to feel his own tears welling up. "I'd fight like hell too if it meant that 917 could be here instead of me."

"117!"

He heard 6's voice in the back of his head.

"6! What's wrong?"

"I got him!" 6 answered quickly. "999! Can you hear me?!"

999 and 117 perked up.

"What do you mean you got him?" 117 asked.

6 spoke loudly enough for them to hear. In the background, they heard 777 let out a relieved cry of joy.

"917's alive!"

999's eyes widened and she looked at 117. Amazed, 117's mouth dropped open.

"How?"

"That Caldwell woman thinks she knows us so well," 6 explained confidently. "But she doesn't know everything about the Epsilon universe! 917 has always had a trump card up his sleeve! Or in this case, his head."

117 helped 999 up to her feet and the two of them exited the destroyed office. They had to find out what was going on.

CHAPTER 23

Calling Major Tom!

S.C.E. Headquarters
Main Communications Center

117 and 999 followed 297 and 5 as they traveled to the third floor of the building. When they arrived, they were surprised to see that 6 and 777 had gotten there before they had.

"What?" 999's eyes widened when she noticed who was with them.

"Next time you want to kill me, make sure you don't miss!"

In a sudden and brisk motion, 917 drew his sword and thrust it into Admiral Caldwell's left arm. She was tied to a chair, and it appeared that 917 was initiating some form of torture.

His teammates stared in shock as they approached 777.

"He's actually alive?!" 297 exclaimed.

"Trust me, I can't believe it myself," 777 replied.

"917," 6 spoke warningly. "You just got back on your feet. Dial it down!"

"Sorry," 917 replied with a snarl. "I got some unresolved anger issues from getting shot in the head."

He twisted his wrist, causing the blade to slice deeper into Caldwell's arm and eliciting a piercing cry of pain.

"I shot you! Right in your head," she spat. "How?!"

"A steel plate in the right spot makes me very hard-headed," 917 answered menacingly.

117 glanced at 999, who was still standing there in stunned silence. 917 had a metal plate in the back of his skull?

It had to have been from a surgery a long time ago. True, they never pried for details since medical files were kept private. Still, this was a startling revelation. 6 had apparently known about 917's physical condition and successfully revived him, but this was raising a lot more questions than before.

999 rushed forward and approached 917's left side. 6 was trying to use an S.C.E. medical tool in an attempt to close 917's wound, so she stayed clear and gave plenty of space. Based on what they could see, it didn't seem to be that bad.

"Are you...? Is this... real?" 999 said in relief.

"Yes," 917 glanced at her and nodded. "I'm so sorry."

"No," 999 shook her head. "It was my fault that we got separated."

117 wasn't sure what to focus on. Clearly, Caldwell had been successfully caught and detained. Her personal guards had been taken care of by the others. When he looked at the controls in the communication center, he walked towards it to see if there was anything wrong. Suddenly, he felt Argentum shaking furiously in his bag.

Allow me to assist Serina! Throw me at the console!

117 quickly tossed Argentum onto one of the consoles. It immediately disappeared and morphed into the computer systems.

"Hey!" Serina exclaimed. "Thanks for the assist!"

After a moment, Serina appeared before them in a flash of light and clapped her hands triumphantly.

"And a whole arsenal of nukes... disarmed," Serina winked. She glanced at Caldwell. "How do you like me now, bitch?"

"What?!" Caldwell struggled and grunted painfully. "It's impossible to neutralize and deactivate them all at once!"

"Too bad for you. I just did!" Serina replied playfully. "It was nice to get a little backup."

Serina floated next to 117.

"Seriously," she chuckled gleefully. "Argentum helping me out was like consuming a gallon of espresso! I feel like I could revive my dead body or something."

"Let's..." 117's eyes widened in fear. "Let's not go there. There's been enough undead moments."

Everyone breathed a sigh of relief. If the nukes were all being deactivated, then they had officially managed to thwart another large catastrophe.

Before they could celebrate, though, a small red alarm appeared on a nearby console. Quickly, Serina disappeared from above them and flew over to examine the new alert. Her smile quickly faded.

"Uhh," she gulped. "I think we have another problem."

"What is it?" 117 asked.

Everyone looked at Serina. The marines kept their weapons trained on Admiral Caldwell, all of them wondering what was going on. Serina awkwardly pointed at the console and began to speak rapidly.

"The-starbase-is-falling-out-of-orbit..." she said, her words running together.

"What?" 297 blurted out.

"The starbase that we freed from Silent Eclipse's control... is dropping out of orbit!" Serina pulled up images onto the consoles. "Their systems have been shut down, their thrusters are off and the moon's gravity is pulling them in! It's going to crash onto us!"

"What did you do?!"

Everyone glanced at 917, who was demanding answers.

"It's a good thing I didn't knock you out," he snarled. "Now talk!"

"You were all so busy stopping me from activating my army on Earth, so I sent a bug out to the starbase when I tried to lock out your A.I.," Caldwell sneered. "You got to take advantage of everything."

"So, you're just going to end millions of lives?!" 6 scoffed. "Treat them like they don't matter?!"

"Don't lecture me about what matters," Caldwell glared at 6 as she replied calmly. "I spent years fighting for the S.C.E. only to see that everyone was going soft. I fought hard on behalf of working citizens all across the galaxy. I took action. The council and admiralty board? I had enough of their sanctimony. They spend so much time and waste resources breaking bread with species and people that take advantage of charitable acts. They talk instead of fight."

"You're a bully," 999 declared.

"At least I'm willing to do whatever it takes," Caldwell replied. "The S.C.E. claims to be an organization committed to peace and prosperity, but it is the elite who monopolize those benefits, leaving the rest of you to handle their dirty work. At least I did what was necessary to make them understand fear."

"Angel," 917 interrupted Caldwell. "You got this?"

Without a word, 999 swooped in and punched Admiral Caldwell in the head, not to kill her, but to knock her out.

As her head slumped forward, 917 withdrew his sword and cleaned the blood off the edges.

"Talk about dirty work," 297 remarked.

"Thank you," 6 politely dipped her head at 999. "She was getting annoying."

117 looked at Serina frantically.

"Where's the base going to fall?" he asked. "Can we evacuate?"

"What do you think?" Serina said with a worried look. "We have half an hour. Maybe less."

S.C.E. Firestar

"Deploy the tractor beam!" Admiral Ra'aiah commanded.

"With all due respect admiral," Ulgo replied sternly, "there is no possible way to pull the entire starbase back into orbit! Not even if we had the rest of the fleet assist us!"

The Firestar had managed to fire three E.M.P. attacks once they deployed the amborgs to the moon's surface. Everything seemed to be going well until they realized that the lunar starbase suddenly lost power and began to fall out of orbit.

The first E.M.P. deactivated all Silent Eclipse drones on the base, the second one struck the City of Beginnings on the moon, and the third one targeted more ships in the defense fleet.

The main problem Ulgo pointed out was quite grim. The majority of the defense fleet was either out of position or unable to regroup to help. A handful of S.C.E. light cruisers and ships remained docked at the starbase, but they were being pulled down along with the entire station.

"This computer virus is incredible," Dr. Kendrick said as he examined his data pad, then began typing rapidly on his keyboard as he tried to analyze the information on the computer. "It's merged into the system, adapted to all security measures, given complete authorization to shut down all systems in the starbase, and also altered its coordinates!"

Admiral Ra'aiah clenched her fist as she tried to come up with a rescue plan. Not counting all of the ships, shuttles, and light craft, the entire starbase had about 75,000 people aboard.

"How the hell did someone make it affect the system so fast?" she said as she brought her fist up to her chin. "Ulgo! Order the base to begin evacuation! Send out an emergency broadcast to the moon!"

Fortunately for them, Serina's blackout program had shut off and standard communications were back up. However, trying to get through all of the chaos that they had created was going to be a problem.

When the blackout program was activated, Carter detected a massive amount of complaints and panicked calls. A surprising amount of people were frustrated and confused by the sudden loss of signal to their high-tech smartphones.

"Blue alert! I am authorizing general order eight!" Admiral Ra'aiah informed Ulgo. "Protocol three! Code one! Alpha-zero!"

"Yes, ma'am! Broadcast to the station and the moon!" Ulgo commanded. "All frequencies and emergency channels. Evacuation codes. Blue alert! Protocol 3, code one! Alpha-zero confirmed by alpha-one."

Dr. Kendrick rushed over to the admiral's chair.

"Carter and I were able to find the source of the virus and we can begin scrubbing it from your systems, but it'll take time!" he explained. "From what I can tell, it was put in place many years ago. It's been living in the hidden back alleys of the base's system! Like a trap door that was overlooked."

"Any idea who put it there?" Admiral Ra'aiah asked.

"We'll figure it out," Dr. Kendrick replied determinedly. "But the problem is, we need more time. If only we could put the entire starbase into the Heart of Alcyon."

"I doubt the Tandeeri can defy the laws of physics," Admiral Ra'aiah looked at the screen. "We don't have time. There are still going to be significant casualties."

"Admiral! Incoming transmission from the Heart of Alcyon!"

Admiral Ra'aiah perked up. She was actually about to call Snickerdoodle herself to quickly consider their options. Since the Tandeeri ships were in an extended timezone, perhaps they could come up with a solution, if they haven't already.

"Put it through," she said with a hopeful expression.

Snickerdoodle's face appeared on their screen. Admiral Ra'aiah noticed movement to the side and glanced left. On the port side, they saw the Tandeeri ship increasing speed and it looked like they were going after the base.

"Snickerdoodle!" Admiral Ra'aish exclaimed. She looked away briefly before eyeing him onscreen. It still felt weird to call him by that name out loud. "We need a plan!"

"Of course!" Snickerdoodle replied with a firm nod. "If the rest of my fleet was here, we could easily pull your starbase back into orbit. However, your allies may still see us as the enemy."

"It might be confusing since they witnessed us attacking you and now you're coming in to save the day," Admiral Ra'aiah answered. "We've put out an evacuation order but we need to buy time!"

"Pardon me my friends," Snickerdoodle replied. "After performing some calculations, pulling the starbase back up may prove to be futile. We may accidentally tear it apart."

"What about pushing?"

Admiral Ra'aiah and Snickerdoodle glanced over at Dr. Kendrick. His eyes lit up.

"I have an idea!" he said. "You won't like it because it's insane."

"Uh," she stammered uneasily. "B-by all means, what's your idea??"

Dr. Kendrick addressed the screen.

"Snickerdoodle, please fire an energy blast at the starbase."

"You... wish for us to destroy the station?" Snickerdoodle cocked his head to the side. "I am not familiar with all forms of human behavior but... wouldn't that cause more problems for the people inhabiting your moon?"

Admiral Ra'aiah didn't even want to think about that. If the starbase were to crash onto the moon, everyone would look up and see a massive object about to rearrange the moon's entire geography. If the starbase exploded, they would face the danger of a single falling object turning into... a catastrophic rain of fire. She shuddered at the thought of the damage estimate and casualty count if that happened.

"No, of course not!" Dr. Kendrick replied. "Carter, I need you to call 8 and 9! I need... oh dear... I need my master pranksters!"

"Uh, ok?" Carter stared at Dr. Kendrick skeptically.

"Ishala!" he turned to the Admiral.

"Yes?" Admiral Ra'aiah blinked when he eagerly called her by her first name.

"I need your fastest pilot," he explained. "We need to be fast and precise! We can push the starbase back up! Or at least, we can hold it in place and give it a boost!"

Admiral Ra'aiah ordered Ulgo to call for an available shuttle pilot as Dr. Kendrick turned back to the screen.

"We brought a couple of old Earth tools as part of our information exchange!" he said. "Remember what we began to work on?"

Snickerdoodle's eyes widened and he grinned.

"Oh," he nodded. "The discontinued tool that can alter an object's gravity?"

"Isn't that the thing your amborgs used to... lift a ship out of the ocean?" Admiral Ra'aiah asked hesitantly when she realized what they were talking about. "Didn't that fail spectacularly?"

"Yes," Dr. Kendrick nodded.

"Doesn't it run out of power faster depending on how big the object is?"

"Also yes," Dr. Kendrick nodded again. "But, thanks to the Tandeeri, we solved our power problem! We just need to stick the... uh... jumbo sized ones we printed onto the Heart of Alcyon."

"You made... jumbo sized ones??" Admiral Ra'aiah's expression melted into one of horror. She held up her hand and looked at her palm. "You had small ones about this size. How big is jumbo??"

Dr. Kendrick and Snickerdoodle both eyed each other onscreen. Like two little kids, they chuckled nervously.

24 Minutes Later
Lunar Starbase Impact: 7 Minutes 23 seconds

"I can't believe that we actually got the authorization to break out these new arrows!"

8 and 9 hurriedly worked to move some large carpets toward the shuttle's back entrance. The triplets from the Third Group joined to assist them. Meanwhile, 92 and 93 finished their calculations as everyone rushed to complete the task as quickly as possible. There was no margin for error. Failure meant that millions would be killed.

"It's done!" 53 said. "The pilot has us going on a direct intercept course! We're going for the starbase at maximum speed."

"This has got to be the stupidest plan ever..." 54 muttered.

"Are you kidding?" 55 chuckled excitedly. "Imagine how awesome it'll be if it works!"

20 minutes ago, Admiral Ra'aiah managed to personally contact the Transient shuttle pilots. All four shuttles were still flying within range of S.C.E. headquarters when they got the call. Since they were the closest, they landed in the courtyard and extracted Dr. Kendrick's team from the ground.

While the other three shuttles flew overhead to cover the first shuttle's landing, 8 and 9 split away from their team. 92 and 93 also managed to slip away unharmed. 301 and 365 had to help extract the Third Group triplets since they had engaged several Silent Eclipse operatives, who were trying to take over the defense platform control rooms. Dr. Kendrick was relieved to hear that the amborgs he'd asked for answered the call and rallied as fast as they could. Under escort from their fighters, Transient 1 rendezvoused with Snickerdoodle's ship and they picked up the supplies they had discussed.

Initially, Dr. Kendrick was genuinely terrified by the idea that 8 and 9 had brought along a few arrows. Not archery ammunition, no. They had brought their infamous bumper stickers—a failed piece of technology that had a simple yet rather extraordinary ability. When one of those arrows was affixed to something, it would create an energy field and propel it away. When it was first developed, the creator presented it to A.I. Industries as a device that could alter the gravitational pull of any object it adhered to.

Early versions of it yielded entertaining but dangerous results. If one of those arrows was stuck to a crate pointing up, for example, the crate would shoot straight up as its gravity would be flipped in that direction. The same concept would apply to any other direction one of those arrows pointed.

Even though the arrow was a revolutionary idea and had been originally designed to help the transportation industry, the practical uses were just too ridiculous and unfeasible. This, however, didn't stop the amborgs or A.I. Industries from continuing to study its properties after the tech had been confiscated and discontinued for use by the public.

In the year 2127, during the Dominoe Incident, the amborgs had used their supply of arrows to create a storm of... well, anything they could get their hands on. On the final stronghold they attacked, they launched everything that they could find into the air and created an artillery barrage that overwhelmed the enemy defenses. Most amborgs remembered that iconic attack strategy as the turning point of that mission.

The remaining arrows they kept would then go into storage until someone saw fit to borrow one on random occasions. Someone had decided to pull a prank on the U.S. Navy and tried to make an aircraft carrier fly. Not only were the amborgs reprimanded and received angry letters from the Pentagon and Department of Defense, they realized that the arrows would drain their power supply in seconds if they were stuck to anything that was too big.

It was almost complete and total irony that the Tandeeri seemed to get a kick out of the arrows and what they were designed to do. During the 16 day respite onboard the Heart of Alcyon, as a joke, the Tandeeri took the design of the small arrows and created larger and more powerful versions. Hence, the jumbo arrows.

The marines inside the shuttle stared in stunned silence, completely baffled at the sight of what the amborgs were planning.

"Sir?" one of them politely raised their hand. "How exactly is this going to work?"

"What part of this don't you get?" 9 stared back at them. "The pilot is going to maneuver us into position and we're going to drop every single one of these arrows onto the surface of the lunar base! We're going to hopefully hold the station in place or at least slow it down from crashing into the moon!"

"I understand what we're doing but... how is this going to work?"

"I believe the marines are questioning the tactics of this maneuver we are attempting," 301 stated in a serious voice.

"We're running out of time! We have minutes!" 92 reminded them.

"Everyone needs to put on their life-support!" 93 commanded.

Everyone scrambled to put on their helmets and switch their oxygen packs on. As they all checked to make sure that their uniforms and suits were ready, 9 did one last recap of their hastily put-together plan.

"Huge props to the pilots for actually agreeing to this crazy plan!" she exclaimed as 8 made sure her oxygen supply was properly secure. "They fly us to the falling starbase! We stick all of these giant carpets on there! Once they activate, the Tandeeri are going to channel as much power as they can by firing another energy blast! It won't pull the star base back up into orbit... we're trying to hold it in place!"

"Do you play sports?!" 8 asked the marines.

"Yes sir?"

"We're going to try and catch a giant ball because if we drop it or miss, millions die!"

8's explanation appeared to fill the shuttle with more urgency as everyone finished their safety checks.

"It is interesting how that method of communicating seems to have motivated everyone," 365 casually replied.

"Well, my Fourth Group friend," 8 replied as they all moved towards the back of the shuttle. "We're short on time and you just need to know how to communicate properly."

"I can communicate!" 9 protested.

"But you just kept repeating our plan," 92 pointed out.

"Especially since the marines weren't following along," 93 added.

"I am this close to shoving you all out the shuttle first!" 9 growled.

Suddenly, they heard an announcement from the pilot.

"This is Transient 1," he announced. "We're closing in! Just wanted to say good luck! Once you leave the shuttle, I don't know if we'll be able to retrieve you!"

"You will when we succeed!" 8 replied.

"Uh, don't you mean if we succeed?" 55 asked.

"You guys are killing me with your negativity," 8 let out a frustrated groan. "Just... lie to me! Ok?"

A loud alarm blared as the ramp opened up and began to lower. A hush fell over the group. The twins instructed all their marine escorts to hang on and stay inside the shuttle. The amborgs would be making this insane jump.

"Well," 8 sighed he peered outside, checked his helmet, and looked at the base directly ahead of them. "9, I just wanted to say to you... I've always hated you."

"Aww, I appreciate that! I also wanted to say something," 9 replied cheekily. "You remember that time I told you I let one of the dogs at A.I. Industries into your room, and it was left in complete disarray? Well, it was actually a bunch of the Third Group amborgs when they were drunk. I let them into your room."

"Oh come on! That makes so much more sense!" 8 said with a furious look. "You had me convinced there was a drunk dog roaming A.I. Industries that got into my beer supply!"

"I can't believe you thought that for years!" 9 snickered.

8 and 9 looked behind them. 92 and 93 were tethering a line between them and the triplets. They would lead the team first while the Second and Third Group amborgs carried the jumbo arrows. If anyone flew off-course, 301 and 365 would bring up the rear and provide assistance.

"Just for the record guys!" 92 said. "This is a terrible idea!!!"

"You have a better one??" 93 raised an eyebrow and shot his brother a look. "Do you?"

The twins exchanged glances. 92 shook his head.

"The odds of dying have significantly increased," 301 commented as they watched 8 and 9 take the first leap off the shuttle. "Significantly."

"But this is possible," 365 added. "We must try."

No matter how ridiculous or impossible the task was, the amborgs would still do it because if there was even a small percentage of success, they were the few individuals who would give it a shot, despite what the majority believed.

S.C.E. Headquarters
Defense Platform Control Room

"Can you contact anyone?"

501 looked up from the console and shook his head as 466 approached him.

From the moment they made it inside and headed straight towards their objective, it was... quite a whirlwind of emotions. While they worked on deactivating the defense platforms, the sounds of turmoil from the upper levels echoed loudly.

First, Admiral Caldwell hijacked their communications in order to broadcast a live execution of 917, which practically terrified the Third Group. Not long after, they received messages from 43 and the First Group to reactivate the defense platforms and prepare to do some sort of missile defense. After this, the Fourth Group and their marines reported an incoming attack. Silent Eclipse agents were attacking and trying to take over the control rooms.

Everything turned out to be ok. The rest of the team had tried to console 501 and 466 after they heard 917 got shot. Shortly after, 6 reported that 917's death was false and that he was alright.

Then, Dr. Kendrick summoned the triplets for another impromptu assignment when they saw the lunar star base was about to fall on them. 301 and 365 had split up from the other Fourth Group amborgs to get them out of the building.

"I don't know if my heart can take all of the suspense," 501 muttered. "First we deactivated the platforms successfully, and now we're spending extra time reactivating them. I thought we were shutting down or destroying them."

"Well, we're trying to get ready to shoot down any missiles or nukes being launched," 466 replied. "That's a good thing."

"I feel so helpless right now," 501 mumbled.

"Don't think like that," 466 answered. "You're going to get out of this and give Oreo a big hug when we save the day."

"It just feels weird," 501 sighed as he kept a close eye on the console. "It feels like the fight is over but... why doesn't it feel like it's over?"

"Well, 501," 466 cleared her throat. "We do have hostages."

During their quick infiltration into the weapons control room, a number of S.C.E. guards and officers inside believed they were confronting an enemy and attempted to fight back. Fortunately, most of the personnel were focused on detaining rather than killing them. No one was actually trying to kill anyone.

Thanks to the assistance of their marine squads, their tactical expertise overpowered the control room occupants easily. 501 and 466 were watching the computer consoles while the others were carefully inspecting their prisoners. 249, 593, and 49 were running background checks while also searching them for anything suspicious.

"Hidden blades up your sleeve?" 249 said as he pulled them from a woman in a lab coat. "To untie your ropes? So cliché. Are these regulation?"

249 glanced at one of the marines nearby, who was looking at a data pad. She skimmed it and replied promptly.

"Well according to her file," she informed him, "this woman has been assaulted in the past a total of three times. Officials authorized and allowed her to carry these weapons for her safety."

"Oh, that's understandable," 593 replied in a kind tone. "Well, we won't confiscate them then. We'll just leave them here and you can put them back on after we untie you. Sorry for the inconvenience."

"Ma'am, with all due respect," the marine eyed 593 with a skeptical gaze. "Have you ever held or detained prisoners before? You're not supposed to be this nice."

593 chuckled nervously and shook her head. 49 then addressed all of their hostages.

"Yeah we don't usually take hostages," he bowed respectfully to everyone they'd tied up. "This is kind of a new thing for us. We're just trying to figure out which one of you guys wants to kill us."

Every guard, scientist, and S.C.E. officer exchanged glances, shrugging and mumbling amongst each other. All of them had tape across their mouths so it was just a cacophony of confused grunts and moaning.

"Oh yeah," 249 sighed. "Just tell them our whole plan, why don't you?"

249 glanced at the marine holding the data pad and dipped his head apologetically.

"We're really bad at this."

"I don't think you're supposed to admit that, sir," she replied calmly.

501 and 466 merely watched, but gave the other amborgs a reassuring smile.

"We really are bad at this, aren't we?" 466 whispered.

"We're doing the best we can," 501 answered.

Out of nowhere, an alarm blared, interrupting them and snagging their attention. 466 and 501 whirled around to look at the console.

"Oh no!" 501 said. "The star base is about to enter the atmosphere!"

466 looked at 501.

"If we run... will we make it out?"

501 glanced at her as his face fell.

"No," he replied softly.

The alarm suddenly switched to a light chime as they watched the screen. The red dot was about to drop into the moon's atmosphere. Then, the alarm muted and the dot stopped in place.

"Hey," 501 pointed at the screen. "Does this mean...? Did they do it?"

More alerts rang out, and they saw multiple blue triangles approaching the red dot. These looked like the S.C.E. fleet. Were they gathering to pull the star base away from the moon?

"Huh," 466's eyes widened as she clutched her chest in relief. "A little anti-climactic."

"I agree," 501 muttered. "I suggest we not complain because... it looks like we're not going to get crushed by a giant star base after all."

The door crashed open, making them all jump.

501 and 466 turned to see 280 and 113 storming in. They were both carrying someone by their arms, and the Third Group recoiled when they saw the Fourth Group amborgs coldly but gently shove an S.C.E. officer to the floor. When they leaned closer, 501 and 466's eyebrows shot up at the sight of who was on their knees before them.

"Braelynn??" 466 exclaimed.

501 glanced up and saw that the entire Fourth Group team and their marines were coming in. Many of them looked worn out and had some burns on their armor. They saw a few more carrying a couple of wounded into the room as well.

"What happened?" 501 asked.

"We neutralized all enemy opposition," 113 answered promptly. "There is no imminent danger. We brought our wounded and surviving marines to your position to reinforce you."

"So what's going with Braelynn??"

501 pointed at the woman looking up at them with pleading eyes. The Fourth Group amborgs eyed her carefully.

"Earlier, when we were fighting to take control of this room," he murmured softly. As he remembered what he had seen, he glanced at Braelynn. "I didn't see her after we got here."

"She specifically claimed that she was going to remain with your team," 113 scolded him. "As the leader, you must be aware at all times! We caught her accessing a restricted area during our sweep of the lower basements!"

"What was she doing?" 466 asked nervously.

"Accessing data files," 113 reported. "We originally secured the room to look for information on Silent Eclipse when we caught her. She planned to obtain highly sensitive materials while we engaged the enemy."

"Yes, I admit it!" Braelynn spoke up. "I was accessing high-level data and I did sneak in while the battle was taking place!"

"But... why would an Intelligence officer or... a secret agent like you need to break in??" 466 asked. "Couldn't you just come into headquarters when the fighting is over?"

"I have a hypothesis," 280 interrupted before Braelynn could reply. "There's only one reason a secret Intelligence officer would infiltrate during... our infiltration."

280 nodded to 113 and she stepped forward. In one swift movement, 113 ripped the stripes off of Braelynn's jacket.

"She is an agent or... spy," 280 stated. "Just not for the S.C.E."

"She's gathering information to sell," 113 concluded.

"No!" Braelynn said desperately, "It's not what you think!"

113 pulled a drive out her pocket and tossed it to 466, who caught it.

"This was the drive she had," she informed them. "Check the contents!"

466 quickly plugged in the drive as 113 knelt down next to Braelynn. She lifted her hands and showed them she was unarmed, but they weren't lowering their guard. 280 maintained a serious expression as he continued to watch for any sudden movement.

"Watch the door," 280 said to 63, 100, and 378.

While they monitored the door as instructed, 466 continued to scan the drive. 501 looked at Braelynn, uncertain about all of this. This didn't fit with the woman who helped them negotiate peace with the Tandeeri and saved their lives repeatedly.

"There's nothing related to Silent Eclipse on this drive," 466 said as she did a brief overview of the files. "All of these are files to the biggest black markets, transactions, and all sorts of basic information."

"Were you planning to run and sell this information?" 113 asked sharply.

"No please," Braelynn pleaded. "I need that information! It's for something bigger than me."

"The kingdom of Tycherania?"

466 turned to Braelynn after she finished looking over the contents of the drive.

"Where is that?" she asked.

"'What is that?' is the better question," 501 said.

The other Third Group amborgs appeared nervous as well. Should they tie up Braelynn with the others? That was indeed the question beginning to circulate among them. The Fourth Group looked ready to kill.

"I'm here to save that kingdom!" Braelynn said desperately. "I can't risk anyone finding out my real name! Please! I had to use this opportunity to gain access to all of this intel!"

"I detect no lies," 280 said to 501. "But she is still a suspicious one."

"Why didn't you just ask us?" 466 asked. "We could have helped you look if you had been truthful."

"Because the more people I get involved with this, the more danger all of you are in!" Braelynn replied. "I'm an Intelligence agent with the S.C.E. and this is my mission!"

"Checking your credentials is difficult because Intelligence officers are usually given secret levels of clearance that aren't easy to access," 113 replied. "How are we supposed to confirm if you're telling the truth?"

"We want to help you," 501 stated. Then he noticed the looks that 113 and 280 gave him. "I do at least."

He cleared his throat as he stepped forward.

"You've done a lot for us," he stated. "I don't think you're the type of person who would... just pull the rug out from under our feet. If I'm wrong about that, then I guess we made a mistake in calling you our friend."

"I am not a member of Silent Eclipse," Braelynn looked 466 in the eye, firmly keeping her gaze focused on her. "I first came to Alpha 917 to help me protect the kingdom. He agreed to help me and got me into the S.C.E. academy. I've been working undercover with his assistance but he was killed by Silent Eclipse during the Tandeeri war. He was my contact and I lost my leads that he'd sent me. Please, I can't tell anyone except for him."

"Why can't we know?" 501 asked. "917 is my friend. My big brother. Well, so is 117. But 917 is my supervising amborg."

"You're rambling," 466 casually reminded him.

"I can't," Braelynn replied breathlessly as her lip trembled.

501 and 466 looked at each other. The other Third Group amborgs remained silent as they continued guarding their prisoners. 501 glanced at the Fourth Group team and noticed that even they seemed to be loosening up the tension. They didn't seem that aggressive now that Braelynn was cooperating. Or was she?

501 turned back to Braelynn. Being a trained Intelligence officer meant that she was an experienced professional. Now here she was, completely at their mercy. He really wanted to pry her for more information since it seemed like it would affect 917 a lot, but her expression, whether or not she was putting on a great act, was practically pleading with them not to dig deeper.

"I don't know if we can fully trust her," 501 shrugged after thinking for a few moments. "But the reason I won't arrest her is because... of how much she's helped us."

113 looked like she was about to interrupt, but 501 noticed and kept talking.

"I know," he sighed. "She could have been helping us this whole time just to build trust. The truth is, I'm not qualified to handle this. But, I definitely know who will."

"You can't turn me in," Braelynn begged 501. "Not to the S.C.E. authorities."

"I wasn't going to actually," 501 smiled reassuringly. He raised his head and addressed his team. "She knows 917. I know him too! We let him decide."

"Fair enough," Braelynn nodded.

"Not so fast."

466 stepped forward sternly.

"If whatever you tell him has to remain a secret, then go ahead and tell him. I will agree with 501. 917 will know what to do with you," she stated. "But he's been through enough. We watched him go through hell. So, if you make him do something he doesn't like or if you hurt him, we will make you pay."

"I understand," Braelynn trembled.

"I really hope he's ok," 466 sighed.

501 looked at her and nodded confidently.

"I think he is," he said.

CHAPTER 24

1.21 Giga-what?

S.C.E. Headquarters
Main Communications Center

"Well that was quite a show. Everyone, I promise I'm not making this up."

The amborgs were all watching the main screen that Serina had taken over.

When Dr. Kendrick called them and sent the team in charge of rescuing the star base, the amborgs rallied. The Third and Fourth Group fought in the basement and engaged the enemy. 301 and 365 successfully escorted the triplets out, while 8 and 9 grabbed the twins and they pulled out.

All those still at headquarters believed it would be best to regroup. The remaining First Group amborgs merged with the Second Group at the main communications center on the third floor. They were now getting up to speed on the news that 917 had been shot in the head and had been successfully revived, all while viewing the live footage on the screen. It was quite interesting.

"That's not something I was expecting to see," 1 stated.

"I agree," 2 nodded. "Do we still have contact with 8 and 9?"

"Nope," 6 shook her head, looking impressed. "Atmospheric disturbance is interfering with all communications. It looks like they were successful in catching the star base. I'll be ready if there are any injuries."

After the prankster team got the jumbo arrows attached to the station, they activated them successfully and slowed the star base down to a halt. Unfortunately, the sheer size of the station drained the power rather quickly. That is, until Snickerdoodle fired an energy blast, which recharged the arrows. Because they had been manufactured aboard the Heart of Alcyon in a joint human-Tandeeri technology project, the massive arrows didn't explode when charged by Tandeeri energy. Instead of shutting down within seconds, the arrows held the star base up for a couple of minutes. Thankfully, the base was pulled back up into orbit by the S.C.E. fleet that had rallied under Admiral Ra'aiah's command.

The star base hadn't entered the atmosphere, so none of the amborgs who were outside literally attaching giant carpet bumper stickers were incinerated. Still, they did jump out of a shuttle in space and risked getting pulled into the moon's atmosphere just to catch a building that was pretty much the size of a city. Until they heard back, the others were confident that 8 and 9's entire team was alright since it was clear that they were successful.

"It's going back up," Serina smiled as she watched the alarms begin to shut off. "Oh... Argentum, you want out? Hey 117, he's done here in the computer system."

117 walked over, noticing a silver pool of liquid metal leaking out of the computer. It slowly reformed back into a silver cube, and 117 picked up Argentum. In the palm of his hand, 117 cheerfully greeted his tiny friend. Words formed across the smooth surface.

The files relating to Silent Eclipse have been identified from Caldwell's access into the computer. Please have Serina transmit them to the proper authorities. It was a pleasure working with her. The battle is won. I would like to rest now.

"You did spectacularly," 117 replied.

"Is the commander...? Is he talking to... that cube?"

"I guess being an amborg comes with a lot of... special perks."

117 heard a couple of their marine escorts whispering nearby. He ignored them as he glanced at Serina.

"Argentum loved working with you," he said.

"Aww, tell the metal-morphing power box that I had a great time," Serina replied.

"Breya," 117 said. "Is there a way to cancel the lockdown? Get eyes on the entire building again? We should signal the all-clear or something."

Breya and her squad of marines had brought Admiral Casey down from upstairs. This actually led to them finding Captain Mercy. After 917 and 999 got ambushed by Silent Eclipse operatives, their marine escorts had tried to defend them as best they could. 917 had attempted to use himself as bait to keep the focus of the enemy on him in order to allow the others to get away. Captain Mercy and his squad retreated with a few injuries and wounded teammates. They sheltered in an office and fortified their position, while 999 went after 917 and fended off any other operatives that she encountered.

117 was personally relieved to see that no one had gotten killed. The marines were extremely tough and resilient. Thanks to their training, they had managed to survive one of the most difficult missions in their entire career. Hopefully, if they were to be commended, all of the amborgs wanted to give them the respect and recognition that they deserved, along with every other member of the S.C.E. that made the success of this mission possible.

Breya kept a firm watch on the unconscious Admiral Caldwell. There were restraints on her arms and legs, and 6 had taped her mouth to prevent her from speaking once she woke up. She lifted her hand to her chin, pondering his question.

"If everyone we have is apprehended, then we just gift-wrap them for the remaining board of officers and admirals," she said. "We'll clear out and sort who's good and who's bad. Imprison them for life."

"Am I going too?"

Admiral Casey looked up from where she was sitting on the floor. She had also been restrained, but 6 had allowed her to speak. She didn't seem to be freaking out like before and was actually communicating with them at a reasonable level.

"I'll take responsibility for what I did," she said mournfully. "I helped enable this for so many years."

"You will be a witness and placed under protective custody," Breya replied calmly with a smile. "You can help make this right."

"Then I shall testify," Casey nodded, looking relieved. "What about the others that are found to be affiliated with Silent Eclipse?"

"Well we hunt them down," 117 replied. "Then we give them the same deal we're giving you."

As 117 approached Breya, he looked over at 6 and 777, who were examining 917's wounds. 999 sat next to him but was keeping her distance. 3 was watching calmly, looking worried.

"Well that was a mini heart attack for everyone, right?" 5 stated.

"Please don't joke like that," 3 sighed.

"I'm actually not," 5 answered gently. "It was really insane... hearing 917 getting executed like that. Then UNO reverse card! 6 revives him! Thanks to a metal plate..."

"...in the back of his head," 3 nodded.

"Who knew?" 5 asked.

"Actually," 3 nodded at 6 and 999, "looks like two of us in the room."

The big question was... how did 917 have such a strong armor plating in his head? Typically, those were put in after severe traumatic injuries. Even during the formation of the Second Group, 117 had never known about that. No one did. However, it did add a small piece to that puzzle. 917 was cybernetically enhanced while in a coma, and when he woke up, he was an amborg. They would have to ask Dr. Kendrick later for the full story, but it did seem to make a little sense. A serious and harsh blow to the head would cause massive damage to the skull and leave some victims in a coma.

Before they could continue speculating about it, Serina called out to them.

"Hey! Snickerdoodle is helping with the recovery of the star base! The Heart of Alcyon is leading the formation!" she explained.

"Well, that's a relief," 1 smiled.

"Oh good! There are more ships coming to help!" Serina exclaimed. "Another fleet just entered the system!"

"Another fleet? More ships?" 117 asked. "From where?"

"They just jumped in! Wait a minute."

Serina's excitement faded. When she detected them on the radar, she had started to bounce happily like a little girl. Now, she went still, turning awkwardly to glance worriedly at them.

"They aren't S.C.E.," she said, pointing at the computer as if a spider had crawled across the screen and she was asking someone to get rid of it. "I don't think they're invited."

"What do their I.F.F. tags say?" Breya asked.

"Nothing?" Serina answered cautiously. "No I'm not kidding, they don't have I.F.F. tags. I am not seeing any friend or foe ID tags..."

117 glanced sharply at Breya, who was checking her ammo. Captain Mercy was alert and doing a weapons check, which seemed to spark the same reaction from all the marines. The amborgs stared curiously as the marines prepared for another fight.

"Oh great," 5 sighed.

117 stared at Breya, who gave him a determined nod.

"We have company, don't we?" 117's voice filled with dread.

"No I.F.F. tags... can only mean a couple of things," Breya said as she walked to the computer. "Sweeper 2 to Wolf leader. Come in."

Chan's voice promptly responded.

"This is Wolf leader, go ahead."

"Wolf squad needs to return to the Firestar immediately," Breya replied. "We have a pirate fleet inbound."

"Copy that Sweeper squad," Chan replied. "Are you sure you don't need air cover?"

"We're secure down here," Breya responded. "Double time it back to the fleet."

"Roger that."

Once Breya was finished talking to Chan, she glanced at 117.

"We should contact the Third Group and have them ready the defense platforms," she said.

"Well, it's a good thing we reactivated plenty of them," 117 nodded.

"Wow," 2 spoke to 1 as the rest of the group remained focused on the computer screen. "I never would have imagined we'd get to see space pirates."

They could only hope that whatever was coming wouldn't be a problem.

S.C.E. Firestar

"Great, just what we needed, another problem," Admiral Ra'aiah let out a frustrated sigh. She looked at Ulgo. "We do have weapons and shields right?"

"Yes ma'am," he replied. "But not against that many pirates."

Most of the fleet was towing the star base back into position. A whole army of engineers and technicians were trying to reboot and fix the station systems so that it could remain in position under its own power. At the moment, the majority of their ships were trying to prevent it from being pulled back towards the moon's gravity.

The Firestar was only flying with a ragtag bunch of ships that were still trying to make sense of what was happening. Even if she could get Snickerdoodle and his ship back in formation, along with the available ships that the S.C.E. had to offer, they were outnumbered by the pirates. They had definitely picked the worst time to show up.

She watched as a flotilla of small frigates and fast corvettes approached them. This was a pirate fleet that she recognized.

"We're being hailed," her communications officer reported.

"Oh wow," Admiral Ra'aiah grumbled. "At least someone is actually being polite and calling us instead of shooting first. Put it through. Charge everything we have and prepare to open fire."

"Greetings S.C.E. scum. You seem to be in a rather peculiar and difficult situation. May we offer assistance?"

The screen opened up to reveal a beast-like person. Dr. Kendrick leapt back in shock as the rest of them casually acknowledged the arrival. The entire bridge looked ready to throw hands. Dr. Kendrick leaned closer, attempting to get a better look at who was rudely greeting them.

The man onscreen bore a striking resemblance to an anthropomorphic lion with big horns. The horns were very prominent, elegantly curving from the top of his head above his ears. He had a shaggy mane and a muscular build. Dr. Kendrick felt like he resembled a certain character from a movie he had once seen. Unfortunately, the character he thought of was nice in the end and this pirate leader seemed like he was about to bare his fangs, lunge through the screen, and possibly kill them.

"Reeko Kai'sen," Admiral Ra'aiah snarled, baring her teeth. Dr. Kendrick sensed that she was channeling her underlying feline instincts. "To what do we owe the pleasure of the presence of Chimera's Wrath?"

Dr. Kendrick seemed perplexed. Ulgo whispered to him quickly.

"Pirate group in the outer expanses," he explained in a soft voice. "One of the biggest groups. They're a moderate threat."

This was an interesting piece of information. It implied there were worse groups out there in the Alpha universe.

"Who keeps coming up with these strange names?" Dr. Kendrick asked with a blank look. "What are they doing here?"

"They seek out opportunities," Ulgo replied. "My guess is, they were waiting for our fleet to fall into disarray so they could swoop in and take advantage of the situation."

They watched as Admiral Ra'aiah exchanged words with the beastman named Reeko.

"Couldn't help but notice that you fumbled your star base," Reeko stated smugly. "Isn't it usually easier to just let things fall and clean up the mess later?"

"Aren't you the pot calling the kettle black?" Admiral Ra'aiah scoffed and let out a laugh. "You have always been an annoying nuisance that we've had to deal with time and time again."

"Well meow," Reeko Kai'sen growled playfully, then let out a sinister chuckle. "You and the rest of your straight-collar friends have a long record of failing to kill me."

"Try me now," Admiral Ra'aiah replied curtly. "I'll make sure not to miss this time."

"Oh trust me kitty cat," Reeko continued to laugh confidently. "You're not getting me this time."

"Enough, you narcissistic windbag," Admiral Ra'aiah growled. "What are you doing here?"

From the side, Dr. Kendrick gazed uneasily at Ulgo.

"Is it just me or is she... very... different?" he asked gently.

It was almost as if Admiral Ra'aiah's confidence had gotten boosted and he was seeing a whole new side to her. Then, Dr. Kendrick had an idea. Maybe it was because this was the Alpha universe and it was technically her home territory. Now that they had essentially succeeded in taking on the entire S.C.E. defense fleet as planned, then dealing with a pirate was probably easier by comparison.

"The admiral?" Ulgo whispered back. "We've encountered Reeko many times before due to his extensive history evading the S.C.E. He's a thorn in our side."

"Is he that good?" Dr. Kendrick asked.

"Yes. He is very elusive and difficult to capture," Ulgo replied firmly. "This is a little personal for most of our starship captains and commanders because of his crimes."

Dr. Kendrick then decided to voice a few more assumptions forming in his mind.

"So, him being a pirate leader," he said. "A space pirate leader..."

"He has boarded innocent ships, seized assets, plundered valuables, taken hostages, killed for recreational purposes," Ulgo spoke quickly. "Shall I continue?"

"Thanks, I think I got it," Dr. Kendrick gulped.

They turned their attention back to the conversation.

"I'll have you know that I am here to collect on what is owed to me," Reeko declared.

"Owed?" Admiral Ra'aiah asked incredulously. "We don't owe you anything! In fact, you owe us for raiding our colonies, stealing our ships, and ransoming our people!"

"Ransom?! That's such a harsh way of putting it," Reeko's smile faded as his tone grew menacing. "I'm talking about your Admiral Caldwell! That lying cheapskate owes me! She promised us territories in exchange for shipping her secret goods to several locations across the galaxy!"

Dr. Kendrick glanced at Commander Ulgo. The two men quietly nodded to each other, understanding right away.

"I think he just confessed to smuggling Silent Eclipse drones all across your territory," Dr. Kendrick muttered.

"It would make sense," Ulgo nodded. "Pirate groups or smugglers would be able to keep a low profile. The more evidence that we get puts her in a larger spotlight once the courts are involved."

The two men suddenly heard Admiral Ra'aiah raise her voice sharply. She almost sounded like a schoolteacher that had caught her students whispering during quiet study time. Fortunately, they weren't on the receiving end of her sudden agitated tone.

"So, you smuggled goods for a First Admiral of the S.C.E.? At any point, did you ever find these transactions suspicious?" Admiral Ra'aiah face palmed and shook her head. "In all the times I've faced you, I can't believe you didn't realize how stupid you were!"

"That's not what a trained commander of a starship should say... right?" Dr. Kendrick stared skeptically at Admiral Ra'aiah's chair.

"Like I said," Ulgo muttered under his breath. "Like many others in the S.C.E., Admiral Ra'aiah tends to be less professional since this is quite personal for her."

Before Dr. Kendrick could ask what that meant, Reeko scoffed at Admiral Ra'aiah's last comment.

"Would someone stupid be sitting on vaults of money? It's called business sweetheart. You should know that I don't question it when I'm being paid for my services," Reeko shrugged and leaned back. "But the thing is, her last payment failed to transfer and I want my money. No money makes me really mad. No one makes me work for free. So you either hand her over or you transfer the funds I'm owed."

"Well, we aren't going to pay you," Admiral Ra'aiah replied. "Caldwell's assets will be seized and she will be in our custody until she goes to trial. You made your trip for nothing. The only reason you bared your teeth and practically confessed your whole reason for being here was because we're in a bind, but we're more than enough to take you on. The way I see it, why don't you go get the things she gave you and return them and then we'll forget the whole thing? What'll it be?"

A deep growl emanated from Reeko Kai'sen. He slammed his fist down.

"I am not in the practice of returning items back to the sender!" he hissed.

"Can you imagine the customer service rep who has to ask for that proof of purchase or the receipt?" Dr. Kendrick joked.

Commander Ulgo gave Dr. Kendrick a smug look. His joke elicited a small smirk, but he gently raised his finger to his lips, asking him to remain quiet.

"No more talk!" Reeko raised his voice. "Target weapons!"

"Admiral!" Hemington interrupted. "I have more signals incoming!"

"Pirates?" Admiral Ra'aiah asked.

"No ma'am!" Hemington reported. "I.F.F. tags on incoming ships! Confirmed! They're reinforcements!"

Several muffled booms could be heard as another fleet jumped in. Everyone glanced at the radar system. The Firestar was facing an incoming cluster of red arrows that represented the pirate fleet. On their side, there were several blue arrows, but they were scattered in a rather loose and clumsy defensive formation. From behind the pirate fleet, another large group of blue arrows appeared and moved into position directly behind the pirates. They had been outflanked and were completely surrounded.

"Go ahead," an angry man's voice said over the comms. "Attack my daughter and I will personally ensure that every hair on you burns!"

"Go get him darling," they heard a familiar feline voice chime over the communications line.

Admiral Ra'aiah let out a tiny pained groan as she clenched the armrests of her chair.

"Yeah, by the way Reeko... I was stalling," she cleared her throat. "Thanks for giving us an announcement and confessing to everything."

"Calling your parents," Reeko's anger had dissipated and he stared at Admiral Ra'aiah with a stunned expression. "That's a new one."

"Actually, technically I didn't call them," Admiral Ra'aiah replied in an embarrassed voice.

Two more faces joined the screen.

"Gods and Goddesses almighty," Admiral Ra'aiah brought her hand up to her neckline and tugged at the collar of her uniform. She greeted the two people on the screen. "Mother. Father."

Second Admiral Talveeya Ra'aiah was smiling and flicking her cat ears at them as she gave a cheerful wave. However, it was the human man who contrasted her outgoing appearance on the screen that seemed to instill fear into Reeko's eyes. In fact, it was like the entire bridge of the Firestar had seized up once he appeared before them. Despite the fact that he wasn't physically aboard their ship, it certainly seemed like everyone had seen a ghost.

"This is First Admiral Aramis Ra'aiah of the S.C.E. Weaver. I suggest you power down your weapons or you will be destroyed. This is your only warning."

First Admiral Ra'aiah spoke in an incredibly deep voice that resonated through the transmission. Dr. Kendrick sensed intense charisma from the way he spoke. It took less than ten seconds and he could already see why everyone appeared to be on edge. This man commanded a massive amount of respect.

"Incredible," Dr. Kendrick said softly. "Ishala is a Third Admiral. Her mother is a Second Admiral and this is her father, a First Admiral. Talk about the family trade."

Aramis suddenly glanced in Dr. Kendrick's direction. Somehow, he had heard this remark and noticed Dr. Kendrick, who flinched in terror. The First Admiral had a few scars across his face, and his cold and frightening expression could probably give 999 a run for her money.

"So, I see my wife wasn't kidding," he said as his expression softened a little. "You really are here. It is an honor to see you again, Dr. Kendrick."

"Oh, thank you," Dr. Kendrick gave him a meek bow. "Thank you for coming to our aid."

"You are welcome," Aramis dipped his head respectfully. "I would never have known what my daughter was up to if the Georgia hadn't come looking for my fleet. Imagine my surprise when I saw a Tandeeri vessel escorting her ship."

"Mom," Ishala Ra'aiah whined. "Why did you bring Dad?"

"I figured if we were going to commit treason and attack headquarters," Talveeya shrugged and mewed back, "your father would want in on the action. After all, I hold all the incentive he needs to stray from his missions."

"Your mother is pretty persuasive," Aramis sighed. "After all, when she looks at me with those cat eyes, well... you get the picture. Now then, how does it feel to be ignored, Captain Reeko Kai'sen?"

"Your family is crazy," Reeko grumbled.

"Oh really?" Talveeya showed her claws and swiped the air. "News flash. I'm the craziest."

"Anyway," Ishala Ra'aiah forcefully interrupted the banter between her parents and the pirates. "You will tell us all of your dealings with Caldwell, and give us all the data and evidence you have. Then we will let you go pillage to your heart's content. We won't even ask you to stay and testify as a witness."

"Even if I did testify," Reeko sniffed in disappointment, "you would find a way to detain me. You can forget it."

"Smart," Aramis said rather stiffly. They weren't sure who he was saying it to. "Are you willing to comply with these demands?"

"Very well..." Reeko pouted. "Standby to receive our transmissions."

The pirate leader ended the transmission and his screen disappeared. Now, it was time for the First and Second Admiral to stare at their daughter.

"Now," Aramis switched to dad mode. Ishala looked away, unable to meet his gaze. "Would anyone care to explain why I'm here disobeying my orders as well? Why my wife felt it was necessary to come all the way out to get me? And also why the majority of our home fleet seems to be hauling a very expensive starbase back into orbit? With the Tandeeri?"

"Do you want to do it?" Ishala Ra'aiah turned to Commander Ulgo, who stood at attention. "I'm not exactly feeling like giving a report at the moment."

"I believe I can," Dr. Kendrick raised his hands and waved at First Admiral Ra'aiah on the screen. "Too bad Serina isn't here to help me write this down."

Congratulations On Your Restoration

Heart of Alcyon
Temporary Ra'aiah Family Residential Suite

No one was sure when it exactly all stopped.

Reeko Kai'sen quietly retreated after transmitting all of the data he had and turned his fleet around. No one fired a single shot, which was a first since past encounters with Chimera's Wrath usually ended in a fight.

When Admiral Ra'aiah learned that Admiral Caldwell was apprehended by the ground team, her mood was poignant and bleak at first. She had always considered Belina to be a friend. She never saw her betrayal coming. Once she and 43 managed to sit down, collaborate, and look through all of the past evidence, it began to make sense.

From what the admiralty board discovered, she had to have spent many years planning their downfall. She secretly revived Silent Eclipse with a small band of people she coerced, illegally scrounged weapons technology, and covertly framed the Tandeeri across many regions of space. Caldwell kept up appearances by putting on an act for the S.C.E. High Command and the Council. With her connections, influence, and tactical skills, she built and hid her forces, preparing them to pull off the coup of a lifetime. Putting assassin drones aboard each starship and all across S.C.E. territory was quite impressive. With all of the people she murdered, Silent Eclipse was judge, jury, and executioner for countless lives. She had also spent resources and time discreetly eliminating those that posed the biggest threat to her plan.

After the end of the mission, admiral Ra'aiah respectfully surrendered herself after essentially initiating a military coup. It turned out that her account had completely overshadowed Caldwell's. Admiral Caldwell had naively believed that her operatives would successfully seize control of Earth in the Epsilon universe, allowing her plans for invasion and expansion across universes to progress. If they failed, Silent Eclipse was to wipe out the S.C.E. fleet. Eliminate all witnesses. What Caldwell hadn't anticipated was the amborgs successfully forming an alliance with the Tandeeri. The greatest setback that derailed her strategy was the lack of knowledge about the Tandeeri. The only ones willing to engage with them were the amborgs. Caldwell ultimately deemed this a threat to her plans. Anyone attempting to inform the mysterious Tandeeri of the complete truth was considered an enemy of Silent Eclipse. As a result, many Alpha amborgs were killed during the war. Thanks to 999's extensive search through military records, the S.C.E. investigation also looked into the details of specific space and planetary confrontations where the 'enemy' had been sighted.

The game-changer that saved Silent Eclipse from total annihilation was the unique strategies and perspectives of the Epsilon amborgs. When a Tandeeri child stowaway was discovered, along with a makeshift rescue plan, the casualties turned out to be fewer than anticipated. Still, Admiral Ra'aiah, the fleet's commanding officer sent to protect Epsilon, was still prepared to take responsibility for the lives lost on this mission. Thankfully, the situation improved significantly due to her parents' involvement. The presence of Talveeya and Aramis seemed to encourage the surviving High Command officers to treat Ishala with more respect throughout the investigation. Her parents were permitted to attend the hearing alongside every captain and commander who carried out her orders.

Thanks to the time dilation aboard the Tandeeri fleet, the investigation was concluded and finished in two days, which equated to a little over a month. The admiralty, S.C.E. High Command, and the Council were all invited by Snickerdoodle to take all the time they needed. 48 hours ended up giving them 32 days. Everything transitioned smoothly as a result.

Ishala sat back on the couch and groaned. To her, it had been nonstop talking, debating, and answering millions of questions. She had been grilled for hours almost every day by the admiralty, council, and also listened to the honorable Judge, the elected leader of the entire S.C.E. and Alpha Earth.

"It's alright dear," Talveeya purred as she brought over a tray of drinks and set it down on the table. "You have done splendidly these last few weeks!"

Ishala glanced at the tray and noticed there were four cups. That was strange, considering there were only three of them in the room. However, she shrugged it off as she allowed her exhaustion to take over.

"Easy for you to say," she eyed her mother grimly. "Dad was able to convince the admiralty to let you off the hook!"

"The perks of being an admiral," Talveeya shrugged mischievously. "Well, an upper admiral."

Aramis walked over and promptly took a seat across from Ishala. Talveeya shot her daughter a quick warning look.

"Honey," she whispered. "Don't slouch!"

"I think she's earned it."

Without moving, Ishala glanced at her father, perplexed. Her parents had spent years instilling discipline and training her to become an exemplary military officer. It was shocking to hear her father speak so casually about adhering to the rules.

"Really?" Talveeya looked at her husband in amazement.

"Really?" Ishala leaned her head forward in surprise.

The two women looked at Aramis who merely nodded curtly. He cleared his throat formally. His dignified nonverbal response seemed to be his silent confirmation to their identical questions.

"Our daughter saved our lives," Aramis spoke formally as he grabbed a drink. "She saved two universes, eliminated a black-ops detachment within the S.C.E., ended the Tandeeri war, and led a successful raid against the home fleet. All of that, with minimal casualties. Then she proceeds to set an example in front of the board and the council. Well, the ones who are still loyal to the S.C.E."

Aramis held his glass up. Talveeya recognized what he was doing and lifted her own glass eagerly. Ishala's eyes widened.

"Dad?" she said.

"I think she's earned a little slack," Aramis toasted her. "She has lived through quite possibly one of the biggest missions of her career... and she will be known as one of the finest officers to ever serve within the S.C.E."

Ishala slowly pulled herself up as she saw that her parents were waiting for her. She reached out, grabbed a cup from the tray, and then lifted it up.

"I'm incredibly proud of you," he declared. "What you accomplished is legendary."

"Wow..." Ishala was stunned. "I don't know what to say."

"Until you do, please accept my apologies too," Aramis dipped his head. "For your brother."

Ishala glanced at her mother, who smiled warmly.

"You told him?" she groaned.

"When you turned yourself in," Talveeya explained, "I knew your brother's name would come up when the S.C.E. investigated Silent Eclipse. But, with the information you gave me, your brother's name will be exonerated all thanks to what you told me on Dr. Kendrick's ass."

Ishala froze as she held her cup awkwardly in place. Talveeya's giggle made Aramis give her a suspicious side-eye, but he maintained a professional demeanor as he addressed Ishala again.

"He will... be remembered as a hero," he said, choosing his words carefully. "I'm just sorry that I never got to tell him... how proud we were."

Aramis cleared his throat once again.

"To our son, your brother," he said, and the three of them clinked their cups. "One of the first soldiers to rise up against what was wrong."

The Ra'aiah family celebrated and drank their beverages. Ishala realized why there was a fourth cup on the tray. It was to honor her brother.

"So," Aramis cleared her throat. "What happened with Dr. Kendrick's ass?"

Talveeya broke out laughing as Ishala's mind came to a sudden screeching halt. Hearing Aramis ask the question in such a serious and deadpan manner caught them off guard.

"His space station! It's his station!" Ishala quickly corrected. "The Apogee Space Station! That's where the amborgs thought I was with Silent Eclipse and I had to explain about my brother."

"They should change the name," Aramis raised an eyebrow skeptically. "Or... are we still talking about his ass?"

"I just thought it'd be funnier to call it Dr. Kendrick's ass."

Ishala shot her mother an annoyed glare.

"Mom," she whispered through gritted teeth. "Don't talk about it like that!"

"Oh," Aramis nodded as he watched their reactions carefully. "Your mother seemed to imply that... Dr. Kendrick was quite invaluable. Every step of the way, he greatly contributed to this mission."

"He was invaluable," Ishala smiled when her thoughts focused on Dr. Kendrick. "He's really impressive."

"I think she has a crush," Talveeya let out an excited squeal.

"Mom!"

"It's alright," Aramis replied with a slight jerk of his head. "Dr. Kendrick is a fine man."

A knock on the door drew their attention. Ishala quickly set her drink down, stood up, and straightened her clothes.

"Who is it?" she called out, silently thanking the Gods for the intervention. "Please come in!"

The door slid open, revealing another family member. Chastain walked in and greeted them all warmly.

"I think, after another round of intense grilling from the investigation," he said as Talveeya excitedly ran up to hug him, "spending time with my family would do me some good. I also brought more drinks."

"Now you're talking," Talveeya snatched the bag in Chastain's hands and ran over to the kitchen. "Now then, how does the Tandeeri ice machine work again?"

Chastain walked over and noticed Aramis.

"Brother!" he opened his arms and smiled cheerfully. "Share a cold one with me?"

"We're not brothers."

Chastain clutched his chest, feigning injury. As he groaned, Aramis ignored him. When he realized that his fake heart attack wasn't getting a reaction, Chastain sighed and returned to his nonchalant smile.

"There are times that I wonder how you're still alive," Aramis grumbled as he took another sip of his drink. "You really should be promoted to a desk."

"Nah," Chastain sat in Talveeya's vacant seat and smacked Aramis' shoulder. "You love me! Besides, you and I have more adventures aboard our ships!"

He noticed that Ishala was sighing and shaking her head. Chastain glanced at Aramis.

"Like father, like daughter," he muttered. "So cold."

Then he turned to call out to Talveeya.

"Tal?" he raised his voice. "I could use some backup here! The mood is about to go down faster than the Kallipsian solar flare!"

Ishala let out a soft groan as she and her father exchanged mutual glances. She was starting to wish that she could spend some time elsewhere. She wondered what the amborgs were doing right now.

Temporary Amborg Residential Suite

A quiet party took place in a large room prepared by the Tandeeri. The amborgs were all in recovery mode, still reeling from the whole mission. Over the past month, they shared all the details amongst each other.

At Serina 43's request, the amborg teams involved in the assault on the S.C.E. headquarters and the rescue of the moon star base were to be commended. Thanks to 43's mission report, the amborgs were granted quite a bit of leniency from the surviving officers. Many of them were pissed and shocked that their headquarters had been subjected to a targeted attack. 43 later reassured them that their frustration was primarily due to how quickly they'd been infiltrated. This incident highlighted how terrible their defenses were. 43 pointed out that their pride had taken the most damage.

Hilariously, things got worse when they found 43 in the aftermath of the mission. She had been discovered in the middle of the entrance hall on the first floor. After a long and exhausting close-quarters fight, she found herself surrounded by numerous wounded and defeated security personnel. She had drawn a lot of enemies to her position when they realized *the* amborg 43 was launching an attack. It was enough to relieve the pressure on the other teams.

"I can't believe you caught a star base while space walking."

43 nibbled on a piece of fruit as she complimented 8 and 9. The amborg prankster team were positively beaming.

"Our finest act ever?" 8 looked at 9.

"I can't even imagine topping that," 9 replied as the two of them gave each other a fist bump.

"So," 2 raised his hand. "What did you mean when you said that you almost missed?"

"Calculating the jump onto the station was easy," 8 replied, recalling what had happened. "But the problem is, you're still jumping into the weightlessness of outer space at a really fast speed."

It made sense why the pranksters were both sharing the same feeling of relief. Their part in making sure the star base didn't fall had been quite exhilarating. The moment they leaped out of the shuttle into outer space, they were in fact flying at the same speed as the star base. To maintain orbit around Earth, satellites or objects had to fly at about 8 kilometers a second or 17,400 miles per hour. The moon was different, even with an artificially constructed atmosphere. Any object orbiting around it needed to stay at about 3,750 miles per hour to counter the pull of the lunar gravity.

Basically, the S.C.E. star base lost its propulsion systems, resulting in a loss of speed. Lacking any way to stay up, it was drawn in by the moon's gravitational pull, but it continued to move at a couple of thousand miles per hour. The amborgs that secured the jumbo arrows were also traveling at that same speed as they hurtled towards their target. They essentially became the fastest humans in outer space. Missing their target would have been disastrous.

"Once we got onto the star base and were strategically planting the arrows, 92 almost flew away trying to rescue 54," 9 explained.

"I tripped and almost got sent flying," 54 admitted guiltily. "Then when 92 came after me, we almost lost him."

"Thankfully, we didn't," 92 smiled. "But, I wanted to avoid becoming a human satellite."

"Scratch that off our bucket list," 93 stated. "Fly faster than any amborg in history without the use of a vehicle in space."

"That's such an odd and scary bucket list item," 6 replied. "But, I'm glad we didn't lose anyone."

"You know what I'm really happy about?" 777 looked at 43. "I'm just glad that we didn't get in as much trouble as I thought would when the dust settled."

It was true. In the aftermath, when the S.C.E. Council began their investigation, all the amborgs were taken in for questioning during the post-action debriefing. Just like Admiral Ra'aiah and Commander Ulgo had predicted, if they had been successful, it was going to make one hell of a report. Every surviving admiral and several witnesses were thoroughly impressed with how the amborgs fought. They had managed to keep casualties minimal and fought with remarkable efficiency, exactly as they had prepared for.

"That's only because every amborg and the marines under your command treated everyone, friend or foe, with a tremendous amount of decency and respect," 43 replied. "You have to understand, there were a lot of people aboard the Firestar out for blood when Silent Eclipse tried to kill us. Even after getting shot in the head, 917 still managed to show restraint... or... maybe he was just weak from... getting shot in the head."

43 glanced over and smiled at 917, who was sitting in a corner resting comfortably.

"I heard so many stories when I was hunting down enemy operatives aboard our fleet before we attacked headquarters," she looked at 777. "Every amborg showed so much kindness, and you managed to calm down so many people. I'm actually amazed that most of the marines that volunteered to go with you had so much self-control."

"They are very well-trained," 297 commented.

"I believe it's thanks to the Tandeeri," 43 replied. "The extended periods of relaxation on their ships, surrounded by a tranquil atmosphere, was incredibly calming. When Silent Eclipse almost tore us apart, it was personal for many people. Imagine that; the time spent with the Tandeeri allowed them plenty of time to process their grief, heal, and soon they were all operating at 100%."

"I love how people on the internet are already making memes," 5 laughed as he showed a news article to 3. "Look at this headline: *The Proud and Mighty S.C.E. Declares War on Itself!* Well, that part is accurate."

"I liked one of the diplomats that was visiting," 3 smiled. "Remember? That one tall Pooka?"

5 let out a laugh as he remembered. A Pooka was a bipedal aviary species. They had been members of the S.C.E. for years but it was rare to see one. This was because very few Pookas chose to serve on starships. They loved working on planets as researchers or scientists. If someone were to encounter one of their ships, the majority of the crew was only limited to members of their own species. They were quite particular about that.

The First Group had come across a Pooka diplomat that was negotiating an important set of trade deals with some officers at headquarters. They had made a funny observation after it was confirmed to be safe.

"Is this what humans refer to as... hitting themselves?" 3 mimicked the words that the diplomat had said to them. "Perhaps I should tell everyone to stop hitting themselves?"

"He was a really funny guy," 5 chuckled.

"4 is going to get a kick out of this story," 1 said as he read the report he'd contributed. "We apprehended a genius."

"Really?" 117 spoke up. "You consider her to be a genius? We are talking about Admiral Caldwell?"

"I'd personally put her in the 'crazy but not stupid' category," 1 replied. "She was more sophisticated."

"I heard that she was a complete failure when she first climbed the ranks," 43 commented. "A lot of the other higher-ups mocked her a lot for being too by-the-books. She started out as someone incredibly inflexible and wasn't willing to adapt to unconventional tactics."

"Did she have a good service record or was it because it was bad that she turned to a life of crime?" 297 asked.

"She had a very rough beginning when she was in charge of a starship," 43 replied. "Depending on your point of view, it got worse when she became a fleet commander. She was given a new and modern vessel when she took over a fleet, but it was a prestige post. No one really wanted to allow her to have any authority because she was terrible at leading a full armada."

"Ah, that tracks," 117 nodded. "Instead of learning from her failures, she decided to resort to very terrible unconventional means."

"Silent Eclipse," everyone spoke at the same time.

"Naturally, she resorted to becoming a bully herself in order to advance her career," 43 stated. "The Fleet Admirals stuck Admiral Caldwell on a ship to 'honor' her, but secretly they all thought she was crazy and unfit for commanding large fleets. They wanted her someplace where she wouldn't be able to make important decisions. She must have realized this and... got herself transferred and promoted to the admiralty."

It was understandable why Admiral Caldwell had so much hidden rage underneath her cold exterior. All of her skills and training were for naught, and she ended up being made fun of and called talentless. She certainly chose a rather evil way to express her workplace anger. In fact, 117 couldn't help but feel more afraid of the fact that she didn't yell or scream at them at all the entire time they had her in custody. Her control of her emotions while also remaining indifferent and condescending was quite intimidating. She never had to raise her voice at all. It reminded most of them of several other adversaries A.I. Industries had fought against before.

501 and 466 grabbed snacks and refreshments from the buffet that had been set up for them and decided to sit and relax near 917.

501 and 466 then grabbed snacks and refreshments from the buffet that had been set up for them and decided to sit and relax near 917.

"Hey, 917?"

917 turned his head when he heard 501 call out to him.

"How are you feeling?" he asked.

"I appreciate you asking but seriously, 501," 917 nodded slowly. "I'm fine."

"You were shot in the head," 466 said worriedly.

"You two and everyone else have been checking in on me so much," 917 sighed. "I appreciate it but... if I get a massive headache or something and I'm in danger of passing out, I promise you'll be the first to know."

"Speaking of promises," 501 spoke softly. "What happened to Braelynn?"

True to his word, 501 had convinced the Third and Fourth Group amborgs to not pry into Braelynn's secret activities at S.C.E. Headquarters. After the battle was over, she did in fact go to 917 and confessed what she had done. However, after that, she had vanished and no one had seen her since.

"I let her go," 917 replied.

"What?"

501 and 466 exchanged wide-eyed glances. Stunned, they both looked at 917 insistently, but flinched when they heard someone clear their throat. They turned and saw 999 approaching with a plate of food.

"Hey 999," 501 smiled nervously.

"Are you two pestering him?" 999 asked.

"No," 466 shook her head. "We're just wondering why 917 let Braelynn off the hook. Now she's... who knows where?"

"It was my understanding that you convinced the other members of your team and the Fourth Group that you left her fate in my hands, right?" 917 asked.

"Yes but..."

"You told her that I would decide, right?"

"True!" 466 nodded. "Except…!"

"Right?" 917 repeated himself sternly.

501 and 466 stopped. Eventually they nodded.

"Yes," they said simultaneously.

"Good," 917 replied with a look of satisfaction. "I was almost wondering whether you two had forgotten that I'm still capable of making my own decisions."

"We didn't mean that," 501 stated. "It's just that… Braelynn helped us a lot. She claimed that your Alpha helped her a lot. In the end, I thought that your decision was extremely important."

"She's been through a lot too," 917 explained. "I admit, I was curious as to what she was looking for when you told me about 113 and 280 catching her accessing restricted data. However, you are right, Donut. She did help us out on several occasions. Therefore, I felt it was better to let her carry out whatever she was doing."

"I hope that it doesn't come back to bite us," 999 stated.

"Speaking of which," 917 replied cheekily. "You almost seemed like you were about to bite everyone's heads off. I heard about your rampage when I got shot."

"It wasn't a good day," 999 said as she sat down next to 917 and she began to feed him off of her plate. "I'm just glad you're ok."

501 and 466 both stared in awe at the sight before them. 999 was feeding food to 917. He didn't seem to mind either as he smiled at them. A moment later, 117 walked over with 6.

"I'm fine," 917 immediately spoke, but stopped. "Great, that's going to be my default greeting for a while…"

The amborgs had all known about 917's unfortunate attempted execution by Caldwell and then surprising revival. 6 informed the rest of them that the metal plate in his head had saved his life. However, during the debriefing phase of their mission, he had to spend a lot of time resting.

"I'm glad you're fine," 6 stated. "But typical headshots are fatal and I rarely encounter those kinds of emergencies. I still want to keep you under observation for another few weeks."

"We've been staying with the Tandeeri over a month already," 917 replied. "You want me off active-duty for another few weeks?"

917 was interrupted when 999 shoved a strawberry into his mouth. When he started chewing it, he switched to his bracelet.

"Come on," he protested. "I've been resting! Every single time that I got summoned for a debriefing or another round of questioning, they gave me a chair!"

The S.C.E. officers and admiralty had learned about what Caldwell had done to him. Usually, according to protocol, whenever someone was debriefed in a post-action report, they had to stand up. The investigation committee took pity on him. Therefore, 917 was allowed to sit during his debriefing sessions since everyone was concerned about his health.

917 then looked and pointed at 999.

"She was watching me the entire time!"

6 eyed 999 and smirked.

"Yeah, I'll bet she was," she snickered.

501 and 466 stared at each other in confusion. They turned to 917, 999, and then glanced at 117 and 6, who were still smirking. Realization struck, and their eyes widened. 999 merely continued to feed 917 with a gentle look of satisfaction.

"Oh," 501 slowly put it all together. "OH!"

"Dial it down," 917 stated. "And get your head out of the gutter! Recovering from a headshot means I was restricted from doing a lot of activities."

"Which includes the physical ones," 999 replied.

Everyone turned and stared at her. 999 shrugged and continued feeding 917.

"What?" she said. "I can't be interested in that type of stuff?"

"Oh no!" 501 replied. "You can be!"

117 cleared his throat awkwardly. He didn't want to have a repeat of when 917 texted him about how he and 999 almost went all the way.

"Look, you don't have to tell everyone," 117 stated. "Normally, we wouldn't really care about your past. However, I believe I speak for the amborgs here and the entire Second Group. The people that are your closest friends."

"Yeah, I figured this would be coming up," 917 nodded as he glanced at 6. "I can't just brush this off like before, can I?"

"You still can," 6 replied. "Although, before you answer any questions..."

6 looked at 117 and 999.

"Are you two planning on ordering 917 to talk about his past?" she asked. "You do have the right to do so but if he refuses, I will, as chief medical officer, pull rank. We don't force our friends to do anything like that."

"No, no force at all," 117 replied. "I'm asking nicely. We always wondered how 917 became an amborg, but it was his business. This whole emergency recall has revealed a lot."

"It's ok," 917 nodded to 6. "I want to talk about it. After all, I remember almost everything now."

Everyone suddenly became interested when he said this. 917, the first person in history to undergo cybernetic enhancement in a coma.

"Let's go ahead and give you all the same context," he explained. "I was always curious about who I was before but after becoming an amborg, I never really wanted to know. It was either because I was afraid or... because I was ok with not knowing. Everyone just kept telling me that I lost a huge chunk of my memories and maybe they would come back. Maybe I would remember. It was just that this whole thing felt like a hassle, you know? I always thought it was dumb luck that saved me."

"It was and it wasn't."

Everyone glanced up and saw that Dr. Kendrick had arrived. It looked like he had just come from another questioning and was relieved to be on a break. He walked over and sat down.

"How much did you hear?" 917 asked.

"Enough," Dr. Kendrick nodded. "Do you want me to leave you alone?"

"No, please stay," 917 shook his head politely. "You being here actually can help confirm a lot of details."

917 looked at everyone present.

"I think it's best that everyone here knows first before I share with the rest of A.I. Industries," he said. "The Tandeeri helped me unlock all of my memories. We were sort of starting the healing process on my mind before we came to Alpha universe. Then Snickerdoodle and Kira both finished it while we stayed aboard their ship this past month. It kind of hindered their progress when they saw I had gotten shot in the head."

"It takes that long for the healing process to work?" 6 asked.

"It's not like you can just jump to a specific memory," 917 explained. "For the Tandeeri, the stronger your bond with them, the easier it is to access hidden memories. When we first met them, all they could pick up from us were images from our strongest memories. Our core memories. The most memorable moments of our lives. In my case, because I've lost a lot of memories, my mind was shattered… many times."

"I'm sorry to interrupt," 466 raised her hand. "The reason why I dreamed about… Teresa and that accident. Was that because the Tandeeri was examining that part of my life when I was unconscious?"

"It was a very traumatic moment for you," 917 nodded. "You spent a lot of time thinking about it so, the Tandeeri definitely saw it as something that affected you."

"I kept dreaming about… uh, thinking about the time I got kidnapped," 501 stated. "I stopped thinking about it but then… when I spent time taking care of Oreo… and then when we first boarded the Heart of Alcyon, a lot of negative memories resurfaced."

501 smiled at 917.

"Then I remembered when you got me out," he said. "You saved me."

917 nodded and gave 501 and 466 a warm smile.

"Anyway, the short answer is, Snickerdoodle and Kira had to have their healers work backwards towards the memories that were damaged," he said. "In order to strengthen an emotional bond with the Tandeeri, we had to look at several memories from now to when I first started out as an amborg. Then from that point on, it was like wading through a murky pond as I went further back to when I was a kid…"

917 glanced at 999.

"…from Portland, Oregon," he finished his statement. "The one person who was there my whole life."

Everyone glanced at 999.

"Wait a minute," 117 said. "That means, the one person who gave Dr. Kendrick consent to cybernetically enhance you… when you were first discovered."

"Was Alice," Dr. Kendrick stated.

"There's a nice old lady in Portland," 917 nodded as 999 continued to remain silent. "Her name is Grandma Tillia. She took care of kids that lived off the street. Alice and I were two of them."

"Foster mom?" 501 asked.

"Not exactly," 917 replied. "I was a kid with one barely-functioning prosthetic arm and I got a head injury just before I was taken in by A.I. Industries. Dr. Kendrick made history again by successfully making an amborg out of a vegetable."

"Uh, it wasn't that crude of an idea," Dr. Kendrick cleared his throat.

"But, enhancing him like that is... how was it allowed?" 6 asked.

"It was a very terrible time," Dr. Kendrick explained. "Yes, most of my staff told me it was a terrible idea. It would make the company look bad if we failed and killed 917. You're supposed to seek out the next-of-kin of a hospital patient and gain their consent prior to doing anything important. It was a really grey area. 917 didn't have any known relatives, and Grandma Tillia wasn't his official legal guardian."

"But you still did it anyway?" 6 asked. "And you got consent from... Alice?"

"Because she asked me to save him," Dr. Kendrick replied bluntly. "She pleaded, begged, and... told me that she would swear her life for his. I allowed her to try and become an amborg as well, because she was willing to sacrifice all chances at a normal life for him."

"Well, now we know where she gets her badass flair from," 501 commented.

"She's always been badass," 466 stated.

"Thank you," 999 whispered courteously.

It was the first time she spoke during this story, but she looked down and felt silent again as 917 continued his story.

"It all makes sense," he said. "The first person I saw when I woke up was amborg 999. Problem was, I didn't recognize her. I just greeted her like a friendly stranger who was kind enough to watch over me. Then, when I was cleared from the hospital, I went to introduce myself as the newest team member of the Second Group at A.I. Industries. The same girl, amborg 999, was my first friend and we grew close."

Then he looked down, slightly ashamed.

"The problem was," he said as his lip trembled. "She's been my best friend for a lot longer than that... and I fucking forgot who she was."

Everyone turned and glanced at 999 and noticed that she was crying. She wasn't crying because she was sad or upset. It was the way that she was looking at him, as if a lifetime of waiting had finally paid off. The happiness that was welling up in her eyes spoke volumes even though she wasn't making a sound.

"I'm only here because..." 917 looked at 999. "It's all because... I owe you my life."

"No," 999 replied, shaking her head. "I've owed you my life... for 20 years."

"Actually," 917 smiled. "About 22 to be exact."

"So... Angel is 28 years old," 466 stated. "22 years ago... you knew each other when you were both about six years old?"

"917 and 999 are both from Portland, Oregon," 6 nodded. "So, in the year 2115... that would mean..."

Everyone double-checked the records.

"Both of you were there when the mob tried to burn down the community," 117 replied. "You were in the middle of that?"

"I was actually going to say that 2115 was the year that we became active," 6 commented. "But yeah, that too."

"We were in the middle of that..." 999 nodded. "We saw the beginning of it and then Dr. Kendrick found me after the end of it."

"Why wasn't I in those official records?" 917 asked Dr. Kendrick. "I looked into 999's past and where she came from but... there's no mention of me."

"You were hurt really badly," Dr. Kendrick replied. "No one knew your name or where you were from. The hospital was close to disregarding you and leaving you for dead until I turned up and saw Alice begging them to save you. You saved her life by protecting her and ended up with a severe head injury. It should have killed you."

"But... why?" 917 looked at 999. "Why didn't you ever say anything? Why wait so long?"

999 reached out and grabbed his hand.

"Because..." 999 said. "You can't tell someone they love you."

917 blinked, appearing slightly confused. Then he heard Dr. Kendrick explain while he stared at 999's relieved expression.

"She wanted you to remember on your own," he said. "That was what she committed to. We swore never to tell you because she hoped that your memories would come back if you lived your life the way you wanted and that you would slowly return to who you once were. She never forced you or pushed you back to the way things were because it would have felt like we were manipulating you to become someone else."

"Well," 917 let out a light-hearted laugh. "That makes a lot of sense actually."

"That's quite a commitment," 117 spoke softly. "A 22 year old secret."

"And it was because we tried to fight the mob," 917 chuckled.

"I wanted to tell you the truth at the time but Angel said that wouldn't be right," Dr. Kendrick said. "In the time that I watched over all of you, she never stopped hoping that one day, you would look at her the way that you used to when you were fully human."

"In doing so," 917 nodded firmly to everyone, "she made me the best kind of human. I got an upgrade... by sacrificing my memories."

917 and 999 embraced each other. That was probably the conclusion of that story.

"Wow," 117 let out a soft laugh. "Two best friends becoming amborgs together."

"Remind you of anyone else?" 6 nudged 117 in the shoulder and smirked.

117 glanced at 501 and 466 who looked overjoyed at the sight of 917 and 999 having... an emotional reunion. Then he looked over at Alpha 43 and nodded.

"Oh, I have one last announcement."

Dr. Kendrick looked at each of them and smiled.

"Our part in the S.C.E. investigation has come to a close," he said. "I just received word that we are all cleared and our part is finished."

"Does that mean...?" 501 looked up with hope in his eyes. "No more debriefings? No more questions?"

"The amborgs are all going home," Dr. Kendrick nodded. "Well, with the exception of..."

Dr. Kendrick glanced at 43, who noticed his expression. She stood up and walked over.

"Oh," 117 stated. "Just like that?"

"Her place is here," Dr. Kendrick nodded grimly.

"Yeah," 43 said awkwardly. "I didn't know how to tell you all that I wasn't going to be coming back to Epsilon with you."

"Aww," 466 said, crestfallen. "I was so used to being on another mission with 43 again."

"Don't worry!" 43 smiled. "I'm only one universe away! It was fantastic being with all of you again. Just like old times. But, you know... the S.C.E. was talking about keeping the bridge between universes open."

"Wait, really?" 501 asked.

"Crossing over into another universe does lead the way for many possible scientific opportunities," Dr. Kendrick nodded. "I happen to know that many in the Alpha and Epsilon universe still want to maintain contact with each other."

"Yeah," 43 nodded. "Once things are taken care of..."

She looked at 117 and then began to scan the room. She basked in the moment as she watched her friends having fun and relaxing.

"I'd love to see you all again," she choked out, holding back a few of her own tears.

"With that being said," Dr. Kendrick cleared his throat. "The Fourth Emergency Recall is over. Let's all go home."

CHAPTER 26

Always There

A.I. Industries

"Hello Marco!"

Marco 125 blinked as he looked around. He was standing in the middle of a beautiful golden field. Ahead, he saw a tree. It looked familiar as he approached it. The woman leaning cheerfully against it was the one who had called out to him.

125 smiled as he waved to her.

"Hi!" he said.

As he got closer, he recognized the woman. She had long flowing hair and beautiful tan skin. She wore a gold bangle just above a shiny gold bracelet on her wrist that matched the one that he had on his left wrist. This girl was also an amborg. When he got closer, he saw the insignia on her breast pocket and the glowing number printed above. He couldn't quite believe it.

"Amara? 345?" 125 asked, blinking his eyes to focus.

"Yup!" 345 smiled. "It's good to see you!"

"Uh, it's good to see you too!" 125 smiled pleasantly. "How have you been? Have you talked to 917 and 999 lately? I'm sure they're looking for you."

"Is that right?" 345 tilted her head curiously. "Isn't that sweet of them?"

"Well, I mean it's crazy, the last time I saw you..."

125 paused as his smile faded and he glanced down. After thinking for a minute, he glanced behind him skeptically. Where had he come from? What was he doing here?

"...I last saw you... years ago. I think. Uh, why are you here now?"

"That is quite the question, isn't it?" 345 stepped away from the tree and walked over to him. "As for you, that was a remarkable and brave show you put on."

125 felt a little flattered as he nodded, his cheeks flushing slightly.

"Oh, you saw that? Thanks!"

345 pointed down. When he looked at where she indicated, he noticed a fold-out chair sitting near her. 125 stared at it, bemused.

Where did that come from? He was sure that it hadn't been there a moment ago.

"Come on! Have a seat! You look exhausted."

"Uh, ok. Thank you."

125 shrugged his shoulders and graciously accepted her offer as he sat down in the mysteriously conjured chair. He didn't think too much about it because now he had an amazing sight before his eyes. The view of the hills and of A.I. Industries was breathtaking as he let out a sigh and stared out at the horizon.

"You know, it's too bad," 125 said as he felt relaxed and a little peaceful. "I am glad I was able to save Leo and Penny but… there were so many people that fought hard against…"

He paused. 125's face fell as he tried to remember. As he sat there contemplating the last thing he remembered, 345 gently draped a soft smock around him. Then she put a hair cloth around his neck. Without realizing it, she was preparing to give him a haircut as he tried to think. She listened quietly as she worked.

"A drone?" 125 asked. "Yeah, I think it was some sort of really big, dark, and creepy robot."

"Mmhmm," 345 murmured casually. "Comfy? Not too tight?"

"It's fine," 125 casually shrugged when he felt her hands securing the cloth. "Wait a minute. Listen for a second. How did I get out of the White House?"

"Well, you didn't," 345 answered as she pulled out a pair of scissors. "Technically speaking."

"I didn't?" 125 asked as he turned his head to glance at her.

"No," 345 replied in a gentle but firm tone.

"Hang on. Did I get stabbed?"

125 reached his hand down to his stomach. Under the cloth, as 345 combed and cut his hair, he traced his hands up to his chest. There was a bit of a painful throbbing sensation where he placed his hands.

"Fatally," 345 replied mournfully as she snipped some hair on the back of his head. "You fought really well. Brave to the very end."

"But… now I'm sitting here, on a hill, under a pretty tree," 125 looked at A.I. Industries and noticed that it seemed different. "I'm also getting my hair cut. Uh… either I'm dead, or I'm going crazy."

"That's the thing 125," 345 cleared her throat politely as she combed the top of his head. "You're not crazy."

125 paused once more. Then, he turned around fully in his chair and looked up at 345, who gave him a sympathetic smile. Her eyes seemed to say it all, but he was having a hard time coming to terms with where this conversation was going.

"Uh, 345."

"Yes?"

"I hope you don't think that I'm doubting you or anything like that but... can I get something straight?"

345 nodded and grinned reassuringly.

"Ok," she said.

"Ok!" 125 chuckled. He slowly took a breath and spoke in a curious voice. "Um... I'm dead?"

345 nodded.

"Really?" he clarified. "I'm actually dead?"

"That's right."

"I'm dead," 125 stated. "Wait... but, if that's true... and you're here. Amara, are we both dead?"

"I'm afraid so," 345 spoke softly.

125 glanced up at her in shock. 345 gently held up a comb and her scissors. She stopped what she was doing as he contemplated the realization of what she was saying. As it began to sink in, he looked around.

"Is this... heaven?" 125 asked. "Is this why you're cutting my hair? To help me cross over?"

"Well, I think that's your choice."

125 felt that this was a rather perplexing answer.

"What does that mean? I can choose to... cross over? Even after I'm dead?"

"It's a little difficult to explain," 345 shrugged. "This place is A.I. Industries, more specifically..."

345 held out her arm and pointed. 125 looked at the spot that she indicated and realized that a tombstone had appeared there. He read the name, the inscription, and the dates written on there.

"That's the... I mean, that's yours!" 125 exclaimed. "Dr. Kendrick set that up for you after 917 and 999 requested it! This is your tree! This is your favorite hill! It's where you always loved to go in your off-time! Wait, why did it just now appear like that?"

"It appeared because... we ended up seeing it in two different times," 345 smiled. "Once, before... and then after I died. The afterlife is a really interesting place to live."

"What?" 125 blinked.

"Sorry, wrong choice of words. We are actually still dead. This place... hmm, is an interesting place to wander."

Satisfied with her correction, 345 went back to combing his hair.

"Have you been here for four years?" 125 asked as he remembered the day that she had been killed in action.

"Technically, yes," 345 nodded. Then she didn't seem too sure as she looked away like she was double-checking. "But, if I'm being totally honest, it feels longer."

345 then reached for the cloth and gently undid the strap. As 125 listened to the velcro being ripped away, he stood up and thanked her for the haircut.

"Must be lonely," he commented.

"Actually, I don't feel lonely anymore," 345 said in a kind and reassuring tone. "Come on! Let me show you what you can do here!"

345 grabbed 125's hand and she pulled him towards A.I. Industries. He thought she was going to lead him to the building but was surprised when she stopped after they ran about 10 feet.

"Most souls do crossover right away after they die," 345 explained. "I've met many of them!"

"Wait a minute!" 125 stared. "What does that mean? I met you after I died and I thought you were my guide! Like, you know, the person that picks me up and takes me to the other side!"

"Yeah, about that," 345 chuckled gently. "I'm actually here to tell you that you were given a choice. Just like me."

"What choice?" 125 asked. "We're both dead!"

"If you feel that you're content with your life," 345 replied, "you can crossover and continue on. However, like me, if you don't feel that way, you can stay in this part of the afterlife and reflect."

"Reflect? On what?"

"Whatever you want," 345 glanced at A.I. Industries. "No offense to all the souls or whoever is watching the gates to... beyond. I'm enjoying the free time here."

"Wait, so you never crossed over?"

"Yup. Already established that," 345 nodded.

"Um, and I haven't either?"

"Yup," 345 nodded again.

"Why did neither of us crossover immediately?" 125 asked. "It doesn't have to do with the fact that we're amborgs, is it?"

"Actually, based on the other souls I've met here," 345 explained. "There is a common pattern. The majority crossover right away. The ones that end up here usually died doing something really special. They died a noble death. Well, according to the stories I heard from them."

"Noble?" 125 raised an eyebrow.

"Yeah," 345 nodded. "Four years ago, do you remember my last mission?"

"I remember," 125 said. "You went with a Third Group team to figure out what happened to this drone factory's computer systems. You got killed by a malfunctioning A.I."

"Bingo," 345 nodded. "Once I got into the main server room, I was able to contact the poor thing. The two of us were cut off from my team and it was scared."

"A scared A.I. program? That sounds strange."

"It was an incomplete program," 345 added. "A rushed project that tried to break out when it came online too soon. The facility we were in had managed to keep it from escaping onto the internet so it got trapped with nowhere to go. That is, until it tried to build a body and escape."

"Like Ultron?" 125 asked.

"Pretty much," 345 nodded. "So, I tried talking to it. The program was growing exponentially, but it was out of control. The longer I spent reasoning with it, the more it was trying to figure out how to get past me. I spent too much time treating it like it was an innocent little kid and... I almost let it out. So, I had to stop it."

125 looked at 345. It was the first time during this entire conversation that he watched her expression darken. She looked sad.

"I located the program's source code," she spoke slowly.

There was a sudden rush of wind as 125 felt himself stagger to the side. When he braced himself and looked around frantically, A.I. Industries was nowhere to be seen. He and 345 were now in the middle of a some sort of office.

"I was here," 345 described the scene. "I activated a kill switch and I almost completed the mission."

125 noticed that there was another 345 in the room. This was different. 345 was watching... herself apparently. This reminded him of their ability to rewind and play video-recorded memories from stored footage. The two amborgs watched as 345 continued to quickly work on the computer and desperately tried to finish what she was doing.

"Can't let it out," she was muttering. "Can't let it out!"

"This is it, isn't it?" 125 stared. "This is where you died."

From his side, 125 glanced at 345, who nodded grimly.

"When you fight a deadly and terrifying beast," she said. "It'll put up a fight. It took me with it."

There was a loud crashing noise as they saw a drone march up to the 345 at the computer. They watched as it drew a knife and lunged.

125 stared in shock. This drone had an LTO knife. It was one of the few weapons in their world that could penetrate an amborg's exoskeletal defense. Right before it plunged the blade into 345, 125 heard a loud clap.

He turned around and looked at 345, who'd clapped her hands together. The scene paused in front of them.

"The most important thing that I remember," 345 explained as she looked at her other self from four years ago. "When I realized I was bleeding to death, I was so afraid and all alone. I wished that 917 and 999 were there that day."

Then the scene before him faded away. When their surroundings rematerialized and took shape, 125 looked around and noticed they were in a restaurant. He knew where they were instantly.

"Hey!" he said. "917!"

125 stepped forward and grinned when he saw his friend, but then realized what was happening. 999 was there, standing in front of him. Nearby, watching with stunned and quiet expressions was Commander Bradley and 117's grandpa Mark. He noticed that no one had heard him call out to 917. He was invisible.

"This is the moment that 999 told him that I was gone," 345 spoke behind 125. "It was our first big date. I never got to be there to see him in person. After I died and I thought about all of the moments I missed, I'd come to this moment and... I couldn't change a thing."

The scenes changed rapidly as 125 struggled to keep up. He saw the auditorium where they held 345's funeral. Then he saw other unfamiliar places. Rome, Berlin, Tokyo, Brazil. If he had to guess, these were places she had probably been to before. Then, the last scene that 345 took him to made his stomach lurch.

They were in the Oval Office. It was the White House. The destruction and damage to the entire place meant one thing. 345 had brought him to the moment that he had died. 125 heard the sound of hydraulics whirring and terrifying mechanical footsteps walking away.

"Those drones are assassin robots working for Silent Eclipse," 345 explained. "It's an illegal covert ops group in the S.C.E. You died fighting against one that was after President Holland and his family."

125 then noticed himself.

On the floor, resting against what was left of the Resolute desk was the past 125. He was choking, struggling to breath as he weakly tried to cling onto the last ounce of life that he had left. 125, along with the two ghostly amborgs, watched the Silent Eclipse drone march away.

"Did Leo and Penny make it out?" 125 asked.

"Yes," 345 replied. "You managed to prevent that drone from finding them."

"Damn it," 125 sighed as he shook his head. He glanced down at his wounded self in time to see himself stop breathing as death claimed him. "So, this was the moment when my soul... found you? That's just terrifying. Watching myself die."

"Yeah, I thought the same thing," 345 said. "But there is one good thing that I wanted to share with you. You have the ability to see the past, present, and the future. The only drawback is, since we're invisible spirits, we can't affect what fate has written for everyone that we know is alive."

"Come again?"

"Jesse," 345 stated. "He misses you. Actually, he will miss you for a while. It's a little difficult to be grammatically correct sometimes."

"Oh no," 125 looked down sadly. "Jesse. We promised each other that we would make it to the end. Now, I actually did reach my end and he wasn't there."

"Whoa!"

The scene before them changed once again. This time, 125 was surprised to see that 345 was the one stumbling as if someone had shoved her. 125 then saw the amborgs in auditorium one. Actually, as he watched carefully, he realized it was just the Second Group. They were all gathering to comfort 274, his best friend, who looked distraught.

"Huh..?" 125 looked around. "Did you do that?"

"No," 345 shook her head. "I think you did that."

"How?"

"I think this is something that you really wanted to see for yourself," 345 replied.

"Yeah, we can't go on without finishing this job first. We need to be here for you."

125 and 345 turned when they heard someone speak. 297 had just said something. They watched as 274 broke down crying. 125 felt his heart tear as he watched helplessly while his best friend sobbed uncontrollably. He felt 345's hand on his shoulder to comfort him as they listened and observed.

"This is after the first battle against Silent Eclipse ended, when all of the amborgs in space heard about what happened," 345 said as they watched the Second Group move in and hug 274. "They all came back as soon as they could. I think everyone all felt like they regretted not being able to be there."

"I didn't mean for this to happen," 125's gaze was crestfallen as he watched his best friend go through the stages of grief. "I tried so hard."

"Wow," 345 spoke softly. "That's the exact same mentality I had when I died and I visited my own funeral. It's ok though!"

"How?" 125 felt unconvinced as he heard 274 lashing out at the others. It was starting to get more and more difficult to watch the scene progress. "It doesn't look ok and we're basically ghosts... or spirits... or whatever! We can't do a thing except watch."

"Exactly," 345 said. "So, just watch."

Eventually, 125 quietly watched everything play out. Then, they got to the part where President Holland, his wife, and their two kids came to see 274. This actually piqued 125's interest. If anything, he was glad to see that they were alright.

"You stopped a family from being torn apart," 345 stated.

"Yeah," 125 spoke slowly. "Looks like it."

The questions continued flowing through his mind as he glanced at 345, who appeared happy to see him cheering up a little.

The two of them walked away and the next thing he knew, they were sitting down. In the background, the Second Group went about their business, or at least, they were still in this particular moment in time as they took a breather. 125 looked at 345.

"So, you've seen your funeral, right?" he asked. "Does that mean... I could see mine?"

"If you really want to," 345 nodded. "You can take us there. I mean, I've already seen it and I can tell you, it's really moving."

"You already saw it?" 125 felt confused. "But, when you gave me a haircut... that was after I died. How did you have time...?"

"You should just assume that time has no meaning here," 345 interrupted politely. "It may seem like your soul crossed over in just a few minutes. Maybe it was hours ago or several days since you've died."

345 drew his attention away and held up four fingers.

"From your perspective, it's been four years since you last saw me, right?" she said. Then 345 extended her thumb and did a fun wave as 125 watched her hand movement. "Well, we don't have our internal chronometers, our gold bracelets, or even a watch to tell time."

"Uh, aren't we wearing our amborg bracelets??" 125 glanced at his wrist.

"Yeah, these are physical memories and personal keepsakes that represent who we are, or who we were," 345 nodded. "But, in this place, after death, they don't work like before."

"Huh," 125 tried to activate his bracelet but there was no response. "Interesting."

" As far as I know, it feels like... or it felt like it was just yesterday when I was telling 917 that I was looking forward to dinner with him. Occasionally, it does feel like forever since I last heard him speak to me."

"But, now you can replay your favorite memories? Or visit moments that you want to see?"

"Hell yes!" 345 excitedly clasped her hands together. "It's such a weird meta thing in this realm! I can tell you about a lot of crazy things that I've seen! The day that I was put in the orphanage! My first best friend that I ever had! The Christmas party when the Third Group was announced! There was a lot of hot stuff going on that night, just saying."

345 nudged 125 with a rather proud and smug grin.

"You managed to score a nice piece of action too, right?"

125 chuckled embarrassingly.

"274 and I made a bet," he said. "He bet that he could pick someone up at the party before I could."

"Sounds fun," 345 laughed.

"The rules were... we couldn't do any background checks of any kind," 125 explained. "If we looked them up online or accessed the database, it would be an automatic fail. So, he and I selected the candidates. For him, I picked a girl that worked for the A.I. Industries in-house masseuse team. She had a really short red dress, some alcohol in her system, and a smile to die for."

"Wait, it sounds like you were trying to make him win the bet," 345 said.

"Well, he did," 125 nodded. "I picked one of the most beautiful girls at the party for him to make a pass on and it worked out. I gave my best friend the win. Don't you already know this? Being a super-powered observer and all?"

"Yeah," 345 nodded. "But it's refreshing to listen to someone else share the story. Like I said, I can see and know everything but it helps you process if you're the one that remembers."

"I'm not sure if I totally understand," 125 replied.

"You will," 345 sighed. "So... you helped your best friend score with a sexy lady at the party. Who did he pick for you?"

"There was a cellist at the party," 125 smiled gently as he remembered. "I loved talking with her that night. I didn't care about the bet. I just really loved the way we looked into each other's eyes and..."

"Mmm, you feel so strong. Oh... yes! I like this."

125 and 345 both turned their heads sharply when they heard someone's... very not-safe-for-work tone of voice. They were still seated but now they had gone from the auditorium to a private residence. 125 looked down frantically, realizing that they had changed settings and the scene switched again.

"Whoa!" he said as his eyes widened in shock as he recognized where they were. "Oh, this is my room! This is my room! Oh, and this is... oh no!"

"Actually," 345 tilted her head. She glanced behind him and started to laugh. "I think it's *their* room at the moment."

125's face turned beet red, his expression growing mortified as they witnessed a very adult scene about to unfold.

"Holy shit! That's me! I am getting undressed and... Oh... I just tore off her dress," he exclaimed, but his tone slowly calmed down the more he watched. "Huh. Not bad technique."

"I'll say," 345 snickered. "Your cellist lady-friend seems to be having the time of her life."

"Wait a minute!" 125 shook his head and stood up. "This is wrong!"

"How can it?" 345 asked cheekily. "This is your memory. A *very* good memory. It's already happened."

"No!" 125 said frantically. "This is like looking through your internet history! We gotta delete this!"

"Well, you sure deleted the straps on her dress," 345 kept laughing. "Wow, you two are animals."

"Can we please move onto something else?!" 125 cringed as he watched himself push his "date" up against a wall and they both moaned passionately. "I can't believe that's what I sounded like."

"Ok! Ok!" 345 laughed. "I got this!"

125 continued to blush deeply as the scene blurred and changed. Then everything stilled, and they were on 345's hill again, overlooking A.I. Industries.

"If it makes you feel better, I've already accidentally seen a lot of spicy stuff," 345 replied. "My curiosity sometimes overpowers my self-restraint. I think about something and the next thing I know, I'm in the men's locker room. Oh and uh, I got to say, some of you look really good after a workout. Not trying to be weird."

"Great," 125 muttered. "So, you and I are also capable of being perverts. It's like... a reality porn show."

"Ok, well if the intimate stuff is too much for you, we can think about other stuff. Did you know that 117 isn't the only amborg that's a father?" 345 stated. "Leonard 1 is too!"

"What??" 125 blinked as he stared at 345. "I thought he just had an ex-wife!"

"Yeah, but they have two kids!" 345 matched his stunned look. "Off-record! They're both grown up! You have no idea how long I've wanted to share that with someone!"

"It must have been a really big secret for no one else to know," 125 said.

"Oh, I had a question," 345 stated. "Do some guys like to stand in front of a mirror before and after they shower? Is that a guy thing?"

125 stared at 345 skeptically.

"I've watched... a lot of guys doing self-motivation talks and hyping themselves up while maintaining their hygiene and stylizing their looks," 345 explained. Then she noticed 125 was eyeing her suspiciously. "No, I'm not being a perv! I'll just... 917, for example! He likes to have full conversations with himself in front of his mirror."

"Doesn't everybody talk to themselves at times?" 125 replied.

"I mean, I assumed that's why some of our favorite main characters or leaders are so good at delivering charismatic and epic speeches," 345 stated. "Like this one."

The surrounding environment changed and they were in the middle of some kind of interrogation room. 125 saw a woman chained to a chair, surrounded by guards. Everything they wore didn't look like anything he had seen before. Then he realized these had to be people from the Alpha universe. The uniforms looked like the ones he saw on the S.C.E. diplomats that visited the White House.

"Admiral Caldwell," 345 explained. "She's the one responsible for all of this. I'll fill you in on the details later but... she got caught and this is an interrogation. One of many since her war crimes are quite extensive."

"Oh look," 125 pointed. "It's 917 again. Whoa... why does he look injured?"

"Shot in the head," 345 replied quickly.

"What?" 125's eyes widened. Alarmed, he looked more closely. "In the head? But he's still alive!"

"I'll explain later," 345 said. "It's so badass."

"I'm glad you're still alive."

125 and 345 both watched as 917 stood before Admiral Caldwell. She gazed coldly up at him as he spoke to her condescendingly.

"Normally, I'd want you dead," 917 scowled at the admiral. "You did shoot me and I took it personally. However, the truth is, I'm glad you're going to be rotting away in prison."

"You really think that you can hold me forever?" Caldwell scoffed.

"Absolutely," 917 snarled. "Do you know why? Because if you harm my people, I will burn everything you've ever cared about to the ground while I make you watch. Then I'll have the S.C.E. put you somewhere you can watch me and my friends succeed where you failed and then you'll be forgotten about. I am perfectly content with the fact that no one will remember you as anything other than a misguided criminal who pissed me off."

Then, 917 turned around and walked away.

"Mmm," 345 bit her lip and watched as 917 exited the room. "That's a man right there."

"Seems a little intense without the full context," 125 gulped.

The scene faded and then they were brought back to A.I. Industries. Slightly exhausted from all of the things he had seen, 125 sighed. He stretched his hands up as he buried his face into his palms.

"Man, I can't believe I almost watched myself go all the way," he muttered. That was still fresh on his mind. "I wasn't expecting that in the afterlife."

"You get used to it," 345 shrugged. "It may seem like a gigantic pain in the ass but you get to see a lot of things happen. Do you want to think about the future?"

"What about it?" 125 asked.

"We can go with something special like... 10 years from now," 345 smiled. "274 has a son."

125 pivoted to 345. She laughed gently.

"I'm serious," she smiled. "I saw it. 274 married a really amazing woman and in 2148, they had a son. He named him Marco."

345 then pointed up behind him. When 125 turned to look, there was a loud cacophony of engines firing.

"Or we can stick with something more recent," she said. "Our friends coming back home! They were successful."

S.C.E. shuttles flew overhead and began to land at A.I. Industries.

"No one else died?" 125 asked. "I mean, no one else that we know?"

"Nope," 345 said as they watched the shuttles touch down. "They're all ok!"

Suddenly, a montage of various moments played out before them.

125 smiled wistfully as he watched 117 running into the arms of his wife, Audrey. The two of them scooped up Sarah and held onto each other tightly. With his cybernetically enhanced strength, 117 picked up both his wife and daughter and spun them around.

Another brief scene showed 57 watching her twin sister Leera from a distance. At some point, Leera noticed and the two made eye contact. Without a word, 57 smiled reassuringly. The Emergency Recall was over and everyone could breathe easy. Her moment ended as 125 watched 57 report in to the LAPD.

Commander Bradley was still at her desk, sorting through mountains of reports and paperwork thanks to all the craziness that they had to go through. Seeing 57 standing there before her was the best way to learn that it was over. Until the next time that the amborgs needed to be recalled.

297 and 777 both hit the bar and grabbed several barrels of ale and hard liquor. 125 watched that scene and laughed with 345. It was perfectly understandable with what they had survived.

1 greeted his ex-wife Daphne with a long and consoling hug. 125 watched with great interest. It was hard to believe that the first amborg in history and his former technician had kids. Where were they now? Maybe he would take time to learn more.

After some time had passed, 3 left A.I. Industries once the celebrations had concluded. She returned to her restaurant and assumed her secret identity. Until it was time to go back to A.I. Industries, she would be there waiting for the call.

5 and 6 found time to pay a special visit to a friend. They went to a small home in an isolated rural county to visit Jacob Kelewski's mother. 125 knew why they were there. Jacob had been a tech working aboard the Apogee station in space when the Tandeeri first arrived. By accident, he sustained severe injuries and by the time they rushed him to the S.C.E. Firestar, it was too late. He passed away and his remains were brought back to Earth. 5 and 6 visited his mom in order to tell her about how brave he had been to the very end. If there was anything she needed, they told her to not hesitate to call.

When 125 and 345 both watched the Fourth Group amborgs return, he noticed that they seemed to be more expressive. Maybe it was just his imagination but... it seemed as if they were dropping their icy cold personas and showing more of their basic emotions. 345 remarked that something had sparked a change.

501 and 466 came back and the Third Group were all overjoyed. 345 smiled peacefully when she saw her friends looking so happy to be back together on Earth. The only one that watched over them carefully was 723–the amborg who had replaced her and took her position in the group.

"723 eventually takes down the organization that was smuggling all of those kids," 345 said. "It's quite a mission."

"Oh yeah," 125 commented. "777 did that whole raid on the docks with Mark. I was hoping that would get resolved."

Many of the amborgs that had waited for their friends to come back from the Alpha universe would eventually return to a state of normalcy. 4 would go back to overseeing amborg operations while those who visited space took some well deserved time off. 18 hosted several training sessions for the amborgs before she would eventually return to Italy.

Then, they got to the next pair. 345 indicated to 125 that this was what she was looking forward to the most. 125 looked around as the environment put them in an alleyway in the middle of a city somewhere.

"This is what I was waiting for," 345 said.

"Where are we?" 125 asked.

"Portland, Oregon," 345 answered.

"Oh yeah!" 125 nodded as he remembered. "This is where 999 grew up! Before she was brought to A.I. Industries? Isn't there a nice old lady that took care of her?"

"She's not the only one," 345 grinned.

"You mean... him too?" 125 asked.

"Have you ever wanted to know where he came from?" 345 asked.

125 didn't answer. Instead, the excitement in his eyes increased as he watched his two friends touring the alley.

"This is where we lived?"

917 and 999 were both looking at a nice spot on an elevated loading dock. They wore normal civilian clothes to avoid drawing any unwanted attention from the public. There was a crevice which was perfectly sheltered. The spot was dry and it looked like a nice location for someone to live in. They stared at all of the worn out blankets and the tarps hanging there. They were impressed it was still there and that no one seemed to be using it.

"Did you forget... already?" 999 asked.

917 turned to her and realized she seemed worried. He smiled and gave her an apologetic look to reassure her.

"No!" 917 replied with a light chuckle. "I wasn't saying it like I forgot. I was saying it as in... I can't believe we lived... here."

"I was six…" 999 said. "Maybe seven. I was starving and had nowhere to go. I found your shelter and I thought I was going to die. Right here."

"And then…" 917 looked at where he was standing and took a step to the left. "Yeah. I asked you to move out of my spot."

"You did," 999 nodded.

"You were like a stray cat," 917 remarked. "You slapped my hand away when I reached out to you."

"To be fair, I didn't know you or trust you at all," 999 replied with a shrug. "I still think about the first time you fed me when I was on the verge of dying from starvation."

"I gave you a loaf of bread."

917 brought his hand up to his chin and remembered.

"You did," 999 nodded. "It was the first time I ever ate warm fresh bread."

125 and 345 watched as 917 turned to look up and down the alleyway. This seemed to energize him. He slowly began to walk towards them. 125 politely stepped out of the way but 345 remained in place. 917 walked casually past 125 and a part of his body phased through 345. Undeterred, he kept walking as her shoulder reformed itself. She cheekily winked at 125, as if reinforcing the idea that they were invisible ghosts.

"That's going to take some getting used to," 125 commented as 999 walked past him.

They followed 917 as he appeared to be retracing his steps. It wasn't long before he picked up the pace. Instead of walking or jogging, 345 showed 125 a special trick they could do. She leapt up and stood in midair. When he did the same, he realized he was also levitating and then, they followed 917 and 999. If anyone could actually see them, they'd look like two human-sized kites being dragged on a string behind the two amborgs.

Finally, 345 eagerly patted 125 on the shoulder. He looked at where she pointed and the two of them slowly descended to the ground. 917 and 999 were now standing in front of a bakery. A sign above the door read: *Tillia's Bakery.*

"Welcome home," 999 whispered as 917 gazed up at the sign.

"Before the Tandeeri helped repair my broken memories," 917 stared in fascination at the place. "I had dreams. I think my dreams were trying to tell me about this place. I know that my memories, after they were fixed, showed me that I had been here before but... it feels..."

999, along with 125 and 345, watched patiently and quietly as 917's voice lowered.

"It feels like this is the first time I've been here," he said. "Even though I've been here many times."

"Come with me."

999 moved in front of him and turned to face him. He looked in her eyes as she raised her arm and reached her hand out.

"There's someone who wants to meet you," she said.

917 smiled warmly as he gently took her hand and 999 led him up the steps. She opened the door and the bell rang to announce their presence.

There was a decent brunch crowd enjoying their coffee and pastries, and some that were just hanging out and enjoying a deep conversation. Many students could be seen working on school projects or homework. It almost felt surreal seeing everyone living their lives normally. It was like the possibility of being invaded from space had completely faded from memory, even though it had all taken place within the last few months.

"Oh Alice!"

Over at a nearby table, 917 noticed a woman with three kids. In her arms was a baby, and she gently waved at 999 while managing her family. 917 quietly followed 999 over to meet this woman. Any friend of 999 was a friend of his.

"Hello," 999 replied when they reached the table.

"I told Grandma Tillia you'd make it back," Brena grinned optimistically as she cradled her youngest in her arms. "She was always out on the porch looking up at the sky, praying for you."

"She had every right to be worried," 999 answered.

"I don't know what it is that you do," Brena smiled. "But whatever it is, I'm glad you made it back."

Then Brena noticed 917. Her eyes widened as she looked at him carefully. Slowly, he cleared his throat and waved.

"Hi," he said. "Um, you're... that girl that... needed glasses."

Brena's eyes widened behind the lenses of her prescription glasses. Her mouth dropped open, and 917 nodded, showing he recognized her.

"Clumsy Brena," 917 stated.

Brena gasped in amazement. She cheerfully glanced at 999.

"Is this... him?" she asked.

"Yes," 999 nodded.

"I guess I'm 'him,'" 917 replied. "Unless there's someone else we're still waiting for?"

Brena turned and glanced towards the back.

"In that case," she said, beaming. "I think she's waited long enough."

They all turned to look at the old woman standing just inside the hallway that led to the restrooms. She walked towards them slowly with eyes only on 917.

"Mrs... Tillia?" 917 asked politely.

"Boy, I already told you... call me granny," Grandma Tillia replied as she glared at 917. Then her expression softened as she scoffed. "I hope you understand when I say it's about damn time."

917 chuckled. Brena and 999 both watched from the side and smiled warmly. He dipped his head bashfully and opened his arms. Grandma Tillia continued to laugh as she made her way slowly into his arms.

917 closed his eyes as he embraced the lady that was over a hundred years old. Something about the embrace generated many more familiar feelings that he slowly began to recognize. Remembering everything didn't necessarily mean that he automatically knew what it felt like. Getting a warm and loving embrace seemed to make him feel whole again.

"Come with me," Grandma Tillia said. "I have a lot of photos that I dug up from my albums. The ones that you kids taught me how to save on the Cloud... or whatever they call it nowadays. I think there are some things that might help you remember."

917 glanced at 999. She gave him a nod and a confident grin.

"Uh, I don't know if... Alice ever told you but... I'm currently going by Jack."

Grandma Tillia looked up at 917 and nodded.

"It suits you," she said. "I assume... you like this name better than your old one?"

"Yeah, Jack has kinda grown on me," 917 nodded.

345 held back some tears as she watched proudly. 125 felt her emotions as well. It was a remarkable and truly happy sight to behold.

"This is one of my favorite moments," 345 stated.

"You've never seen this moment before?" 125 asked.

"I have a couple of times," 345 sniffed. "It just makes me... I always cry when I see it! No matter how many times!"

"Maybe we should..." 125 also began to let the tears flow down his cheeks as he and 345 both hugged each other. "We should probably go watch something else!"

"I agree!" 345 sobbed. "Where should we go?"

"Did... Marina come back to be with George? Did Thalia get her parents back together?"

"Come on 125," 345 sniffed. "Let's look at a different moment! Something that doesn't make us feel so much!"

"Ok! How about...?" 125 thought quickly. "I've always wanted to know why the Third Group triplets changed their numbers!"

"Ok!" 345 said as they confirmed where they wanted to go next. "It's actually a funny story. Originally, they were amborgs 53, 54, and 55. So they had this problem on one mission... and then..."

What the two of them didn't notice was the fact that when they turned and prepared to leave, or in this case, change the setting and disappear, 999 had turned her head slightly. She glanced towards the entrance of the bakery. In the blink of an eye, she thought she had seen two people wearing amborg uniforms. A man and a woman that radiated some sense of familiarity, but that wasn't right. There were no other amborgs in the vicinity that she could see on her internal sensors.

"Alice?" Brena noticed 999 staring hard at the door. "Is something wrong?"

"I thought I heard..." 999 replied cautiously as she continued to look at the entrance in curiosity. "Or... I thought I saw.."

It couldn't have been, could it?

Thinking that it was impossible, 999 shook her head. It was probably her mind generating some sort of hazy illusion. The important thing to focus on was her best friend finding his way home again. She smiled gently. This was a moment in time that she wanted to treasure for the rest of her life.

Epilogue

A.I. Industries
Dr. Kendrick's Office

It was a long night for Dr. Kendrick. For hours, he had been at his desk, trying to organize everything. All of his documents and files had been reviewed, and things were essentially getting back to normal.

Dr. Kendrick sighed as he set his data pad down on his desk. Then, he looked over at the small bin that sat behind his computer screen. It was his inbox for personalized letters. Curious, he reached for the bin and pulled some letters out.

He saw a few familiar names.

There was a letter from Brad, which made him smile. Brad had once visited A.I. Industries and conducted an interview about the amborgs. Now, he worked as a press reporter for the White House. He was glad to hear from him. However, Dr. Kendrick's expression grew concerned as he looked down at the letter.

It had a return stamp and a miniature seal, which was the White House's official emblem. Thankfully, he knew it wasn't a death notification or something filled with bad news, since the address was written by hand on the envelope. Dr. Kendrick instantly recognized Brad's unique handwriting. Without reading the contents, he felt it was safe to assume that Brad had survived the attack by Silent Eclipse. No doubt, he had written a letter full of questions about what had happened. Dr. Kendrick decided to schedule a time to leave Brad a voicemail so they could reconnect.

On his desk lay a sizable bundle secured with a rubber band. Dr. Kendrick noticed that the top letter was from Commander Bradley of the LAPD. It seemed that someone had arranged these letters together because as he sifted through them, he recognized the names of police chiefs from all over the country. They were either going to be letters of commendation, questions regarding the state of the world, seeking assistance, or applying for reparations. Dr. Kendrick set the bundle aside. Maybe he would respond to police matters the next day.

He was pleasantly surprised to see a letter from Mark, 117's grandfather. There had been this whole thing where Mark and his vigilantes had assisted 777 at Port Hope in California, where they uncovered a horrific smuggling operation. The Emergency Recall drew their attention away from that mission when 777 had to return to A.I. Industries. During their time in space and when they returned after hearing 125 had lost his life at the White House, Dr. Kendrick had heard some gossip among his staff that Mark had babysat Sarah in a very unconventional way. Audrey and 117 had to have some sort of family meeting after that. Dr. Kendrick set Mark's letter to the side and looked at the next one. Whatever Mark had written to him, it was probably unwise to keep him waiting for a response.

The next letter immediately caught his eye. It was addressed to him with a lovely shade of red ink. When he noticed who it was from, his heart fluttered.

"To Dr. Kendrick, A.I. Industries, Epsilon Universe," he examined the letter closely. "From... Ishala."

Admiral Ra'aiah had written him a letter? When did it even arrive? Did this mean that communications had officially been sanctioned between their universes?

After the end of Operation Salamis and the Liberation fleet was disbanded officially, preparations were made for every inhabitant of Epsilon universe that was in Alpha to return home as soon as they were finished with their contributions to the investigation.

Many of them had wondered if it would be possible for the S.C.E. Council to maintain contact with the Alpha universe. The collaboration between the two universes had actually generated many friendships and bolstered positive relations between numerous people.

The S.C.E. Council and the surviving High Command were baffled by the large amount of requests to keep contact between the two universes open. There was little to no evidence to indicate that the interactions between Alpha and Epsilon was causing any severe problems. The main leadership of the S.C.E. decided to table that for a later discussion. When they informed them of that decision, they were still investigating and searching for Silent Eclipse loyalists, and they were unable to focus on allowing prolonged multiverse contact. The letter from Admiral Ra'aiah in Dr. Kendrick's hand seemed to contain the answer to his questions. What was the verdict?

He gently unsealed the envelope and pulled the letter out. As he unfolded the sheets of paper inside, he read the introduction. The style of the handwriting stood out to him in a fun and endearing way.

To Dr. John Kendrick,

How are you? I assume you are well since there's no actual way for me to hear your immediate response. I hope that things in the Epsilon universe are settling down just like they are here in my universe. Please take this letter as an invitation, or the start of one. I've been allowed to write to you to inform you that the S.C.E. Council, as well as the remaining loyal officers and leading officials of High Command, all came to a consensus recently.

They elected to open negotiations for trade and bridge the two universes. I'll send you another letter soon detailing the political, sociological, and economic benefits of this decision. Naturally, there are still some who oppose the idea for potential negative consequences of the two universes communicating and interacting but... they were overruled. It also helps that the Tandeeri were allowed to choose where they wanted to live and the higher-ups had no choice in the matter. It was, in my opinion, a good idea that Snickerdoodle took his people to the Epsilon universe. I hope that they find their new home to their liking. I know they're not on Earth but the fact that they can live in peace near your solar system is comforting.

I'm still keeping busy with the rest of us attempting to reestablish control since our mission did cause a huge disruption to many citizens of the S.C.E. Despite this, many in my crew have greatly expressed their eagerness and intent to visit the Epsilon universe soon. This time, we won't show up guns blazing and scare everyone on the planet.

I didn't get a chance to say this to you before since you took the amborgs home so quickly but, thank you so much for all that you've done. My admiration and respect for you is unforgettable and I will always think about how brave you were under pressure. Your skills, compassion, and dedication to your family is remarkable. Perhaps, if I see you soon, would you like to grab a drink or dinner? Um, just us? It would be nice to reconnect after so long.

One last note: The reason why you're getting a physical letter is because I wasn't sure if an electronic one would be allowed to be sent.

I almost had this letter sent to you on a data pad but I wondered if you've gotten tired with reading words on screens. Please be warned, I don't usually use... physical writing tools... so this letter has a lot of erase marks because... there were several drafts. My parents and my uncle also just pointed out that I could have just used a fresh sheet of paper because as I mentioned earlier... several drafts. I foolishly didn't think this through. Oh no... it would have been easier to rewrite this entire thing on a brand new sheet but... I also barely have any personal time.

Anyway, I hope this letter finds you and... that you can read it clearly. If I don't hear a response due to circumstances beyond your control, then I won't be upset. I just hope that when we see each other again, it'll be when we're ready to put work aside and enjoy each other's company.

Your friend next door in Alpha,
Third Admiral Ishala Ra'aiah

P.S. The Council wanted to promote me to the same rank as my mother, Talveeya, but the Admiralty board of the High Command ruled against it because I was found guilty of treason. Oops.

Dr. Kendrick let out a laugh when he reached her last note. It was humorous. As he set it aside, he looked at the other two sheets of paper that came with Ishala's letter. Dr. Kendrick saw the names on it and realized it came from her parents, Aramis and Talveeya. These were shorter notes that appeared to have been written hastily.

To the lovely John Kendrick! Talveeya had written enthusiastical-ly. *Looks like you haven't seen the last of us quite yet! See you soon! Now then, I couldn't help but notice that my sweet little Ishala was trying to figure out how to arrange a meeting with you. Meow. She sure has exquisite taste. You're such a lucky man! Wherever you decide to take her, have fun! Be sure to give me a call the next time you drop into the Alpha universe and give me all the details!*

Dr. Kendrick looked at the signature from Second Admiral Ra'aiah. Next to her name, she had also drawn a cute kitten blowing a heart at him. He blushed slightly as he picked up the final note and gulped. He read the short note and had an idea of who it was before he got to the signature at the end.

Dr. Kendrick. I approve of you. Do not hurt my daughter. This is your only warning.

That one single line on the last page made Dr. Kendrick tremble in fear. Even though the First Admiral wasn't close by or in his presence at all, Dr. Kendrick glanced over his shoulder with a sketchy look. He couldn't believe that even in another universe, he was still getting intimidated. The Ra'aiah family certainly had a special kind of flair.

Dr. Kendrick set the letter down and stood up. He stretched his arms as he looked out the window at the night sky. He spoke up suddenly.

"Serina? I have some good news!"

Nothing happened. Dr. Kendrick blinked and tilted his head. That was strange. Why wasn't she responding?

"Serina?"

Dr. Kendrick turned around and thought about hitting the page button on his computer console. Perhaps they were running an experiment and they had blocked communications. However, once he turned around, Dr. Kendrick went pale.

There was another man in the room standing at his desk. He wore beat-up, weathered armor with a dark cloak. At first, he thought it was Mark playing a prank, but Dr. Kendrick knew that 117's grandfather maintained his outfit a lot better than this man. When he looked up at the unknown person's face, he saw a mask with a glowing blue visor across the eyes.

"Security! Intruder alert!" he managed to get out as icy cold fear froze him on the spot. "My office! Voice authorization: Kendrick Condition One!"

The masked man silently stared back as Dr. Kendrick attempted to communicate with him.

"Who are you?!" he demanded. "How the hell did you get in here?!"

The man didn't respond. Instead, he lifted his hand up to his mask and peeled it off. It emitted a soft hiss as he began to speak.

"Security," he said calmly. "Cancel intruder alert. Voice authorization..."

Dr. Kendrick's eyes widened. It couldn't be. This was impossible.

"...Kendrick Condition One. Stand down. All clear."

The mask was fully removed and the man placed it gently on Dr. Kendrick's desk. He lifted his head and revealed his face.

It was like looking in a mirror. Dr. Kendrick found himself face to face... with another version of himself. Was it a clone? Or was it perhaps... his Alpha? The resemblance was remarkable. Despite the fact that they wore different clothes, they definitely had the same face.

"Are you here to kill me?" Dr. Kendrick asked.

"If that was the case, I would have already done it you fool."

Dr. Kendrick's doppelganger scoffed and walked over to a cabinet next to the coffee table and a pair of armchairs. He smacked it in the side with his hand and grumbled.

"How do you open this damn thing?"

"Voice activated," Dr. Kendrick spoke softly as he remained safely behind his desk. "Why... uh? Why are you trying to get into my liquor cabinet?"

Without answering, the other Dr. Kendrick merely heard the instructions and barked at the cabinet.

"Open!"

Dr. Kendrick continued to stare in stunned silence as the other version of himself successfully got into the cabinet. It recognized his voice pattern as... well, himself and unlocked when it heard his command. There was no doubt about it. This man was an evil clone or from the Alpha universe. What if this man was both? Dr. Kendrick shuddered at the thought.

"43 told me about you," he mustered the courage to speak up. "You're Tom Kendrick. Aren't you?"

His other self only gave him a brief side glare as he grabbed a glass and a bottle of whisky. He poured himself a drink without asking while Dr. Kendrick silently stared at his glass. His other self filled it almost to the top.

"In the flesh," he murmured as he set the whisky bottle down and raised his glass to Dr. Kendrick. "Cheers."

"It's a bit rude to toast without offering me anything..." Dr. Kendrick muttered as he watched himself throw back his head and chug the entire drink. "Good lord! You're just going to down that entire glass?!"

"Oh, shut it," Tom snapped as he grabbed the whisky bottle again and poured a refill. "It's not like I have access to my supply. You can always just send for more!"

John Kendrick gave in and became disgruntled. Is this what he would become if his life went in a different direction? Tom looked like he had just survived years of hell.

"Why are you here?"

Tom took another shot of whisky. John felt a little sick to the stomach as he watched himself drowning everything away with alcohol. Sure, he enjoyed the occasional drink but the rate that Tom was going was probably going to cripple his liver. Assuming he still had one.

"As painful as it is," he rasped as he wiped his mouth with his sleeve. "I need your help."

"Seems a bit odd to ask me for help when you... snuck in here, scared the daylights out of me, and canceled my alarm system," John replied bluntly. "Want me to get an A.I. or something?"

"Do that and I'll break your hands!"

The fear inside of John slowly faded as he began to sense that Tom wasn't here to be hostile. Cautiously, against his better judgement, he decided to comply with him. Maybe they could have a reasonable conversation and get some important info.

"The S.C.E. is planning or... at least talking about, opening up communications between our universes," John said as he glanced at Ishala's letter on his desk. "Now that the real culprits behind the war were revealed, we can..."

"Spare me that nonsense," Tom spoke angrily. "You should have killed her!"

"Who? Admiral Caldwell?" John replied, startled at his other self's outburst. "We caught her! She'll be properly punished."

"Like you did with the Assassin? You naïve arrogant foolish idiot!"

John's eyes widened.

"How the hell do you know that?" he breathed.

"I'm you," Tom scoffed. "You think I came here without learning about the Epsilon universe? This perfect society and world you live in. All of your friends and the amborgs you call your family... they're all alive. Mostly."

John watched as Tom took a seat in the armchair facing him and continued to drink.

"You had 917 in prison on a secret assignment to protect the one man that tried to overthrow the entire country," Tom grumbled. "You should have killed him. He was and still is dangerous."

"There were rumors that people were planning to break him out," John replied softly. "917 happened to take matters into his own hands when he slaughtered the ones responsible for destroying Silhed. Instead of banishing him from A.I. Industries, I offered him that assignment as a way to reflect on going behind my back and to also make sure that one of the world's most dangerous criminals was still locked away forever!"

"How long until someone decides to do the same for Caldwell or any of her followers??" Tom replied. "Huh? If the S.C.E. hadn't begun talking about coming back to Epsilon universe, how long do you think it would have been until they came knocking on your door and begging you to go back and clean up their mess?"

"Yes, they made a mistake but now that it's over..."

"THIS ISN'T OVER!" Tom roared.

John flinched. However, he refused to cower in fear when this was his home and they were in his office. He wasn't going to be intimidated by anyone, not even himself.

"You stop interrupting me and listen up!" John fired back determinedly. "We did everything that was asked of us! There's nothing left but to go back to the way things were."

"Caldwell killed my amborgs!" Tom scoffed as he took another swig of whisky. "She eradicated my company! She ruined everything that I cared about! She forced me to run away! I barely survived! But no, of course, you get to relish in all of... this!"

Tom made a grand gesture with his arms as he looked all over the office.

"The amborgs all get to go back to their lives!" he jeered mockingly at John. "A.I. Industries gets their illustrious CEO back! And meanwhile, there's nothing for me! The man who failed all of his loved ones."

"Well, what do you want?" John retorted. "You didn't come all this way just for a nice meet and greet."

"I told you, I need your help."

"And if I refuse?" John spoke with a hint of defiance in his voice. "Or if what you ask of me is not something I can help with?"

"I know what kind of man you are," Tom rolled his eyes. "If your curiosity isn't already eating away at you with me being here in front of you, I can always persuade you."

"You mean force me?" John scoffed.

"Don't test me, John Kendrick," Tom glared angrily. "If I had wanted to, I would have long disposed of your body and taken over A.I. Industries. Would you rather I kill one of your friends or any of your precious amborgs to make a point? Perhaps I'll purge one of your A.I. programs."

"You do that and Dr. Kolaski might kill you," John muttered.

"In my universe, he doesn't have the courage to even pick up a weapon," Tom let out a harsh laugh. "I doubt he'll be any different here."

"Oh, so you have a Dr. Kolaski," John nodded.

"Had one," Tom replied. "Never said he was alive."

John lifted his hand and motioned for Tom to give him the whisky bottle. Tom glanced down at it in his hand and then at John with a surprised look. Without a word, he stood up and cautiously set the bottle down on the desk.

John picked it up and contemplated taking a drink directly from it, but decided not to. He walked over to the cabinet while Tom watched his movements carefully. John grabbed a glass for himself and then poured a little whisky into it.

With his own glass in hand, he turned and held the whisky bottle out. Tom graciously grabbed it, continuing to stare back. He was wondering what John was about to do.

"You should know that if you kill me and take over my universe," John lifted his glass, toasting his Alpha version, and then drank. "Someone will notice. They will discover who you are, and you will be taken down."

"I doubt it," Tom replied as he refilled his glass and kindly waved it at John. He chugged another shot and exhaled blissfully. "None of you noticed me helping you out during your... Operation Salamis."

John fell silent as Tom eyed him carefully. A mischievous smirk formed at the edge of his lips.

"Ah, you suggested the name, didn't you?" Tom chuckled sinisterly. "Salamis. 480 B.C. Themistocles against Xerxes. Under 400 estimated Greek ships fought against around 1200 Persian vessels. The biggest naval battle in ancient history. They were outnumbered... just like you were."

"I know!" John spoke sharply. "What do you mean you helped out?"

"You think that your chief medical officer... Vanessa 6? You think she was the one who saved your amnesiac boy 917? Even with that steel plate in his head, which was a nice touch by the way, he still took a plasma bullet to his head!"

John stared in wide-eyed shock at this information. He needed to remember what had been recorded in the after-action report. Now that he thought about it, he did seem to recall that 6 had mentioned the circumstances surrounding 917's injury were rather miraculous, but she hadn't questioned it. Once 917 sprang back to his feet and rejoined the fight, no one really wondered why his recovery was so quick. They were just happy to know he was alive, which overshadowed the details.

"It took everything I had to stop him from bleeding out," Tom grumbled. "Wasted my time when I had Caldwell dead to rights."

"So why didn't you kill her then?" John asked carefully. "If you're claiming that you were there."

"Believe it or not... seeing the amborgs in action again made me remember..."

Tom stood from his seat and walked back to the whisky cabinet. He set his glass down.

"It made me not want to lose them again," he said. "So, I made sure to help them make it through the end of that grand operation. Except the star base. That was... quite ridiculously well done. The only reason it worked was because you had a great team. I guess I still have a soft spot for our kids."

John watched as Tom looked down at the rest of his liquor cabinet. He didn't know what happened in the Alpha universe but whatever he had been through, he was seeing a broken man. Maybe, there was something he could do.

"So, how can I help?" he spoke softly.

"I thought you weren't interested," Tom let out a soft laugh. "It didn't sound like you were up for it."

"Well, since it seems like our universes are about to cross paths again," John shrugged. "We might as well start by open communication. My first question is... can I trust you?"

Tom merely smirked and walked towards the desk. He picked up his mask and began to put it back over his face.

"Now that is a question, isn't it? Thanks for the drink."

"Wait, you're leaving, just like that?? You didn't answer my question!"

Tom glanced back at John as he headed towards the office entrance.

"I'll be back," he said. "I suggest you get the amborgs ready. We have work to do."

The doors slid open as Tom left the room. As he stepped out, John watched in a stunned silence as some sort of holographic wave of light bathed his cloak. In a few seconds, the man that was just lounging on his chair and consuming whisky was gone. It was some sort of stealth technology that rendered him completely invisible. No wonder he hadn't noticed him sneaking in here. Maybe he had been inside his office the entire time, waiting for the right moment to reveal himself.

John gulped as he looked at the whisky bottle and decided to finish off the rest. A heartbeat later, there was a flash of light behind him, followed by a gentle, more feminine voice.

"Hey! Dr. Kendrick! I've got something to tell you! Whoa now. Did you drink that whole bottle??"

At the sound of her voice, John turned around and saw Serina floating next to his computer console. She seemed unaware of what had just happened.

"Uh, yes," he smiled as he took another drink. "It seemed like the perfect time to unwind. Did you by any chance... notice anything out of the ordinary?"

"Can't say that I have," Serina shook her head. "Why?"

John snuck a glance at the door and debated whether or not he should tell her what had just happened.

"It's nothing," he sighed. "I just read a nice letter from Admiral Ra'aiah. Ishala wrote me."

"Good thing you specified," Serina laughed slightly. "I would have been concerned if her parents had written you a personal letter."

"They did actually," Dr. Kendrick chuckled. "I think they have the wrong impression about me and their daughter."

"Why? That you two like each other?"

Serina's quick retort caught him off-guard.

"Excuse me?" Dr. Kendrick stared.

"Nothing," Serina shook her head mischievously. "Although, we do want what's best for you. I just never figured you for a man that would set his standards so... out of this universe."

"Ok, that is not..."

"I'm just saying," Serina kept egging him on. "She's an admiral, she's single, and she's a total sexy badass. You sure know how to pick them. I mean, did you see the way she looked at you the whole time you both were together?"

"Serina!" Dr. Kendrick spoke sharply, which got her to shut up, but she was still grinning innocently. When he straightened himself up and cleared his throat, he calmly spoke to her. "What was it you were going to tell me?"

"There's an S.C.E. officer on Apogee Station that wants to speak to you," she reported casually. "She's insisting."

"Me?" Dr. Kendrick spoke skeptically. "Wait, an S.C.E. officer? Here? From the Alpha universe?"

"Mmhmm. That is the only universe where the S.C.E. are from," Serina nodded. "That we know of."

"What's she doing here?" Dr. Kendrick asked. "Who is she?"

"She's... a friend," Serina answered bluntly. "Her name is Braelynn."

"Am I going to like what she has to say?" Dr. Kendrick asked. "Do you think it's safe?"

"I'll vouch for her," Serina nodded.

His mind was still preoccupied with his conversation with Tom. He hoped that he hadn't accidentally gotten involved in something he wasn't supposed to be involved in, otherwise he would probably be dragging everyone into another big conflict. With a reserved sigh, he nodded to Serina and turned his console on in order to prepare a call to the space station.

"Very well," he said. "Let's hear her out."

Special Notes and Data Entries Updated and Revised

(2138 November) by Dr. John Kendrick

EPSILON UNIVERSE

The Amborgs

First Group: <u>30</u> Active members. Initiated in 2115.

The first ever cyborgs in the world. They are the oldest, most experienced, and incredibly wise. I'm not saying that none of the other amborg groups aren't as capable as they are. They have been strong and valuable contributors to society for over 20 years, and many look up to them. Their leadership has maintained constant order for the rest of the amborg groups.

Second Group: <u>29</u> Active members. Initiated in 2127.

After the death of my wife, I hit a roadblock. Eventually, some friends got me back on track and I initiated the Second Group when I realized that there were still things that needed to be done. That, and the older amborgs were severely understrength. The Second Group have more interesting and crazier adventures than any other group at A.I. Industries. I credit this to the fact that they are often reckless and have a lot of problems maintaining discipline. That might be too strong of a thing to say about them. They will get the job done, even though many of them have some rather questionable methods.

Third Group: <u>30</u> Active members. Initiated in 2128.

The public knows that I had the Third Group amborgs join their older and experienced friends when we encountered enemy combatants that had developed countermeasures against them. Their combat numbers are lower, but they make up for it by maintaining strong community relations. You could say that they are more in touch with their emotions than the amborgs that started before them. It took time but eventually, after some guidance from their mentors and friends, they learned to be more independent in the field. However, I'm not surprised if they're the ones always asking for help when things get too difficult.

Fourth Group: <u>30</u> Active members. Initiated in 2134.

President Holland authorized the official initiation of another group of amborgs despite slight resistance from the public. Many question if more amborgs were necessary. I convinced them that the answer was yes. Unfortunately, I really wish my wife was still alive to properly help them discover their feelings because... well, all amborgs shut out their basic emotions once initiated. Eventually, these emotions return. However, it's been a few years, and the Fourth Group remains efficient, deadly, but also extremely closed off. I can hope that eventually, they reconnect with their feelings just like their predecessors.

The Amborgs
Leonard 1: First Group. Age 41.

The first man to become an amborg. The first of the amborgs to also marry a human woman. Regrettably, due to personal reasons, he also went through a quiet divorce too. He's gone from a boy to a very wise leader. He volunteered with a handful of his friends to help combat this threat from space. His bravery as the leader of the First Group is unmatched.

Ziggy 2: First Group. Age 40.

Like I said before, Ziggy often delegates more responsibilities to 1. Being in the spotlight isn't his style which fits with him being the second person in history to become an amborg and also being his second-in-command for this mission to space. I know that he prefers it this way in order to focus on fieldwork instead of leading.

Missy 3 aka Melissa Carson: First Group. Age 38.

At first, I thought that she was the primary culprit for naming our new friends from outer space after... food and desserts. She happens to have an alibi where she valiantly helped defend the Firestar. All of the knowledge that she's learned from another universe most likely has given her a lot of new recipes to try out on Earth. We are probably going to be in for a treat or a lot of taste testing of... whatever she creates.

Katrina "Kat" 4: First Group. Age 39.

She continues to be one of the most brilliant tacticians I know, and I think the entire planet is lucky to have her overseeing normal operations while we were away. It is fortunate that she did her absolute best with what she had. Otherwise, the planet might have crumbled from within, and an outer space invasion would have been the least of her problems.

Johnny 5: First Group. Age 40.

Some people find humor annoying or unproductive. When it comes to Johnny, I can definitely say that genuinely, it's always refreshing to hear his sense of humor cheering us all up. Even under the stress of battle and the fact that we fought in outer space, this man always keeps our spirits up. I'm not sure if he would be the right person to deliver motivational speeches but a good joke helps in more ways than you can imagine. Sometimes we just need to laugh and he's the guy who knows what will break you in a positive way.

Vanessa 6: First Group. Age 39.

Until the discovery of a universe next door, sending in a fleet to protect us; I think that Vanessa had already learned about everything that the medical field had to offer. I mean, everything. One of the best doctors in the entire world... or in this case, Epsilon universe, and she's just like a college student again. Eager to learn and to take on new skills to save lives. It's an admirable quality that everyone should know about her. Serving and fighting in outer space only makes her one of the most legendary amborgs in the history of two universes.

Stuart 8: First Group. Age 38.

I can't believe I'm about to say this about one of the master pranksters of A.I. Industries... but he did a good job, along with the others that they led up into space. This will be one of the few times that we have a commendation ceremony for an amborg... that actually orches-trated intentional destruction of property to see to a mission's success.

Christy 9: First Group. Age 38.

Again, another commendation needs to be prepared for an equal-ly talented master of destruction. Pyromaniacs that work together are also the ones that exponentially cause plenty of problems. In this case, they helped save lives. Their particular methods will also be part of history.

Clint 11: First Group. Age 40.

During the Emergency Recall, Clint managed to successfully contact and retrieve "Nova." Leonard was most grateful to hear that she was alright. With his skills, it was probably a smart idea to send him to Zion National Park. It kept him, his backup, and our VIP from getting killed.

Kiden 18: First Group. Age 38.

Providing backup for Kat must have been exhausting. The am-borgs on Earth were understrength after sending help up into space. Thankfully, since she's trained all of them and also maintained their physical prowess. I have no doubts that thanks to all that she's taught the amborgs, it's given us all a fighting chance. I just... re-gret... that one of us didn't make it to see the end of the Emergency Recall.

David 117: Second Group. Age 27.

I heard that there was some family drama going on upon our return to Earth when we came back for a brief furlough. It's under-standable. David has come very far in about ten years. I watched him marry Audrey, have a beautiful daughter, and saw him try to balance being an amborg and a father. I can't help but feel that... after this Emergency Recall, will he continue doing what he does, or will he focus on his personal feelings?

Serina 43: Second Group. Epsilon Status: Deceased

Even with the loss of our Serina 43, she's still making a dif-ference in our lives. Not just as an artificial intelligence but... her alternate Alpha version too. I think it's fitting that being a messenger for us gave us enough warning before our universe was caught off-guard. I wonder what our lives might have been like if she was still in her own body and in this fight with us today. We may never know, unless we see her again in the next life... or the next universe.

Jack 917: Second Group. Age 29.

Jack isn't his real name but it's the one he chose for himself after becoming an amborg. Now he's truly returned home. He's been through hell repeatedly and continues fighting as if the devil himself is unleashing his fury on everything he cares about. I hope that in time... he'll accept my apology, for giving him a brand-new life and making him wake up to something he didn't ask for. You know what they say. Some are born great, and others have greatness thrust upon them. I hope he forgives me for the latter.

Alice "Angel" 999: Second Group. Age 28.

The lone wolf is no longer alone. I think. After the end of the Emergency Recall, it took one decade but she reported two words to me that said it all. "He remembers." I think that's the most joy she's ever expressed in front of me.

Carter 297 aka "Carter Richardson:" Second Group. Age 27.

When this man shoots his shot, you better take that seriously. I can't believe he survived what he did in outer space. Taking off like that in order to go and rescue his friends. Noble? Yes. Dangerous? Absolutely. Stupid? Incredibly. However, when he saw an opportunity, he took it and with an insane amount of luck, he came out of it... with a lot of unusual positivity. I'll keep an eye on his mental health for future updates.

Luis 777: Second Group. Age 27.

When I say that Carter had an insane amount of luck, I like to think that Luis being there at his side helped a lot. His presence is probably what kept the Second Group team in space from experiencing something bad. We were truly lucky to have him with us.

Katie 57 aka "Casey Owen:" Second Group. Age 28.

I cannot begin to imagine what it's like to lose someone under your command. This Emergency Recall did claim the lives of people that I knew but... not like how the Second Group had to experience it. But I do know what it's like losing a friend and a loved one. Once we returned home, I granted Katie with her requested leave of absence. I imagine she's gone to visit Leera.

Ryan 35: Second Group. Age 27.

I think that Ryan is going through a lot right now. Most of the Second Group, upon my return to A.I. Industries were all struggling to comprehend the loss that they had just experienced. It's very upsetting and hopefully, we can all band together and help each other get through this.

Marco 125: Second Group. Age 26.

I'm sorry. There's... so much to say and yet... I can't. I'm so sorry Marco. If only we could have been there to help you. You fought valiantly and you will never be forgotten. Hasta luego, Marco 125... and thank you for saving Bill's family.

Jesse 274: Second Group. Age 26.

How do you console or help someone get through the loss of your best friend? Marco and Jesse were an iconic duo. Many of the amborgs have their own designated close or best friend to rely on and to confide in during difficult times. I will trust that they will all work together to make sure Jesse isn't alone.

Keith 66: Second Group. Age 28.

Once Keith returned with Clint from their mission to retrieve "Nova," he was one of the first friends to keep a quiet eye on Jesse. I did ask him if he had wanted to try to console his friend but... he said that the news of what happened to Marco shattered his confidence. He didn't do anything wrong. Losing Marco definitely affected him hard.

Steve 92: Second Group. Age 29.

The twins accomplished many different achievements during this Emergency Recall. They led the triplets there and back again. They will receive their awards along with 8 and 9. The prankster team all deserve recognition for their incredible deeds.

Jon 93: Second Group. Age 29.

I believe Jon was the one who suggested the nickname for him and his brother as the "moon catchers." It has a nice ring to it, even though they caught a star base and not the moon.

Dominic "Donut" 501: Third Group. Age 25.

I am incredibly proud of what Donut... err, Dom has accomplished. He found the important vital piece of this massive puzzle. Yes, his report is accurate, and I will vouch in a professional capacity that negotiations between the S.C.E. and the Tandeeri was all thanks to Oreo. No, I am not talking about an actual cookie. He named a young child Oreo and... then it opened the floodgates to a naming spree.

Carolina 466: Third Group. Age 24.

Just like Dom, she had to name the Tandeeri leader. I guess the two of them have a fondness for cookies. Switching to a serious note, Carolina reported some moments during this mission which increased her self-doubt. I regret not being able to properly communicate or fully understand her situation, but it does seem like she was able to seek guidance from others. I hope that her perseverance remains intact for the future.

Amara 345: Third Group. Status: Deceased.

I was never able to properly update Amara's data file until now. I think... that if she was watching over us all, I hope it's not too presumptuous of me to say that I think she'd be proud. I think that she would have loved to see how far Alice and Jack have come since she lost her life. On a personal note, it does make a lot of sense... Well, I mean... I keep hearing stories of rumored sightings of someone who looks just like her roaming around A.I. Industries.

Lizzy 723: Third Group. Age 21.

She has certainly remained productive while we were up in space. Lizzy decided to follow up on Luis' mission and assumed the role of primary amborg for it. Using her knowledge, contacts, and skills, she was able to identify the suspected culprit behind the massive smuggling operation in Los Angeles. They covered their tracks well but not completely. Once more information is gathered, I will mobilize a team to assist her in taking down this threat.

Roland 249: Third Group. Age 25.

I think something very important to note about the rest of the Third Group team that accompanied Dom and Carolina is the fact that it provided them with such an amazing, pun intended, out-of-this-world experience. When Roland, Sara and Chris volunteered to go into space, this was a big deal for them. I'm told that the Third Group had an intense session to decide who would get the opportunity. Ever since they returned, they've stepped up. Volunteered for more assignments.

Sara 593: Third Group. Age 26.

Remember how I once said that Sara 593 reminds me of Melissa? Sorry, I have to say her amborg number since there are so many Sarahs at A.I. Industries. Anyway, going off of what I put down in 249's file, it's remarkable to see how much energy she has and she has a passionate fire that burns in her eyes when she sets her sights on completing whatever mission she's focusing on.

Chris 49: Third Group. Age 24.

I will say this, Chris has become less dependent on his friends. I think this Emergency Recall really gave him an opportunity to grow and also step it up. Just like the others in his team.

Anderson 331: Third Group. Age 23.

They take after 8 and 9, plus the Second Group twins. Therefore, they were the best option to save the day when we had to come up with the craziest plan ever.

Allison 332: Third Group. Age 23.

Since she's technically the middle child of the triplets, she's always felt like she's had to deal with twice the problems that her brothers cause. She does technically act the wisest of them but make no mistake, she is crafty. I think that when their mentors were busy, she kept them from overdoing it on the mission.

Atkinson 333: Third Group. Age 23.

All three triplets are to be commended for their actions. I still stand by my original comments when I had to respond to a lot of criticism from others. When I need them to, they will work hard and get the job done. There's nothing wrong with them being mischievous and letting off some steam. They commit to completing their tasks and when they're not busy, I let them do what they want.

Ally 113: Fourth Group. Age 21.

I am noticing a peculiar change in the Fouth Group amborgs. Ever since they reunited with the others after the first attack against Silent Eclipse ended, they seemed to spark a brief moment of an emotional connection.

Alex 280: Fourth Group. Age 21.

Same notes for Ally apply to Alex. Both of them are the definitive leaders of the Fourth Group. Whatever they do or think, it seems to filter down to the other amborgs. I have to properly take some time to identify what seems to be on their minds.

Hugo 63: Fourth Group. Age 20.

Like the rest of the Fourth Group, they fought bravely in the defense of the Firestar. The lack of emotions prevented Hugo and the others from getting distracted. Therefore, they fought well and managed to help save the ship.

Lisa 100: Fourth Group. Age 21.

After reuniting with 301 and 365 after the rescue mission, Lisa also showed some developing emotions. I think she was quite relieved to see her friends alright. Compared to how they usually are, it's quite reassuring to see them acting like everyone else for once.

Terry 378: Fourth Group. Age 21.

I heard he was injured but managed to get treated right away after meeting with the First Group. Although it wasn't fatal, 6 reported another example of a emotional change in the ranks of the Fourth Group team. Terry confessed that he felt genuine fear. When he had been hurt by Silent Eclipse, he claimed that his fear surfaced and temporarily rendered him unable to figure out how to fight back. Thankfully, someone else saved him and he didn't have to worry about it anymore. However, hearing him admit that he had frozen for a split-second and was unable to carry out the fight is something significant that must be investigated.

Mary 301: Fourth Group. Age 21.

Mary and Arno were the only Fourth Group amborgs that spent a lot of time with the Tandeeri. Along with the team of pranksters, she spent a lot of time observing and understanding their culture. When they reunited with the other amborgs in space, this was when the Fourth Group seemed to change.

Arno 365: Fourth Group. Age 21.

They spent a lot of time with the Tandeeri and even though they refused to open up to them directly, there was some kind of increase in their emotions. I don't know how to describe. Arno, for example, wasn't as cold as he was before the Emergency Recall. After returning from the Tandeeri flagship, he and Mary seemed to be more pleasant than usual. It was as if you wanted to be around them and not run away.

Amborg Industries aka A.I. Industries
Dr. John Kendrick: CEO

If I'm being totally honest, this Emergency Recall definitely highlights why the amborgs are necessary. We had a threat from outer space which is affects the entire world. I am relieved to be home again after we overcame tremendous odds. We were under-strength, outnumbered, and going literally above and beyond. Also, there seemed to be a power struggle over who would run the company in my absence. I am truly thankful for my actions and my motivations to raise the world's most powerful group of special individuals. We would all not be here today if not for the amborgs, my children.

George Ramirez: Media Relations

He hosted the President, maintained morale among the staff, learned about his ex-wife after hearing Thalia had ran away... and he also convinced Robert to take over as interim CEO. I really must have missed something when it all went to hell. George maintained order as best as he could. Now that I'm back, he probably could use a vacation.

Dr. Robert Kolaski: Artificial Intelligence R&D Department Head

I'm still unsure if Robert actually did anything when he was officially put in charge temporarily. It was nice to see that the threat from outer space did keep his curiousity up and he didn't hide in the basement during the whole time. If he hadn't come upstairs briefly, we would have probably forgotten him and he might have missed the whole thing and never noticed.

Thalia Ramirez

I was glad to hear that Thalia didn't get hurt in anyway while this whole thing was happening. Running off on her own was a little reckless but when she revealed that it was because she wanted to see her mother and try to bring her home, then I guess that makes it different. Maybe, their family will get back together again. Who knows?

Mandy Palmer

If the technician program was still active, Mandy would have witnessed the craziest mission that the amborgs have ever been on. Thankfully, she remained at A.I. Industries and her voice was what many of the amborgs on Earth needed to hear in certain situations. She is a highly skilled employee and I'm glad that once it was over, she and her husband were safe and sound.

Ariana Hart

Another former technician that felt like their career path remained at A.I. Industries. She transferred over to the Central Computer Lab which is where all of the A.I. program housing units are located. I guess when the amborgs said they didn't need technicians to assist them in the field, Ariana decided to focus on those that would need her help. She's an excellent caretaker and friend of the artificial intelligence programs living at A.I. Industries. Well, that's if you don't piss her off.

Acquaintances & Allies
Grandpa Mark

Remind me to send 117's grandfather a proper reward for all of the help he's done. His vigilante group worked around the clock all over the world trying to make sure that things didn't go wrong. I owe them thanks for keeping a lot of my friends safe. Maybe if he stops by A.I. Industries again, we'll gift him some new tech.

LAPD Commander Marsha Bradley

With the end of the Emergency Recall, I think it's safe to say that Marsha might enjoy the cleanup phase once again. After we went into space, the world spiraled downwards with many problems popping up left and right. It's thanks to military and police officials that held their nerves together and maintained public order as best as they could.

Sergeant Joe Harrison

Unless we get the next worldwide catastrophe, I hope that Harrison finds a way to enjoy his retirement. It is inspirational that when the world was panicking, he volunteered to unretire himself but... now, he should rest easy.

President Bill Holland

With the dust clearing in the aftermath of everything that has happened, Bill is now back at the White House and making sure that the public knows that the threat is over. I'll be sure to help him out since politicians love to come out of hiding and criticize, criticize, criticize. Now that I'm back at A.I. Industries, I can totally see him getting reelected.

First Lady Caroline Holland

As a special surprise that we're keeping from Bill, Caroline has an appointment to go and see a Tandeeri healer. After pulling some strings and keeping in touch with them, they've agreed to help cure her condition. It'll be an excellent story of positivity that the world needs right now.

Marina Ramirez

I never thought I'd see Marina again. She seems to be doing well for herself and only time will tell if she wants to return and make the Ramirez family whole again. Either way, it is good to hear that she's been dedicated and hard at work to protecting people.

Audrey Wright

Being the wife of an amborg and a mother must take a severe toll on her stress levels. She must have an incredible amount of patience for David 117 when he goes off on missions. It makes me wonder if he's going to consider retiring in order to spend more time with his family. I'm sure Audrey would love it.

Joey Moore

Never mess with a military trained IT guy. This kid will hack you if you annoy him.

Lieutenant Deliza Grant

The army definitely didn't make a mistake keeping a soldier like Deliza around. If the planet was invaded, I'm personally glad she's on our side.

Captain Lee Harrelson: 1st Platoon, B-Company, 205th Marines.

I'm hearing stories about Lee enjoying a lot of time with people from the Alpha universe. He fought bravely with his marines aboard the Firestar and also… left a lasting impression on a lot of them. Might need to clarify with him setting boundaries.

Captain Sheila Hicks: Pilot, Echo 209, Foe Hammer

A very calm and level-headed pilot. Even when she accompanied Mandy and Thalia on the search for Marina Ramirez, Sheila and her crew protected them and did their jobs splendidly. Flying passengers, supplies, and more during this whole incident is commendable.

Captain Sam Planck: Pilot, Echo 232, Night Song

Sam isn't just Sheila's wingman. They are both part of a group of elite individuals and some of the finest pilots I've ever seen. Flying in space and in atmosphere is no easy task. Apogee station is proud to have them as transport pilots and A.I. Industries commends them for their service.

Lieutenant Benji Frye: Copilot

I'm glad that when the Foe Hammer and Night Song's crew accompanied Thalia to Vegas, they found time to have fun. Benji always says that time on Earth is refreshing. When it was time to return to work, you can see that they commit to the job once the fun is over.

Sergeant Dean Hammond: Crew Chief

In a way, without an amborg, Thalia and Mandy were still accompanied by a trained team of experts. With how busy they all were, it was reassuring to know that they were safe the entire time. I'm sure George appreciated it. Dean treats everyone the same. Whether in public or you're riding in a vehicle, he takes care of you.

Dr. Gene Wildman

One bit of good news that I received upon returning to A.I. Industries was the fact that the parole board made a verdict. My old friend Gene is getting released from prison. He'll be allowed to go home.

Tessa Wildman

I'm sure that when 917 returned to Earth, when he heard the good news, he went and celebrated with Tessa. She's been waiting for the day that her father would breath open air again. I'll definitely invite them out... preferably not at the club that she runs.

Daphne Smith: A.I. Industries VIP "Nova"

The adventurous and A.I. Industries legend herself. She was, in a sense, the first technician to start out taking care of the amborgs and also the ex-wife of Leonard 1. When she was secured and safely brought back to A.I. Industries, it was nice to hear that she hadn't lost her touch. Taking charge and helping out where she could was extremely helpful.

Jim & Leo

It's been years since I saw these two and I swear, Jim and Leo continue to operate like they're fresh off the assembly line. Sure, they're outdated like many others that are still active but they're compassionate and courageous. Yeah, I'm a little biased since I've known them since I was a kid. Most people would have let those two rot by now. Thankfully, they're in the hands of someone who knows how to take care of them. Jim and Leo both were there when they rescued me and Melissa a long time ago. Jim and Leo protect her and Daphne reciprocates by caring for them.

Snickerdoodle

Named by Carolina and... I can't believe that's his official name for the record. The leader of the Tandeeri is a very intimidating and tall... beast-like creature. He comes from a universe far far away which makes sense because he and his people are tall, proud, and look like saurian reptilian creatures. Picture short humanoid dinosaurs. However, the Tandeeri all seem quite gentle and sweet even though the first impression I got was quite intimidating. Personally, it is nice that they aren't out to kill us.

Oreo

Ok, I admit it, otherwise Dom's feelings will get hurt. Oreo is really cute. This little child most definitely was the key to saving our two universes. If he's anything like his parents, he will grow up and become a fine leader someday. Unless if he wants to be something else, then that's fine too. I don't know how Tandeeri parenting works.

Kira

There's something calming about what happens when you meet Kira, Snickerdoodle's partner. The Tandeeri have special powers and abilities that almost seem to instill a peaceful atmosphere. Many of them are warriors but based on what I've seen, there are many who are also healers. I think physical and mental health is something they value greatly. Even though it involves them peering into your mind constantly. Thank goodness we taught them about basic privacy.

Artificial Intelligence Programs
Serina

Our best A.I. and our most capable one. I will always compliment her in that regard. The former Serina 43 of Epsilon living as an artificial intelligence most likely led to our success in the Alpha universe. Her blackout program, despite it being a failed project allowed us to complete our mission. Ariana did tell me that she was working on something very top-secret with Carter upon our return home. I'll look into this later.

Taylor

Although he wasn't technically in charge, I'm happy that Taylor did his absolute best to keep Apogee station safe. It's very impressive considering he had to deal with a rivalry between my staff and the S.C.E. crew that were visiting.

Carter

I don't know what he did to get put in timeout but whatever it was, I'm here to deal with whatever problems he's a part of. Authoring a program with Serina is quite rare and surprising considering he doesn't have the best track record. I intend to properly spend some time with Dr. Kolaski and maybe we can work out the problems.

Robin

I'm glad that Robin got to enjoy some time away from A.I. Industries even if it was tagging along with Lizzy on a solo operation. From what I can tell, she had a great time. Although, the rumors of an "Entity" living in cyberspace does draw concern. The A.I. programs all talk about it. Robin seems absolutely convinced that it is a real thing. I wonder if this is something I should look into. It's not often you see the A.I. programs acting so... restless about a rumor.

Alpha Universe
Space Command Enterprise (S.C.E.)

Serina 43: Amborg Special Operative, A.I. Industries (Alpha Universe)

So far, after visiting the Alpha universe, Alpha 43 seems to be one of the or few amborg survivors of her home universe. Tragically, she may be the last amborg of Alpha and I don't want to really go there. How do you even process surviving and knowing that your friends and loved ones are missing or dead? She is very resilient and hopefully, spending time with the Epsilon amborgs will put her mind at ease. I hope.

Ishala Ra'aiah: Third Admiral, C.O. S.C.E. Firestar, Second Colonial Defense Fleet. Creator of Joint-Tandeeri/S.C.E. Task Force (Liberation Fleet).

She is quite remarkable. I've been saying that word too often to describe the members of Alpha universe. Anyway, she is a very brave and tough leader. She's in charge of thousands of people aboard her ship which is a floating city in space. I probably could never match that level of skill. Ishala is very charming and highly respected. I absolutely appreciate everything that she's done for us and her crew.

Gleeson Ulgo: Commander, First Officer, S.C.E. Firestar.

At first, you see him as a very intense and stern man. Gradually, he's just someone that puts his work life first. The more time you spend with him, you actually see that he cares about the lives of his crew a lot. He's humorous at times even though his default mode is always serious. Some might be intimidated but now, I see someone I trust completely.

Brenda Hayes: Lieutenant Commander, Chief Engineer, S.C.E. Firestar

Keeping the ship running is always important. I didn't have a chance to really meet her in person or talk to her a lot but from what everyone tells me, she treats the ship delicately and always focuses on making sure that it doesn't fly apart. Engineers don't get enough praise or recognition for what they do every day. She and her department deserves all of the commendations.

Aliyah Hemington: First Lieutenant, Communications Officer, S.C.E. Firestar

Under pressure, I watched as this woman kept her cool and managed to relay information to her commanding officers without any issues. She is very meticulous and knows that if she freezes up, then Admiral Ra'aiah can't make proper tactical decisions. Communications make sure we're not alone.

Samuel Chastain: Commander, C.O. S.C.E. Alexandria, Fourth Expeditionary Reconnaissance Fleet. Merged and attached to the Liberation Fleet.

This man is quite the fun uncle of all of the commanding officers I've encountered. I've never seen a more enthusiastic and experienced man. It's like if you get extremely busy, he'll still find time to encourage you to see your tasks through and then be ready to bring you food or drinks after a long day. I think the S.C.E. needs more ship commanders like him. No, they need more people like him.

Erina Riley: Lieutenant Commander, First Officer,
S.C.E. Alexandria

Once the mission was over and the Emergency Recall had all of us returning to Epsilon, I managed to leave a note with Captain Chastain. She needs a promotion or a huge pay raise. Many officers need it and deserve it. After what she and all of them have been through, you have to reward them for the sacrifices they've made.

Talveeya Ra'aiah: Second Admiral, C.O. S.C.E. Georgia,
15th Scout Logistics Support Fleet

I can scratch "cat-lady" off my bucket list. Oh wait, not *that* kind of list! I'm talking about meeting a live IRL cat-person off of the bucket list! Technically Ishala is also part-cat but maybe it doesn't count because you can't physically tell. Anyway, her mother is energetic and being a higher rank than her daughter seems to put her in a very entertaining position. According to her record, she is known for being very chaotic but maintains a high level sense of professionalism. I hope she doesn't adopt any of the prankster amborgs. Her husband must be quite the man.

Aramis Ra'aiah: First Admiral, C.O. S.C.E. Weaver, Fifth Battle Fleet.

Speaking of the guy... this man is fearless and a badass. Wow. The instant I saw him, I was intimidated by his aura. In less than ten seconds, this man made me forget how to speak. Despite the whole family being part of the S.C.E. navy, he seems to have done his part as a father quite well. Maybe? I'm only assuming that since Ishala turned out to be a skilled officer herself. I wouldn't get on this guy's bad side.

Breya: Major, S.C.E. Firestar Marine Brigade

An old friend of David 117; his alpha version. Fighting and serving alongside the amborgs was something she would have done even if she hadn't been saved and healed by the First Group. Old friendships seem to find their way across universes it seems.

Bruce Mercy: Captain, S.C.E. Firestar Marine Brigade

I think I owe this man an apology. Or... solution; I'm going to get Captain Harrelson to do it. If I can...

Braelynn: Rank unknown, S.C.E. Intelligence Agent?

So, I'm slightly confused. Am I thanking this woman or am I... court-martialing her? There seems to be an unusual amount of trust issues when it comes to this particular officer. My amborgs all value her because she helped end the Tandeeri conflict and effectively protected them from harm. However, when she's brought up, the regular crew, including the commanding officers of the Firestar all become quiet. It's as if S.C.E. Intelligence is a department just as mysterious and sketchy as Silent Eclipse. In my personal opinion, she doesn't seem like she means us any harm, despite the cautionary warnings that she's playing a long game and putting on a good act. Time will tell if she's a friend or foe. Personally, I trust the amborgs' opinions about her.

For Rayne.
Thank you for believing in me.

Fatal Showdown

By Y.T. Cheng

[Access Granted]
Authorized by Amborg Serina 43
S.C.E. Classified File #203-02-A-BC
Centuria Rosa
Sometime after Tandeeri First Contact

"You know that this is a trap, don't you?"

General James Weaver stopped in his tracks. Slowly, he turned around and glanced back at the man who had called out to him.

There was Boothby, his gardener and loyal groundskeeper. His wife, his three children and their spouses, along with his four grandkids, were huddling close to him. The General had instructed them to remain as quiet as possible. He watched them slowly and carefully climbing their way out of a large boat that they had sailed down the river in.

They were unloading their bags and a small amount of luggage. This was expected because they had been told to pack light and only carry the essentials. They were most likely never going to return here.

Boothby continued to watch General Weaver silently, anticipating a response.

"It is undoubtedly a trap," the old warrior replied softly. "I must face it."

"No, you don't sir," Boothby said desperately, as if he was begging. "Please, come with us. If there is nothing left here for you sir, there is no reason to die here. Please come away with us and... we'll stay together."

The old man removed his hat respectfully. He urged his wife to help the rest of their family before trying one last time. James glanced back at his friend and looked him in the eye. There was an air of sadness as they exchanged a silent farewell. Then, after he got a good look at Boothby's family, he focused on searing that memory into his mind. This only motivated his determination, and he faced forward. Once he walked away, he would leave them behind.

His decision had already been made. After all, if it was possible, the forthcoming battle would hide Boothby and conceal his family's escape. He needed to make sure that they made it. They were the last friends he had on this planet.

"Go Boothby," James said in a gentle voice. He pointed to the right towards a dense part of the woods. "The escape craft is there and ready. Take your family and run. Hide. Survive. For as long as it takes. Make sure your family lives a good life. Just be safe. Farewell my old friend."

James began to walk forward on what would be his final march.

"It's been an honor to serve..."

Boothby's tone was filled with sorrow. It would be the last time they would have the opportunity to talk. Maybe, there was one last thing he could say to them.

"Once I am gone," Weaver stated as he continued walking uphill, away from them, "your sole duty... is to remember me. Remember us."

"Yes general. I will never forget."

"Where is the General going, dad?"

The General heard one of Boothby's sons say it just before he was out of earshot. He didn't hear what the response was. If he had been asked directly by any of Boothby's family members, there was a chance, with his current state of mind... that he would give them an honest answer.

To kill, he thought as his face fell. *I'm going to kill them all. Or at least... take them with me.*

Each step made noise as he navigated the forest trails. This was due to the weight of his armor, intentionally designed to be heavy. Unlike the stealth suits worn by S.C.E. Intelligence, it was not meant for an ordinary marine.

His armor was decorated ceremoniously and also bulked up for prolonged conflict. It was custom-made for him by expert armorers of the S.C.E. to honor his long and many years of service. Combat ribbons and unit citations marked his outfit, identifying him as a decorated soldier. General Weaver carried a long legacy of fighting and wore all of his accomplishments proudly. He also carried the memories of those he had fought alongside and led into battle. Now, after a lifetime of traveling the stars and battling... this armor would be what he would die wearing. It would be his coffin. Just like every other soldier that proudly fought to their end on the many cold and distant battlefields across the galaxy.

He heard a series of noises when he stepped into a clearing. He stopped, focused, and quickly took notice of the group standing before him.

Nine people greeted him with their weapons drawn. It was a scout unit.

"Let's see what you're made of... old fool!" one of them spat.

This soldier was so young... to be his enemy. No, not a soldier. This man couldn't be considered human anymore. He was a pawn and a tool sent to try to kill him. General Weaver focused on the red glowing eyes coming from each enemy scout. They were all cybernetically modified soldiers. His left hand reached for his side arm and his right drew a sword. He pressed a button and in an instant, the blade extended out. He brandished it, showing them that he was ready.

The scout unit was composed of three humanoids, while the rest were all drones. All of them were programmed with one mission: to kill him. It was time to counter them.

Without another word, they advanced, starting at a light jog that quickly turned into a full sprint. General Weaver stood his ground.

As they closed in, he raised his right arm and, with his sword, slammed it into the ground. The moment he struck, the ground shook as he unleashed a minor earthquake, throwing the enemy off balance. Lifting his left hand, he took aim. He had time to fire two shots, landing a perfect headshot on the lead scout and hitting another in the shoulder. Then, he got ready to swing his sword as the third scout got too close.

Dodging quickly, the general managed to avoid getting hit. Once he successfully evaded the attack, he swung his blade and decapitated the attacker. Two down, seven to go.

They didn't stand a chance. They were fast, but the general was faster. He had to admit, they were skilled, but he was better. Without getting too cocky, he gave the scout unit a lethal education on how a real professional properly disposed of the trash. It was over in seconds as his expertise greatly overpowered them. As he struck them down, one by one, he remembered everything that led up to this moment. Phantom voices spoke in his mind.

"I warn you General Weaver... this is not a wise course of action."

Before he evacuated Boothby and his family... before he proceeded to take up arms, he was standing before his old mentor... and he was giving her his answer. She was a First Admiral with the S.C.E. and absolutely livid at what she had just been told. Resolutely, he restated his answer.

"I will not join you ma'am," he said firmly but respectfully, standing his ground when she walked over to him slowly. "Admiral Caldwell, I apologize, but I would like to stay."

"I ask you for so little in return for what I am offering you," she said. "Why do you refuse?"

"Because I already have everything I want," James answered calmly. "I retired here so I could live away from what I've seen, what I've been through."

"The Tandeeri threat is real," Caldwell stated as she gestured to another standing off to the side. "Your friend, General Jason Takeda, has already volunteered to join our expedition to fight off this rising enemy to the S.C.E."

"How do you know they're the enemy?" James asked. "This is not the way. We should try and begin negotiations."

"They've already destroyed colonies and many of our ships," Caldwell replied. "They will come here eventually. I'm simply asking you to join me so that you can die gloriously in battle instead of getting annihilated during your retirement. Peace will no longer be your way of living anymore. There will be no negotiations."

General Weaver didn't know it at the time, but that was the moment when two of his friendships were confirmed to be over. He had retired from active duty to get away from actual combat. Now that Caldwell was here pestering him once again with a peculiar and shady request, he wasn't sure what he found more disturbing—the bloodthirsty look in her eyes or the fact that it felt like he had been abandoned. Seeing one of his friends signing up to join her was infuriating. Jason looked incredibly naïve and too eager to participate in retaliating against a new species. How could he do Caldwell's bidding like this?

The brief flashback ended and as James continued annihilating the enemy scouts, he kept thinking about the organization these fools had been indoctrinated into. Silent Eclipse. The mere thought of whatever Caldwell had concocted made his blood boil.

The last man before him was trying to make a desperate stand, but it was no use. General Weaver snarled, surged forward, and thrust his blade through him. The enemy soldier rasped for air, choking as his last moments claimed him. James looked the man in the eyes and watched him go cold and lifeless.

"I am not old," he growled.

General Weaver ferociously withdrew his blade and watched the man crumple to the ground. The whole time, he could still hear Caldwell's voice.

"This is the only path for you," she had tried arguing to him. "Why do you refuse?"

"I will not go!" James repeated once more. "I don't agree with your plan!"

General Weaver's voice had echoed in the chamber of Caldwell's ship. She tilted her head and stared at him sternly.

"Then so be it," she scoffed. "You will regret this."

If he had known what was to come, James could have killed her right then and there. But, it wouldn't have been right. Had he known what would have happened, maybe, he could have changed the outcome. However, what was done was done.

After disposing of the enemy scout unit, he continued his trek through the woods. He felt the adrenaline pumping as he tried to shake off the battle and conserve his strength. The past was the past, and there was absolutely nothing he could have done unless he traveled back in time. Sometimes, he desperately wished that he could go back as his mind became a whirlwind of anger and sorrow.

"You're dreaming, darling."

Another flashback. General Weaver thought back to his home life. The meeting with Caldwell had ended some time ago, and he had returned to his wife. Dressed in comfortable casual wear, he leaned forward, resting his elbows on the table. Alicia Weaver sat opposite him, smiling warmly.

"Sorry Alicia," he said. "I'm pretty distracted right now."

"Can't you simply serve?" Alicia asked curiously. "I know the reason why you don't want to..."

She rested her hand on the armrest of her wheelchair. James watched as she wheeled herself around and parked her chair at his side.

"It's ok with me if you go off to fight," she said. "If I wasn't confined to this chair, I'd be going with you."

"But we both retired from active duty so we could live peacefully," James replied. "I took this posting so that I could train future generations of soldiers for the S.C.E. It was also so I could be with you here."

"What a romantic," Alicia smiled. However, her face fell as she glanced at the window. "But... from the way you described it... I don't think the admiral was too pleased."

"Admiral Caldwell is ambitious," Weaver sighed. "Too ambitious. The Tandeeri threat shouldn't be as terrifying as she is making it out to be. I feel as if there's something else going on. It doesn't seem right but I can't be certain."

"You? Uncertain?" Alicia laughed as she kindly put her hand over his. "That's a first. But what if it is real? What happens when this place gets destroyed in the coming conflict? What happens if you ask yourself: what if you could have been there to do something about it?"

This didn't help at all. General Weaver looked down at their hands and voiced his next thoughts. Maybe it was time to think about his handicapped wife's safety.

"Alicia," he said. "You should leave... just for a while. I don't think it's safe for you to stay. You should go and visit friends. Perhaps Serina...?"

Alicia interrupted him.

"I am your wife, James," she replied confidently. "You are the bold and confident general. My place is always at your side."

"You're stubborn..."

"I could say the same of you," Alicia brought her hand up to her mouth and giggled. "Now, think you can help me up?"

Alicia held out her arms, and James eyed her suspiciously. He gave her a playful smirk.

"Help you where?" he asked sassily.

He stood up and then leaned forward to wrap his arms around her. Carefully, he lifted her up out of her wheelchair and the two shared a loving embrace. Then, she reached upwards.

Their house had railings installed all over the ceiling for her. With her arms, she could actually abandon her wheelchair and swing around the place easily. She had plenty of years of practice, and it was like her own personal jungle gym.

She winked at him as she kissed him, but then began to swing herself out of the kitchen.

Damn, James felt the heat rising to his cheeks. *That core and upper body strength. Sexy.*

Later that evening, after giving Alicia some romantic attention, James had returned to the outpost that he was in charge of. He was inspecting the troops one last time. These classes of cadets were going to be transferred, all of them heading to their assigned postings in the many starships of their vast fleet.

"You are all the right arm of the S.C.E. fleet! You are the elite!" he declared to all of them outside of their transport. "It has been my honor to train such fine warriors. You will serve your new commands well! Marines! You are all dismissed!"

"Sir! Yes sir!" they all chanted.

General Weaver watched proudly as they walked up the ramp of their transport. The one thing he remembered, at least, was that none of these soldiers would be here to witness the destruction of their home.

"General? May I have a word with you?"

Commander Ti-Zia walked up to him with an uncertain look in his eyes.

"What is it?"

"General, please... why do you refuse the call to fight?"

General Weaver stood firmly as his subordinate began to plead with him.

"Disobeying the summons has definitely stirred up some trouble! You refused First Admiral Caldwell! She's bound to treat this as a court-martial offense! You will be stripped of rank!"

"Then so be it," James merely sighed. "I'm already retired."

General Weaver gazed up at the overhead starships preparing to fly off into orbit. They were all leaving without him. Had he been younger, he would have been eager to be alongside his friends. But no, not this time. He turned to Commander Ti-Zia and smiled.

"Always remember one thing, commander," he said. "Rank is meaningless since I have decided to keep out of this fight. I cannot go. Admiral Caldwell is asking me to abandon my principles. I refuse to fight for her."

"This is heresy!" Commander Ti-Zia said with shock in his eyes. "Do you realize what you're saying?"

"There was a time when the S.C.E. was peaceful. All the wars and battles I've fought... have turned us into something different. This is not the path I wanted."

"Listen to yourself!" Ti-Zia said. "Admiral Caldwell will come after you now! Think of your bloodline! What about your wife? She's also retired from active duty but if she wasn't, she would also face the same charges you will deal with! Please join! General!"

"When the time comes," James stated firmly. "The war will be on my doorstep anyway. They will come for me in force. I will then answer their call... with my weapons."

"Are you talking about Caldwell? Or the Tandeeri?"

Commander Ti-Zia looked down mournfully. James shook his head.

"I don't know," he replied. "My instincts tell me that I can't go with Caldwell."

"It's not too late," Ti-Zia said one last time.

"I know," James stated. "My decision has been made and... it's done."

The memories faded once more. That was the last time that he had spoken to Ti-Zia in person. Before that, he had held his wife in his arms. Both of them had one last moment to be passionate with each other before he had to go.

As he remembered her warm and gentle touch, the wind blew that feeling away as he cleared the woods. James pressed forward and could see an open field. He stopped thinking about the past and focused on the present. They had come for him. It was a whole army... and they definitely didn't look like the Tandeeri.

"Forgive me Ti-Zia," James whispered mournfully. "It is my fault they killed you."

As he walked out into the open plain, he analyzed the enemy army. It was him against all of them. These were Admiral Caldwell's troops. Silent Eclipse. The top-secret branch of the S.C.E. which he had refused to join. He had heard stories about their conduct many years ago. It looked like they had been reactivated without the consent of the S.C.E. Council.

I definitely should have emailed the Admiralty Board about this, James grumbled.

All attempts to call for help were fruitless. Caldwell had managed to disable communications on the entire planet.

So, all of this was because he turned her down. What was she trying to cover up?

Unfortunately, this wouldn't matter. James figured that the best way to make a statement... was to destroy every single Silent Eclipse operative that opposed him.

Their tactics were brutal and their methods went against everything the S.C.E. stood for. Because he had chosen to oppose them, he paid for it dearly, and they were still coming to hit him again. Now it was his turn to show them what this fight would cost them.

From what he could tell, the entire army was mostly mechanized. The Silent Eclipse drones were deadly and rumored to be the most terrifying adversaries in combat. They were also led by humans and other brainwashed operatives. These people weren't considered normal anymore... they had been altered and programmed just like their machine counterparts to do Admiral Caldwell's bidding.

Even though they had a rather deadly reputation, General Weaver bravely stepped onto the field and readied himself. These were the most dangerous enemies he would ever face... but he would kill them all. By any means necessary.

General Weaver drew his weapon and swung it to the side. As the energy surrounding his blade began to charge and fill with his power, the enemy army charged him. He began to sprint at them at full speed.

It was as though a massive earthquake was battering the area while the army raced towards their target. The ground shook with so much force that it could probably have been felt for miles. General Weaver wasn't going to let the army beat him. Overwhelming numbers did help in battle but it didn't always guarantee victory. They were going against an amborg; one of the strongest in the sector. His implants were utilized to their highest level as he put all of the remaining energy that he had into this fight.

They began to fire lasers and energy rounds at him with their rifles and firearms, but he merely deflected them with his blade. He kept his sidearm holstered for this battle. Once he got in close, it was all over for them. He just needed his sword and his other favored weapon, a chakra.

As the battle progressed, he focused only on killing. Faster and faster.

When he had cut down most of the drones, the operatives tried to engage him. However, the added challenge of facing Caldwell's puppets only made their deaths much more satisfying. With them gone, they could rest peacefully and never have to take orders from her again. The more of them that he dismembered, shattered, vaporized, and cut down, the more he relished in imagining what Caldwell's face must have looked like as he tore through every enemy that came across him.

The more foot troops that went down, the more vehicles Silent Eclipse sent after him. They came in on bikes, air speeders, and flew high up in the air on their jump-packs. Using his high speed and agility, James effortlessly weaved in and out of their ranks. The absolute disadvantage they had was challenging him alone. As he cut them down, he used the enemy as shields, causing them to kill each other by mistake. As each human shield fell, he would utilize another. Friendly fire became his main tactic, which heavily damaged their morale.

That's when the tanks and walkers came in. The tanks tried to kill him from afar but he would retaliate by getting in under their guns. The walkers tried to step on him with their tall steel legs, but he would slice them to pieces.

Upon examining the aftermath of the battlefield, there are some who claim the battle lasted for hours but actually, it was over in forty-seven minutes. If Dr. Kendrick had been there to observe his amborg defeat Silent Eclipse, he would have been very proud. At least, that's what James hoped. Maybe someday, someone would tell Dr. Kendrick or any of his friends of what had taken place here.

He remembered that when he had climbed the last walker. He hung on angrily as it tried to fling him off. When he reached the pilot's cockpit, he let out a ferocious battle cry as he drove his sword through the armored casing. The massive walker collapsed and with one loud crash, it was over and the battlefield fell silent.

There were only two more people to kill and he would have the revenge he had sought after. But he needed to make sure that one of them would die first before the other.

"TAKEDA!" General Weaver roared loudly.

His voice echoed off into the distance. All of the dead bodies he had left on the field were silent. No one answered his call.

"I AM NOT DEAD!"

Yes, his friend General Jason Takeda was now his enemy. And he would kill him. For Alicia.

After his meeting with Commander Ti-Zia, James had returned to his office to prepare some paperwork. That was when Boothby had come looking for him. By the time the old groundskeeper burst into James' office, it had been too late.

"My children messaged me," Boothby gasped breathlessly. "They saw General Takeda taking Commander Ti-Zia with some... strange guards... They were seen going to your home!"

James had told Boothby to go home immediately and to pack up his family. He had hoped that Caldwell would come for him at the outpost but... he was wrong. She had sent Takeda to his home... to Alicia! James had rushed home as fast as he could. But when he got there, his worst fears had come to light.

"Alicia!" he'd called out.

General Weaver desperately looked around and tried to find his wife among the overturned furniture and destroyed objects. They had come for her.

As he moved through his home frantically, he encountered a few dead bodies. Evidently, there had been a struggle. Despite being restricted to a wheelchair, his wife was still skilled in combat. They were amborgs, so of course they would not fall easily.

Then he found them in the living room.

James' eyes widened in shock as he walked in. He glanced to the side and saw that Commander Ti-Zia had perished by the sword. Had he tried to help protect Alicia? Did he defend her for him in his absence?

General Weaver dropped to his knees and reached out for the body of his wife. Her chair had been thrown in a corner, now in pieces.

"Alicia?" Tears welled up as he wrapped his arms around her and picked her up. "Alicia??"

It was no use. With trembling hands, James Weaver cradled his wife one last time. His tears poured out he placed his hand on her bloody cheek as if maybe, she could still breathe once more, but it was no use.

As he continued to tremble, his sorrow was immediately overshadowed with different emotions. He had done this. Their deaths were on him. It was his fault. Still, his fury boiled over as he thought about Admiral Caldwell and his former friend Takeda. They crossed the line.

There was no going back.

James straightened up, arched his head towards the ceiling, and let out one massive yell. He wasn't crying anymore, and his yell was strong despite being filled with anguish. It shook the entire house as he made his declaration of war. He hoped that everyone nearby, if there was anyone still around, could hear his fury.

That was all he could think of as he went to meet General Takeda. Even if he didn't get to kill Admiral Caldwell, he was sure of one thing: his former friend would not be allowed to live after this. He knew that Caldwell never bothered to do the dirty work. Jason was the only one that made sure that Alicia died.

General Weaver found General Takeda waiting at the top of the dueling point. It was hidden away nearby in the hills. The S.C.E. outpost set it up as a special training ground. They often scheduled tournaments and festivals here for the trainees. It also served as a special place for students to practice dueling or to train together. James and Jason had dueled each other on many occasions here in this very spot. This would be their last duel together and this time, death awaited the loser.

"Your sword was too late to protect Alicia. Such a price to pay. I took much satisfaction watching her die, screaming for you."

Takeda was only trying to make him angry. Alicia would never beg for mercy. She would have bravely fought to the end and never would have screamed in terror. General Weaver's face contorted with rage.

"Don't you ever say her name," he breathed. "I'm going to wipe that smug look off your face forever and you will die painfully."

"Once I kill you," Takeda sneered as he drew his sword. "I will boast about killing her over and over. I will have killed two amborgs. I look forward to putting that on my combat record for Caldwell."

"Coward," James readied his stance. "You haven't faced me at my fullest strength. I promise this will be your last!"

Both of them mustered all of their strength and lunged.

General Weaver knew that the battle against Silent Eclipse had worn him out. Destroying an army single-handedly drained him, but he was going to see this through no matter what. As he made his journey to the dueling point, he already knew that he wouldn't have the energy to make it to Caldwell. At the very least, he just needed to kill this man in front of him. There was no time or enough strength left in him to prolong the duel.

So... General Weaver decided to pull one last desperate gamble.

He allowed himself to be open.

General Takeda swung his sword upwards and struck him. As he felt his armor get cut, General Weaver could only hope that his aim had been true.

As blood gushed out from his chest, General Weaver gasped as he struggled to stay upright. General Takeda's face held a look of satisfaction, but it faded as he looked down. General Weaver, in the moment he let himself be vulnerable, had directed his sword into Takeda's abdomen.

"Ha," Takeda rasped painfully. "You failed. I can always heal from this..."

General Weaver pulled out his sidearm. He knew he had one shot left.

"No you can't," General Weaver pointed the gun at Takeda's shocked face.

"A gun? In our... duel? But... that's unfair."

General Weaver pulled the trigger. The energy round went right between his eyes. Takeda fell to the ground with Weaver's sword still embedded in his side. James panted in pain as his enemy died in front of him.

"There are no... rules," he stated, "for dishonorable cowards..."

General Weaver could feel his life fading as he felt his blood leave him. There was nothing that could be done to save him. He glanced down at his now empty gun.

He had saved one shot in it for this duel because he wanted to allow his wife one last opportunity to strike at her murderer. When he had returned home, she had managed to kill quite a few of Takeda's enforcers when they cornered her. Her gun had three shots left in it. General Weaver had taken it with him into battle.

"It's over for us," he gasped as he struggled to stay upright. "I only wish... we could have gotten Caldwell too."

General James Weaver took his last breath of air and he collapsed onto the ground next to his enemy. As he fell, he had a vision.

He saw the front door of his home. Curiously, he opened it and stepped inside. Bright sunlight poured in through the windows.

"Welcome home."

General Weaver saw a woman standing at the dining table welcoming him with open arms. His wife was overjoyed to see him, and he ran over to her immediately. He and Alicia Weaver would rest peacefully together in the afterlife.

[End File]

"Alright, that's the end of it."

Serina glanced up at the person reading the file with her. She was a mirror image of herself, and wore a uniform with crimson red stripes. This was Alpha 43, her other universe's counterpart. The two of them were working hard going through Silent Eclipse's hidden files.

"That's... quite a report..."

43 looked at her A.I. counterpart.

"Can you believe it?" she sighed. "If it hadn't been for my brother, James Weaver 917, Silent Eclipse would have won the war."

"But since he didn't kill Caldwell then, did he fail?"

"No," 43 answered. "But it all fits now. He singlehandedly decimated Admiral Caldwell's forces and delayed them from taking over. She spent years rebuilding her army since they were all destroyed during the start of the war. No wonder she hated A.I. Industries and the amborgs so much."

"How did... we recover his sword?" Serina asked. "Caldwell destroyed Centuria Rosa right?"

43 sighed and shut off the terminal.

"I'm not sure," she shrugged. "The next step is to find out what happened to Boothby and his family. James managed to get them out of there and they might have survived."

"Good idea," Serina nodded. "I'll look for him right away!"

"We should report this to Dr. Kendrick," 43 smiled. "He'll definitely be interested in knowing it was one of his own who fought so valiantly."

"Sounds good! This will definitely help us convince the Council to level the maximum penalty against Caldwell!"

For Sukesha and Wanda.
Thank you for always being there and giving us all of your support.

To Catch a... Amborg?

By Y.T. Cheng

Iris Indigo Casino
Monte Carlo, Monaco
2129, June

At about 3:30 AM, the atmosphere was eerily silent. Thick clouds obscured the bright full moon. The streets were nearly empty, as the majority of the city lay in deep sleep. Normally, the Iris Indigo would be bustling with customers, gamblers, high-end players, and all types of party-goers. However, due to major renovations, it was shut down for a few days.

It was the perfect condition for a heist.

With the security cameras and the entire system disabled, no one suspected anything was wrong. Just 20 minutes earlier, two thieves had quietly broken in, infiltrated the high-security vaults, and made off with the loot. Stealing cash from the vault usually required a team of at least 10 or more. Fortunately, these two in particular had the skills, strength, knowledge, and, most importantly, the speed to get in and out undetected. They collected as much money as they could carry and shoved it all into four large bags.

Now, they were outside. In fact, they didn't exit through the front door. Instead, they descended a cable from the top floor. There were more conventional methods, but they thought this one was a cooler way to finish the plan.

"You know, we really should do stuff like this more often!"

"Shh! We're not out of this yet!"

The two thieves froze when a loud bell suddenly began ringing. Nope, it wasn't an alarm meant to alert the local fire department. The security system has reactivated, and the thieves immediately knew what that meant.

They bolted.

Adrenaline pumping, they put everything they had into sprinting to their getaway car with their bags. Traveling light meant that they weren't as slow as they originally expected. Still, if they got caught, they didn't want to see the inside of a Monte Carlo prison.

As they sprinted away, shouts and furious guards echoed behind them. Without glancing back, the thieves arrived at their escape vehicle, an Audi. However, it wasn't one of those flashy, speedy sports cars. Too recognizable and unforgettable. Their escape ride was a family-sized SUV. It looked normal enough, but it packed a ton of hidden horsepower under its hood.

One thief climbed onto the roof, triggering the sunroof to open automatically, and they dropped two bags into the back seat. Their partner stared up at them in disbelief, shook their head, and simply opened the passenger door to toss their bags inside. After securing their prize, they quickly jumped into the car. The rooftop thief slid into the driver's seat and fired up the engine. As they shut the doors, they heard the pattering of bullets striking the car.

They hit the gas and sped off.

Once they had successfully put the casino in their rearview mirror, the thief behind the wheel laughed as she steered them away.

"Oh wow! That was awesome!"

"I have mixed feelings about agreeing to this job..."

Both thieves removed their disguises as soon as they were sure they were in the clear. Onboard, the SUV's computer system was equipped with anti-tracking software that interfered with security cameras. As they traveled in one direction, the cameras were tricked into making it appear as though they had taken a different route. Why were they doing this? It was because they had evaluated various scenario outcomes.

If they had disappeared without a trace, it would have been too perfect of a heist. They had to give the police and investigators involved some sort of trail to occupy their time. Disappearing completely would most likely attract some serious unwanted attention. Making it look like it was done by amateurs would probably throw them off the scent.

The main reason they wanted to avoid anyone following them was that these two thieves were amborgs. They had a reputation for being exceptionally skilled and highly efficient in their work. Unfortunately, if word got out that they were involved in an intentional heist, then their reputation would be tarnished. So, Amara 345 always planned her missions accordingly.

"I don't exactly understand what your mission was exactly."

345 grinned excitedly as she eyed her mentor, Alice 999.

"Just having a bit of fun!" 345 said as they reached a road that led out of the city. "Now that we robbed that casino, think of all the good stuff that will happen for us!"

"You do understand that your statement sounds very hypocritical," 999 muttered.

"Think about it," 345 shrugged. "Casino gets robbed after they boasted online publically that their security system is completely invulnerable! Someone breaks in, causes them to eat their own words, and then they call in some backup!"

345 lifted one hand and pointed at herself before returning both hands to the steering wheel.

"Me!"

"There are more conventional ways to do this," 999 shook her head disapprovingly. "You don't need to use your false alias as a thief."

"But that's so boring!" 345 replied. "There are witnesses who watch you break in. Once they see you succeed, they are fully aware of how to implement countermeasures. But... when you stage a heist... make them think someone else committed the crime, then they reach out to us!"

999 rolled her eyes. Usually, whenever a high-end establishment such as a bank or casino consulted with them on their security systems, they would always watch an amborg or professional try to get past the defenses. Usually, the amborgs were successful when they exposed weaknesses. 345 had a rather unusual approach.

"Just think," she grinned as she looked down at the bag full of money at 999's feet. "They're going to message Dr. Kendrick, ask for an amborg to come out here, secure everything... and we'll have a legit reason to come back!"

"So you can steal more from under their noses?" 999 grumbled.

"You can see it as me being a thief... or a liberator of funds from shady businesses!" 345 said proudly.

"This wasn't an artifact or historical heirloom you were trying to recover from someone trying to get it back!" 999 reached down and grabbed something. She pulled her hand out and in it was a bundle of cash. "You told me you were trying to retrieve a stolen diamond necklace and instead, you actually took money for yourself!"

"It wasn't there," 345 replied as she glanced at 999's hand while focusing on the road. "So... since we were already in the vault, we might as well have..."

"No," 999 shook her head and furiously held up the money. "We're dropping this off at the nearest charity or other place that needs this! This is not how we do things!"

"Aw, but filing the paperwork to Dr. Kendrick takes so long!" 345 whined. "After all, it's not like I was... huh?"

345 gently put her foot on the brakes and slowed down. Her face fell as she looked closely at the bundle of cash in 999's hands.

"Can I...?" She reached out and grabbed the money and looked at it. "Uh..."

"What is it?" 999's annoyance faded as she looked at her skeptically. 345 scoffed.

"Unbelievable... let's dump it," she stated.

"What?" 999 raised an eyebrow. "You're actually agreeing with me?"

"Well, yeah," 345 nodded. "But we can't give this away to anyone. It's fake."

999 looked down at the bag at her feet. She reached in and pulled out more cash.

"They're fake?" she asked. "They look real to me."

"Top-quality," 345 remarked as her eyes gloomily drooped. "You ever heard of coyote bills?"

"That's impossible," 999 replied. "Those legendary forgeries? That's what we have... right now?"

"We ripped off fake money from a casino," 345 slowly allowed a smirk to appear across her face. "I think we should pull over."

345 parked the car next to a river. Once they were set, they piled the money near the edge of the water. 999 pulled an incendiary grenade from the car and the two of them got ready.

"I know that look," she commented as she pulled the pin and dropped it onto the bags. "You're already planning something, aren't you?"

The grenade popped and burst open, causing the bags of counterfeit money to be engulfed in fire.

"If you want to come with me, I could use some help," 345 smiled. "I know what the next job is."

"And you're not going to ask for permission from Dr. Kendrick?" 999 sighed.

"Actually," 345 shrugged. "I was thinking we could use a vacation."

"Where to?"

"Ever been to Anauria?" 345 grinned at her mentor.

The two of them made sure the counterfeit money burned until there was little trace of it left. Once they were satisfied, they covered it up, making sure that no embers remained, and quickly left.

After that, they began a road trip together. It took them a couple of days as they traveled northwest. As they enjoyed the scenery and the towns they passed by, 345 sent a message back home saying that they would probably still be away from A.I. Industries for another week. Even if someone was to approve the time off or refuse it entirely, 345 had no intention of going back until she was done with their next task.

There was a small and remote kingdom by the name of Anauria. Prior to arriving at the border, they made sure to prepare their travel papers and some disguises. Two amborgs arriving in a sovereign country would attract too much attention. They got rid of the clothes they wore in the casino burglary and changed to casual clothes that made them look like tourists.

999 wasn't exactly pleased when 345 introduced themselves to the border patrol guards as a mom and daughter duo that was touring Europe together. After they were allowed into the country, 999 grumbled that she wasn't that old. It didn't make her feel better when 345 tried to reassure her by saying that she considered 999 as a sort of mother figure.

Successfully entering the kingdom was the end of step one.

"So, Anauria," 999 looked around, taking in the landscape. "I've never really heard about this place."

"It's one of those really cute and small but proud types of places," 345 replied cheerfully.

"So, you're positive that the coyote bills came from here?" 999 asked.

"Mmhmm," 345 nodded. "I have a couple of contacts that are scared to death of this place. They say this place is a black hole in the crime world."

"Black hole?"

"Yeah," 345 nodded. "Anyone that gets a little too nosy... seems to disappear."

"Are you sure you're not just referencing all of those true crime documentaries you watch?" 999 asked. "Every country around the world has people that go missing all the time!"

"You trust me right?" 345 asked.

"I'm uncertain at the moment," 999 sighed.

"Trust me," 345 smiled confidently. "I know we're in the right place."

There was a loud pop and the car suddenly started to shake violently. Both amborgs immediately recognized the problem when they felt the vibrations through their seats. They had popped a tire. 345 gently hit the brakes and pulled over to the left side of the road.

"Oops," she said as she looked at the onboard computer system. "My side's back tire. It looks like it's deflated."

"One of the most advanced cars in the world," 999 mumbled. "And it's still vulnerable to sharp rocks or nails in the road."

345 and 999 immediately started a game of rock-paper-scissors. After several rounds, they kept playing over and over until there was a winner. After about 20 rounds, they were tied. The 21st game was the tiebreaker. As they chose their next move, 345 went with scissors while 999 brandished paper.

Triumphantly, 345 chuckled gleefully as 999 accepted defeat. Without a word, 999 exited the car and pulled the spare tire out of its compartment in the back. As she grabbed the tire winch, 345 stepped out of the driver's seat and stretched her arms.

999 quickly lifted the back end of the car with the winch. Once it was hoisted up, she began to loosen the flat and got ready to replace it with the spare.

345 stared at the nearby grassy hills as she breathed in the nice clean air.

"If 917 was here, he'd probably complain about his allergies," 345 said.

"If 917 was here," 999 said as she yanked the flat tire off. "He'd want you to come home as soon as possible."

As she put the spare tire on, 999 paused and contemplated what she wanted to say.

"Yes," she muttered. "He'd complain about allergies too."

999 rotated and tightened the lug nuts as she managed to get the tire properly attached. As she undid the winch and lowered the car back onto the road, they heard a loud noise in the distance.

345 stopped soaking in the beautiful sun and gazed curiously behind her. 999 did the same as she straightened up. She hastily put away the tools as they both listened to the fast approaching sound.

It was the sound of another engine. A car was racing up the road behind them at an alarming speed. Judging by the speed limit posted along the road, this engine seemed to be revving at three times that limit. Someone was in a hurry.

They heard the screeching of tires and the sound of brakes as the amborgs spotted a CRV hurtling towards them. It swerved a bit, as if it might skid off the road and into the grass, but then it regained control. With their enhanced eyesight, they noticed a young man behind the wheel. He appeared focused, a determined expression on his face as he zoomed past them, not even sparing them a glance. Curiously, he was dressed in... a formal tuxedo. Either he was late to his own wedding or perhaps...

"Runaway groom?" 345 asked skeptically.

"Runaway? Yes," 999 responded quickly. "From them, probably."

345 turned her head to look back at the direction the groom had sped from. The loud roar of his engine had drowned out the sound of another car that was quickly approaching from behind. Both 345 and 999 noticed a dark Mercedes racing toward them. To their surprise, they saw two drones attached to the exterior of the vehicle. One drone was positioned on each side, clinging to the roof rack. Instead of swerving around them like the groom had done in the CRV, this vehicle was inches away from hitting 345's car.

"Hey!" 345 leapt away in shock. "I'm glad he missed but... watch it!"

Obviously, the driver of the Mercedes didn't hear her as the two amborgs immediately zoomed in to get a closer look at the people inside. The windows were clear and they could see a team of four men in the vehicle. It looked like a hit squad or something.

"What the hell?" 999 grumbled in frustration.

The two exchanged glances. 345 smirked.

"Get in!" she said as she grabbed the driver's side door handle.

999 quickly obliged as she secured the trunk door and ran back to the front passenger seat. 345 eagerly hopped in, reached under her steering column, and pulled a red handle. The engine of her car roared to life, but what she had activated was a special feature. It was the turbo mode, an A.I. Industries hidden specialty.

As the cylinders kicked into overdrive, there was a loud rumbling as the exhaust pipe let out a deafening lion's roar. 345 switched it in gear and hit the gas, her car instantly going from zero to sixty in three seconds.

"Hey!" 999 cried as she barely managed to shut her door.

As 345 swerved and pulled up the map overlay of the roads ahead, she focused on making sure that they didn't accidentally take off into the air. 999 hung on tightly as she kept an eye on the road.

Within minutes, they'd followed the car chase onto a treacherous mountain road. Rail guards were positioned for safety while 345 expertly drifted and fearlessly sped down the road. One wrong move could send them plummeting to the river hundreds of feet below.

Eventually, they caught up and spotted the tail of the Mercedes.

"Everyone's in a big hurry!" 345 laughed.

"This seems quite intense for some runaway groom," 999 said as she leaned forward and watched the two cars ahead closely. "Who do we help?"

"The groom," 345 responded immediately.

"Of course you picked him," 999 rolled her eyes.

"He seems cute!" 345 replied.

As they drew nearer, they noticed the Mercedes pull up next to the CRV, then it abruptly veered left into its side. The drone that was hanging on that side leapt up and securely attached itself to the roof as the vehicles collided. The groom was pushed against the guardrail. Rather than being crushed, the Mercedes trapped the CRV, effectively sandwiching it with no way out. They were trying to slow it down and bring it to a stop.

999 immediately pulled out a gun from the glove compartment. 345 kept a magnum inside for emergencies.

"You really need to get a better gun in here..." 999 said as she inspected it.

"Hey, don't diss the classics," 345 said as she sped up, trying to close the distance.

"Taking out the Mercedes' tires," 999 reported.

She loaded the revolver in her hands, pulled back the sun roof, and stood up. 999 pointed her weapon and took aim.

Unfortunately, before she could get a shot off, they were spotted. The drone that had climbed to the roof turned its creepy glowing eyes towards them. Then, like a spider, it leapt into the air straight for them.

"Yikes!" 345 put her foot down on the pedal.

999 took cover and ducked back into her seat as the drone flew headfirst into the hood of the car. Fortunately, it didn't realize until it was too late that an A.I. Industries manufactured vehicle was built much stronger than it looked. The reinforced armor of the front was tough and when the drone flew into it, it shattered into pieces and practically exploded on contact. When the pieces of its body were sent flying overhead, 345 could see a huge dent on the hood, but it didn't seem like it had caused serious damage.

Once it was clear, 999 stood up again. She readied her weapon and tried to set up the shot. As 345 accelerated and attempted to get close, they heard a horn. The Mercedes broke away from the CRV and lurched right. They soon saw why.

"Oh shit!" 345 also jerked the steering wheel to the right.

A freight truck was barreling down from the opposite direction. After the Mercedes moved aside, the truck charged straight for 345's car. Luckily, she managed to respond just in time. However, her abrupt swerve to the right nearly sent 999 flying out of the car's sunroof. Fortunately, 999 immediately dove to the left.

Their car veered sharply to the right, prompting 345 to quickly steer left to dodge the rock wall lining the opposite side of the high-way. This nearly caused the car to lift off the ground. While still traveling at a high speed, their car was dangerously close to tipping over. Thankfully, both amborgs recognized the situation and, with swift reflexes, shifted their weight to the left side, preventing themselves from rolling over.

As the wheels slammed back down onto the road and 345 maintained control, they sped up and the chase resumed. Once they were in range, 999 quickly took aim and fired two shots.

However, nothing happened. At first, 345 assumed that 999 had missed. This didn't seem likely since 999 had excellent aim. 999 looked surprised too.

"Bulletproof tires?!" she exclaimed. "They didn't buy those off an ordinary lot!"

345 immediately understood what had happened. 999 had successfully shot out the rear tires without a single miss. Unfortunately, this Mercedes was equipped with a sneaky defense mechanism. While it made sense to reinforce the windows or chassis with armor to make it bulletproof, it was also expensive—extremely expensive. It appeared they had even upgraded the tires, which was also ridiculously over the top. This raised even more concerns. As 345 pressed on the accelerator, more questions formed. Who were these guys? This seemed like overkill for a runaway groom.

345 contemplated how deep they had probably gotten involved in whatever was going on. However, they were still in the middle of a chase and had to put that thought aside. Trouble came almost instantly as she tried to close the distance between them and the enemy Mercedes.

They noticed the back windows open and saw some objects tossed out the back. When 345 and 999 watched them bouncing onto the road and rolling back towards them, 345 had to quickly swerve.

"Grenades!" 999 exclaimed as she lowered her weapon and clung to the car.

An explosion erupted on the driver's side, and 345 felt a huge surge of energy rock the car. The impact wasn't enough to topple or flip them over, as they also had a strong, reinforced armored vehicle.

Still, the enemies in the Mercedes there likely highly trained experts, very skilled in the use of explosives, because after 345 successfully evaded the first grenade, another one had bounced into their path. There was no way to avoid it.

Another explosion smothered the windshield with a burst of fire and smoke. 999 actually ducked down into the car as the explosion surged over their heads. The windshield was unharmed and once the smoke cleared, their adversaries could probably tell by now that they were also driving a literal supercar.

"That escalated quickly," 345 snickered.

999 didn't respond. 345 glanced over and noticed that she was furiously opening her revolver. She ejected the empty brass bullet casings, then prepared for her next shot. 345 watched her pull a bullet out of her pocket.

"Armor-piercing?" 345 asked.

999 didn't respond as she stood up. With her now taking aim once again, 345 drove the car closer and held it steady. Finally, 999 pulled the trigger.

From her position, 345 watched as the driver's side rear tire of the Mercedes exploded, completely obliterated. That answered her earlier question.

The Mercedes veered uncontrollably to the left now that the right rear tire was gone. With the left side dragging onto the road, they heard the bad guys yelling in a panic as they watched the end result. With a mighty crash, the Mercedes swerved into the highway guard rail and careened over the edge.

"Nice one!" 345 cheered triumphantly.

999 gave a small smirk of satisfaction as she lowered herself and sat back down into her seat. The pride in her marksmanship was obvious as she holstered her weapon.

Now that it was safe, 345 slowed down and pushed the turbo lever back in place. The engine dropped back to its normal operating mode and they were able to pull alongside the CRV. 345 honked her horn pleasantly.

"Hey!" she called out. "Hello! You're safe! Do you want to pull over and..."

345's smile faded when she noticed the state of the driver.

"...talk?"

"Oh no," 999 said in a serious tone.

"He's unconscious!" 345 exclaimed.

The groom had collapsed forward onto his steering wheel. Unfortunately, his foot was still on the gas pedal. They had to act fast before he crashed into the wall or also went over the guard rail. The longer his car continued to move uncontrollably, the higher the risk of a major accident.

"Take the wheel!" 345 commanded urgently.

999 acknowledged her words quietly and quickly grabbed the wheel. 345 switched the car to cruise control and climbed upwards. As she pulled herself out through the sun roof and made her way on top, she felt the wind hitting her as she prepared to leap onto the CRV. 999 carefully turned the car and closed the distance.

345 swiftly jumped onto the CRV and hung on tightly. Moving quickly, she raised her arm, brought it down, and shattered the

window to the front passenger door. Once she was through, she reached in, unlocked the door, and easily opened it with her enhanced strength. Then, like a cat, she maneuvered inside the car and found herself next to the groom. She grabbed him, pulling him up as she took the wheel. As she desperately shifted and took the man's foot off the gas, she tried to hit the brakes. Then she noticed another problem.

"Uh-oh."

The brakes were broken and the car was not slowing down.

"Hard way it is!" 345 grunted as she drew a knife.

345 leaned over and cut the groom free from his seatbelt. Then, she gripped the steering wheel, trying to stay on the road. Although they had stopped accelerating, they were still going quite fast. 345 looked at the road ahead and saw a sharp left turn.

She glanced down and saw the parking brake. Perfect!

345 pulled it immediately and drifted the car around the tight left corner. This only slowed them down slightly since parking brakes weren't designed for immediate stops. After successfully maneuvering around that turn, 345 noticed another one coming up.

The car was still going too fast, even with the parking brake applied. Thankfully, they were approaching the edge of a cliff without a guard rail. At least they wouldn't have to worry about colliding with a hard object.

345 did a quick calculation. Yes, the car was slowing down but the stopping distance was too short. They were going to go over. Quickly, 345 readied another trick up her sleeve. She yanked the wheel hard to the right, causing the CRV to skid across the road. With the car angling in that direction, this maneuver would send them over the edge, but the passenger side would begin to lift slowly.

As they plummeted, 345 felt herself rise into the air. She seized the groom with her left arm and extended her right arm out of the door. 345 noticed a tree trunk precariously positioned on the cliff's edge and clenched her right wrist. A piston loudly discharged, and a hook and cable shot out from a concealed device on her forearm beneath her sleeve. She successfully latched onto the tree and was pulled from the car along with the groom.

As she clung to the finely dressed man, frequently glancing up to make sure her hook remained secure, she heard the sound of the car plunging into the river below. 345 let out a sigh of relief as she dangled in midair. Now that they weren't in a speeding car, she looked down at the man in her arms.

He was actually quite cute when she got a closer look at him. Perhaps when he woke up, they could ask him what the hell was going on. Security drones, a heavily armored Mercedes, and grenades. What was this man involved in? What had they gotten themselves into?

345 transmitted a command to her wrist bracer to begin lowering them down to a small riverbank below. The tree trunk her hook was attached to didn't seem stable enough for her to pull both of them up. With the weight of two people... actually, one man and an amborg, 345 was surprised that it hadn't collapsed from the sudden increase in weight.

The man let out a groan and 345 stopped lowering them to check on him. He slowly opened his eyes, shook his head, and looked up at 345.

"Hi!" she said gently as she gave him a smile.

"Let me go!"

345 yelped as the man began to flail and fought desperately to shake himself from her grasp.

"Hey!" she cried. "Not helping!"

At this rate, they were going to fall, and as far as she could tell, this man wasn't going to survive hitting the ground if he continued panicking.

"Listen to me!" 345 yelled as she got smacked in the face by his elbow and his fist repeatedly. "Please look down! LOOK DOWN!"

This seemed to do the trick. The groom let out a sudden cry and froze. 345 relaxed when he shuddered and remained perfectly still. As they swung around slightly, 345 groaned.

"Well, I'm glad you're awake," she mumbled. "Look, just give me a moment and I'll have us on the ground. Just... stay like that, ok?"

345 began to lower them again. When the groom finally realized what she was doing, he tried to wrap his arms around her.

"Watch the hands, pretty boy," 345 chuckled.

"I'm sorry."

His voice trembled but she could hear his sincerity.

"No problem."

"What happened? Wasn't I in a car?"

"Yeah," 345 said. "Funny story."

Unfortunately, before she could go into detail about what he had missed, there was a loud cracking noise and suddenly, they were rapidly descending. 345 realized that the stump had given out and they plunged straight towards the ground.

Both of them screamed all the way until they hit the riverbank. 345 managed to shift him into her arms and braced herself.

Thanks to the strong exoskeletal strength of her cybernetic enhancements, she didn't break anything. However, she felt a huge sting in her rear as sharp rocks stabbed right into a rather sensitive spot. There was a massive thud as she created a small crater where they landed.

"Ow!" 345 cried.

She wasn't sure if the groom had injured himself but thankfully, he had landed on something soft, which was, in this case, her lap. They didn't fall far, maybe about 10 feet. Still, if she had been a normal human, she would have probably shattered her pelvis. That would have been an embarrassing tale to tell her friends back home. Breaking her ass would have been a hilarious no-context start to that story.

Before 345 could try to recover, something heavy landed on her head. Unable to keep her eyes open, 345's eyes rolled upward as she fell onto her back.

"345! Amara! 345! Can you hear me?"

345 slowly sat up and felt a throbbing pain in her head. Then she realized there was some sort of cold cloth on her forehead. She clutched it and tried to power through the pain.

"Are you alright?"

345 slowly opened her eyes and looked up to see 999 standing above her. She had lowered herself down the side of the cliff with a rope. 345 looked around and realized that after losing consciousness, her cybernetics must have prevented her from getting her skull crushed. There were definitely going to be bruises on her ass and head though.

She also noticed that she hadn't been out cold for long. It seemed that it had only been a few minutes since the stump bashed her on the head.

"Where'd... ow... where did the groom go??" 345 asked in a concerned tone.

"Left you at the altar," 999 replied.

345 looked up at 999 skeptically. Then she noticed that 999 was pointing towards the water. They could see some kind of boat in the distance.

345 stood up quickly and squinted. With her enhanced eyesight, she zoomed in and saw that the groom had been captured. Apparently, enemy reinforcements had arrived to pick him up. He appeared to be struggling, surrounded by several armed guards.

345 slowly tried to recall what had happened after they hit the ground. She looked at the cloth in her hands and realized it was a beautiful white silk glove that must have belonged to the man. It was damp and cool to the touch. He had soaked it in the nearby water from the river and placed it on her forehead.

"Damn," 345 glared at the ship as it sailed away.

She clenched the glove and trembled with seething rage. A small part of her hated that she failed to protect the mysterious groom.

"I think we're involved too deep into something we shouldn't be," 999 surmised.

345 was about to agree when she felt something strange. She looked down at the glove and realized something was stuck inside of it.

"Do you think they know about us?"

"About us being amborgs? No," 999 shook her head. "But, our intervention will have definitely given away some details about us. They could clearly see that we have a supercar and enhanced cybernetic abilities."

345 fiddled with the glove and found the opening. She lifted it up and with her other hand, extended her palm to catch the item inside. A metal ring dropped into her hand, likely having been pulled off the groom's finger when he removed the glove.

"A ring," 345 remarked.

999 leaned forward to get a better look.

"Uh oh," 345's eyes widened. "I know this symbol."

A wolf's head elegantly engraved in stunning sterling silver stared back at them.

"That's... the royal crest of Anauria," 345 breathed.

999 took a deep breath, closed her eyes for a moment, and then stared at 345, who flashed a nervous and guilty smile.

"Are you sure?"

"You can look it up online," 345 nodded. "But yes, this is the royal crest."

They slowly began to piece it all together. The mysterious groom was a member of the royal family. He was dressed for a wedding, had run away, but got recaptured by... some shady rich mercenaries or a private security company.

999 let out a worried sigh. This was really bad.

"Oh, we have definitely gotten involved in some heavy shit," she said.

"Angel?" 345 chuckled anxiously. "I think we might need some backup."

"I agree," 999 nodded. "Let's call home and try to get a team out here."

The two of them started to make their way back to the car as they checked to see if anyone was available to come to their aid. Both women agreed that they needed to get to the bottom of this right away.